THE SHEPHERD KINGS

OTHER HISTORICAL NOVELS BY JUDITH TARR

Lord of the Two Lands

Throne of Isis

The Eagle's Daughter

Pillar of Fire

King and Goddess

Queen of Swords

White Mare's Daughter

THE SHEPHERD KINGS

JUDITH TARR

A TOM DOHERTY ASSOCIATES BOOK
NEW YORK

THE SHEPHERD KINGS

Copyright © 1999 by Judith Tarr

This book is printed on acid-free paper.

A Forge Book
Published by Tom Doherty Associates, Inc.
175 Fifth Avenue
New York, NY 10010

Forge® is a registered trademark of Tom Doherty Associates, Inc.

Library of Congress Cataloging-in-Publication Data

Tarr, Judith.
    The shepherd kings / Judith Tarr.—1st ed.
        p   cm.
    "A Tom Doherty Associates book."
    ISBN 0-312-86113-3 (alk. paper)
        1. Egypt—History—To 332 B.C. Fiction.   2. Ahmose I, King of
Egypt Fiction.   3. Hyksos Fiction.   I. Title.
PS3570.A655S47   1999
813'.54—dc21   99-21930
                                                                    CIP

First Edition: June 1999

Printed in the United States of America

0 9 8 7 6 5 4 3 2 1

THE SHEPHERD KINGS

PRELUDE

.... THE FOREIGN KINGS ....

ON THE DAY the world changed, Iry escaped her nurse to play in Huy the scribe's workroom. Huy never minded. If he was busy writing in his sunlit corner, palette and pens to hand and roll of papyrus on his lap, Iry would play in a corner of her own, and be very quiet, and for a reward, when he was done with his writing, he might tell her a story. He told marvelous stories. Or better yet, he would let her draw a word, or even two, on a bit of scrap.

Words were wonderful. They looked like beasts or birds or even people, waves of water or hills or houses or the eye of the sun, but they meant so many different things. Iry wanted to be a scribe when she grew up, though that meant she would have to grow up to be a man, and that, her brothers told her haughtily, was not possible.

Iry's brothers were dreadfully haughty. They were all older, men or almost men, and they had all gone away to war with Father and the levies from the villages and their cousin Kemni. They looked down from a great height on small fools of sisters. Brothers were like that, Kemni said. Kemni was as old and as full of himself as they were, but he was much less haughty. Iry liked Kemni; she was sorry he had gone off to war instead of staying and keeping her and Huy company.

Today, quite a long while after Father and the others had gone, Iry played quietly in a patch of sun while Huy frowned and muttered over his papyrus. On it he was writing the accounts for the holding, full of tiny crabbed columns, and his eyes were not what they had been. Sometimes he asked Iry to look at the scrap he was copying from and tell him what the words or the numbers were, so that he could write them on the great heavy roll in his lap.

He had not done that today. Iry had watched him for a while, admiring the way the sun shone on his bald brown head. Then she had engrossed herself in a game. She had brought her youngest brother's wooden army with her, a forbidden pleasure but Huy never said anything, and built a house of papyrus scraps. Some of the army lived inside, being lords and servants. Some were outside practicing in the fields. The great prize, the wooden chariot that Father had brought back from the foreign kings' city, drawn by wooden horses, she set to galloping past the fields as fast as the horses—and her hand—would go. She liked to make the chariot go fast on its rattling wheels. The terrible figure in it, the foreigner from the land called Retenu with his brush of black beard and his fierce painted scowl, rocked and swayed as the chariot raced. Iry would have liked to make him fall out and break his neck, but that would get her a beating when her brother came home.

She settled instead for stopping the chariot and standing the chari-oteer in a field, and letting the Egyptians with their spears and wooden swords practice killing him. The Retenu were bad men, Father said. They had swept into Egypt when Great-Great-Grandfather was young, and taken the whole of the Lower Kingdom, and made themselves kings. "Kings!" Father would burst out in the evening when he had had a little more beer than Mother liked to see him drink, pacing the dining hall like a leopard in a cage. "They are no kings. They are in-terlopers—invaders—foreigners."

"Conquerors," Mother would say in her cool sweet voice, but with the hint of a smile. She always smiled at Father's fits of temper. "They do rule us, after all. Yes, even you."

Father used to snarl and fret and seethe until she coaxed him into her calming embrace. But then, not too long ago, he had stopped snarl-ing. Word had come: the king, the true king, the Great House of Thebes, lord of the Upper Kingdom, had mounted an army and come down the river to take back the Lower Kingdom. Father had lit up with joy. So had Mother, but visibly less so when Father gathered the levies and his sons and his sister's son who had come bearing the news, and marched away to the war.

He was coming back soon. The Great House and his armies—in-cluding Father's part of it—had come to Avaris, the conquerors' own city, and set about taking it. Everybody expected the war to be over after that, and the Retenu driven back into the far cold country where they belonged, and Egypt would be the Two Lands again, both Upper and Lower.

Iry let her wooden soldiers kill the bearded Retenu. He lay stiff at their feet, still scowling his terrible scowl. She regarded him with a frown of her own. Retenu should not have funerals so that they could live forever beyond the horizon; they should die like dogs, Father said, and wither away to dust and be forgotten. But if she embalmed him and wrapped him, he could be a proper Egyptian corpse. Then she could give him a funeral of surpassing solemnity.

As she looked about for something that could serve as mummy-wrappings—her own clothing not being possible, since she wore none, and nothing else either but the amulet about her neck and the blue luck-bead about her middle—people began to make a great commotion outside. Servants ran back and forth, shouting, and some of them were shrieking.

Iry sat very still. At first when she went missing, her nurse had carried on appallingly, but now everybody knew where to look. And she had not done anything before she came here, to get people so upset— not at all like the time she had let the heifer out because she lowed so piteously, and the bull had happened to be in the nearest field, and had broken down the house gate to get at her. Iry had come straight from her nursery to Huy's workroom. To be sure, she had the wooden army with her, but the one who would object to that was far away, fighting with a real and fleshly army.

No, this uproar was not for her. She had never heard anything quite like it. She left the army where it was, safe in its patch of sun, and found that Huy had done the same with his papyrus. She did not know why, but she slipped her hand into his as she came up to him. His fingers were thin and surprisingly cold. They went out together to see what there was to see.

✦ ✦

It was a messenger, a man with a white and haunted look, and his arm bound up in a filthy bandage. He had come down the river in a boat, running from something terrible. Iry knew him. He was her father's master at arms, Pepi who liked to bounce her on his knee and sing her silly songs. There was no silliness in him now.

"Lost," he was saying to the people in the courtyard just inside the outer gate, "all lost. We had Avaris, and the Lower Kingdom. We *had* it. But the Retenu were too clever for us. They sent word to their allies in Nubia, away to the south of Thebes, and had them start a war there, a greater one than we could wage here. The Great House had to turn back or lose it all, Upper Kingdom as well as Lower. He's fighting his way south."

"But maybe," said Teti the steward, "if he leaves his lords who are of the Lower Kingdom behind, and lets them fight—"

"No," said Pepi, with sharpness he might not have used to a man of Teti's rank, but he was clearly exhausted. "We're not enough."

"At least," said Teti's wife, "we'll have our lord and his sons back. Maybe the Retenu won't notice that they were gone. Maybe—"

"The Retenu know," Pepi said. His voice was flat, so flat the words seemed to have no meaning. "They're dead. All of them. They died in the retreat from Avaris. A company of chariots caught us on our way to the boats. It mowed them down. The rest of us who survived were allowed to retrieve their bodies. The embalmers have them. When the embalming is done, they'll come back. The Retenu don't mind giving honor to enemies who have fallen. And giving—" Pepi's voice broke. "Giving their belongings to the one whose chariots killed them."

Huy's hand gripped Iry's so hard she nearly cried out. But she bit her lip and kept silent. Not everyone understood what Pepi had just said. But Huy did. He said it for them all. "All of us. All of us here in the Sun Ascendant—we belong to the Retenu?"

"To a Retenu lord," Pepi said. "When our lord comes back in the funeral boat, the Retenu will bring him. He'll see to the burial. He'll take the holding. He'll be our new lord."

"We can't do that," Teti's wife Tawit said in her strident voice. "That's ridiculous. We were never conquered—we were left alone, except for the tribute."

"That," said her husband dryly, "was before our lord took arms against the foreign kings. We're booty now—captives."

"I won't be," said Tawit. "I refuse. I'll leave."

"And go where?" Teti asked.

That quelled her, though she stood and simmered, and Iry knew she would burst out again later. But not now. Everyone was asking questions, battering poor exhausted Pepi with words. He answered as much as he could, but none of it mattered to Iry except the one thing, the main thing. Father was dead. Her brothers, Kemni—dead. There was a new lord coming. A foreign lord, a bearded and scowling Retenu, whom she could not kill as she had killed the wooden charioteer.

She could try, she supposed. She was only a child, and only a girl, but her will was strong. Everybody said so. *Headstrong*, they said, and *stubborn*. She was not going to give in to the foreigners, any more than Tawit would.

Or Mother. Mother was in the women's house still, because Mother would not come out in the court like a vulgar servant. She must know what Pepi's message was. Mother knew everything. Mother would not give in to the Retenu. No, not ever. Nor would Iry. Not in her heart, or in her spirit. Not anywhere that mattered.

HORUS

THEY DANCED THE bull in the court of the sun.

There were three of them, two whip-slender youths and a maiden as slender as they. The bull was vast, looming and terrible, dappled white and red like seafoam flecked with blood. His horns were long and curved and deadly sharp.

The dancers danced to the beat of a drum and a skirling of pipes, a rhythm as old and yet as young as the morning of the world. The bull's snorts cut through it, and the soft thunder of his hooves in the raked sand. He was swift for all his bulk, and deadly strong.

The youths and the maiden danced a ringdance about him, the two youths with set intensity, but the maiden smiling, sweet and wild. It was she who broke the ring at the moment of the bull's lunge toward her, flew into a handspring, caught the spear-keen horns and whirled and spun and vaulted over his back onto the waiting shoulders of the taller youth.

The bull grunted, cheated of his prey. The wall of the bull-court loomed in front of him. He thundered to a halt, spraying sand; wheeled and spun with terrible speed.

The smaller youth, jealous perhaps at the girl's bravado, leaped in close as she had done. But he had leaped too soon. The bull's horn caught him in the air. It pierced him as if he had been made of linen, pierced and tore.

The bull tossed its head, grunting at the sudden weight trapped on its horn. The youth's body convulsed. But he made no sound. Nor could he move, even to grasp the horn that stabbed him to the heart. He slid down the horn onto the bull's head and shoulders, lying there as if at ease, staring open-eyed into the pitiless face of the sun. He was not dead, not yet. But death lay upon him as he lay upon the bull. The bull bellowed in sudden anger at his ungainly burden, reared and twisted and flung it lifeless on the sand.

✤ ✤

Kemni started awake. In his dream he had not been the bulldancer, and yet in his waking he could feel the agony of the horn in his own vitals, ripping through them, rending the life from him.

He lay gasping, running with sweat—and not alone because the night was warm. His throat was raw. Had he been screaming?

If so, no one had heard, or troubled to come. Slowly the world came back to him, and with it memory. He lay in his bed in the palace of Thebes, in his cell of a room that he had managed, one way and another, to fill with possessions. One such, the lamp painted on its side with a many-armed and coiling sea-creature, burned low but steady. It made great shadows about the carved and painted chest in which he kept his clothes, and the plainer chest of his weapons, and the box atop it that held his treasures.

His eyes rested on none of those, but on the lamp itself. It had come from Crete, or so the trader had assured him. Was that then why he had dreamed a Cretan dream tonight?

He had heard how they danced the bulls before their gods, and seen pictures painted, but never in life. Yet he could smell the sharp sweat of the dancers, and the heavier, muskier reek of the bull, and the dry hot scent of sand—and over it all, the stink of blood and riven entrails.

He sucked in a breath. It brought him nothing more terrifying than the pungency of his own sweat and a hint of perfume from the maid who had been in his bed when he fell asleep. She was gone. He was all alone. He and his dream.

He sat up, fighting the urge to protect vitals that no bull's horn had ever gored. His head ached abominably. Of course the winejar was empty. He had drunk the last of it with the girl—what was her name? He did not recall that he had ever asked.

He stumbled to his feet, clutching the jar to his chest, and went somewhat foggily in search of wine.

It was the black hour before dawn, when even the servants slept, and only the night-guard struggled to remain awake. He had walked these ways before in the whispering dark, by the slant of moonlight across a courtyard and the flicker of a torch in a passageway. Spirits of the dead and those who slept like the dead fluttered and chittered overhead.

He had no fear of those. They were only air. Nightwalkers he did fear, drinkers of blood and eaters of souls, but he was protected: amulets of no little power hung about his neck.

He had never been able to find one that was proof against the dreams.

Wine never prevented them, but it softened the blow afterwards. He found a jar in the nearer storeroom, and it was nearly full of the strong sweet wine that came over the sea. Not much of that came as far as Thebes since Lower Egypt was taken by foreign kings—and all the gods curse them. But this was the palace, and this was the princes' house within it. For them, never aught but the best.

Someone was waiting for him as he came out of the storeroom with the filled jar, a shadowy figure lounging against the wall. Unless the *ka* walked of its own volition while its master slept, this was a shape Kemni knew well indeed. "Gebu," he said.

The figure straightened, bringing itself into the light of the torch by the storeroom's door. It was a young man, though older than Kemni; taller, a

little, and broader, a big man as men went in Egypt. He reached from the jar
and took it from Kemni's unresisting hands, and sipped. His brows went up.
"Since when," he inquired, "did you have leave to dip from *that* jar?"

"Since a dream of mine saved the prince-heir's life," Kemni said. "And
what are you doing awake at this ungodly hour?"

"Tracking you," Gebu said. "So it was another dream?"

Kemni nodded. It was not cold, not even near it, and yet he shivered.

"Drink," Gebu bade him.

Gebu was a prince, though not the heir. Sometimes it pleased Kemni to
remember that. And now, remembering it, he thought it best to obey.

The wine was strong, unwatered. It dizzied him a little. Gebu's hand steadied him, and guided him out of the passage and into a courtyard full of moonlight.

This was the court of blossoming trees, some long-gone prince's fancy that
had endured for later princes' pleasure. The air was heavy with fragrance. The
moon turned every blossom to silver, and every shadow to blackest black.

Gebu sat Kemni down under a tree, in a cool wash of moonlight. "You've
not dreamed in a while," he said.

Kemni drew himself into a knot about the winejar. "No," he said from
the midst of that shelter.

"Tell me."

Kemni raised his head. This was not the king's heir. But he was a prince,
and a power in this place; and, which mattered more than the rest, Kemni's
friend and battle-brother. For that, Kemni did not put him off. "It's nothing
much. Really. No one we know died."

"Tell me," Gebu said again.

"I dreamed," Kemni said, "that I was in Crete. I saw them dance the
bulls. One of the dancers died. He leaped too soon, you see. The bull caught
him on its horn."

Gebu frowned. "Crete? Bulls? You never dreamed outside of Egypt before."

"I am not a prophet!"

That came out of Kemni's heart. Futile as it was, it comforted him a little.

"I dream dreams," he said. "Sometimes they signify something. I always
know—there is a difference to those that the gods send me. But I am not a
prophet."

"You are not a prophet," Gebu said with the air of one who obliges a
friend. "But—Crete? Why would *their* gods vex you with visions?"

"Gods know," Kemni said sourly. His fingers tightened on the winejar. It
was brimming full still, but he had no stomach for it, suddenly. He set it down.

"This one you should tell my father," Gebu said.

Kemni shook his head firmly. "No. No, I will not."

"Then I will," said Gebu.

"No," Kemni said. "Then all the world will know—"

"That you dream dreams?" Gebu shook his head. "Not if we do it properly. Come now, you should sleep. It will be daylight soon enough."

+ +

Kemni had no intention of sleeping, particularly with Gebu standing over him. For a while he did not, though he shut his eyes to gain himself a little peace. He did not want to be known as a dreamer of dreams. People had a way of expecting things; and of prophets they expected prophecies. The dreams came when they came. Kemni did not invite them. He did not particularly welcome them. They were a gift, he supposed; but a gift edged like a sword.

In spite of himself he slid into sleep. The dream came back in fragments, scattered and incomplete. The horror of it had drained away. It was merely strange.

+ +

The Horus, the living god, the king, Great House of Egypt, lord of Upper Egypt and all lands tributary to it, was in a splendid mood this morning. He had slept well, with the assistance of a concubine of surpassing skill. There was no disaster to vex his morning's ease, no trouble that kept him from preparing a hunt upon the river. They would embark in a fleet as soon as might be, armed to hunt the riverhorse, with bows and nets to catch fowl for the pot, and even lines for such as had inclination toward fish of the river.

But at this hour, still close to sunrise, Ahmose the king lingered over his breakfast. He dined alone but for a small army of servitors, unattended for once by any of his lords or by the tribe of his sons. It was a luxury a king could seldom afford, and one that his son Gebu did not long allow him.

He was not visibly troubled to see that one of his sons, nor vexed by Kemni's intrusion, either. He smiled at them both and beckoned them in, and bade them take what they would from the table spread before him.

Kemni found that he was hungry. He had broken bread with the king before, though not, to be sure, in the palace of Thebes. Ahmose was not one to stand on ceremony when he did not see the need. He was a warm man, for a king. He was at ease among mere mortals, and even among commoners.

Sitting with him, eating subtly flavored cakes and fine wheaten bread and cold roast goose, Kemni began to feel like himself again. Perhaps after all it would not be so ill if Ahmose knew of Kemni's gift. Kings took gifts, and used them. It was their way. But Ahmose would use it as he judged best for his people.

His son Gebu favored him for looks, though Ahmose was not as big a man. He had inherited the kingship from his brother Kamose a hand of years before, after Kamose died in battle against the Nubians; he had been past the bloom of youth when he took the crown. Nonetheless he looked hardly older than his son. He was strong, and young in his strength.

One did not begin a conversation with the king. One ate one's breakfast with unfeigned relish, washed it down with good Egyptian beer, and waited for the royal majesty to speak.

Which he did, but only after both young men had eaten and drunk their fill. It was a courtesy, one of many that marked this lord of Upper Egypt. He said, "Now, sirs. Tell me what brings you here."

Kemni hesitated. Gebu shot him a glance, but he could not find the words that he should say.

Gebu said them for him, with admirable patience in the circumstances. "Kemni my brother in blood, whom I love, is a dreamer of dreams."

Ahmose's brow went up. It was not surprise, Kemni noticed. "So I hear," the king said.

Gebu nodded, equally unsurprised. "In the night, he dreamed the bull dance."

The king's brow climbed higher. He turned the force of his stare on Kemni. Kemni stiffened against it. "Tell me," he said.

Kemni told him as he had told Gebu, word for word. It was no easier in the second telling. The king listened in silence, offering no word, no response at all, only that level dark stare. Flat, Kemni would almost have called it, but only as deep water is flat; because human eye has no power to pierce beneath its surface.

Ahmose, after all, was king and god. Kemni, mere mortal that he was, could only speak as he was commanded, and hope that it would satisfy the king.

And so it seemed to. When Kemni had told the last of it, the young dancer slain, the bull triumphant, he fell silent. Ahmose was silent, too, tugging at his chin, pondering the tale that he had heard.

At length he said, "The bull was victorious, you say. What of the other dancers?"

"I don't know, sire," Kemni said. "I only saw the one who died."

"Indeed," the king said. He glanced at Gebu. Gebu's brows went up. The king nodded.

"Now?" the prince asked.

The king inclined his head.

Gebu had caught Kemni's arm and tugged him up and out of the king's chambers before he could say a word, or think to resist. Only when they had passed the outermost guard did Kemni manage at last to dig in his heels. "What—"

"Just come," Gebu said.

"Not till you tell me where."

"Not here," said Gebu. "Follow."

It was that or be dragged bodily, with the aid of a massive Nubian guard. Kemni went where he was led, biting back the rest of his protests.

✦ ✦

He had gone that way before, and often enough, too: out one of the back ways of the palace, into the less savory portions of the city. They went in no more state than they ever had on night rambles in search of bad beer and willing women, and no escort but one another. Kemni would have been better pleased if he had been given time to put on something other than his best kilt. At least, he reflected wryly, he had put on few jewels and only his third-best wig, since it was likely he would be hunting the riverhorse with the king once his audience was done.

It seemed he was hunting something else altogether; something that made its home down by the river. Not far from here, traders moored their ships. Their crews found women and beer and lesser entertainment behind the low doors and the weatherbeaten walls. The streets were ripe with the reek of their passing: piss, stale vomit, the fierce stink of dung both human and canine.

At this hour of the morning, only a valiant few braved the light and the rising heat. Swarms of flies beset them. A pack of dogs, all ribs and mangy hide, jostled past and vanished into a lesser alleyway, in full cry after the gods knew what.

Kemni had begun—not to be afraid, no. But to wonder if he done something to anger the king. Why else had he been brought here to this odorous underbelly of Thebes, if not by way of punishment?

When Gebu paused, Kemni nearly collided with him. He ducked through a leather curtain into a house like every other along that cesspit of a street, into darkness absolute.

He froze, but Gebu had him by the arm again, tugging him into a space that he could not see. Then, with the rattle of a bolt and the slide of a latch, out suddenly into daylight again.

Daylight and the scent of flowers; the glimmer of sunlight in a pool. Kemni stood blinking, astonished, in a courtyard such as he might expect to find in any lordly house—but not here, in this poorest quarter of the city.

They paused only long enough for Kemni to get his bearings, before Gebu tugged at him yet again. They passed under the colonnade into shade and almost-coolness, then up a stair and into a long airy room.

Kemni stopped short on the threshold. Before he could stop himself, he laughed.

He was standing inside his own lamp from Crete. The same many-armed sea-creature coiled and undulated along the wall, in a great gathering of its kin. No bulls here. No slender supple dancers.

One of the shadows moved. Kemni suppressed a start. This was not his dream come to life. It was an older man, thicker-bodied, tanned to leather by years of wind and sun. But the shape of him, broad shoulders, slender waist; the long-nosed, large-eyed face; and the hair bound in a fillet and trailing in ringlets over his back and shoulders, all spoke vividly of the dancers in the dream.

He moved like a dancer, too, light on his feet, soft and quick as a cat.

There were others behind him, quiet men with the look of well-trained servants. He took no notice of them, nor did Gebu. It was Kemni's oddity that he noticed everyone, even slaves.

Gebu advanced past Kemni with an air of unfeigned pleasure. The Cretan's face reflected it: sudden smile, quick clasp of hands. "Naukrates," Gebu said. "I thought you might have sailed before this."

"You knew I didn't," said the one called Naukrates, "or you'd not have come looking for me."

Gebu laughed and spread his hands. "Very well then. I hoped you'd still be in the city."

Naukrates spread his hands and bowed, a graceful, foreign gesture. "And what is it that I can do for you?"

Gebu glanced back at Kemni, who had chosen to remain near the door. "This is my brother in blood and battle, a lord's son of Lower Egypt. His name is Kemni."

"Kemni," the Cretan said. His tongue softened it, gave it a lilt that was more pleasant than not. *Kemeni,* it sounded like. It was a greeting, and a welcome.

He made no move, but as if he had given a signal, servants padded in, soft on bare feet, bearing chairs, a table, jars and cups and bowls: all the makings of a small feast. Kemni marveled a little that a house so evidently deserted, unguarded, undefended, should after all be so well tenanted.

Foreign secrets. The wine was foreign, too, but the food was familiar enough. Whoever the cook was, Kemni would have wagered silver that the man was Egyptian.

Proper manners required patience. One had to eat though one had eaten one's fill with the king; drink, and speak of nothing, and dance the dance of strangers meeting. One did not ask what one was itching to ask, nor indicate through glance or shift of body that one was ready to leap out of one's skin with impatience.

Naukrates was the captain of a ship from Crete. He told tales of the Great Green, the sea that flowed at the bottom of the world, and all its ways and its creatures, and the peoples who lived along its shores. They were wonderful tales. And through them Kemni saw something else.

This was not a simple merchant captain. That he was here, that he had passed the barriers the foreign kings had raised on the river south of Memphis, spoke for a determination beyond the ordinary. The wealth of this house, the number and quality of servants, made Kemni suspect that here was one of rank perhaps equal to Gebu. He had the air, the calm expectation that when he spoke, men would listen; and when he commanded, men would obey.

Rather subtly, so that at first Kemni was barely aware of it, the current of conversation shifted. They had been speaking of trade, and of navigating the river of Egypt. It was inevitable that they speak of the foreign king who squatted athwart the delta of the river, and ruled the trading-houses of Memphis.

"Once we were the Two Lands," Gebu said: "Upper Egypt, which was Thebes and the long narrow valley of the river; and Lower Egypt, which is Memphis and the Delta. Two lands. Two worlds, as it were, Upper Egypt as narrow sometimes as a man can walk in an hour, bounded by the desert; and Lower Egypt with its green marshes and its damper airs.

"And now only Upper Egypt is ours. Lower Egypt belongs to the invaders out of Asia, the lords from Retenu. Half a score of years ago we took it back—but we lost it as soon as we had won it, because we could not hold it all, not against both the foreign kings and the kings of Nubia."

"I suppose," said Naukrates, "that one could simply endure."

"One could," said Gebu.

"Or one could . . . act on it."

"One might," Gebu said. "And how would that serve you?"

"Simply enough," Naukrates answered. "Egypt has always been rich in trade. These foreign kings are willing enough to take what we offer, but they close off the greater wealth of Egypt, and the trade that comes with it, from places far away on the world's edge."

"Gold," said Gebu. "Ivory."

"Elephants and apes and fowl like living jewels." Naukrates sighed. "The foreigners trade with Nubia, to be sure. But the tribute their king demands is ridiculous."

"Any king's tribute is ridiculous, if you ask a trader," Gebu said.

"His is more ridiculous than most," said Naukrates. "He looks to the land, to the kingdoms of Asia, and to the trade that comes from the sunrise countries. He thinks little of us who come from the sea."

"Whereas we who sail in boats on our river that can be as broad as a sea—we understand the trade that comes in ships from across the Great Green."

"Just so," Naukrates said.

Kemni listened in silence. He was beginning to see, perhaps, what this signified.

Crete lay far away, an island in the Great Green. Between Thebes and Crete lay not only water but the whole broad stretch of Lower Egypt. And Lower Egypt was held captive by kings out of Asia.

Not all of Lower Egypt lay passive under the conqueror's heel. Kemni knew that—perhaps none better. He was the son of a lord from Lower Egypt. His father had bowed his head to the invader. But Kemni had not. Kemni had taken arms with his uncle, his father's brother, likewise a lord of the conquered kingdom, and gone to fight for the king of Upper Egypt. The uncle had died for it. Kemni had lived, but he had not gone back to his lands. Gebu had brought him to Thebes and made a prince of him, and cherished him as a brother.

Crete was a great power on the sea. Its ships and its fighting men were a wonder of the world.

Suppose, thought Kemni, that Upper Egypt had not had to fight alone.

Suppose that it could ally with Crete, and crush the foreigners between. Then might it not at last, after a hundred years, succeed in taking back what belonged to it?

✦ ✦

While his thoughts wandered, so had the conversation. They were speaking now of gods and of wonders, of dreams and visions. But before Kemni could open his mouth to speak, that too had shifted. Now Gebu said, "You sail soon, I suppose."

Naukrates nodded. "We've lingered here overlong. I'd like to be home for the dancing of the bull. We do that, you know, at the year's end."

"Yes," said Gebu, in Kemni's silence. "When you go, can you take a passenger?"

Naukrates shrugged slightly, a very Cretan shrug: expressive of much, not all of it clear for an Egyptian to read. "I might," he said. "Can he pay his passage? Or should I put him to work?"

"He can pay," Gebu said, "but he might be of use. He's not a bad sailor, as men go in Egypt."

Naukrates' brow went up. Kemni knew what the sailors of Crete thought of Egyptians and their boats. Children playing in puddles, he had heard one of them say once.

And why, wondered Kemni, was Gebu seeking passage to Crete? Not rebellion, surely. Not running away from his father and his people and the war that, Kemni was sure, was coming soon.

Embassy. Yes. And how subtle, and how secret. If the king in the north learned of this before the Cretan ship passed the last port of Egypt, he could capture and destroy every man on it, and the alliance with it.

Then Naukrates said, "So you fancy yourself a sailor."

His eyes were not on Gebu. He looked Kemni in the face.

Kemni felt a perfect fool. Of course he was the one they were speaking of. Why else would he be here? He was well enough loved, but he was hardly privy to the king's secrets. Unless he could be of use.

After rather too long a pause, he gave Naukrates such answer as he could. "I fancy myself well enough, but I'll never pretend to be a sailor on the Great Green."

The Cretan's dark eyes glinted. "What, a modest Egyptian? Has the world ever seen such a thing?"

"The world may want to know why I go to Crete," Kemni said.

"Because the gods chose you," said Gebu. "Do you refuse? You can if you like. It's a long way to go for little more than a dream."

Kemni stiffened at that. "And did your father pray for a sign, then? And I was his answer?"

"That's between my father and the rest of the gods."

Kemni's breath hissed between his teeth. "You want me to leave Egypt."

"Leave Egypt, go to Crete, speak with the king in the Labyrinth. And," said Gebu, "come back with a token of the alliance. A living one, if promises be true."

"They are true," Naukrates said. "For a compact such as this, the only true bond is living flesh."

"A wife for the king." Gebu sighed a little. "I asked to be given the task, you know. But the gods asked for you."

"One dream," Kemni said. "One vexatious nightmare. Can you say you've never had any such thing?"

"I never dreamed of this," said Gebu.

"Very well," Kemni said crossly, and no matter what the Cretan captain was thinking. "I'll go. But promise me something."

"Whatever you like," Gebu said.

"When I come back," said Kemni, "don't simply make me rich. Give me horses and a chariot, and let me learn the way of them."

Kemni had never seen Gebu so flatly astonished. "Horses? Why would you want *that?*"

"So that I can conquer the conqueror," Kemni said.

"Well," said Gebu after a pause. "I did say *anything*. I'll speak to my father. If it can be done, he'll do it."

"That will do," Kemni said, then caught himself. But Gebu did not rebuke him for presumption. He only laughed and cuffed Kemni's ear, and called for the wine to go round again. "In your honor," he said, "and in honor of the embassy."

.... **II** ....

K EMNI MUST HAVE been mad. Even if the king had commanded it, to agree to sail in secret out of Egypt, to speak for the king before the king of Crete—Kemni had no subtlety. He could fight a battle, sail a boat, amuse a prince. But embassies were for the wise, and for great lords and princes. Not for the adopted brother of a lesser prince.

All he had was a dream. It seemed a fragile thing on which to hang the fate of Egypt.

But it was decided. The king said so. "The gods chose you," he said when Kemni tried to protest. "They will guide you. Trust in them."

Kemni had no choice. The king had spoken. And Naukrates the Cretan was sailing in the morning.

Kemni would go alone. He might have had a servant, or a guard, but he declined. It was a secret embassy, after all, and must be hidden from the Retenu.

And that too, perhaps, was why he had been chosen. A lord of higher rank and position might have insisted on a greater show. The offer of a guard or a single servant would have insulted such a personage. And the proper entourage of a great lord would have been recognized long before it passed the ports of the Delta, and his embassy and his secret been uncovered, and all of it destroyed.

This was not battle of the field, man to man and the gods must choose the victor, and yet battle it was. That it must be fought in secret was a great shame, but never as great as that Egypt herself lay divided, and a king out of Asia ruled over the half of it.

✦ ✦

In the end, Kemni rode on the back of anger: anger at the foreign king, and anger that he should be driven out of Egypt in his own king's name, to beg yet another foreign king to aid in the winning back of Lower Egypt. Anger sustained him when he could not bid farewell to his friends or to any of the princes but Gebu; even when he received nothing from his king at parting but a box that proved, on his opening it, to be filled with pieces of silver. That was wealth—but hardly enough to win the favor of a king.

He left the palace quietly, casually, as if he had gone out merely in search of amusement, and made his way through the waking city, down to the quays and the ships.

The ship from Crete, like Kemni's own embassy, was made to seem less than she was. Her name, he had taken the trouble to discover, was *Dancer*. She was worn, the painted eye on her prow much faded with waves and weather, the sail once purple now dulled to a cloudy grey. Her crew of black-ringleted sailors took little apparent notice of Kemni as he stepped none too ineptly aboard, but they were aware of him. He could feel it on his skin, and in the space between his shoulderblades.

Naukrates the captain was notable here not in his splendor—he affected none—but for that he stood under a canopy on the deck, and all the others looked to him for their orders. Not that they did that often. They had the air of men who had served long and well under the same captain, on this same ship. Everything on her was familiar, and every man had his place and his purpose.

Kemni had no part in this smooth working of men and ship. He found himself shifted quickly and irresistibly to a space near *Dancer*'s horned prow, up against a heap of stowed cargo. There, it was clear, he was to stay, and forbear from interference.

It was well for him that he had so little pride to lose, he reflected wryly as he made himself as comfortable as he could amid the boxes and bales. In so little a semblance of lordly state, on a ship that had evidently seen better days,

Kemni sailed out of the harbor of Thebes. No crowds cheered him on. No great lords of Egypt saw him on his way. He went as any common traveler might go, unmarked and unregarded.

And that was exactly as the king had wished it. Kemni endured it for no other reason. He was still angry. He meant to stay so, for Egypt's sake, until he stood in front of the king in Knossos, and spoke the words that his king had given him to say.

He would not need those words for yet a while. He settled therefore and determined to be invisible, cargo as the boxes and bales were cargo, riding the river away from the city that had been home to him for the past hand of years. He did not look back. Thebes was as clear in memory as he would ever need it to be.

His eyes fixed on the river ahead. The water was full of boats. Every fisherman was out, it seemed, and every trader, and every man or woman of whatever degree, who had any need at all to be out and about. He saw a flotilla of funeral boats with women wailing, carrying the stark encoffined dead to a tomb on the western bank. He saw a lord in a bright barge with a boatful of musicians in his wake, making the air sweet with the sound of pipe and timbrel and harp. He saw traders of several nations, each in his own manner of ship: Nubian, Egyptian, Asiatic. But only his was a ship from Crete.

The river ran strong and deceptively slow, in this its season of waiting before the flood that would spread it wide over the valley of Egypt. The day dreamed its way into evening, and thence into a night of bright stars. They did not beach the ship even here in Ahmose's kingdom, but sailed nightlong, riding the river down toward the sea. Kemni would have slept among the cargo, indeed had fallen into a drowse, but a hand on his shoulder brought him suddenly awake.

He blinked up at a face he knew, but where he had known it, or how, he did not just then remember. It was a Cretan face, and young, all eyes and black curls. At first glance he could not have told if it was male or female; but when he sat up and the Cretan drew back, he saw well enough that it was a man, or boy rather, naked and brown and irresistibly cheerful.

He babbled at Kemni in his own language, quick and light as water running. When Kemni simply stared, he sighed a little—just enough to be perceptible—and said slowly, with an atrocious accent, "Captain says come. You come. Yes?"

"Yes," Kemni said. He rose and stretched, working stiffness out of neck and shoulders and back. The Cretan boy grinned at him. He grinned back, as a lion grins, baring fangs.

The boy laughed. "You come," he said.

✦ ✦

Naukrates the captain sat at ease in his cabin under the deck, in the gentle rocking of water, by the light of lamps that burned sweet oil. There was no gleam of gold here, no blatant luxury, but to eyes that knew how to see, this was a great lord's place, and no doubt of it. The lamps were made of bronze, simple work but exquisitely fine. The coverlets on the bunk built into the curved wall of the hull, the cushions that made it comfortable, were somewhat worn but beautifully made, the work of a fine needle: noble surely, perhaps even royal. Another such weaving covered what must be a sea-chest of respectable size; and what was in that, Kemni could guess.

It was serving as a table now. Kemni had not expected a king's banquet, but this was a fair feast for a ship that made no pretensions to luxury. The wine was Cretan, and very fine. The bread was well milled and baked just so; and there was oil to dip it in, rich and pungent-sweet, pressed from the olives of Crete. The roast duck and the platter of fishes from the river, each cooked in a different herb, would have been reckoned elegant enough even for the king. And there were onions, too, and lettuces, and bits of green to cleanse the palate, and after those, cakes made of honey and spices.

Kemni sat back at last, full almost to bursting, and belched his appreciation. "My compliments to your cook," he said.

Naukrates smiled. "He'll thank you, I'm sure."

"Even though I'm an Egyptian, and therefore worth little?"

"Ah," said Naukrates. "You understand us too well."

"Egyptians think the same of Cretans," Kemni said. "It's the way of the world."

They sat for a little while in silence. Kemni watched the lamps sway as *Dancer* rolled gently on the current. He could hear the sounds of a ship at night: men snoring, rigging creaking, the soft pad of the watch on the deck above his head. Warm wind wafted through the port. Someone was playing on a flute, very soft, very sweet.

"Tell me now," said Naukrates, "why you were given this charge."

"I, of all who could have been sent?" Kemni spread his hands. "I look to be of little account, don't I? Even for an Egyptian."

"I think there is more to you than one might think." Naukrates reached for the winejar and filled both their cups. He took up his own, but did not drink at once, turning it in his fingers instead, watching Kemni over the rim of it. "Tell me who you are."

"My name is Kemni," Kemni said after a pause. "My father was a lord, not a great one but respectable enough, up in the Delta past Memphis. Our family lived in that holding, which we called the Golden Ibis, since before there was a lord in the Two Lands.

"Then came the foreign kings, whom we call the Retenu. My grandfather fought them, but was defeated. He kept his holding, held it and ruled it as best he might, but paying tribute to a king who was never born in Egypt. When he went to the Field of Flowers, where no doubt he received a just and ample reward, his son took the lordship after him. That was my father. He was a quiet man, little inclined to contest an overlord's will. He married late. I was born when he was already old. He may still be living; I don't know. I left him when I was old enough to fight, went with my mother's brother to offer myself to the king in Thebes.

"He took us as his servants, as was right and proper. And we fought in battle against the invaders. We won—we were triumphant. We took the greater part of the Lower Kingdom, and laid siege to their capital, to Avaris itself. My uncle died there with a Retenu arrow in his heart. I was wounded. Maybe I should have died. But the gods were watching over me. I never knew I was hurt: after my uncle fell, I fought my way through a wall of enemies and found myself back among my own people. We fought till there was no one left to fight; and then I found myself back to back with a man who looked at me and said, 'Great Horus, they've spitted you like an ox!' "

"And had they?" Naukrates inquired.

"Almost," Kemni said. "I was lucky. The spear hadn't pierced anything vital. I was a pitiful object for a while, and my new battle-brother had much to do to look after me, especially after we broke the siege at Avaris and ran clear south to Nubia to defend the kingdom's borders, but in the end I was as well as ever. By then I knew that my comrade in arms was one of the king's sons, and one way and another he'd taken me into his house. There I've lived since, and served the king as I may, and I suppose prospered. But I've never gone back to the lands that should have been mine. I've been branded rebel. The Retenu would slaughter me on sight. Not that I care for myself, but my mother, my father if he still lives—they would suffer if I came back."

"So you have clear cause," Naukrates said, "to want the invaders gone."

"Oh yes," said Kemni. "Yes, I have cause." It was an old anger, that one, honed and polished like an antique sword. "I told my battle-brother once that I would do anything to drive the Retenu out of Egypt. Even—yes, even leave Egypt."

"Egyptians never leave, do they?" Naukrates said.

"Why should we want to?"

The Cretan shrugged, half-smiling. "We sail the world over. Home is here," he said, and struck his breast lightly with his fist, over the heart. "The land we come from, it is beautiful, but our souls yearn for the sea. We're sea-people, children of the wind. We ride on the wave's breast. When we come back to Earth Mother, we come as her beloved, to rest for a while before we go back to the sea."

"All that we are is in Egypt," Kemni said. "The Red Land that borders it. The Black Land that is the heart of it. And the river that makes it all one. It is all we need, and all we ever look to need."

"What strange people you are," said Naukrates.

"No stranger than you," Kemni said.

"Only promise," said Naukrates, "you'll not wither and die out of sight of your Egypt. I'll be hard pressed to explain that to your king—or to mine."

"I hope I'm a stronger soul than that," Kemni said a little stiffly.

"Ah. I've offended you." Naukrates did not sound unduly troubled. "Then let me offer further offense. Embassies prosper by the talents of their interpreters. If you would be pleasing to the great ones of my country, you would speak to them in their own tongue."

"Would you ask that," Kemni asked, "if I had been a great lord in a golden barge, with armies of servants?"

"No," Naukrates answered promptly.

"Well," said Kemni. "Well then. I'll have little enough else to do, I suppose."

"We'll find uses for you," Naukrates said, "and while we do that, we can teach you to speak in words that the sea will understand."

+ +

Kemni had never heard of such a thing before. To be turned into a pupil, like a small boy in the scribes' school—except that his teachers were many, indeed most of the sailors on the ship, and his schoolroom was the ship itself, riding down the river toward the conquered country. And thereafter, if the gods were kind and the conquerors sufficiently blind, out upon the sea, the Great Green that he had heard of but never seen.

There was no sharp line between his king's lands and the lands that bowed to the conqueror king. Much had remained the same: the villages and towns, the cities spread along the river, the traffic and commerce of Egypt. But as *Dancer* sailed northward, Kemni began to see signs of the invader. A donkey caravan winding along the river's edge. A robed and heavy-bearded man sitting uncomfortably in a boat, being rowed the gods knew where. And most striking of all, a troop of chariots racing from Black Land into Red Land, with a glitter of spearheads and a bright gleam of armor. Whether they were riding to the hunt or to a battle, Kemni did not know. He would have given heart's blood to learn the answer; but he could have no part of it. Not now. Not by his king's decree. He must preserve his secrecy until he had passed out of Egypt.

He kept to such shadows as there were, and did his best not to seem conspicuous. One brown wiry person must seem very like another, though his hair was cropped close and not grown out in ringlets. He lent a hand where he was needed, and learned the words that went with whatever he did, and managed, after the first long day, to be much too busy for boredom, and much too exhausted in the nights to do more than sleep. Dreams let him be. He was doing as the gods bade; they kindly left him to it.

THEY CAME TO Memphis on a day of heavy, humid heat. The Cretans were gasping in it. Kemni roused to it, for he had been born in this country, bred in it, raised and nurtured there. This city had been his city, this world his world.

And he could not walk in it, not if he would do his king's bidding. He had to lurk and skulk and hide here more than he ever had before.

They would linger in the city for a day and a night, and depart on the second morning. Naukrates had cargo to unload and cargo to take on—for this was truly a trading voyage, whatever else it might also be. He could hardly conceal a ship of this size or fashion, nor did he intend to try.

Because the riverside was crowded, and because they preferred to remain afloat where they were not so vulnerable, they rode at anchor and ran boats to the shore. Kemni kept to the cabin as much as he could bear to. Even he found the air close there, the heat oppressive, and no breeze to cool it. There was a fan, and water sweetened with wine, for such relief as those might give. And he was glad of them when the harbormaster's man came in his gilded boat to inspect the ship and its cargo; for that voice, high and somewhat affected, and that self-consciously ponderous step on the deck were terribly familiar. Ptahmose had been a frequent guest in Kemni's father's house: kin in somewhat distant fashion, and keenly interested in the holding's fortunes. If Kemni had been a daughter and not, thank the gods, a son, Ptahmose might have hinted at marriage.

And now he was the harbormaster's servant, and no doubt his coffers were well lined with silver and with foreign gold. Kemni clung tightly to the shadows and prayed that neither Ptahmose nor his trampling company of guards would carry on their inspection belowdecks.

But he seemed content to loiter above, drinking Naukrates' wine and eating the cook's fine cakes. Kemni knew well how fine they were: a napkinful had found its way down to his hiding place. The cook, who loved no one, disliked Kemni less than most.

After an endless while, Ptahmose and his men removed themselves from the ship. Naukrates went with them, or close behind them. There was no urgency in it, that Kemni could hear or sense.

He was sweltering in the dim box of the cabin, but he did not leave it just then. He lay on the bunk. Perhaps he slept. He might have dreamed; but he did not choose to remember.

When he sat up with a start, the heat had abated a little. The cabin was dimmer than ever. *Dancer* was as quiet as she could be, a sunset quiet.

He came out carefully, keeping to shadows. The deck was all but deserted. Most of the crew had gone ashore. Those who remained were quietly watchful. No ordinary sailors, those. Kemni knew the look of fighting men.

Naukrates might seem unconcerned, but he was well on guard. Kemni eased a little, seeing that.

His frequent place on the deck had altered. Some of its familiar boxes and bales were gone. Others had taken their place. Kemni found a shadow to rest in, with even a whisper of breeze, and no more stinging flies than strictly necessary. It was almost pleasant.

As he lay there, quiet but alert, like the watch, some few of the crew came back—early, from the greetings they received. He could understand a little of it, not every word but enough. They had met a friend, or an ally, or someone equally well disposed toward them. They were bringing that one to the ship. And indeed there was a stranger among them, a figure as shadowy as Kemni tried to be. It was wrapped in a mantle even on such a night as this, its movements almost soundless, slipping through the kilted or naked crewmen. They gave way as it passed, as men would to one of greater rank than they.

For a while Kemni wondered if Naukrates had come back, for some reason in disguise. But this was a smaller figure, lighter on its feet, and quicker, too. Before he was fully aware of its intent, it was standing over him, a shrouded shadow, and deep within the darkness, a gleam of eyes.

He hoped the stranger could see more of him than he could of—her?

Yes, her. It was not anything he saw, but his skin knew, and the marrow of his bones. She did not move like a woman, nor stand like one; she had a man's sure step and his arrogant carriage. But he could not, once he knew, mistake her for anything but a woman.

She spoke in the Cretans' language. Her voice was low, but it was clear. "This is the one?"

The captain of the watch had come up behind her. "Yes," he said.

"He looks harmless enough," she said. "Tell him he will dine with me."

"I will dine with you," Kemni said. His tongue was not as quick as his ears, yet, but he could say that much, and even be understood. "But first, tell me who you are, and why I should do what you tell me."

"Because I tell you," she said.

Kemni's brows rose. Egypt had its fair share of imperious women, but he had never seen one quite as imperious as this.

No one else seemed startled or even amused. The sailors conducted themselves as if this were only as it should be; and in Crete, who was to say that it was not?

Kemni, who was a guest in this place, determined to conduct himself as a guest should do. This woman, whoever she was, did not dine below as the captain did. For her they raised a canopy on the deck, and lit it with lamps, then closed it in with hangings of fine Egyptian linen, covered over with plainer, duller stuff to deceive any eyes that might see. And when all was ready, they let Kemni in.

He entered a space that though small, seemed as wide as a palace. The linen hangings, the lamps hung or set with cunning intent, balanced light and shadow in ways that were almost magical. There were two couches set facing one another, spread with the faded splendor that Kemni had seen often in the captain's cabin, and a low table between.

She reclined on the couch farthest from the entrance. He did not know why he had expected a woman of years perhaps equal to Naukrates'. She had moved like a young woman in her heavy mantle, but the authority of her voice and the arrogance of her carriage had bespoken, to him, both age and power.

If she was as old as Kemni was himself, he would be astonished. She must be kin to Naukrates: her face was much like his, if softened somewhat by youth and by her sex. Naukrates was a handsome man, in his Cretan fashion. She was a handsome woman, though not, he decided judiciously, beautiful. Her face was too strong for that, her stare too direct, straight and keen as a man's.

Though that was no man reclining there, dressed in the fashion of a lady of Crete: long, many-tiered and flounced skirt of richly woven fabric, belted close and high about her narrow waist; and vest of like weaving, trimmed with gold and pearl. It left her breasts not only bare but beautifully and strikingly so, lifted high and arrogant, flaunting them before the world.

Women in Crete were proud to be women—that, he could well see.

She studied him with perhaps more intensity than he studied her, though she must have seen all of him that there was to see, outside by the cargo. As if she wanted to know him, or to understand what he was. He understood nothing of her, nor even knew her name; but he was not about to let it trouble him.

She might be an enemy. He could not tell. He rather doubted that she would betray him to the foreign kings. Not out of any care for embassies or alliances, but because such a course might bring harm to the captain of this ship, and to its crew.

All this passed in a moment, though it seemed ages long. Kemni sat on the couch opposite her, not waiting to be invited; waiting to see what she would do.

She did nothing. As if his sitting had been a signal, the cook's boy brought food and drink, no better or worse than Kemni had dined on with Naukrates. He was hungry. Though neither of them had yet spoken a word, he took bread, broke it, offered her a half. She accepted it without visible hesitation.

They ate in silence as they had begun. It was an odd silence, almost comfortable, as if they were friends and not utter strangers. He did not even know her name.

When they had both eaten all that they would, and the winejar had been filled again, but neither moved to pour from it, at last, she spoke. "My name is Iphikleia," she said—in his own language, and not badly, either.

"Iphikleia," he said. Or tried to say. His tongue stumbled from beginning to end—worse than Naukrates' struggle with Kemni's own and simpler name. "Mine is Kemni."

"Kemeni," she said, as the captain had. She inclined her head. "You're not what I expected."

His brows rose. "Oh? And what did you expect?"

"Someone older," she said.

"Someone of more power and presence in the world?"

She shrugged. It did fascinating things to her breasts. "A king chose you. He must have had a reason."

"It seemed sufficient to him," Kemni said. "For me . . . I would rather be in Thebes, hating the foreigners and waiting for the next battle against them."

"This is battle," she said. "Never doubt it." She shifted suddenly, speaking words that meant nothing, until his lagging mind put sense to them: Cretan words, spoken somewhat slowly, as if she wished to be very clear. "There is no place here for children or fools. I hope for your sake that you are neither."

"And are you the captain," Kemni asked in the same language, "to say who is permitted on this ship?"

Her eyes widened slightly. "You speak our language well."

"Well enough, for an Egyptian." Kemni met her level dark stare. "Naukrates is your father, yes?"

"My uncle," she said. "My mother's brother."

"And he lets you command on his ship?"

Kemni's incredulity pricked her pride: he saw her lips tighten. "He is the captain," she said stiffly. "He sails the ship. I own it."

"Do you now?" Kemni had heard of women owning boats before. But a whole trading ship? And this of all that sailed the river of Egypt— "You were in Memphis," he said. "What were you doing in Memphis?"

"Is that any affair of yours?"

This was too subtle for his stumbling Cretan. He shifted back to Egyptian—swiftly and rather pleasantly gratified to see in her the same moment of confusion as she had caused him, when she shifted languages without forewarning. "As long as I serve the king who rules in Thebes, any stranger who has tarried in Memphis is a matter for suspicion. What were you doing in this city? Were you, perhaps, forging alliances with the foreign kings?"

"You sit on my ship," she said, low and level. "You accuse me of treachery. If I were what you fancy I am, I would have had you seized and taken long since."

"Not if you hoped to learn my king's secrets," Kemni said.

Her lip curled. It was a beautifully molded lip, painted with great artistry— and why he should even care for that, in this that was as keen as any battle he had fought with spear or sword, he could not imagine. "I doubt that you are privy to anything but the few words of a king's message. A dancing ape could do as well, or a singing bird."

"And do apes dance the bulls, then, in the courts of the Double Axe?"

She had moved before he knew what she had done. Her fingers were strong about his throat, strong and strangely cool, like bands of bronze. Her face filled all his world. Her voice was a whisper, like the hissing of wind in reeds. "Do not ever," she said. "Do not ever, even in anger, even to vex the likes of me, speak so of that dance. Do you understand me?"

He understood. But she had stung his pride, and he had no fear of dreams; even dreams that came from the gods. "Was it you I saw, then, taunting the young men, till one died trying to match your leap?"

She went still. No, that had not been her face; he had known it even as he said it. But close. Very close. As if that one had been her blood kin. The lines were much the same, though hers were not as exquisitely drawn, nor near as beautiful.

Her hand drew back, slowly, as if she hated to do it, but some force compelled her. "So," she said in a new tone, a cold tone, but empty of anger. "So. That is who you are. I should have known."

"Known what?"

Of course she did not answer. She returned to her couch, but did not recline there in comfort. She sat as a woman might sit in Egypt, carefully upright. "Be aware," she said, "that the gods may speak through you, but they add nothing to your wisdom. You will be judged as you are—not simply as the gods' instrument."

"I should hope so," Kemni said a little sharply.

She took no notice. "Presume nothing," she said. "And know this. We have as little need to love your king in the south as the king in the north. And the king in the north stands athwart the gate to the sea. We do whatever we must do, to keep that gate open."

"Including betrayal of the king in the south?"

"If it should suit us," she said. "At the moment it does not."

"Then why were you in Memphis?"

He pressed too hard; he knew it. But he could not seem to stop. She was driving him half mad: her odd, too-strong beauty, her impudent breasts, her mind that was as keen as a blade and more relentless than any man's.

She did not leap again, nor did she threaten him. She said in a voice that might have been thought mild, "We are a trading people. We trade wherever trade is to be had."

"In secret? Shrouded from the world?"

"Not all trade is conducted under the sun. Not even most of it."

Kemni felt his eyes widen. "Smuggling—what?"

"You, for one," she said with a flash of wit that he had not expected. "I was not in Memphis."

"Do you ever give up?" she asked him.

"No," he said.

"Then we'll continue to mistrust one another," she said. "Go now. Sleep as you can. We sail with the first light of morning."

Almost he challenged again her right to say what was and was not done on this ship; but she was, after all, the owner of it. "You must be a very great lady in Crete," he said.

"And you are a lord of little enough note in Egypt," said Iphikleia.

He laughed. It did not take her aback as he had hoped, but it did lessen a little the twist of scorn in her lips. "And that, princess, is truth. But I do serve my king. That much you can believe."

"I do believe it," she said.

+ +

She let him go then. He would have liked to imagine that he had left her, but when he walked out of that place of light into the dark and odorous night, he did it because she allowed it. He stumbled below and fell into the bunk that had been given him, and lay unmoving, but still wide awake. Not even in front of the king in Thebes had he been pressed so to his limits, or been wrung so dry.

This was not a king. This was something perhaps more than a king. And a woman, and young, and gods, it had been a long and barren while since he tumbled that pretty maid in Thebes.

The god Atum, some said, had begotten the world and all creatures in it, one night when his wife denied him her body. Kemni could have done no more or less than a god might, if he could have moved at all. His whole body felt as if it drifted under deep water, his mind wound with confusion like a riverbed with weed, and thoughts darting through it, too quick to catch.

He knew that he was dreaming. It was not prophecy, not this; no god sent it, nor goddess either. And yet it was as vivid as the living daylight—a paler light than was in Egypt, fully as clear and yet far softer. Light in Egypt was white, so bright it blinded. This was mellow gold. It illuminated a great work of hands, a white palace that sprawled and stretched over a strange green country girdled with the sea. Every tower and summit was surmounted with the image and likeness of the bull, his horns that clove the blue-blue sky.

Kemni flew above them, high as the falcon against the sun. This was his dream-soul, his bird-soul, the *ba* that would endure past the body's death; that could fly free when his body slept, and seek out new places, strange places, places that he had never been in waking life. He soared through the blue heaven, looking down on the horned towers; and indeed, from so high, they seemed a great herd of snow-white cattle, jostling and lowing amid the craggy summits of their island.

Then as one may in dreams, he had plummeted to earth, and somewhere cast off his wings, and become that other face of his soul, the *ka*, immortal image of his mortal self. He walked through the courts of that white palace. Cold courts, empty courts, courts bereft of life or warmth. On every wall was painted a single image: the double axe that, like the bull's horns, was sign and seal of royal Crete.

Round and round he went through that maze of courts, deeper and deeper. There seemed no end to them. *Labyrinth,* they called that palace: House of the Double Axe. That was not an ill word for a maze, or for paths so convoluted and turns so numerous that the mind, dizzied, lost all sense of where it was or where it had been.

And yet he persisted, because this was his dream, and he had a great yearning in his belly to see the end of it. That end, when it came, was as he had somehow expected: a great and echoing hall, a forest of pillars, and a march of images in bronze and silver and bright-gleaming gold: great-horned bull, double axe, taking turn on turn down the length of the hall.

But Kemni was not to pause there. His dream drew him with winged ease past the bulls and the twin-bladed axes, toward the great golden throne, and then past it, through a door cunningly hidden behind the tall chair.

And there was the heart, the center of the Labyrinth. It was a room of some little size, though small after the hall without. The walls were painted, not with bulls, not with axes, but with men and women, youths and maidens, crowned with garlands, dancing in a long skein. The many lamps that illumined them gave them the semblance of life, so that they seemed to move, to toss their ringleted heads, to whirl in a shimmer of laughter.

The living form amid them seemed less lively than they. It was a single figure, seated on a low couch, hands resting quietly on knees. It did not move, seemed not even to breathe. Only its eyes were alive. Dark eyes, large in the narrow face, fixed on him with a fierce intensity.

He knew that face; knew those eyes, and those high impudent breasts, and that body in its tiered skirt and its embroidered vest. As if she had only waited to be recognized, Iphikleia rose to face him. She held out her arms.

He moved toward her; but stopped, breathing light and fast. What he had taken for armlets of ornate and subtle artistry, had stirred and roused and lifted narrow serpent-heads. Forked tongues flicked. Jeweled eyes gleamed.

Serpents in Egypt were sacred, but they were deadly—as gods could all too often be. No priest or priestess would dare to wear them like jewels, or stroke them as they coiled about her arms, and smile over their heads at Kemni.

That smile was sweet and terrible. Whatever fear had roused in him, suddenly was gone. In its place was a white and singing exultation. It came from nowhere and everywhere. It took sustenance from her eyes.

The snakes coiled and slid up her arms, over her shoulders, down about her breasts. They circled them, lifting them briefly even higher, as if to say, *See! See how beautiful!* And they were beautiful, as beautiful as the moon.

Twin moons. Twin goblets carved of alabaster, tipped with carnelian. The serpents left them, perhaps with regret, down the sweet curve of her belly, girdling her tiny waist and the sudden flare of her hips. She had, somehow, forsaken her garments. She stood all naked, like an image in ivory. Her only covering was jeweled serpents.

They joined about her middle, circled it and settled and were still; save one that, wicked, dipped its head down and for an instant, too swift almost to see, kissed the dark-curled thatch that shielded her sex.

Kemni's breath caught. He would have given—oh, worlds—to be so blessed. But he could not move. He dared not. He had known when he saw her in the waking world, that she was more than simple woman. That would have been difficult to mistake, once he had seen her appear out of the shadows of Memphis and take the ship with the sure hand of one who owned it.

But this was more. This was a thing of gods and mysteries. Whatever his manly parts cried out to him to do, and they cried out most piteously, his wiser spirit knew that whatever he did, he did only by her sufferance.

She beckoned. Her smile had warmed to burning. *Now,* she said, he thought, the air itself murmured.

He did not take her. She was not one to be taken. He approached her as one approaches the shrine of a goddess, bowed down before her, worshipped as she should justly be worshipped. He drank her like wine. He folded his arms about her and sank down to a floor that had, in the way of dreams, become as soft as water.

They floated there, drifting on a warm and surging tide. She opened to him. He plunged deep. She sighed like a wave drawing back from the shore. A wave as warm as blood. He sank into it, deeper and deeper, stronger and stronger, hotter, more urgent, till all the world had shrunk to that single awareness.

It narrowed to a point, a pinprick of blinding light; and burst, and blazed, and consumed him.

IV

KEMNI WOKE IN the dark, rocked still on the wave that had borne him in the dream. It faded inescapably into waking: the dimness of his own space under the deck, his bunk under him and the planking of the deck just above. From the quality of the dark, it was still night without, but *Dancer* had come alive—softly, quietly, but unmistakably. Men ran hither and thither, voices called not far above a whisper.

He crept out blinking into starlight and wan moonlight and the bustle of the ship getting under way. The moon rode low, casting deep shadows over the westward bank of the river. The old tombs of kings rose there like mountains sheathed in silver.

No one ever sailed at night, unless he had strong reason. Kemni made his careful way toward the captain's place on the deck.

Naukrates was not there. His niece Iphikleia stood where he was accustomed to stand, ordering the sailors with the perfect presumption of authority. They obeyed her without a murmur.

"Where is he?" Kemni demanded of her. He was still more than half asleep, or he would have been more circumspect. But he was rather fond of Naukrates. "You can't be leaving him behind!"

She ignored him. Even in his half-dream he could sense the urgency, see how the sailors labored to ready the ship and cast it off.

"What is this? Why are we going at this hour?"

Still she paid him no heed. He was not fool enough to strike her, or to shake her till she looked at him. He squatted at her feet, where she must step over him if she moved, or fall.

The anchor slid up, hand over hand. Softly, almost silently, the oars slid out. Iphikleia raised her hand. The oars poised. Her hand dropped. The oars bit water. *Dancer* trembled like a live thing, shook herself, and leaped suddenly ahead.

Kemni clung to the deck at Iphikleia's feet. He was waking now, roused by the movement of the ship and the wind in his face, damp and almost cool in this hour before the sun's coming. He was aware, rather sharply, of her presence; of her body in the tiered skirt and the scrap of vest; and above all, that she must not know where his dreams had taken him.

He drew up his knees and clasped them, and hoped that that would be enough. One thing the woolen robes of the Retenu were good for: concealing a man's more rampant moments. The Egyptian kilt had no such capacity.

Dancer was moving quickly now, riding the strong slow current of the Nile. The oarsmen had not slackened once they reached the middle of the stream. This was urgency, as if they fled something.

"What?" Kemni asked suddenly. "What are we running away from?"

He had more than half expected to be ignored again, but Iphikleia answered him without taking her eyes from the oarsmen. "Questions," she said.

Kemni considered that. When he had considered it adequately, he said, "It may get interesting, if we have to traverse the whole of the Delta with . . . questions on our heels."

"That is what my uncle is doing," she said. "Assuring that questions are answered, or never asked."

"And dying for it?"

"One hopes not," she said.

And he heard that austere tone, looked up at that still face, and remembered her warmth in his dream, and the sound of her laughter. This waking woman never laughed. He was sure of it.

✦ ✦

Sunrise found them a respectable distance downriver from Memphis. They relaxed a little then, shipped oars and raised the faded sail and traveled in more leisurely fashion. If foreign eyes looked on them, there was nothing to remark on, no urgency to be seen. But the men were never far from weapons, and the woman who had taken the place of captain did not step down, or even sit.

She was waiting for something. Battle? Somehow Kemni did not think so.

The river's traffic thickened as the day brightened, till the rising heat and the sun's glare drove all but the most determined to shelter on the bank. A wind had caught the sail. There was little for anyone to do but keep the sail trimmed, and snatch what rest he could.

At the height of noon, when the air was like hammered bronze, and even the stinging flies had gone in search of refuge, a small boat pushed off from the bank. One man stood in it, a slender brown man in a scrap of loincloth, with another scrap wound about his head.

Kemni would have recognized a Cretan even in ignorance of this one's name and face. The wide shoulders, the narrow waist, the round-eyed face and the utter ease in that whippy little craft, were unmistakable. But no one pursued him. No one cried treachery from river or shore.

Naukrates had begun somewhat downstream of the ship. He was able, almost, to wait for it to catch him; to fling himself at its side as it slid past, and clamber aboard.

He was welcomed without ceremony, but something on the ship had changed. It was, Kemni thought, whole again. Iphikleia could command and be obeyed, but Naukrates was the captain. Without him, *Dancer* had lost her head.

He did not linger on deck, nor waste time in idle chatter. He spared a moment for a long, sweeping glance that took in the whole of the ship. It seemed he found it good, or at least not terrible. With the slight flicker of a nod, he turned on his bare and filthy heel and went below.

✦ ✦

Kemni gave him time to bathe, dress, even rest. But when the sun had visibly descended toward the western horizon, he left the deck himself. No one stopped him. He was a little surprised at that.

Naukrates had been asleep: his face had that rumpled look, and his bunk matched it. But he was up, dressed in his accustomed kilt and gnawing the end of a barley loaf. He had had a cup or two of wine, from the look of it. He poured one for Kemni even as he slipped into the cabin, and thrust it across the table.

Kemni sipped for courtesy's sake, but he was not thirsty for wine. "You traveled fast," he said, "to catch a ship sailing wind and current, that left you behind when it set off."

"Chariot," Naukrates said, "and the gods' blessing." He stretched a little painfully, and rubbed a shin that must be aching. "The Retenu learn to ride in chariots before they walk, but for those of us who find more comfort on land or on a ship's deck—ah!"

"And what were you doing in a chariot?" Kemni wanted to know.

Naukrates laughed. "I do like that about you, Egyptian: you speak as quickly as you think. What do you think I would be doing in a chariot? Working treachery against you and your king?"

"That is possible," Kemni said, "but I find it difficult to credit. That's not your way. You'd have killed me long since and fed me to the crocodiles, if you wanted to be rid of me."

"I might surprise you," Naukrates said with an edged glance. But then he said, "Not every chariot in the Lower Kingdom belongs to a conqueror. And not every team of asses bears a foreign brand. You should know that, lord's son of the Lower Kingdom, if anyone should."

"I know it," Kemni said. "I wanted to hear it. So you were talking with Egyptians who have no cause to love the king set over them. Was that also why your ship fled so suddenly?"

"We had word that certain officers of the king might have a mind to visit in the morning. We weren't in a hospitable mood."

"Or in a mood to let them see Egyptians among the Cretan crew." Kemni tasted the wine in his cup, realized he was thirsty after all, drank deep. When he emerged from the cup, there was bread in front of him; and after all, he was hungry. Between bites of the rock-hard crust, he said, "You might have done better to linger. When a man runs, he may be thought to have reason."

"We had reason," Naukrates said. "A summons from Crete, bidding us return before the dancing of the bulls."

Kemni opened his mouth to point out that that summons had come before *Dancer* left Thebes, but he let the words go unspoken. One never argued with convenience. "Who was coming to nose about? Would it be a certain Ptahmose?"

Naukrates inclined his head.

"So," Kemni said. "How did you know he knew me?"

"One can converse of many things," Naukrates answered, "while suffering a lordly visitation."

That was all the answer Kemni would get. He was not altogether content with it, but it would have to do. That there was more in train here than he had been told or shown, he had known since he took ship. He was serving his king as his king wished to be served. He was not asked or expected to offer an opinion.

+ +

They might not be pursued, but neither were they of a mind to draw more notice than they could help. When the river divided in the wet green expanse of the Delta, divided and divided again, Naukrates chose branches that took them past the lesser cities. Avaris, the foreign kings' own capital, they never saw at all. That would be tempting fate.

Kemni could feel the conqueror's hand over this land: oppressive beyond mere humid heat. Fields that had been rich with barley and emmer wheat were all stripped now, grazed to the ground by herds of asses and, less commonly, the larger and more elegant horses. Sometimes he saw them coming down to the river to drink, or moving swift or slow on some errand best known to themselves.

He should hate them. They were the conqueror's wealth, his weapon and his strength. But they were beautiful, strong and swift, and they, in themselves, meant men no harm.

A weapon, he thought as he leaned on the rail watching one such herd— horses, those were, startled into a gallop by some stirring in the reeds—cared little whose hand wielded it. Egypt could master the chariot, and the beasts that drew it.

He was not the first to think such a thought, but no one had acted on it, not as Kemni meant to. And he would, he swore to himself. When he had done his duty in Crete. When he had come back to Egypt. He would tame the enemy's horses and capture his chariot. Then Egypt would be as strong as the Retenu, and as invincible in battle.

·············· **V** ··············

THE DELTA WAS both deep and broad, a great land and a rich one. But it came at last to an end, and emptied its many waters into the sea.

Kemni had never seen the sea. He had never traveled so far north, nor followed the river to its end. He had not expected to smell it first, long before he saw it. It was a strange smell, pungent, heavy with salt. Almost he hated it. Almost he loved it.

The gods had brought him so far unchallenged, and except for the night departure from Memphis, unthreatened by any who might know his face. Now he dreamed of flinging himself from *Dancer*'s prow into the river of Egypt, his river, the only river in all the world that was as great or as blessed.

He could not leave Egypt. Egypt was in his blood, set deep in his bones. Away from it, he would wither and die.

But his king had commanded him. He must do as he was bidden.

As to the ease with which they had come so far, they were not thanking the gods yet—not till they had passed the last point of land and sailed out upon the open sea. They went with care, with weapons near to hand, and watchers at prow and mast, scanning the green thickets of the banks. The only sound was the buzzing of flies and the slip of water against the hull, and far off the lazy roar of a riverhorse.

Kemni kept the place he had been keeping as often as not, near the captain's post. He was knotted tight. If he let himself go, he would spring for the side and leap into the water, and never mind the crocodiles. Almost he caught himself praying that the enemy would appear, a whole army with chariots.

And if the enemy did come, what could they do? They might shoot at *Dancer*, but the ship would not stop for them, nor slow. They had no fleet of their own.

Kemni could look for no such rescue. The land of Egypt slipped away behind them, swifter it seemed, the nearer they drew to the sea. Then, as if between one breath and the next, it was gone. The great slow swell had taken them. The sky had opened, and all the horizon was water. There was no land. No Egypt. Only the vastness of the Great Green.

It was not green. It was blue; deep pure blue like lapis, studded with the white of foam. Directly beneath the ship was a memory of the land: a broad fan of mud-brown, the gift and tribute that the river brought into the sea. But all too swiftly they sailed out of it into waters both deeper and purer.

Kemni clung to the deck and fought the urge to howl like a dog. All about him, the Cretan sailors had eased their vigilance. A certain grimness that had lain on them was gone, melted away in the sun. They were home, and free at last.

He had been home, and was no longer. There was an emptiness in his spirit. He thought, rather distantly, that he could die of it.

A hand fell on his shoulder. He tensed against it, not caring whose it was, until he heard the voice over his head. It was clear and a little cold, and unmistakably Iphikleia's. "Drink the wind," she said. "Fill your soul. Remember where you come from. That will never leave you, not as long as memory endures."

She was not being kind, or gentle. She was telling him that he must be strong. He looked up into her face. She seemed to be taking no notice of him at all. Her eyes were on the horizon. The sun was in them, and the wind, and the cold kiss of spray.

"The gods live beyond the horizon," Kemni said. Where that came from, he could not precisely have said, but it happened to be true. "The horizon never changes, no matter where one stands."

"Yes," she said.

She offered him nothing more, but nothing less. It was convenient for her, he supposed, to keep the Egyptian king's messenger from running mad and trying to swim back to his own country. And yet he owed her a debt. She had, with so few brief words, taught him to see clearly, and given him courage to face the vastness of the world.

It was very great, this world, and very empty, a waste of water and sky. There was nowhere to anchor, no shore to rest on when the sun sank and the stars came out over the breast of the sea. These Cretans sailed by sun and stars, with a fair wind blowing. The sea-gods were pleased, they said, glad to have them back again after so long on the river of Egypt.

✦ ✦

Naukrates had long since come to himself again after that wild chariot-ride of his to catch his ship before she left him far behind. The first night at sea, he played host on the deck to Kemni and Iphikleia and one or two of the more lordly sailors. Kemni need no longer keep his head low, nor hide that he was not of these people. He found the habit rather dismayingly hard to break; but once he had broken it, he felt as if a weight had fallen from his shoulders. He put on his third-best wig and his second-best kilt and his collar of gold, and was a lord again, for a while.

Iphikleia had put on finery, too, as they all had, and painted her breasts as she had her lips, as if to taunt him with what he could dream of but never hope to have. She maintained her air of cool distance, her haughty stillness, even with her uncle—though he twitted her for it, and teased her with stories of her hoyden youth.

"Wild as a gull you were," he said in the warmth of the wine, "running where you pleased—even into the king's high council and among the priest-esses when they sang their rites. But mostly," he said to Kemni with a flicker of laughter, "she was out in the hills, chasing the cattle and the sheep and driving the shepherds to distraction. She heard how people ride horses, away in the east of the world, and decided that a cow would make a fine mount for a Cretan child. She fashioned a saddle for it of an old fleece and bits of leather and strappery, and made a bridle out of knotted cords, and chose herself not any cow, but the Lady's own heifer. White as milk she was, and her horns were like the young moon, and the priestesses fed her the finest barley and garlanded her with flowers.

"And this child undertook to make a horse of her. The heifer was as tame as a new lamb, with all the worship she was given—and that was fortunate, because if young insolence had taken it into her head to tame one of the bulls . . ."

"I was rash," Iphikleia said, "but I was never stupid. I chose the one most likely to be amenable. And she was. She was hardly easy to sit on, not like a horse whose back is made to hold a rider, but she was willing enough to suffer me. She would even go where I bade her, and stop, mostly, when I asked. She was a quite reasonable mount, when it came to it."

"Until the priestesses caught you," Naukrates said. "Gods and goddess, how they carried on! It's a wonder they didn't demand your living heart torn from your breast."

"No; only my living body to dance the bull." Iphikleia shut her mouth with a snap. This, her manner said, touched on things not fit for strangers to hear.

But Naukrates was not minded to spare her. "Yes, they laid on you a hard sentence. But you danced the bull with the Lady's blessing. Then there was nothing for it but to make you one of her own, to keep the rest of her cattle safe from your ambition."

Iphikleia set her lips together. She had no lightness of spirit, Kemni could see, and least of all when it came to herself. And yet in childhood she must have been all lightness, all air and wickedness. It was rather a pity that she had grown out of it, and so completely.

In the night again he dreamed of her, a slender minnow of a girl with her breasts scarce budded, riding a milk-white heifer. It was a chaste dream, as his others had not been, and yet when he woke he was aching with desire. He gave himself such relief as he could, and swore an oath in the dim closeness of his cabin: when he came to land, he would—oh, yes, by the gods he would—find himself a willing woman, and love her till she cried for mercy.

✦ ✦

They were five days at sea, and four nights of dreams that Kemni would sooner not remember. And as the fifth day rose toward noon, with a brisk wind blowing, and the sailors stepping lively, singing and dancing amid the ordered clutter of the ship, the cry rang out: "Land! Land ho!"

It was only a shadow, a cloud on the horizon. But it grew as the day unfolded and the sun climbed; and as the sun began to sink, even a stranger's eye could see the shape of the great island. Rocky promontories crowned with green, and scattered among them the gleam of white: cities of men, and palaces, and white temples set high on sheer cliffs. The first one of those that Kemni saw, he thought it must be the place they were seeking, the sacred palace, the house of the Double Axe, the Labyrinth of the king of Crete.

But it was a temple—to a god of the sky, Iphikleia said. The house of the Double Axe lay inland, round the far side of the island. They were days from landfall after all, must sail full round that mountain in the sea, before they came to the harbor of Knossos and began their ascent to the Labyrinth.

"Take pleasure in it," she said at Kemni's visible dismay. "We'll sail by day, rest by night in villages. Crete will give us its warmest welcome, with no haste to lessen it."

Kemni bit his lip and kept silent. Iphikleia knew what he was thinking: her painted brow arched. But she too held her peace.

✦ ✦

Kemni did his best to do as she had advised him. The days were brisk with breezes and pungent with salt. The green ascents and rocky summits of the island drifted past, wafting toward them a rich scent of earth, so very different from that of the sea. At night, as she had said, they drew up on shore—blessed land, however stony underfoot. Slender brown people came, brought food, drink, music and song. Kemni went to sleep to the sound of waves and the voices of these strangers singing.

They came to Knossos at last on a fair day, with a fair wind blowing them toward the harbor, and the sun just coming to its zenith over the steep crags of the island. In sight of her own city, even cold Iphikleia had warmed a little: eyes wide and bright, red lips parted, yearning slightly forward where she stood on the deck.

This to her, to them all, was home as Egypt was home to Kemni. He found it very strange, so stony and yet so green, and cool—almost cold to his Egyptian blood, like Iphikleia herself. The Cretans were well content in their kilts and their tall boots. He in his kilt and bare feet was all one great shiver. The wind whipped the warmth out of him, and the spray kept it away.

But when *Dancer* had come to land, when it slid up on the shore, he cared for nothing but that he should stand on solid earth again, and no need in the morning to clamber aboard ship, no need to sail further, not till he went back to Egypt.

All of his shipmates had leaped down, every one, swarming over the sides, whooping, singing, dancing on the best of the earth their mother. There were people waiting for them, dancing too, and singing: women, men, children, what must be half the people of this island, all come together to welcome them home. They even welcomed Kemni, caught his hands and whirled him about and dropped him dizzy to the sand. Kemni minded not at all. He embraced the earth; he kissed it. He would have made love to it, if he had been a little wilder.

It was not his own earth, his Black Land, nor yet the Red Land that bordered it. But it was earth. It would suffice.

············ **VI** ············

K EMNI ROSE AT last, well dusted with sand, staggering on ground that did not rock and sway like a ship's deck, and found himself the center of a circle of stares. Every idler and hanger-on in this port seemed fascinated by his sandy and unstable self.

And there before them all was a woman of beauty to break the heart. She looked, somewhat, like Iphikleia; but all Cretans looked like one another. She was smaller, a delicate handful, and her breasts were even sweeter. He could have circled her waist with his two hands.

Iphikleia he dreamed of, and burned for when he woke. This was beyond
dreaming. This, he would die for.

She must be a goddess, or a goddess' image. And yet she regarded him
with such a look of pure and wicked delight that he caught himself grinning
like a fool. She laughed, sweet as water bubbling from a spring, and brushed
the sand from his shoulders. "Oh!" she said. "Such a lovely gift the sea has
brought to me. Where do you come from, beautiful man?"

"He comes from Egypt," Iphikleia's clear voice said from just behind him,
"and he comes from their king."

"All the better," the stranger said. "Come, beautiful man! Come to the
palace with me."

Kemni did not think he could have resisted, even if he had wanted to. She
had taken him by the hand, easy and trusting as a child, but no one of all those
about looked on her as such. They were as dazzled as he was, and as helpless
against her.

Of all the ways he had thought to come to the palace of the Labyrinth,
this was the least conceivable: walking hand in hand with this most beautiful
of women, listening to her light sweet chatter. He was dimly aware of a city
about him, white walls, streets paved with smooth stones and glimmering
shells, flashes of bright color everywhere his eye happened to glance: a tumble
of flowers down a wall, vivid paint along a portico, a gleam of gold in shadow.
And everywhere there were people, slender, with black ringlets worn long, and
wide dark eyes. But clearest then and always to his memory was her face lifted
to his, for she came only as high as his chin, and her voice running on.

"My name is Ariana," she said. "I was born up there, in a high white
room that looks out past a spire of stone to the sea. I have the sea in my blood.
Is it true what they say, that Egyptians have sand there, and river mud?"

Kemni laughed before he thought, half amused, half taken aback. "That
is one way of putting it," he said.

"You speak our language very well," said Ariana. "Iphikleia taught you, I
suppose. She's a fine teacher."

"She is very . . . severe," Kemni said.

Ariana's laughter rippled to the blue heaven. "She likes people to think
that. It comes of being such a scapegrace as a child—she tries to make up for
it by being the most dignified of women. But I know," said Ariana, "that she's
really as wild as ever. Did she run about Egypt as she used to run about here?"

Kemni opened his mouth to deny that, but shut it again. He could not
help but remember how she had come onto the ship in Memphis, slipping
aboard under cover of darkness, and refusing to say exactly where she had been
or what she had been doing.

"You see," said Ariana, skipping a little as she led him on up the steep
narrow street. "Never believe her when she frowns and threatens lightnings."

"Not even when she speaks for her gods?" Kemni asked a little wickedly.

"She speaks for Earth Mother," said Ariana, "but you'll always know when she does that. You have eyes that can see."

Kemni stilled—a great deal within, a little without; but she tugged him onward.

"Come, beautiful man! We've a fair walk ahead of us."

They were almost to the top of what, he realized with dizzy suddenness, was quite a steep ascent. The white houses marched away below them to the blue gleam of the sea. The way leveled ahead, but then began to climb again, up and up to a dizzying height.

They would not, thank all the gods, be compelled to walk so far or so high. People were waiting, servants with bright curious eyes, standing beside an elegant and gold-bedecked chair such as, in Egypt, kings and great lords rode in before their people. Ariana stepped neatly into it, arranged her tiered skirts, and smiled at Kemni. "Well? And are you coming?"

Kemni had ridden in such a chair a time or two, for honor or for the weakness of a wound. One had carried him away from the battle for Avaris, until he was laid in one of the king's boats and carried half-conscious down the river. But he had never ridden so, face to face and knee brushing knee with a woman as beautiful as a goddess.

Her chatter relieved him of any need to be good company. It washed over him as the servants lifted the chair onto strong shoulders and began the climb to the Labyrinth. It was long and in places so steep he clutched the sides of the chair and prayed, while Ariana laughed at him.

Yet at length it came to an end. The sun had begun visibly to sink. The bearers were panting, their sweat pungent and yet rather pleasant. And there above them was a wall, white as seafoam, white as the clouds that scudded in the blue heaven. All along the summit of it were the images of horns, sharp white curve like the new moon, or like the horns of the bull that they all worshipped here. And along its face was carved or limned or painted the *labrys*, the double-headed axe.

There was a gate just ahead of them, wide and high and crowned with the horns of the Bull, that were like the horns of the moon. Guards stood on either side of it, tall as men went here, broad and strong, armed with the double axe.

Kemni's middle tightened. He was a poor object to be seen in a palace, crusted still with sand, no wig on his close-cropped head, and a kilt that had seen the worst of wind and salt. But Ariana was his guide and his defense.

They bowed as the chair passed, those tall guards in their high helmets; bowed to the ground. It might be for Kemni, but he rather thoroughly doubted it. Ariana rode past them with her head high, prattling on as if she passed this gate and these guards every day. And so she must. She was a power here, or he had lost all sense of courts and kings.

Such strange power, this beautiful child who went abroad all unguarded, and took a fancy to a stranger, and brought him with her through the gate of the Bull, into the house of the Double Axe.

✦ ✦

Kemni was no stranger to palaces. He had walked in that of Memphis and that of Thebes; even in that of Avaris where the Retenu ruled. He had walked on pavements that were old in the dawn of the world.

This palace was not old as an Egyptian would think of it. If anything it was rather raw with newness. Nor was it as vast as that of Thebes, as lofty or as deeply weighted with awe. And yet it had its own power, and its own unmistakable majesty.

It was a maze within, a great gleaming ramble of buildings all over the summit of that high hill. Ariana knew it as Kemni had known the thickets of reeds outside his father's house, every twist and complex turn of it. She led him unwavering though he was all turned about, to a house among the many, set amid a garden. There was a pool to bathe in, and servants to wait on him, and a bed to rest in if he should be so minded. There was even a wonder, water that flowed into basins at the turning of a lever, to wash in or to relieve oneself: remarkable, and a great game, to watch the water flow and stop, flow and stop.

She left him there alone and made it clear that he was not to follow. But she had promised to come back for him. He clung to that, here where there was nothing that he knew, and nothing that was his own. Everything of his was still on the ship, as far as he could tell.

If this was a plot, a conspiracy to separate him from his own people, catch him alone and so destroy him, it had succeeded admirably. He could huddle in a corner, stiff with fear, or he could let himself be waited on by these deft and bright-eyed servants. They were all young, youths and slender maidens, dressed alike in a scrap of kilt, with their long hair caught up in a scarlet fillet. They were not slaves—that much he could tell, as bold as their eyes were, and their commentary as they cleaned and shaved and made him presentable. They did not, perhaps, know that he understood their language, or if they did, they did not care.

In Egypt he was reckoned good to look at, though he had never reckoned himself a beauty. Here they cared less for perfection, and more, as they averred, for the whole of a man's self. For some reason beyond his fathoming, perhaps only because Ariana found him beautiful, they were delighted with him. They loved the warm red-brown of his skin, so different from their olive darkness. They were a little taken aback at his hair, cropped short for comfort under a wig, but they marveled at his long dark eyes. They marked the shape of him, how he was not so wide in the shoulders nor so narrow in the middle as they, but wide enough and narrow enough to be pleasing. And they had a great deal to say of his manly organ, which he had never reckoned to be anything remarkable—but they did not crop the foreskin here for cleanliness and for sacrifice to the gods. They pointed and stared and giggled, and one bold creature took it in her hand and fondled it as if she had every right in the world.

He could grow angry if he tried, or if they persisted. But they went on to other wonders, dried him and wrapped him in a kilt after the Cretan fashion, and put tall boots on his feet—more marvels there, as narrow as those were. Elegant, they said. That was the word they repeated to one another. He was elegant, as if that were a great virtue.

He did not feel elegant. He was clean and dressed and tidy, but he felt oddly rumpled and annoyed. He was not accustomed to servants who spoke so frankly over a lord's head—or over his nether parts.

They invited him to rest in the wide bed, in a room full of the song of the sea—strange, that, for the sea was rather far away, out of sight if not of scent and sound. But he was not minded to do their bidding in that. He went out instead into the garden. On that side a parapet walled it. Kemni found himself atop a high terrace, looking down a steep descent to the rocky defiles and brief levels of inland Crete. It was a wild prospect, strange and not particularly hospitable, and nothing at all like his own country.

He shivered. He had not been truly warm since he left the Delta of Egypt. Here, even in the sun, the wind was chill. It sang from the sea, and the sea's cold heart was in it.

Soft warmth fell about him. He spun, startled, to find Iphikleia standing behind him, and a mantle about his shoulders, wool the color of sea and sky, lined with cream-pale fleece.

She was even more forbidding after the bright memory of Ariana, and even less delightful a companion. But she had brought the mantle, as no one else had thought to do. He wrapped himself in it, savoring the warmth, and yes, the beauty of it, too. "This is a mantle for a king," he said. "I thank you."

She shrugged a little and came to stand beside him, resting her hands on the parapet. "We can't have you taking your death of cold before you even speak with the king," she said.

Such concern for his welfare, he thought wryly. "And when will I speak with the king?" he inquired.

Again, she shrugged. "When the king is ready, he'll summon you."

"Ah," said Kemni. He knew kings. "And what am I to do with myself while I wait for him?"

"Anything you like," said Iphikleia.

"Murder? Rapine? Murrain among the cattle?"

Did her eye glint at the sally? He never could tell, with her. "Anything within the laws," she said.

"Then," he said, "will you be my guide? I'd like to wander a bit, if I may."

"I am not a servant," she said. "I doubt you know what I am."

"A priestess," he said. "A princess. I come to speak for the king of Egypt. I may be far beneath you in myself, but my king is rather above you."

"Is he?" She lifted her chin. "Very well. I see how ignorant you are of our ways—and your accent is still abominable. You might ask for wine and be given a chamberpot. I'll play guide. Come."

Gracious she was not, but he was not looking for grace. He wanted the knowledge of one who had run wild over these hills as a child, and who had not—whatever she might wish him to think—forgotten a fingerbreadth of it.

In her company he was considerably less diverted, and considerably more inclined to notice where he was and what he was looking at. And yet he was aware, always, of her presence, like the warmth of the mantle on his skin. She did not call him beautiful, nor much of anything else either. But she knew where the best wine was, and the most splendid view of the island and even, distantly, the sea; the finest avenue of noble houses and the richest pasture of the famous cattle. She even knew where there were horses.

There were not many. Kemni counted four handfuls of them, mostly mares and foals. The stallion was old and much scarred with ancient battles. But they were horses, and they were sacred. "They belong to Earthshaker," Iphikleia said with a gesture that averted evil from the name. "He accepts the sacrifice of the Bull, and cherishes the dance. But we call him Lord of Horses. He was given them, you see, long ago, before ever our foremothers came to this island, by his mother who made them."

"I had heard," Kemni said, "that he made them."

"So men would have you think," Iphikleia said. "No; Horse Goddess made them. He had them from her as a gift. They bless this land. They embody his promise: that while they live and thrive, his hand will never fall on us."

"They protect you," Kemni said. He watched the horses in their field, as they grazed and played and—yes, over yonder, mated. "They threaten us. The Retenu—"

"The Retenu have turned them into a weapon," she said. "But a weapon serves any hand that can wield it."

"Yes," he said. "I've thought of that. By the gods, I've thought of it. But now, in front of them, to dream that we can wield this one . . ."

"Are you afraid of them?" she asked him.

"No," he said. And that was the truth. They were large, but oxen could be larger. They were not as gentle as oxen, but neither were they as fierce as crocodiles, or near as deadly.

She walked past him into the field. Some of the horses raised their heads. One or two of the youngest came to investigate, bright-eyed with curiosity. She greeted them as one who knew well their ways, walking at ease among them.

Kemni had never seen horses so close, except in battle. These were not coming at him to destroy him. They took little notice of him in the main. They were animals, that was all, engrossed in their own concerns.

"Could I learn," he asked with beating heart, "to understand them?"

"You could try," she said.

"Then I shall," he said. He spoke with more courage than he actually had, but he did not try to take the words back once they were out. Iphikleia's glance betrayed how well she read him.

Better she read this than what he dreamed of nights. He sighed faintly. She was in among the horses, smoothing manes, scratching necks, fending off inquisitive noses. He gathered his courage and plunged in behind her.

It was difficult. He could not help but remember how he had known horses, drawing chariots in battle, trampling the bodies of his own people. His uncle, his uncle's sons, had died beneath those hooves and those cruel wheels, crushed and torn till the embalmers were sore taxed to restore them to a semblance of their living selves. When he found them past the Field of Flowers, if he should be so blessed, he hoped that they would have been healed; or their life everlasting would be a poor and tormented thing.

These were not horses of war. Cretans did their fighting on shipboard. Their horses were sacred beasts, cherished, pampered, and driven only in festivals. They were peaceable creatures. They smelled of grass and sea-salt, clean air and something rather pleasant that was all their own. His hands lingered on smooth necks and rounded rumps. Their manes were thick and tangled. He worked the knots out of one, a dun mare with a dark colt at heel. The colt nibbled at his mantle, snorting a little at the scent of wool and fleece.

"You need less to understand these horses," Iphikleia said, "than to master them. Understanding is easy enough. Mastery may be beyond you."

"I can try," he said, "if someone will teach me. Since it seems I'll be cooling my heels for a while on this most splendid of islands."

Her brows arched. "Ah. After all, you have a courtier's speech. Who would have thought it?"

"Not I," he said. "Find me a teacher and I'll let you be."

"We shall see," said Iphikleia.

.... **VII** ....

K EMNI DINED ALONE in the house that, it seemed, he had been given. Servants waited on him and fed him royally, but none of them was inclined toward conversation. He thought of demanding company, of asking that he be shown to Naukrates' house, or taken to some gathering of the court. But he was more weary than he had known, with all his travels, and then tramping hither and yon about the island.

Iphikleia was gone, she had not deigned to say where. She had simply left him at the door, just at dusk, and gone wherever it pleased her to go. She had not waited to be invited in, nor given him occasion to ask.

Certainly he could not quarrel with the dinner he was fed, or the wine that went with it. Both were superb, prepared and served with impeccable grace. Nor were they excessively strange. Someone perhaps had made an effort to feed him as he was accustomed to be fed.

When he had eaten and drunk his fill, a servant with a lamp led him to the bedchamber. The man made to help him undress, but Kemni sent him away. He could perfectly well shed kilt and belt and boots by himself, and fall onto the broad expanse of the bed.

It was too broad, and much too soft with cushions and coverlets. He could not sleep in such luxury; he had never known it.

Something stirred amid the coverlets. He started and half-leaped to his feet. Light laughter followed him.

There was a woman—a girl—in the bed, tousled and heavy-eyed as if she had been sleeping, but bright enough, and laughing as she rose up out of a nest of cushions. She was utterly exquisite in the Cretan fashion, with her big round eyes and her masses of curly black hair and her waist so tiny he marveled, even as taken aback as he was. He could see every bit of it. She was as bare as she was born.

Well, and so was he; and the nether part of him knew what to do about that. His loftier self scrambled its wits together to demand of her, "Who are you? What are you doing here?"

"I am Ariana," she said. "I've come to keep you company."

He glared at her. "You are not Ariana. I know her, and she is not—"

"I am Ariana," she repeated. "The Ariana sent me. Therefore I am—"

He shook his head. He had fancied himself well in command of this language, after so many days under Iphikleia's tutelage. But this made no sense. "Ariana? *The* Ariana? What—"

"We are all Ariana," she said. "All who serve the goddess in the Labyrinth. The Ariana bids us come and go. She bade me come to you. Do you not want me? Will you disappoint her? She so hoped that you would find me pleasing."

Kemni struggled with fogged mind and sore distracted body, to understand what she was saying. "Ariana—is a title? An—an office?"

She nodded happily. "Yes. Yes, a title. The Ariana likes you. She calls you the beautiful man." She narrowed those big round eyes, and tilted her head. "Yes, you are good to look at. Will you come now, and let me keep you company?"

Kemni had never, in years of dallying with maids and servants and the occasional, desperately daring lady of quality, been approached quite so boldly or with such vivid intent. He could not move, nor could he speak.

The girl—this one of what must be many Arianas—shook her head and sighed. "The Ariana said you might be silly about this. She told me to tell you that you can't have her, it's not permitted, but you can have as many of us as are minded to play with you. Would you like more? Am I too few?"

"No!" cried Kemni. "Oh no. I didn't—I don't—I've never—"

"Ah," she said. "Poor beautiful man. Come here."

She said it so imperiously, and yet with such warm and bubbling amusement, that he could not help but do as she bade. She was almost child-small in his arms, but no child was so supple or so wickedly skilled. She teased and tormented him, casting him down and rising above him, just touching him with lips and breasts, till he arched in a near-convulsion. But she would not let him spend his seed. Not yet. She gentled him, calmed him, nibbled here, stroked there, till he lay in a quivering stillness.

He was all helpless against her. She rode him as if he were a ship on the sea, great waves rolling, lesser ones surging and ebbing, and no release, though he was ready to groan with the sweet pain. She had him in her hands, stroking, tugging till he gasped, and laughing all the while. "Oh!" she said. "Such a great tall man you are!"

He shrank at that, or tried; but she would not suffer that, either. Her tongue flicked. His body snapped taut.

Then, and only then, she had a kind of mercy. She mounted him, took him inside of her, hot sweet pleasure, and rode him long and slow, till he was all one great throb of desire. He had no mind, no will, no self. Only the heat that was between them, rising and rising, no end to it, no relief, no consummation. She would torment him until he died. And he was powerless to resist.

Death. Yes. A little death, swelling till it burst, a great ringing cry that made her laugh aloud.

+ +

He fell from the summit into sleep that was like black water, deep and bottomless. If he dreamed, he never afterward remembered it. No dream tonight of Iphikleia, nor of dancing the bulls, either. And yet, in the grey interval between sleep and waking, he remembered. He knew whose face Ariana—the Ariana—wore. He had seen her in the first dream, that dream that had brought him here, the dream of the bulldancing. She had been the maiden who danced the bull, for whom one of the youths died, because he could not bear that she should best him.

And had the youth worn Kemni's face? He did not think so. It had been a Cretan, he was sure of it. Not an Egyptian. Not Kemni nor any of his people.

He took the memory with him into daylight, full morning and the slant of sunlight across that ridiculously vast bed. Someone, a servant most likely, had opened shutters on a blue brilliance of sky.

He yawned hugely and stretched. His body ached all over, but it was a pleasant ache. Even the one below his middle, where he felt as if he had been pummeled with fists.

There was no mark on him, even there. He might have dreamed it all, except for the imprint of her body in the cushions, smaller and narrower than his own, and a faint, elusive scent that spoke of her.

He rose gingerly. All of him seemed to be where it belonged. He had not been so thoroughly pleasured since—no, not even since Gebu and a pack of lesser princes had taken him on a grand campaign through the underbelly of Thebes. He had thought himself a man of skill and wide experience. He had been a child, a babe at the breast.

He was rising to the memory of her, and gasping with it, because yes, oh gods, he ached. Chill wind off the mountaintop cooled him enough to go on with; and there on the windowledge he found a jar of watered wine and a loaf wrapped in a cloth, and a bowl of olives cured in brine.

He ate perched on the ledge, prickle-skinned with cold but glad of it. His heart had risen and begun to sing. He was not in Egypt, not at all, and yet he was glad—to be here, in this place, on this of all mornings in the world.

✢ ✢

His bright mood clung to him as he dressed and went out, determined to find the horses' field and, if it were possible, someone there to teach him what he wished to know. A god must have guided him. He wandered not too hopelessly amid the mazes of the palace, turned on a whim and found himself in a gate that opened on the tumbled hillside. It was a postern of sorts, faced away from the city. There Kemni got his bearings, took a deep breath and ventured the road that narrowed to a path, turned and twisted and wound among the hills and hollows.

And there, as he had hoped, was the herd that he had seen yesterday, grazing round the bubble of a spring. Someone was there already: a figure in well-worn leather, harnessing a pair of horses to a chariot.

It was a woman, and no mistaking it. He braced for Iphikleia's clear hard glance, but froze as the dark head lifted. It was not Iphikleia.

Ariana—the Ariana, the mistress and model for them all—laughed merrily at his expression. "Beautiful man! Are you shocked?"

"Startled," he said.

"And was she pleasing, the one I sent to you?"

He was blushing. He could not stop it; the more he tried, the hotter his face grew. "She—she was pleasing. But—"

"I can't, you know," she said, light and calm as ever. "I'm for other uses. But my servants are delighted to take my place."

"I would never expect a princess," he said, "to—to—"

"She never said you were shy," said Ariana. "Come here, beautiful man. Don't you want to learn to drive a chariot?"

Her shifts were too quick for him. He could see nothing for it but to be obedient, since after all she was the Ariana.

✢ ✢

A chariot was an odd unstable thing, rolling and shifting underfoot, lurching as the horses fretted in their traces. Ariana held the reins lightly with strength that made him stare. She was like a blade of fine bronze, slender and seeming frail, but fiercely strong.

He had no such strength, and no grace, either. He clung to the chariot's sides, rocked more strongly than on any sea. The horses were not moving swiftly, he knew that, but it felt as if he flew upon the wind.

She rocked against him, warm solidity, and somehow, in the shifting of the chariot, he found his hands full of the reins. They were a living weight, the horses tugging, that on the left markedly stronger than the right. The chariot began to veer. He tugged hard to the right. The chariot lurched side-wise, and the right-hand horse flung up its head.

Kemni gasped. Ariana laughed. "Straight on," she said. "Soft now. Light, but be firm—don't let go. Yes, yes, that's so. They'll go straight enough, if you but ask."

He had steered boats enough, balancing the oar with a mingling of strength and delicacy that had been natural to him since he was a child. This was somewhat like it. But a boat was not a live thing, though it might often feel so. Horses had minds of their own, more by far than wind or water.

It was more difficult than he had ever imagined, and yet he could feel that, with time, it might become easy. If he had such time. If the gods gave him the gift.

The horses had dropped to a walk while he struggled in the tangle of reins. That was a mercy of theirs, and he was glad of it. He found that he could steer well enough, at that slow pace. He could stop, too, and make the horses go again, with Ariana's guidance.

She stopped him then, though he would have gone on and on. "Enough," she said. "Tomorrow we go on."

She would not be shifted. Her will was as strong as that slender body of hers. Nor was she done with her instruction. The horses must be unharnessed and rubbed down, the chariot put away in what must have begun its life as a cave, but had been shaped and built and raised until it was a rather well-hidden but capacious stable and storehouse. There was much to do indeed, and when that was done, she took him with her into a palace that, somewhat to his surprise, had come alive.

Maybe it was only that he had not been taking notice. There were people everywhere, of every station, on every imaginable errand; and of course the inevitable idlers and hangers-on, loitering in comfort and pronouncing judgment on the world as it passed them by. The palace in Thebes had been much the same. The people here wore different fashions and spoke a different tongue, but they were indisputably courtiers.

Kemni, in the company of one who was a great priestess and perhaps a queen, could not but attract notice. He recognized the signs: sidelong glances, veiled murmurs. Within the hour, he had no doubt, the intrigues would begin.

People would court his favor. Factions would swirl and shift about him. He would be expected to play the game as it was played in every court of the world.

Ariana must know this. Her taking him through these most public portions of the palace could not but be a signal, and a message that courtiers could well interpret.

It had begun, he thought: the dance that he had come for. He drew a breath and straightened his shoulders, and did his best to put on a brave show. He could do no less for his king, or for Egypt.

VIII

K EMNI, WHO HAD spent his first evening all alone amid the strangeness of Crete, advanced toward his second as the new darling of the palace. So quickly a man's standing could change, when a great lord or a queen made him a favorite.

He knew. He had come to Thebes the battle-brother and protected friend of Gebu the prince. It seemed to be his fate, to ride the wake of princes.

Here, that served his purpose well, and would, he hoped, further his king's cause. He set himself to be pleasant, and to learn names and faces, as many as his head could hold. They all seemed to know who he was and why he was there. So: that was not to be a secret here. He had wondered, when he was left to his own devices, if he should lie low and take care not to be seen.

But people were frank in their questions, and remarkably well apprised of matters in Egypt. They knew of the Retenu, and of the Great House, and of the need that Egypt had for allies to win back the Two Lands from the conquerors. "They have no power on the sea," said a lord of the same age and stamp as Naukrates. "All their wars have been fought on land, with chariots. If a fleet came at them up the river, and another down it, with an army embarked on each, they might be caught in the pincers. Then Egypt would belong to its own king again."

"So my king thinks," Kemni conceded. "And yours? Would he agree?"

The lord shrugged. "Minos takes his own counsel. We can only advise."

"So it always is with kings," said Kemni.

The lord nodded, sighing a little as men did at the ways of those set above them. They parted in amity, each to go his way: the lord on some errand of his own, Kemni to explore the palace further, and to learn the ways and faces of its people. He was not brought before the king, nor did he ask to be. That would come in its time.

He dined in a hall that seemed half a garden, with a portico that opened on a green and pleasant place. Sweet airs wafted in. Revelers drifted out, then in again, in no order that he could discern. The wine was strong and sweet, the tables laden with wonderful things. Flowers bloomed in painted splendor on the walls, and in scented beauty on the tables and trailing over the portico. One was expected, Kemni saw, to crown oneself with them, and to breathe their fragrance, which held back for a while the dizziness of the wine.

In Egypt they did as much, and crowned themselves with cones of unguents mixed in fat. And as the evening went on, the fat melted in the heat of the revelry, and released its scent over the revelers' heads and shoulders. There was no such fashion here. There was no Egyptian but Kemni, no foreigner at all, only the lords and wanton ladies of Crete.

Oh, so wanton. They had no shame and no shyness, nor any fear, it seemed, of retribution. Kemni had hardly sat to eat before wicked hands crept under his kilt and closed about his manly member. They gripped just hard enough to hold him where he was, and stroked and teased until he was ready to cry aloud, then left him as wickedly as they had come, trembling violently, aching and unsatisfied.

Nor could he say a word. In Egypt women could be reckless, particularly if they were warm in wine, but there was always the looming shadow of father or brother to keep the young men honest.

Here there seemed to be no such check on them at all. As far as he could see, a man did not ask a woman for her favors, but waited for her to ask him—and when she did ask, he had little choice but to oblige her. No one seemed concerned for any woman's honor—not the men, and certainly not the women themselves.

But Kemni was not a Cretan. He extricated himself as best he might, not without a sense of tearing reluctance, and went in search of the house that had been given him.

There was someone in his bed. He could not say he was surprised—nor could he deny that he was relieved. She was not the same who had been there the night before, though very like her. She grinned at him from amid the cushions, and informed him with evident satisfaction, "I won the toss tonight. Am I not prettier than my sister?"

She was certainly pretty. Kemni wondered briefly if he should be annoyed that the sister priestesses were gambling for his favors. It was flattering, in its way, but hardly comfortable to think of.

"You are Ariana, too," he said. "Yes?"

"Of course." She bounced up out of the cushions, as bare as she was born, with her impudent little breasts and her pointed kitten-face. They did not have cats here—he had seen that. With such creatures as this priestess, he doubted that they felt the lack.

She was wilder than her sister, and wickeder, too. She did not even wait for him to be ready. She fell on him where he stood, kilt and wig and golden collar and all, and laughed as he rose suddenly and rather painfully to meet her. She was on him and he inside her, her legs wound about his middle, her breasts brushing his breast, each touch of those small hard nipples shocking him as if he petted a cat in the dry desert wind. He fancied he saw sparks between them.

All his life in Egypt, where the dry wind and the fierce heat were as perpetual as the roar of the sea was in Crete, and he had never played at love with a woman till the sparks flew. She traced his body in little tingling shocks, half pain, half pleasure. Last of all she touched lips to lips with a jolt that wrung a cry out of him, and sent the seed bursting in a hot irresistible stream.

He sank down panting, struggling not to fall. His knees had turned to water. This Ariana went down with him, still joined to him, though he was limp and shrinking inside of her. He slipped slackly free as they tumbled on the floor. Her hair trailed across his face. He gasped, and sneezed.

She rose above him, laughing. "Dear lovely man. Has anyone told you how delightful you are?"

He could not see what was delightful about his graceless sprawl on the floor, but he had never claimed to fathom a woman's mind. He lay and gasped and took what refuge he might in silence.

She swooped closer. Her long hair veiled them both. "Remember," she said. "If a woman asks, always give her what she asks for. But never try to take it from her."

"I—had suspected that," he managed to say, between struggles for breath.

"Wise man," she said approvingly. "You'll do well among us. For a stranger."

He was too weak to protest. She was rousing him again, which he would have thought impossible; but Cretan women were great masters of this branch of the magical arts. In a very little while he had no will at all, and no mind for aught but the things that she was doing to his body.

✦ ✦

The days filled quickly, with the horses, with the Arianas, with the court and the palace. Kemni did not pause to reckon the passage of time. One did not, when one waited upon kings. He saw the king once or twice from a distance, and once stood in a doorway and watched him dispense his justice. Minos was a Cretan; that was all he could really see, a middle-sized man, broad of shoulder, narrow of hip, with black hair going grey, and, rare to vanishing among these people as among Egyptians, a black and curling beard. He sat in the hall of justice beside a tiny woman, no larger than a child, but no child had ever possessed so very womanly a body. She could not but be the queen, the lady of the bulls, mother and mistress of this palace and all who dwelt in it.

Kemni was not summoned before them. He saw other embassies, bearded and robed princes of Asia, wild sea-raiders, coal-black Nubians—and one that made Kemni stare till his eyes were nigh starting out of his head. They were giants, half again as tall as a tall man in Egypt. Their skin was the color of milk, and their hair was yellow as gold; their eyes were the blue of lapis. They came, a servant said, from somewhere far to the north of the world, and their language was as barbaric as their manners.

Next to those, Kemni was utterly ordinary. And yet he was the emissary of the Great House, the son of Horus, the lord of Upper Egypt. And he was losing patience.

One night, after yet another Ariana had come and wrung him dry and gone, with some little commentary on how many of her sisters waited their turn with the man whom their mistress reckoned beautiful, Kemni raised his aching body in his bed, and struck the cushions with his fist. "Enough," he said. "Enough of this waiting. Tomorrow I speak with the king, or never speak with him at all."

There was no one to hear, unless it were the ghosts and the night spirits. But Kemni had sworn an oath to himself. He meant to keep it.

He slept deeper than he had thought to sleep, and woke later, well past dawn, with the sun slanting bright across the tumble of the bed. His breakfast was waiting as always, his clothes laid out, and no servant to be seen. One would come if he called, but he had made it clear long since that he preferred to endure his mornings alone.

There was someone waiting for him when he came out, an elegant personage who could hardly be a servant, not with that lofty manner and those golden armlets. He carried a staff of ivory topped with golden horns, cradling it as if he cherished it. As no doubt he did; for it marked him a king's messenger.

Perhaps, after all, the night spirits had heard Kemni's vow and chosen to convey it to those who might fulfill it. He greeted the messenger with courtesy, and with such grace as he had. It fell short of perfection: the man's lip curled ever so slightly.

Kemni shrugged, making no effort to hide it. He was a fighting man and a prince's friend, not a great lord. Such as he was, he was. His king had judged him fit for this errand. It was for the king of Crete to make a like judgment; not for this underling. For that, however haughty his bearing, he was.

The messenger sniffed audibly. "You are summoned," he said baldly, without embellishment, "to the king's presence."

Kemni nodded. "Lead me," he said with equal simplicity.

✛ ✛

Even so early, the king was about his duties, seated in the hall of justice. That hall, for this palace, was almost small, on a throne made of the great curving horns of bulls. Its seat was woven of their hides and spread with their skins, red and white and black, spotted and pied and subtly brindled. Another was set beside it, and the queen sitting in it, that child-small woman with skin like cream and beautiful rich breasts, and hips as broad as her waist was tiny. She was not young, but that mattered little. Her beauty was of a sort which would never fade, merely grow finer as she grew old.

He could see Ariana in her, in the wide bright eyes and the delicate features. She smiled at him with warmth that he had never looked for in a queen. He blinked, dazzled.

It came to him, rather slowly, that he had come here to speak with the king, not to gape at the queen. The king did not seem disturbed by the lapse. He was smiling slightly, neither as warm nor as welcoming as his queen, but amiable enough, as kings went. He rose, which was a great honor. One of the servants who stood about, the inevitable attendance of kings, hastened to fetch a chair. It was lower than the king's, Kemni noticed, but not so very much lower. He was being accorded great honor.

He acknowledged it with an inclination of the head. Here, after all, he was not merely Kemni the commander of a hundred; he was the voice of Egypt in this foreign kingdom.

When he had sat and been given wine in a golden cup shaped like the head and horns of a bull, he sipped the rich sweet vintage and waited for the king to speak. As he waited, he took in the room in quick glances. It was a high and airy place for all its smallness, the walls painted with images of sea and sky. Except for the two royal seats and his own carved chair, there were no furnishings, only a bank of lamps and a painted image: one of the mother goddesses that he had seen throughout the palace. They all looked like ladies of the court, dressed in the height of fashion, their waists cinched tight with golden girdles, their faces painted with white and rose, carnelian and malachite. And they all wielded the serpents that were sacred here as in Egypt, brandishing them like living swords.

The goddess in this hall of private audience wore a skirt embroidered with gold and silver, and a vest studded with jewels. Her smile was sweetly serene, her serpents seeming almost to hiss, so lifelike had the sculptor made them. Her face was Ariana's face, and the face of the queen. But then, they were the living goddess. That much Kemni had come to understand.

The king spoke as Kemni's eyes rested on the goddess' image. He spoke of small things: greeting, welcome, inquiry as to Kemni's comfort in his palace. Kemni answered as one does in courts, with patience hard learned, and suitable inconsequentiality. It was a dance, each step prescribed, a graceful circle that came round, at last and at the king's whim, to the purpose for which Kemni had been sent here.

He tried not to look relieved when the king shifted the conversation to Egypt and its bearded invaders. Often in this dance of courts, it might be days before a king came to the point. This king of Crete was almost precipitous; and well for Kemni's peace of mind that it was so.

"My captain and my sister's daughter tell me," said Minos, "that the north of Egypt grows restless under the Retenu."

"It would seem so," Kemni said: with a spark of interest that Iphikleia was, it seemed, of higher rank and family than he had thought. "The south—Upper Egypt—feels a turning of the tide. But not enough. We can muster armies, and more if the lords of Lower Egypt will join with us, but the Retenu are strong. And they have chariots."

"It might serve you to muster your own force of chariotry," Minos said.

Kemni nodded. "Yes. Yes, I had been thinking the same. But if we're to acquire herds of horses and asses to pull them, or train men to drive them, we need time. More time than any king is minded to spare. I suppose a few of the northern lords may have taken up the art; we can search and find them, and try to win them over to us. But to win this war, my king believes that we need something the enemy doesn't have."

"Ships." Minos sat back stroking his rich curled beard. "Tell me what you could do with ships. You can't fight a sea battle with men in chariots. There's no reasonable way to spirit your armies to the sea, where our ships could take them on and sail up the river into your enemy's cities."

"But," said Kemni, "if we brought our armies down the river in our own boats, and you sailed up it with your fighting ships, we could crush the enemy between us."

"That is supposing that the enemy would sit still to be crushed," Minos said.

"He is sure of his supremacy," Kemni said. "And he has no fleet."

Minos frowned. "It would be a great undertaking. We would have to fight our way through the Delta. Memphis would be too far, too hard to win. Avaris . . ."

"Avaris is the king's own place, and the heart of his kingdom. If we took that, we would have Lower Egypt."

"So easy? So simple?"

"We did it before, half a score of years ago. But we lost it, because we had to defend our backs. This time we are prepared for that. And, lord king, consider. For all his power, the enemy is few. He rules with his chariots and with the force of his weapons. Cut off his head, the city and its king, and cut open its belly—its bond to Asia—and the rest will wither and fall away. Even those who won't fight for us against the Retenu would rise up with good will and help to destroy their remnants."

"You hope for a great deal," said Minos. "Much relies on fate, and on the element of surprise. Apophis may not believe when he hears of twin fleets sailing against him—but if that disbelief passes too quickly, we could lose the war."

"Victory is never absolutely certain."

"Indeed." Minos regarded Kemni with a level dark stare. Just then, and vividly, Kemni saw Ariana in him. "Tell us what we stand to gain from this. What Egypt gains is obvious. Why should Crete shed its blood for Egypt's sake?"

Kemni did not answer that at once. He needed to find the words, and then to frame them with care, so that this king would hear and understand. He had not been having great difficulty with this language—Naukrates and Iphikleia had taught him well—but he had to be certain that the words he chose were the right and proper ones.

At length he said, "Egypt gains more. That I cannot argue. But for Crete, there is the friendship of the reunited kingdoms, and the wealth, and the great power that Egypt holds. My king is prepared to offer you portions of his own tribute, shares in his mines of gold and copper and precious silver, and a part of his trade with the nations of the world. Crete has great power on the sea, riches and strength that all the world knows—but Egypt has more, on land and on the water. My king offers you a part of that."

"Tempting," Minos conceded. "Very tempting indeed. Still, gold may be poor payment for the lives of all our young men."

"That is a risk you take," Kemni said. Probably he should not have said it, but he never had been able to prevaricate.

"So," said Minos. "Go now, and take your pleasure as you will. I make you free of the palace and the kingdom. Whatever you ask, it shall be given you. I have so commanded it."

As dismissals went, it was thorough and strikingly gracious. Even if Kemni could have mustered arguments against it, he was not inclined to try. He bowed as if to a great prince of Egypt—though not quite as to his king—and did as he was bidden.

················ IX ················

AN ENVOY'S TASK was to wait, even more than to speak for his king. Kemni waited, he thought, with reasonable patience. He played as he had before, danced the dance of courts, and took the freedom of the island. Everything was as it had been, but the king's word eased his way remarkably. All doors were open to him, and people gave him anything that he asked. If there was a delicacy he favored, it was given him without his asking. He had his mornings with the chariot, and his nights with what seemed an inexhaustible succession of Arianas. In between, he found ample to amuse himself, if he was minded to be amused.

The thing that Naukrates had come back for, the great festival of the Bull, came at the time of the new moon. Perhaps preparations had been in train since Kemni arrived, but he had not known to look for them. But there was no escaping the sudden inrush of people into city and palace, the gathering of ships in the harbor, and the burgeoning of the market to fill, it seemed, every square and corner of the city.

Three days before the festival, they brought in the bulls. Priests and priestesses had gone out days since, found the herds where they wandered amid the tumbled hills and crags of inland Crete, and called on the gods and on the Mother Goddess to choose the best and the most holy. Those, they had separated from the herds, brought together and driven down toward the sea.

People had been waiting for them since before dawn. The way that they ran was old, and had been hallowed to the bulls since the first king sat his throne in Crete. All along it, people waited, dressed in festival finery, with garlands and banners, music and song and the sound of laughter that seemed, more than any other, the truest music of this kingdom.

Kemni came down into the city in a great crowd of the younger courtiers. They had insisted that he keep them company—for luck, they said laughing, because he was a foreigner and a king's messenger, and the gods would bless them for his presence. He had his doubts of the gods' care for his mere and mortal self, but he was eager to see the bulls. He was glad enough to be led and danced and cajoled out of the palace and toward the city, and thence to the far side, where a steep and winding road made its way down from a rocky height. It seemed rather too narrow and ill trodden to support the coming of the great bulls of Crete, but everyone was waiting along it, and fully expecting the bulls to appear.

His companions vanquished a flock of rival lordlings to seize a coveted place: where the road began to level, just before it entered the outskirts of the city. The city wall was farther on. Here were little fields and farmsteads, taking advantage of what tillable ground there was. They were set well to either side of the narrow road, with ample room for crowds to gather—and for the bulls to run.

Kemni had seen on the way there, how wise people kept to the roofs and balconies of the houses. But here there was no high ground. They were all level with the road, and Kemni was in the front, thrust there in the passage through the throng.

He wondered, briefly and unbecomingly, if this might not be a plot: to dispose of the Egyptian king's emissary at the horns and hooves of the sacred bulls, and so free King Minos from the need to consider his proposal. But that was not like anything Kemni had heard of Minos. The Cretan king was a wise man, and just, and as honest as a king could afford to be.

It seemed a long time before Kemni felt a shaking underfoot. He thought little of it at first, until the hum of conversation faded, and silence spread in a long wave through the gathering of people.

Now he could hear it: a low rumbling, and a sharp cry that must be one of the drovers urging the bulls onward. With breathtaking suddenness after so long a wait, the first great shape breasted the hill. Its horns were vast, nigh as long as a man. Its hump loomed against the sky. It plunged down the slope, a white bull patched with red, like foam shot with blood. Its brothers thundered in its wake.

Any man of sense would have stayed well back from the herd, and let it pass unhindered. But there were fools in every crowd, and sacred idiots. These were young men, and sometimes a slim bare-breasted girl, running alongside the bulls, leaping to touch their sweating sides, to tug at their tufted tails. When one touched a bull, he cried out—or she: "Gods' blessing! Gods' blessing on all my kin!"

Kemni was not a fool. He was not mad. He was not even Cretan. And yet, as the leader of the bulls passed him in a great pounding of hooves, in snorting and in the strong musky reek of his hide, Kemni was running, running like a mad thing, light as air and too utterly terrified to stop.

The bulls took as little notice of him as they had of anyone else. And yet those horns were as sharp as spears, and those hooves could trample a man to a bloody pulp. All he needed was to slip, or to misjudge his step.

Still he ran. The first of the bulls had passed him. He was in the middle, and in their midst, running between two great snorting beasts, one spotted with red, one with black. The wind of their passage bore him up. He could run, he thought, forever, sustained by the strength of the bulls.

He reached out easily, because it seemed to be time. His hand brushed a hot damp hide. The bull did not flinch or shift away. He let his hand rest there, running light, running easy. He said nothing. The gods' blessing lay on him like the sun's warmth.

It came to him, distantly, that he was trapped, surrounded by bulls. While he ran with them, he was safe enough. If he flagged or faltered, they would not stop for him, nor move aside.

He must run, then, and trust in the gods to protect him. They had brought him here. They could keep him safe.

He had passed into the city, through the gate with its echoes and its sudden dimness. The throngs were thicker here, hanging from roofs and balustrades, sometimes dropping among the bulls, and always leaping to touch, or to run with them.

But only Kemni had run so far, or stayed with the bulls so long. The walls of houses closed in, then drew away again: a square of the city, narrowed and thick with people, but the sky was wider overhead.

His breath sobbed in his throat. His lungs were afire. His knees dared not buckle.

A new madness struck him, a thought that he almost feared to think. But it pricked at him. It tempted him. His eye slid toward the great ivory sweep of a horn, and toward the swell of a hump. This was not a horse—there was no level place to rest.

Iphikleia had done it. She had chosen a gentle heifer. This was a wild bull. And yet . . .

Just as he had entered the herd, he watched his hand reach out, grasp a horn, let the force of the bull's advance swing him onto the neck behind the heavy head. There was room there, just, between hump and horns, a place to rest if one were truly mad.

And so he rode the whole long way from the city to the palace of Minos on the neck of a black-spotted bull, no more or less unwelcome than a bird perched on that vast swell of back. People stared, he supposed. He did not try to see.

Then at long last the world went still. The bull stood, sides heaving, in a wide court.

Kemni slid from his neck, staggering as his legs found their strength again. The bulls were not all motionless. Some fretted, tossing their horns, stamping, uneasy to be confined within walls.

He walked away from them unscathed. There were people, of course there were. He did not want them to stare so, or to murmur; only to let him pass, find a quiet place and collapse and find his breath where he had long since lost it.

But that grace was not granted him. He had committed sacrilege, he supposed. Could they put to death a foreign king's envoy?

The eyes on him, once he gathered his wits to notice, did not seem appalled. They were more—speculative? Curious? Amazed?

Some of them he recognized. Iphikleia, of course. Ariana—the Ariana, and an escort of bright-eyed wicked girls whose faces he remembered rather well. Kemni did not forget a face, particularly if it had hovered close to his through the whole of a night.

Ariana looked him up and down. "Beautiful man," she said, "you do know how to make an entrance."

"I suppose I'll die for it," he said.

"No," she said. "If the bulls chose to let you live, it's not for any human creature to question."

Kemni felt the breath rush out of him, and most of his strength with it. Firm small hands held him up: Iphikleia, no more gentle than she ever was, but blessedly there. She kept him from shaming himself. She knew; she had done it herself. "Go and rest," she said. "When you wake up, maybe you'll be sane again."

"I'm sane now," he said. "Whatever I did—the gods—"

"The gods, yes," she said. "Now go." She sent two of the Arianas with him, "And not to keep you awake, either. Mind you sleep. Do you understand?"

"Perfectly, great lady," he said.

She made a sound of disgust. "Oh, go. Go!"

✦ ✦

Iphikleia was as salubrious as a dash of cold water in the face. But she had commanded that he sleep, and sleep he did; nor would the Arianas suffer him to dally with them before he slept. They bathed him—teasing him unmercifully—and dried him and tucked him in bed, and left him there, already more than half asleep; though his manly parts would gladly have roused the whole of him to quite another occupation.

He dreamed of bulls, a great heaving herd of them. Bulls running. Bulls grazing. Bulls mating, mounting the smaller, gentler cows, driving home their seed, dropping sated to the trampled grass. He dreamed that he was a bull; that he courted a fine speckled cow; that she ignored him, but the way of her disregard invited him to pursue her.

It was a hotter passion than men knew, and swifter. A man could linger, could draw out the pleasure. A bull knew no such thing. Once he had mounted, the rest was irresistible: thrust and thrust, and the burst of it, all at once, with force that emptied him of thought or will or self. There was nothing in the world but this. There could be nothing, nor ever would be.

+ +

He woke with a start. The light was all wrong, the shadows twisted. Somewhere amid confusion, he found memory.

It was evening, the sun not yet down but near to it. He had slept much of the day away. His body ached: his legs in particular, but his nether parts, too. He had joined in wild passion with the coverlets.

He rose stiffly, cleansed himself and dressed, and reflected that, come morning, he should ask the servants to shave him. But he would do, for a while longer.

He peered at himself in the disk of polished bronze that lay on a table near the bed. He never did that; he trusted servants to keep him looking presentable, and women's eyes to assure him that he looked well enough for the purpose. This evening he had an odd desire to be certain that the face he wore was his own; that he had not grown the horns and muzzle of a bull.

It was much the same face he had last seen reflected in bronze. There was nothing remarkable about it. It was Egyptian: narrow, long-nosed, full-lipped. His eyes were long and dark, painted with kohl and malachite against a sun that did not shine here; but habit was strong, and fashion inescapable.

After so long in Crete, looking at rounder, softer faces, and seeing every man and woman with a waist-long curly mane, this crop-headed, sharp-featured face was strange. He did not see the beauty in it that all the women claimed to see. There were handsomer faces in Egypt, and great beauty among the women.

But he was content with it. It was his face, and not the bull's head that he had half feared to see. With a sigh and a shake of the head, he went in search of a congenial dinner.

+ +

Kemni's place in the palace had not changed because he had ridden the bull. He was still the stranger, interesting because he was foreign, and fashionable because he had the Ariana's favor. The bull only proved what they had all been saying: that Kemeni the Egyptian was anything but a dull guest.

Kemni the Egyptian, doomed to be fascinating, attended the bulldancing as the Ariana's guest. She had sent her servant for him—a man, somewhat to his disappointment, but perhaps that was as well. He did not need distraction before that of all festivals in Crete.

He had dressed in his best, as if he went before the king; and after all, it was a god he honored, the great Bull who was the image and servant of the Earthshaker. In wig and kilt and gold of honor, he followed his guide through the mazes of the palace, to a part of it that he had not seen before.

Except in dreams. This was the court in which he had sat so often in the spirit, the court of the Bull: great open space, and ranks of benches ascending in tiers, and below them, clean white sand, raked level, waiting for the dancers. He sat where his eyes had been in the dream, just above the sand, with the wall below and the crowds of lesser watchers above. His seat was softened with cushions, his head canopied against the sun. Great lords and princes sat about him.

But not the king. The king sat across the court under his own golden canopy, with his queen beside him. There were older lords, ladies in jeweled skirts and tall headdresses, and servants with fans and sunshades and jars of wine and platters of sweets. Here on Ariana's side were the younger folk, the priestesses, the lords' sons and younger brothers, warm already with wine, and passing round a gluttonous array of sweets and spiced cakes.

Kemni could not eat or drink. Since he came into this court, he had felt odd, as if one or more of his souls had wandered apart from his body.

Ariana was not there. Another priestess sat in the tall chair of ivory inlaid with gold. It was, Kemni realized with a shock, Iphikleia. She was clad as if she had been a goddess, even to the serpents wound about her arms. Kemni thought them the work of hands, until one of them stirred and lifted its head, questing toward him with a flickering tongue.

He sat still on his scarlet cushion. The rite had begun below: the mournful cry of horns made of great shells of the sea, and a processional of priests—men, for Earthshaker was a men's god, though both men and women honored him in the dance. They wore the horns and hides of bulls, and came as bulls would come, stepping slowly, stamping, snorting, pawing the sand. Behind them came the dancers, slender youths and maidens in kilts wound and belted tight. These laughed as they passed into the court, spun and wheeled, leaped and somersaulted, like acrobats in a market in Egypt.

There was a wild joy in their coming, a gladness that Kemni understood: he had felt it when he ran with the bulls. Today one of them, or more, might die. Or they all might live, conquer the bull and honor the god.

Three by three they leaped and danced and whirled about the court, and three by three they paused, first to salute the priestess, and second to salute the king. With prayers and chanting and moaning of horns the priests blessed them; and then, abruptly, they were gone. The court was empty. Servants ran to rake the tumbled sand, to smooth it once more, as if no foot had ever sullied it.

The court stilled. All the hum and babble of gathered people, the ripple of laughter, eruptions of song, fell silent. Everyone, it seemed, drew breath together, and held it.

A drum began to beat. Pipes skirled. Horns sang their moaning song. The bull came.

Kemni knew him. He was the pied bull who had carried Kemni into the palace. He seemed even vaster in that court, and far more deadly, as he loomed in his gate.

The dancers' gate faced his, opening beneath the priestess' seat. For a while Kemni could not see them, though he knew they had come out: the crowd had drawn taut, and the eyes of those on the far side were fixed below him. The bull saw them. His head lowered. His ears flicked. He pawed the sand.

With sudden motion, all three of the dancers leaped into the center of the court. Kemni had not known that he was holding his breath. But they were not the dancers of his dream. These were two maidens and a youth, somewhat pale even at this distance, and intent on their dancing. First they tempted and tormented the bull, to lure him out of his gate. And when he had come, slowly, dubiously perhaps, they began the dance proper, the leap and spin and somersault over those long curved horns.

The bull was placid as bulls went, as Kemni had discovered when he rode it into the palace. It seemed almost to indulge the dancers; to spin and circle and gallop massively from end to end of the court, with dancers leaping weightlessly over and about it. There was a kind of beauty in it, an ease and almost safety that might have pleased the dancers, but the crowd was growing restless. When the bull had circled thrice, the dancers joined forces to drive it through its gate. It went as if it had been a tame thing.

The dancers took their bows and the less than avid approval of the crowd, and whirled and leaped and tumbled out. Again the servants came out to rake and smooth the sand. Again there was that breathless waiting: the sun beating down, the crowd breathing as one, the bull coming forth and the dancers coming to meet him.

Seven times they danced the bull in that court, seven sets of dancers, seven bulls for the honor of the Earthshaker. For Kemni who knew none of the finer points of the art, it grew monotonous. Some dancers won more approval than others: most often, he thought, because the bull was wilder, his will more malevolent. For some of the bulls, as with the first, this seemed almost a game, a thing they did for the amusement of it. But for others, this was battle. The dancers, tiny leaping things, were like gnats: annoying, then irritating, then maddening.

At last, when the sixth dance was done, Kemni gathered wits to ask one of his many questions. He addressed it to the priestess beside him, but Iphikleia answered from her throne, where she had sat unmoving through all that long burning morning. "The bull's anger makes the dance more deadly. Earthshaker cherishes it the more for that. And if there is bloodshed . . ."

Kemni nodded. "Then if the bull is placid, Earthshaker withholds his blessing?"

"No," said Iphikleia. "The dance is always holy, and always blessed. Blood makes it stronger, that's all."

There had been blood already: a dancer in the third dance had caught herself on a horn and so pierced her hand. But she had spun free and her fellows had diverted the bull, and she had continued the dance, leaving a bright trail in the white sand. All the others had escaped unharmed. They were not, it was clear, expected or even asked to sacrifice their lives to the god.

The last dance began just as the sun reached its zenith. The court throbbed with heat. It was warm enough even for Kemni, as warm as Egypt. For the first time since he had sailed past the Delta, he was not shivering with perpetual cold.

There was a difference in this dance. The drums and horns seemed louder. Voices joined them, a deep, slow chant like the surge and swell of the sea. It was Earthshaker's hymn, invocation and blessing, and a promise that here, at the end of the dance, he would find his greatest favor.

Kemni had forgotten to breathe again. The light, the heat. The stillness of the gathered people, the great circle of faces rising up the sides of the court.

With the inevitability of a dream, the bull came out from beneath his gate: a great bull, speckled white and red like seafoam flecked with blood. And the dancers when they came, two youths, a maiden laughing, wild and eerie-sweet.

Kemni the dreamer had not known her. Kemni the waking spirit, king's emissary to Crete, knew her well indeed. The Ariana danced below him, danced for the honor of the god, dared death to win his blessing for her people.

In his dream she had lived, but one of her fellows had died. Kemni could not move to cry warning, though every step unfolded as he had seen it while he slept, far away in Egypt.

This was not why he had come—to save the life of a boy who had consecrated himself to a god. And yet this had brought him here. This had marked him from all who might perhaps better have gone on his king's errand.

He could only watch, barely breathing, as the dance played itself out under the pitiless sun. A god could not be gainsaid, nor his sacrifice denied. No matter how a mortal might dread it, and yearn to stop it.

The boy was one whom he had seen here and there about court and palace. They might have shared a banquet together, or gone in company on an expedition to the city. Kemni did not remember his name. There were so many like him among the youth of the court.

He danced well, but without wisdom. Ariana seemed to care little for danger or death. And yet her skill was great, her control remarkable. People murmured at it, marveling—how close she came to those terrible horns, and

how effortlessly she evaded them. Her taller partner was nearly as skilled—
Kemni could see that, after six full dances. The smaller boy had not danced
before, someone behind Kemni whispered to someone else. He danced well,
but he took risks he should not have taken. He should have left them to the
others, hung back somewhat, protected himself with caution.

But caution was seldom a young man's virtue. And Ariana taunted him
with her art. She leaped when the bull was nearly upon her, leaped and whirled
and came lightly to rest on the shoulders of the taller dancer. The bull plunged
onward. He was one of the great ones, the ones made mighty with a terrible
anger. The curve of his hump was like the swell of the sea. His hooves thundered like the crash of waves on the shore.

The boy flung himself as if into the sea, and like the sea, the bull took him
and broke him and cast him up on the sand.

In the dream Kemni had awakened as the boy died. But this was no dream.
He saw the body fallen, the slow seep of blood, the deep and terrible silence.

It shattered. It burst in a vast wave of sound, a roar from every throat in
that place: men, women, even the bull. But Kemni was silent. He owed no
loyalty to Earthshaker. His gods were of another place and kind.

The sacrifice was made, the victim carried away in great honor. Those who
had watched him die left the court in quiet that partook a little of grief, but
much more of exaltation.

·············· X ··············

THE DAY AFTER the dancing of the bulls, Kemni was summoned again
into the king's presence. It was a day of quiet after the great festival,
a day as it were of atonement, of mourning for the one who had died,
and invoking the gods and the great goddess to bless the land and
people of Crete.

Earthshaker had blessed them that morning, as the people thought of it.
Kemni had just risen, and was reaching for the jar of water lightly sweetened
with wine, when the earth heaved and shifted underfoot. The jar began to
topple. He snatched it, too startled yet to be afraid.

The earth had moved. He shook his head, sure that he had dreamed it;
but the spatter of spilled wine belied him.

It was true, then. In this country, on this island in the sea, the earth itself
could shift and stir as if it had been water.

The Cretans had taken it as an omen. Earthshaker was pleased with his

sacrifice. Kemni, more shaken than at first he knew, obeyed the king's summons without reflection, and with little expectation of what he might hear
or say.

✦ ✦

King Minos received him this day, not in any hall of audience, but in the court
of the bulls. Kemni hesitated at the entrance to which his guide had brought
him, blinking at the blaze of sun on sand. No blood sullied it now. All that
had been taken away when the sacrifice was done.

The king sat at ease and in little state, on a bench that, the day before,
had seated a common man of Crete. A single guard attended him. There was
no other escort, no witness but the servant who had guided Kemni to this
place.

Kemni had learned long ago not to question the whims of kings. Therefore
he was not astonished to be received with such lack of ceremony. But the
place—he could not burst out with the question, however strong the temptation.

The king knew. His eye glinted as he said, "Come, man of Egypt. Sit. I
trust it's warm enough for you here?"

"It is very pleasant," Kemni said. The king seemed comfortable enough
himself, though his brow gleamed with sweat.

Kemni sat on the bench just below the king. Minos gazed out over the
sand. "You dreamed the dance," he said. "Did it happen as you remember?"

"Exactly," Kemni said. "I couldn't—if I could have stopped it—"

"No one should ever try to stop what the gods have ordained." Minos
spoke mildly, but his voice held the hint of a growl.

Kemni bent his head.

"Earthshaker chose you," Minos said. "And Earth Mother—she blessed
you. It seems they see some profit for us in this venture your king proposes."

"Perhaps," said Kemni, a little unwisely, "they believe that Egypt and
Crete together will be a great power in the world."

"Perhaps," the king said. "And is it insult or great gift that your king sees
no threat in us? We could conquer you once we drove out the conquerors."

"You might try," Kemni said.

The king laughed, startling him. "Ah! Well and swiftly countered. Yes, we
might try, but for what? We have no great yearning to rule a people who
despise us. And your river—it is very great, no one denies it, but never as great
as the sea."

"We cherish our river," Kemni said, "and admire your sea."

The king smiled. "So. We are safe from one another. Will you pay a price
for our aid in your war?"

"Only ask," Kemni said, "and if I can't grant it, I can take it back to my
king, and he will decide."

"You must grant it now," said Minos. "Here, where the gods have brought you."

Kemni had not felt alone or terribly far from Egypt in some considerable while. It had been a kind of mute endurance, and a refusal to fall prey to the sickness that could fell a man far from home.

But now he felt it, in this court, in this audience that had nothing of formality about it, and yet was everything to his embassy. Thebes lay at the other end of the earth. Any choice that Kemni made, he made alone, with the whole fate of Egypt resting on it.

Minos knew that. He might wish Kemni to end his embassy now, to confess that he lacked the power or the will to speak for his king. Kemni was young, with little wisdom and less skill in the arts of princes. Perhaps his presence was an insult—gods, dreams, and all.

He must not waver. He must trust to the gods who had brought him here, and to the indulgence of his own king, that whatever bargain he struck, Ahmose would honor it.

"Tell me your price," he said levelly.

Minos might be amused. He was not struck dumb with admiration, Kemni could see that. He stroked his beard as he seemed to like to do when he would draw out a moment. "This is not my price," he said after a while. "You should know that. I am king in Crete, but there are others higher than I. They ask this of Egypt, if Egypt is to have our aid in its war."

Who asks? Kemni almost asked aloud. *Your gods?* But he was silent.

"You are asked," said Minos, "to confirm this alliance with blood as well as gold. To make a marriage, man of Egypt, between your king and a royal daughter of Crete. Will he do that? Can he do it?"

For a long moment Kemni could not answer, nor think of an answer. He had been envisioning terrible prices: mountains of gold, armies of hostages, blood of princes poured out in the court of the bulls. But this—he almost laughed aloud.

"Lord king," he said, "royal marriages are a frequent consummation of great alliances. If that is all the price you ask, my king will pay it gladly."

"Ah," said Minos, "but will he pay it as we ask him to pay? This will be no concubine, no last or least of a flock of wives. If he takes to wife one of our royal ladies, she must be a queen. She will accept no lesser rank."

That was perhaps difficult. But still, not impossible. Unless . . . "She cannot be the first of the queens, the Great Royal Wife. That office belongs to a lady of Egypt."

"Queen Nefertari," said Minos. Which proved that he knew sufficient of Egypt and its rulers, and could pronounce that great lady's name with a reasonable accent, too. "Yes, we know of her. Our lady will not ask to displace her. But to be second to her—that, she will expect. Will your king allow it? Will his Great Royal Wife?"

"That truly is a choice that they should make," Kemni said.

"We ask you to make it for them."

Minos was not going to yield in this. That was all too clear. If Kemni agreed, he might face the wrath of his king—but worse by far, that of the Great Royal Wife.

He had seen Queen Nefertari, of course; she sat beside her husband, who was also her brother, in court and at festivals, and shared in the ruling of the Upper Kingdom. But he had never spoken to her, nor had she singled him out for her attention. She took little notice of the crowd of young men about the princes.

Now he feared, if he chose wrongly, she would fix him with the terrible and burning sun of her regard. Stronger men than he had withered in it, and even, people whispered, died of it.

He had a sudden, vivid recollection of her face as he had seen it once, caught in the lamplight of a banquet, in an expression as close to unguarded as a queen might ever permit herself. She had been a little weary, perhaps a little ill. In the distraction of a troupe of firedancers, she had let her head droop somewhat, and rested her cheek on her palm. She was beautiful as royal ladies were expected to be, in the perfection of paint and wig, gown and jewels, that befit a queen. And yet, in that moment, she seemed almost mortal.

The memory did not comfort him. Queen Nefertari was a great force in Egypt, some said greater than the king—whispered, even, that Ahmose wore the crown, but Nefertari ruled the kingdom.

Whatever Kemni agreed to now, she would judge. This more than any was a woman's matter: the bringing of a rival queen into the palace over which she ruled.

Nevertheless, her lord—and therefore, Kemni realized with a small, chill shock, she herself—had sent him here. He had been given the power of an envoy, and the discretion to make such bargains as he might. They should have sent a wiser man, or one more fit to decide such matters. But they had not. He was all they had.

He drew a breath, steadying himself. "Very well," he said. "I speak for my king, and for my king's Great Wife. I accept that price for your aid in our war."

Minos inclined his head. Kemni could not tell whether he was relieved or dismayed. "Then it is done. My clerks will write it as it should be written, and those will witness it who properly should. In the morning on the third day from now, you sail for Egypt."

So sudden. So complete. Kemni should have expected it, and yet it took him by surprise. He had come to think that he would live out his life in this foreign country, speaking a language not his own, even coming to forget the accents and the cadences of his native Egyptian. Foolish, but he did not have to be wise just now; only obedient. He bowed to the king as to a lord of Egypt, and accepted his dismissal with suitable grace.

But before Kemni took his leave, Minos raised a hand. "Wait," he said.

Kemni paused.

"Come to dinner tonight," Minos said. "A servant will fetch you when it's time."

Kemni bowed again. This was an honor, but no less than he deserved. He was allowed to leave then, to claim the day for himself—to cherish the knowledge that, in three days' time, he would be sailing back to Egypt.

✢ ✢

Kemni dined with the king that night, and with the queen, and with the great ones of the court. But Ariana was not there, nor was Iphikleia. Kemni did not know why he should care that either was absent. Nor, after he had been so honored, did any new Ariana come to his bed. For the first time since he had arrived in Crete, he slept alone. He wondered if he was being punished for some infraction. Perhaps for failing to appear for his morning in the chariot, because he had been summoned to the king instead? Surely Ariana had known of that. Ariana appeared to know everything that passed in the palace.

Somewhat out of pique, but also because he was expected in the clerks' court for the signing and witnessing of the agreement between Egypt and Crete, Kemni did not go the next morning, either. And again he slept alone, without message or explanation.

The next morning, the morning before he was to take ship for Egypt, he went out as he had so often. He did not expect to find anyone in the horses' field, not by then. But he wanted to see the horses one last time. He had brought a packet of honey sweets for the pair of bays, who had learned long since to come to him for their tribute. He had grown fond of them.

They were waiting for him as he came up the path into the field, with an air of having waited excessively long. He laughed through a startling catch of tears, rubbed their ears and noses, and fed them the sweets that he had brought. Not until his palms were empty and licked clean did he see who sat beyond them, perched on a jut of stone, knees clasped to leather-tunicked chest.

She had not brought out the chariot, though she was dressed to drive it. Nor did she greet him, or seem to see him at all, until he set himself in front of her. "Good morning," he said civilly.

She regarded him almost without recognition. He had never seen her so remote. Even Iphikleia was warmer toward him than this—and this was Ariana, his bright companion and his instructor in the art of chariotry.

Maybe it was the bulldancing that had done it, the death of the boy who had tried to be as reckless as she. Kemni did not flatter himself that she grieved for his departure. He was a diversion, no more. When he was gone, she would find another.

He told her so, with boldness that he hoped would make her smile.

She frowned as if he had spoken in Egyptian, which she knew nothing of. "Diversion? Another? Why would I want to do that?"

"To amuse you," he said. "To give you pleasure."

"Ah," she said, and slid into her reverie again.

He wondered if he dared shake her. But she had already made it clear that a man did not touch her—not without her leave. He settled for a shrug, an audible sigh, withdrawal in the horses' company. They were glad enough that he was there, and they acknowledged his existence, too. They were, at the moment, better companions than Ariana.

When he came back from visiting the whole of the herd, she was gone. She had never explained the oddity of her mood, nor had she waited to say goodbye. He told himself that he should not be disappointed. She was a princess and a great priestess. It had been more than he ever dared expect, that she had given him so much of herself. Now, as he had said to her, she would go on. She would find herself another occupation to while away her mornings. Or maybe it would be enough that she drove her chariot alone, racing the wind in that high green pasture.

The rest of his farewells were easier, perhaps because that one had been so unexpectedly difficult. He would not be sorry to go, because he was going home. But he had been happier here than he would ever have expected, more at ease and more—yes, more at home. He was proud of that.

⁂

One more lonely night, sleeping fitfully in a bed that seemed suddenly strange, and then, at last, it was time. A fair dawn, a brisk wind blowing southward to carry him home. His few belongings were packed and taken away to the ship. He put on his best clothes, his gold of honor, and the blue mantle that had been given as a gift, to keep him warm against the chill of the morning.

He had come in with little attendance but great honor, with Ariana as his guide. He left in a surprising crowd. Most were faces he knew, people he had dined with, drunk with, hunted and played and danced with. They were his guides and his companions on the long steep way to the harbor. They sang; they played on drums and pipes and the stringed instrument that they called the lyre. They gave him a royal leavetaking.

The ship was waiting for him—familiar, faded yet strong beneath: Naukrates' swift *Dancer*. Kemni caught himself grinning at the sight of her. And yes, there was the captain himself on the deck, regarding the crowd with lifted brow. When his eye caught Kemni, it brightened. Glad, no doubt, that at last his ship could catch the tide.

But they were not to leave quite yet. As Kemni boarded the ship, a further disturbance brought him about. An even greater crowd was coming, with even more noise. People were blowing the sea-horns, long moaning cries, and singing, and clapping their hands. They danced as they came, tumbling like bull-dancers, wheeling and spinning, dizzying the eye.

Kemni had never seen such a procession. Everyone in it seemed to be a bulldancer or a priestess, or both. He half expected to see a bull among them, but the god's great servants were safe in their high pastures now that they had performed their office.

The center of that uproar was resplendent in gold, aglitter with precious stones. She came in the wealth of a kingdom, high-crowned with gold, stepping lightly, delicately down to the water. So brilliant was she, and so potent in her presence, that one almost failed to see who rode behind her in gilded chairs borne on the shoulders of strong young men: the king and the queen themselves, come to bid farewell.

But not, or not only, to Kemni. Ariana, and Iphikleia all but unnoticed in her shadow, boarded the ship with the air of one who did a great and courageous thing, and who wished that everyone would stop remarking on it.

The king and the queen stayed on the shore. Kemni was still not certain what was happening, though he knew he should have been. Ariana was sailing on the *Dancer*. That much he could see. She must be going on a pilgrimage.

She was even more abstracted than she had been in the horses' field. Kemni might almost have thought that she was drugged. Her face was white, her eyes all but blind.

And yet, as she mounted to the deck, with Naukrates reaching to lift her up, and Iphikleia supporting her from behind, she came alive. She looked down at the people on the shore, and round about at those on the ship. She shuddered just visibly, or shook herself. The life flooded back into her face. She held out her arms, then spread them wide.

The people cried aloud. There were words in it, mingled almost out of comprehension. But from them Kemni gained a sort of meaning.

Indeed, she was going away. She was going to Egypt. She was going—

He could not speak here. Not now. He bit his tongue till it bled.

At last the farewells were done. At last, with grinding reluctance, the Cretan king and his people would let their princess go. The ship cast off, men from shore and sailors from the ship setting hand and shoulder to the hull, sliding it smoothly into the water. Kemni clearly felt the shift from earth to sea. *Dancer* was alive beneath him. The water bore her up. The oars bit, pulling her out into the harbor.

Music followed her, and song, and people calling like the crying of gulls. Their princess was leaving them, going away to be a queen in Egypt.

✦ ✦

"You weren't supposed to come *now*." Kemni was trying not to rail at her, but not succeeding. They were well out to sea, the sail up, the oars shipped, and *Dancer* skimming before the wind. The women had put off their finery and put on more practical garb. So too had Kemni, taking a few moments' respite on the sea-chest of a cabin that had been his own on the voyage to Crete. He was rather surprised to have it, and undismayed to discover that he would share it with the captain. The women, of course, had the captain's cabin with its greater space and comfort.

Now they were all on deck in the sun and the spray, the great green expanse of Crete skimming past. Ariana was much restored to herself, now the thing was done—now she had set sail for Egypt.

Kemni should not have said what he was thinking. But they had been passing round a jar of wine, and the sun was strong and the spray was cold, and this was Ariana. "You were supposed to wait till the war was over, then come in suitable state to seal the victory. What if the Retenu get rumor of this? You'd be a hostage beyond all others. And if—*if*—we pass them undetected and come as far as Thebes, how will you manage? Queens reckon their rank and estate by the number and quality of their attendants. One attendant, however royal, however holy, will serve you poorly in the queens' palace."

She sipped wine and appeared to listen, but she offered no response. She was doing it to madden him, he was sure.

"Listen to me," he said. "What good does it do you or any of us to come to Egypt now, in secret as it must be, and when you come to Thebes, if you come there, to be married without full public ceremony, or the enemy will know what's transpired? What are you looking to gain?"

"Time." That was Iphikleia, answering with her wonted lack of patience for Kemni's profound male idiocy. "Wisdom, maybe. Advice in your king's ear, from someone who knows all the secrets of Crete. A queen is a pretty thing, and a wedding is a pleasant festival. But Egypt needs more. Egypt needs us."

"You, too?" Kemni demanded. "What, you'll offer my king two queens when he looked for one?"

"Not likely," said Iphikleia with a slight curl of the lip. "He'll take this one and be more than glad of her."

"He might have been gladder if she'd brought her horses," Kemni said.

"Horses can be had," said Ariana, speaking at last, and as clearly as ever. She was back among them in truth. "Egypt does need me, you know. I know the fleet, I know how it sails and where, and what signals it answers. I know horses, I know chariots. Being a wife I may not know, but I can be priestess and queen. Now teach me," she said. "Teach me while we sail. Teach me of Egypt."

"I should teach your captain to set you off at the first port," Kemni muttered.

She laughed. "You will not. Now begin. I would know everything. All you can think of—and as much of your language as I can learn. I taught you the chariot. Teach me Egypt."

Kemni might upbraid her, and he might disapprove highly of what she did, but in the end, he could only obey her. She would, after all, be his queen.

INUNDATION

THE RIVER FLOODED early that year, taking almost by surprise the priests whose task it was to predict the rising and falling of the waters. One day, it seemed, the river ran low and slow. The next, it roared in flood, spreading wide over the parched land. People fled, but they laughed as they ran, and sang, for this was the wealth of Egypt, the life and prosperity of the Two Lands.

"It's a plot," Ramerit said as she heaved up a great basket of soiled linen. "Thebes knew of this days ago. But did it tell any of us, up here past Memphis? It did not!"

"Well," said Nefer-Ptah, who despite her utterly Egyptian name was utterly and imposingly a Nubian. "You can hardly expect them to give us anything here. Not as things stand."

Ramerit sniffed. "They should have told us."

Ramerit had never been a reasonable person. Iry, who was not particularly reasonable either, but who at least knew when to be quiet, went on bundling linen into the baskets. If she worked quickly, she might be able to escape while Ramerit and Nefer-Ptah were occupied with arguing over rebellion in Thebes.

Iry did not want to think about rebellion in Thebes. She ducked her head till the straight black hair hid her face, and bent more assiduously to her work. As she had half dreaded, the two womenservants were at it full force. They would dredge up every slight against both halves of Egypt, all the way back to King Salitis who came roaring in his chariot out of the north and seized the whole of Lower Egypt for himself and his sons and his lords and lesser kings, and all the way forward to Ahmose who was king now, away south in Thebes where Egypt was still Egypt.

She loaded the last basket while they were but halfway between the kings, ducked even further and slid and sidled and, in a breathless rush, was gone.

No squawk of outraged discovery pursued her, for once. She escaped the breathless closeness of the linen-room, darted down the dim and odorous passage that led to the kitchen, and slipped out the door into the sudden and blazing brilliance of the day. The heat was heavy, oppressive, but she was naked as any sensible creature would be here, but for the blue bead on its string about her hips, and the amulet of Bastet that hung between her young small breasts. She stopped to embrace the light and heat both, with a pleasure as pure as any animal's.

Like a cat, she thought with a little purr in her throat. As if in answer to what was half thought, half prayer, one of the cats that deigned to live in this house came and mewed and wove its sleek spell between her ankles. She bent down. The tawny back arched to meet her palm.

As she straightened, a hand stroked her back precisely as she had stroked the cat's. She had arched to meet it before she thought; and certainly before she saw who did it.

She hissed and recoiled. Her least favorite tormentor grinned at her and, in the moment of her startlement, wheeled her over and against the wall. She was trapped in the cage of his arms, breathing the musk of him that said, inescapably, *foreigner*. And no matter that she had been bound to these conquerors for the past two hands of years.

This son of the conqueror was remarkably callow, in her opinion, and intolerably determined to be the light of her life. She looked into his broad high-nosed face with its patchy young beard, and considered spitting at it. But that would only make him laugh. Milord Iannek was the least easily offended of men, and the most difficult to be rid of.

Iry sighed deeply and determined to be as nothing: a breath of wind, a shadow on the wall. It was not easy, with hot and none too fragrant breath on her cheeks, and tall thick-muscled body looming over her. He had grown since last he trapped her against this wall. He was—gods, he was almost a man.

Under the heavy robes that he affected, that were a matter of pride to these Retenu—and no matter that the sun of Egypt could kill a man wrapped to the eyes in wool and leather and furs—she still could feel the rod risen and grown hard in her honor. It did not match the rest of him, which was tending toward the burly; it was a slender wand of a thing.

But eager. Very eager. Not for the first time, Iry was glad of his swathings of garments. If he had been wearing a proper Egyptian kilt, he would have had it off and her on the tiles in the blinking of an eye.

He certainly was thinking of it, robes or no. She bared her teeth at him. "*Little* man," she said. "Let me go."

"Not likely," he said. "And not before you give me a kiss."

"That's not all you'll ask for," she said.

"It's a beginning," Milord Iannek said.

"You only want me because I won't have you," she said.

"I'll always want you, my beautiful one," he said.

She snorted. "Go chase Ramerit. She's prettier than I am, and she loves to hunt ducks in the reeds."

"My duck mates for life," he sighed, "and he has chosen you."

"Then he'll pine away unrequited," Iry said.

He swooped to seize his kiss, whether she would or no. She ducked, slithered, slid—and was free. Quick as a lizard from the hawk, she darted for cover.

Milord Iannek's laughter followed her. He was never offended, not even by her cruelty. Nor, gods help her, was he ever deterred.

✦ ✦

This time no one barred her escape. She had nowhere in particular that she wanted to be, except that it was elsewhere—away from duties; away from importunate lordlings. She went where her feet led her, guided by the slant of a shadow, the angle of sunlight on a wall. She knew every cranny of this place, this house of the Sun Ascendant in the green country north of Memphis. How not? She had been born here.

The bitterness had shrunk to a tightening in the back of her throat. If she tried, she could remember as vividly as yesterday, though it was ten years gone and she had been a small girlchild, how it had been to be lady and mistress here, and not menial and slave.

But that was past. Her father had joined in rebellion against the Retenu. He had died for it, he and his sons. His wife and his daughter had gone to the conqueror.

The conqueror had a name. She never called him by it. She never looked him in the face, either, or acknowledged his existence, though when he visited this one of his several estates, she was expected to wait on him. It was an amenity of the house, to be served by a slave who had been a nobleman's daughter.

He had been gone since the last Inundation. No one had missed him greatly. Teti the steward, preoccupied with skimming the cream of the estate, would have been delighted never to see the overlord at all. Milord Iannek, who seemed to spend an inordinate amount of time cooling his heels in the country for one infraction or another, was a minor annoyance—however much he might vex Iry.

She found herself atop the wall, leaning on the parapet above the eastward gate. There was supposed to be a guard up here, but Teti only troubled to post one if the lord was in residence. No one would dare invade this house, not since it had passed into the hands of a lord of the Retenu. It lay wrapped in its lands not far from the road between Memphis and the foreign king's city, but not so near that many were minded to turn aside. There were richer pickings to the south of it, great and noble houses, houses whose wealth had not all frittered away into a shabby gentility.

That had been so before Iry's father died. She had no shame of it. Her mother, the Lady Nefertem—that was a different matter. But Nefertem kept to the women's house, and never ventured into the sun lest it darken the perfection of her skin. She would never follow her daughter up so high, nor know of it either, unless one of the servants was minded to tattle.

Nefertem was a slave, too. Somehow she managed to forget it, except when the lord was in the house. Then she served him as a woman of great beauty must serve her conqueror—not as Iry did, pouring his wine and tasting his dinner, but in the inner room.

Milord Iannek would have liked to make the same use of Iry, but he lacked his father's authority. Which was well for him, and well for Iry, too.

She leaned on the parapet and gazed out across the lands that had belonged to her family for a thousand and half a thousand years. They were shrunken now, covered over with the river, an expanse of water as broad, said those who knew, as a sea. The river had risen even since this morning. At its fullest extent it would stretch almost to the house, and naught between but a thin rim of dry land.

The heat was heavy, like a wash of steam across her body. No breeze rose to cool her skin. She did not mind, much. She was born to this. And it was more pleasant than Milord Iannek's hot breath and scratchy wool, by far.

As she lingered there, half-dreaming, a cloud of dust caught her eye. She watched it idly, thinking little of it, though travelers on this road were few. This one moved fast, and ran four-footed.

Retenu. Only one of those would come in a chariot, at the gallop, behind a team of horses.

Iry hated horses. Every good Egyptian did. Horses were a weapon; were the enemy. With horses and with their cousins the long-eared asses, the foreign kings had trampled the armies of the Two Lands, and killed its princes, and ruled where none but men of Egypt had ever ruled or thought to rule.

She hated horses. And yet she could not take her eyes from them. They looked like antelope, more or less, but larger, heavier, stronger. They had no horns. They had manes that streamed on their necks, and tails that flowed long behind them. They were terrible, and they were beautiful. And swift—oh, so swift. Like a bird on the wing, like a fish in the river. No man could outrun a horse. The cheetah could do it, and the gazelle—but even they were hard pressed to hold the lead.

These were fine horses, and fast. The chariot behind them was of the lighter sort, a racing chariot. A messenger, then, and in a great fever of haste. He nigh ran through the gate. It opened in the last instant to let him thunder in.

Iry atop the gate, unnoticed and unregarded, heard perfectly clearly what the messenger said to Kamut, who happened to be manning the gate. He spoke in bad Egyptian, worse even than most, but it made sense enough. "Master's dead. Where's the Lord Iannek?"

Milord Iannek was nowhere to be found. Iry could have told them where to look, but she was crouched above the gate, transfixed with shock.

The master dead. The conqueror, the invader, the slayer of her father. Dead. Big black-bearded man with a laugh that boomed through the house, and a rod, the servants said, as long as a child's arm. Iry hated him even more than she hated horses. Horses were animals, and innocent. He had known exactly what he did when he killed a rebel and the rebel's sons and kinsmen, and seized the rebel's lands and wife and daughter.

✢ ✢

Now he was dead. Killed not in battle, the messenger said over wine and bread, nor on a hunt, but in bed with one of his concubines.

"She wore him clean out," Nefer-Ptah opined, much later, when they all should have been asleep. But the house was in an uproar. Milord Iannek had been found at last, too coincidentally abed with the buxom Tuty—which rather proved Iry's judgment in such matters. He was summoned to the king's city, and without delay, too. Which meant that the servants must be up all night gathering his belongings, including his women and his dogs, and readying them for the journey.

Iry never asked questions where anyone else could hear. It was a matter of pride. But Nefer-Ptah had been her nurse before they were slaves together. With her, Iry could stoop to be curious. And for once they were alone, folding robes and tunics and packing them in boxes by the light of a bank of lamps. "Why is he summoned to the king?" she asked. "Don't they bury their dead where they fall?"

"Right on the spot," said Nefer-Ptah. "But now there's the estate to settle. King Apophis will have called all the sons together to tell them who inherits."

"What, won't it just go to the eldest son?"

Nefer-Ptah shrugged. "You'd think so, wouldn't you? But with kings one never knows. I heard the firstborn was killed in some suitably ignominious fashion, and the rest have been at each other's throats since they were born."

"How many of them are there?" Iry asked.

"Three or four dozen," said Nefer-Ptah, who seldom troubled herself with mere numbers. "Who knows? Too many."

"*One* would be too many," Iry said, "if they're all like Milord Iannek."

"Ah, little bird," said Nefer-Ptah. "He's not so bad."

Iry did not dignify that with a response. Nefer-Ptah laughed deep in her throat and clapped the lid shut on the last of his lordship's tunics. There was still the formal robe to pack, which Iry had been leaving for last.

But she paused. "Do you think he'll get it?" she asked. "Will he be lord over us all?"

"Not likely," Nefer-Ptah said. "He's too young. And he's always getting in trouble. And," she said, delivering the crowning blow, "he won't exert himself to make friends at court."

"His mother might do it for him," said Iry, who was not an utter innocent in the ways of courts.

"His mother is dead," said Nefer-Ptah. She took the state robe from Iry's heedless fingers and smoothed and folded it more quickly and much more acceptably than Iry could begin to do. "No, you don't need to worry. He won't ever be more than a frequent nuisance. Maybe not even that, if the place goes to a brother who's no friend of his. Then won't you be glad? You'll finally be rid of him."

"Pray the gods it be so," Iry sighed.

And yet in spite of herself she could not help a small, fugitive pang of regret. Not that they might be losing their unwelcome visitor. No. Of course not. But whoever came after him—if anyone troubled to come at all—would be different. And different, in Iry's experience, was never better. Usually it was worse.

·············· II ··············

MILORD IANNEK WENT away in the morning, much earlier than he would have been most pleased to do. But the king's messenger was insistent. His majesty wished to resolve this matter quickly. He would not wait upon laggards, nor look kindly on them when they deigned at last to appear.

The lordling's departure left a great quiet in its wake. Iry had not even known till they were gone, how many people he had brought into the house, or how very noisy they had been. There was hardly anyone left. A few servants, the cook, the gardeners. Teti the steward and his household, who kept to themselves in the main, and made no incursions on the lord's quarters or those of his ladies.

It was almost like being free again. Iry's duties were few and none too onerous on the whole. Much of the time, she could do as she pleased. That, chiefly, was to bedevil Huy the scribe to teach her what he knew. Huy was old and going blind, and he had no sons or kin; they had all died long ago in some forgotten pestilence. He loved nothing in the world but his palette and brushes and the inks in their bright array. He could see them still, in a dim and shadowy fashion, though that was fading fast. He did not remember, or did not profess to remember, that Iry was a slave now. He called her "young mistress," and treated her with a courtly respect, as if she had been a great lady.

At first she had tried to remind him of the truth, but as he persisted in his conviction, she let him be. It was pleasant to sit in the room that he had been suffered to keep when newer, younger scribes came in to do the accounts for Teti. It was small but very well lit, with a linen fan to keep it cool, blowing in breezes from the garden.

Iry kept the fan wetted down with water from the jar when she was there, and tied its cord to her foot and so kept it swaying as she read and wrote and listened. Huy was not a man of many words, unless they were written on papyrus. But sometimes he was minded to tell a story, and then he was well worth listening to. Iry would write as he spoke, for the practice, and because so few of his stories were written anywhere in the scrolls that heaped the room and overflowed into the hallway. Those were all household accounts, legal records, dull and daily things that seemed, to her, to be a great waste of papyrus.

But his stories were wonderful. Stories of kings and gods, great adventures from long ago, battles, magic and wonders, priests' arts and princes' exploits— and much of it, as he averred, as true as the record of the barley crop from the farthest south field.

"Probably truer," he said a day or two after the Inundation had reached its height. There had been a festival in honor of the event, a small enough thing in so diminished a household, but there had been wine and barley beer and enough song to give everyone a headache the day after. Iry's head was pounding: she had indulged in a whole jar of wine, because Teti's daughters had dared her to do it.

Huy was oblivious to her scowl and her tight-set lips. Of course he would be; he was nearly blind. "Barley crops are as large, sometimes, as the steward wants them to be. Or, often enough, as small."

"He skims a share, you mean," Iry said. "Everybody knows that."

"And do you know what the lord used to do to him, if he was found out?"

"Cut off his ears and his nose," she said, "and set him to work in the privies."

"So you would think," said Huy, rubbing his long crooked chin. "But oftentimes, if he was more useful than not, the lord would turn a blind eye, but manage to skim a half of what the steward skimmed. And so a sort of balance was kept."

"I like stories of Horus and Set better," Iry said. "Lords and stewards are dull. And a little sordid."

"That's the world of the living," said Huy. "The world of gods, and the world of the dead . . . now those are different."

"I'd rather be there than here."

"You would not," the old man said.

"And why not?" Iry demanded. "Look about you! Or remember—what a world this is. Foreign kings in Lower Egypt, and the king in Upper Egypt bows his head to them. The king, the god, bowing to foreigners. And here— and here—"

"Ah," said Huy as he always did when Iry touched on the way of things in this house, breaking it off before it was well begun. "A rebel, are you? Will you run away to Thebes, and learn how to fight like a man?"

Iry hissed at him. "If only I could! I'd wield a great sword, and I'd slay the enemy in his thousands. But I can't do it. I'm only a girl."

"A woman can do a great deal," Huy said in his gentle voice, "if she puts her mind to it."

"Yes," Iry said bitterly. "And if she puts the rest of her body to it, too. I won't do that. Mother does it—Mother hasn't any choice. I have. I won't give it up."

"That's a brave thing," Huy said, "if perhaps not wise."

"I don't want to be wise," Iry said. "I'm not sure I can be brave. I just want—"

She trailed off. He waited with patience that he must have learned in youth, when he was one of the royal scribes.

When she spoke again, it was not to finish what she had begun. It was to say, "Tell me about Set again. Set and Osiris."

Huy's brows rose slightly, but he did not try to return to what they had been speaking of before. "Set was the enemy of Osiris," he said in the singsong tone of the taleteller, "brother and bitterest enemy. Some say there was cause: some slight, some sin committed. Others say no, it was simpler than that. They were rivals, and Set was jealous of his brother, who was the elder and the stronger and by far the more beautiful, and who—perhaps most unbearable of all—had wooed and won their sister Isis, and taken her for his bride.

"And there came at last a day before the days of this world, when Set could bear it no longer. He tricked his brother, tempted him with a wonderful thing, a chest of gold and precious stones, which would belong only, Set declared, to the one who could lie in it, and whom it fit exactly. That one, of course, was Osiris. But the box was wrought with a dark enchantment, that cast him into a sleep; and Set and his allies sealed the box and cast it into the sea.

"But Isis found the box, hunting far and wide over the earth, and undertook to bring Osiris back to life again. This, Set found even less endurable than the rest. He seized the body before it could be revived, and hacked it in pieces, and flung it all along the valley of the River.

"Still Isis would not give up, nor would she give way before the dark god. She yearned for the bright god, the beautiful god, her brother and her lover. She hunted as she had before, but with even greater purpose, to find each and every piece, and bring them back together, and make them live again."

"And that is just what she did," Iry said, impatient suddenly with this tale that she had known since she was a child—and never mind that she had asked to hear it. She was all at odds this morning, cross-grained and ill-tempered. "She gathered every part of him, every one—all but the one, the manly organ. Even that at last was brought to her, when she had all but despaired; and she did with it what woman should do, and conceived and bore her son Horus. And he avenged his father and cast down the dark god—but lost an eye in doing it, so that now the eye of Horus that sees is the sun, but his blind eye is the moon." She shook herself, impatient, twitchy as a cat. "I don't know why I want to remember this. The Horus in Thebes lies too solidly under the heel of the foreign Set. Rebels fight, and rebels die. Or are taken into slavery."

Huy sat where he always sat, in his crisply starched linen kilt that Nefer-

Ptah put on him every morning, with his shaven head gleaming in the bright clear light of the room, and his eyes staring placidly into their private dark. "Memory is a gift of the gods," he said.

"Memory is a curse," said Iry.

She left him after that, none too graciously. Later, she would regret that. Now, she was too irritable to care. It was late in any case, and her one duty of the day was waiting.

⯈ ⯇

Iry's mother was still, to everyone in this house, the Lady Nefertem. Her lord was dead, her body enslaved, but like Huy the scribe, she seemed impervious to the world's changes. Even the foreign lord had found himself unable to oust her from her apartments, though he had been firm enough in claiming her bed. His own women, when they were in the house, had found accommodation elsewhere.

The rooms were as they had been for as long as Iry could remember. The scent of her mother's perfume, a rich mingling of musk and flowers, wafted out long before she reached the door. The Nubian on guard in front of it was the same massive eunuch whom her father had given her mother in honor of some forgotten occasion, as huge and impassive as ever, like a guardian carved of gleaming black stone. His eyes glinted on Iry as she approached. He never said anything to her, nor did his face change expression, but his eyes always smiled. She always smiled back.

But not today. She scowled and stalked past, mad at the world and no good reason why. Her head still ached, and her back had decided to join it; and there was a griping in her belly. She was not falling ill. She refused.

The Lady Nefertem was holding court as she did every day at this hour. She had bathed and been anointed, and taken the chair in her receiving-room. No ladies from other estates came now to visit her or to share gossip, but Teti the steward's wife never failed to be in attendance, and her daughters with her. They babbled like a flock of geese, and not much more brain to share out among them than one goose was gifted with, either.

They welcomed Iry with shrieks that fair split her skull, and dragged her to sit in the midst of them. Iry never could understand why they were so enamored of her, even when she was in a presentable mood. Probably, she thought sourly, because she was the Lady Nefertem's daughter. That counted for something in this house, foreign conquerors or no.

That lady had acknowledged Iry's coming with a regal inclination of the head, and gone on calmly addressing the steward's wife. When the daughters' uproar had died down, Iry was able at last to make some sense of it. "Yes, this unguent is perfectly wonderful for the skin. Here, try a bit of it. Soft, yes?"

"As a baby's behind," said Tawit, who was not precisely genteel. Unlike her daughters, she knew it, accepted it, and let it be. She studied her plump brown hand next to the Lady Nefertem's slender ivory one, and sighed. "I swear, my lady, you look younger every year. That's the gods' gift, I'm sure; or I'd be a beauty, too, for all the potions I've slathered on my face."

Lady Nefertem smiled faintly—the most expression she ever allowed herself. Smiles, as she frequently admonished Iry, caused wrinkles, and wrinkles were not to be borne.

Tawit went on robustly, not even slightly deterred by the lady's silence. "Ah well, my lady, we're as the gods made us. These bones can be content with that."

Tawit's daughters were all named for beauty: Nefertem after the lady, Nefertiri, Mut-Nefer, Neferure, Nefer-Maat. Nefer-Maat, the youngest, pinched Iry's arm till she gasped, and said in a tone of great annoyance, "*Iry!* You aren't *listening!*"

"She is now," said Mut-Nefer with a little too much relish. "Iry, haven't you heard? We have a new lord."

"Should I care?" Iry wanted to know.

"I'd think you'd want to," Mut-Nefer said.

Iry sighed in exasperation. "It's Iannek, then."

"Oh, no," said Nefertem-the-younger. "Not hardly."

"Not hardly," her youngest sister echoed her, giggling and clapping her hands at her own wit.

Mut-Nefer rolled her eyes at them both. "No, it's not Iannek. He's much too young. It's someone else—an older brother. He's been abroad, they say. Away far away, beyond even the foreigners' own country."

"Really?" In spite of her determination not to be interested, no, not in the slightest, Iry could not help but state the obvious. "If he's been away, how could he have influenced the king and his ministers, and won his father's holdings?"

"That's the wonder of it," Mut-Nefer said. "And the foreignness, too. He fought for it."

"*Fought* for it?"

Mut-Nefer grinned at Iry's incredulity. "Yes. He came back, and another brother was claiming the inheritance. But his father chose him, and the king agreed with it. The other brother challenged, of course—how could he avoid it? The king had to let them settle it by combat. He won. He killed the other one and took the lordship."

"No," Iry said.

"Oh yes," said Mut-Nefer. "That's how they do it."

"Maybe they'll all start fighting at once, then, and kill each other off," Iry said nastily.

"You are bloody-minded today," Mut-Nefer said. Her sisters giggled in chorus.

Silly nits. Iry wished her head would stop pounding and her belly would stop cramping. As if it could matter at all which of the Retenu called himself master of this place—and therefore of Iry. They were all the same. Foreigners. They did not belong in Egypt. They did not, before the gods, belong in the world.

······· III ·······

NO WONDER THAT Iry had been so conspicuously ill. At last and rather excessively late, her woman's courses had come upon her. She was first and most powerfully aware of it when she went to rise from the cushion she had been sitting on, and reeled dizzily. Nefer-Maat, beside her, let out a little shriek. "*Iry!* You're *bleeding!*"

"Of course I'm not bleeding!" she said crossly, till Nefer-Maat snatched up the cushion and thrust it in her face. Then she could hardly deny the evidence; it was darker than heart's blood, a dark and secret thing, a thing she suddenly—overwhelmingly—did not want.

But there was no denying it. Late, unlooked for, and with an unwarranted amount of pain and sheer irritability, Iry had become a woman.

If she had had any sense at all, she would have recognized it when it began, and seen to it before it became the talk of the house. The new lord was a great matter for speculation, but Iry was an actual, living presence. Her cherished anonymity and frequent invisibility was, she hoped briefly, gone.

The women made a great fuss over her, with pads and possets, petting and pampering. Worst of all, the Lady Nefertem was roused to action. For the first time in recent memory, she not only recalled Iry's existence, she remembered that Iry was her daughter.

The Lady Nefertem as distant, regal personage was more comforting than not. She sat in the heart of the house as the goddess Isis sat in the heavens, remote and vaguely benevolent. The Lady Nefertem as mother was frankly alarming. She hovered. She fretted. She summoned flocks of servants to stand about and yawn and grin at Iry behind the lady's back.

Iry wanted nothing more than to crawl into shelter like a wounded cat and nurse her misery till it was gone. But the Lady Nefertem was having none of that. She took the place of honor beside her own bed, in which she had insisted that Iry be laid, and with her own fine white hands applied cooling cloths to Iry's brow.

The cloths were clammy, and the herbs and spices in which they had been steeped were cloyingly potent. Even at that, they were better than the potion, which, from the taste, must be made of ox-dung and river water. Iry gagged and flung it across the room.

The cup, her mother's best one, carved of chalcedony and rimmed with gold, clattered to the floor but did not—mercifully—break. The horrid concoction sprayed wide. The great bulk of it found purchase on the hem of a heavy woolen robe.

The whole roomful of chattering women fell abruptly silent. A hawk among the pigeons, Iry thought. A lion among the gazelles. A great broad-shouldered black-bearded man with a sword at his side and a staff in his hand, and eyes—such eyes—

The Retenu were dark men, bigger and hairier than Egyptians, but dark-eyed as any human creature should be. This one—she thought of the hawk again, and of the lion. His eyes were light, almost gold. They were fixed on her, and she knew that he was perfectly aware of the stain on his hem and the stench that wafted up from it. But he was, just then, much more interested in the perpetrator of the stain.

He wanted to kill her, she supposed. Or rape her. Retenu always wanted to do one or the other. At the moment she was too intensely annoyed to care. "What are you doing here?" she demanded—forgetting every scrap of discretion she had learned in ten years of slavery, and forgetting the audience, too.

He raised a brow. He had a nose like the curve of the new moon, or like a falcon's beak. What the rest of his face was like, she could not tell. His beard was thick, and grew high up on his cheeks. Maybe he was smiling. Maybe his lips were set in a thin line. There was no way to see.

But his eyes—those smiled. Mocking her. "What am I doing here?" he echoed in reasonably passable Egyptian. "Serving as a target for practice, it seems. Shall I move a little closer? Would you like another missile?"

That pricked her temper even more deeply than before. "Who are you? How dare you come in here?"

"How dare I indeed," he said, with a glance that took in the whole of the room and everyone in it—even the Lady Nefertem mute, staring. At that one, he paused. Both brows went up. The tawny eyes went briefly, truly gold, as if dazzled by the sun.

He inclined his arrogant head to her, as he would never have dreamed of doing to Iry, and said in a voice much softened and gentled, "I beg your pardon, madam." As smoothly then as a servant in a palace, he backed through the door and drew it shut, with him on the other side of it.

Once he was gone, the room erupted. Iry clapped hands over her ears and buried herself in sheets and cushions. But there was still no escaping the uproar, or the hands that plucked her out. They belonged to several of the five Beauties, and every one of them seemed to be shrieking at the top of her strong young lungs. Out of the racket, she managed to distinguish one intelligible fragment: "Iry! *What was that?*"

Iry shook herself free and struggled to her feet. Against such numbers, she needed every advantage she could get. One of those was height: she was a good handbreadth taller than any of them. "That was one of the Retenu. What was he doing here? He should have been plaguing Teti, not ogling the women!"

"The new lord must have sent him," Mut-Nefer said. "That was a noble-man's dress, and a fine sword, too. And that staff—he's no servant, that one. Now he'll be telling the lord what a sharp-tongued slavegirl he has. If you escape with only a whipping, you'll be fortunate."

"Hush," Tawit admonished her daughter. "Let's not be prophesying trou-ble before it falls on us. If there's one Retenu in the house, you can wager there's a whole pack to follow. We'd best be ready for them."

That shook them all out of their silliness—though it could hardly silence them. Tawit gathered them together like a goose her goslings and herded them mercifully out.

There was still the Lady Nefertem, and those of the maids who had noth-ing to do but wait on her. The lady had not moved through all the fuss and flutter, nor seemed to take particular notice of the invader past that first, in-credulous stare. She had a gift of not seeing what she did not wish to see. It must serve her strangely in the lord's bed. It spared her a great deal of suffering otherwise, as far as Iry could tell.

Iry had no such luxury. She could stay here; her mother would pamper her and cosset her and drive her mad, but she would not have to face another pack of invaders. A new lord—the old one had been tolerable only in his frequent absences. What if this new one was worse?

She had to know. She escaped easily enough, between her mother's lin-gering silence and the maids' incapacity to do more than stand and gape at whatever passed by them.

+ +

The house was in mighty disarray. An army of Retenu had invaded it, and no warning but itself; no messenger had come ahead of it.

That was deliberate, Iry was sure. A truly canny lord would do such a thing to test his steward; to see what his house was like when he was not there to oversee it.

Teti could be lazy and he was not entirely honest, but he kept the house in decent order. It was clean, the storehouses were as full as they could be in this season, the servants found their places soon enough and bent themselves to duties that they had hoped to be free of for yet a while.

Iry's place was between kitchen and banqueting hall, wherever she hap-pened to be needed. In taking herself to it, she managed to go the long way about. The men's quarters were humming, as she had expected; there were Retenu everywhere, beards and robes and voices speaking their barbaric tongue. She spoke it, though she did not like to. They were saying nothing much worth listening to, except the lord's name: Khayan. And that he was there; he had not sent them ahead, he had come himself.

And he had horses. A whole herd of them, whom Teti was beside himself to find housing for. One of the Retenu, as Iry slipped past, said in exasperation, "Fool of an Egyptian! What's that field we rode past on the way in? It will do."

"That is the eastern barley field," Teti protested. "If we lose that, we'll lose the fifth part of our harvest."

"Now it is the field for the horses," the Retenu said. "Tubal, see to it."

Another Retenu dipped his head and ran to do as he was bidden. Teti looked ready to shriek aloud, but clearly remembered where he was and who faced him. He swallowed the cry, though his face twisted; and turned his back on the foreigner; and betook himself elsewhere.

So too did Iry. She did not want to see the horses, but somehow the way she chose brought her to her vantage atop the gate. The herd had been kept contained just outside of it, warded by men in chariots, and by something else that she had not seen before, nor imagined: men riding on horses. Sitting on their backs. Sending them hither and yon as if they had been hounds on a lead.

She stood astonished in the hard bright sunlight, forgetting to crouch low lest she be seen. But no one looked up or called out. The herdsmen were occupied with the horses.

So many horses. The old lord had had a number of them, as great lords did; but most of the beasts that had come with him on his visits were asses. Many, many long-eared asses to draw chariots and bear burdens and walk in caravans.

This new lord had only horses. Some were familiar in color and shape, red or brown or dun. But those that ran in the center, like a current of clear water in a mud-sullied river, were the color of clouds and mist and rare, precious rain: white, silver, grey. Some were dappled like the moon. Some were dark, but sheened with silver.

They ran together, surging like wind-ripples on the river, pale manes streaming. Iry had never seen anything so strange, or so strangely beautiful. She watched them all the way down the road and over the hill to the eastern field. Even after they were gone, she stayed where she was.

She hated horses. Her cousin Kemni had died under trampling hooves, broken by the wheels of chariots. She had seen his body when they brought it back. The embalmers had done what they could, but there was no disguising how broken his limbs had been, or how his skull had shattered. There had been no face to bid farewell to, even as shriveled as the embalming would have made it.

Still she could not forget these horses. Horses of the moon; horses of cloud and rain. They were not of earth as the others were. They were of another country. The gods' country, maybe, though not such gods as she had ever known.

It was a long while before she came down from the gate. Even then she might not have left, but she heard rough male voices and the tramping of booted feet. The new lord was posting a guard on the wall. She slipped round and down by another way, and came at last to her proper and servile place.

✦ ✦

The new lord had brought a great riding with him, and his own cooks and servitors, too, which put Rahotep the cook severely out of countenance. "I share my kitchen with no one," he declared in the face of the robed and portly Retenu who would have made himself lord of the hearth and the bread-ovens. "Find yourself another kingdom. This is mine."

The lord's cook retreated in such order as he might. Maybe he would find a place in the women's house. Or he would settle to a life of ease, and take it as a gift of the gods.

Once freed of the interloper, Rahotep returned to what he had been doing, which was the preparation of a feast for the new lord and his following. They were all men, he was assured. "But there are women coming," said one of the house servants, come in late and breathless and full of news. "A whole houseful of them."

"What, are they pausing here on their way to Memphis?" Nefer-Ptah inquired. She was not one of those whose place was in the kitchen, but everyone passed through there if she could; all news came there, and every rumor in that part of the Delta.

"They're not pausing," the servant said. "They're staying."

"No," said one of the undercooks, who had finished preparing a brace of fine geese and set them in the oven to roast, and taken a few moments' rest. "What would they stay here for?"

"They're all staying," the house-servant said. "The lord's making this his chief estate."

"What's he doing that for?" Nefer-Ptah demanded, voicing Iry's own thought. "This isn't the least of his holdings, but it's far from the greatest, either. Why would he want to stay here?"

The servant shrugged. "That's what they're saying. He wants to live here."

"He's mad," Nefer-Ptah said.

Iry considered taking umbrage, but she rather agreed. And if the lord made his home here—farewell to freedom, and to long easy seasons while the lord made his home elsewhere. Even if he was out and about his lands, serving his king, fighting in wars, his women would be here, meddling, giving orders and treating the servants like—gods, like servants.

It was ill news, all things considered. She frowned as she pondered it. So did everybody else. It was remarkably quiet in the kitchen after the house-servant left. Amid the scents of bread baking, meat roasting, sweet cakes cooling by the hearth, no one spoke more than he must, or lifted his eyes from his work.

She did what needed doing. She plucked fowl, ground spices, kneaded bread. She had forgotten the aches in her body, and what they meant, too. There would be no festival for her now, no celebration of her newborn womanhood. She was a slave again, and of no consequence.

It did not matter. When she closed her eyes, she saw moon-colored horses. When she opened them, the world was a dim and shadowy thing, and the people in it frail and without substance, like souls that had not quite found their way to the land of the dead.

When at last all was ready, when the feast was laid and the Retenu brought in to it, Iry's place was in the procession of maids with the wine. They all wore garlands about brow and waist, and their long hair free, and no other garment or ornament. Iry, the last and tallest, was to wait on the lord as she always had. That was Teti's own order, relayed by his daughter Nefer-Maat, with much giggling and silliness as she did it. "Father says to put on your best manners, and be charming if you can. This lord's softer than the other was. He might be kindly disposed toward you."

"I know the kindness of the Retenu," Iry muttered. "I neither want nor need it."

Nefer-Maat did not hear, or else she did not understand. Iry was glad enough of that. Teti was trying to do well by her, in his way. She could hardly fault him for that.

She took her place at the end of the procession, cradling the tall pitcher of copper inlaid with gold, and hoping her garlands would stay in place and not slip down to her eyes or her knees. She had no illusion of beauty, except what every Egyptian woman had: long dark eyes, fine-boned face, slender long-limbed body. Her breasts were small and her hips little broader than a boy's—though that would change, Tawit had assured her, now she was a woman.

That was its own inconvenience. The twist of wool that she had been given felt odd, uncomfortable in its secret place. If it failed, she would be worse than ashamed. Retenu were peculiar about women's matters. They had some notion that a woman in her courses was unclean, and should be kept apart from men. Which Teti should know—and if he did know it, and if his wife and daughters had told him of Iry's condition, then he played a deeper game than she would have thought him capable of.

No. Teti did not know, or was not thinking. Iry could defy him, but she was minded to do as he bade her. She wanted to see this new lord. To know what sort of man traveled with so many horses, and such horses, at that.

They waited a long time to be given the signal, but that was as it always was. The passage in which they waited was close and ill-lit and suffocatingly warm. Iry leaned against the wall and hoped the dizziness would pass. Her eyes must be clear and her mind unclouded when she entered the hall. This was her enemy, her new lord and master. If she was to know him, she must have wits enough to study him.

The other maids chattered incessantly, oblivious to her silence. They had all been slaves or servants before Iry's father died. Iry had little to say to them, or they to her.

They could hear the sounds of revelry beyond the wall, louder when the door opened for servitors to come and go. Retenu believed in making a great noise when they feasted—for luck, they said, and to honor the giver of the feast. Not that they would see Teti as any such. He was a servant, that was all, a mere Egyptian. Any honor they gave, they gave to the new lord of the house.

It was time. The babble of voices swelled and faded. Iry heard the rattle of the sistrum and the beating of the drum, the signal for the wine to come in. She straightened her wilting garlands and her wilted self, and raised the heavy pitcher to its proper and elegant angle.

She never did this for the foreign lord. She did it for herself, and for her family. That was older than these outlanders could ever imagine. And in all that time, it had never, not once, bowed its head to a lord who was not Egyptian.

She could keep her pride, whatever else she lost. That straightened her back and squared her shoulders. She walked into the hall that she knew so well, with its painted frescoes of lords and ladies feasting and dancing. Burly bearded men sat at the tables now. The scent of flowers struggled against the pungency of sweat, the lingering odors of roasted meats, spiced sauces, beer and barley bread.

Some of them at least had had the sense to put on kilts—far better in the heat than wool and leather. They were not beautiful to see, not in the slightest. Even their shoulders and backs were black with hair. Iry could understand, from that, why so many kept their robes. They did look better clothed, even with cheeks scarlet and beards wet with sweat.

The procession advanced slowly to the beating of the drum. A semblance of silence had fallen. Surely these Retenu knew the custom; and just as surely they were inured to the sight of naked maidservants. Still, she supposed it remained a novelty. Their women did not dine with them, nor walk about save in robes and veils.

Such a hideous life those women must lead. Iry was glad of her bare skin in the heavy heat of the hall, glad too of the garlands that sweetened her nostrils with fragrance. The men at the tables were a blur of bearded faces, heavy brows, eyes glittering out of the shadows. There was one in the lord's place, in the high seat, a black-bearded man like any other. But when she met his eyes, she almost laughed. Golden eyes. Falcon-eyes.

Oh, of course. Of course that had been the new lord, invading the women's quarters, looking on those too of all his possessions. Who else could it have been?

He would not recognize her. She had been lying abed, rumpled and snappish; not walking with all the pride she could summon, bearing a pitcher of the best wine.

And yet as he met her glance, she saw again that sunlit laughter, and—yes—the spark of recognition. She flattened her own stare against it.

He was no more dismayed by her intransigence now than he had been then. She had not her mother's gift of reducing men to stumbling incoherence. They only laughed at her.

She bowed to him as if to a king—low to the point of insolence. He saw that, too. Retenu were not supposed to see such things. With set teeth and tight-drawn lips, she filled his cup with wine.

He lifted the cup, saluting the hall—but with a tilt that turned the salute on her. His people cheered and hammered on the tables, and drained their own cups of wine.

He did not even sip. "Taste it," he said with a slant of the eye at Iry.

"What, are you afraid of poison?"

"Should I be?"

"No," said Iry. She plucked the cup from his fingers and drank a hearty swallow. It was wonderful wine, the best indeed, sweet and dizzyingly potent. It made her reel a little as she set the cup back in his hand, so that her fingers brushed his: a brief touch, with a spark in it, a crackle that made her recoil.

He caught the cup before it fell. "I asked your name," he said.

"I know yours," said Iry.

"You could hardly avoid that, could you?"

"And why would you care what my name is? You must have a hundred slavegirls, here and elsewhere."

"But only one casts a full cup at my feet, and follows it with the sharp edge of her tongue." He was grinning at her, a white glint in the shadows of his beard.

She bared her teeth in return. "So what will you do? Have me impaled on a spike?"

"Oh, no," he said. "You're much too entertaining. Come to my rooms tonight."

"No," she said.

Ah; at last. She had taken him aback. "No?"

"No," she said—and with beating heart, too, but there was no unsaying it. She did not want to go to him after the feast was over. No matter how quick his wit, or how wicked his smile.

He could force her. He was lord and conqueror. She knew that. He knew it, too: she watched him think of it. But he said, "Someday you'll summon me to your bed."

"I don't think so," she said.

He only smiled.

THE LORD KHAYAN took another of the maids to his bed that night, one he chose at random, Iry rather thought. A man must have a woman in his bed, after all. She doubted that he was greatly grieved that that woman was not Iry. She had piqued his fancy, for a moment. Then he had forgotten her.

That was perfectly to her liking. She left the hall once her pitcher was empty, and went to her bed in a cubicle not far from the kitchen.

That was not exactly a slave's place, but no one had yet contested it, nor did anyone dare to try. The room was tiny but it was hers, and she had it to herself. It was her refuge, the one place where no one pursued her. She kept her few belongings there, her eyepaints and brushes, her wooden comb, a little box of odds and ends and bits of treasure, all in a larger box that stood beside the plain wooden bed with its lashings of worn leather.

Tonight the sheets were clean, and the lamp newly filled with oil and burning with a clear yellow light. Nefer-Ptah, who had been her nurse when she was small, was sitting in the lamplight like an image carved of black stone. She had the gift of sleeping upright, which served a slave well, and which Iry had never been able to acquire.

She also had the gift of waking instantly when the one she waited for set foot on the threshold. Iry stopped there, frowning; not angry yet, but prepared to be. "What are you doing here?"

"Child," said Nefer-Ptah, "that's no way to thank me."

"What, for this?" Iry demanded, taking in the sheets and the lamp with a sweep of the hand. "For that I do thank you. But why?"

"Because I wanted to," said Nefer-Ptah. "And because someone should remember what day it is for you."

Iry's eyes pricked with tears. She was tired, she told herself, and all her aches were coming back. That was all it was.

"I'm glad it happened as it did," she said with an edge of sharpness. "I was going mad with all the fuss. I'd much rather people fussed over *him* than over me."

"Would you really?" Nefer-Ptah did not sound dubious, merely interested. "He is pretty, isn't he?"

"He looks like all the rest of them. All hair and vaunting arrogance."

"He's young," Nefer-Ptah said. "Much younger than you would expect.

He's not the eldest son by a fair lot of years. It must have been scandalous when he came back from the east, and his father named him the heir over all the elder sons who had stayed near him."

"That's probably why he did it." Iry stepped round Nefer-Ptah and dropped to the bed. "Do you mind terribly? I'm tired."

"So you are," said Nefer-Ptah. "Here, roll over."

Iry glowered, but did as she bade. In a moment the strong deft hands were kneading and stroking the tightness out of her shoulders and the ache out of her back. She sighed and wriggled and gave herself up to it.

✢ ✢

She woke much improved, though in dire need of the twist of wool that waited on the chest beside the bed. She stretched and yawned hugely and sighed. This being a woman was a nuisance, she could already see.

It was the fate the gods had given her. She sighed and suffered it, in a house that had come alive again, humming with the presence of a foreign lord and all his following.

His women came that day, having taken time to settle his affairs behind him—that, Iry learned later. On that day she only knew that there was a new hubbub at the gate, more horses, more chariots, armed guards, and creaking, trundling wagons with canopies both plain and embroidered. In the wagons behind the teams of oxen rode the conqueror's women: robed, veiled, hidden from any eyes that might see.

It came to her only slowly that not all the guards were bearded, and not all of those were fresh-faced boys. Fresh faces, yes, but soft and sweetly rounded, and under the leather tunics the faint but unmistakable curve of breasts. These were women, one or two riding on horses, the rest in chariots drawn by horses, with swords and spears and bows, and an air of fine and high insouciance.

They were not such women as Iry had ever seen before. Some were dark, but some were fairer of skin under the darkening of wind and weather. One had hair the color of her horse's coat, like old bronze. Another's eyes were familiar: paler than eyes should be, almost gold. She had a nose like the arc of the young moon, and a way of turning the head that reminded Iry all too vividly of the Lord Khayan.

His sister, Iry would wager, or his very close kin. She had not her brother's warmth. She was as hard and keen and cold as a swordblade, sweeping past Iry in the shadow of the gate and springing from the back of her tall dun horse. Even before her feet touched the ground, she was calling out orders in the conquerors' tongue, in a tone that expected all nearby to leap up in obedience.

Iry chose to be invisible. Lords and servants were one thing; they need trouble her only as far as she chose to let them. Women who strode about like men—that was another thing altogether.

They would want the women's house. And the Lady Nefertem had not surrendered that to any woman whom the old lord brought with him. He had learned to leave the rest of his women behind when he came here. This new lord had had no such teaching.

Iry considered each of several things that she might do. After a while, as the invasion sorted itself out and the parts of it began to disperse, she set off toward the women's house.

She was just ahead of the Retenu, but she made no move to walk more quickly. She found the women's house in its morning order. Maids were cleaning the central hall, sweeping and scrubbing. Others were out in the courtyard with the vats of water from the river, washing linens and running up the stair to the roof, there to spread them to dry.

The Lady Nefertem was awake and completing her morning toilet. She did not acknowledge Iry's arrival: she was greatly preoccupied with choosing between two grades of malachite for her eyes. "The darker, I think," she said to her maid, "though the lighter may be more appropriate in this season. Or perhaps . . . the lapis? For variety?"

Iry made herself comfortable in a corner. She had always taken a peculiar pleasure in watching her mother make herself beautiful. The raw beginning, the face all cleansed of paint and upheld to the light of day, was as exquisite and yet as unfinished as a sculptor's sketch in clay. Then layer by layer the maids painted and adorned it. First the cheeks and brow, smoothed to the whiteness of alabaster; then the blush of the high cheekbones, and the lips drawn full and red, and the eyes made long and brilliant with kohl and, after a last discussion, the darker malachite. And when all that was done, the selection of the wig. That too was a matter of great moment, a high affair of state. The plaits, the curls, the straight glossy wig like a helmet—even the Nubian wig with its cap of tight curls, which was not in fashion, but the Lady Nefertem might be inclined to make it so.

She shook her head at length and laid that aside, and chose the wig of many plaits, with its fillet of blue beads and gold bound with golden flowers. It was a more formal wig than she used to prefer in the mornings; but Iry knew better than to think that her mother was altogether oblivious to the doings in the house without. Her gown was one of her best, too, of fine white linen cut so close to her body that it had to be sewn on, and when she would be free of it, her maids would cut the stitches. It concealed nothing of her beauty; not her lovely round breasts with their rosy nipples, nor the gentle curve of her belly, nor the black triangle of her sex. Concealment was no part of it. She was better than naked; she was beauty heightened, and made more wonderful for the thin sheen of gauze between it and the world.

Iry sighed a little. Beauty was not her gift or her art. She had no patience for it. But her mother was a great master. She had a gods-given talent, too, for the exact moment; so that she was ready, dressed, wigged, painted, and set in her regal chair in the room of the waterfowl, when the foreign women entered the women's house.

They came in like an invading army, which was no more or less than what they were. She of the yellow eyes led them, and the rest of those in tunics, who had ridden on horses and in chariots; then the chattering flock of those in veils. And last of all, as if the others had been the vanguard, a circle of veiled women, and one in their midst who walked slowly, as a queen will, or a woman of years and august presence.

They could not all fit into that one small chamber. The bold ones in the lead scattered to rooms beyond, and most of those in veils, too. But the rider with the falcon-eyes, and the circle of veiled women, did not retreat. Nor did she of the veil and the high head, who must have looked to claim such a chair as the Lady Nefertem sat in, but found herself with nowhere to sit but on the floor.

She stood therefore, and from the glitter of eyes within the veils, she did it with no good grace. She spoke in the language of the Retenu, high words and haughty. "Who are you? How dare you sit in this house as if it were your own?"

Iry could have told her that the Lady Nefertem spoke only Egyptian, and probably should have. But no one else saw fit to do it, either. The Lady Nefertem sat in silence, ignoring the words that meant nothing to her ears, as she had always done and as she would always do.

The silence went on for a great while. The foreign women glanced at one another, and rustled a little, but their lady's stillness forbade them to speak. The same held for the Egyptians; they knew better than to utter a sound.

When it was considerably more than evident that the Lady Nefertem was not going to break the silence, the foreign lady snapped, "Someone speak to this creature in words that she can understand."

Iry thought about it for some little time. No one had stepped forward to speak, and no one seemed inclined to. She did not like the way the Retenu was glaring at her mother. Retenu did not control their tempers well. And when they grew angry, they were given to killing whatever got in their way.

In such a case, it was not greatly wise for Iry to speak; but her mother, after all, was her mother. She said in Egyptian, without rising or leaving her corner, "Mother, the woman asks you what you are doing here."

The Lady Nefertem raised one perfect brow. "I live here," she said.

Iry bit her lip. It would not be wise to laugh. No, not in the slightest. In Retenu she said, "This is her house, madam."

The foreign lady spun about in a whirl of veils. How she bore them, Iry could not imagine. They must suffocate her. And that, no doubt, was the root of her ill humor, even more than the insolence of those whom she reckoned but slaves. "*Her* house! How dare she?"

"Perhaps," said Iry mildly, "because it is." She looked the woman up and down, bold to insanity and knowing it, but she did not care. "May I ask who you are?"

"You may not!" That was the woman who had ridden the dun horse, outraged and with hand clapped to swordhilt, as if she had been a man.

But the other woman—who Iry thought was older, though it was difficult to tell—spoke with surprising coolness. "I am your mistress here. And who is this?"

"Our mistress here," Iry answered. "Are you his mother or his wife?"

The eyes within the veils widened slightly, startled; taken off guard. "I am neither. I am his elder sister. I keep his house for him."

"He has no wife?"

"Who are you to ask such questions?" the rider demanded. "I shall have you flogged."

But the other had paused, as if something in Iry's voice, her manner, even her impudence, struck her as greatly interesting. "He has no wife," she said.

"Well then," said Iry. "He'll not get this one."

"And can she not speak for herself?"

"She doesn't choose to," Iry said.

"This is outrageous," said the rider. "Maryam, let us dispose of them both!"

"I think not," said the one called Maryam.

As if she had made a momentous decision, she let fall her veils. Her face was not beautiful, but neither was it ugly. It was, for these people, rather ordinary: strong-featured, solid-chinned, with an arched nose and thick black brows. She had not inherited the golden eyes that marked her brother and her sister. Hers were dark and direct, fixed on Iry with a hard, clear stare.

"Tell me your name," she said to Iry.

Iry did not see any profit in defying her. "My name is Iry," she said.

"How refreshingly brief," said Maryam. "And who is this one?" She tilted her head at the Lady Nefertem.

"This is Nefertem," Iry said, "the lady of the house." She did not see that this foreigner needed to know what the Lady Nefertem was to her. There was little resemblance, everyone agreed. Iry took after her father, who though handsome enough had not boasted of great beauty.

This Maryam did not seem inclined to ask if Iry was the lady's kin. She studied the Lady Nefertem, who ignored her with queenly disdain, sitting still and expressionless as she could do for hour upon hour. Where her mind was, or what she did there, Iry could not imagine. It must have been pleasant enough: her mouth bore the hint of a smile.

"She goes far away," Maryam said as if to echo Iry's thought. "Or does she merely lack the wit to understand what passes in the world?"

That too had been a thought of Iry's, but bitter with shame. That shame fed anger, and anger escaped in a spit of words. "She is not the fool here. Now get you gone. The old lord's women had a place allotted them. Ask Teti the steward; he'll show you the way to it."

"But," said Maryam levelly, "this is the women's house."

"This is the Lady Nefertem's house," Iry said. "You will have a house of your own. You'll find it's adequate. Some might even call it luxurious."

"And if we choose to take this one?"

"You may try," Iry said.

"Enough!" cried the rider, so sharp that even the Lady Nefertem swam out of her reverie to stare. "Maryam, if you will not silence this slave, I will."

"No," Maryam said. "No. I'll speak with our brother. And," she said with a glance at Iry, "if he bids us cast out these monsters of insolence, then we will do it."

The rider snorted. "Khayan! When has *he* ever gainsaid a woman?"

"Egyptian women," said Maryam.

Her sister only laughed.

But Maryam, it was clear, had made up her mind. She summoned all those who had come in with her, and sent them out again. She went with them; but first she paused, looking long at Iry's face, as if to remember it.

Iry neither flinched nor looked away. She had never been so wild before, or so careless of her own safety. Was this what it was to be a woman? How strange. She had seen such things in boys who became men, but when a girl became a woman, she most often shrank and dwindled into herself.

Whatever the cause of it, she would live for yet a while. The Retenu were gone, the women's house clean of them, though how long that would last, or what would come of it, Iry could not foresee.

················· **V** ·················

THE NEW LORD'S sisters and the rest of his women—maids, servants, and concubines—took up residence in the lesser house, apart from the women's house though connected to it by a garden. If they voiced their complaint to him, Iry did not know of it. Maybe, when they saw the house, they had seen the wisdom of silence. The women's house was inescapably Egyptian. This one had been made new by the old lord's chief wife, built and ornamented in the Retenu fashion: heavy draperies, heaps of carpets, furnishings that would not have been amiss in a tent in the desert. To a Retenu it would be both beautiful and luxurious, though Iry found it suffocating.

And so they settled, each in his place, with no more disruption than one might expect of a house full of Retenu. Iry undertook to be as invisible as she had ever been: belated prudence after the beginning she had made, but, she hoped, not too late.

For a while it seemed she had succeeded. No one troubled her. She performed such duties as she had, and evaded that of pouring the lord's wine in the evenings, trading that office for a daily stint in the laundry. It seemed a fair exchange, and a safe one.

She saw him often enough, from a prudent distance. He had informed a scrupulously expressionless Teti that since he intended to make this the chief of his houses, he wished to know every corner of it, and every corner of the estate, too, all up and down the river. Every morning, when it was as cool as it could be in this season, he rode out in his chariot to visit this village or that. Every afternoon, in the cool of the hall, he sat to hear petitions and judge disputes.

These were matters that Teti had always seen to, under Iry's father as well as the Retenu who supplanted him. This young lord had ambitions of ruling in every aspect of his domain: great foolishness in Iry's estimation, though he seemed to think it a great good deed. Certainly he seemed pleased with himself when she saw him.

Teti was not so pleased. In front of his lord he maintained a mask of decorum, but when he went home to his wife, he was . . . difficult. That was the word she used.

"Difficult," she said to the Lady Nefertem at their morning audience, shaking her head and glaring at the daughters who would have elaborated on the word. "He's always been the one to say what comes and goes in these lands. Now he has to stand aside while that interloper does it. Really, lady, if this goes on, I'm afraid he'll turn rebel."

"Is it rebellion to serve the true king?" the Lady Nefertem asked, so soft and yet so clear that Iry doubted she had heard it. But they were all staring, Tawit and the five Beauties, and even the maids. The lady seemed as impervious as ever. She smoothed one of the many pleats in her gown, then pleated it again, meticulously, till it was folded to her satisfaction. Then she said, "There are too many Retenu in this house. We should be rid of them."

"That . . . won't be easy," Tawit said with what, for her, was considerable caution.

"What, are you a coward?" the lady asked her.

"No, lady," said Tawit. "But prudent, and fond of this skin, however unlovely—that, I am."

The Lady Nefertem sniffed delicately. That was all the commentary she offered, and all she needed to offer.

Tawit did not linger long after that. Iry felt a small shiver down her spine as the steward's wife swept her daughters ahead of her, out of the room and away. If Tawit's conception of prudence extended to informing the foreign lord that the Lady Nefertem entertained thoughts of rebellion, then none of them was safe. Not the lady, not any who waited on her. And not Iry, who was, after all, her daughter.

Iry was not afraid, not precisely. The time for fear had passed when she knew that the man to whom she had been so rude was the new lord of the house. He had done nothing to her then—less than nothing. He was a soft man, complacent. He did not think that any Egyptian, still less an Egyptian woman, could be a match for him in wit or will.

She would like to see him fall, struck down by an Egyptian sword. That would be sweet, and more than sweet. And if every Retenu in Egypt was driven out, and Egypt was made whole again under its true and proper king—that would be sweetest of all.

＋ ＋

Tawit did not betray her lady, or if she did, nothing came of it. Perhaps the Retenu were contemptuous; or perhaps they were simply distracted. They were awaiting yet another arrival, one of much more moment than the arrival of the lord's sisters and his women.

As greatly perturbed as they were, Iry would have expected an overlord at least, or the king himself. But it was no mere male who advanced upon them, and no mere king. The one who came in a wagon as a woman of respect and standing, a wagon drawn by milk-white oxen and escorted by a company of women on the backs of horses, was no lesser eminence than the lord's own mother.

The Lord Khayan himself awaited her in the outer court, standing with his young men as he would have done for the coming of the king. His sisters waited, too, with their veiled women: a royal welcome.

The wagon creaked and grumbled to a halt. One of the oxen shook its broad white head, scattering flies. The mounted women sprang from their horses' backs and stood as guards stand, fanning out from the wagon to the lord and his men. It only needed a clamor of trumpets; but there was no music but the lowing of an ox.

There was a pause. Iry, watching from the shade of a pillar, admired the way in which this foreign woman drew every eye to the curtain behind which she sat. Only when she had complete silence, when even the oxen had stilled, did the curtain draw aside. She was in shadow still, a dark figure, black-robed, black-veiled. She rose slowly, with grace that the Lady Nefertem would have admired, and took the guard's hand that reached to her, and stepped down on the broad back of a second.

Oh, she was regal, that one. She was not particularly tall, for a Retenu; Iry was little smaller. Yet she held herself perfectly erect. She accepted her son's deep bow and his kissing of her hands as no more than her due, and let her daughters perform their own obeisance.

Iry held her breath, waiting for the woman to demand that she be taken to the women's house. But when she was led away to the lesser house, she said no word. She had not spoken at all, that Iry had heard.

That was great power and presence, to stand silent and reap such respect. Iry's mother could do it, too; but she simply did not care. This was a keener mind, Iry suspected, and a sharper awareness of the world.

+ +

With his mother in residence, the Lord Khayan was all too obviously determined to stay in these lands of the Sun Ascendant and be lord of them. As to why . . .

"The horses," Pepi said. Pepi had been a master of arms in Iry's father's day. He had taken a great wound in battle when his lord died, and been sent home; and so remained in the Lower Kingdom when the rest of the army had marched away from its victories to a slow defeat.

Pepi was an oddity. He was not afraid of horses. More: he liked them. He had kept the stables for the old lord. The new lord had his own master of horse, but Pepi knew the ways of the house and of the stables that the old lord had built. He knew how to make himself invaluable; and he listened wherever he could, and remembered what he heard.

Not that Iry would venture to that realm of snorting monsters. Pepi and old Huy the scribe were friends—unlikely enough as a pairing, the frail old scribe and the stocky old warrior, but firm enough for all that. They liked to sit together in the mornings, sharing their bread and beer.

That morning Iry had a little time to herself before she had to set to work scouring soiled linens. She had not visited Huy in an unconscionable while, and she had a craving for one of his stories.

She found him not greatly inclined to tell a story, but Pepi was full of gossip from the men's side. "The lord is a master of horses," he said, "one of the great ones of the conquerors. He'll be the king's own horsemaster, it's said, when the old one dies. Did you see the horses that he brought with him?"

"I did," said Iry. She did not mean to speak, but it seemed she could not help it. Just the mention of them brought back memory: clouds about the moon, and white manes streaming. "They weren't . . . like other horses."

"Ah," said Pepi with a lift of the brows. "You saw *those*, did you? Those are something beyond the ordinary run of horses. But of ordinary horses too he has a great number. He's to breed horses for the king's chariots. Those he's brought with him are among the best to be had."

"But what does that have to do with his insistence on living here?" Iry demanded.

"Much," Pepi answered. "These lands, he says, are admirable for the raising and keeping of horses. The grass is rich, the fodder ample. The fields are broad and well watered. And the road is near, but not too near; it's easy to run the herds of young stallions up to the king's city when it comes time to break them to the chariot."

"There are other places that would serve as well," Iry said.

"But none as well situated, or with as large and suitable a house." Pepi drained his cup and belched comfortably. He reached for the jar to fill his cup again. "No, he's not leaving at any time soon, except when he's called to wait on his king. He likes it here."

"How can he? We detest him."

"Do you think he cares for that?"

Iry set her lips together and glowered in silence. Pepi patted her hand with beery familiarity. "There, there, child. It's a nuisance, but it's the gods' will. And maybe, after all, it won't last so long."

"Are you a rebel, too?" Iry asked him.

He stared at her as if she had begun to babble nonsense. She thought he might say something, but he drained his cup of beer instead. When he was done with that, the current of conversation shifted—deliberately, she might have thought, if Pepi had been a clever man. But Pepi was not clever. He was blunt, he was honest, but clever—no.

Iry did not press him. No Egyptian bore well the lot of the conquered. Everyone dreamed of driving out the Retenu and paying tribute to a true king again. And those who acted on it died or were sent into exile. That lesson she had learned from her father and her brothers and her kin.

She left the two old men to their beer and their memories. She should be tackling the day's heaps of linen, but she found herself wandering down through the courtyards to the gate. It stood open at this time of day and with the lord in residence and the country at peace—if there was war, it was far away to the south, where Egypt was still Egypt. The guards stood at ease, lazy yet alert. They took no particular notice of Iry, though she walked past them into the open air.

She had not stood outside of these walls in longer than she could remember. It was the same air, the same sun, but strange, because there was no end to it. No walls to close it in. Only the thick moist air of the Delta, and the River retreating, leaving the black earth behind that was the wealth of Egypt. Egypt was Two Lands, Upper and Lower, south and north, yet it was also Red Land and Black Land, raw dusty desert and rich growing land.

She stood in the Black Land, and the Red Land was far away. The fields stretched before her, bright already with new green. The River flowed high still, but in a little while it would return to its lesser banks, and leave the Black Land for men to till.

The road underfoot was much worn and rutted with hooves and chariot wheels. Human feet never trampled it so badly, nor the feet of oxen either, bearing their burdens to and from the lord's house. Horses and their long-eared cousins were marking the land as nothing else had done before.

When she had her bearings, and the dizziness of open space had gone away, she turned her face toward the hill to the north and east. Even before she had reached the summit, she knew where the horses were. She could hear them: snorting, stamping, shaking the earth as a herd of them sprang into a gallop.

Horses did not run like gazelles. They were heavier, more solidly bound to earth. But those who were running, the horses of the moon as she had come to think of them, had a power and a grace that she had seen in no animal before. They skimmed the ground. They danced on it. They seemed to laugh as they ran, tossing their heads, kicking up their heels.

She could almost imagine that they ran for her. She stood atop the hill, and they ran below her like a streamer of cloud in a strong wind.

The others, the darker ones, the reds and browns and blacks and duns, grazed or ran in their own herds. But she had eyes for none but the moon-horses.

One of them curved away from the sweep of the herd, running lightly up the hill. It was darker than some, dappled like the moon, with a broad forehead and a great dark eye. Its mane was blue-silver, its tail blue-white. Its little ears were pricked, intent on her.

Iry reflected, distantly, that she might do well to be afraid. There was no human creature within sight. The herdsmen were gods knew where. She was all alone between earth and sky, no wall and no defense against the creature that approached her.

And yet there was no fear in her. The dark eye was mild. The ears were up, alert. With such an expression, Iry might greet a friend.

She was no friend to this creature of the outlands. She willed herself to turn away, but her body chose not to obey her.

The horse slowed as it drew nearer, till it was standing still, just out of reach. Its nostrils flared. It was breathing lightly, and sweating lightly, too, a warm odor, pungent but not unpleasant.

She had never stood so close to a horse before. She had never wanted to. It was larger than she had expected, but smaller than she had feared: chin-high in the back. Its head rose above her own, longer and wider by far than any gazelle's.

Her hand reached out. She did not will it; it did it of itself. The horse did not shy away. Its neck was smooth, flat and warm, and very strong.

The great head turned. Iry froze. The horse brushed her arm with its nose. Soft nose, not at all harsh as she might have expected, and warm, with a tickle of breath.

She was not afraid. She was *not* afraid. This huge creature, this enemy of her people, was gentle, soft in its touch, and strangely amiable. It meant her no harm.

She still hated horses. But not this one. She stroked its neck and its big flat shoulder, and then, daring greatly, leaned against the curve of the barrel, pressing her face to the warm pungent back. It smelled of grass and dust and horse—a good smell. It comforted her.

As she rested there, a great knot unraveled in the center of her. She had not even known it was there until it was gone. An ache that had been part of her for longer than she could remember, was all smoothed away. It came to her, but slowly, that her eyes had brimmed and overflowed.

Tears? But whatever for?

For everything. Her father and her kinsmen dead. Her mother gone all remote and strange. Her world broken and left where it lay: her freedom taken from her, her body relegated to the lot of a slave.

She had not wept since her father marched out to his death. Now she wept for it all: every moment of the years between, and every grief, and every humiliation. All on the warm and steady shoulder of an animal that belonged to the enemy.

When she was wept dry, she lifted her head from the horse's shoulder. The horse blew gently, ruffling her hair. She laughed painfully. "Why," she said, "you're like a cat."

The horse did not dignify that with a response.

A horse like a cat. Such a thought. Iry entertained it nonetheless. Cats were divine, everyone knew that. Horses were anything but—except for these with their coats like the moon. Iry stared at her thin brown hand on the pale neck, and looked from that into the soft dark eye. "I don't understand," she said.

The horse did not mew or purr like a cat, and yet she could see well enough what it thought. What was there to understand? The world was as it was. Iry should simply accept it.

"No," she said. "I don't accept. I don't endure very well, either."

Then that was as it was, the horse said with a tilt of the ear. Oh, yes, it was very like a cat. Just as mystifying, and just as maddening. And like a cat, it had wanted her here, for gods knew what reason; and now that it had her here, it would not tell her why. It simply asked her to accept.

She would not play such a game. Not unless she knew the stakes. She thrust herself away. The horse made no move to stop or keep her.

She walked down from the hill—quickly, but she did not run. She was proud of that. Nor did the horse follow. It had set her free—for the moment. And if it summoned her again—when it summoned her again . . .

She turned her mind from that, as she had turned her back on the horse. The house was waiting, both refuge and prison. She was almost glad, just then, to go back to the life of a slave.

K HAYAN CAME IN dusty and sweaty and reeking from his morning with the chariots. He had nothing in mind but a bath and a clean tunic, and a cup of wine maybe, and something other to eat than the endless Egyptian barley bread.

When the ambush fell on him, he was taken off guard. He reeled against the wall.

His attacker laughed, sweet as water in the desert. She wrapped strong slender arms about him and trapped him there against the wall, with her breasts against his breast and her hips against his hips and the strongest part of him, just then, rising high between.

"Barukha!" he gasped. "What are you—"

"Tormenting you," she said. For proof, she nibbled his ear. He yelped. She laughed.

"Should you not be waiting on my mother?" he demanded—not as harshly he wanted; there was too little breath in him.

"Your mother has maids enough in attendance," she said. "She'll not miss me for a while."

"And when she does, and if it gets out, and if your father and your brothers hear of it—"

"My father and my brothers are safe in Avaris," she said, "waiting on the king. They'll never know what we do here." She paused. "Are you a coward, then, my beautiful lord?"

"I am not!" he burst out; no thought in it, either.

And at that, too, she laughed. "You are so lovely," she said, working fingers beneath his robe, weaving them into the curly hairs of his chest. "And who would have thought it? Such a great gawk of a boy you were, all knees and elbows. Your mother's people made a man of you."

He bit his tongue before he betrayed secrets. But in the safety of his mind, he laughed a little bitterly. *They* would never make a man in the way she meant.

She knew nothing of the people who had guested him and suffered him to ride with them, afar away in the east. Nor would he be the one to tell her. "You have grown," he said, for something to fill the silence. "You have grown—beautiful."

And so she had. He had known her when she was a child, too young to conceal herself in veils, with no more shape to her than a peeled twig. That image, now, one would never think of in relation to her. She was all, and entirely, a woman.

He could see it perfectly clearly. She was veiled, oh yes, but those veils were of Egyptian weaving, gauze as fine as spidersilk, revealing far more than they concealed. Her face with its full cheeks, its ripe lips. Her shoulders, so sweetly rounded. Her breasts—such breasts, milk-white beneath the frost-white linen, the rose-red nipples erect, taunting him. His hands had found the rich curve of her hips, the narrow waist above, and below—

He pulled away. "This is dishonor!"

"Dishonor is what I say it is," she said with a suggestion of edged bronze beneath the sweetness. "Come here, my lord, my beautiful one, my lion of the desert. Am I not beautiful? Are you not the most splendid of men?"

"I'll be the most thoroughly emasculated of men, if your father gets wind of this."

"Oh you coward!" She looked ready to spit on him. She seized him instead, and got a grip on his robe, and with strength that made him stare, rid him of it.

He stood like a plucked goose, naked but for his loincloth, and caught all flatfooted. "Barukha—"

"Khayan," she said, mocking him. "I can scream now, and the guards will come. You know what they're going to think."

"I think you may scream regardless," he said tightly, "when you have what you want of me."

"I might," she said. "Won't you gamble? Am I not beautiful?"

"You are glorious," he said with a kind of despair.

"So then," she said, capturing him again, and somehow she had lost her veils. She was as naked as she had been born, but for the golden bells that swung from her ears. They chimed softly, oh so softly, as she mounted him—even standing there, with him braced against the wall, and no more will or resistance in him than in a stallion broken to the bridle.

They began so, but they ended in the bed, as was more proper—though what could be proper about a lord's daughter dancing the oldest dance with a man not her husband, Khayan could not for his life's sake imagine.

Once there was no escaping it, Khayan gave up the fight. Fear made it keener—that much was true. And she was no maiden, either. He was not, by then, astonished to make the discovery. Barukha had always been wild, even as a small big-eyed child trailing after her brothers.

She had had excellent teaching. But then, so had he. Honor among his mother's people was a strong thing, as strong as the life that bound blood to bone, but it was not the same honor that his father's people knew. In that world, a woman would indeed do as this one had done. Had she known it, then? Had she trusted in it, in laying her ambush?

For a while then, all thought vanished. Her lips, her hands, traced his body in lines of fire. He found her hot secret place, and plunged deep. She gasped; then she laughed. "O beautiful!"

He had no words. If he had, he might have cursed her—or blessed her. Beautiful. Yes, beautiful. And oh so deadly dangerous.

✦ ✦

They lay in a tangle, breathless. She was laughing—she lived her life in laughter. He was rather perfectly spent. But he could not fall into the sleep that lured him so irresistibly. "Where—" he managed to say. "My servants—"

"Now you notice," she said. Her fingers tangled in his hair, tugging lightly, not quite enough to rouse pain. "They'll be back in a little while, and ready for your bath, too. Don't you feel marvelous? Aren't I a wonder?"

"You are horrifying," he said. "What do you want of me?"

"Ah, suspicion." She rose over him, smiling down, swooping to kiss him: brow, cheeks, lips. "Do you know," she said, "it's strange to kiss a bearded man, now. Egyptians all shave their faces."

"You've been consorting with Egyptians?"

She grinned, wild as a boy. "Oh! I've shocked you."

"If your father knew—"

"My father wants to marry me off to someone dull, suitable, and preferably elderly. Then I'll bear him a son, and he'll oblige us all by dying, and my father will have his lands and wealth, and I'll have a regency to keep me occupied. It's a sensible plan, don't you think?"

"I may be dull," said Khayan, "and for all I know I'm suitable, but I am not elderly."

"No," she said tenderly, stroking her breasts against his breast till he was nigh mad with the mingling of annoyance and pleasure. "You are not elderly. I'll not marry you, my beautiful lord. But if you would like to sire my son . . ."

"What, are you leaving tomorrow to marry some ancient?"

She laughed. "Not likely! No, I'll be here for a goodly while. I'm your mother's servant and her pupil. I'm to learn whatever she can teach."

"Why?"

She shrugged. It did wonderful things to her breasts. "I asked. She consented. It seemed a useful thing, to know what she knows."

His eyes narrowed. He was wide awake, and that was no small feat, either. "You came to serve the goddess?"

"I came to wait on your mother," Barukha said. She had not answered him, precisely.

"And I'm what? Diversion in the afternoons?"

"If you like," she said. She curled against him, head cradled on his shoulder. "I've always wanted you, ever since I knew what it was to want a man. When you came back from the east with the Mare and her people, and won the lordship from that lout of a brother—what a wonder that was. And what a pleasure. I knew I'd have you then. Whatever it took to win you."

"Very little," he said, more wry than angry. "Tell me your father didn't have something to do with the delegation of princes who persuaded me to fight for the lordship."

"Did he need to?"

"I'm the foreign woman's son, the one who went away, who came back on another errand to find his father dying and a war ready to break out over the spoils. I'm hardly the most likely of choices."

"He chose you," she said.

"And how did you know that?"

"Your mother told me." She drew idle swirling patterns on his breast and belly. "There were sons ahead of you, and not a few of them, either, and one who was sure he would be lord. But your father named you the heir."

"He was half out of his head," Khayan said sharply. "And he was well out of patience with the vultures flocking to the feast. They were already squabbling, though he was still alive to hear it. I came in, he rose up, he pointed to me. He said, 'That one! That one is my heir!' He only did it for spite."

"Maybe," she said. "A man can be both spiteful and wise."

"Wise?" Khayan nigh choked on the word. "I had to kill three brothers whom I barely knew, and one of whom I was almost fond, when they challenged me for the lordship. And now I have blood on my hands, and enemies among my own kin. He'd have reckoned that a fair price, I suppose, for going away for so long, and living among my mother's people."

"You didn't refuse to take the lordship," she said as her hand wove and spiraled downward. "You could have done that. You could have gone back into the east again once you'd brought the Mare to her priestesses, and been free of it all."

"So I could," he said.

"But you didn't."

"No," he said. "I didn't."

"So," said Barukha.

"So," he said. "Tell me what you want of me."

"You," she said.

"That can't be all of it," he said.

"It's more than enough." Her hand closed round his shaft, which was waking again at last. "A widow is allowed to choose her husband. Maybe I'll choose you."

"And if I don't wish to be chosen?"

She smiled and did something astonishing with her fingers. He gasped in shock and sudden pleasure. "Imagine this," she said, "whenever you want it."

He could not answer. She had shocked the words out of his head—again. She was a witch, no doubt of it. Her spell was on him, too strong for any escape.

✦ ✦

Khayan was not at all surprised, that evening, to be summoned into his mother's presence. He had left Barukha with more reluctance than he liked to admit, and gone to the duties that he had taken on himself. When he came back to his rooms, she was of course gone, and the servants were all in attendance as if nothing had ever happened.

But there was a messenger waiting, a shy boychild who spoke the words in a rapid singsong: "My lord your lady mother summons you at once if you please."

Khayan did not please, but he knew better than to refuse such a command. He went as he was, in the robe he had worn for sitting in judgment, with the staff of lordship still in his hand.

None of the women had settled in what was, he had been assured, the women's house. That was the province of that strange and very beautiful woman who had been lady of these lands while they were still in the hands of an Egyptian. His own women—such as they were, for he had no wives and precious few concubines; most of those who had ridden with him had belonged to his father, and had nowhere else to go—his own women had taken up residence in a lesser house, but one, they professed, much more to their liking.

Once he had entered it, he could see why. No wide bare Egyptian spaces here. No walls crawling with vividly colored images: beasts, birds, flowers and trees, and human shapes, too, drawn in the strange twisted way that was the fashion of this country. All the walls in this house were decently curtained, the floors carpeted. The scents were scents of home: incense, musk, roasting mutton. Egyptians were all too fond of complicated and difficult perfumes, and bread and barley beer, and profusions of strangely scented flowers.

The guards on the door here were women, daughters of the eastern tribe from which he had too lately come. He yearned for it with sudden and fierce intensity. They greeted him with bold eyes and no more respect than they reckoned any male deserved. There was a surprising degree of comfort in that.

Here, in this world, he was not a lord of creation, or even of these lands. He was the son of his mother. That set him moderately high, but not as high as one of her daughters.

She kept him waiting for some little while. That it was to humble him, he had not the slightest doubt. He set himself to be patient; to refrain from any display of temper. He sat in a room hung with dark draperies, but one of them had been looped up and away from a window. There was little enough to see beyond: a covered colonnade, a dazzle of sunlight in a courtyard—brilliant even so close to its setting. The room was cooler than the air without, but warm still.

Not for the first time, Khayan considered Egyptian dress, or lack thereof. A linen kilt, one's head and face and body shaved smooth, a wig for grand occasions. Ornaments in profusion to mark a man's standing in the world. No heavy, scratching wool, no sweat-sodden weight of leather to bear one down.

Some of the lords in Avaris had succumbed to temptation. Khayan could well see why. The sun could flay skin little accustomed to it, but for idling about under canopies and in palaces, it was a thoroughly sensible garment.

He ran fingers through his thick curly beard and sighed. Some things a man would be hard pressed to give up. If it meant that he kept the rest . . . well, and so be it.

A step brought him about. His sister Maryam stood in the doorway. His smile was swift, broad, and altogether unselfconscious.

She smiled back, warmly. One forgot, then, her unfortunate resemblance to their late father: the solid features, the thick sturdy body. Her eyes were beautiful, and her smile. She had her share of pride, as all his family did, but she tempered it with grace.

"Ah," he said. "My favorite sister. And are you keeping well here?"

"Very well," she said. "This house is pleasant, I do admit it. It's not so ill after all to have our own place, apart from the Egyptians."

"It's as bad as that?"

She shrugged. "No one ever conquered them before. They don't know how to endure it."

Khayan frowned, though not at her, nor particularly at what she had said. "That's true, isn't it? They hate us. They call us the Hyksos, the Foreign Kings, and the people from Retenu, which is what they call Canaan, and 'vile Asiatics.' They won't call us by our names. Any of them. As if, in refusing to acknowledge our names, they refuse our existence."

"Yes," she said. "They have a great belief in the power of names."

"Have they cursed us, do you think?"

"I'm sure they have." She took his hand and held it in her own, and smiled up at him. She was much smaller than he was; a fact that always subtly amazed him. She had been nigh a woman grown when he was born. Now he was a man, and she but a smallish woman nearing middle years, unmarried and some would think unregarded. But Maryam was no such feeble creature as that.

"We should go," she said to him. "Our mother is waiting."

He nodded. She led him inward, into the realm of shadows and half-lights, subtle scents and soft voices, that he had always thought of as the women's country. He felt large and ungainly there, creature of sun and wind and open places that he was.

The Lady Sarai was waiting in the heart of her domain. They had set up a loom there, and she and her women wove a fabric of wondrous complexity, colors mingled so subtly and with such artistry that the eye could barely begin to encompass them. He looked, the quick dart of a glance. But there was no sign of Barukha.

He had come prepared to fret greatly over that most maddening of women, and to face the accusation of dishonor. And yet, in Sarai's presence, all of that ceased to matter. She was not thinking that of one of her servants. Perhaps she seldom thought of Barukha at all.

Khayan let out a barely perceptible sigh. He had not been summoned here for that, then. Sarai had another use for him. He set himself to be wary, to watch for ambush, but in that quarter at least he was safe.

Sarai looked up from her loom. He was the child of her age, he and his sister Sadana who had been born in the year before him. After him had been no more.

And yet, as she sat at the great loom, with only the lightest of veils over her hair and none concealing her face, she seemed no older than her daughter Maryam. Her hair was ruddy still, barely touched with grey. Her eyes were as clear as they had ever been, wide amber eyes that she had passed to her son and her younger daughter.

For all the terror of her presence, when she looked up from the loom and smiled, he was as besotted as any raw boy must be with a queen. "Khayan," she said. "Come. Sit by me."

There was room, because her women saw to it that there was. It was not so unfamiliar to sit at a loom, or to take his turn with the shuttle, either.

When he had added a finger's breadth to the pattern, Sarai said, "You've labored mightily to be lord in this place."

He stared at the fabric stretched out in front of him, as if a response had been woven into it. But it was only colored thread. "I've done what I may to fulfill my duty," he said.

"You're not loved for it."

"Love has little to do with it."

"Yes," she said. She wove her own stretch of cloth, then paused again. "Why do you trouble yourself?"

"How can I not?"

"Not and be Khayan." She petted him as if he had been a fine hound. "Yes, child. As futile as it is, you will go on doing it. But have a care. No Egyptian in this country is friend to one of us."

"What, none?" he asked. He was not mocking her, not exactly. He had been away, after all. Much could have changed. Though, it seemed, little had.

"We are all enemies," she said. "Egypt has not accepted us in a hundred years. I doubt that it ever will."

"Does that matter, as long as we rule it?"

"As long as you rule it," she said, "no."

He narrowed his eyes. "What, Mother? What have you heard?"

"Nothing," she said.

"Then you summoned me simply for the pleasure of my company?"

"May not a mother do that, when her son has been away for most of the years of his manhood?"

"She may," he said. "But you have never yet done anything for a simple reason. What is it? Rebels in the house? Murderers under the beds?"

"No more than there ever are," she said. "No, I've another thought entirely. The Mare."

He raised his brows. That was a great thing and a mystery, a deep matter of gods and their servants, and he was part of it. He had been sent in childhood to his mother's people, far away in the sunrise countries, to grow to a man where men were not taught to be arrogant lords of the world, but obedient servants to women and the gods. His father had not objected; this was a younger son, and the mother who sent him was high in the lord's favor.

Then when Khayan was grown to manhood, he was given a task, chosen over the women of the tribes—most of whom felt themselves far more suited to it than a mere and youthful male—to bring into the west the living image of the tribes' great goddess, Horse Goddess herself. That was the moon-white Mare. Her predecessor, the goddess' elder image, was dead. The Young Mare would go where the elder had gone, away into Egypt, there to bless the conquering kings with her presence.

It was the will of the Mare herself, the elders had said, that Khayan be her escort into the west, nor were they at all pleased to say it. But since the Mare was what she was, her will was to be obeyed, and never questioned.

The elders had been in much dismay, even in their obedience. The Mare before this had left the east when she chose her priestess who would serve her till she died, had gone through all the lands of the west until she came to Egypt, and there made it clear that she would stay—a shocking thing, and a great loss to the tribes, for the white Mare had lived in the east since the dawn of the world. Then too soon she died, and her servant died with her, felled by some fever of this pestilent country.

That had been a tragedy, but not unbearable—until the Young Mare in the east had made it clear to the priestesses that she also would go into the west. More—that she would take her kin with her, the herd of moon-white horses. Horse Goddess had departed from the tribes, taken her living presence and the blessing of her regard from the people and bestowed it on their distant and somewhat estranged kin.

There had been great mourning and weeping, and a great rite of grief and parting, but no one presumed to stop the Mare or to bind her. One did not bind a goddess.

Khayan stood now in front of his mother, who was a queen's daughter of the tribes, and said, "What is it? Hasn't the Mare chosen her servant?"

For the first time since he could remember, his mother looked less than perfectly serene. A frown marred the smoothness of her brow. Her lips were tight. "No. She has not."

Khayan blinked. "But the Mare always chooses—" His eyes passed swiftly over the room. "Where is Sadana? Has something happened to her?"

"Sadana is out drowning her sorrows," Sarai said. "Riding, as she always is."

"But not on the Mare." Khayan shook his head. "But, Mother, she was supposed to be chosen. No one ever doubted that she would. That was why they let me go—because they thought I'd take the Mare to my sister. She was the priestess' acolyte. She was to be the chosen one."

"The Mare passed by your sister in the rite as if she were no one at all."

"That's unheard of," he said.

"The Mare does as she pleases," Sarai said with calm that must be hard won. "Yes, I thought that my daughter would be chosen. I never thought that she would fail."

"How could she fail? She's *your* daughter."

"The Mare doesn't care for that," Sarai said.

"Gods," said Khayan. "What this must be doing to Sadana— She hasn't come to me at all."

"And what could you do if she did?"

"Comfort her," he said. "Console her."

"That's not a thing she'll take from a man just now," Sarai said. "And from you least of all."

"Still," he said stubbornly and not too wisely. "Why wasn't I told sooner? You must have known this soon after I brought the Mare back."

"We delayed the rite when your father died," she said. "Then you were chosen heir, and there was a great to-do over that. It wasn't till you'd left to come here that we did what had to be done."

"And the Mare chose no one."

"And the Mare chose no one," Sarai said.

Khayan bent to the loom. The simple labor helped him to think. This was not a thing of the men's side, not at all, but Khayan was his mother's son. For the Mare to choose no one was unheard of. Or else . . . "Is there a candidate you could have presented but didn't? Someone you never thought of, or thought of and discarded?"

"We presented every woman of suitable age who was within our reach," Sarai said. "She ignored them all."

"Then there's one you forgot," he said.

"What, one of our eastern cousins?"

Khayan shrugged. "Maybe. Or some lord's wife or daughter who wasn't able to be at the choosing. I rather doubt that every lord with women of suitable age would have sent them, the Mare's servant being what she is, and living as she does, free and unveiled before the people. Wouldn't it be like some of them to hide away their kinswomen, and lie to the searchers? Not every man is as obedient to the gods as the people in the east."

"We did think of that," Sarai said a little dryly. "This has never happened before. Always, at the choosing, there has been one chosen from among those presented—however many or few those might have been. This Mare would have none of them."

"It's said," Maryam said, daring greatly to speak in front of their mother, "that this is a message and an omen. This country has no love for us. We should leave it."

"And yet I've heard," Khayan said, "that when the Old Mare came here, *that* was an omen, a token of great favor. Horse Goddess had blessed my father's people and chosen them to be her own."

Maryam bent over the loom as he had done just now, but her hands were still, making no move to add to the pattern. "Who knows what the gods think? If the Mare has no companion, then Horse Goddess' rites can't be celebrated. The men have their own gods. They claim that horses are theirs, but all the wise know that without Horse Goddess we lose the greater part of our strength."

"There are precious few men of such wisdom in Egypt," their mother said with a suggestion of weariness. "No, my son, and nor are you. But the horses have always spoken to you. If you might go to the Mare—"

"She won't choose me," he said a little too quickly.

"No," said Sarai, "she'll not choose a man to be her one great servant. But she might reveal somewhat to you that she has declined to reveal to the rest of us. She chose you, after all, to be her guardsman."

Khayan opened his mouth, but shut it again. He could hardly argue with such logic. It was women's logic, Mare's logic. He bowed to it.

VII

KHAYAN COULD NOT go out at once to confront the Mare. Night had fallen while he spoke with his mother. The daymeal was long since spread, and he had been absent from it. There was a sizable repast waiting for him in his chambers, and a lissome woman in his bed— not the astonishing Barukha, somewhat to his surprise. This was one of the maids, an Egyptian, with smoky eyes and smooth bare limbs and no modesty at all.

He ate what was laid out for him, and took the maid, too, because she was willing—or so she pretended. She lacked Barukha's liveliness, but not the skill. She was very skilled, even with a man too tired and preoccupied to do her justice.

She soothed his body. His mind was not so easily comforted. It spun back and forth, round and about: Barukha, his mother, his sisters, the Mare who would not bind herself to a human woman. Nor would Khayan, either, but that was half laziness, and half circumstance. He did not want a wife. He did not want to exert himself to the degree that a wife required. Nor had one been presented to him, Barukha notwithstanding. Barukha had made it clear that he would have to wait for her. She wanted that old and wealthy man first, to make her a widow, and therefore free to choose. Then she would come to Khayan.

And all the while his mind rested on her face and voice, the maid stroked and fondled, bringing him erect in spite of himself. He woke with a small start to awareness of her face, little pointed Egyptian cat-face, long Egyptian eyes. The lips smiled but the eyes were dark, dark and cold.

He gasped. She mounted him and rode him as one of his own sisters would ride a stallion, still with smiling mouth and empty eyes. That was Egypt. Yes. That was all this country to a lord of the conquering people.

＋ ＋

It was a full hand of days before Khayan could do his mother's bidding. He could not escape his duties, nor would he shirk them. When he woke in the morning, the steward Teti was there with his list of things that the lord should do. After Khayan had done as many of them as mortal flesh could bear, the dusk was closing in and the daymeal was spread and waiting.

One such duty was presented to him the day after he spoke to his mother. His summons there had put him in mind of that other house, the women's house proper. He remembered all too vividly how he had gone into that house that first day, fresh with the delight of his bright new lordship, and found a huddle of Egyptian women round one of their own who was ailing. That one had flung a cup at his feet, full of something perfectly foul; most sane and sensible of her, he had thought then. She had done well enough since, he had undertaken to discover. She had served him wine that very night, though not on the nights thereafter.

She was but one of the slaves. But the one who had made herself the center of that room—that one was no more a slave than she could well bear to be. Teti would not speak of her unless pressed, and then in tones of barely muted awe.

The Lady Nefertem. She had been the lady of this house while it was an Egyptian holding, wedded to its lord who had died in a rebellion against King Apophis. She had been enslaved as was proper, but that fact had never impinged upon her consciousness. She had kept her house, her place, her servants.

Khayan's father had not been a weak man, but he had had a weakness for strong women. And beautiful women. Khayan remembered well the face turned to him in the dim light of the sickroom, the ivory pallor of it, the lines as pure and clean as carving in white stone. There was beauty such as he had never seen, exquisite in its perfection. It knew itself completely, accepted itself utterly. It did not even trouble to be vain.

Khayan could not see that it was reasonable for a lord of his people to live in a house still half in Egyptian hands. Particularly since, if certain rumors were true, the winds of rebellion were blowing strong again. It was enough that the steward of the estate was a native man: that needed one who spoke the language, and who could make the slaves and servants and the farmers in their fields work for their lord. There was no need and no sense in suffering the women's house to remain an outpost of the enemy.

Therefore, between his morning's travels out and about and his afternoon's sojourn in the hall of judgment, Khayan turned toward the women's house.

He was not stopped, no more than he had been on the first day. But his coming this time was no surprise. He found the hallways open to him, the guards submissive. And in the heart of that brilliantly colored and strikingly bare house, he found her.

She was sitting in a chair of carved ivory, an ivory image herself, sheathed in the translucent gauze that Egyptian women called clothing. Her wig was severe in its simplicity, straight black hair cut to frame her face. It shone like a jewel in that setting. One almost forgot the body so barely hidden by the gown, the breasts rose-tipped and half bared, the dark triangle in the curve of her lap.

Almost. Every fingerbreadth of her was exquisite. The face merely crowned it, still and cold in its perfection.

She did not acknowledge him, though he stood in front of her, towering over her. He was huge in that place, outsized, looming and awkward. Her maids cowered away from him. She did not even seem to see him.

"Nefertem," he said.

The sound of her name should have roused a flicker at the least. But she was lost in her own strange world.

He did a thing he would never have done if she had seemed even slightly aware of him: he reached and took her chin in his hand and tilted it up. It moved like a child's toy, with lifeless obedience. The eyes so lifted to his were blank. She might have been carved in stone, for all the life or soul he found there.

Again, if she had seemed alive, he would not have done what he did. He swept her off her chair. She resisted him not at all. Her maids fled shrieking; none even tried to fend him off.

There was, in the pattern of such houses, a room beyond this one, and a bed on a platform, draped in gauzy veils. He let her fall to it. She made no move to protect herself, simply lay as he had cast her. Save that she was warm, and her breast rose and fell as she breathed, she might have been a dead thing.

Khayan stood over her in a kind of despair. A proper man of his people would take her now, take her and master her, and make himself truly lord of this place.

Khayan was his mother's son. He had grown to manhood in the east, in a tribe ruled by a woman. He could not master a woman in such a fashion.

Almost he turned and walked away—fled, to give it its honest name. But he had his own kind of stubbornness. Rape he would not—could not—commit.

So let it not be rape.

Carefully and with deliberate slowness he put off his robe and his tunic and his loincloth. She never moved. He resisted the temptation to arrange her limbs, to make her more comfortable.

He lay naked beside her. He was fiercely, almost painfully aware of his height, his breadth, his pelt of black curly hair—all so alien to that ivory slenderness. What she thought of him, if she thought at all, she betrayed no sign.

But of course. His father had had her. That had been made clear to him. Cold as a fish, she must have been. But the old man had had no such foolish compunctions as Khayan had. He would take a woman if he reckoned she needed taking.

Khayan would take her, too, but in the way that suited him best. Gently, barely perceptibly, he stroked his hand down that still and lightly breathing body. It did not quiver. Nor did he retreat. He stroked her as if she had been a filly he wished to tame, over and over, gentle, steady, and perfectly persistent.

However far away a woman's mind might wander, her body could not ignore forever the persistence of touch. Her skin warmed under the drift of gauze. Her nipples tautened. Did her breath quicken? Of that he could not be certain.

He rose over her. She was as remote as ever. Her wig had not moved in all this while. Was it perhaps, after all, her own glossy black hair?

The paint masked her face in odd ways: made her eyes long and strange, shaped her lips into a perfect bow. It was like kissing a painted image, and yet the flesh beneath was warm. "Lady," he said in her own language, breathing the word. "Lady, you are beautiful."

Beauty without life; without living response. He would rouse it. He made a vow to himself. She would wake and see him, and know him for her lord.

Arrogance. He laughed suddenly, dropped to the bed beside her and propped himself on his elbow and said, as if she would respond, "My father never touched you, did he?"

To his astonishment she replied, "He never dared."

"So," said Khayan. "You're not a lifeless thing."

She did not move, did not glance at him. But her words were clear enough. "You will never master the Two Lands."

"I'll be content to master you, lady."

"You may try," she said.

"Did he talk to you, too?"

"In his own language," she said.

"Did you answer?"

"Sometimes."

"Are you sorry I can understand you?"

"They say you were far away, living among a people we never knew. Where did you learn to speak the language of the one true people?"

"I was born in Memphis," he said. "My nurse was Egyptian."

"Pity," she said.

"It did corrupt me," he said.

How strange to be lying here naked beside the most beautiful woman he had seen in his life, and she not moving, not a muscle, except to speak in that soft, clear voice. He had gathered, from words dropped here and there, that her beauty masked a mind of no particular acuity or wit. Lying here, listening to her, he rather doubted it. It was not a mind like other minds—but it was keen enough.

She moved suddenly, taking him off guard. She rose over him as, a little before, he had risen over her. Her hair hung down, hovering just above his cheeks. Her white breasts swayed. Her eyes were alive, glittering like the eyes of the cobra that to these people was sacred.

The cobra was a goddess. She protected her people. Some she devoured— but that was the way of divinity.

The Lady Nefertem raked long painted nails down his cheek, his throat, his breast. He lay utterly still.

She kissed him. Her kiss was fire. Songs sang of such things. He had never believed in them. Kisses were wet, warm, and yes, arousing. But fire?

This was fire. It licked his limbs with pleasure close to pain. It brought his rod springing erect, so sudden and so fierce that he gasped.

Her fingers closed about it. Bands of heated bronze, holding it close, not tight, but with a hint, a glimmer of cruel strength.

She smiled. Her smile was sweet, remote, and not a little mad. "Now who is master here?" she asked him.

"Why, you are," he said, and not terribly unwillingly, either. "But out there, where the world can see, I am. For that world's sake, I can't let you rule in this house. I hope you can understand."

"What is there to understand?" Her fingers tightened on his rod. He set his teeth. She began to stroke him, slowly, with skill to find each separate point of pleasure or pain.

"You are not my master," she said. "You are not master in the Two Lands. We will cast you out, foreigner: you and all your kind."

"I could have you put to death for that," he said—gasped, for she was doing marvelous, terrible things with those clever fingers.

She laughed. It was true laughter, sweet and achingly pure. "You? You could never harm a woman."

"But certain of my men could."

"Surely," she said. "And you would never set them on me. Your heart is soft, foreigner. You have no cruelty in you."

"You don't know that."

"I know you very well indeed," she said. Stroking, stroking; sending ripples through his body, till he was near convulsed—just on the edge of bursting, but never, quite, past it.

A woman could still, after a fashion, think, even in the midst of this oldest of dances. With what little was left of his wits, Khayan regretted that part at least of being a man. He was entirely in this woman's power, and well she knew it.

Maybe she thought to break him so. If he had been as other men of his people, so might she have done. But he was his mother's son. He had learned these arts in the arms of women more skilled and colder-hearted than this one could begin to be. As they had taught him, he gave himself up to it; he let himself be mastered. So he protected his spirit; so he kept his heart whole, though she did with his body as she would.

At last she let him go—a release so welcome that he groaned aloud. She laughed at him, sweet rippling laughter like water running.

He astonished her: he laughed with her. She fell silent, staring. He would dearly have loved to collapse into sleep, but that would not be wise at all. He rose—staggering slightly, which he hoped but doubted she would not see—and smiled at her. "You are rather skillful," he said. "For an Egyptian."

He gathered up his clothing, shrugged into the robe and bundled the rest under his arm, and left her there. What she was thinking, he did not know, nor overmuch care.

VIII

WHEN KHAYAN HAD bathed and put on fresh garments, he summoned Teti the steward. The man came with reasonable dispatch, as he should have done: he would have been waiting with the rest in the hall of judgment for Khayan to begin the day's deliberations. Khayan would do that, oh yes. But first he had a task for his steward.

Teti was a small man as all Egyptians were. Unlike some who seemed to bake and dry in the desert heat till they left little for the embalmers to do when they died, he was in good flesh, firm rather than soft, with a solid belly and broad bull's shoulders. He walked with authority, and carried himself as one who matters in the world.

There was in fact a remarkable lack of servility in this place. The Egyptians called it the house of the Sun Ascendant, a grand name for a minor lord's holding. Certainly its people conducted themselves as if they believed in it.

Khayan sat in the chair that he had made his own, conspicuously at his ease, and regarded the steward of the Sun Ascendant. The steward waited patiently. He had served three lords now, two of them foreigners, and remained alive, unmaimed, and in full possession of his office. He had well learned the virtue of silence.

"Teti," Khayan said. "You will do a thing for me."

The steward bowed his head in its heavy wig. His collar glittered. It was a massive thing, made all of beads, blue and white and green and red, and here and there a gleam of gold.

"You will go," said Khayan, "and take the woman Nefertem, and conduct her to my lady mother. This is a gift, you will tell her, to do with as she pleases."

Teti had been still before, but not as still as this. His cheeks had gone grey. Khayan saw well his heart's trouble. He was servant to this master, had accepted this lordship and therefore bound himself in obedience to it. And yet he had an older loyalty, and a deeper awe.

Khayan had no intention of sparing him this. A lord could not be a lord without his people's obedience. That lesson he had learned from his childhood.

"Go," he said. "See that it is done."

Teti bowed again, so low that Khayan could not see his face at all. He backed out so, as if from a king.

Khayan pondered briefly the wisdom of sending one of his own men to be certain that the Egyptian obeyed. But that would confess to weakness. He rose instead, stretched the knots and stiffness out of his body, and went to judge whatever disputes had need of his judgment.

✢ ✢

Teti came into the hall while Khayan was in the midst of a lengthy, tedious, and profoundly confusing debate between two farmers over the value of an ox. It was not that either of them actually owned the ox, so much as that they appeared to share it with a third farmer, who was present but not involved in the dispute. As far as he could understand, they were perfectly agreed as to who had the use of it at which time and for what purpose. The disagreement seemed to have something to do with who was to feed the ox, and who was to repair its stable, which was in need of a new roof. But it was all tangled up in a great number of other things, from the marriage of one man's daughter to the shrewishness of their neighbor's wife.

Khayan would dearly have loved to halt the proceedings, send the fools away, and hear Teti's news, if there was any. But that was not a lordly thing to do. However long the disputants driveled on, he must hear them out. Then he must, as best he could, issue a judgment.

Teti had taken his proper place beside and somewhat behind Khayan's chair, which by accident or design set him just out of Khayan's sight. Khayan could feel him there, the heat of his presence; hear the soft hiss of his breath.

The dispute went on and on. The sharing of the ox and the repair of its stable had delayed the wedding of one of the farmers' daughters. Why that should be so, was still not entirely clear. It seemed she did not wish to marry while her father was embroiled in a quarrel with the uncle of her intended.

Khayan's head had begun to ache. As feuds went, this one was remarkably bloodless, but it was also remarkably complicated. And the shadows marched across the floor of the hall, growing longer and ever longer. He thought he could catch a hint of fragrance: meat roasting, bread baking for the daymeal.

At last, as the light shifted over toward the mellower gold of sunset, Khayan struck his staff on the floor. The babble of argument barely slowed. He rose. He did not lift his voice, but he made certain that it could be heard. "I have heard enough."

He held his breath. They could ignore him, easily. But something in his voice brought them up short and stilled them, so that they turned all in a gaggle and stared at him.

He let his breath out slowly. "Very well," he said. "You will continue to divide the use of the ox according to your older agreement. You will feed him on alternate days. You will both repair his stable. And," he said, "your children will wed on the next day of good omen."

"But that is tomorrow!" one of them gasped—the girl's father, Khayan seemed to recall.

Khayan smiled. "Then you had best get to it, had you not?"

That rid him of them, and handily. Any others who waited must wait another day; it was far too late to hear them. Khayan beckoned to Teti. "You come," he said. The rest he left behind, all but the one of his young fighting men whose turn it was on guard.

On most days Khayan would have gone back to his rooms to prepare for the daymeal, but he had had enough for the moment of roofs and walls. He went to the stable instead.

That might not have been the wisest choice of places to take an Egyptian— they hated horses, and feared them unreasonably—but Khayan's mood was too contrary to care. There in the open sandy courts, in the smell of horses and cut fodder, he could breathe; he could think.

He went in among his own horses, his team of duns that he had bred and raised and broken to the yoke himself. They whickered at his coming, there in the space that they shared, crowding together to take the bits of barley cake that he had brought. He smoothed forelocks, rubbed broad brows, murmured into ears that cocked to catch his words. The language he spoke to them was the language of an older people than his father's, the language of the eastern tribes.

Almost he forgot the Egyptian hovering in the doorway and quaking when the horses glanced at him, but waiting doggedly upon his lord's pleasure. He turned in the embrace of his stallions, and saw himself for a moment as an Egyptian must see him: surrounded by monstrous creatures and nigh over-whelmed.

The vision made him smile. "So tell me," he said more warmly than he might have done in other company. "Did she go quietly?"

Teti's lips were tight. He was angry, and taking care that Khayan knew it. "Yes, my lord," he said. "She went quietly."

"Tell me," Khayan said.

A more taciturn man might have set his lips and refused, but Teti had no such gift of restraint. He hated to speak to this foreigner, he made it clear, but speak he did. "She made no protest," he said. "She bowed her head and did as you bade her through me."

"And when she came to my mother?"

"I did not go in," Teti said severely. "I sent her with your lady mother's guards."

Khayan's teeth clicked together. Ah: revenge. It was petty, but it must be sweet.

Let him enjoy it. Khayan would go later, and see how that haughty lady fared among women of her own ilk, if not of her own tribe and nation.

"You've done well," Khayan said to Teti. "You may go."

The man departed with visible relief. Khayan lingered in the warmth of his horses' regard. Moon had a tangle in his mane; Star had cut his foot. Khayan tended them with care and without haste, for the simple pleasure of it.

But his mind could not stop spinning. He was born in this country, under this immensity of sky. He loved it. He had yearned for it in his years away, for all the beauty of the eastern lands, for all that they had bred his mother and her mothers before her. When he came back to Egypt, he had wept for joy.

And its people hated him and all his kind. A hundred years they had been in Egypt, and Egypt had never forgiven, never forgotten. No foreign king had ever sat the throne of Egypt, until Salitis of Retenu. Every king after him had been hated the more.

"And yet we are solid here," Khayan said to his stallions. "We've taken root. We belong here."

They who had been foaled in the broad grasslands of the east, had no care for such things. Horses did not take root. Horses went where the good grazing was, and where their master wished to be. The grazing here was good indeed, and he was here. In the way of horses, they were content.

✣ ✣

Khayan did not, that night, go to his mother or inquire after the welfare of his gift. Let them settle with one another, he reflected as he sat to the daymeal with the men of the house. There was a guest this evening: one who greeted him with a whoop and a rib-cracking embrace.

"Iannek!" he said when he could speak again. "When did you come here?"

His brother grinned at him. "Just now," he said, "and yes, the king let me go. He was tired of my moping about, he said. He told me to go somewhere where I'd learn to smile again."

"Here?"

Khayan must have sounded more dubious than he knew. Iannek slapped his shoulder, not lightly, and laughed. "What can I say, brother? I missed your somber glower, your foreboding frowns, your—"

"So," Khayan said. "Who was she this time?"

Iannek's face fell, betraying him, even as he said, "Who was she? What makes you think it was a woman?"

"Because I know you," Khayan said. "If you could keep it sheathed even half of the time, you'd be a much happier man."

"I'd rest better," Iannek admitted. "But happier? No, brother. Not that."

"So who was she?"

Iannek ducked his head and mumbled it. But Khayan's ears were keen. "Prince Kastan's seventh wife. But," he was swift to add, "he hadn't even looked at her since their wedding was over, and his other wives were cruel to her, and—"

"You were cuckolding the king's favorite brother?" Khayan could not say he was surprised. What did amaze him—"And you were allowed to go away free and unmaimed?"

"Well," said Iannek. "I left quickly. If you take my meaning."

"You were encouraged to make yourself scarce while the king pretended to be unaware of you." Khayan sighed. "He must love you. He'd never do this for another man."

"It's my charming smile," Iannek said. "He says I remind him of himself when he was younger."

"He was never that bad," Khayan said, with a growl in it. "So now he's inflicted you on me. What does he want me to do with you, besides clip your wings?"

Iannek shrugged. "Ignore me? I'll behave myself."

"Swear to it."

"Well," said Iannek. "I'll try."

"Swear," said Khayan.

Iannek wriggled and muttered and fussed, but Khayan was unrelenting. At last the young fool said, "I swear."

"Good," said Khayan, no doubt to his brother's great relief. "Come, dinner is waiting. Sit by me; tell me all the gossip from court."

Iannek eyed him sidelong, maybe looking for further signs of lordly sternness, maybe incredulous that Khayan of all people should care for court gossip. Khayan did not, not really; but a lord had to know who was feuding with whom near the king. That much he had learned while he was himself at court.

Whatever he thought of the matter, Iannek was willing enough to share roast ox and stewed duck, and more than willing to chatter on about this lord and that, this feud, that alliance, so-and-so married into thus-and-so's family, some young idiot dead in a knife-fight in the streets of Avaris, and now half the young idiots at court were hot to follow his example.

"Delightful," Khayan said to that. "They'll kill each other off, and spare the rest of us the trouble."

"Oh, no," said Iannek. "They're not killing one another. They're hunting Egyptians. Egyptians killed Samiel. So now everybody's out to get revenge."

"I'm surprised they aren't hunting in native coverts," Khayan said dryly.

"Oh, they're doing that, too," Iannek said. "But mostly they go to the towns, or even down to Memphis. Some of them are bringing back the right hands of their kills, like old Egyptian warriors."

"What, not their rods, too?"

Iannek stared.

Khayan shook his head. "They all must be as ignorant as you. The old Egyptians would bring back the right hand and the rod—so that the king knew it was a man indeed that had been killed, and not a woman."

"That's barbaric," Iannek said.

"Yes," said Khayan.

Iannek was immune to subtlety, or to irony either. "Well, and a hand is enough, these days. It's quite a fashion in some circles. Not mine," he was quick to add. "I'm not a great one for hunting men."

"That's well," Khayan said. "Nor am I. War is one thing. This—the Egyptians hate us enough as it is. This will tip them straight over into rebellion."

"Ah," said Iannek with a tilt of the head, "rebellion. They're always rebelling. We'll put them down, we always do. Even the time they took Avaris. And that will give us a nice war."

Khayan shook his head. There was no reasoning with a mind as simple as this, and little profit in trying. He applied himself to his cup and bowl and plate, while Iannek chattered on, wandering mercifully away from tales of Egyptians hunted like animals toward the safer ground of yet another family feud.

+ +

Khayan's men were not in fact any older than the pack of young rowdies that ran with Iannek, but they were horribly dull in comparison. Khayan had chosen them for their sobriety and self-discipline—not easy virtues for any young horseman—and for their skill with horses. If he was to increase his herds, and that on Egyptian land, with Egyptian labor as much as might be, he needed men who could conduct themselves with restraint.

No such requirement accompanied Iannek's following. Most, from what Khayan could gather, had attached themselves to the young lord for a lark, or because, like him, they had reason to vanish for a while from the king's city. They were a restless, troublesome lot, idle and fond of brawling.

When they discovered that the wine was not free for the taking, and the beer was handed out at the kitchen door by a large and humorless personage who was immune to every threat, from pleading to outright force, they howled like dogs. They actually tried to storm the storehouses—only to find themselves face to face with grim men and sharp spears.

None of the maids was safe from them. Khayan had, as soon as Iannek was well settled, seen that they were moved into his mother's house of nights, but these young rakehells were at them from dawn till dusk. Never an hour passed, it seemed, but that he heard a shriek and a scuffle, and saw a bruised and tousled girl running from a bellowing male. Or he would walk round a corner and stumble into a pair of them going at it with good will, maid as well as man. That he never tried to stop; but the other roused his temper, sometimes to an injudicious degree.

He had to make order in this house, if he was to continue ruling it. And had he not thought the same of the Lady Nefertem? He had hardly dealt with her when this new plague of disorder fell upon him.

Maybe she had cursed him, at that. Egyptians were great masters of magic, everyone said so. Not that he had ever seen anything more wondrous than a charlatan in the market of Memphis, turning staves into serpents and water into wine. Still, he had not been in the temples, nor seen the great rites of which people whispered. Who knew what that lady might have done? Her will was as remarkable as her beauty, and she hated his kind with a perfect hate.

If that was so, then she was laughing at him now. He could not cast these ramping fools into his mother's clutches, no matter how he might be tempted. He could send them away—but Iannek was his brother, and his burden as lord of the house.

He would bear the burden somehow. He pondered it as he rode out of a morning—could it be a mere hand of days since he spoke with his mother? It seemed a great deal longer.

He had intended to ride out past the horses' fields, to ride the eastern border of these lands, and to visit the village that sat between this estate and that of the Oryx, which belonged still to an Egyptian lord. That one kept to himself, Khayan had been given to understand, and did not either vex or commune with his overlords. He had beautiful daughters, it was said, and sons even more beautiful, and they were all kept as close as royal ladies.

One day Khayan would visit this lord and see if the tales were true. Tomorrow, maybe, unless his house found better order in between. He might even, he thought a little wildly, inflict himself on his neighbor for a day or three, taxing that lord's hospitality as his brother's following taxed his own.

But not this morning. He was alone but for a pair of guards following in a second chariot. Even beyond the gate he could hear the start of the day's uproar: voices raised, yelling for wine; snatches of drunken song left over from the night before; and the squeal of a woman set upon by what sounded like a hungry mob. He almost turned back at that, but the next voice that sounded was that of his own captain of guards, a great beautiful bull-bellow that made Khayan laugh aloud. Ah: so they had gone after Bashan's woman. Not wise of them. Not wise of them at all.

And he was free of them, for a while. He glanced over his shoulder at his guards. They looked as glad to be out of that uproar as he was. He grinned. They grinned back. "Race you!" he called out.

They grinned wider. Melech the charioteer whipped up his fine strong bays. Daleth his brother clung to the side of the chariot and whooped.

Khayan was already somewhat behind. Star shook his head in the traces and snorted. Moon squealed in rage. He could never bear to lose a race. Khayan gave them rein and braced his feet. They leaped from trot into gallop.

The wind whipped his face, sharp-edged with sand. He laughed at the small stinging pain. The heavy tail of his hair lifted and streamed out behind him. His tunic flattened to his body, pressed as tight as a woman's embrace. "Faster," he sang to his stallions, his golden-coated, black-maned beauties. "Faster!" They stretched their stride.

Melech's bay mares were flat to the ground, racing at full speed. Khayan's duns were still at their ease. He shortened rein a little, held them level with the mares, though Moon snatched at the bit in protest. "Not yet," he crooned to them. "Not . . . quite . . . yet."

The hill was still ahead, the long low ridge that divided the house and its lands from the farther fields. Just as the ground began to rise, Khayan slackened rein. Moon needed no urging. His yokemate was of one mind with him. They had been racing Melech's bays. Now they raced the wind itself.

They breasted the hill far ahead of the others, still fresh enough to object mightily to his bidding that they slow. But Khayan hardened his heart. They had still a fair distance to go, if they were to go at all. He brought them to a fretful and jigging walk, and sang them into calm, though not into full acceptance. They were too high-hearted for that.

In slowing them he had turned and run along the hilltop for a little distance. When they would walk at last, he turned again, angling somewhat down the hill. The herds spread out below, all his horses, those that he had inherited from his father, and those that he had acquired since he came back to Egypt— and most beautiful of all, if least numerous, those that, like his duns, had come all the way from the east of the world.

Most of those were duns, too, and bays, and blacks. But the Mare's herd ran near them as always, greys all, from dark filly-foal to cloud-white queen. Khayan could never see them without remembering the land that they came from: windy fields of grass rolling toward the sunrise, and the sky's vault over them, and Earth Mother's spirit breathing through them.

These were the Mother's children, her beloved, Horse Goddess' own. Their foremothers were foaled in time out of mind, long and long ago in the dawn of the world. It was still strange to see them here, under this sky that had never known their like, before gods that wore the faces of beasts and birds, but never of horses.

They seemed well content in this land to which they had asked to be brought. The heat troubled them little, that he could see, though their lesser kin suffered in it, fell ill and too often died. The sun beat on their pale coats and left them as cool as ever. Their wide nostrils breathed deep of the air, though it burned like the blast from a furnace. Their dark eyes gazed easily into the glare. They gleamed in it like bright metal, or like snow on the mountaintops, far away on the world's edge.

They grazed now in their herd, moving slowly over the broad field. In time they would come to the water-passage that ran from the river, the stream that men had dug and filled to keep these fields green. Then they would drink, and wander away again.

The stallion walked behind them, he of the great white neck and the streaming mane. He was beautiful; his ladies less so, with their sagging bellies and their air of great weariness with the world. And yet any horseman, once he cast eyes on them, could not easily turn away. They had no match in the world, and well they knew it.

At last Melech and his bays came level with Khayan. He greeted his guardsmen with a glance and a nod, and said, "Daleth, come here. Drive my beauties down by the road, and wait for me past the last of the fields. I'll walk there in a while."

The brothers glanced at one another and rolled their eyes. This was one of their lord's oddities, to walk among the horses—most peculiar, to their minds, and no matter what the arrival of a chariot drawn by a pair of stallions would do to the delicate balance of nations within the fields. A man afoot in a tunic of fine-tanned horsehide, smelling of horses, scarce alarmed even the shyest of the foals.

He passed among them with a deep pleasure that he knew nowhere else. The horses raised their heads at his coming, drew in the scent of him, blew softly but knew no fear. The young ones came to him, and some of their elders, too, so that he might rub an ear, a neck, a shoulder. It was a royal progress of sorts, if he could be so arrogant as to see it so.

Horse Goddess' children did not stoop to come to a man, however great he might reckon himself in the world. Their foals were less circumspect. The youngest, the lovely colt with the star on his brow, called out in a shrill whinny. He led the others in a grand charge. Khayan waited for it, fearless and full of a sudden, piercing joy. They swept around him but never touched him, swirled and circled and came to rest all about him. They blew warm breath into his hands; they slipped warm necks under his arms. They nipped, or made as if to try. He laughed and pushed them away.

The star-browed colt was closest and most persistent. When Khayan moved away at last, the others wandered off, but he followed. If Khayan paused, he made certain that Khayan's arm rested over his back. He was a most determined colt.

The mares watched with wise dark eyes. Horse Goddess was in them all. But she who was most truly divine, she who had been born at the full of the moon in a Great Year, a year of the women's mysteries, was nowhere among them.

Still trailed by the colt, though the colt's dam called to him, summoning him, Khayan went hunting the Mare. She could not be difficult to find: a moon-colored coat among the black and brown and dun, dappled like the moon, and a mane like a fall of bright water.

And yet he searched far through the herds that he had brought to this place, and beyond them, and saw no sign of her. Not until he had almost turned back in despair, when he had come all the way to the river, where it shrunk nigh to its smallest extent. The grass there was newer than elsewhere, soft and vividly green. Great stands of reeds grew there, and the fans of papyrus that were so precious in Egypt. Birds fluttered and called in the coverts. A little distance down the river, a riverhorse surged to the surface, breached and rolled and gaped its great maw at the sky.

Khayan was parched with thirst, but he knew better than to drink from the river. Demons of sickness lived in that water, and worse yet for one who stooped to drink, crocodiles lurking, lying in wait for prey. They could sever a man's head from his shoulders with one swift leap and snap, and leave his body for the vultures to find.

He shook his head at his morbid fancies. He had a waterskin hung on his belt, and clean water in it, too. He paused to drink, sipping as one learned to do in the desert. Though he was parched—fool, to come so far in the sun and never touch his waterskin—he fastened it up again with much of its contents intact. He kept the last sip on his tongue, rolling it, savoring each vanishing drop.

Beyond a tall thicket of papyrus, something moved; something pale. He stilled with a hunter's instinct. Softly he advanced.

She was there, past the thicket, grazing in the rich grass. Nor was she alone.

At first Khayan did not see the figure sitting in the shade. It made him think of a young deer, though it was indisputably human; and incontestably female, too, for in the manner of young Egyptians of whatever station, it was as naked as it was born.

It—she—rose up out of the grass as he watched, went to the Mare and tangled fingers in the pale mane and leaned against that strong shoulder as if she had done such a thing many times before. And very likely she had.

She *was* Egyptian. Her slim brown body, her straight black hair cut level with her brows in front and cropped to the shoulders behind, her long painted eyes and her narrow pointed face—those had never ridden out of any eastern tribe. And yet she kept company with a horse—with the Mare—as if she had been born to it.

He was standing in plain sight, yet she was not aware of him at all. She was half turned away from him, intent on the Mare, plaiting a string of flowers into her mane. It was so utterly a thing that a woman would do, and a young one at that, that Khayan bit his lips against laughter.

Just as the colt betrayed him, he slipped—again with hunter's instinct—into the cover of the thicket. The colt whickered and trotted toward the Mare, aware at last, perhaps, that he was far away from his mother.

The Mare flattened ears and snapped at him. He veered, mouthing submission. Had he had speech, he would have been crying for mercy.

"Lady!" the Egyptian said—clear, sharp, and in his own birth-tongue.

"Why did you do that? Here, little one, where did you leave your mother, then?"

The colt was no fool: he knew when he had found an ally. He insinuated himself into her arms much as he had done to Khayan, and with the same success, too. She lacked a certain skill, but she knew where to rub, and she did it with a good enough will. She had none of the fear, and certainly none of the loathing, that he had seen in every other of her people.

Khayan drew back further into hiding. She intended, plainly, to seek out the colt's dam and return him to her. It would not be an arduous search: the mare and a handful of her herdmates were a little distance behind him, following the wayward child since he would not follow them.

The reunion was as touching it could be among horses. The colt dived for his mother's teat. She nipped him sharply on the rump as he passed, by way of rebuke. The rest crowded toward the rich sweet grass.

The Egyptian was Egyptian after all: she flinched a little as the horses surrounded her, drawing back against the Mare. And the Mare shifted until she stood between the girl and the rest of her herd. Guarding her as a mare guards a foal—or a human whom she has made her own.

················· IX ·················

KHAYAN HAD MUCH to think on. He had found his chariot and turned his stallions and driven back to the house of the Sun Ascendant, gone as far as his bath and let himself be attended in it, before he remembered that he had been riding to the eastern village.

That would wait as long as it must. So too the day's judgments in hall.

"Put them off," he said to Teti the steward.

Teti would not ask why, and Khayan had no intention of answering. Nor would he put on the robe that his servant had laid out for him. He demanded and received a tunic of linen: Egyptian fabric, outland fashion. It was cool, which was all that mattered to him then. Cool and unobtrusive.

He needed the steppe: the endless sea of grass, where a man could ride forever and never meet another human soul. What he had was here: a stiff little box of a garden, and a pool with fish drifting lazily in it, and an arbor of green branches under which a man could sit and try to dream that he was free.

His mind was still in great part by the riverbank, watching the Mare with her—her!—Egyptian. He could with no difficulty remember the Mare before her, who had been old when he was young; but they were long-lived creatures. The woman who belonged to her had been of no age in particular, a small plump woman of great power among the priestesses of Horse Goddess. Had her ascent to eminence been a shock to those who knew her?

That, he rather doubted. She was of an old line out of the east, if not of the oldest. Her breeding was as impeccable as the Mare's.

This . . .

An Egyptian. A slender fawn of a girl, whose face he had reason to recognize. She had been ill when he came into the women's house, his first day in his new lands. She had poured his wine that night, hale as if she had never suffered any sickness; and then he had no memory of her.

And no wonder in that, if she had spent her days with the Mare.

"Melech!" he called.

His guardsman, who had been hovering in clear hopes of not being seen, crept out from behind a pillar and bowed. "My lord?"

"Fetch my master of horse," Khayan said. "And then, if you please, put yourself to bed. You were up half the night playing my nursemaid. It's time you gave someone else a part in the game."

Melech grumbled at that, but he was obedient. Khayan settled to wait. A servant brought wine kept cool in a deep storehouse, and a platter of the cook's whimsies: little cakes, spiced fruits, nuts rolled in honey. Khayan had not known he was hungry till he looked at the platter and saw that half of it was empty.

His master of horse appeared while there were still cakes and fruit to offer him, and most of the jar of wine. Jerubaal had been born in Byblos, but his ancestors had been horsemen since the dawn time, riders, charioteers, masters of horses. He had the look of his kind: thin, wiry, dried to whipcord by years of wind and sun. But for the worn leather tunic and the curly black-grey beard, he might have been an Egyptian.

Jerubaal did not stand on ceremony with the man whom he had first known as a naked, toddling child. It was he who had caught the very young Khayan on the day he decided, all on his own and eluding his nurses, to visit the horses. Khayan had gone in among the mares and played for a long while with the foals, and fallen asleep with his head on the shoulder of an equally tired colt. The first face he had seen when he woke was Jerubaal's, younger then and much less grey, but as narrow and humorous as ever. "So, little prince," the man had said then. "Chosen your stallion already, have you?"

Today, a good score of years since, Jerubaal sat beside Khayan and poured himself a cup of wine. He would have been in the stable at this time of day, when it was too hot to work the horses: mending harness, trimming hooves, grooming horses. He seemed glad enough to have been called away; he did not ask why, nor trouble Khayan with chatter. Like his horses, he had the art of silence.

Khayan basked in it for a while, sipping the last of his wine and regretting, somewhat, that last honeyed cake. He was almost sorry to have to break the silence; but the day was slipping away. "So," he said, soft in the stillness. "Tell me about the Mare."

"Ah," said Jerubaal. He took his time with the rest of it, savoring a sip of wine, a spiced nut. "So. You saw."

"I saw," Khayan said. "Who is she?"

Jerubaal shrugged. "Gods know. Not one of ours."

"I think you know," Khayan said.

"Well," said Jerubaal. He toyed with his cup, turning it in his long gnarled fingers. "She's a slave in this house, but time was when she was a lady in it. She's the rebel's daughter—the old lord who was killed fighting for the southern king."

"Is she?" Khayan did not trouble to berate himself, but he paused to be rueful. He should have discovered who the girl was the day he came here, when he found her the center of so much attention. Of course a mere slavegirl would not be granted the gift of the Lady Nefertem's regard.

"Jerubaal," Khayan said, out of that thought. "Is she the daughter of the woman who fancies herself lady here?"

"So I've been told," said Jerubaal. Which meant that he had discovered it to be the truth.

Khayan sat back against the cool stone of the wall, running fingers through his beard, tugging at it. The small pain kept him on edge; helped him to think. "Does my lady mother know?" he asked at length.

"Not from me," Jerubaal answered.

Perhaps therefore she knew it from no one. And surely, if she had, he would have known it. "When did you first see her with the Mare?"

Jerubaal frowned, counting on his fingers. "Well, my lord. Four—no, five days ago. She came wandering in among the horses, scared half out of her wits but walking like a woman bewitched. The Mare found her."

Khayan sat bolt upright. "The Mare? The *Mare* found *her?*"

Jerubaal nodded. He poured another cup and drank it down, as if he needed what courage was in the wine. "She came to the horses, but I'd wager it was a summons. The Mare went right up to her, touched her and herded her where the Mare had in mind to go. She didn't have the look of one who does such a thing of her own will."

"Was she afraid?"

"No," said Jerubaal. "Not of the Mare."

"The Mare called her," Khayan murmured. "Gods. My mother is going to be appalled."

"It is irregular," Jerubaal said.

"Irregular." Khayan snorted. "It's absolutely unheard of. This is an *Egyptian.*"

"So what will you do about it?"

"I don't know." Khayan sprang to his feet, unable to bear another moment's stillness. He paced in and out of the sun, from welcome shade to searing blaze and back again.

"This is a women's thing," Jerubaal said from the sanctuary of the arbor. "Why not leave it to the women?"

He spoke wisdom, as he usually did. But Khayan was oddly reluctant to do the thing that would free him from the whole affair. He had done as his mother had asked; he had inquired of the Mare, and received an answer. He had only to send word to her, and the rest was in her hands.

So simple. And so difficult. He stopped and spun. "Tell no one of this until I give you leave. See that your men do the same. Will you do that for me?"

"For you," said Jerubaal, "I'll do it."

Khayan nodded. Jerubaal drained his cup of wine, belched appreciatively, and took his leave.

Khayan lingered, though the day was dwindling. He had never kept a secret from his mother before, or from any woman. It was strange. It might anger Earth Mother. But not, he thought, Horse Goddess.

She had her reasons. What those were, were not for a mere man to know.

But he could certainly do his best to discover them.

+ +

In the morning Khayan rose before dawn, harnessed his horses with his own hands, and slipped out through a gate guarded only by a yawning young recruit. The recruit leaped to attention when the guttering torch showed him his lord's face, but Khayan bade him be at ease.

It was almost cool at this hour, when the stars had just begun to fade, and the very first of the light woke on the eastern horizon. The Egyptians had a god for this most mysterious of hours, the god of the first dawn: Khepera, Ra of the Horizon, who wore the face of the dung beetle, rolling the burning ball of the sun into the sky.

The earth was waking about him: birds calling, fish leaping, a riverhorse bellowing from the middle of the river, echoing over the water. He thought then and poignantly of first dawn among his mother's people, wind in the sea of grass, and a clear eerie voice rising over it: the Mother of the tribe, waking first as she did every morning, and going out to sing the sun into the sky.

Her song came to him as he drove his horses into the waking morning, words so old that all meaning was forgotten, and music ancient beyond human memory. He could not sing it aloud—that would be blasphemy. But it hummed through him. It sang in the reins, in the lightness with which his stallions took their bits, and caught the rhythm of the wheels over the uneven ground.

The horses were in their morning clusters, grazing where dew had fallen. He found the Mare's people down near the river, and the Mare grazing with a handful of her sisters. The youngest of those was a still a yearling and inclined toward silliness, but the rest forebore to encourage her.

Khayan hid his chariot in a bed of reeds, unharnessed his stallions and hobbled them apart from the herds. They would do well enough, if Horse Goddess was kind.

He had brought wherewithal for a day of lying in ambush, but of weapons only his short sword and his bow and quiver. He was not hunting to kill. Simply to see what he might see.

✦ ✦

She came just at full morning, striding as all these Egyptians did, even on the pavements of palaces: the gait of a people who had trusted to their own feet from the dawn of the world. Among Khayan's people, only the lowest walked so; and among his mother's people none did at all. They were all riders and charioteers.

Now that he knew who she was, he tried to see something of her mother in her. Apart from slenderness and darkness and a certain grace, which most Egyptians had, there was little. She was good to look at in her way, but not as the Lady Nefertem was—not a glorious and luminous beauty. She favored her father, perhaps.

She was rather unexceptional, truth be told. A girl or young woman of the conquered people, naked and sleek as a fish, with a blue bead on a string about her middle, and painted eyes. And yet as she came, all the Mare's people lifted their heads, and some whickered, welcoming her. She stroked necks and shoulders and rumps as she passed through them, fearless of them as she was not of other horses. Them she knew. Them she trusted.

The Mare waited for her on the herd's edge, too proud to mingle with her sisters and aunts and cousins. The girl seemed unsurprised by that. They met somewhat as lovers meet, in a kind of breathlessness. The Mare lowered nose into the girl's palm. The girl rested her head against the Mare's neck. And so they stayed, for a while, until the Mare remembered herself and went back to her grazing.

Khayan watched them the whole morning long. They did nothing of great interest, nothing wild or striking or magical. They lingered in each other's company, that was all. And at noon, as the sun touched the zenith, the girl bade the Mare a reluctant farewell, and walked back over field and hill to the house. She had never seen or sensed Khayan at all, though the Mare was well aware of him. The girl lacked a hunter's instinct, or a horse's. She was a simple mortal woman, that was all. Nothing more, if nothing less.

✦ ✦

Still he did not seek out his mother, or his sisters either. He was outraged, that was it. Appalled, and somewhat blackly amused. For the Mare to choose a foreigner, that was unheard of. But such a foreigner. No beauty, no brilliance, no royalty of lineage. Her ancestors had never known the Mare's people, had never known horses at all.

In the evening he asked that the Lady Nefertem's daughter wait on him. The one whom he asked, one of the understewards, rolled his eyes rather like a startled horse, but did not muster the courage to contest his lord's command.

The girl, however, was another matter. When the wine came around, she who brought it was a lissome Egyptian beauty, but she was not the one who went out every morning to keep company with the Mare.

Khayan endured the daymeal with less than his usual patience. Nor was he assisted by the boisterousness of his brother's following. They had got at the wine well before they came into the hall, having mounted a raid on the storeroom that would not, he swore to grimly to himself, be repeated. Those who fell over face-first in the roast duck were bearable. The rest bade fair to raise a riot.

Khayan left them to their folly—and bade the guards secure the entrances. Any that had in mind to wander off would find himself confined till morning. Or perhaps even longer, if Khayan happened to forget that he had shut the lot of them in the hall. With, he could not help but note, a dwindling supply of wine, but enough bread and meat to sustain them for a respectable while. Maybe he would simply leave them there. It would be inconvenient for banquets, but for peace in the house, it well might be worth the sacrifice.

✦ ✦

A lord did not usually make it his business to know every cranny of his house. But Khayan was not the usual sort of lord. He knew where the servants slept, and where they took what ease their duties left them. It was a useful thing to know when one was lord of a conquered country.

The girl, whose name, he had discovered, was Iry, had a room of her own. It was tiny and airless and boasted few comforts, but it signified much. A mere serving girl should not have her own place—no more than a fallen lord's wife should rule over the women's house as she had done when her husband was alive. They were all rebels here, subtle but unmistakable.

He brought a lamp with him from the hall to illumine the darkened passages. As much as he knew of the house, he had not walked often in the servants' corridors. They were narrow and dark, and their walls were of plain mudbrick without adornment. No march of painted Egyptians here, no beasts or birds or thickets of papyrus, no strange-faced gods watching over those who passed. When a door stood open, the light of his lamp showed a bare box of a room, and sometimes a huddle of bodies in it, servants sleeping in a heap like puppies, men together or women together or, once or twice, a man and a woman wound in one another's arms.

He trod silently as a hunter will. He had left his robe outside the hall, and kept only the tunic beneath. His feet were bare. He stalked his quarry to its lair, and found it—waiting?

Sitting on a bed that, though utterly without elegance, was more than most servants could claim. A lamp burned on a table beside the bed. She looked like one of the images that Egyptians so loved to set in tombs: cross-legged and utterly still, with eyes as dark and flat as stones.

He paused in the doorway. The room was tiny; if he entered it, he would fill it. She regarded him in silence, with neither surprise nor fear. He saw then how she was like her mother. She had that same air of pride that nothing could break, and obstinacy that nothing could shift. Whatever she did, she did of her own choice. No one had ever compelled her, or ever truly would.

He smiled faintly. Indeed; how like the Mare.

It was still an outrage. He glared at her. She stared coolly back. "You were not in hall tonight," he said.

She did not speak. Her shoulder lifted just visibly: the suggestion of a shrug.

"Are you not my slave?" he demanded of her.

"I do not choose to be," she said.

"Have you always been so defiant?"

"No," she said.

"Then why?"

Another shrug, a little clearer this time. "You're softer than your father was," she said.

"You think so?"

"He'd have had me brought to him by force, and made me kneel and beg his pardon."

"Ah," said Khayan. "I did think of that. But it's such a usual thing for a lord to do. I try not to do the usual."

"You are soft," she said.

"And you are your mother's child." He paused. "I gave her to my mother. What would you do if I did the same to you?"

She neither paled nor flinched. "I would do whatever seemed wise."

"Even if that were to serve her?"

"I might," she said. Her head tilted. "Are you going to take me before you send me there?"

"Why? Do you want me to?"

For the first time he saw a flicker of emotion. What it was, he could not be sure, but there was no mistaking it. Had he startled her? Amused her? Even dismayed her? "You are a strange man," she said.

"I'm my mother's son."

"Yes," she said.

There was a silence. Khayan considered leaving, but he had not said what he came to say. She could not escape: there was only one door, and he filled it. She lay back and propped herself on her elbow, at evident ease. She was naked as she always was, and as innocent of immodesty as a newborn child.

She made him think of his mother's people—and that was a dangerous thought; dangerous to his outrage.

"I saw you," he said. "Among the horses."

She did not move. Had she tensed a very little? "Is that a forbidden thing?" she asked.

"Do you think it should be?"

"You don't seem to approve," she said. "Why? Because I go out? Because I don't labor in the house from dawn far into the night?"

"No," he said. He paused. He asked her, "Do you know what horse it is that calls you until you come?"

There: at last. Visible, and honest, stiffening, and eyes wide in the narrow face. "How do you know— What do you mean? Is it a sacred horse?"

"Sacred," he said, "yes. As you knew. Didn't you?"

"And my presence defiles her." She did not sound bitter; merely reflective. "You've come to forbid me. She won't like that. What will you do when she calls me again, and I go?"

"No," he said. "Oh, no. She can't be defiled, nor is she ruled by any human creature. If she chooses to trouble herself with you, it's not my place to permit or forbid."

"I don't think I believe that."

"Believe it," he said. "That is the Mare. She does as she pleases. And it seems that she pleases to take you for her servant."

"Is she a goddess?"

"No," Khayan answered, "and yes. Horse Goddess lives in her. But Horse Goddess is more than simple flesh."

"Of course," the Egyptian said, dismissing that whole great mystery with a toss of her head. "So she wants me as a sort of priestess. Why *me?*"

"If I knew that," Khayan said, "I would never have had to come here. It's unheard of."

"Ah," she said in sudden understanding. "That's what you don't approve of. But she doesn't care, does she? She wants what she wants."

"She is the Mare," he said, with a faint and, yes, exasperated sigh.

"And your mother is going to be even less pleased than you. And your sisters. The fierce one, the one who rides about and wears a sword—she'll try to kill me. Won't she?"

"She won't dare," he said.

"But she may threaten." Iry seemed not at all dismayed. "I see how awkward it all is."

"It's worse than awkward. It's appalling."

She laughed. She was not mocking him, not really. Her laughter was infectious. He had to struggle not to echo it. "I do think I like you," she said. She sounded surprised. "Will you teach me to ride the Mare?"

He bit his tongue on his first answer, which was a resounding *"No!"* Instead he paused, drew a breath, and when he was calm, asked her, "Why do you want to do that?"

"*I* don't want to," she said. "She wants me to. But I don't know what to do."

Ai, he thought. The Mare was not going to have mercy on any of them, he could well see. "Mostly," he said with some care, "one learns from the horse."

"I think I'm too old for that," she said. "And too afraid."

"Why do you ask me? I should think you'd be afraid of me, too."

"Of course I'm not afraid of you," she said. "And if it's you teaching me, who can stop me? Whereas if I asked someone else . . ."

Khayan did laugh then, a little incredulously. "Gods," he said. "You and my sisters . . . they'll hate you for being Egyptian—and for being so like them."

"Then will you teach me?" she asked.

"I suppose I had better," he said, "or the Mare will never forgive me."

She did not clap her hands or indulge in any other style of girlish delight. She lay there, that was all, and gave him the gift of her smile.

· · · · · · · X · · · · · · ·

KHAYAN TOOK THAT smile away with him. It was as warm as sun on one's face after a long and bitter winter among the tribes. Her body had done little to arouse him, but that smile, in all its innocence— that he could not forget.

He went direct to his bed, yawning, tired suddenly to the bone. Servants were waiting up for him, ready to undress him, bathe him, comb out his hair. He waved them all away. He wanted to sleep. He wanted—yes, he wanted to dream of that smile, and of that odd quick wit and those calm dark eyes.

His bed was occupied. He saw, at first, only the long sweep of back, the curve of buttocks, and the broad flare of a woman's hips. Then she stirred, rolling lazily onto her back, arching it. Her breasts were beautiful, round and full; the nipples huge, deep red like the lips that curved in a smile of greeting.

It was meant to allure, that smile; and maybe in another hour it would have. But he was fresh from the memory of a different smile altogether. "Barukha," he said, flat and unwelcoming. "What are you doing here?"

She pursed those ripe red lips and frowned, but coyly. "Why, my lord! What do you think I'm doing?"

"Vexing my rest," he answered, making no effort to soften the snap in his voice. "I didn't summon you."

"You did not," she said. "And a fine state of affairs that's been, too. I had to practice every art of intrigue I had, to escape your mother's clutches. She guards me more closely than my brothers ever have."

"Does she?" He turned toward the door, opened his mouth to call the guard.

"My lord!" she half-sang behind him. "Summon a guard and I tell him what I'll tell my brothers—and your mother. You ordered me here. You compelled me to lie naked before you. You—"

He turned back to face her. Her smile had taken on a hint of triumph. "I understand you," he said. "Good night, madam. Sleep well."

He hoped that she was suitably nonplussed to be left alone in his bed. She was welcome to it, for all the good it did her. Even if she chose to tell the tale that she had threatened—he took care to sleep where no one could mistake his presence: in the guardroom, among his own chosen men. They greeted him with pleasure and a careful lack of curiosity, offered him the best corner and a cup of their middling bad wine, and let him into their game of stones and bones.

He was, he realized as he lost resoundingly to a downy-cheeked stripling of a guardsman, as happy as he had been in a considerable while. Even with a beautiful woman abandoned in his bed, and his manly parts aching with the deprivation.

When he slept at last, rolled in a cloak and secure against the wall, in the warm redolent snoring company of his own people, he dreamed not of Barukha lolling in his bed, but of another woman altogether. She lay in her cell of a room, fixing him with her level and unflinching stare, until suddenly—dazzlingly—she smiled.

+ +

Once again Khayan rode out before dawn. This time he brought a companion: Iry still more than half asleep, dragged protesting from her bed and flung into his chariot. She clung blindly to the sides, her eyes clamped shut, as the chariot lurched and rattled from rutted road to plowed field.

It came to him belatedly that she must be terrified. "Have you ever been in a chariot before?" he asked her.

At first he thought she had not heard. Her eyes were still shut tight. Then she shook her head, a sharp jerk of the chin.

"Here," he said, shifting easily, balancing on the rocking floor. Her hands were locked on the chariot's sides. He wound the reins about his middle and pried her loose. Before she could clamp on again, he had shifted her from behind to in front of him, secure between his body and the foremost rim. She was as stiff as a stone.

He shifted the reins till they were in both his hands again, and his arms bracing her, holding her easily between them. Her head came just to his chin. She did not use heavy perfumes as so many did in Egypt. The only scent she wore was her own, light and clean, with a faint pungency of fear; but that was fading.

Her hands slid down his arms, so light that at first he did not think what it meant. She had let go her deathgrip on the .rim. She was reaching for his hands—no, for his hands on the reins. Not trying to take them. Simply resting there, small and cold, but warming slowly.

He was aware as he had not been in too long, of the living tension in those lines, the feel of the horses' mouths at the end of them, their eagerness held softly in check, their bright will that they placed at his disposal. It was a gift, and a great one, but worn thin with use. He had been taking it since he was a child, born and raised among the horses.

To her it was all new. Her fear had melted into wonder. At any moment, she would ask if she could take the reins; but he was not about to let her do that.

Not yet.

He had misjudged her, perhaps. She did not ask anything. She rode with him, that was all, in among the fields of horses, and stood by while he unharnessed his stallions and hid his chariot away. When he had done that, she said, "Wouldn't it be easier just to ride one here, and never mind the rest?"

He considered several answers. In the end he chose the most obvious, and the most immediate. "Then you don't need me to teach you? You ride already?"

"Of course not," she said.

"So then," he said. "Come. The Mare is waiting."

That distracted her, as he had hoped. She turned away from him with almost insulting eagerness, and went in search of that one of all the horses.

He sighed a little as he followed. A woman could want a man quite as fiercely as a man could want a woman. She could also conceal it, and often would, if it suited her purpose.

He did not think that this one was concealing anything. He was nothing to her but an intrusion upon her world, and, for the moment, a set of skills that she could use. He still had not gone to his mother, and certainly not to his sisters. He had gone out, truth be told, in secret, and he was proceeding in secret. As if he, the lord of this domain, the master of his kin, should need to hide anything—least of all from his mother and sisters.

He would speak with them when the occasion presented itself. For the moment he had a pupil, and she was waiting upon his instruction. He had brought with him a bridle and a saddle-fleece, and other things bound up in it for the tending of the Mare.

She was grazing in her wonted place. At sight of the two of them together, she snorted softly, but did not take alarm. No more did she recoil from what he carried. She was no stranger to them. Far away in the east, Horse Goddess' priestesses had raised her and taught her what she should know. It was expected that she be ready when she chose her own servant—as it was expected that the servant be ready for the choosing.

This was utterly irregular. The Mare cared not in the slightest. She greeted the Egyptian with the soft sound that mares make to their foals: a flutter of the nostrils, a low whicker in the throat. Iry took the beautiful pale head in her arms and laid her forehead on the broad forehead, and rested briefly there, with an air of one who has come home.

Just as Khayan was about to lose patience, Iry straightened, and the Mare sighed and drew back a little. Khayan unrolled the saddle-fleece and took out the wherewithal for grooming and tending the Mare, and set them in Iry's hands. "Now," he said, "begin."

He did not mean to be merciful. No more did he mean to be unjust. She would learn as a boychild learned among his father's people, first to tend the horse, then to put on the harness in its proper order—or, here, bridle and saddle-fleece. He showed her how to brush and polish the coat, and to comb the mane and the long, tangled tail, and to pick out the big round hooves. And when the Mare was gleaming, and only then, he showed Iry the way of bridle and saddle.

And when the Mare was saddled and bridled to his satisfaction, he taught her how to take them all off again, and smooth the back and head and ears, and grant the Mare her freedom.

Iry did it all as she was told, without a murmur of protest—until he said, "Now let her go."

Then she said, "I'm not to ride her?"

"Not today," Khayan said. "Not until you are perfect in these lessons."

"And what if that is never?"

"What, are you retreating now, foreigner child?"

"*You* are the foreigner here," she said: an unguarded utterance, startled out of her by an altogether unexpected flash of temper.

He was almost sorry to see her master herself again quickly. "I am not retreating," she said then. "I am asking."

"You will learn," he answered, "because it's I who teach you."

"A little bit arrogant, are we?" She turned her back on him—quite shocking in a slave before her master—and set off toward the place where he had hidden the chariot.

"*Not* so fast," he said. And when she stopped and, as if against her will, turned, he pointed with his chin toward the bridle and saddle-fleece and the rest. "You will look after that," he said, "and carry it. Now begin."

She rolled everything together with dispatch and with impressive skill, bound it and tucked it under her arm and looked him in the face. And waited.

He turned on his heel and set off where she had been going. Not till he was well turned away from her did he allow the grin to break loose. He had always had a peculiar fondness for the less docile of his pupils, man and horse both.

But to her face he must be as stern as ever lord and preceptor should be. He set her to work with the chariot, too, and the much greater complexity of its harness. If he tired her out, so be it. If her mind could not absorb it all, then that was a pity; because he would expect her to know it when next she came out with him.

She would not ride back with him. "I can walk," she said.

He opened his mouth to object, but wisdom silenced him. It was full morning now. If he rode back with this of all women in his chariot, all the household would know that something was afoot. Or, more aptly, ahorse.

He held his tongue therefore, sprang into the chariot and took up the reins. Iry was on her way already, walking easily with her long stride. She did not glance up as the horses trotted past her, nor meet Khayan's gaze. She might have been alone under that endless Egyptian sky, for all the notice she deigned to take of him.

✦ ✦

Khayan should have known better than to think that he could conceal anything from his mother. That very day, the day he began to teach Iry to ride the Mare, he received a summons into her presence. Two such, so close together, did not bode well. He had a brief, wild thought of disregarding it, but lord of the domain or no, he had no power to match that of the Lady Sarai.

He chose therefore to go at once, leaving Teti the steward to settle yet another tedious and tangled dispute. Teti's lot was lighter, perhaps, but Khayan had hopes of escaping sooner.

His mother waited for him in her place of audience. She was alone but for a single servant. That servant made Khayan pause the fraction of a step, then sigh ever so faintly and advance to stand before his mother.

Iry did not know why she was there. Khayan would have wagered silver on it. She seemed bored and considerably annoyed, though she was hiding it rather well. Khayan wondered what his mother had been doing to vex her. Nothing, most likely, beyond having summoned her and kept her standing there with empty hands and no visible task.

Iry was no better a servant than her mother Nefertem. Khayan bit back a smile before either of them saw it. He bowed to his mother as was right and proper, and waited to be acknowledged.

She looked him up and down. "My son," she said. "You are well?"

"Most well," he said serenely. "And you, lady mother? Do I find you well?"

Had her brow twitched? "Very well," she replied. "Your domain: how does it fare? Are your people pleased with you?"

"No more or less, lady mother, than they believe they should be."

"Ah," she said. And let him stand there, waiting upon her pleasure.

He was content to wait. He did not even mind that he had been left to stand, with no chair fetched for him, nor any to fetch for himself. He had been sitting for much of the time since noon. He was rather glad to be on his feet.

At length Sarai said, "I asked you to discover a thing for me, not long ago. Did you discover it?"

Khayan was almost taken aback. That was striking directness, and very sudden. But it was like her. He answered honestly, "Yes. I did."

"And what did you discover?"

"I do think you know," he said.

"And why do you think that?"

"Because," he said, "you are my mother, the Lady of the White Horse people."

"And why did you wait so long to tell me?" she inquired.

"Because I am a coward," he said. "And because it seemed too preposterous to believe."

"And yet it is so," she said.

All the while they tested one another like warriors in a battle, neither glanced at Iry. Khayan was aware of her, keenly. She had roused a little when his mother asked after his people, but had subsided once more into boredom. She did not know that they spoke of her. How could she? Her people knew nothing of the Mare, or of the Mare's servants.

And now Sarai turned to her and said, "Girl. Who are you?"

Iry stared at her, astonished. "Who— What does that matter?"

"Answer my question," Sarai said, cold and clear.

Iry shrugged in something very close to insolence, and said, "I am your son's slave."

Sarai's hand swept that nonsense away. "Don't play me for a fool, girl. I know what you and your mother are in this house. Tell me who you are."

"If you know what I am, you know who I am," Iry said. By the gods, she was fearless. Perhaps it came of caring nothing for her life. It was worth so little, after all; slave that she was.

"I would prefer that you tell me," Sarai said.

Iry shrugged again. One must indulge the old, her gesture said, and the feeble of wit. "My name is Iry. I am the daughter of the Lady Nefertem and of the Lord Meren-Ptah, who rests now among the justified of Osiris. They were lord and lady of the Sun Ascendant, children of children of the first lord and lady, of kin who have ruled here a thousand and half a thousand years. And who," she demanded with a flash of heat, "are you?"

Sarai laughed, sweet and clear as a girl. "Oh, girl! What a spirit you have! *My* name is Sarai. I am the daughter of Sadana, the daughter of Sarai, the daughter of Savita, the daughter of Sadana, daughter of the daughters of the granddaughters of Sarama of the White Mare's people, who have ruled in the east of the world for a thousand and a thousand and yet again a thousand years. And so, child, since my line is older than yours, suppose that you put aside your impudence and answer me a question."

"Ask it," said Iry, undismayed, and not visibly awed by lineage so demonstrably ancient. No doubt, in Egypt, it was reckoned merely venerable.

"Do you know what the Mare is?" Sarai asked her.

She frowned. "So that is what this is for," she said. "She's a goddess—a goddess' image. Your son told me. He said you would be angry."

"That is not exactly what I said," Khayan interposed.

But they were not listening to him. As always when women dealt with women's matters, the mere male was forsaken and forgotten.

"Why would I be angry?" Sarai wanted to know.

"Because I am Egyptian." Iry spoke as to a child.

Sarai's eye sparked at that, but she forbore to be provoked. "That is irregular," she conceded. "More than irregular. Do you understand what you have done?"

"I suppose," Iry said bitterly, "you want me to stop answering when the Mare calls me, and let someone proper do it instead. I could try. But when she calls, I go. I can't help it."

"No one can," Sarai said. "No, you don't understand. The Mare chooses her servant. None of us has a say in it. What it means . . . girl, it is an omen. Never in thrice a thousand years, and in years beyond count before that, has the Mare chosen any but a daughter of one kindred. It was regarded as a great omen when the last Mare brought her servant into Egypt, and a greater one when this Mare brought her kin to live here. Now she has not only chosen a servant of another clan and kindred, that servant is not even of our people."

Iry's head had come up. Perhaps in spite of herself, her eyes had begun to blaze. She knew what sort of omen that was.

"We will fight this," Sarai said. "Be well aware of it. The Mare may be telling us that Egypt is truly ours; that we have taken it as she has taken you."

"Or," said Iry, almost too low to be heard, "that we will take it back, and drive you out." She paused. Sarai let the pause stretch. Iry said, "You can't get rid of me, can you? If you kill me—what will the Mare do?"

"That would be sacrilege," Sarai said. "No one will kill you. But because the Mare has chosen you, you belong to her, and therefore to us. There is much that you must learn, and much that you must do, duties, obligations, offices that you must fill."

"And if I won't?"

"You will," Sarai said with terrible gentleness. "You begin now. Part of the day, you belong to the Mare—and to my son, who has taken on himself the task of teaching you to be a horseman. The rest of the day, and the night, you are mine. You will do as I say, when I say it, without question."

"I will be, in short, a slave."

"You will be a priestess," Sarai said, "whether you will or no. This is the Mare's doing, her choosing. For her you do it. For her you suffer it, and perform it as best you may. Any less dishonors her."

"I'll run away," Iry said. Was she perhaps growing frightened?

"The Mare will bring you back," said Sarai. "Endure it, girl. You're hers now, and have been from the moment you answered her call."

Iry lowered her head. It only looked like submission. Khayan saw how she glared up under the black fringe of her hair. "Do I have to wear a robe?" she asked: startling question, and he thought she knew it.

"When you are among my people," Sarai said, "you will observe the proprieties. For the rest, you may do as you please."

Iry kept her head lowered. She would be among Sarai's people now, and not her own—that much she had to understand. But she said nothing. One might almost think that she had surrendered to necessity. Except for those eyes. There was no submission in them.

And people said that Egyptians were servile. Khayan would have laughed if he had been alone. As it was, he made his escape as soon as he might, and perhaps cravenly left Iry to his mother's mercy. It was justice of a sort, as insolent as that child was, and as thorough a stranger to submission. Sarai might never teach her to submit—but, like the Mare herself, she might learn to obey.

THE TWO
LADIES

K EMNI SAILED INTO Thebes on a morning of blessed, searing heat, somewhat after the Inundation of the Nile had crested. They had fought their way upriver, laboring under oar and sail, and thanking the gods that the foreign kings had not known or stopped them. Even so, they had crept through Memphis at night, sailing by the stars, and trusting to the ocean-width of the river in that season. The cargo that they carried was far too precious to risk.

Kemni had been heart-whole again from the moment he passed the first green reedbeds of the Delta. Here at last, in the royal city of the Upper Kingdom, he was home. He had never been gladder to see those towering walls, or to look out on the bare bleak hills beyond them. His eyes had looked on a foreign sky, and his body known the chill of an outland air. If he never left Egypt again, he would be more than content.

Ariana came up beside him as he stood on the prow. If he could have braved the crocodiles, he might have leaped into the river and swum to shore. But he was prudent. He yearned, but he kept to the ship.

He glanced at her. She did not speak, not at first. She was rapt, staring at the city that would hereafter be home to her. The voyage had seemed easy enough for her. She had not pined visibly for Crete, nor, once she had taken ship, fallen back into that strange, remote stillness which had so alarmed him. Her laughter had brightened that whole voyage.

He was heart-glad to be home, but he would be sorry to lose her to the queens' house. Not that she had ever tempted him, or allowed him to take liberties. He had not even presumed to dream of her. But he had had long days of her company, and long evenings of her stories and songs, jests and sallies and wickedly clever games. A voyage that might have been unbearably tedious had been remarkably pleasant, even with the need to skulk and hide as they passed through the foreign kings' lands.

And now it was ending. She said to him, "Promise me something."

"Anything I can," he said cautiously. "If it's honorable."

She made as if to strike him. "Oh, you! Of course it's honorable. Promise you'll be my friend when we're shut up in the palace."

"I'll always be your friend," he said.

"Of course you will," she said a little impatiently. "That's not what I meant. I meant, my *friend*. Someone who comes to visit me, and keeps me company, and—"

"The king might have something to say of that," Kemni said. "The queens don't have the freedom that a princess has in Crete."

"Why not?"

They had spoken of this before—never so directly, but she knew perfectly well how a queen was expected to conduct herself. She had never objected to it before.

He did his best to answer her question. "Queens are more than mortal. Queens are divine. As are kings. They live as gods do, constrained within the bonds of rite and ceremony. They can't sully themselves with mortal men."

"I am not an Egyptian queen," Ariana said; and for an instant he saw all the arrogance of divinity in her. He remembered, then, that she was an image of her own great goddess.

But that was not a goddess of Egypt. "You are Egyptian here," Kemni said, "if you marry the king of Egypt."

She set her chin and firmed her lips and said nothing. He knew better than to think he had won the skirmish. He could never win a battle with a goddess.

✦ ✦

Thebes opened its arms and gathered them in. *Dancer* came to haven at last, weary and tattered but indomitable as ever. Kemni bade farewell to her with genuine regret.

Her cargo he had thought to leave behind, but Ariana had no such intention. "We go together," she said. "All of us." She would not even hear of his sending a messenger, nor wait for the harbormaster to come, but swept him off the ship, with Iphikleia silent in their wake—but Naukrates held his ground. He had to stay with his ship. Even the Ariana of Crete could not shift him.

She sighed and shrugged and left him, but made him promise to come to the palace the moment *Dancer* was inspected and secured. He agreed to that, or at least did not disagree.

Kemni almost envied him. Any wise man would have sent a messenger to warn the king of what came to trouble his peace. Kings did not like surprises. And such surprises as this . . .

If Kemni had been fortunate, Ahmose would have been elsewhere, traveling about his realm or hunting down the river. But the king was in residence. His guards stood at the gate in all their finery. His chamberlains barred the way within, and swept them smoothly and irresistibly to the house of the foreign envoys, which just then was not, quite, bursting at the seams; and there left them to cool their heels in royal luxury.

Or so the chamberlains imagined. Kemni had in mind, once they were left to their own devices, to go in search of the Prince Gebu. Gebu would win them entry, he had no doubt of it.

But Ariana had no intention of waiting quietly for Kemni to arrange matters. She fixed the chief of the chamberlains with her haughtiest glare, and said
in ragged but serviceable Egyptian, "You will take us to the king. You will take
us now."

"Madam," the chamberlain said with a curl of the lip that took in her sea-
worn clothing, her salt-stiffened hair, and her demonstrably foreign origin,
"the Great House of the Two Lands will grant you audience in the proper
time and with the proper ceremony. Until that time—"

"That time is now," said Ariana. "You will take us to him."

The chamberlain so far yielded to desperation as to cast Kemni a look of
appeal. Kemni, who was only more acceptable than she in that he was male
and Egyptian, knew better than to be flattered, but he was amused. "Lady,"
he said, "at least wait until we've bathed and made ourselves presentable.
Would you have the king of Egypt think you a raw barbarian?"

"The king of Egypt, everybody says, is a reasonable and sensible man."
Ariana folded her arms over her breasts and glared at them all. "I will speak
with him now."

Kemni shot a glance at Iphikleia. She offered him no help. The chamberlain's face had set in the immovable obstinacy of his kind.

Kemni sighed heavily and said to Ariana in Cretan, which he hoped the
chamberlain did not speak, "Lady, if you please, let him go. I know a better
way."

"What?" she demanded in the same language. "To wait till we're all ancient? You know we won't be let in as we are, not unless we do it quickly."

"Will you trust me?" he shot back. "I live here. I have a little influence.
Once we're clean and fit for anything but sailors' company, I'll see that we're
granted audience with the king."

"Promise that?"

"Promise," Kemni said with only the slightest quiver. If Gebu was not in
the palace, or if he was not inclined to serve Kemni's purpose . . .

Ariana need not know any of that. She glowered still, but she said, "Very
well. You do what needs to be done. I," she said with a toss of her head, "shall
wait for you in the bath."

"I'll bathe myself," he said, "by your gracious leave. Even Gebu, who
happens to be my friend, might be more pleased if I were cleaner."

She sniffed audibly, but she did not forbid him. Therefore, and rather
wickedly, he bathed first, in royal Egyptian luxury, with servants who knew
truly the art of making a body clean. They shaved him and anointed him and
clothed him as befit a prince, with ornaments that widened his eyes somewhat,
for they were rather above his deserts. He had not worn so much gold before,
a collar so weighty that the servants grunted a little as they lifted it, and armlets
as heavy as shackles, and a belt like the spreading wings of a vulture, each
feather enameled with green and red and blue. He fought the frequent urge
to stroke it as he went in search of his battle-brother.

Kemni had come in a stranger with a pair of foreign women, of little regard and less importance. But now, agleam with gold, in a kilt of the finest linen and a princely wig, he attracted stares and whispers. He recognized many of the faces, but few seemed to recognize him. Of course; Kemni the commander of a hundred had never affected such state. And he had been gone half a year and more. Gods knew what rumors had risen in his absence.

It was strange to be thought a prince. He was not sure he liked it.

He was however seeking one who was a prince in truth, and trusting to paths and patterns that were half a year old. Prince Gebu was in residence, said a lordling who had hunted with Kemni many a time, but looked on him now without recognition, blinded by the gold and the finery. He was burning with curiosity, Kemni could see, but he was too polite to ask the name of one who must surely be too august to be unknown.

A lord of the Lower Kingdom. The whisper ran ahead of him. It was true enough.

Gold and finery won him through where sea-stained near-rags would never have done. He entered the princes' house, in among that warren of alliances and squabbles, riots and revels and tangled intrigue. It was not home, but it was close enough.

There they knew him. People here were accustomed to piercing the mask of gold and paint to a man's true face. "Kemni! Kemni's back from the dead!"

Half the princes were here, it seemed, or came quickly as word went out. They crowded around him, embraced him, pummeled him, gave him the welcome that neither the city nor the greater palace had known to give.

It was all he could do not to burst into tears, break down and howl. But that would sully his beauty. He embraced and pummeled and roared happily back at the lot of them.

They herded him into one of the halls, where there was always wine to be had, and whatever else a young male fancied. Today it was a flock of girls in wilted garlands, and the remains of a roast ox. None of the girls was as pretty as Ariana, but they were all beautiful, if only because they were Egyptian.

But he could not dally with them, however much he yearned to. He put them aside regretfully, and raised his voice above the tumult. "Gebu—where is Gebu?"

It took a while, and a great deal of shouting back and forth, but at length someone had an answer: "He's serving his time in Amon's temple."

"No, he's not," someone else said. "He finished that yesterday, don't you remember? He's waiting on the king."

"So much the better," Kemni said.

They objected strenuously, even after he promised to come back and finish celebrating his return. But he had to speak with the king.

He had more escort than he strictly wanted, but as he passed the gate of the princes' house, the princes and their following went back to their revelry. None went with him to find the king. That would be dull, they said. Ahmose was holding audience or settling disputes or counting grains of barley with his scribes, or some equally deadly royal pursuit. Gebu, fresh from his season of priesthood, would no doubt find it stimulating, but they were made of softer stuff.

"Ah, to be home again," he said. They laughed and made as if to bathe him in wine, but he escaped with his splendor intact.

+ +

Ahmose the king was not, after all, going over accounts with his scribes, or even receiving embassies. He was taking his leisure in the royal menagerie, enjoying the sight of his latest acquisition.

Kemni stopped short on the edge of a space like a garden of grass. Half a dozen horses grazed there, a stallion and a harem of mares. They were taller than the herd in Crete, by a little, and lighter in the body; more delicate, closer in semblance to the gazelle than to the ox. They were all red, the stallion black-maned—a bay; the rest lighter, red-maned or even fallow gold.

"Where in the name of all the gods did you find *these?*"

Kemni had forgotten where he was, or who would hear him. Ahmose answered from beyond the horses, where he stood with Gebu and a pair of guards. The guards looked as if they were defending their king against a horde of crocodiles, standing with spears at the ready, glaring at the placid horses.

"Good day, my lord Kemni," Ahmose said. "Welcome back at last from your journey. I trust we find you well?"

"Very well, my lord king," Kemni said with belated civility. He would have gone down in obeisance, but Ahmose's upraised hand prevented him.

"No, no," the king said. "Be at ease. Do you like my horses, young lord?"

"I like them very much indeed," Kemni said. "But, majesty, what—where—"

"They come from Libya." Ahmose stepped past a startled guard and held out his hand. One of the mares lifted her head and sniffed lightly at it. When she found nothing to eat therein, she snorted and went back to her grazing. "You did ask to be paid in horses. Did you not?"

"Not—" Kemni stopped. He had asked to learn to drive a chariot, that was true. He supposed that would be to be paid in horses. "But, sire, these aren't for me."

"They might be," Ahmose said.

He was waiting. Kemni lacked the subtlety of courts; it struck him belatedly, what he had been asked, albeit without a word. He nodded, but he frowned a little. Ahmose's brows went up a fraction.

Kemni resorted to words again, too quickly perhaps, but he hoped he would be forgiven. "There is . . . something. A price."

Ahmose waited as eloquently as before.

"A marriage," Kemni said. Ahmose was not dismayed: no doubt, as Kemni had, he had expected it. But he might not be expecting the rest. "The king of Crete gives you his daughter, a lady of very high rank. He asks that she be made a queen."

"That . . . might be arranged," Ahmose said.

"I told him so, sire," said Kemni. "But . . ."

"But?"

Kemni breathed deep, steadied himself, said it. "She's here, my lord. Minos' daughter. She took ship with me."

"What, and all her attendants? And not one of our spies said a word of it."

"Because, sire," Kemni said, "she came alone but for a single attendant. It's irregular. I told her so. But, my lord—"

"How very interesting," Ahmose said. And that was not a thing he said often, Kemni could see: Gebu, who had been hanging back as was proper, was a little wide-eyed. "And what reason did she give for this great departure from tradition?"

"She said," said Kemni, "that you need her now, and now is when she must be here." His eye slid toward the horses. "Sire, she knows how to drive a chariot."

"Ah, does she?" Ahmose was interested indeed. He was almost lively.

"She has taught me somewhat of the art," Kemni said.

"I see," said Ahmose, "you've wasted little time."

Kemni bowed his head. It was little and late, but he did not want to seem more forward than he had already.

A hand fell on his shoulder. He started and almost flinched. The king had touched him, with his own hand, and shaken him lightly. "Young lord," Ahmose said, and his voice was warm, "you have done well and more than well."

"Even if I couldn't keep Ariana—the princess from breaking with all proper conduct?"

"We shall see what she considers proper," Ahmose said, still warmly. He was amused. Very much so. "Come. Take me to her."

"But—"

"I too," said Ahmose, "may depart from proper conduct."

It was worse than improper. It was appalling. But it was a royal command, and Kemni was the king's servant.

Still, he ventured to say, "My lord, if it were I, I would summon her here. And let her know that there are horses."

Ahmose considered that. Kemni held his breath. Then the king said, "Yes. Yes, that is wise. Kamut—go to the house of the foreign embassies. Fetch the lady from Crete."

The smaller of the two guards bowed low and ran to do his master's bidding. While they waited, Ahmose called in servants, and had a canopy set beside the horses' enclosure, and a table, and wine and dainties. It was all done

and waiting long before Ariana appeared, and somewhat after Kemni had begun to fear that she would refuse the summons.

⊹ ⊹

But Ariana was no fool. She knew where Kemni had gone and what he had
hoped to do. She kept the king waiting, but not too long. Just as the sun
slipped visibly westward from its greatest height, she came, with Iphikleia for
escort and shadow. The guard Kamut, who had been sent to fetch her, trailed
like a lost dog, visibly smitten.

She was wrapped in a mantle of linen like an old woman, with a fold of it
over her hair. But as she approached down the path of raked sand, she let it
slip and fall.

Kemni heard the gasp beside him. Gebu had never seen a Cretan lady in
her full glory. It was, Kemni agreed, a marvelous sight.

Ariana had brought a small bag with her, Kemni had known that. Out of
it she had conjured wonders. The embroidered skirt, the jeweled vest, he knew;
he had seen them in Crete. The jewels were of rare quality. The paint of face
and breasts, he supposed, was Egyptian, but what she had done with it was all
Cretan. Her hair was washed and dried into ringlets, plaited and coiled and
caught in a fillet. She was the very image of her own goddess, even to the
serpent armlets—jewels for once, and not living creatures.

What Ahmose thought of her, Kemni could not tell. The king's face was
a royal mask, expressionless and still. Nor could Kemni tell what Ariana
thought of the king of Upper Egypt. He was not a young man or a greatly
beautiful one, but she had never struck Kemni as the sort to care for such
things.

They regarded one another with a remarkably similar expression, or lack
thereof: still face, dark eyes, no word spoken.

It was Ahmose who broke the silence. "Lady," he said. "I welcome you
to Egypt."

She inclined her head. She was as haughty then as Iphikleia could ever be,
but Iphikleia's eyes did not glint so, nor did a smile touch the corner of her
mouth. "My lord," she said in better Egyptian than Kemni had imagined she
knew. "I am most pleased to stand in your presence. And so soon. Is he not
a marvel of a courtier, this ambassador of yours?"

Kemni's cheeks burned. They were not supposed to speak of him. He was
not supposed to be there. He should be invisible, intangible, forgotten.

But this was not in any way a proper meeting of god-king and royal bride.
Ahmose said, "He has served me well, do you not agree?"

"Most exceptionally well," she said. She tilted her head toward the horses.
"Is this his reward?"

"Would you like it to be?"

"Does it matter what I like or dislike?"

"I should be pleased to have pleased you," Ahmose said.

"Then," she said with lovely composure, "I should like it if he were to become a lord of horses. Have you chariots, my lord?"

"They are being made," Ahmose said.

"Tomorrow," she said, "I shall see them."

"As you wish," said the king.

She nodded briskly. "I thank you. So, my lord: are we agreed? Do you pay all the price my father sets?"

"You wish to be a queen," the king said. "You must know that you cannot be Great Royal Wife."

"So I was told," said Ariana. "That suits me well enough. What I would do is best done without excessive press of duties. But authority—that I must have."

"And what is it that you would do?"

She tilted her head toward the chairs set by the table. Ahmose bowed, granting her leave. She sat with delicate care, as a cat will, smoothing her skirts, accepting wine in a cup of chalcedony set in gold, and nibbling a bit of sweet cake.

When she was well settled, and when Ahmose had sat also and the others arranged themselves as befit their rank or their sense of what was proper, she said, "You want the whole of your kingdom back. My father can help with his ships and his mariners. You have armies, I'm sure, all ready to strike. What you lack are chariots. These horses are a beginning, but you need more. Many more. If horses aren't to be had, then find asses, preferably trained to the yoke already. I will need, for this beginning . . ."

She paused, as if reckoning numbers in her head. "Let us begin with three-score good chariot teams, and a hundred men willing and able to learn a new way of war. Give me this man to command them, and full discretion in equipping and paying them. And—"

"And?" Ahmose interposed. "There is more?"

"There is always more," Ariana said. "Do you want to win this war?"

"I am going to win this war."

"So then," she said. "Give me all of that, and give me the rank and the authority to command as I must. And with that, a house, and servants who can be trusted. An estate would be best; a holding with fields of grass, not too close to a city, nor too near a road. We'd not want the enemy to know what we do there."

"What you ask," Ahmose said, "is to be made lady of a holding, and given full power to rule therein as you please. Do you wish to be queen as well?"

"We should marry as soon as may be," she said. "All this will be easier for a queen than for a lady of rank. But we'll not make the wedding public. When your war is won, then you may take me to wife with all suitable ceremony."

"You have everything laid in order, I see," Ahmose said.

"Yes," she said, apparently oblivious to irony. "How not? You've waited a hundred years to take back the Lower Kingdom. Your brother took it, but let it go. Won't you both take it and hold it?"

"Won't I indeed?" said Ahmose. His eyes were laughing. "My lady, it seems to me that your father gave me a very great gift in you."

She raised her own eyes to his face. Kemni saw how he started a little, as if he had not known till just then, what brilliance was in her glance. "I gave myself," she said. "I asked to come."

"Why?"

Such simplicity. She smiled at it. "Because I wanted to."

"And why did you want to?"

He was not going to let her go until he had an answer that suited him. She answered gravely, though there was laughter still in her eyes. "My people are seafarers. They came out of the east long ago, came to the sea and knew it for their own. I was born a princess, and would be priestess by my lineage; and our goddess chose me to be the chief of her servants. But my heart knew that there was more she asked of me. When you sent this man to be your messenger, because he dreamed a dream and I was in it, I knew my goddess was speaking to me. She was calling me to Egypt.

"More usually," she said, "she calls us to herself. We dance the bull, and he takes us. But the bull spared me. I was to come here. And so I have come, my lord, and so I will stay. You will not refuse me."

"I am king and god," said Ahmose. "I do no man's bidding."

"But," she said, and the laughter rippled in her voice, "I am not a man."

He laughed himself, deep sudden startled laughter. "Lady!" he cried. "Oh, lady! You may never command me. But I may choose—and I choose to do as you wish."

"Of course you will do it," she said with great composure. "How can you not?"

"How indeed?" Ahmose took her hand. "Very well, my lady of the sea-people. I will take you for my queen, and you will make us horsemen. Only win our war for us, and you may have anything else that your heart desires."

"Anything?" she asked with an arch of the brow.

"Anything," he replied, "but to be my Great Wife."

"Oh," she said, shrugging. "Well. No. Not that. But when the war is won . . . I will remember."

"Yes," he said. "Remember."

K EMNI RECKONED HIMSELF lucky to escape unnoticed and even unscathed from that audience of the king and his new queen. But he
was not to rest in peace for more than a night. In the morning, as
he slept off a good night's revelry in the princes' palace, a chamberlain dragged him bodily out of bed. He was dressed, wigged, and at the
trot before he woke enough to demand, "Who are you? Where are you taking me?"

"You are summoned," the chamberlain said. And that was all he would
say. Kemni considered digging in his heels and refusing to move, but he had
come too far already. No doubt the king wanted him. Or Ariana, perhaps. He
was being herded in the direction of the queens' palace.

Yes; there it was, with its gates carved and painted like the fans of papyrus,
and Nubian guards on either side of it, gelded to make them safe for the
warding of women. The chamberlain surrendered Kemni at that gate, handed
him over to a woman of noble girth and severe expression, who looked him
up and down as if he were an ox she had in mind to slaughter, and clearly
found him wanting.

He had begun to suspect, and to dread, who had summoned him here.
Ariana could not have shifted herself as yet to the queens' palace; she was not
yet a queen. But there was one here who could command any and all of the
servants in this house and in the greater one. Who ruled among the women,
and who was great lady and queen of all this kingdom.

Queen Nefertari received him in a hall of lofty pillars, where sun slanted
in long golden shafts through a scented gloom. It was cool in that high airy
space, and quiet but for the liquid trilling of birds in a golden cage. All along
the walls marched processions of dancers, young girls and beautiful, whirling
in the abandon of wine.

Their living images sat or stood or reclined about the steps of a dais. Some
were naked but for a bead or an amulet or a garland of flowers. Others were
dressed in linen as sheer as a cloud over the moon. Those in their way were
more alluring than their sisters who were naked.

The queen sat above them on a throne of gold and lapis and chalcedony.
Her gown was as sheer as the sheerest, just barely concealing the beauty of her
body. Her breasts were high and pointed like a girl's, her nipples large and
rosy-dark, blushing beneath the gauzy linen. Above them she wore a great

collar of gold, and a golden headdress in the likeness of a falcon's wings spread to embrace her head and shoulders. The falcon's head rose above her brow, its eyes of crystal glittering on Kemni as if it were a living creature.

He was no stranger to beauty in royal women, who had sailed from Crete with Ariana and her cousin Iphikleia. Ahmose Nefertari, queen, Great Royal Wife, was not, if he acknowledged it, as fair of face as they, nor as rich of body. And yet she was beauty pure, and beauty whole. She was queen and goddess, great lady of the Upper Kingdom, matched and mated to her king and god.

He fell on his face before her. It was nothing he thought to do, nor was it required. It would have been enough simply to bow to the floor.

"You may rise," she said above his head. Her voice was low, its music subtle. It practiced no artifice. It was simply itself.

Kemni rose obediently to his knees.

"Come closer," the queen said.

He rose fully to do that. But when he had reached the foot of the dais, he went down again to his knees, and sat on his heels, eyes fixed carefully on the floor.

"Look up!"

He had done it before he thought, full into her face. The dark eyes in their mask of paint were nigh impossible to read, and yet he thought they might be amused.

"You *are* good to look at," she said as if to herself. Her voice rose slightly. "Tell me, Kemni, once of the Lower Kingdom. Did you bring back a princess from Crete for my husband's sake, or for your own?"

Kemni gasped as if she had struck him. He was taken utterly aback, or he would never have said what he said. "Are you jealous, lady? Will you make me pay the price for it?"

She did not rise up, did not call her guards to destroy him. She sat as still as she had before, and said in that deep sweet voice, "A queen cannot afford to be jealous. Now answer my question."

"I brought her for Egypt," Kemni said. "Because it might win us back the Lower Kingdom."

"And for yourself?"

"Lady," Kemni said steadily, "I am not a prince nor a great lord, but I am an honorable man. That is a daughter of queens. She is meant for a king."

"She will have a king," said Nefertari. "And she will do what she came to do. But she will not be Great Wife in this or any other kingdom."

"She understands that, lady," Kemni said. "I told her father so, and I told her. They both accept what must be."

"Do they?" Nefertari leaned forward slightly. "Do you trust them?"

Kemni stared at her. "Lady, does it matter what I think?"

"Yes."

He drew a breath. He did not like it that kings and great queens were interested in him. It was like walking past a nest of crocodiles. One wanted to be quiet, to be invisible, to be ignored. The attention of kings was not a comfortable thing, nor at all a safe one.

But he had attracted the attention of this queen, and she was waiting for his answer. He gave it as best he might. "I . . . trust them as far as it serves them to be our allies. We have much that they want. They'll be faithful to their promises."

"But?"

"There is no 'but,' " Kemni said. "When Ar—when the princess marries our king, she will promise to be faithful to him, to serve him, to stand beside him in all that he does. She'll keep that promise."

"But will her father?"

"Minos is honorable, lady," Kemni answered: "as honorable as a king can be."

"So innocent," she murmured. "And yet . . . Ahmose thinks highly of you. Ahmose is not a fool."

Kemni certainly hoped not, but he knew better than to say so. He stood silent, leaving the queen to her pondering. Her eyes rested on him as if she needed, somehow, to remember his every line.

She reminded him of Iphikleia. It was a startling thought, and perhaps a little shocking. Iphikleia had the same brittle and brilliant temper, and much the same ruthlessness of mind. Kemni wondered, perhaps presumptuously, if Nefertari had been a hoyden in her youth. Somehow he doubted it; but he would never have believed it of Iphikleia, either.

He hoped that he would not dream of this, his queen and goddess, as he still did of the Cretan priestess. The thought made him blush—just as Nefertari looked into his face again and said, "I give you a charge, Kemni of the Lower Kingdom. Go with her as she asks. Learn from her. Watch her, and guard her. And if she makes a move to betray us . . . do as you must."

Kill her, that meant. Kemni could expect no less from this of all the queens.

"Do you trust me to do the utmost?" he asked her.

She looked him in the face. "Can I?"

He could not lie to her. "I don't know," he said. "When we were in Crete, she was my teacher and—if I may be so presumptuous—my friend. If she betrayed Egypt . . . I don't know what I would do."

"Honest as well as honorable," Nefertari said. "Yes, I trust you. As my husband does; and as, I think, does she."

He bowed low. For a long moment he feared that she would keep him there; that she would torment him further. But she let him go.

His departure was not quite like flight. He walked erect, with shoulders back, out of that long hall, down the corridors and through the courts, and out through the lotus gates into the glare of the sunlight.

✦ ✦

There he stopped, and his knees nearly betrayed him. But he steadied them. It had not been so long an audience, nor so terrible. And yet he was wrung dry, as if he had fought a whole day's battle, and been wounded in it, too.

And now he was bound to her, as he was bound to the king, and to Ariana. Three bindings, three loyalties. Nor were they all the same. If one came into conflict with the others . . .

He could not think of it now. He had much to do with his new duties, to be horsemaster and pupil to Ariana. That began as soon as he could muster his wits and his spirit, for she was determined to inspect the workshop where men undertook to build chariots for the king.

It was set apart within the great walled city that was the palace, not far from the armories, and from the king's forges. Shieldmakers labored nearby. Smiths wrought swords and spearheads, axes and daggers. The clamor was astonishing, and yet it had in it a rough music.

Ariana had come already to the chariotmakers' shop. Her escort was small: Iphikleia, the Prince Gebu, and a pair of Nubian guards. The king was not present. He was much in demand elsewhere, and could not, even to amuse himself, tarry overmuch with this interesting foreigner.

It was as well. The palace, thus far, had noticed little of the Cretan ladies but that they were present as ambassadors—striking, unusual, but how unusual it was, no one seemed as yet to have guessed.

Ariana's presence here in the workshop that was kept secret by being set openly among so many others, was neither greatly public nor greatly hidden. She had dressed herself as an Egyptian woman, modestly and plainly, but there was no disguising the tumbled curls of her hair. She had caught them up in a fillet, to keep them away from her face.

The workmen had paused at her coming, but when she did nothing, simply stood near the door, they went back to their work. They were building the body of a chariot. The wheels rested against the wall, already made. Ariana wandered over toward them. She frowned slightly as she examined them, tracing the curve with her hand, measuring, judging.

Egypt had not used the wheel before, except the potter's wheel. It was a new thing, and strange; but these artisans were gifted in creating exactly what the eye could see. They kept their model before them: a war-chariot won from the enemy. There was still a dark stain inside of it, the blood of the charioteer who had died to give Egypt this prize.

Kemni shivered a little. As much as he wanted to be a charioteer, he still had that old fear, the horror of Egypt for the enemy's great weapon. Even knowing what it was like to ride in a chariot—he had not ridden in a war-chariot. That of Crete had been smaller, lighter, less visibly deadly.

This he must learn; must master. He stroked the bronze that sheathed its rim. This had conquered Egypt. Now Egypt would conquer it. And if the gods were kind, the Lower Kingdom would belong again to its proper king.

✦ ✦

"You must work faster," Ariana said to the king. "And you must work with greater care. It's not a toy you make, nor a work of art. The wheels must withstand rough ground, stones, the bodies of the fallen. The axles must be strong, and slow to break. The chariot has to be light enough for two horses or two asses to pull, but strong enough to carry the weight of a man. If you were wise, you would steal yourself a chariotmaker, and make him teach you all he knows."

"And how are we to do that?" Ahmose inquired.

It was evening of what had been a furnace-hot day. The king had invited Ariana to dinner, and Ariana had brought both Iphikleia and, somewhat to his surprise, Kemni. They had come braced for a court banquet, but it was only the king and a few of his sons, and, quiet as a cobra in its lair, the Great Wife Nefertari.

Ariana had shown no dismay at sight of that of all women. She had done reverence as one should to a queen, and greeted the princes civilly, and settled almost at once to the thing that had been engrossing her since, that morning, she visited the workshop. She barely waited for dinner to be done or for the wine to be drunk.

Now he had asked her what to do, and she was glad to answer. "There are chariotmakers in plenty among the enemy. When his armies travel, they take a few with them, to repair the broken chariots and if necessary to build new ones. Surely a party of enterprising men could abduct one or two and persuade them to divulge their secrets."

"Surely one could," Ahmose agreed. "And would you be the one to give it its orders?"

"If my lord so wished," she said demurely, "yes. Of course. They'd want to be certain that it was a master chariotmaker, and not an apprentice or a servant. And more than one would be useful."

"Then would you persuade these prisoners to do as you ask?" Ahmose inquired. "Might they not simply refuse, or persist after torture had ruined their usefulness?"

"I'd not need torture, my lord," Ariana said. "Do I have your leave, then? May I do it?"

"You may do it," Ahmose said.

She clapped her hands, as delighted as a child. "Thank you, my lord! I'll begin tomorrow."

Ahmose smiled. He was not besotted with her, Kemni did not think, but he found her highly diverting. Nor would he be averse to seeing her in his bed. That much Kemni could see.

What Queen Nefertari thought . . .

Kemni tried to read her, but she was too greatly skilled in hiding behind the mask of a queen. She was studying this child with whom she must share her husband; studying and pondering. But she was letting nothing escape. It was all hidden behind that beautiful and royal face.

Ariana seemed oblivious. She drank her wine and ate eagerly of the sweets that had come in with it, chattered and laughed, and charmed the princes utterly. Their father might not be enthralled, but they quite visibly were. Even Gebu, who was known as a man of some seriousness, and not easily swayed by a woman, was hanging on her every word.

✢ ✢

When the king had made it clear that he was weary and would take himself to bed, the princes offered themselves as escort to Ariana and her silent shadow. They might have been glad to bear her company past the door of the house where she was staying, but she laughed and bade them all farewell, and left them panting like dogs outside a door both shut and firmly barred. They looked ready to bay like dogs, too, but settled for a headlong expedition into the city. "For," they said, "the night is young, and so are we."

Kemni did not go with them. Nor did Gebu. The two of them walked together toward the princes' house, not speaking, until they had passed the gate. Then Gebu said, "Don't go to bed yet. Come in and talk to me."

Kemni sighed faintly, but he was not yet asleep on his feet, nor had he drunk more than a cup of the king's good wine. Queen Nefertari's presence had kept him too much on edge. And so, if he would admit it, had his nearness to Ariana.

Gebu's chambers were quiet, his servants asleep, all but one who came padding out with wine, then went gratefully back to bed. Kemni sat cross-legged at the end of the prince's bed as he had many a time before, and Gebu half-sat, half-lay at the head, and they passed the winejar back and forth.

For a while they spoke of nothing in particular. But Gebu's mind was on other things than the quality of the wine or the reputation of a dancing girl. After a while he said, "That is a very unusual woman."

"Very," Kemni said a little dryly.

"You sailed with her," said Gebu. "You drove a chariot with her. Was there . . . anything else you did?"

Kemni considered taking offense. He should. It was not a question even a prince should ask, even in friendship. But this was Gebu, as close to Kemni as a brother. For that, Kemni answered and did not challenge him to a fight. "There was nothing else we did. She was not allowed, she said to me. She meant of course that she was meant for a king. And so she is. She's much too high for the likes of me."

"And yet she thinks a great deal of you," Gebu said.

"What makes you think that?"

Gebu grinned at him, though he had not said anything amusing, that he knew of. "What, are you blind? She looks to you for any number of things. She'll want you for that expedition, you can be sure of it. When she sends you out, take me with you."

Kemni had been annoyed, and perhaps a little bored. But this astonished him. "You want to come on *that* venture? What in the gods' name for?"

"Why, don't you?"

"Whoever goes will have to be stark mad. Or desperate for glory."

"You don't think I'm either?"

"I think," said Kemni, "that you are the king's son of the Upper Kingdom, and you can hardly risk your life in such a wild scheme."

"And yet you will."

"I'm to be her master of horse," Kemni said. "She won't send me out to get killed before I even begin."

"Are you sure of that?"

Alas for Kemni's peace of mind, he was not. But he could return to the other, the important thing. "You can't go. Your father won't let you."

"So we won't ask him." Gebu met Kemni's incredulity with a bland stare. "Come, brother. You're tired of traveling, I'm sure; you went all the way to Crete, and you've just now come back. I've been in Thebes since the gods know when. We haven't had a battle or a skirmish in a year. We go hunting once in a great while, and we went up the river once to Abydos, and worshipped Osiris. Except for that, all there's been to do is a round of less than onerous duties, a great deal of more than onerous reveling, and rather more boredom than I can easily stomach. We'd all be happy to start a war if it would vary the monotony."

"We'll have a war," Kemni said, "once we're ready for it. But, brother—"

"Brother," Gebu said, "if you don't take me with you, I'll take myself."

"It's likely I won't go at all," said Kemni.

"You'll go," Gebu said. "And I'll go with you. Now, are you going to keep all the wine to yourself, or do I get a share of it?"

Kemni opened his mouth, but shut it again, and passed the winejar in silence. He had not thought Gebu could be such a fool. Truly, it must be dull in Thebes, if even that most calm-minded of men was demanding to be taken on an expedition that could get him killed.

If the gods and Ariana had any sense, Kemni would go nowhere but to the estate that Ahmose had promised his bride; and someone else would risk his neck on that wild errand. Kemni could but hope.

When the jar came back to him, he drank so deep that Gebu protested. His head whirled with so much wine so quickly; some distant part of him knew that he would rue it in the morning. But he did not care. He was too much vexed with kings and queens—and yes, with princes, too. He was happy enough, just then, to take refuge in wine.

III

A HMOSE THE KING, Great House of Egypt, Lord of the Upper Kingdom, took to wife Ariana daughter of Minos, priestess, mistress of
the Labyrinth of Crete, on the seventh morning after she had come
to Thebes. It was nothing like the great royal festival that she had
promised him after his war was won. They went separately to the temple of
Amon that was near the palace, each with a small escort—and one of Ahmose's
companions was his queen, the Great Wife Nefertari. They had gone, as far as
anyone knew, to pay respect to Amon and to pray for the kingdom's prosperity.
Ariana in her turn was known to be taking in the sights of the city, and happened, just at that hour, to have paused in the temple.

And so, in one of the inner chambers, they came before the high priest
and spoke the words that bound them one to the other. With all the trappings
of state ceremonial stripped away, it was a simple exchange of contracts, and
a speaking of vows that were both binding and brief. A plain man of the city
might marry a woman equally plain, with the same words and gestures.

Ariana did not seem to care that the rite was so short. Ahmose, as always
in her presence, was clearly diverted. Perhaps, Kemni thought with a rush of
daring, he was as bored as his son Gebu. Even a king might succumb to te-
dium, after all; and Ariana was anything but tedious.

Once the words were said and the vows and the contracts written and
signed and sealed and laid away in the high priest's own coffer, the king and
his new queen went again their separate ways. Ariana professed no regret at
the lack of a wedding feast, though her husband said as they parted, "We will
dine together. It's not the great feast that it should be, but it will have to
suffice."

"We'll do our feasting later," she said, "when your war is won. Good day,
my lord. Look for me at evening."

Ahmose left then, but as Ariana lingered, waiting for it to be prudent to
follow, a voice spoke out of the temple's shadows. "Wait," it said.

It was no goddess speaking, and no spirit, either. Queen Nefertari moved
slightly, so that they could see her standing by one of the great pillars that
held up the roof. Kemni had been sure he saw her depart with the king. Had
she worked a magic, then? Or had he seen only what he expected to see?

Not that that mattered. She was here, with a single maid for company, and
she faced her fellow queen with no air of either awe or friendliness.

Ariana greeted her with respect, as was fitting, but neither shrank nor cowered. She was not afraid. She even smiled a little. "Thank you for coming to this wedding," she said in her voice that was so light, and so much like a child's.

And yet she was no child, and Kemni thought that Nefertari knew it. The Great Wife inclined her head. She did not speak. She might be hoping to discomfit Ariana with silence.

But Ariana had never been discomfited in her life. She went on as if there had been no pause, nor any expectation of an answer. "I hope we may not be enemies. There's much we both may do to help our husband, and much he needs of us, if he's to be the king he was meant to be."

"And you expect," Nefertari asked coolly, "to accomplish such a thing?"

"I was sent here to do it," Ariana said, "and to help you. Your gods love you, lady. They've made you a great queen, and will make you greater."

"You flatter me," said Nefertari.

Ariana shrugged. "It's the truth." She looked about her with interest, and began to wander a little. As if she could not quite help herself, Nefertari followed. Their way was curving and sometimes circuitous, but it led toward the outer gate.

Neither was dressed as a queen, but as a lady of substance. They would not be recognized unless they wished to be. Kemni was sure they both knew it, and rather reveled in it. One might have thought them allies, if not friends; though that was not, at least yet, what they were.

Ariana would alter that, he thought. He well knew the allure of that light prattle. It was difficult to resist her.

Perhaps a woman might find it easier, but she was very charming. Nefertari said little, letting her run on.

When they reached the gate where Nefertari's chair was waiting, Nefertari did not offer to share it with her fellow queen. Ariana bade her farewell with no sign of offense, and went back on foot as she had come, as a sightseer in this city of kings.

※ ※

How Ariana fared on her first night as a king's wife, Kemni did not want to know. But the god or spirit who vexed him with dreams was not minded to leave him in ignorance. He dreamed that he hovered as a winged spirit above the king's great bed. And there below him was Ariana, more beautiful than ever in her nakedness, dancing the old dance with that man who was as old as her father.

He did not want to be angry, or to feel the sting of jealousy. But over that too he had no power. He had bedded an Ariana nigh every night in Crete, but never this one; never the one who had sent them all.

Even in his dream, watching her coax that tired aging man to rise and love her as a man should do, he wondered if Nefertari dreamed also, or if she lay awake, brooding over this stranger who had come to trouble her world.

+ +

Kemni's world had been troubled since somewhat before he met Ariana, who was now a queen of the Upper Kingdom. She did not keep the state that one would expect, nor retreat into the world of women's secrets. A bare three days after she had become one of Ahmose's queens, she left to take possession of the estate she had asked for. It was some considerable distance down the river, and much closer therefore to Lower Egypt, north of the holy city of Abydos.

There was nothing to mark it out from among the many such noble estates along the river; and indeed, any who rowed or sailed past would see fields of barley and emmer wheat, villages of farmers, and up past the river's edge, the low rise of wall that was the house itself. But behind it, where one would expect the tilled land to give way to barren desert, the earth had obliged Ariana's purpose by curving and folding and shaping itself into a broad low plain that, by a happy accident, received a finger of the river's flood in season, and out of season was sustained with greenery through the offices of a watercourse such as farmers were used to maintain for the nourishing of their fields.

There Ariana brought the horses that the king had given to Kemni, on none other than the *Dancer* of Crete. They traveled uneasily, but scarcely more so than the sailors, who lived in imminent terror of a hoof bursting through the hull. But Ariana went with them, whispered and sang to them, and calmed them enough that they could endure this great indignity.

There were servants waiting for her, chosen by the king, and, he had promised, a greater herd of horses and long-eared asses, all that his kingdom could muster. There also had gone a number of his apprentices in the art of chariotmaking. They seemed little enough to begin a great war, but she professed herself content.

There was no change in her since she was made a wife. Sometimes a woman bloomed; sometimes she gained a bruised look, like a flower battered by the wind. Ariana remained herself. She did not weep or pine to take leave of her husband. He seemed more moved by the parting than she: lingering a fraction longer than he might have done, and following her with his eyes as she embarked on her uncle's ship.

As far as the world had need to know, he was bidding farewell to that odd embassy, honoring it with his royal presence. People would remark on that; would wonder at it and spread rumors of it, but they would not, if the gods were kind, stumble upon the truth.

And when the ship cast off from the harbor of Thebes, Kemni left again the city that he had come to consider his own. This time he was not alone among the mariners of Crete. Prince Gebu came with him, and a company of the prince's guards and servants. They were going on a lark, they professed, for life in Thebes had grown unbearably dull. Since that was in fact the truth, they did not need to stain their spirits with a lie—even a lie in the king's service.

"We'll pass the judgment all the sooner once we die," Gebu said as they

sailed past the outer edges of Thebes. He had not lingered nor yearned backward as Kemni would have liked to do. His face was turned unfailingly toward
the northward stretch of the river. Kemni had not seen him so bright or so
eager since—by the gods, since the last battle they had fought in. And that
was years past.

"You should have gone to Crete," Kemni said.

Gebu lifted a brow. "What, I?"

"You," said Kemni. "You're the king's son. You know the words to say,
the things to do. I did nothing but stumble. It's the gods' own miracle I never
fell."

"It seems to me," said Gebu, "that you did better than stumble. That you
flew." He tilted his head toward Ariana where she stood by the prow. She was
a marvelous sight, dressed again as a Cretan lady, with her lovely breasts bare
to the sun of Egypt. A maid—new gift from her husband—did her best to
shade her with a canopy, but she was in no mood to be protected.

"The gods called you for her sake," Gebu said. "She has a great fondness
for you. She'd not have taken so to me, I don't think."

"Do you know that?" Kemni demanded.

Gebu shrugged. "My belly knows it. So does yours, or you'd not be blushing like a girl. That embassy needed you. This one . . . well, and this one, too,
but for once I can trail behind and share a little of your glory."

"Don't talk like that," Kemni said. "It's not fitting."

"Ah, poor child," Gebu said without sympathy. "I've made you wriggle.
And well I should, when you're being such a fool. Chin up, little brother, and
strut a little. You're a power in the kingdom now, whether you like it or no."

"I don't think I like it," Kemni muttered.

"You'll learn," said Gebu.

+ +

The estate was called Bull of Re, which Ariana reckoned fitting, and Kemni
found a little disturbing. It was too much like the dream that had begun it all
for him, and the bulldancing. But it was a pleasant place, a house of an older
style, now out of fashion but Ariana declared herself charmed by it. The odd
twofold nature of it, estate like any other before, hidden valley behind, pleased
her immensely; and more so when she saw the valley populated with herds of
horses and asses.

She was less pleased with her apprentices' attempts at chariotmaking.
"Men's lives ride in them," she said. "They must be perfect."

But she was not ready, yet, to steal the enemy's masters of the art. There
was much to do with the estate first, and its inhabitants both animal and human. There were a handful of chariots in various states of repair and disrepair,
that would suffice for training the horses and asses. There was harness to be
made, men to be trained; and of them all, only the Cretan women—both—
able to guide and teach.

"You learn quickly," Ariana said to Kemni. "Now learn as you've never learned before. Learn swift, learn well. Live, eat, breathe this that we teach you. Then teach it to whoever else will learn."

Kemni did not trouble to protest. Ariana would not have heard him. She seldom commanded anyone, but she asked in ways that no mere mortal could refuse. When she bade him learn, learn he must. He was given no other choice.

The king had sent a company of men to the Bull of Re, picked young men of the royal armies. Some Kemni knew; of those, a handful had been in his own company of a hundred, when there were battles to fight. They were his, they all said. The king had sent them to serve the Cretan women, but they would look to Kemni for their orders.

It was a rebellion, quiet and rather touching. But Kemni could not let it go on. He faced them in the courtyard of the wing that would be their barracks, the whole lot of them dressed and armed for inspection, and said flatly, "I'll be your commander. But your obedience belongs to the queen."

"*The* queen? Queen Nefertari?"

Kemni met the eyes of the man who had spoken. He was an insouciant young thing, a lord's younger son from the look and bearing of him, with a glint of gold in the ornaments that graced his person. His name, Kemni recalled, was Seti. It was a name somewhat out of favor in this part of Egypt: the foreign kings had taken the god Set for their own, and imbued him with the powers of their own king of gods.

This Seti had an air of one who relished a fight. Which could be a good thing, or could be a terrible nuisance. Kemni met him with a bland stare and the suggestion of a smile. "Here, in this place, there is only one queen. That queen is the Ariana of Crete. That is a great lady, my friend, and a priestess, and a living goddess. She may not be our goddess, but she is our queen."

"She holds herself high," drawled Seti. Others near him nodded. Some grinned lazily at Kemni.

Kemni knew the look of a manpack when he saw one. He let his smile widen a fraction, just enough to show a gleam of teeth. With no more warning than that, he kicked Seti's legs from under him and knocked him flat. As Seti lay winded, stiff with shock, Kemni said, "You will speak of her with respect."

Seti, unlike Kemni, did not appear to learn quickly. He drew himself up painfully, licking blood from a cut lip. "Respect?" he said. "But why?"

"Because," said Kemni, sweeping a blow that knocked him flat again, "I said so."

Seti bowed to that. He did not appear to resent Kemni's rough handling; if anything, like a dog that learns to welcome its master's kick, he was glad of it. It proved to him that where he offered obedience, he offered it to strength.

Kemni suppressed a sigh. The manpack would go where its leader led. The rest, if he was fortunate, would follow Ariana for herself, and not simply because her commander of a hundred was heavy with his fist.

He faced them all as he would have done on a battlefield. "You are sworn to serve the king. Your service to him resides now in your service to this lady from Crete. Any who fails in that, answers to me."

That satisfied them well enough. Kemni swept them with a last, raking glance, turned on his heel and stalked away as a commander of a hundred could not but do.

+ +

"Hail the hero! Hail the conqueror."

Kemni jumped nigh out of his skin. In the sudden blind dark of his passage from blazing sun of the courtyard to shade of the colonnade, Iphikleia's voice sounded eerily clear. Her mockery lashed him like cold sea-spray.

It took all the strut out of him, and most of the self-satisfaction, too. "Sometimes," he said, "you might leave a man one or two of his delusions."

"Why would I want to do that?" she asked.

He should be raging at her. And yet there was something so bracing about her, and so unlike anything else he knew, even Ariana, that he could only laugh a little painfully, shrug and sigh and say, "Yes. Of course. Why should you trouble yourself?"

"It's not good for a man to indulge his fancies," she said. One or both of them turned at the same time, and they walked together down the colonnade to the gate. "Men are so strong, you see, in the body, but so weak in the spirit. They're like bulls: everything they are has to do with rutting."

"Oh, come," he said. "There's a little more to us than that."

"Why, surely," she said: "when there are women to teach you discipline."

"Sometimes I think you do that just to see if I'll take the bait," he said.

They paused in the gate, blinking at the light of the larger courtyard, but not quite too dazzled to see each other's faces. Was she smiling? No, he *was* dazzled. Or was it her smile that was doing it?

Gods. She did not know what he dreamed of—still, so often that it had become an old familiar thing. She in her royal rank, her sanctity, and her unshakable conviction that the world was hers to command, could not possibly be dreaming as he was dreaming. That would be far beneath her.

He did not even like her. She did not ask to be liked. Neither did she particularly want to be.

And perhaps, he thought, that was a mask she wore. When he dreamed her, she was a warm and laughing armful, warmer and merrier even than Ariana. It was always a shock to see the waking woman, and to come face to face with her coldness.

She did not seem so cold now. The pause stretched. It was cooler in the gate than in the sun, and there was a faint waft of sweetness from the tattered but indomitable garden. Kemni was wanted in the stable, where the first of the horses had come in to be trained. But it was oddly pleasant to stand here, saying nothing, doing nothing, simply and comfortably at rest.

She touched his arm, light as the brush of a feather. He started a little. Almost he might have doubted that she had done it, but his arm burned as if she had brushed it with fire.

She stepped past him, out into the sunlight. He thought of holding back, or of speaking. But he did neither. They walked across the court to the stables.

✦ ✦

There was a terribly great deal to learn, and terribly little time to learn it. Many of the horses, Ariana said, showed signs of having been trained to the chariot before; as they would have expected, since most had come as prizes of war. That made matters somewhat simpler. So did Ariana's ruthless assessment of Kemni's recruits on their first day in front of her, and her dividing them into companies, each with its duties as well as its daily lessons. Seti the insolent, Kemni happened to notice, was chosen among the first. She did not appear to care if a man was ill-mannered, if only he learned what she had to teach.

Seti did have a gift with horses. With them he put aside his air of eternal ennui. They responded in kind, and even granted him respect: not an easy thing to earn, with those self-willed beasts.

Kemni had to learn all that his men did, and command them, and look after them, and still wait on Ariana and assist both her and her cousin in their study of the language of Egypt. He rose before dawn and fell abed long after sunset, his head buzzing with all that it was being forced to hold. So much to learn. So much.

And in sleep he had little rest, either. Iphikleia haunted him. He knew her so well, as she was in dream, that he could have been her husband of a dozen years. Though if husbands had of their wives what Kemni had of Iphikleia, marriage was a blessed state indeed.

Now that Kemni was in the house of the Bull of Re, he dreamed that he came together with Iphikleia there. The room they trysted in did not exist outside the dream—he had looked; but there was no chamber that opened on the garden, and that had on its walls a fresco of the bull-dance. The girl who danced the bull was painted in Ariana's likeness. The young men were not those whom he had seen in the dance. One could have been Naukrates a score of years past. The other was Kemni, odd with his Egyptian face and long painted Cretan ringlets, preparing to dance the bull as that one had who had died for it.

Kemni refused to take that as an omen. It was a dream. Dreams could be treacherous.

This night, not long before the time of the river's flood, he had come to the chamber first, naked as he always was, and rampant with it. Often when he came before Iphikleia, he lay in the great bed ornamented with the horns of bulls. But tonight he was restless. He paced the room, slowly at first, then more quickly, swift strides, sharp, almost angry.

She was very late. She never came so late; she was always hard on his heels, and eager. But tonight he paced for long and long before he heard that step without.

He stopped—by chance or design, in the shadow of a pillar. She walked blindly through the door, dressed as always in the many tiers and flounces of a Cretan lady. Even in dream she was not as simply beautiful as her cousin Ariana. Her beauty was a subtler thing, slower to strike the senses, but much more lasting.

She did not appear to see Kemni. Nor did he move to greet her. He hung back, gritting his teeth against the aching in his loins, and watched her. She paced for a while as he had, frowning, biting her lip. Just as he gathered himself to speak, to ask her what so troubled her, she stopped abruptly and spun. "Goddess!" she burst out. "This has to stop. I can't bear it."

There was no answer, no stirring in the air, no flicker in the corner of the eye. Iphikleia flung herself onto the bed, headlong as a child. "I can't let him know," she said. "He'll laugh. He may even hate me. Every night, to steal his spirit because I—because I—" She buried her face in cushions.

Was she weeping? Iphikleia, crying like any mortal woman? It did seem that she was; or else she was laughing till her body shook, racked as if with sobs.

It had to be laughter. Iphikleia was not a woman who wept.

She sat up at last. Tears ran down her cheeks; but one could weep with laughter. She wiped the tears away, a sharp gesture, more like her waking self than most of what she did here. "I can't tell him," she said as if to someone standing over her, someone who taxed her with her deceit. "I can't. My beautiful man, my Bull of Re—if he knew, he'd never forgive me."

He had to move then, or not at all. He came strolling as if he had come from the twilight of the garden, yawning and stretching, with his rod so stiff he dared not touch it lest he cry out in pain.

She did cry out—but not, quite, in pain. She flung herself into his arms, bearing him backward, eating him alive with kisses. Her body was fever-hot. He could only defend himself as best he could, and hold her till she calmed. She took him inside herself then, rocking slowly, startling after the wildness that had come before.

She was weeping—truly weeping. He kept on holding her, settling to the slow rhythm that she had taken, which was like a slow swell of the sea.

She was slow, too, to come to the height of it. He tried to hold back, to slacken, to slow, but there was only so much a man could do. He let go almost guiltily, with a gasp that made her cling even tighter.

She held him inside her for as long as she could. He tried to babble apologies, but she was not listening. She was rocking him still, holding tight. If a spirit could wander beyond even dream, hers had done it.

Often after the first fierce heat of passion they would lie together, talking lazily of this and that. Tonight she had no speech in her. She was so real in his arms, so warm and solid, and so strangely sad.

If it was possible to sleep in dreams, they slept in one another's arms. Even after he woke, he could feel her there, a living presence, as if she had been there in truth. But he was alone. The dream faded as it always did, but for a lingering presence, like a scent of her that wafted for a while through the room, and slowly vanished.

IV

I PHIKLEIA IN DAYLIGHT was as she always was: remote, forbidding, but willing enough to teach him what she knew. Of course she had not changed. She knew nothing of the world he walked in while he slept. How could she?

And yet he caught himself eyeing her sidelong as he harnessed one of the horses or mended a bit of harness or taught a group of his recruits, with her help, to catch and groom a horse. His wild boys had learned at once, and thoroughly, to keep their hands to themselves. One was still nursing the scar of her knife through his hand.

Kemni could well imagine what she would say if she knew what his dreams were like. He must not imagine that he knew her, simply because the gods brought the image of her to his bed every night. This living woman was a stranger, nor cared to be aught else.

When the horse had been captured, groomed to a sheen, and let loose again to roll in the wallow that the herd had made near the stream of water from the river, the recruits were dismissed to another duty. Kemni had duties himself, and so no doubt did Iphikleia. But he was minded to linger for a bit, and she had paused to reckon the count of horses in this particular herd.

There were the same number that had been in the valley before the lesson began, and that had been there the day before, and for days before that. More would come, the king had promised, but it would take time to gather them all together and herd them toward the Bull of Re.

Somehow, when Iphikleia turned to stride back toward the chariot that brought her from the house, Kemni happened, just then, to turn himself. They collided, she with a gasp, he with a sudden hammering of the heart. She fit into his arms just as she had in dreams—perfectly. For half a breath's span he held her, and she rested her weight against him.

They stiffened in much the same instant, and drew carefully apart. She sprang into the chariot and gave the restive horses their heads.

Which left Kemni to walk, and it was some small distance. He shrugged and sighed. He had trusted to his feet long before he ever set foot in a chariot. He could trust to them again.

It was a rather pleasant walk, for a walk in the full glare of the sun. He had water at his belt, to quench his thirst. And as he came in sight of the house-wall, Prince Gebu rose lazily from the stone on which he had been sitting, and said by way of greeting, "So, brother. What *did* you say to her?"

"Nothing," Kemni said. "Why? What is she—"

"She rode in like the wrath of Set," Gebu said, smiling at the memory. "She ripped the harness off the horses and put them up with every hair in place, slammed through half the house, and locked herself in the women's quarters. We thought you must have threatened to make her laugh."

"I didn't do anything," Kemni said. Which was not exactly the truth, but surely she could not be as angry as that, simply because, by accident, he had touched her.

✦ ✦

Wisdom would have kept him well away from her. But he was not particularly wise, and he needed her to help him teach his rebellious recruits to put together a heap of jumbled straps and lines and bits of bronze, until it showed itself to be a chariot harness. Maybe she would forget her temper, if he determined to ignore it.

In any ordinary great house that had become home to a queen, no man would have dared to walk into the women's quarters without escort. But women in Crete lived more freely than ladies in Egypt. Kemni's presence set a flock of maids to fluttering and screeching, but they were silly fools who had seen him there a myriad times before. Gebu would have said that they did it to catch Kemni's eye. Kemni rather feared that that was the case.

It was fortunate, then, that Gebu had had occupations of his own that kept him from following Kemni into this place. Kemni extricated himself from the gaggle of girls, and went where they managed, amid their flutter, to direct him.

Iphikleia had sought the deepest part of the house, and the highest: a room of somewhat surprising size and spaciousness, at the top of a steep and narrow stair. It might have been a guard's post once, or a tower to shut a treasured daughter in, that no touch of the world should sully her. Kemni rather favored the latter. Guards might not be as enchanted with the painting of the walls as a young girl would be: forests of reeds, flocks of ducks and geese, a riverhorse lifting its head from the river, and a pair of ibises dancing amid the reeds. It was much faded, and peeling in patches, but it had still a dusty beauty.

Iphikleia perched in the deep embrasure that hinted at a guardroom after all, though it might serve to torment a prisoner with so narrow and so distant a vision of the world beyond. Iphikleia had turned her back on that, and drawn into a knot, glaring at the world.

The force of that glare rocked Kemni back a step. Perhaps he should have waited after all.

And yet, he had come this far, and he was winded, and his temper was just a little frayed. A servant must endure all the vagaries of his masters. That he had been taught. That he had done his best to do, even if it galled him.

Even the best of servants might fail of his duty. Kemni was a simple mortal creature; and he was vexed out of all patience, waking and asleep. He glared straight back at her.

"Go away," she said.

He did not move. "You're wanted below," he said. His voice was cold.

"I said," she said, "go away."

"No," said Kemni.

At first perhaps she did not believe her ears. "You—no? That is an order!"

"And I'm not taking it." Kemni leaned against the wall, arms folded, as insolent as he knew how to be.

Which was not very; but it seemed to be enough. She flew out of the window-embrasure and fell on him with force enough to knock the breath out of him. They tumbled in a heap, Kemni beneath. He hardly held her, and yet she struggled, cursing him for everything he was and was not.

He slapped her. She stopped, startled into stillness. Her face was just above his own, her eyes wild, but slowly coming into focus. They fixed on him. Something in them went strange. She bent down and deliberately, carefully, set her lips on his.

It was just like his dreams. In them he had not been flat on a dusty floor, with the throb of bruises to keep him wide awake. And yet the rest was the same, her warm and supple body, the brush of her breasts across his breast, the taste of her mouth, which was like sweet wine. She knew just where to kiss, just where to nibble, and exactly where to stroke him till he arched like a cat.

There was no thought in it at all. She had tugged his kilt free, letting it fall where it would. Her own had vanished somewhere. He knew exactly when to lift his hips, and when to take her hands in his hands and guide her down.

There was one difference. A difficulty. A barrier that he had broken before he knew what it was. And when it was too late, when the thing was done, he could not stop; he could not even slow, though his heart was cold with a kind of horror.

But she had taken him as he would have thought no maiden would know to take a man. If she knew pain, she betrayed no sign of it. She took him with a kind of wild joy, with abandon that swept him with it, cold heart, gibbering mind, and all the rest.

She would not let him go till she had had the whole of him. There came a point, deep in the heart of terror, in which, he discovered, it no longer mattered. Then the terror was—not gone. But transmuted. It was almost plea-sure, and just short of pain. It was—exquisite. Just as she was. Exquisite.

She brought herself to the height of pleasure again and again, but held him just short of it, till he was nigh to screaming with that sweet torture. Then at last, with a slow sweep of those wondrous hips, she let him go. He cried out, utterly without will.

And when it had passed, when his body had ceased its throbbing, his rod fallen slack, he lay as limp as sea-wrack. She knelt astride him, gasping, running with salt sweat. Her skin was hot and slippery where it touched his. Runnels ran down between those lovely breasts. He could not help himself; he took them in his hands. They were just as they should be, fever-hot, firm yet soft, the wide dark nipples waking, tautening at his touch.

The lower part of him was spent, but his hands had still their strength. They left her breasts, running down her sides to the sweet curve of her hips, and slipping in beneath. She arched, with a catch of breath—just as, one night, he had dreamed it, dreaming all the places that her body most loved to be touched. Just as in dreams, she gave herself up to it, head thrown back, long hair trailing down. She rocked lightly against his hands, then more firmly, her breath coming faster, faster.

It caught. She throbbed against him. He was rousing, long before he might have expected, and just as she subsided in his hands. With the hint of a sigh, she sank slowly down. Her body lay along the length of his. It was familiar to the point of pain. Even its imperfections, just as he had dreamed them: the faint soft down on her lip, the mole on her shoulder, the scar on her palm where she had, on a child's dare, lifted a still-searing blade out of a forge.

He kissed the marred skin there. Her fingers curved along his cheek. She had gone quiet, nestled body to body, just as—*just* as—

"That's why," he said suddenly. "You dreamed. You dreamed, too."

She tilted her head to stare into his face. "You—" She shook her head. "You didn't."

"I did," Kemni said, half in terror, half in exultation.

"You dared?"

"No more or less than you," he said with a flare of temper.

It caught her by surprise. She almost shrank before it. Almost. "You never said a word," she said.

"Nor did you."

"How could I? You would have despised me."

"I don't despise you now."

She shook her head. "That's not what I meant. I don't know what I meant. This should never have happened!"

"If you command me," he said carefully, "I will forget. And it will be as if this had never been."

"No," she said. "No. I don't want to—" She pulled away from him, lifting herself to her knees, bending over him. Her hair brushed his belly. His skin quivered; his rod roused itself once more, valiant to the last.

She took no notice. Her eyes were on his face. She took it in her hands. Her fingers were cold and a little unsteady. Almost they made him forget all his resolve, and his determination to do nothing that she did not ask.

"I don't want to forget," she said. "But if there is no other way you can endure this—"

"I want to remember," he said.

"Swear it."

"I swear," he said.

She sighed faintly. She did not look comforted. She looked—wild. This must have been what she was when she was younger: this fierce eagerness, this almost frightening delight.

"You hide it," he said slowly, "because it's too much; it's too strong. It scares people."

She did not seem to hear, or if she did, to know what he meant. She stooped and kissed him till he thought he would die for want of air, then let him go so suddenly that he gasped. "Beautiful man," she said. "Beautiful, beautiful man. Tell me you want me. *Me*, not some royal vision."

"I don't dream of loving your cousin," he said. "You . . . if you are absent from my sleep for even a night, I find myself yearning after you."

"Why?"

How very like her that was. He almost laughed; but she would not have welcomed that. "Gods know. I'd have thought I had more hope of becoming her lover than of becoming yours. You were always so cold."

"No," she said. "Never cold. Never for an instant."

"But—"

She silenced him with a finger to his lips. "When I first saw you, bundled on *Dancer's* deck like a part of the cargo, I thought you the most distressingly beautiful man I had ever seen. I was incredulous that no Egyptian had seen and recognized you. You turned every man on the ship to a shadow. Surely anyone with eyes could see what you were."

"Most people," Kemni said, his voice somewhat strangled, "don't have . . . your kind of eyes."

"They don't, do they?" She stroked his cheek, and the curve of his brow. "You don't know. You don't believe it. And maybe that's best. A man who knows his own beauty can be insufferable."

"But I am not—"

"Yes," she said. "Yes, doubt me. It's charming."

"Better charming than insulting," Kemni said. She had claimed back her hand. He felt oddly bereft. "I . . . you tried so hard to shut me away. I could have hated you."

"I wanted you to," she said. "I swore an oath, you know. When I was young. I would never belong to a man. That's why—" She blushed—Iphikleia, blushing; impossible, and yet there was no mistaking it. "That's why I never took one to my bed. It's expected, you know. It's even encouraged. Unless you are the Ariana; then you send your servants to men you fancy, and preserve yourself until you can wed a king.

"But I would become no man's possession. I swore that when I was nine summers old, before my breasts had even budded."

"I rather doubt," Kemni said, "that I can hope to possess you. You are not a possession."

"All men want to own their women," said Iphikleia. "They can't help it. Bulls, stallions—they do the same. The lion owns his harem of ladies. But I will not be owned."

"It would be presumptuous of me to dream of it," Kemni said. "You are royal, and a goddess' beloved. I'm as mortal as man can be."

"Beloved Egyptian," she said, half scornful, half tender. "Your land is full of gods. Your kings are gods. I'm a very ordinary thing here, yes? And you wonder why I find you so astonishing."

"You are never ordinary," Kemni said. "Whereas I—"

"Perfectly extraordinary," she said. "I won't marry you, do you understand? I won't parade this in front of the world. But I'm not going to let you go—awake or asleep. Can you endure that?"

"Do you give me a choice?"

"You may walk away," she said, with a flash of her old, cold self. "I won't stop you. But I won't call you back. Not now, and not after."

Such a choice. She was still in most respects a stranger. But somehow, by the gods' will, they had shared their dreams. The Iphikleia he knew on the other side of sleep, the Iphikleia who lay in his arms and managed still to glare at him, was as dear to him as life. That other one, the cold and haughty priestess, was a mask.

He spoke to the Iphikleia of the spirit, the bright, fierce presence that was, he was certain now, the truth of her. "I won't walk away. For your honor and for your name's sake, I'll not strut this union through the streets. The rest of it will be as the gods will."

"And the goddess," she said. "Always the goddess."

He bent his head in respect, as to a queen. Iphikleia caught it in her hands again, pulled it down, and rolled him up against the wall. There, and headlong, she took him all anew, so fierce and yet so sweet that it was almost beyond mortal bearing. Then when he thought that now, surely, he must die, for there was nothing more to do in this world, she let him go. She kissed him and stroked him and left him, and went to be, once more, the Iphikleia that all the world knew.

V

KEMNI REELED THROUGH the rest of that day as if he had been struck a blow to the head. That night he did not dream; his sleep was as dark as deep water.

Until he woke, at some hour between midnight and dawn, to wicked fingers teasing him, coaxing his manly parts to rise and greet this incalculable creature who had made him her own. He was deep in her before his eyes had even opened, savoring the scent and touch and taste of her, and her presence here, waking, in his bed.

They said that a new-plucked maidenhead was more pain than pleasure; and that a woman had to learn the first steps of the dance before she knew what joy it could be. Iphikleia had known it in the spirit long before she knew it in the flesh. She took an honest delight in it. She even laughed, soft and rich, as she tried a twist and stroke that made him cry out. "*Ai!* Woman, you'll kill me."

"Maybe someday," she said. "But now I want you alive."

She wanted him more than alive. She wanted him inexhaustible and insatiable. But he was not a woman, to be so blessed of the gods. He gave her what he could, and she professed herself satisfied with it.

And when there was nothing left of him but a limp rag, she held him in her arms and kissed him softly, and said, "Ariana is sending you to steal a chariotmaker from the Retenu."

He had known that. Of course he had. But—"You tell me that *now?*"

"When should I tell you?"

He opened his mouth, but he was not a perfect fool. Instead of the rush of protest, he asked simply, "When?"

"As soon as you may."

She was cool, calm. Another woman would have wept, or tried at least to seem sad. But this was Iphikleia.

"I suppose she'll want to see me in the morning," Kemni said after a while. Then: "Does she know?"

"There's little my cousin does not know." Iphikleia played with his hair. "Are you ashamed of me?"

He looked up startled. "I should be asking you that."

"No," she said. "I'm a foreign woman. My rank and where I come from matters little here. And you are the king's trusted servant."

"I'm not—"

"Stop that," she said. "It's not fitting for a man to imagine himself less than he is. You were born to a lesser lordship. You've grown to more. Do you think the king will let you slink and hide, now he's discovered how useful you can be?"

"Probably not," Kemni said a little ruefully. "I am convenient. And I do take orders well."

"And fulfill them well."

He shrugged. "You," he said, "should flaunt yourself at the king's son. He's pleasant, charming, and completely to be trusted. And he's of rank to match yours."

"I like him," she said, not at all disconcerted by this new shift of his. "He is pleasant. He has no gift for any language but his own, and he'll never understand horses."

"He wants to understand them," Kemni said.

"But he has no gift for it. They cry out to him with every flick of the ear, and he's as deaf as the earth underfoot."

"He'll learn."

"One can hope so," she said.

"So," he said. "While I'm gone risking death to bring the king a chariot-maker, will you be warming his bed as you warm mine?"

"I don't have to answer that," she said.

"No," he said.

She kissed him. Her lips were fire-warm. They woke him rather thoroughly. He drew her down. She was ready for him, and more than ready.

✦ ✦

Ariana gave Kemni three days to gather his wits and his companions. He could not take an army, but neither could he go alone. A party small enough to escape notice, but large enough to capture and hold a prisoner or, better yet, prisoners—fishers on the river, with a small fast boat and a clutter of nets and cargo. No one noticed fishermen or farmers. They were everywhere, naked sunburned men who knew better than to draw a lord's eye.

Kemni chose from among his own hundred, men who knew how to wield net and line, and who were wise enough to be circumspect. One of them was Seti. He was wild and he was insolent, but he was a fine sailor, and Kemni thought he might be more sensible than he wanted to seem.

The others were quieter men, wiry-thin even for Egyptians, the better to seem poor fishermen and not king's soldiers. They stripped naked or wrapped their loins in a bit of rag, took care to go unshaven and unwashed, and embarked on the boat in a fine state of redolence.

There was someone waiting for them. Kemni sucked in his breath. "Don't begin," Iphikleia said. "You need someone who knows a good chariot from a bad one."

"This isn't a ship from Crete," Kemni said. "You can't hide as I hid."
"I'll do well enough," she said. "Now may we go?"

Kemni turned to Ariana, who had come down to the river with them. She spread her hands. "I don't command her," she said. "If she wants to go, she goes."

Nor could Gebu help him. Gebu was on the boat past Iphikleia, somewhat less filthy and unshaven than the rest, but a creditable fisherman nonetheless. He grinned as Kemni glared at him. "I can't take you both! What if you're captured or killed? Two kings will be after my hide."

"Then you'd best protect us, hadn't you?" said Gebu. "Come, brother. Time's wasting."

Kemni's careful plan was crumbling about him. He had had every intention of sailing in, doing what he must, and escaping unrecognized. With a Cretan woman all too obviously perched in the bow of a fishing boat, and a royal prince less than perfectly hidden among the crew, Kemni would be as difficult to notice as an ibis in a flock of geese.

He was bound to go. He had given Ariana his word. And she would not order these interlopers off the boat.

With a deep sigh, he bade farewell to his Cretan queen, and lent his shoulder to rest of those that slid the boat from the bank into the water. He was the last to clamber aboard, drawn up by eager hands, just ahead of a crocodile's sudden snap.

That was omen enough to begin with. Kemni chose to regard it as hopeful, in that he had escaped unharmed. The crocodile, cheated of its prey, lashed its tail in temper and vanished beneath the water.

The boat rocked in the wave of the crocodile's passing, but steadied as the men aboard it dug in the oars. They rowed out into the middle of the river, raised the sail to catch the bit of wind, and let the current carry them downstream.

Kemni had taken the steering-oar. It was easy work, needing no thought. The wind was almost cool, the sun fierce, but he was born to that. Iphikleia, he saw, had sunk down in the curve of the prow and drawn a mantle over herself. She looked, even from so close, like a bundle of nets.

As much as he disliked to admit it, it was possible they would escape undetected. Neither Iphikleia nor Gebu was a fool. And yet . . .

He shut the thought away. It was some while before they would need to creep and hide. They were still in the Upper Kingdom here. For the game's sake he had determined that they should be fishermen indeed, and wield net and line as they went. What they caught they would eat, or if there was enough, they could trade in the villages for bread and beer and other, more varied provisions.

It was not like sailing on the *Dancer* of Crete. This was a smaller boat, cramped, with few amenities. Every finger's breadth of space was put to use.

At night they drew up on the bank, set up camp and a watch and slept as they could. The weapons they concealed in bits of baggage and folds of net were not the weapons of simple fishermen—Kemni had yielded to sense in that much; they carried the swords of warriors, short spears and hunting-lances, and bows with arrows set ready to hand.

But, except for those, they lived and camped as what they seemed. There were no elaborate pavilions, no flocks of servants. Even Gebu had to fend for himself. People were willing to wait on him, but their numbers were too few and their duties too many.

He insisted that he did not mind. "It's a grand lark," he said to Kemni, the third night downriver from the Bull of Re. They were traveling slowly, but not as slowly as Kemni had feared. The river's current had grown swifter. It was coming to the flood early this year.

In a day or two or three, they would pass into Lower Egypt. Then they must be more circumspect, and pray the gods that what they looked for could be found soon. Kemni half feared that they might have to sail as far as Avaris.

But that was ridiculous. There were strongholds of the enemy much closer than the royal city. In one of them, there would be makers of chariots.

Iphikleia professed to know where some might be. "And how did you know that?" Kemni inquired.

"This way and that," she said. She was not fond of Egyptian beer, but they had brought no wine. Fishermen did not drink it. She sipped, grimaced, began to set the cup down.

Gebu caught her hand, held it. "No," he said. "No, lady. Wine, one sips. Beer, one drinks down as quickly as one can. Here: shut your eyes, and drink deep."

She did not at all appear to mind that he had touched her. She did as he advised, screwed up her face and squeezed her eyes shut and drained the cup in a swallow. She gagged, gasped, coughed, but opened her eyes and said in somewhat breathless surprise, "It's not so bad!"

"You see?" said Gebu. "It's not a taste to linger over. But taken quickly, without pause to think—it's rather splendid."

"It . . . does grow on one," Iphikleia admitted. She went back to gnawing at her share of barley bread.

Kemni watched them narrowly. Gebu was sitting close to her, as someone had to; it was a tight circle round the fire, well back from the river with its threat of crocodiles. Kemni had found a place somewhat apart from them, between Seti and a tonguetied young man who regarded Iphikleia in awe. Gebu the prince affected him not at all, but Iphikleia in her shabby mantle and her redolence of fish was an object of veneration.

She was suffering Gebu to sit very close. He touched her often, by accident as it seemed, but Kemni knew that art as well as any.

It should not matter. Iphikleia was not Kemni's possession. She had barely glanced at him since she set foot in the boat—as if what they had had was left behind in the Bull of Re.

And now she favored the prince. Had she lied, then, when she said that it was not Gebu she fancied? Or had she changed as a woman could do, and turned toward him after all?

Fruitless thoughts, and futile here, where every eye could see and every ear hear what passed between any two of them. If he indulged in jealousy, he must do it alone—and know it for folly.

"This is splendid," Gebu was saying in response to a murmur from Iphikleia. "I've never fended completely for myself before. It's refreshing."

"I'm glad you think so," she said.

"Oh yes! Do you know how truly wearing it is to be royal?"

"I never found it wearing," she said, "but I ran away often. I even sailed in ships. I came to Egypt more than once."

"You see?" said Gebu. "It dragged at you. You escaped it as often as you could. That gift wasn't given me—till my battle-brother helped to set me free."

"He helped you, too?" Her voice was cool. "He's not happy with his gifts, I don't think."

Gebu laughed softly. "No, he's not. My poor brother. So blessed, and so reluctant."

Kemni stopped his ears with the rough sack that was all the blanket he had, and tried to sleep. They chattered on through the night, as far as he knew, as friends will, or friends who would be lovers.

It was fitting. They were of like rank. Kemni was markedly lower in station than they, honored of the king or no.

+ +

Such thoughts had no place and no purpose in the burning daylight. Kemni could not keep them away in the dark, and suffered rather too much loss of sleep thereby. But when the sun was in the sky, he fixed on what was his to do: sail the boat, command the men, see that the fishing went on as it should. The river was running even swifter now, and rising higher. The flood was coming, the great Inundation that would spread the water wide across the land of Egypt, and leave behind it the rich black earth that was the wealth of the Two Kingdoms.

He began to think that perhaps he had been less than wise to venture the river in a fishing-boat with the water rising. But it was a sturdy boat, made of reeds bundled together in the ancient way, born on this river and begotten of it. It gave to the surge of the river as a boat of wood might not have done, and rode with it, borne lightly atop it.

There were fish in plenty, though the nets had to drop lower, and dredge deeper. Kemni chose to continue trading the catch in towns along the river, though that grew more dangerous the farther north they went. They gathered

gossip in that way, and news, and rumors that ran swifter than the river. One
such persisted, and grew stronger as they drew nearer to Lower Egypt: that
war was coming. The foreign kings and the king in Thebes would meet in
battle as they had ten years agone.

"And why would either of them trouble to do that?" Seti drawled in the
marketplace of a town not far south of Memphis. Seti had a good ear; he could
mimic dialects with ease, though he was not as quick with languages as Kemni
was. He managed, at every town, to speak in the accent of the town before
that, so that people would think he had come from just upriver. It was wonderfully clever, and well he knew it, too.

"So," he said in the dialect of a day's long sail upriver, "tell me why war
should come now. It's been years since the kings fought. And isn't old Apophis
getting on a bit? He's not the young lion he used to be."

"Neither is Ahmose," said one of the idlers in the market, while an as-
sortment of wives and servants haggled over the fish. "They've both got grown
sons. But that never stopped a king, that I ever heard of."

Kemni was occupied with a supremely contentious harridan and her even
more contentious servant, but he kept half an ear on the conversation, and half
an eye on Gebu, who had flat refused to stay with the boat. Days of sun and
sailing had given him a rough and suitably common look, but he had lifted his
head at his father's name. Those eyes had never belonged to a simple fisherman.

Seti, whose air of worldly ennui passed here for youthful foolishness—
though the women tended to like it; it charmed them—snorted at the king's
name. "Ah! Ahmose. He's younger than Apophis, but I'd have hoped he was
wiser. Why would he fight a war he can't win?"

"How do you know he can't?" another of the idlers demanded.

Kemni had sold the harridan a basketful of fish, each one selected with
exacting care and endless haggling. He left the next buyer to another of the
crew, and busied himself between Seti and Gebu, brushing flies from the fish,
and shifting the bit of sail that shaded them from the sun.

Seti had stopped even pretending to help with the selling. "So tell me how
Ahmose can win a war against the Retenu."

"By fighting it," the idler answered, speaking as if to an idiot child. "He
sits in his big house away upriver, eats off his golden plates and shits in his
golden pot, and wishes he could be lord of Two Lands instead of one. I tell
you, man, if he got up and dropped the girl he's bouncing on his knee, took
up his sword and called his armies and got to work, he'd be king of everything
before the flood came to the full."

"That fast?" Seti's voice was deeply and mockingly awed. "And what
about the king downriver in *his* big house, with his chariots and his herds of
asses? Won't he have something to say about it?"

"Oh," said the idler. "Him. He's so busy with his hundred wives, he
doesn't have time to bother with a war."

"But his two hundred sons," said Seti, "might find a war well worth the trouble. It's hard these days, being a king's son of a warrior people. No women to rape, no cities to pillage. Give them a war and they'll be glad to take it."

"Surely," the idler said, "and so would good Egyptians. I've got kin up by Memphis. They've been eating ass manure for years, and hating every bite of it. Give them a king to fight and an army to join, and they're ready to march."

"That's not what my father says," Seti said.

"Your father's old, isn't he? Sure it's made him wise, but has it made him brave?"

"Bravery's for young men," Seti said. "You're that brave down this way?"

"Braver!" declared the idlers in chorus.

Seti shook his head. "I hope you'll say the same when the Retenu come to conquer you."

"They already did that," the chief of the idlers said. "We wore them out, here. Down the river where they're still strong—they'll need a harder hand."

"We could all be kings," drawled Seti, "if we were as wise as you."

"Laugh all you like," the idler said. "I'm telling nothing but the truth."

✣ ✣

Gebu told the tale by the fire that night, where they all had come together in the boat's shadow. He was alight with it. "They will fight. They *will*."

"They say they will," Kemni said. "They're near enough to the enemy here to feel his breath on their necks. Those who live under his sway may be less willing to endanger themselves and their kin."

"You were willing," Gebu said.

Kemni shook his head. "I went because I was bored and I was angry, and I was wild to fight foreigners. My uncle and my cousins were all killed. We were all that had the will to fight."

"And maybe the years have changed even your people," Gebu said. "Talk like that in the market—we never heard such a thing before, even when we won this kingdom under my uncle Kamose."

"We were never simple fishermen before," said Kemni. "Princes don't hear what the people talk of. It's not reckoned dignified."

"Do you think that of me? That I've lost my dignity?"

Kemni laughed in startlement. "No! No, of course not. I only meant—"

Gebu waved that aside. "I hear more than people know. They do sometimes talk when I can hear, or forget how near I am, and tell one another the truth. We learn, we princes, to gather knowledge wherever we may."

"Such a life," Iphikleia said. She leaned against the hull, wrapped in her mantle. If it troubled her to spend every day in hiding, she was not admitting to it. She managed somehow to be clean, to keep her hair in order, to look much as she always had.

The sight of her made Kemni's heart beat hard. She was as oblivious to him as she had ever been. Her eyes were on Gebu, as they so often were. "A palace is a world in itself," she said. "It's hard to remember what other worlds there are."

"Unless one determines to remember," Gebu said.

"Yes," she said. She stared into the dark beyond the fire's light, frowning slightly, as she did when she was pondering matters too deep, no doubt, for a mere mortal man to understand.

When she spoke again, it was to no one of them in particular. "This serves us. When we come back, my lord, it would be well if your father knew; if he sent his men here to muster an army."

"And north of here?" Kemni asked. "What of the people in the foreign kings' power?"

"When we've seen them," she said, "and heard what they say to one another, we'll know."

"I think you know already," he said.

She did not answer that. He had not expected her to.

·············· **VI** ··············

M EMPHIS WAS THE gate of the Lower Kingdom, but Retenu power stretched somewhat to the south of it. Kemni did not want to go as far as that city where he was known, not if he could find what he looked for in another, lesser city.

As he had while he sailed on *Dancer*—and not so long ago, either—he saw how the land changed even as it remained the same: how the land began to fill with foreigners. The people seemed much the same, but they were not as bold as their kinsmen to the south. They kept their heads down and their eyes veiled, and did their best to escape the notice of their foreign overlords.

Kemni and his crew were not remarkable, there, in wishing to be invisible. Everyone slunk and crept past the Retenu. It was expected.

That served them; but they would have to move soon, find a nest of Retenu, and search for the makers of chariots. Kemni's knowledge of that country was years old. Those who lived in it were closemouthed and wary of strangers. It was only wise where any man might be a spy, and the lords were all outlanders, all enemies.

And yet where there was beer there was hope of loose tongues. And Kemni had fish to trade, and barley, and a bolt of middling fine linen that he had taken from that harridan in the south, in return for a basketful of fish. He steered the boat toward a town that he had known when he was young, but that, he hoped, would not know him in this disguise.

The gods were kind, in their way. The town had grown since he was a child: it had added a temple to the Retenu god, whom they called Baal and men in Egypt called Set; and near the temple, on an outcropping of rock over the river, had risen a wall of stone and a low tower. Men were building it even as the boat made its way to the shore below, hauling stone and raising the wall higher.

Someone foresaw a battle. Although, Kemni thought, Retenu were always prepared to fight. They lived their lives in expectation of war, ate it, slept in it, breathed it. Everything was war. There was no glory in peace, nor any hope that a man's name would be remembered.

This had been a lively town when Kemni knew it. It was hectic now, and bursting at the seams, between the new fortress and the new temple. Its market was as large almost as a city's, full not only of the wonted barley and beer, bread and meat, onions, greenstuff, bolts of linen, amulets, potions, herbs and eyepaint and scent; but richer things too, a coppersmith, even a goldsmith and a seller of jewels, and a thriving market in slaves.

There the Retenu seemed mostly to be: big, bearded men in elaborate robes, with their hair plaited and their beards curled, and no women with them. Their women lived locked behind walls, less free than the slaves who stood naked on the block.

Kemni, pausing outside the slavemarket, saw how fiercely they battled one another for possession of a single woman: a creature of surpassing strangeness, milk-fair of skin, with hair the color of copper. Her face was not particularly beautiful—its features were blunt, her lips overfull, her nose too small and upturned at the tip. But her hair was wonderful, and her skin. Her body was overly rich for Egyptian taste, her hips broad, her thighs heavy, and her breasts as white and nigh as large as twin lambs. The Retenu slavered at the sight of her. Kemni saw one, near the edge of the throng, slip his hand beneath his ro● and begin to rock gently. He had called out a price, but it was long since overwhelmed.

Someone jostled Kemni from behind, and cursed him for blocking the way. He moved on past, caught in the crowd. Somewhere behind him was Seti, and Gebu. He could not see them; they were lost. But they knew where he was going, to the market and in search of a beerseller's stall. They would find him. Or not. They all knew where the boat was; that much he could trust in.

So many people. Kemni had been living like a prince, if he was honest about it. He had forgotten what a crowd was like, how irresistible its currents could be, how manifold its voices. Haggling mostly, and snatches of song; the cry of a child and the shrilling of a woman at her feckless man. And, buried within it, the bray of an ass.

He had not even thought before he turned toward that one sound among so many. Asses were the wealth of the Retenu, their honor, and their royal sacrifice. Where asses were, must be chariots. And if there were chariots . . .

He slipped under and over and through the press of people, working his way to a side-current, and thence to a street that made its twisting way inward through the town. The crowds were much less here, and quieter, except for the pack of children that howled past like hounds on a scent. Kemni plucked his bag of barley grains from clever fingers, and smiled sweetly into a grubby young face. The child grinned, gaptoothed and unrepentant, and sprang in pursuit of his fellows.

Somewhat more wary but still intent on his own hunt, Kemni strode swiftly down the street. It went on rather longer than he had expected, with several bends and turns. More than once it crossed another street, lesser or greater, but none of those led where he had in mind to go.

Then at last he came to it: a broad open space, a square bounded by the low mudbrick houses that were everywhere in Egypt. It was, he saw with interest, not far at all from the new temple, and just below the fortress that was rising on its jut of hill.

The market here was a cattle market, as it must have been for time out of mind. But one side of it was given now to lines of long-eared asses, and to clusters of bearded Retenu settling bargains in their guttural language.

There were no horses. And no chariots. These were pack-beasts for caravans, Kemni could see: some were sold in their pack-gear, some even laden, their burdens sold with them. Kemni wondered if the buyers knew what they had bought, or if they took what luck brought them. Certainly they must hope for better fortune than those who had died or been lost, leaving their beasts to be sold in the market.

No chariots. But the fortress rose on its hill, its walls half-finished, but already warded with a gate and guards. Kemni had hoped for a lord's estate with its open gate and people passing in and out. This was a stronghold, a house of war.

And yet, its gate was open. People passed in and out. Most were Egyptian, of every rank and station. The lord must be in residence, then, and his following with him.

Kemni hesitated for a moment. But he was alone—no sign of Gebu or Seti—and unarmed and nondescript. Surely he could walk in with any of the other unarmed and barely noticeable commoners, see what there was to see, hear what he could hear, and come out again with none the wiser.

It seemed wise enough, and safe enough, though he might have been wiser to find his companions and tell them what he intended to do. But they would insist on coming with him; and three men together, with one who was not skilled in concealing the manners and bearing of a prince, would attract far more notice than one man alone.

His feet decided somewhat before his wits did: he was walking around the edge of the market, casually, not slinking or creeping as if he had something to hide. He was but one of many of his kind, unmarked by gold or fine garments or a retinue, and therefore scarce to be marked at all.

And yet, as he passed between the two tall bearded guards under the half-finished gate, his back tightened. They could not know that he was different from any other small wiry red-brown nonentity. He wore no jewels, put on no airs. He was nothing to them. Danger came armed and in multitudes, not single and weaponless.

The guards never even seemed to see him. He forbore to collapse with relief once he had passed them; they would see and, perhaps, begin to wonder. He walked on instead, with but the hint of wobble in his knees.

He had been in Avaris of the kings, even walked there briefly as a conqueror, and in lesser holdings of the Retenu, long ago and in his father's company. He had walked in a fortress or two, the high house of a man who claimed lordship over Kemni's lands and people. This was much the same: part palace, part encampment. It had few of the graces of the Egyptian palace, though to be sure, this was unfinished, and rough with it. Workmen were clambering over the wall as he walked briskly past, fitting stone to stone and raising the wall high.

A stable would be set against that wall, most likely, or just outside of it. As indeed it was: just outside, a square of mudbrick buildings, and the very earliest beginnings of their like in stone, and a broad court of smoothed sand marked now with the ruts of chariot wheels. A handful of shaggy young men were playing at battle, whooping and clattering about the court, whipping on their teams and making a great show of hairbreadth turns and sudden skidding stops. None of them drove horses. This lord perhaps had none, or did not choose to indulge in those larger, swifter, but more costly and more delicate creatures.

But Kemni was not here for the horses. He sidled along the edge of the court, in and out of shade and sun. He did not see any Egyptians here: a flaw in his plan, but he was not ready, yet, to retreat. Perhaps, if no one expected to see an Egyptian there, no one would see him.

It was a thin hope to rest a life on, but it was the best Kemni had. He would not withdraw. Not yet. He had to see where those fine and gleaming chariots had come from.

They well might have come from Memphis or Avaris. He had no honest right to expect that there might be a workshop there. And yet he went on. He found the storage for fodder; the stable proper, where asses stood or lay in company, some tied to the wall, some left loose; what must be the quarters for the stablemen, empty now but full of their clutter. And then, when he had begun to wonder if he would ever find it, the place in which they kept the chariots and the harness. It was much larger than he had expected. Men worked there, repairing—no, building a chariot.

Kemni shrank as deep into shadow as he might. His hand had risen to the amulet of Amon that he wore on his breast, and clasped it tight. The gods were with him, oh, indeed. In the first place of the enemy to which he had come, to find what he sought . . .

And well he might find it, but to make use of it—that was not so simple.

No lord of the enemy would be so much a fool as to leave his prized artisans for any passerby to steal. These would, he suspected, be housed above their workshop, close to the heart of the stable, and in full view of the guard atop the gate.

But at night . . .

Kemni itched to go. Still he lingered, watching and listening. He understood their language, if he set his mind to it; he had learned it long ago, as one learns all one may of one's enemy, the better to do battle against him. They were speaking of little that mattered, and nothing that need trouble him. Except that one said, "I'll be glad when this one is done. It's well past time we saw Avaris again."

"Tomorrow," another said. "Now quick, finish that wheelrim. Soonest done, soonest over—and we've a journey to prepare for."

The first man sighed. "And none too soon for me. The next time the king sends us out to build chariots for one of his pets, he can leave me at home. I've had a bellyful of these lordlings and their 'Do this, do that, do somewhat else of no use whatever, but great pleasure, because it makes the king's men leap to our bidding.' "

"Ah," said the second. "Well. That's lordlings for you. We're gone in the morning, thank the Great God; and we've left good work behind us."

"We have done that," his companion agreed.

Kemni thrust his fist into his mouth and bit down hard. Tomorrow? They left tomorrow? But that meant—

He could not run. He must walk out as casually as he had come, and make his way past the guards, and pass with maddening slowness through the crowds in this town that had ambitions to become a city.

It seemed an endless while before he came to the boat, and found it all but deserted. The two men who had drawn guard-duty were loitering about as if they had nothing more pressing to do. Iphikleia was not in any of her wonted hiding places. He could not dare to hope that she had hidden herself too cleverly for him to find: it was not a large boat, nor blessed with many recesses in which a grown woman could conceal herself.

She was gone, the gods knew where. Kemni could see no profit in searching for her. He hated himself for that practicality; but he was a practical man. He paced and fumed and fretted, till one of the men on guard, sauntering past, slapped a jar of beer into his hands. He nearly dropped it. It was heavy: full almost to the brim. It was good, too, well brewed and not too sour, with just the proper taste of barley and a hint of the bread from which the beer had been born.

He could not drink himself into a stupor. He sipped—just enough to dull the edge of his anxiety, and no more. When he was beginning to be comfortable, his men began to straggle back. Some were well gone in beer. Others looked as if they would have liked to be.

Last of all, Gebu came, and Seti behind him, looking inescapably like a man of rank and his servant. They glowered at Kemni. "Where did you get to?" Gebu demanded. "We hunted high and low for you."

"I'll tell you," Kemni said. "But first—where is Iphikleia?"

"Here," she said.

He nigh jumped out of his skin. She was sitting on the boat's rim, wrapped in her shabby cloak, with bare dirty feet and her hair in a tight plait. She looked like a child, and not one of rank, either.

He most certainly had not found her on the boat. She must have come up the other side, and waited till he was off guard before she made herself known.

He set his teeth and throttled his temper. "And where have you been?" he inquired.

"Here," she said.

"You have not."

She lifted her chin. The urchin was suddenly a princess, haughty and cold.

He grinned at her. He would rather have snapped his teeth in her face, but that would not be proper. "Well; and you're here now, and no armies on your track. I'll presume that you haven't done anything excessively deadly."

"How generous of you," she said.

"Isn't it?" He turned back to Gebu, deliberately putting her out of his mind—or as much as he could ever do, when sometimes he felt as if she had, somehow, captured one or more of his souls.

They were all in place at the moment, and he had no time to waste. The sun had begun to sink. "I've found what we're looking for," he said without preamble. "It's up there, in the fortress."

Faces that had brightened when he began, fell quickly at the end of it. "We'll never get into or out of that," Seti said for them all. "Not without an army."

"No," said Kemni. "We won't. It's strong even half-finished, and it's crawling with men. "But we won't need to storm the fortress. The gods are with us. These chariotmakers—they're not the lord's own. The king lent them to him. And tomorrow—tomorrow they go home."

"Home?" Gebu frowned. "To Avaris?"

"So they said," Kemni said.

"But that means—"

Kemni nodded.

Gebu's scowl vanished. He flung arms about Kemni and whirled him in a brief, headlong dance. "Brother! Little brother! What a wonder you are!"

Seti was not so quick to credit it. "You think they really will leave tomorrow? Well; and if they do, how will we follow? I'll wager silver they'll go in chariots."

But Kemni had been pondering that for all that long afternoon. "They'll go on land, I'm sure. They're Retenu; they hate boats. But the river's running fast. We can keep pace well enough. Let them travel well away from here, until they're in the empty places—then we can fall on them and capture them all."

"I don't think there's room in the boat for that," Seti said.

"We'll make do." Iphikleia had not softened her expression at all, but she had spoken for Kemni. That would do, he supposed. She slid down from the boat to the bank, and said, "You're sure they're what we need."

"I'm certain," he said. He was still, carefully, patient.

"Well then," she said. "Someone should watch to see them leave. Even tonight—they might go early. And if they do—"

"I'll go," Seti said. "Only feed me first, and give me a jar of beer. It will be a long night, whatever comes of it."

Kemni had thought to go himself. But he did not need Iphikleia's long look to understand that he could not both spy on the fortress and set his men in order. He bent his head toward Seti. "Eat," he said, "and go. And the gods protect you."

·········· VII ··········

NONE OF THEM slept overmuch that night. Soldiers learned to sleep wherever they paused to rest, but this was something other than war. They had known that they were deep in the enemy's country, but it had meant little.

Now they began what they had come to do. If they failed, they failed their king. Even if they succeeded, they could be found and killed, and Ahmose— and his Cretan queen—would not have what they needed to win the war.

Kemni could torment himself with fears. Or he could lie wrapped in his blanket and try not to think of Iphikleia. She slept on the boat as always, a shadow among the shadows of its cargo. Whatever they had said or done at the Bull of Re, it was gone and forgotten here. He was no more to her than any of his men; and less, perhaps, than Gebu the prince.

He lay open-eyed for an eternity of starlit darkness. The town slept. The river was rising: the boat had been drawn up away from the water, but now it lapped just short of the pointed bow. If they did not cast off by full morning, he judged, the river would do it for them.

When his bones felt the first hint of dawn, when the night was darkest, the air full of whispers and unseen passings, he rose softly and walked the edges of the camp. It was a frequent boast hereabouts that neither crocodiles nor lions of the desert dared trespass within the town. Kemni was watchful none-theless. Not only beasts could be a danger here.

Seti had not come back from watching over the fortress. Kemni hoped that meant the Retenu had not left yet, and not that Seti had been captured or worse. It was quiet round about, no company of guards approaching to take them all prisoner.

He perched on a heap of flotsam just past the camp, clasped his knees and waited for the dawn. Slowly, infinitely slowly, the darkness paled. The east, over the barren hills of the Red Land, came clearer little by little, under a pellucid sky. The stars faded. Away in the beds of reeds, now all but sunk in the river, a bird began to sing.

+ +

They were all up and fed and girded for the day, somewhat before the sun climbed over the horizon. Seti still had not come back. Kemni was half minded to wait for him; but urgency ate at his belly. "Get the boat in the water," he said to his waiting people. "We'll fish downstream this morning, and see who rides on the northward road."

They were glad to obey. All this journeying had been adventure of a sort, but this was what they had come to do. There was a lightness in their move-ments, an eagerness; even a snatch of song, quickly cut off—till Gebu said, "No, no. Sing. Sing. We're honest fishermen, setting out to bring in the day's catch—not spies creeping about by night. Sing!"

They sang therefore as they slid the boat into the water and clambered aboard, and set off down the river. Their songs reminded Kemni rather more vividly of a guardroom than a fishing boat, but he doubted the enemy would know the difference.

The river was fractious this morning, the steering oar strong in his hands. The flood was rising fast. He had to hope it would not keep him from the bank when the time came.

For the moment it was well; they needed no oar or sail, simply rode the current, fishing with lines off bow and stern, and pulling in what the lines caught. They watched the east bank, idly, as it might seem.

Boats passed them as the morning brightened into full day. Some hailed them; others were too full of their own importance. None held a cargo of chariotmakers bound for Avaris. On the bank meanwhile, there was somewhat less coming and going, but enough. Twice, bearded men rattled past in char-iots. People on foot came and went—came, mostly, at this hour, walking to market or to business in the town. A noble passed with his retinue, perched aloft in his gilded chair.

That could have been Kemni, and should have been Gebu—if this had been the Two Lands of the old time, or of the new one that Ahmose hoped to begin. Filthy and reeking of fish, unshaven, ragged, and beneath any great one's notice, they rode the river down toward Memphis.

At midmorning Kemni began to edge toward the eastward bank. The reeds were thick here, bulrushes and tall fans of papyrus. They hid a flock of geese, which fled honking and flapping, and with care, the boat itself. The men, armed with knives and sickles, cut a path through the reeds, those who cut leaning down over the boat's sides and prow, held tightly by their fellows. The crocodiles were not hunting here this morning, it seemed; there was no sign of them. Kemni murmured a prayer to the god Sobek, who wore a crocodile's face, that his children should let them be, for the winning back of the Lower Kingdom.

When the cutting and pruning was done, the boat rested in a clearing in the reeds with its prow up against the riverbank. They anchored it there. No one could see them from the river, nor from the land either. They were perfectly hidden.

Kemni slipped from prow to land and ghosted up the bank to be certain. Even before he had emerged from the reeds, the boat and its people were invisible.

He paused on the edge of the thicket. Oh, the gods were kind: the reeds gave way to bare sunburned earth, the Black Land bleached almost white by heat and sunlight. He could see how far the river was wont to rise: where the richer earth of the river's gift gave way to the sand and stones of the Red Land. There, on the edge between the two, ran the road to Memphis.

There was no one on it just then. Fresh droppings marked the passing of an ox or oxen, a farmer most likely. None of the foreigners' donkeys had passed by this morning. They were still behind, then—if they were coming at all.

Kemni must trust that they would. He settled behind a screen of reeds, as if he were hunting waterfowl and not men. He was aware that someone had followed him, but he did not look to see who it was. It must be Gebu. No one else would be bold enough to leave the boat without Kemni's leave.

The other slipped beside him, in under his arm, and said in a voice that was anything but cool, "Oh, you clever man!"

He tensed to recoil from Iphikleia, but his arm tightened about her instead. She turned in the circle of it. Whatever she did, however she did it, she was naked, her mantle spread beneath her, and his loincloth suddenly, magically vanished.

Some part of him snarled at her, and upbraided her for sparing him not even a glance between the Bull of Re and this thicket. And what, he almost asked, of Gebu?

But his body knew no such folly. It fell on her like one starving. She caught at him with sudden fierceness, wrapped herself about him and drove him deep inside her.

He gasped. She was eating him alive. Kisses, love-bites, one after another, everywhere that she could reach. She rode him as if he had been a ship on a high sea, deep strokes and long, drawing him almost—almost—to the summit, but sinking away. She tormented him. She sapped him of wit and will. She conquered him as utterly as the Retenu had conquered the Lower Kingdom.

Then at last, when he was ready to scream at her to end it, she let the tide take him and cast him up gasping on the shore.

When he could breathe again, he said, "I think I hate you."

"I'm sure you despise me," she said. She dropped down onto her mantle, arching her back and stretching like a cat. Her body was limned in light and shadow, bars and blades of dark and gold.

Memory struck like a blow. Kemni scrambled to hands and knees and peered out through the screen of reeds.

The road was deserted. He let his breath out slowly.

Iphikleia's hands smoothed and stroked his back, rubbing away the tightness, winning from him a soft groan. He stilled it quickly. She laughed in his ear, and nibbled it.

He pulled away slightly, coming somewhat to himself. "You never even looked at me," he said.

"Of course I didn't," she said. "Did you want a whole boatload of snickering spectators?"

He could never best her in a war of words. And yet he had to say, "You looked at Gebu often enough."

"Ah! You're jealous."

"Do I have reason to be?"

"No," she said. She slipped from his back to lie beside him, chin on fists, gazing out at the road. "Mind you, I like him. He's well-spoken, he's charming, he's just as a prince should be. But I don't dream of him."

"I'm surprised," Kemni said.

He meant it honestly. It seemed she took it as such. She shrugged a little, a shift of warm bare shoulder against his. "Would you be happier if I did?"

"No."

"So," she said. Then: "Listen."

He opened his mouth to ask what she meant by that, but his ear had caught it also: a distant sound like the braying of an ass.

She shifted beside him, a small flurry that ended in her being wrapped in her mantle again. He should find his loincloth and put it on, but he paused, listening. Another bray. A murmur of men's voices. The hollow clatter of hooves on the hard-beaten road; rattle of wheels.

It could be another party of Retenu on its way to Memphis. Kemni remembered to breathe, to calm himself. He rose then, softly, and wrapped his loincloth and fastened it tightly. A brief flash of vanity regretted that he could not do this thing in a clean kilt and a shaven face; but it would serve him better to be thought a mere brigand. Brigands were not hunted in this country as a lord from the Upper Kingdom would be.

"I'll tell the others," he breathed in Iphikleia's ear. She nodded, keeping her eyes on the road.

His men were waiting. They were not precisely atwitch with eagerness. Most seemed asleep or nearly so. But when they heard the news he brought, they woke abruptly.

There were no orders to give. Those were all given long since. He slipped back to the place where he had been. Iphikleia was gone from it, the gods knew where. Not, he trusted, to betray him to the enemy.

It seemed a long while before the company rounded the curve of the road. When at last it appeared, it was less than Kemni had expected. There were only two chariots, each with two men in it, and a string of laden donkeys, and a handful of men on foot: servants, those must be, and nearly all Egyptian. One of them—

Kemni bit his lip till it bled. Seti. Seti striding briskly with the rest, as innocent as if he had been all he seemed, and no one eyed him oddly or asked him who he was.

And what if . . .

No. They were too calm. No one looked about him, or seemed to care that he might be ambushed. There were guards, but they idled behind, half a dozen on foot and one in a chariot driven by a curly-headed child. Kemni saw and heard no more than that. Nor was there any signal from his men who had been given the charge, that an army waited in hiding.

It was arrogance. Or the Retenu did not believe that Egypt truly could rise up against them.

Whatever the cause of it, Kemni took it as a blessing, and a sending from the gods.

They were level with him now, idling along, laughing and singing. Kemni raised the signal: a clear shrill call like the falcon's as he stoops for his prey.

There was a breathless hush. Even the Retenu paused a fraction, and their laughter stuttered. Just as it smoothed again, the earth erupted.

Kemni's men had seemed few enough when he mustered them. But falling on the Retenu from every side, armed with swords and knives and spears, they seemed as numerous as the king's own armies.

They took the Retenu utterly by surprise. Kemni himself leaped on the captain of the guard, pulled him out of his chariot and wrested his sword from him, and cut his throat before he could muster breath to cry out.

The young charioteer had reined his team to a halt, turning them, whipping them on. Kemni leaped aside, fell and rolled, landed somehow on his feet and within reach of the chariot as it flew past. He leaped as he had once before, saw the chariot pass, knew a moment's sinking despair before he half fell, half staggered into the lurching, rattling thing. The child kicked at him. He stumbled against the chariot's rim. The child pulled hard on the rein. The chariot veered. Kemni staggered again, but forward, into greater safety. For a breath's span he had his balance. He snatched, heaved, thrust the child out; and seized the reins just before they snapped loose.

These long-eared creatures were little like the soft-mouthed horses he had driven under Ariana's tutelage. Their mouths were like forged bronze. He cursed and hauled them about, with a briefly chagrined reflection that he, a man grown, could barely master them, and that infant had driven them as easily as if they had been made of air.

But they yielded to him at last, and consented grudgingly to turn. The battle was over. All but one of the guards were down. The two chariots stood still, with Kemni's men at the asses' heads. Iphikleia stood in one, kilted like a man of Crete, and no mantle to be seen.

It was the sight of her, perhaps, that had astonished the Retenu into immobility. She was a wild beauty, with her black hair streaming over her white breasts, holding her team still with effortless strength.

Kemni muscled his own pair of long-eared demons to a halt beside her. The former passengers lay on the ground, with Kemni's men standing over them, and a spearpoint resting lightly on each throat.

He had seen them both in the workshop. But the one who had seemed to command them stood in the third chariot. As far as Kemni could see on a face bearded to the eyes, he was deeply affronted and not even slightly afraid. "Take your hands off my bridle," he said to the man who held his team's heads.

Gebu smiled at him, sweetly insolent. He did not speak the language of the Retenu—he would not stoop to it—but the tone was clear enough.

This foreigner bridled at the smile, which was indeed provoking. It was the smile of a prince in the face of an upstart underling—and such a prince, filthy, unshaven, and dressed in a scrap of rag. "Bandits! You—slave. Tell them to take that pack-donkey yonder, and let us go."

The slave he spoke to was Seti, standing amid the scared huddle of servants, surrounded by half-naked and ill-shaven men with bright and well-kept weapons. Seti was as cool as Kemni had always seen him, as well he might be; he had nothing to fear from these brigands.

He did, it was clear, understand what the foreigner had said. "Tell them yourself," he drawled with wonderful insolence.

The foreigner sucked in a breath of pure outrage. Kemni intervened before he could collapse in an apoplexy; he was, after all, the whole cause and purpose of this venture. "I thank you," he said in that guttural tongue. His own command of it was rough, but it was serviceable. "We'll take the donkey—along with the rest."

"Just the donkey," the foreigner said, pivoting to face him, speaking slowly as if to an idiot child. "Just one donkey. We take the rest. We belong to the king; we go to him in his city. These are the king's donkeys."

"Are they now?" Kemni smiled as sweetly as Gebu had. "Better and better." He tilted his chin at his men who were waiting. They were delighted to oblige: falling on the foreigner and his mute, staring charioteer, plucking them from the chariot and binding them and stringing them together on a lead, like a train of asses in a caravan.

Kemni disliked to abandon the chariots and their trained teams, but they could not escape on the road. As difficult as it would be to row and sail upriver against that powerful current, they must do that. And there was no room in the boat for chariots. Nor, for the matter of that, for as many men as they had captured.

The three from the workshop, they must keep. "Kill the rest," Seti said.

Kemni raised a brow. "Were they as irritating as that?"

"Somewhat," Seti said. "You can't let them live. They'll run straight to the nearest foreign lord and set him after us."

"I don't think so," Kemni said. He went to stand over the servants where they had been ordered to sit, all of them huddled together, watching him with wide, frightened eyes. "Listen to me," he said. "We're going to leave you here and vanish. We'll bind you and strip you, as if we were bandits. But we won't kill you—if you promise one thing."

They stared at him. Not one seemed possessed of wits enough to speak.

"Promise me," Kemni said, "that you will tell those who found you that bandits ambushed your caravan, killed your masters, and made off with their possessions."

"That isn't the truth?" one of them asked.

"It's what you'll tell anyone who asks," said Kemni.

They all nodded vigorously. Kemni eyed them in some doubt still. Slaves would say whatever they thought their masters wanted them to say. But he had taken precautions. None of them had seen the boat, or could know of it. If they told their tale of bandits, men would scour the hills in search of men afoot or in chariots—and never think to look for a boatful of fishermen on the river.

But for that to succeed, the chariots and the caravan must be disposed of. If someone could lay a trail that led into the desert.

Kemni had decided almost before he paused to think. They had thought to capture and abduct a single man, not three of them—four; Gebu had caught and held the young charioteer, who was calling his passenger *Father*. A son?

A hostage. Even as Kemni formed the thought, Gebu acted on it. He laid the flat of his knifeblade against the child's throat, and said to the eldest and tallest of the Retenu, "Come with us. Or he dies."

In whatever language either of them spoke, the gesture and the tone were unmistakable. The foreigner's face darkened. He nodded sharply.

Gebu smiled. "Thank you so kindly," he said. He handed child and knife to the man who stood nearest—who happened to be a deeply contented Seti—and as easily, as effortlessly as a prince could do, set about ordering the retreat into the reeds. "And as for the chariots—" he began.

Kemni spoke before he could go on. "I'll take them up into the hills."

"But—" said Gebu.

"If we leave them, people will look for us. If we shatter them and sink them in the river, there are still the beasts to think of. They'll make their way home if they can. I can take them far away, far enough that when they do return, it will be far too late to betray you."

"And then how will you go home?" Gebu demanded. "No, no; best we sink them with the chariots. By the time the flood brings them up, if it does, we'll be long gone."

"There's no time to do all that," Kemni said. "It's only the gods' good fortune that no one's come down the road since we began. Go quickly, my lord. Take these men back to the Bull of Re. I'll come when I can, or send word if I can't."

Gebu's eyes narrowed. "Oh, will you? And what are you plotting, O my brother?"

"O my prince," said Kemni, "I'm plotting nothing but to rid us of these chariots, and to go back home as I can."

"By way, perhaps, of Avaris?" Iphikleia inquired.

Kemni shrugged. "Maybe. Maybe I'll go where I'm moved to go, and listen, and watch, and see what there is to see. If the Upper Kingdom is ready to cast off its yoke—then so much the better for my king."

"Brother," said Gebu, "there is no need for you to—"

"I know," said Kemni, "that your father is not altogether cut off from this kingdom. But a man known to him, trusted by him, admitted to his lesser councils—how many of these are here?"

"What will you do, then? Raise a rebellion?"

"I might try," Kemni said.

Gebu shook his head. "No. You'll get killed."

"We'll get killed if we wrangle here. Go, my lord. I'll come when I can."

Kemni braced to fight again, but his ears had caught what he looked for long before now: the sound of feet on the road. He sprang into the chariot that was nearest, and scrambled up the reins. One of the men tossed him the rope that bound the packbeasts in their long string. He looked with despair on the second chariot. If he could fasten that somehow to the packbeasts' string . . .

Iphikleia sprang into it. "Go," she said. *"Go!"*

Kemni bit his tongue and wound the lead about a post in the chariot's rim, and whipped up the team. They responded with admirable speed. The packtrain, by the gods' blessing, saw fit to follow.

They had to cling to the road for some distance. Something flew at Kemni. He ducked. It thudded into the chariot. A—robe? And one of the tall hats that Retenu sometimes wore. He had no beard to go with them, but from a distance, he might pass for a beardless boy. He struggled into the robe, which reeked heavily of old wool and new sweat, and pulled the hat down over his ears.

Iphikleia, behind him, was likewise clothed. If he looked as outlandish as she did, then all their stratagem was of no use.

But no one met them. The passers behind were all on foot, except for one with an ox: farmers and men of the villages, carefully oblivious to the Retenu ahead of them. Gebu and the rest were gone, vanished in the reeds. Kemni prayed to any god who would listen, to keep them safe and bring them back whole to the Bull of Re.

An almost unconscionable distance from the thicket of reeds, the road begot a side way, narrow and rather steep but not impossible for a chariot. Or so Kemni hoped. He urged the team up it. The packtrain scrambled after, and Iphikleia in their wake.

It was brutal going for a chariot, but too narrow and steep to turn back. With every bruising jolt, Kemni prayed that wheels and axle would hold. The team strained, slipping and scrambling, but kept their footing by some miracle of the gods.

The track narrowed even further, and seemed minded to shoot straight up the cliff. But just as he had despaired, when he knew there was nowhere to go—up, down, sidewise, into the sun-shot air—the track breasted the summit and came out on a long level.

Kemni stopped there, content simply to breathe. The packtrain stood with heads hanging, till first one and then another bethought itself to nibble the thorny scrub that dotted the plain.

There was a skin of water in the chariot, and a bag that proved to hold bread, cheese, a packet of dates. The packbeasts were laden with more water, more food, and a gathering of varied riches: tents, bedding, a whole great packful of robes and linen tunics.

Iphikleia seemed in better state than Kemni: fresher, and less whitely terrified. "We should go farther," she said. "A day's journey. More if we can. If we can find a place with ample grazing, the herd might not leave it for days."

"I had been thinking that," he said. "It's been too many years since I was in this country, but as I remember it, there is such a place at not too great a distance. If we're not fallen on by bandits, we'll come to it in a day or two."

She nodded. She had sipped from a waterskin in her own chariot, but laid it thriftily away after two brief swallows.

"You shouldn't have come," he said. He had not meant to say it; he knew it was futile. But it slipped out.

She took no notice of it. She had set her team in motion once more. Up so high and so far from the road, they had no need to run. In a while they would quicken their pace. Now, they walked, chariots and packbeasts, across that high and barren level. No living thing stirred upon it save a vulture circling high against the sun. The heat was stunning, staggering—wonderful. Kemni stripped off the reeking foreign robe and cast the hat on top of it on the chariot's floor. Soon, if he was wise, he would put on robes and a mantle from the pack of garments. But for a while he reveled in the force of light and heat on his bare shoulders.

Iphikleia had wrapped herself in her ragged mantle once more, swathed like a desert tribesman; and well she might be, with that milk-fair skin. She was not a child of the sun as he was. The sea was her father, and a cold and distant island her mother.

She endured this that must have been as hot to her as a forge, silent and uncomplaining. If he had been a god he would have sent her winging back to the Labyrinth, to those cool airy halls and those blinding white walls, and everywhere the horns of the Bull that were also the horns of the moon.

But he was only mortal, and this was his own country, his Egypt; his Lower Kingdom. The pace he set was swift but not so swift as to exhaust the beasts. He had no desire to kill them; simply to lose them for a while, till Gebu was safe with the prisoners, far away in the Upper Kingdom.

Lose them therefore he did, riding toward the slowly sinking sun, across the barren land and the bare land, the Red Land that was like a sea of stone, endless and waterless. When dark came, they made camp, spreading rugs and fleeces under the stars. The tent they left in its pack, but they brought out a small feast, and likewise the bedding, and a jar of wine fit for a king.

There was even water to wash in, if they were profligate. Kemni washed off the worst of the dust and river-mud, and felt almost clean for the first time since he had left the Bull of Re. He ate in great comfort, drank sparingly of the wine.

Iphikleia was silent—had not said a word, now he stopped to think, since the morning. She did not seem ill. He took her in his arms to be certain. She came without resistance. Her skin was cool, her brow unfevered. She warmed for him, and quickly too.

There under the stars, far away from any human thing, protected by firelight and starlight and Kemni's prayers to the gods of earth and sky, they danced the oldest dance of all. They danced the stars into dawn, and the sun into the sky. And when it was morning again, they went on, westward and ever westward, till memory of green and scent of water were gone.

WHEN KEMNI HAD almost despaired, when he was certain that he had lost them beyond hope, the line of hills struck his memory. There, two close together like plump sisters, and a long slope of sand and scree, and wonder of all wonders, a glimmer of green. The spring that he remembered was there where the two hills met, pure water bubbling from the rock. It trickled into a pool, overflowed and tumbled down a narrow headlong bed into an oasis in the desert.

It was, if one were honest, a poor and barren place; but in this wilderness it was rich. It had water; grass, sere now and dry but ample for the beasts; and even a bit of shelter, an overhang of rock that was not quite deep enough to call itself a cave.

They turned the beasts loose there and let them graze on the yellowed grass. The packs and chariots they hid under the rock, all but the little that they would take: food, clothing, water for the journey. It would be a long way back afoot, long and perilous.

But before they embarked on it, they rested. A day; two. Three. There was no time here, no urgency; no press of the world and its troubles. They were out of the world, and out of time, as if they had been taken away beyond the horizon into the land of the dead.

And yet they were still vividly and fiercely alive. Kemni rose from proving it, the third morning—and never mind what it did to his body to be so suddenly deprived of its pleasure. "We have to go," he said.

She did not frown or stiffen or protest. She rose, much more steadily than he had, and washed in the stream, and put on the robes that she had set aside days since. Then, while Kemni scrambled belatedly to follow suit, she set her pack at her feet and waited.

He would hate her, when he had leisure. Three days' bliss, and she conducted herself as if they had never been.

That was Iphikleia. He could let it drive him mad, or he could suffer it, since there was no changing it. With a faint sigh he shouldered his own pack. "It's a long walk," he said. "Shall we begin?"

✦ ✦

Long indeed, and dry, and burning hot in the day, but icy cold at night. They traveled in the almost-cool of the mornings and in the somewhat lessened heat of the evenings, and rested in the middle. Their water dwindled. Kemni found his way to one of the oases that he remembered from a campaign long ago. It was still there, the well still good. They drank deep and long, and slept well after a livelier loving than either had looked for when they stumbled parched and spent into the oasis.

Kemni woke with a small start. He had gone to sleep in the shade of the oasis' palms, with his mantle over him to block out the harsh light of noon, and Iphikleia in his arms. It was daylight still, but softer, the sun hovering low. The heat was breathless, and the air utterly still. Iphikleia slept at a little distance in a tumble of dusty black hair, creamy bare shoulder, ragged brown mantle.

Wind there was none, but there was ample stirring in that green and pleasant place. Asses—a whole herd of them. For a dazed moment he knew they had followed him from that hidden place to the westward. But none of them had had caparisons like this, or been attended by bearded men in embroidered robes.

It was a caravan, and not a small one, either. Packbeasts, chariot teams, men afoot and in chariots—it could have been an army, so large was it, and so well armed. It was coming from Nubia, perhaps—the Retenu traded with that nation, the better to discomfit the king in Thebes. There were great tusks of ivory bound to some of the packs, with armed men on guard. And in those chests and boxes might be gold, or ebony, or spices.

They had not seen Kemni or his companion, or else had reckoned them of no account. The place Kemni and Iphikleia had chosen was somewhat away from the well, up a slope, in a grove of date-palms. Unless someone had a fancy for green fruit, he was hardly likely to trouble himself with either the place or its occupants.

So Kemni told himself. Two people alone, with no visible weapons, would be little threat to such a caravan. And if they were bait for a trap, he doubted the caravaneers would be greatly concerned. It would take an army to capture this caravan.

They seemed intent on making camp, ordering their ranks, securing their defenses. The beasts were strung together in lines, the chariots set in the middle like a wall about the heaps of baggage, with men on guard, armed and watchful. Kemni would have divided those heaps of treasure and scattered them a bit, rather than gathered them all together for the ease and comfort of robbers who might fall on the caravan, but he was only a soldier. He knew little of managing caravans.

He was glad, then, that he had not yielded to temptation and brought a donkey to carry the packs. A donkey would have raised questions that he had no desire to answer.

He lay a while longer, breathing carefully, holding off the rush of panic. He was nothing to draw their lordly eyes, nor need he be.

A soft sound brought him about. Iphikleia was awake, lying on her stomach, taking in the caravan as Kemni had done just now. Her brows were knit, but they always were when she first woke from sleep.

Still—"Trouble?" he asked her, just above a whisper.

She did not answer at first; he thought she was not going to, until she said, "No. No trouble. Unless . . ."

"Unless?"

She slanted a glance at him. "Unless we yield to temptation."

"Temptation? What . . . ?"

"Tell me you don't want to go down and eavesdrop."

"I don't," he said. "They're merchants, not princes. They'll not know any secrets that we can use."

"Can you be sure?"

"I'd prefer to find my way alive and undetected to Memphis, and do my listening where Egypt and the Retenu meet."

"Noble of you," she said. "Merchants know everything, you know. And love to talk about it."

"So what would you do?" he asked with an arch of the brow. "Walk up to them and ask them what they know of rebellion in the Lower Kingdom?"

"That would be foolish, wouldn't it?" She rose lazily, and stretched. The mantle slipped from bare shoulders. He would happily have fallen on her and done what a man does most joyously, but her eyes were not on him. She restored her mantle, slowly, and not too snugly, either.

Kemni turned to follow her gaze. There were three of them, one of the armed guards and two in embroidered robes. The guard was ageless as those heavily bearded men always seemed to be, but the two in robes were young. One was beardless but for a shadow on his lip; the other's beard was a thing of wisps and patches. Their eyes were huge.

"Good evening," Iphikleia said in Egyptian.

"Good evening," the older boy replied, as if in a dream, or as if he could not help himself. His accent was not too appalling.

Kemni's fists clenched. He hated to hear the Retenu speak his language. Why, he did not know; it should not matter. And yet it did.

Iphikleia, who could hardly have been troubled by such a thing, said in a sweet and rather baffled tone that was utterly unlike her wonted self, "Is that a caravan? Is it yours?"

"Oh, yes," the boy said. "Oh—oh, yes. My father's, that is. Our father's. We're just coming up from Nubia. We're going to Avaris."

"We're going home," Iphikleia said. "Is that an elephant's tusk?"

Kemni could have killed her. If she had kept quiet and kept her face hidden, they might have escaped invisible, or been disregarded, which was just as much to be desired. Now not only were they visible, they had faces that these Retenu would remember.

She managed, with her wide-eyed curiosity and her fascination with everything, to be brought back to the heart of the caravan with the older boy for her guide. The younger one and the guard gathered dates from the trees. Kemni, who was still apparently invisible, elected to go with Iphikleia after he had scrambled together their belongings and shouldered the lot of it. It was a pitiful small bundle by now, and he a disreputable vision, no doubt, unshaven and filthy and all but naked.

She was beautiful even in that state, and more adept than he could have imagined, at seeming to be a silly chit of a girl. "We ran away," she said, her light chatter the image of her cousin Ariana's—and she looked a great deal like that mistress of enchantment, too, just then. "Father wasn't happy at all with us, and he was threatening to have my Ptahmose beaten for daring to touch me. But Mother and the aunts are fond of him, and they've been working on Father; and now he's letting us come back. I'm so glad. It's very adventurous to live in the desert. But it's terribly hot, and terribly cold, and so very dry."

Kemni, or Ptahmose as he was to be, kept his head down and his shoulders bent. Let them think him of no account.

"You don't think," the boy was saying to Iphikleia, "that this might be a trap? Your father may simply be luring you back so that he can give your man his beating."

"Oh, no!" said Iphikleia in tones of great shock and surprise. "Father would never do that. He likes Ptahmose, he really does. He just says he isn't good enough for me."

"Jubal!"

The boy started. The man who had called to him was sitting under a canopy near the well, sipping wine and overseeing the settling of the camp. It must be his father or close kin: the noses were the same, great leaping arches, and a certain angle of the head, an inclination to the left, that was rather striking to the eye that troubled to see.

"Jubal," the man said in the Retenu tongue. "Who are these people?"

"This is—" The boy blushed crimson. Of course he did not know her name. But he mustered his wits rather well, if Kemni had in mind to be fair. "This is Ptahmose from a village by the river," he said, "and this is Ptahmose's bride. They're going home to their kin."

"Indeed," said the master of the caravan. His eyes were keen, taking in the two of them; narrowing slightly as they passed over Iphikleia. She smiled sunnily at him and let her mantle slip to bare a shoulder and a round white breast. His eyes glazed. If he had recognized the Cretan face and form in a woman who claimed to be of Egypt, all that vanished in the light of her beauty.

"Good evening, great lord," Iphikleia said. "Is this your caravan? Do you have any horses? When you were in Nubia, did you see elephants?"

The master understood Egyptian: he blinked, taken aback perhaps by her boldness and her utter lack of concern for the modesty that Retenu prized so highly. But he spoke in his own language. "Jubal, my son, this is a charming little she-cat. Take her, see her fed, give her a trinket. Then do what you like. But be sure, when morning comes, that she doesn't follow you. These creatures can be all too persistent."

"Take—" Jubal was still blushing. It was not at all becoming; it made his face appear diseased. "Oh! But I couldn't—"

"Of course you could," his father said. "Go, enjoy yourself. But remember what I told you."

"Yes—yes, Father," Jubal stammered. "Father, I—"

His father had already forgotten him, absorbed in some matter involving one of the packs, a skirmish between packbeasts, and the safety of a delicate burden.

Kemni would have lingered to discover more, now that there was no help for it, but Iphikleia tugged him with her, deeper into the camp. People glanced at their master's son and his ragtag foundlings, but aside from a spark of interest at Iphikleia's still ill-concealed charms, they seemed altogether unconcerned.

Arrogant. So thin a story would never have deceived an Egyptian. And he certainly would have recognized that this woman was as much a foreigner as the men she moved among, chattering as lightly as Ariana could ever have done, and with as little regard for either sense or consequence.

They were taken to a tent—a pavilion indeed, of noble size and airy height—in the camp's heart, not far from the chariots and the heavily guarded baggage. Servants moved in and about it. There were not, somewhat to Kemni's surprise, any women in evidence. Everyone here was a man. They took their pleasure where they found it, then.

Iphikleia must have heard what the master said to his son. She was remarkably unconcerned.

Kemni could not share her trust in the harmlessness of fools. The boy was callow and terribly awkward, but he was half again as large as Kemni, and though he was soft, he looked strong. And if he met with resistance, he had an army of guards to help him, and a whole caravan to bolster his courage.

Iphikleia continued to play her part, to exclaim and coo and clap her hands over the smallest things: the wine in its jar, the cups of hammered bronze, the necklace of blue beads that Jubal produced with a flourish and clumsily fastened about her neck. Her astonishment was overplayed, Kemni thought sourly, but no one else seemed to think so. Jubal was profoundly smitten. He had a look Kemni knew well, like a calf who has just discovered the beauty of heifers. When he put on the necklace, he hardly dared touch her; each time his fingers brushed her skin, they recoiled as if from a flame.

Just as he was about to draw them away, she caught them. They happened to have paused just above her breasts, where the sweet swell began, and where—as Kemni well knew—the skin was as soft as new cream. She smiled. "It's so pretty," she said. "May I really keep it?"

"You really may," said Jubal, stammering and stumbling but managing, in the end, to get it out. His eyes had fixed on his hands, and on what was just below them. His mind must be lower yet, if he was even as much a man as he seemed.

Iphikleia shifted a little, as if by accident. The boy's big raw-looking hands slipped inevitably, and irresistibly, to cup her breasts.

He recoiled as if she had burned him. She smiled, brilliant and vacuous. "Do you have rubies?" she asked. "I always loved that word. Rubies. They're red, people say. Like blood. Are they really?"

"Yes," Jubal said as if she had snatched him out of a dream. "Yes—yes, they're red. But we don't—we only have gold. And ivory. And something— here!" he said, scrambling away, rummaging in a box that rested against the wall of the tent. He muttered as he did it, cursing the length of the search, but refusing to give it up until a last and heartfelt curse broke into a hiss of triumph. "Yes. Yes!"

He turned with the thing in his hands. It was enormous and rather gaudy: great nuggets of gold polished and rounded, and even greater lumps of amber, each the color of honey, and in each one the dark fleck of a winged and many-legged creature.

Kemni thought it hideous. But Iphikleia clapped her hands and crowed. "Oh! *Oh!* This must be a king's ransom."

"Actually," said Jubal, "it was. A Nubian king. He fell on our caravan just after we'd finished trading for the gold and ivory. It was a very good battle. We won. My father captured the king and dragged him behind his chariot, till the king and all his people begged for mercy. We took this as ransom, and all the gold from his wives and sons."

"Why," said Iphikleia, wide-eyed, "you must be as rich as . . . as kings."

"We're as rich as traders," Jubal said.

"So much gold," she said, stroking the smooth heavy nuggets. Her fingers lingered over the amber, as if she cherished its warmth.

"You can keep it," Jubal said.

She squealed like an idiot girl and clapped her hands. "Put it on me. Let me see it!"

It looked quite as ghastly on her as Kemni had expected, but she professed herself delighted. Jubal was blind with young lust, or else he truly had no taste. He seemed pleased. He would not be so full of his own generosity, Kemni was sure, when his father discovered what treasure he had given away to a chance-met stranger.

That stranger ate and drank everything that was set in front of her, or seemed to; and encouraged the boy, eagerly, to match her cup for cup and bowl for bowl. Kemni, forgotten, ate sparingly and drank less, but was not fool enough to refuse it all.

Iphikleia relaxed greatly as she ate and drank. As she relaxed, her mantle slipped, till it had fallen to her waist. The ugly necklace, which would have looked well enough on a great bull of a Nubian, gleamed over her breasts. Jubal could not take his eyes from them.

Perhaps he had not seen such a sight since he was a child at his nurse's breast. Women of the Retenu lived hidden, and as far as Kemni knew, spent their lives wrapped in robes and cloaks and veils. Iphikleia, utterly easy in herself and well aware of her body's beauty, must be a revelation to this child of robes and modesty.

A revelation and a growing obsession. Kemni had determined already that there were weapons in the tent, and seen where some of them were. In his own pack was a sword and a dagger—and if the Retenu found those, the questions would be difficult, to say the least.

He could only sit poised, ready to leap, and hope that Iphikleia knew indeed what she was doing. Jubal had a look that Kemni did not like. Young bulls had it, and young stallions. There was nothing of intelligence in it.

He lunged suddenly. Iphikleia giggled. He crouched blinking, baffled. She sat just out of his reach. He groped toward her. "Oh, no," she said. "You have to ask."

"I don't—"

"Yes, you do," she said sweetly. "What would you like to touch?"

"I want to—touch—your—"

"This?" She held out her hand, turning it, making it a dancer's gesture. It circled and swooped like a bird in flight, until it settled, oh so softly, on the curve of her breast. She stroked it, long and slow. Jubal's eyes were rapt.

Kemni had not known that those robes could show anything of the body beneath. But this was a man of noble proportions after all, or a boy so engorged that he must be in pain. Almost Kemni pitied him. He was no match for this priestess from Crete; no mere man was.

She began to sing, low and honey-sweet. It was a wandering song, wordless, moving as her hand moved, round and round. Her body swayed with it. Supple as a serpent, alluring as no serpent had ever been: white breasts, round hips, dark secret place that Kemni knew—oh, very well indeed. And this child wished to know it, too; dreamed of it, yearned for it.

She dared him to dream. She dared him to hope for what was no man's to take, and only hers to give.

Kemni set his teeth. She was weaving a spell. He had not even noticed that Jubal's guards were gone. And when had they left? He was alone with Iphikleia and the boy in that dim and airy space, lit by a lamp that seemed brighter than it had before. The sun was setting beyond the tent's walls. Night was coming.

Iphikleia swayed toward Jubal, and then away. He swayed less gracefully after her. She brushed the fingers of her free hand against his face, ruffling the patchy young beard. He quivered. She drifted away again. He gasped. She swayed closer than before, brushing his breasts with her breasts. He looked ready to faint.

This time she did not withdraw. She hovered, just touching. Her song had sunk to a murmur, but sweeter, more enchanting. She stroked his face, long and slow, as she had stroked her breasts. His eyes had shut. His head fell back. She brushed his lips with a kiss. He collapsed with a sigh and lay still. On his face was an expression of pure amazement.

Iphikleia rose from her knees, sought her mantle, wrapped it close. "Come," she said. "Before anyone catches us."

Kemni could hardly be startled at the restoration of her usual self, but she had caught him off guard. He could only think to ask, "Is he dead?"

"Of course not," she said impatiently. "Quick! Do you want them to find us here?"

"No, but I—"

"He dreams," she snapped. "He thinks—you know what he's thinking. You think it yourself often enough, but I suffer you to do it awake as well as sleeping."

Kemni plunged to the heart of that. "You *enspelled* me?"

She dragged him out, pack and all, under the back of the tent and into merciful darkness. There were no guards here, and lights were few.

Kemni's own feet carried him once he had begun. Escape was all his world; escape, and the shadow in front of him.

These merchants watched closely for any who might seek to come into the camp. They never looked for two who sought to go out. Iphikleia slipped behind a guard, almost close enough to touch, and ghosted out into the desert, a shadow upon shadow, all but invisible under the stars.

················ **IX** ················

K EMNI FOLLOWED IPHIKLEIA because he was only half a fool, and because he could think of nothing better to do. They traveled in silence even after they had left the oasis behind in its fold of the barren hills. When Kemni stopped to relieve himself of what little wine he had drunk, she did not pause. He had to stretch to catch her again.

After a long while he shattered the silence with a word. "Iphikleia."

She did not pause. He did not know if she heard. But if she had, she would hear the rest of it, too. "Iphikleia, you laid a spell on that child. And if you did it to him . . ."

"Are you telling me I shouldn't have done it?"

"No! I'm telling you—"

"You're telling me I did the same to you. I did not. The gods did that, man of Egypt. Your gods and mine."

"Can I believe you?"

"I don't lie," she said. Her voice was flat.

Kemni bit his lip. The going was deep, a long slope of sand. For a while he needed all his breath for that. But his mind raced on, a churning in his belly.

Past the hill of sand they paused. It was deep night, and chill. Kemni wrapped himself in his blanket, sipped water from the skin that he had filled at the oasis, and let his body rest for a little. It ached. His eyes were gritty, and not only with sand. The caravan had robbed him of his sleep.

Maybe he dozed for a while. He woke with a start. Iphikleia sat near him, a shadow against the stars.

"Tell me why you did it," he said. "Why did you torment that child?"

She started, which gratified him. But her voice was cool, unruffled. "He might not call it torment. As far as he will ever remember, he had great pleasure of our meeting. Then I left, because the night was calling, and my kin were waiting for me. Would you rather I had let us be known for what we are?"

"Now we're known," he said. "They'll remember our faces."

"The faces of peasants," she said.

"The face of a sorceress."

She laughed, as clear and cold as only Iphikleia could be. "Whatever that child remembers, it won't be a Cretan priestess and her Egyptian companion. His father bade him take his pleasure and dispose of us. As far as he knows, he did exactly that. There's no more he need remember."

"Pray the gods that's so," Kemni said. "But that necklace—how could you let him give you such a thing? His father may not care for us, but he will come after us for that treasure."

"He will not," said Iphikleia. She turned so that he could see her in the starlight. There was a necklace about her neck: blue beads, dark in the night. No gold. No massive amber.

"But where—"

"It's in the child's hands," she said, "where it will catch him trouble enough, but nothing that need concern us."

Kemni subsided reluctantly. She had always got the better of him; she always would. He was a fool to think otherwise.

Then she did a thing that melted his anger altogether. She slipped into his arms, warm and solid and blessedly real. "Beautiful man," she said, "someday I may ask another man to love me, because it's needed or because my heart calls to him. But not tonight. Not that child. I gave him dreams. He'll never have more."

"Do I have more?" Kemni asked a little bitterly.

"Stop that," she said, but without temper. "You're very pretty when you sulk, but it wastes time. Wouldn't you rather have this?" Her kiss was long, deep, and dizzying. He took it as an answer: all the answer he needed, and all the proof of what was his.

→ ←

They came down out of the Red Land into Memphis, just as the river crested in its flood. From the desert it seemed that all the green land was becoming a sea, and men had taken to it in boats, or sought refuge in houses set apart from the water.

The city in flood season, before the heat and damp and stinging flies had frayed everyone's patience, was one long festival. Time was, when the Two Kingdoms were whole, that the king himself had come down the river to serve as priest at the rite of the river's cresting. Now the king of the Retenu made an excursion out of it. What the priests of Ptah thought, none of them was saying. The river brought its blessing no matter who sat the throne of the Lower Kingdom. In that, no doubt, they took such comfort as they could.

The city hummed with joy. But there was a frenetic quality to it. Tempers were brittle. Drinking bouts ended in battles. Packs of young Retenu prowled the streets, hunting whatever prey presented itself. The women who sold themselves for riches were worn ragged. Those who sold themselves for less, or simply to eat, had more custom than they could handle; and sometimes, if they were unfortunate, they died.

Kemni and Iphikleia came into this hive of men on the day of the flood's cresting. Even as they made their way through drunken throngs, the Retenu king stood beside the priests of Ptah as they measured the river's height, marked it in the book of years, and blessed it with the great rite. Kemni had no desire to see that great bearded outlander next to the shaven priests, nor to hear him speak the ancient words in his guttural accent.

Iphikleia was leading him. For lack of greater inspiration, he let her. They looked of even less account than they had before the caravan: after so many more days in the desert, they were filthier, more redolent, and even more ragged.

He kept an eye alert for a face he recognized, whether from long ago or from the caravan. But they were all strangers, all those people who jostled one another amid the white walls and the walls of mudbrick, between the river and the desert.

She was leading him through a quarter he knew, though not well, nearer the river than the palace, where traders had their houses, and foreign embassies, and travelers from abroad. The streets were a little quieter here, the throngs less excitable. The markets were shut, the shops closed to the world, in honor of the holiday. Those who were out and about seemed intent on business nonetheless, or simply on being seen.

He, who had no interest in that at all, shrank and slunk and tried to keep to shadows. But Iphikleia was walking with her head up, albeit wrapped in her mantle, nor showing any great concern for secrecy.

Just as he was about to remonstrate, after she had been all but run down by one of the packs of half-grown conquerors, she turned abruptly down a side way, then down another. That one led to a small square, hardly larger than a courtyard in a minor lord's house. There was a cistern in it, and a trough for watering animals. The house that faced it was like every other house in the city: blank walls, barred gate. All its light and life, if it had any, would be within.

She set hand on that tall and forbidding gate, and slid a bar that he had not seen. A smaller gate opened within the larger one. She slipped through. He hastened to follow before it shut in his face.

He had expected a house like that in Thebes to which Gebu had taken him, when he first dreamed of dancing the bull. That had been poor and rather small beside this one, and deserted; but here were flocks of servants, Cretans all, and masters who kindly let the newcomers be until they had been scoured clean and rendered fit for decent company.

Kemni had forgotten what pure luxury was in a bath. Hot water, scented oils, strong skilled hands scraping away the filth and the accumulated vermin. They shaved him as he asked, all over, as if he were a priest going into the temple. There was no other way to be truly clean; and it was a sort of consecration, a beginning of—who knew what.

Clean, then, and tingling—and yes, stinging where the razor had gone too deep—he rested a while on a couch covered with soft rich weavings. There was a kilt waiting for him, a wig, and eyepaint, and ornaments if he wished. Maybe he did. He pondered it, lazily.

While he pondered, he dozed. It was cool in that room, and dim. It invited sleep.

A shadow bent over him, a waft of scent. He blinked up into Iphikleia's familiar face. Familiar not from days in the desert, but from the time in Crete, when she was lady and priestess, and one of the great beauties of the island. Her hair was washed and combed and piled on her head in the fashion of a Cretan lady; her face was painted, and her beautiful breasts. She wore the many-tiered skirt and the embroidered vest that were so wonderfully alluring to Egyptian eyes.

She looked down at him in—dismay? "What did you do to your hair?"

He ran his hand over his shaven skull. "Lice," he said. "It will grow back."

"I do hope so," she said tartly. "You look—" Her eyes narrowed. "You don't look terrible. But you look . . . strange."

"Clean," he said. He stretched again, and yawned vastly. "Ah, lady. Whatever I hoped for in Memphis, it was never such a wonder as this."

"What, were you thinking to find a gutter somewhere, and beg us a loaf of bread?"

"Not as bad as that," he said. "I've a little silver. We would have been in reasonable comfort."

"But this is better." She sat beside him, demurely as she must in those clinging skirts, and began, still demurely, to run her hand down his clean smooth body. His manly organ rose to meet her. She smiled. She teased it, running her finger round the base of it, and up, barely touching, and yet the touch rocked him.

She drew away, which won from him a groan of protest. "We're wanted in the hall," she said.

She helped him dress and prepare, not without further torment—but he was ready very quickly even so, in a kilt of fine linen, and belt and pectoral, and a wig in the style called Nubian, short close curls bound with a bit of golden wire. He looked well enough, and fit to face a king.

⚜ ⚜

It was not a king he faced, though it was a lord of Crete. Naukrates rose from his seat in a long pillared hall, hands outstretched—greeting not only Iphikleia but Kemni with the embrace and the kiss of kinsmen.

There were others in the hall, men and a woman or two, with a look and an air about them of the high ones of the Labyrinth. Kemni did not know any of them, but perhaps he knew their kin.

They were in Memphis, Naukrates said as he settled Kemni beside him, as traders and wanderers. There was an ambassador in the king's court in Avaris, but he did not know of this other gathering. "And that serves him well," Naukrates said as servants brought wine and dainties, "for if we do anything that the king would disapprove of, he can truthfully swear that he knew nothing of it."

"So," said Kemni, "you know why we're here."

"We had word from upriver," said Naukrates. "Your brother came safe home, and all his cargo with him."

Kemni allowed himself a long sigh. He had trusted in it, but to know—that was a great relief. "If you can send word," he said, "if it pleases you—"

"It's done," Naukrates said smiling. "They'll be glad to know that you've found us."

"It wasn't as mad a venture as they thought," Kemni said. "We were safe enough."

"It would seem so," said one of the others—a woman, weathered and wind-seared like the men, and kilted as they were. Her name was Dione. She was captain of a ship, Kemni had gathered when she was presented and named to him: a great rarity, but not wholly unheard of. She had the manners of a man, brusque and practical; she affected none of the graces of the Cretan ladies he had known. She looked him up and down in frank appraisal, and said, "The Ariana is not greatly pleased with you."

"I didn't think she would be," Kemni said a little wryly. "Now tell me I was a fool to have done it."

"No, not a fool," she said. "Reckless, but it had to be done. For the rest . . . we have our spies here, but we are foreigners. A man of this country may be better suited to this task you've set yourself."

"And yet you don't approve."

She shrugged. "It's not for me to approve or disapprove. The Ariana would prefer to keep you safe."

"I'll not stay away long," Kemni said. "I only wanted—"

"Yes," Dione said. "You saw your own country, and you hated to leave it."

"That wasn't—"

"Of course it was," Iphikleia said. "I'd have done the same." She sipped from her cup, and nibbled something both green and pungent: a grape leaf wrapped about a bit of meat and onion and cooked in the lees of wine. Kemni found that taste too strange for his stomach. He had settled for the bread and cheese, and the sweet cakes, and the fruit stewed with honey.

It was a feast, of which he was wise enough to eat sparingly, for he had been on short commons for some considerable while. Having vexed him sufficiently with their perception of why he had taken on this journey, they settled to other matters: trade, ships, gossip of the courts, both in Crete and in the Lower Kingdom.

"Apophis is complacent," said one of the men, whose name Kemni had not caught in time to remember. "His kingdom is secure, his sons are no more murderous than they ought to be, and he's certain that the king in Thebes is properly cowed. They say he's thinking of demanding tribute in some fashion, or even taking the kingdom; though he wonders if it's worth the trouble."

"He'd be a fool to do that," Naukrates said. "Even if he's had no word of rebellion in the south, he can't but know that he'd have to fight to keep whatever he took."

"He knows that," said Dione. "His sons are at him constantly, or he'd not trouble himself at all. They want a war."

"We can give them one," Kemni said, "if they're only a little patient."

"Patience is not a virtue these people cultivate," Dione said. "Tell me, kinsmen: did you hear what happened to old Iannek?"

"What, the lord who married a woman from the horse-people?" She nodded; Naukrates frowning slightly. "I heard he'd died. What was it, poison?"

"Hand of the gods," Dione said. "No, that's clear enough; there's no scandal in how he died. But did you hear who took the lordship?"

"I know his eldest son was carrying on as if he were the lord, well before his father died," Naukrates said. "What was the man's name? He wasn't another Iannek, was he?"

"No, that's one of the younger sons." Dione drained her cup, reached for the jar, filled the cup to the brim and drank deep again. She was not even slightly soft about the edges, though Kemni had counted three cups, and this was the fourth. "It's been the talk of the court. All the sons came to their father's deathbed—even the one who went away."

"What, the wild horsewoman's son?" Naukrates sounded mildly astonished. "I'd thought he was exiled."

"Not at all," said Dione. "He went because his mother sent him—to be taught properly, she said, and that ruffled a few feathers, as you can imagine. He came back, it's said, not long before his father died. It's not clear exactly what happened, but after the old man died, his eldest brother challenged him— maybe not even for the lordship; maybe for a woman, or simply for that he'd been away so long, and it was thought he'd be weak. But weak, he was not. He killed his brother in the fight. Then some of the others challenged him. When the dust had settled, all his brothers were dead or cowed, and he was lord in his father's place."

"Imagine that," Naukrates said. "A son of *that* people taking a lordship in this country. I suppose he brought horses with him?"

"Horses," Dione answered, "and more than horses. He's let it be known that he's taking one of the estates his father left him, and settling his herds on it. Rumor has it that he'll settle in the Sun Ascendant."

Kemni had been listening rather idly. The lord Iannek he knew—too well. That had been the Retenu who called himself overlord in Kemni's native country. He had been glad to hear that the old monster was dead. But this new and younger one—if rumor was true, he had chosen the holding that Kemni knew best next to his own Golden Ibis, the holding that his uncle and his cousins had held before they died fighting for the Great House in Thebes.

He had been calm. He was proud of it. Even if this she-captain saw truly, and he had come back into the Lower Kingdom as much out of love and longing for it as out of desire to aid his king, he had not let himself think too long or too deeply on what he saw about him. This was his country, his homeland, surely. And he would fight to the death to restore it to Egyptian hands.

Yet when these Cretans spoke of the Sun Ascendant, that small and yet lovely holding, with its fields both many and rich, he knew the piercing pain of yearning to be home again. In his own country, among his own people, speaking the dialect that had won him mockery in Thebes.

They must all be dead, all his kin. No word had come to him of his father or his mother, except a rumor that his father was dead. His uncle, his cousins were dead in battle. Their holdings—his holdings—would be in Retenu hands. Those hands: the hands of this stranger who had lived among the tamers of horses.

"His name is Khayan," Dione was saying. "He's terribly young, though he's no child. He has his mother's spirit, they say. If that's so, he'll be the very plague to cross."

"And he's a horseman." Naukrates seemed to find that fascinating. "I wonder . . ."

But he did not say what it was that he wondered. No one asked. Kemni thought to, but held his tongue. The conversation wandered elsewhere, leaving Kemni to his silence and his thoughts.

.... **X** ....

T ELL ME WHAT a horseman is," Kemni said.

Iphikleia turned from taking her hair out of its many elaborate curls and plaits. She had left the hall when he did, and come to the room he had been given, nor did anyone remark on it or seem to find it objectionable. Women's belongings had appeared among those that had been given to Kemni, and the bed was spread and scented with herbs, as if for a wedding.

She was much too casual for a bride, but quite as beautiful as a bride could be. She paused with her hair tumbling down over her shoulders, her paint softened with the hours' passing, and all her skirts in a tousle, now she need not take care to keep them in order. Kemni had had a little to do with that. More than a little.

She answered his question in her own time, a little thoughtfully, as if she needed to consider, herself, what it was that had drawn Naukrates' attention. "Among these people, a horseman is more than simply a man who has horses. Asses are sacred, and are the root of their power: strong legs, strong backs, greater speed than a man can muster. Horses are something more than sacred.

"These people of the Retenu are not, in themselves, horsemen. They were lurkers in barren places, savages with a gift for trade, fierce fighters who dreamed of ruling kingdoms. They tamed the wild ass and made him their servant. They learned to conquer, and then to rule. In time they built cities, and made them great. But they knew little of horses.

"There are, far to the east of their old cities, cities older yet, now sunk into dust; and people who ruled once in those cities, but left them long ago, and settled in tribes far away from other men. Women rule these tribes. They have little use for men, it's said, except to use them as the mare uses the stallion: to breed her in her season, and thereafter to let her be. Their men and their sons live in remnants of the ancient cities, while the women wander with the herds.

"Sometimes—not often, but not seldom, either—men or women of these tribes wander westward. Your Retenu have always welcomed them, and been a little in awe of them, because they've mastered horses. They brought the chariot into the west of the world long ago, and taught the Retenu to drive their own beasts, and made them great conquerors.

"If this Khayan is a horseman," she said, "or the son of a horseman—or a woman rather, since it's his mother who comes from the tribes—then it's most interesting that he was allowed to inherit his father's lands. Horsemen are objects of awe and veneration, but they are not given rank or power. It's said they refuse it. I think not. I think the Retenu keep it from them, in fear of them. They have great powers, it's said; great magic. They command the winds, and the grass will grow for them. And of course, the horses are their servants—though it's said that's not so; it's they who serve the horses."

Kemni pondered all the sides of that, as much as he could between the wine and her beauty. "So," he said, "if this horseman has been allowed to take his father's place, he must have some power that no one's speaking of. Or his power is so negligible that no one fears him, even knowing what he is."

"He is young," said Iphikleia. "But young needn't be harmless. He did battle for his place—"

"He was challenged," Kemni said. "He'd have had to fight or suffer loss of honor. Honor is a terribly important thing to his people."

"But why was he challenged? What purpose would that serve? He was a younger son. He needn't have been a threat at all."

"I'm sure there was a reason," Kemni said. "But that's not what intrigues me. Why is your uncle so enthralled with this? It can't have a great deal to do with the war. This Khayan is only one lord of many, and not among the highest. Most likely he's weak—he'd have to be, as young as he is, and as recently come to his seat. Why does it matter to a lord of Crete, that the lord of a smallish holding comes from that particular tribe?"

Iphikleia frowned. "It's an oddity. My uncle has always been interested in oddities. You never know, he'll say, when a small thing will grow into force enough to topple a kingdom."

"He doesn't think this is a small thing," Kemni said.

"What, have you spoken with him?" she asked with a twist of mockery. "Maybe it's only because we're kin to the horsemen, very long ago and far away—to the women who ruled the ancient cities before men came with horses and changed the world. Our ancestors grew restless, wandered westward, and in time found the sea. His ancestors lingered in the sea of grass. We take an interest, still, in our remotest cousins."

Kemni shook his head. But he could not find words for the niggle in his belly. Maybe it was only that this horseman had taken his own kin's house and lands, and become, if he wished to see it so, his own overlord. It struck too close. It mattered too much.

Everything here mattered too much. When he sailed through the Lower Kingdom to Crete, the river had borne him up. He had kept at bay his yearning for the land, for the country that was his own. But once he set foot in it, when he had left the fishing boat to capture a maker of chariots, its spell had fallen on him. This was his own land. This was his mother, his beloved. He belonged in it, though if he were known, he could die.

He was not doing this for his king, though it might serve his king's purpose. He was doing it because he had come home, and because he yearned, to the very heart and soul, to make this land his again, free of any foreign invader.

Iphikleia turned back to her toilet, taking her time about it, transforming the ornate beauty of the day into a simpler and, to his taste, even more potent nighttime splendor. She cleansed the paint from face and breasts, and combed out her long curling hair, and put aside her ornaments and her garments and came to him as she had in his dreams, naked and gleaming. Her skin was soft, scented with sweet oils. Her hair smelled of flowers.

They came together almost gently, without haste, and without great urgency. The whole of the night lay before them. She seemed preoccupied, somewhat, but not so much as to turn away from him. Her touch was gentle, a little abstracted. Her kisses wandered aimlessly. When she took him into herself, it was as if she could not help it, but neither was she desperate to end it. They rocked together, just enough to keep him aroused, but not so much as to bring it to its summit.

It was peaceful, in an odd way. Quiet. Comfortable—but not, gods be thanked, dull. There was fire beneath, banked but clear in memory.

She woke it suddenly, startling him, so that he laughed; then gasped. He had never meant to be taken so completely off guard.

They slept in each other's arms, or feigned to. Kemni kept his eyes shut and his breathing slow. He was pondering, still, thoughts without words, scattered memories, fragments of dreams that he had all but forgotten. Dancing the bull. Driving a chariot. Standing under a wind-tossed sky in a sea of grey-golden grass, as a herd of horses grazed and mated and played about him. He had not seen such horses in the waking world: pale horses, grey or silver or white. They glowed like the moon in that dream-softened light.

He woke with a start. That was not a dream he had had before. It lingered, without fear but with a kind of intensity that made him—almost—groan aloud. The gods were toying with him again.

He would go. He lay beside the soundly sleeping Iphikleia in the cool of dawn, and knew that he did this for no king, though perhaps for a god—which god, he did not know. He would go toward Avaris, toward the foreign king's city. And if he happened to pause in his own native country, to see what lord now ruled it—well, and that would serve his king well enough, when all was considered.

SOWING

T HE LIFE OF the Mare's servant was both utterly familiar and utterly strange. Iry lived as she had always lived, in the house that had been her ancestors' for time out of mind. Even that she was enslaved to a lord of the Retenu: that had become the way of her world. She hated it, but it was inescapable.

And yet, in a way she barely began to understand, she had become one of these foreigners, these people from Retenu. She would think of them in no other way. Names were power. A name remembered conferred immortality. A name forgotten was a death beyond death.

She would forget the name they called themselves. It was a petty revenge, and probably useless: she was a slave, after all, and they were kings. But it gave her pleasure.

These who called themselves rulers of the Sun Ascendant were foreigners among the foreigners. The lady Sarai and her daughters were of another blood, blood of tribes far away in the east of the world. They had great power and great magic. They spoke direct to their goddess of horses, who was also, to them, all that was of earth. She was somewhat like Mother Isis, but her rites were older, and wilder.

They were rites of windy grassland and open sky, cold clear spaces that ran forever into a blue horizon. There were no gods beyond that horizon. The gods were in the earth beneath and the sky overhead, the wind and the sun, and the rain that fell out of the sky. Blood was their sustenance. Life was their mystery, and death its continuance. They ran on the hooves of horses, and fell with the rain.

And greatest of them all was Horse Goddess, Earth Mother, the Lady of all that walked and swam and flew. She wore the likeness of a white mare, among many others. A mare—the Mare—was her living self among mortals. And the Mare, of her nature, required a servant. That servant, for some incalculable reason, was Iry.

Iry was not made for the rites of cold and empty places. She was of Egypt, and Egypt was Red Land and Black Land, desert and rich black earth, heat like hammered bronze, and light so vivid it seared the eye. Blood was not its sacrifice. A handful of barley, a garland of flowers, delighted the Mare far more than blood that made her snort and stiffen, or flesh of sacrifice that she would not, of her nature, touch.

But these women would not hear such things. Sarai did not bear alone the burden of Iry's teaching. Her elder daughter Maryam took on herself, or was given, the task of transforming an Egyptian slave into a foreign priestess.

She was there in the morning, the day after Iry came into Sarai's power. Iry had been interested to be given, the night before, a room of her own above the garden, and a small mute maid who insisted on waiting on Iry as if Iry had been a lady. Which she had been once, but now she was a slave. She had lost the habit of being served.

And in the morning she woke on the rather ample bed, in the pale-gold light of morning, and looked into a face without beauty of feature, but with wonderful eyes. They made her think of the Mare's eyes, dark and strong and rather wicked. They were not merciful, or kind. But neither did they bear her any malice.

And that she found fascinating, even half asleep. "You should hate me," she said.

"Why?" said Maryam. "What profit would there be in that?"

"Hate isn't for profit," Iry said. "And I should not be what you all think I am."

"You should not, but you are. The Mare is wise," Maryam said, "and a goddess. She cares little for our understanding. Only for our obedience."

Iry rose, because it irked her to lie abed with this foreigner standing over her. The little maid was waiting, and another who must have come with Maryam. They had orders to bathe her and anoint her and clothe her as these people reckoned fitting. The robe at least was linen, and therefore less unbearable than the swathings of wool that Iry had dreaded. It was simple, without ornament: a votary's robe. They combed and plaited her hair, and when she was all seemly, delivered her into Maryam's hands.

And hard hands they were, too. There were no horses for Iry this day. Khayan, it seemed, was gone, and likewise his sister Sadana, the one who rode horses and bore arms like a man. The one who should have been the Mare's servant, but the Mare had chosen otherwise. There was a crocodile down the river, and it had been snatching infants from cradles, and had taken a woman who had been working in the fields some distance from the water. Very sad, and very urgent, but Iry could not help but suspect that Sadana had been removed, with care, from Iry's vicinity.

Meanwhile Iry was to learn the ways of a woman of the tribes, ways that often made little sense, but were tradition. The keeping of the house, which in the east would be a tent; the feeding and ordering of its people; the weaving and embroidering of robes and all that went with it, from shearing the sheep to dyeing the wool to spinning the thread: all that, she was expected to know. And the works and days, the festivals, the rites of each sunrise, each sunset; the rites of new moon and full moon, shift of the seasons in a country that knew neither heat nor river's flood, the great sacrifices and the lesser, with the choosing of beasts and offerings for each, and the words one spoke or sang, the music, the dancing, the song . . .

She fell into bed that night in exhaustion such as she had never known. Her head felt as if it would burst with all that she had been given to learn. Her belly was knotted, as if she had gorged on a feast of strange meats and stranger spices.

And this was to be her lot every day, for as far ahead as she could see.

She could run away. The thought tugged at her on the edge of sleep. Run—where? Thebes? Anywhere in the Upper Kingdom? Oh, indeed, if she had been a man she would have done it years ago, and died too, no doubt, as her father and her brothers and her cousin had; but she would have died free.

And what then would the Mare do? If Iry fled, would she follow? That would bring the wrath of the Retenu on the Upper Kingdom, and no mistake.

She was bound here; bound to the Mare. And yes, to her mother and her people in the Sun Ascendant, though she had seen none of them in all that day. She could have been shut away in another world, for all she saw or knew of her own. Nor had she been given a choice in the matter. Gods never troubled with such things. Nor should they; and neither should mortals resist them. Yet Iry could not help the small stab of resentment.

That resentment must be nothing to what drove Sadana. She was being kept away. That was evident when, after a handful of days, the lord Khayan came back without her, but with the crocodile's head and hide for trophy. His sister, he said, had gone hunting gentler quarry, she and her warrior women.

Iry kept quiet. Now that he had returned, she was let out of the house, away from a teacher who stood over her like a guard on a temple. She would have gone regardless, because the Mare was calling her; but Sarai had made it clear: Iry was to go in his company. What that meant, Iry well knew. The secret was out. There would be no hiding, and no concealment. Iry would be seen next to the lord, and marked for what she was.

How that served Sarai or for that matter Khayan, Iry did not know. Her mind was not deep. She was no master of intrigue, nor skilled in the ways of courts. She did as she was bidden, because it suited her fancy.

He was waiting for her in the stableyard—a lord waiting for a slave; how wonderful. Her step caught on something as she came out into the sunlight— the hem of her damnable robe, surely. He seemed much larger than she remembered, which was absurd; much broader and more imposing, and yet, oddly, much less foreign.

His yellow eyes widened slightly at her approach. Of course: she must look different. Her hair, the garment that had been forced on her—but no one could compel an Egyptian to forsake her eyepaint, even to be a priestess of a tribe from beyond the edge of the world.

There were people about. Some were Retenu. More were Egyptian. They were staring. She quelled the urge to slink and hide and dive into shadows. There was no shame in this. She could hold her head high, and be proud of all that she was.

She stepped into the chariot without a word. Nor did Khayan speak, though he seemed to bite back a word of his own. With a slight shrug, he took up the reins and urged his horses forward.

This was her world, her Egypt: river and reeds, fields of black earth growing rich with the new crops, and the sun beating down and the heat rising up, blessed and familiar. She stripped off the robe once they were out of the house, let it fall to the floor of the chariot, and let the wind of their speed cool her body.

Khayan slanted a glance at her. Amused? It seemed so. She tossed her head like the Mare in a temper, and gripped the chariot-rim, eager enough, almost, to leap out and run on her own two feet. But the horses were faster.

Out among the horses, nothing had changed. The Mare greeted her as if she had been there every day: disappointing, a little, but it suited the Mare's humor. It was preferable to a royal sulk, which Iry had been more than half expecting.

The lesson proceeded as always: chariotry, management of horses, and at last, saddling and riding the Mare. For that Iry could not go bare. "You'll regret it richly," Khayan said. Was he blushing? No, of course not. Not that arrogant young lord.

He had brought, among the other things that came with him every day, a garment such as Iry had seen Sadana and her women wear. It went on a leg at a time, and fastened about the middle. Trousers, he called it, or them. "They're all the fashion among the tribes," he said.

They were not at all beautiful, were in fact rather well worn, but they fit well enough. And they were indeed useful for sitting on a horse. Iry had not expected much of what that was like. To be up high, oh yes, but there was a living, breathing, shifting weight beneath her. It moved in a slow and rolling rhythm, a little like a boat on the river.

She was not to clutch and cling. Khayan made that bitterly clear. She must sit quiet and let the Mare carry her. That should have been easy, and yet it was astonishingly difficult.

If Khayan was laughing at her, he hid it well. He was patient as always, but never indulgent. She must do as he asked, exactly, or he made her do it over and over and over again. She had protested when they first began, and more than once. Every time, he had said, "I am far more forgiving than the Mare is."

That was true. The Mare expected perfection of her servant. Nothing else was worthy of her.

Iry's time with her was too brief. All too soon, Khayan ended the lesson as it had been ending of late, with both of them retrieving and harnessing the chariot-team. Then when they were in the chariot, he handed the reins to her.

She had driven often enough, out in the field. He had never allowed her to drive back to the house. That too was proof that the secret was secret no longer.

The horses were stronger when their heads were turned back toward their stable. Stronger and more willful, taking the bits in their teeth, tugging hard against her hands. She was not their lord, and they knew it.

But he had taught her well. She had not his strength, but she knew how to set her weight, and how to twitch the reins out of clenched teeth, to slow the team, to master them until they advanced at the pace she chose. She was too preoccupied to be proud of herself. And yet there was a deep and thrumming joy in it, in the wind in her hair, and the reins in her hands, and the horses stretching, eager, toward home.

+ +

They could not keep Sadana away from Iry forever. No more could they keep Iry from her own people. But they could manage it for a goodly while, and so they did: long enough that Iry felt herself becoming a foreigner, growing accustomed to the damnable robe, speaking the language, thinking in it—gods help her, shaping her thoughts in a language that she hated to the very blood and bone.

And all for a white Mare, an imperious, heedless, headstrong creature who cared not in the slightest what her servant sacrificed in order to belong to her. Iry was hers. That was all that mattered.

And Sadana was not—and that mattered altogether too much.

Iry the slave would have had her spies and her allies. Iry the novice priestess had nothing but herself. She was cut off from her old friends, her old fellows. Her mother, who lived in that house, she never saw. She had always kept to herself; she would not have minded, so much, if she had not needed her spies to tell her when Sadana was coming.

Because there were no spies, Iry could only wait and try to be wary. That was wearing, but no more than anything else that was laid on her.

And after all of that, when Sadana came back, Iry had no warning. As she had the first morning in Sarai's house, she woke to a stranger standing over her. This time it was not Maryam; it was Maryam's wild sister, looking even wilder than Iry remembered, as if she had come straight from her riding, in a gust of wind and sand and horses.

She was staring down at Iry without expression, and without a word. There was no weapon in her hand—that much consolation Iry could take.

Iry thought of sitting up. It would make her less vulnerable. But it would be a confession, that she thought she was in danger. She stayed where she was, therefore, yawned and stretched and blinked sleepily at her guest, and said, "Good morning. Did you come back just now?"

"Before dawn," Sadana said tightly.

"Ah. Then you rode through the night."

"It was cooler."

Iry sat up then, not to defend herself, but to set her head level with Sadana's. She was the priestess, the Mare's servant. Her rank must be higher. And this was her country, which made her even stronger. She had no need to slink and hide and be afraid.

She was not a warrior, either, or a master of bow and spear. She did not know how to fight as men fight.

She said, "If you kill me, you'll gain nothing."

Sadana's brows went up. She was very haughty, that one. "Why should I want to kill you?"

"I would," Iry said.

"They said," said Sadana slowly, "that you were . . . different."

"I am Egyptian," Iry said.

Sadana's fists clenched. The anger flared then, swift and fierce. "Who are you, that she should choose you?"

"If I knew that," Iry said, "I would know how to refuse it."

"You would refuse the Mare?"

Sadana was outraged. Iry knew better than to marvel at it. These people were strange about their goddess. Why should Sadana be any different?

"I was not raised to worship her," Iry said. "I was raised to hate her. I never wanted to belong to her."

"No one refuses the Mare," Sadana said.

"I don't want to," Iry said. "And as you say, I can't. Are you going to oppose me at every turn, or will you give your goddess her due?"

"What you have should have been mine."

"Surely. But the Mare chose otherwise."

"I do not understand it," Sadana muttered. "You have nothing. No beauty, no wit, no power. You are a child. You have not even a child's wisdom. What magic did you work? What plot is this?"

"No plot of mine," Iry said. "If the gods are conspiring against you, then that is their will. I have no part in it."

"That is a lie."

"I never tell lies," Iry said.

Sadana snorted in disgust, very like a mare, and turned on her heel. Iry made no effort to call her back. It was war. That much she had known already. This was no ally. Her life was in little enough danger, perhaps. But her souls?

Ah; and these people thought that a person had only one soul. Iry had seven. But she could not spare even one of them, except to wander in a dream, or to speak for her before the gods.

Maybe that was what she must do. Send her winged *ba,* or the *ka* that was her image and likeness, to speak to Horse Goddess in her own distant country.

Maybe Horse Goddess would let her go, and give Sadana what she yearned for.

Maybe Egypt would be reunited, too, and the Retenu driven out. Who knew what might happen? For the gods, anything was possible. Anything at all.

·········· II ··········

K HAYAN WAS A lord among lords of this conquered kingdom. It should be of little moment to him what intrigues the women wrought, or how they waged their shadowy wars within the house that he allowed them.

But before he was a lord of men, he was a child of the White Mare's people. Women's wars were the great wars; the more so if they had to do with the Mare herself.

The Mare went her own way. The Mare's servant would have liked to—that much Khayan could see. No doubt his mother could, too. His mother missed nothing. She had no mercy either, nor cared to find any. She had set Sadana to teaching the girl to shoot a bow—futile, it might have seemed, except that the child had been taught long ago to shoot at birds in the reeds; and she remembered. Perhaps even then the gods were preparing her for what was to be.

Khayan wondered, daringly, at his mother's setting Sadana such a task. Had she no fear that an arrow might fly astray? Surely they all reverenced the Mare, and were taught from youth to cherish the Mare's servant. But this was an Egyptian. She was impossible—outrageous.

"It is amazing," Barukha said from the depths of his bed, one breathless hot night. Khayan had not invited her there. He had come in from the hall to find her so, naked as an Egyptian, with her long hair newly washed and scented with musk, and a garland of flowers about her brows. The scent of musk and flowers, in that heavy heat, was overpowering.

But she seemed oblivious to her own potent allure. She was musing on the Mare's new servant. "So ordinary," she said. "So unexceptional. Cast her into a crowd of her own kind, she vanishes. There is nothing remarkable about her at all."

"You've been talking to Sadana." Khayan had had dreams of casting aside the swathings of his robes and falling asleep in such coolness as was possible. But Barukha had other intentions. She had taken from him all that she wanted, with great relish but little care that he be satisfied. Then, as heedless as only

Barukha could be, she turned to the thing that had been occupying her mind as it had everyone else's.

"Sadana finds her ordinary, too? She bites the throat of anyone who talks to her, these days. Her riders walk well shy of her."

"I can imagine," Khayan said. He propped himself on his elbow. The sweat of his exertions was drying, if slowly. It cooled him a little.

Barukha stroked lazy fingers down his breast, raking nails lightly through the curly hairs. Her touch made him quiver.

She smiled at his response, but did not choose, just then, to take it further. "Sometimes I think," she said, "that for the Mare, any Egyptian girl would do. Surely that one has nothing to recommend her but her tribe and nation."

Khayan was not inclined to argue with her. In a little while she had tired of her musings—and, it seemed, of him. She left him where he lay, took up the dark robe that had covered her and slipped away into the shadows.

Khayan rolled onto his back. It stung: she had raked him with her nails. He sighed. If he had been a man as other men, he would have cast her out of his bed when he found her in it. But he was his mother's son. She had taken of him what she would, and he had allowed it.

He ached and his back stung, and he was not satisfied. He sighed and finished it, without pleasure, then went to the bath that was one of the great luxuries of this house. Servants could fill a great basin with hot water, but for such times as this, the broad tiled pool with its floating pads of lotus and its dance of bright fishes was a wonder and a marvel.

The water was cool on his fevered skin. It washed away the sweat and the stains, and soothed the heat both without and within. When he was as clean as he could be, he floated in a half-dream, in the light of the one small lamp.

He was not dreaming of Barukha. Once she was gone, she was gone. The face and body that lingered in his memory were quite different.

Khayan did not know when he had begun to find Iry fascinating. In teaching her what she hungered to know, what she needed in order to serve the Mare, he had learned that she was not ordinary at all. She understood horses. She understood people, too, though she seemed unaware of it.

And while she was not beautiful, she was . . . interesting. She was tall for an Egyptian. She had the leggy grace of a young filly, and an ease in herself that he, child of robes and modesty, could envy.

When he had first seen her robed as a priestess, after so often clad in nothing but a blue bead on a bit of string, he had had all he could do to conceal from her how greatly she had aroused him. It was well for him that she was an innocent, or she would have had cause to mock him.

Then, when they had come to the horses' field, she had stripped off the trappings his mother had imposed on her, and become again the naked Egyptian slave. But to him she had changed utterly. The garb of his own people had given him eyes to see her.

That was perhaps not a fortunate thing. As a slave she was his to command.

As the Mare's servant, she could command him. She who had been far below him was now far above.

He swam from end to end of the pool, not far but far enough, then back again, over and over. It took him out of himself, out of mind and will and worry.

And when he could swim no more, he climbed out and lay on the cool damp tiles, till his heart had stopped hammering and his breath came slow and deep again. He felt clean, as he had not felt in a long while; clean and cool. Blessed, blessed coolness.

Someone was kneeling next to him, taking shape out of lamplight and shadow. He knew she was a dream. She would not be here, not at such an hour, watching him gravely with those long Egyptian eyes. She was naked as she best preferred to be, as modest in it, and as comfortable, as a lady of his people in all her robes and veils. Her high small breasts, her girlish-narrow hips, were charming rather than beautiful, pleasant rather than alluring. And yet something about her made him want to do all the things to her that he did not, in his heart, greatly desire to do to Barukha; but Barukha insisted.

There was no concealing what he felt. He was as naked as she, but for him, who had modesty, it was nakedness indeed. And when a man wanted a woman, no one could ever mistake it.

She did not seem to notice or to care. Of course; to her it was a common thing.

She was more intent on the rest of him. Her hand crept out and brushed his breast, just where Barukha had stroked it not so long ago. He shivered more deeply now than he had then. That was real touch, real warmth of flesh. Real and living fingers taking in how different he was from men of her own people, how much broader, taller, stronger; and marveling at his curly pelt.

"Like an animal's," she said.

"I am a man," he said a little stiffly.

"Surely," she said.

He thrust himself up, scrambling away from her. "What are you doing here? How did you get in? What do you want?"

She shrugged. "This was my house," she said. "I know every corner of it."

"But what—why—"

"I couldn't sleep," she said. "I heard you in here. Do you do this often?"

"No!"

"You should. Your people aren't made for this heat. You won't dress for it, either."

"Can you see me in a kilt?"

Her head tilted. Her eyes narrowed. "You would look . . . not so bad. Your shoulders are smooth. And your back. Some of them, they look like apes out of Nubia."

He drew himself up, affronted. "They look like men of the people."

"Not my people," she said.

"They are now."

Her lips tightened. He thought she might deny it, but she said, "I like you better this way. You're quite—yes, you're beautiful. I didn't expect that."

"You think I'm ugly."

His voice must have been flat: her lips quirked. "I think it's hard to tell. All those robes, you know. And so much . . ." Her hand brushed his beard. He stiffened. No one did such a thing except a lover. And a lover only did it by his leave.

But this strange child did not even know that liberties she took. "I wish I could see your face," she said.

"You see my face."

"I see," she said, "a pair of eyes like a falcon's, and a nose like the curve of the moon. And then, nothing. Is it ugly? Is that why you hide it?"

"I am a man," he said.

"So I noticed." Her eyes had slanted in a direction that made him blush like a girl—and be glad indeed of dim light and beard high up on his cheeks. "I think you may not be ugly," she said. "I think you may be too beautiful for your own comfort. You are, aren't you?"

"You've been talking to my sisters," he said. His voice had a growl in it.

"They do call you the beauty of the family," she said.

"Can't I be that without looking like a girl?"

"You do not look like a girl," Iry said. "How strange you people are, to worry so much about being a man, and to be so afraid of seeming like a woman. I don't think your mother or your sisters would be happy to hear you."

Khayan's teeth clicked together. No. Indeed they would not. Among their people, a man could have beauty, and be much sought after for it, too. But . . . "A man to them is a man. He doesn't try to turn himself into a beardless boy."

"That's to be cool," she said, "and clean. The heat would trouble you far less if you cultivated less fur."

"I am what I am," he said.

"Surely." She smiled at him, which was always disconcerting. "I try to hate you. But you're very hard to hate."

He could shift quickly, if she insisted. That much his sisters had taught him. "Why would you want to do that?" he asked her.

"Don't be a fool. You know what you are here."

"My kin have been lords here for a hundred years."

"And mine were lords here for many times a hundred years. We'll take it back, lord of the Retenu. You can be sure of that."

He shivered in the warmth of the night. She spoke calmly, not threatening, simply telling him what must be.

"I will do all I can," he said with equal calm, "to prevent that."

"Of course you will." She swooped toward him before he could recoil, and brushed his lips with hers. Then, as if her temerity had put her to flight, she was gone. Not even a hint of her presence remained.

⁓ ⁓

He might have dreamed it. In the morning she was as she always was, no shyness, no mention of what had passed between them in the night. He began to be certain that it had been a dream.

Then, as the morning's lesson ended—sooner than usual, because he had a court of justice to attend, and after that must receive a gathering of men from the region—just as they were done with harnessing the horses, she brushed his hand with her fingers. It was quick, and almost not to be felt; and yet his hand stung as if she had brushed it with a flame.

She did not speak of it. Nor, he discovered, could he.

He tried to put it out of his mind—to forget it, not to mull it over and over when he should be hearing petitions, judging disputes, and coaxing the headmen of the villages to speak to him as if he were their lord and not their enemy. Maybe that was why she did it. Because he was the enemy. Or else because—

Oh, no. She cared nothing for him. How could she? If it was not hostility that made her do such a thing, it was innocence. She found him interesting, as if he had been one of the horses. There was no more to it than that. And he should not try to make it matter more than it did.

The headmen left soon enough, but much later than he would have liked. He barely remembered what he had said to them. It must have pleased them in some way: they did not rise up to smite him, and they left with what seemed like good cheer. Some were even smiling. He sent a prayer of thanks to whichever of the gods had deigned to speak for him.

He would have liked to go apart and maunder further, but too many people had need of him. First there was Teti the steward, who had matters that must receive the lord's approval. Then there was his master of arms, and his master of horse, whom he must satisfy. And after they had left him, there was Iannek.

Iannek had been quiet of late, for Iannek. A good number of his following had wandered off in search of greater amusement than Khayan's backwater could offer. Those who remained were kept in hand, if sometimes with difficulty.

And that was Iannek's trouble. "It's dull here," he said. "Don't you do anything but trudge from duty to duty?"

"Is there anything else a lord should do?" Khayan inquired.

Iannek snorted. "What a stick you are! And here I'd thought you were a man of spirit. You used to be, before you went away to be a tribesman. What did they do out there, geld you?"

That startled laughter out of Khayan. "Good goddess, no! They like their stallions all present and accounted for."

"Ah!" said Iannek with a sudden awakening of interest. "Did you really . . . ? Did they . . . ?"

"You would love to know," Khayan said.

"Torturer." Iannek wandered about the hall where Khayan had been sitting for what seemed an eon of days. Most of the servants were gone, and all of the men of substance. The few servants who remained were busy with small things: sweeping the floor, wielding the fans that cooled the hot still air, fetching wine for Iannek to drink. He sipped warily, and scowled: it was the same heavily watered wine that he was always given. "Water is for fish," he muttered. "A man drinks wine."

"This man drinks it to excess," Khayan said. "Come, think of it as a gift: you can drink to your heart's content, and still be standing when you're done."

"And what good is that?" Iannek drained the cup, grimacing as he did it, and poured it full again. "Tell me what it was like, being a stallion among such mares."

"I will not," said Khayan.

"You *are* a stick." Iannek flung himself down at Khayan's feet, ignoring the perfectly acceptable chair that had been set nearby. "Gods, it's dull here!"

"So leave," Khayan said.

Iannek rolled an eye up at him. "You know I can't do that."

"Why not? You could go to Memphis. Vex our uncles and cousins. Cut a swath through the maidservants there. In fact," Khayan said, "I'll send a messenger to Uncle Samiel this very day, and tell him to expect you."

"Oh, gods," Iannek groaned. "Not Samiel."

"Why? Don't tell me he has reason to clip your ears, too."

"He'll clip more than that. He has the most beautiful—the most exquisite—the most astonishing concubine. She comes from somewhere nobody's ever heard of, where everybody devotes his life to the arts of the bedchamber. And such arts! Brother, if you could even begin to imagine—"

"I think I'm glad I can't," Khayan said dryly. "Not Samiel then. And probably not Memphis. What of one of the cities south of it? Or even Nubia? Nubia might be interesting enough for you."

"Ach," Iannek said, "no. Nubian women have teeth in their nether parts, everybody knows that. Take one of them—*snap!* It's the geldings' paddock for you."

"That's nonsense," Khayan said.

"Do you know that for certain?" asked Iannek. "Do you really, brother?"

Khayan smiled in a way that he knew would vex his brother extremely. "I'll wager I know who told you that. She was most accommodating to those she wanted. Those she didn't . . . she told a tale. Such white, white teeth she had. And when the tale came to the point—*snap!* And away the poor fool would run."

Iannek blushed furiously amid the patches of his still uncertain beard. "I'll kill her. I'll hunt her down and kill her."

"I'd like to see you try," Khayan said. He sat back in his chair of office, lazily, diverted for the first time that day. He was greatly indebted to his brother for that, though he would never have let Iannek know it. Iannek was troublesome enough without that knowledge to wield over Khayan.

"So," Khayan said when the silence had stretched sufficiently. "Nubia?"

"It's beastly there," Iannek said. "It must be. It's even farther from any-where interesting than this is. Don't you think we could start a war? Or sack a few cities? It's been ages since we fought the Upper Egyptians."

"Not today," Khayan said, "or tomorrow either. A war takes a little time to prepare."

"I know that," Iannek said crossly. "But a raid—that takes no time at all."

"It takes very little time to die, either," said Khayan. "Well; since you won't go to Nubia and I won't let you sack any cities, would you do a thing for me?"

Iannek eyed him warily. "It had better not be peaceful."

"It probably won't be," Khayan said, "though it might be quiet as often as not. But it will give you ample to do, if you do it properly."

Iannek still was not won over. "What is it?"

"You do know that the Mare has a servant," Khayan said.

Iannek's brows leaped toward the fillet that bound his hair. "It's true, then? It's an Egyptian?"

"You've seen her," Khayan said. "Everybody has."

"Yes," Iannek said. "Of course. But they're saying it's a plot. Or a mystery. Something the women are doing to discomfit the Egyptians."

"The Mare chose," Khayan said. "No human creature compelled her."

"And it's . . ." Iannek shook his head. "That one thinks she's mistress of this place, or her mother does. They both do."

"They were once," said Khayan.

"It seems the Mare wants to make the young one so again." Iannek sighed and stretched, easy as a cat on the floor at Khayan's feet. "She has a tongue on her, that one. I used to try to get her to kiss me, but she never would."

"You never tried to force her?"

Iannek sat bolt upright. "What do you take me for?"

"A young rakehell who had to leave the king's court abruptly because of an outraged husband. Who dares not go to Memphis because of outraged kinsmen. Who—"

"Those ladies were willing," Iannek said with an air of injury. "Some were more than willing. I've never taken a woman who didn't want me."

"I would hope so," Khayan said mildly.

"You don't want me to touch *her*," Iannek said. "Not now. I'd be sitting on the haft of a spear, and the head of it coming out my mouth, if I did such a thing to the Mare's servant."

Khayan kicked him, not too hard, but hard enough to make him grunt. "Idiot! Of course I'm not asking that. I'm asking you to look after her. Keep her safe. Fend off the fools and the madmen. Protect her from anyone who would harm her."

"Even in the women's house?"

"She lives there," Khayan said.

"But your mother—"

"I'll settle it with her," Khayan said. "Will you do it?"

"That's a great charge," Iannek said a little slowly. "What's a young rake-hell doing taking it on himself?"

"Maybe the young rakehell simply needs something to occupy his mind."

"Have you asked her what she thinks of that?"

Khayan's teeth clicked together. That part of his brilliant scheme had not occurred to him. Nor should it have occurred to Iannek. Iannek, like all blessed fools, was only clever when no one wanted him to be.

But he was a fool, and a happy one. "I thought not," he said. "Don't worry, brother. I'll charm her till she begs me to be her servant."

More likely, Khayan thought, she would flay him with her tongue till a wiser man would have screamed for mercy. But Iannek, whose wisdom was entirely of the accidental sort, would reckon it all a grand lark. It would keep him busy, which was what mattered; and it might even keep Iry safe.

················ **III** ················

S AFE FROM WHAT?" Iry had given Iannek the flaying he professedly expected; and he had taken it in good part, and refused adamantly to stray from her shadow. He was like a large, shaggy, and irritating young dog.

Iry was not fond of dogs. She was even less fond of lords who thought she needed protecting. "And from what?" she demanded of Khayan. "I'm your holy priestess. Who would dare touch me?"

"I should think you understood courts," Khayan said. He had been harnessing his stallions when she caught him in the stable, some time before he could have been expecting her. But he had seemed if anything rather relieved to see her—and to receive the sharp edge of her tongue. He had been expecting it, too, then.

"I understand courts," she said. "But this is no palace."

"No?" He paused with a bridle in his hand. "You live in the women's house, and you can say that?"

"Sadana," she said. The name recalled the woman: set face, bitter eyes, teaching that yielded nothing to any resentment. Sadana had been commanded to teach Iry the bow, therefore she did. She did it well. She made no effort whatever to gain Iry's liking or even her respect.

"Sadana will do nothing to me," Iry said. "She hates me with a perfect hate, but the Mare chose me. She'll not go against the Mare."

"Sadana is no danger to you," Khayan said. "And I did say courts. Royal courts. The king has asked to see the Mare's new servant."

Iry's back stiffened. Her skin went cold. "The king? Apophis?"

"Not Ahmose," Khayan said dryly. "Yes, Apophis."

"In Avaris?"

"He could come here," Khayan said, "but that's not overly likely. We're going to Avaris, yes. I have duties to the king in any case, and so do you."

"Not to that king," she said from far down in her belly, where the cold was deepest.

"Then think of it so," he said: "the king has duties to you." He bridled his horses while she pondered that, and harnessed them to his chariot.

Before he was done, and while his back was turned, she was gone. She shed her robe before she left the stable, thrust it into a chest with a heap of saddlecloths, and slipped into the shadows. She did not greatly care where she went. They would find her in the end, of course; and she would find the Mare first, and no doubt Khayan.

Khayan. She set that thought aside until she had found a place to cherish her solitude. It was a small garden in a corner of the outer wall, a space of little use to anyone, but someone long ago had planted a date-palm as on an oasis, and set a pool at its feet. The palm gave little enough shade, but the rustle of its fronds was pleasant, and the water was cool as she laved her face and her feet.

Then the thought she had left aside came back to haunt her. The water reminded her, the feel of it on her skin. Moonlight, and another such escape from constant vigilance. And Khayan lying in a pool of that cold light, glistening with water, his beard and his thick hair curling with the wet. He had looked like some great and beautiful animal. She understood then why these Retenu swathed themselves in robes—not to hide their ugliness, but to veil their beauty. Then nakedness was a different thing, not a simple matter of course, but a marvel and a gift.

She had not been able to help herself. She had had to touch him. He had not seemed to mind it. Maybe he thought it was a dream. He had been close to sleep. His skin was softer than it looked, and his hair, too, not rough as she had thought it would be.

She wanted to touch him again. That would not be wise at all, she knew it, but wanting knew nothing of wisdom. He was a foreigner, a conqueror. She hated him. And yet . . .

It was strange to think such things, and of that one of all men. Other women did, she knew it very well. In the women's house, as among the servants that Iry had been, that was all they did seem to think of. Except the lord's sisters—they were above it, or maybe immune to it. His mother?

No, Iry would not let her thoughts take such a path. The lesser women, the servants, the women of rank or family who attended Sarai, were entirely caught up in it. One of them—Barukha, that was her name—crept out most nights when she thought no one was watching, and crept back toward morning, tousled and heavy-lidded and smelling of something a little rank and a little wild, and to Iry's nose, a little repellent. It was not like a cat in heat, at all, but the feel of it was the same.

Barukha was a lord's daughter. Such things were forbidden her, Iry had thought; certainly in daylight she acted as if that were so.

They were not forbidden the Mare's servant. Iry had asked—seeking an answer of Maryam, who was the most inclined to give clear answers to odd questions. The Mare's servant could do whatever she pleased. That was her privilege, as it was the Mare's. She could marry or not marry, love a man or many men or no men at all—even love a woman, if she so desired.

Iry did not want to love a woman. A man . . . she had never wanted that, either. Not when all the men she could have were bearded Retenu, or Retenu slaves.

It was so strange, this thing that she had become, on the whim of a white Mare. She was still herself. She was still Iry. But there was so much inside of her now. So many words in that language she hated, and in the beginnings of another language, an older language, that of the Mare's people. So many things to remember. So many secrets; so many mysteries. All entrusted to her because of the Mare.

They reckoned themselves masters of intrigue, and yet they trusted her, Egyptian born, with knowledge that no Egyptian had ever had. Knowledge that, if she wished, could turn against them—could betray them. She knew the names of their gods, and the powers that were given them. There were rites and magics that could sway all these people—and she was learning them. She had little enough yet, but given time, she could wield it as she chose, against whom she chose.

She turned her hands palm up on her bare brown thighs. So much power. She had been born to be lady of a holding. Then she had been made a slave. Now, she was—why, she was as powerful as a queen.

Her fists clenched. No. Not that. Not yet. She was too young still. She knew too little. All she had was the beginning of an understanding. If she lived long enough, she would be a woman of great power and wisdom. But now, she was but a child, with a child's strength.

A shadow fell across her. She looked up, not particularly alarmed. She had heard the scrabbling, and the sound of toes and fingers finding purchase on the wall. Silly. There was a small gate only a few dozen paces away, which the guards never troubled to watch.

She said so. The shadow against the sun, which was Egyptian, male, and somewhat unsteady on its feet, said rather crossly, "It was barred on the inside."

She narrowed her eyes against the glare. The voice reminded her of something, or someone. She could not think who it might be. The face . . .

The world tilted, then righted itself. She could not breathe, suddenly; then, with equal suddenness, she could. "You died," she said. "I saw your body. I saw your face."

His face. There had been no face, not on that one of the bodies that came back from Avaris. Horses' hooves had shattered it beyond the embalmers' power to restore.

Then maybe—then surely—the man they had buried with all due rites had not been Kemni at all. She did not trust her feet, but she had to get up, to see him better. To look into that face which she had thought destroyed.

Yes. It was Kemni. He was older, of course. Taller; broader. Much darkened with wind and sun, unshaven and not particularly clean, and very much alive.

"You grew," he said, which she was thinking, too. But he would be more startled than she: he had been a man already, if very young, when he went away—she thought, to die; and she had been a child, her breasts not even budded yet.

He frowned. "It is you. Isn't it? Iry?"

She nodded. "Kemni," she said. "Cousin. How—"

"I was with your father and your brothers. I saw them die. I would have died, too, but one of the princes saved me and carried me away. They must have found someone else near your father and taken him for me. There was such confusion: battle, retreat, bitterness and anger. I never came to myself till we were well south of Memphis. By then your kin were long gone, sent back to this place, and I was safe—so they told me—in the Upper Kingdom. I thought you all must have been killed, since your father was a rebel. The Retenu were in no forgiving mood when we left them."

"My mother wouldn't stand for that," Iry said. She was calm again, she thought, until she started to sway. He caught her before she could fall. His hands were warm and strong. He *was* alive.

"But I heard," he said, "that a foreign lord had taken this place."

"One did," Iry said. "One took it when he died."

"And your mother? The Lady Nefertem?"

"Alive," Iry said. "And well."

His eyes closed for a moment. He looked as she felt: as if he dared not let go of himself, or he would howl like a dog. When his eyes opened again, he said the thing he must most have dreaded to say: "My kin? My father?"

Iry answered him baldly, because there was no way to soften the blow, not really. "They died. No, no one killed them. Your father took ill of a wasting sickness. Your mother lingered long enough to see him to his tomb; then she went to it herself. There was no one to take the Golden Ibis then; so the foreign lord took it. He has a steward there now, a cousin to our Teti. It's well enough looked after, all things considered."

Kemni sank down on the raked sand. "I was going to go there first. But I couldn't. I couldn't bring myself to—"

"No." Now that he was not looming over her, Iry could see him more clearly. He had a rangy look, as if he had been walking far and long, but he was strong, and well enough fed. Except for the dirt and dust and the scurf of beard, he looked as if he had been prospering. The sight of him was peculiarly terrifying, and strangely exhilarating. As if the dead could walk, or what was gone could live again.

But this man was patently not dead, and no spirit walking, either. "You've not been living in the Red Land," she said.

He was glad to change the subject, she could see. "Thebes," he said. "I've lived in Thebes."

"Ah," said Iry.

"And you?" he asked.

"I've lived here."

"Are you well? Are you—?"

"I'm well," she said. "I suppose I know why you're here. Who sent you? The Great House?"

He nodded.

She had meant it for mockery, somewhat. But he was not laughing. "Really? The king himself?"

"The king himself." Kemni drew himself up a little. "I'm battle-brother to one of his sons. I serve . . . one of the queens."

"You're raising a rebellion." She did not know why he should stare. It was obvious. "If anyone catches you here, you'll hang from the wall by a hook."

"Why? I'm just another slave."

"Slaves in this house," she said, "are clean."

He glanced down at himself, as if he had not even noticed his condition. "Well then; I've been laboring in the fields."

"That's farmer's work," she said. "House-slaves don't stoop to it."

He glowered at her. "You were always difficult. Couldn't you have changed even a little?"

"No," she said. And that was a lie so blatant, she wondered that he did not rise up and strike her with his fist.

He had not changed at all, except to grow taller and wider and more full of himself. He had been a cocky young thing when he ran wild between his father's house and his uncle's. He was still cocky, and not so very old, either. "Tell me where I can find a bath," he said, "and a razor that's not too blunt."

"You're staying here?"

"For a while."

"That's not wise. At all."

"Probably not," he agreed. His brows quirked. "Bath? Razor?"

She should have sent him on his way—back over the wall for choice, or to one of the few people in this house that she trusted. But she could not bring herself to let him go. He was a memory from years past, a name and face that she had made herself forget, except when it was time to remember the dead. Now he was alive again, warm and solid and rather redolent.

It was mad, what he was doing. If one of the Retenu caught him, he was dead, as she had warned him. And yet he quite likely had the right of it. Retenu could not tell one Egyptian from another. Bathe this one, shave him, make him fit for decent company, and he would vanish among the rest of his numerous and unregarded kind.

But first she had to get him to that bath and that razor. She took him on roundabout ways, down passages that she hoped were little used, through the chains of courts and houses to a room that most in the house had forgotten.

There, as she had hoped, was Huy the scribe, aged and blind but still keen of wit—and by the gods' grace, Pepi the master of the stable was with him, sharing a jar of beer for old time's sake. Iry hesitated before she passed that door. She had not been there since she was taken away to be the Mare's priestess. If they looked on her with hatred, or worse, with contempt, she did not know if she could bear it.

But Pepi greeted her with a broad gaptoothed smile, and Huy's face lit like a lamp, even blind as he was. "Little one!" the old scribe cried. "Oh, child, we've missed you."

"And I you," she said a little thickly. "Are you well?"

"Very well," Huy said, "now you're here again. Pepi, move your creaking old bones, we have a guest."

"Two guests," Pepi said, eyeing Kemni narrowly. Iry could not tell if he recognized her cousin, until he said, "Well. Well and well. So the dead do walk. Where've you been, boy? Lying in a furrow for the birds to peck at?"

"Close enough," Kemni said with a hint of laughter. "Your lady brought me here, I think, to make me fit for human company."

"I'm sure," Pepi said dryly. "Here, boy. We'll see to that."

Iry could leave then; should have left long since. But now she had come this far, she could not go. Huy was so glad to see her, so transparently happy, that she lingered. She had a sip or two of beer from the jar. She heard one of his stories. He did not ask her to tell him one in return, asked nothing of what she had been or done. He was simply content that she was there, in that hour, keeping him company.

When Kemni came back, he was much altered, and much for the better. He was clean, shaved, and visibly content. Iry was a little startled then, to realize that he was good to look at. Rather more than good, if truth were told. He had been pleasant enough as a boy. The man had beauty, and no little share of it, either.

Surely he knew it. Equally surely, he did not let it go to his head. He sat where Pepi showed him, took the cup he was given, and tore into the loaf of barley bread with controlled ferocity. As strong as he was under the lingering marks of wind and weather, he had not been on short commons for long; but he must have eaten poorly for the past day or two or three.

When he had eaten a third of the loaf and drunk half the cup of beer—wise man; he knew not to gorge a starving stomach—he sat back and belched politely, and said, "Ah. Now I feel a proper man again."

"You do look it," Iry said. "Now tell me true. You really are gathering forces for a rebellion?"

He glanced at the two old men. Huy sat in his wonted blind serenity. Pepi was deep in a fresh jar of beer. Iry knew better than to underestimate either of them, but they did look vastly harmless.

Kemni tilted his head a fraction. He said, "Swear for all of you, cousin. Swear that you will say nothing of this to any Retenu."

Iry's brows rose. So: he was not such a fool as he seemed. "No Retenu will know of this," she said.

"Good," said Kemni. He paused. Then he said, "I'm not raising rebellion yet. But I'm testing the waters."

"And what are you finding?" she asked.

"Discontent," he answered. "Anger. A great deal of laziness and no little cowardice; but people would be glad to be free of the conqueror."

"Even the laborers in the fields?"

"They say," he said, "that one king is as bad as another, but if they must have one, they prefer one who doesn't pasture his blasted donkeys in their best barley fields."

Pepi snorted, coughed and choked on a mouthful of beer. While Huy pounded his back, Iry said, "It's horses here. This lord is a horseman."

"So I'd heard," Kemni said. "He's . . . not as badly disliked as most. Because he's new, I suppose. And soft."

Iry agreed that Khayan could be perceived as a soft man. He had put no one to death yet, nor hung anyone from a hook to feed the vultures. But she did not make the mistake of thinking him weak. "He's strong enough," she said.

"You know him, then," said Kemni.

Pepi looked as if he would say something to that, but Iry's glance silenced him. "Everybody knows the lord in this house."

"And you?" said Kemni. "What are you to him? Has he—"

"He's never laid a hand on me," Iry said. And that was true; and she surprised herself by almost—almost—minding it. "He has women of his own, and he seems content with them. His mother comes from a tribe far to the east, a tribe of warriors who are women, and who ride horses. He grew up among them. He'd never touch a woman against her will."

"Even a slave?"

"Any woman," Iry said. "Women are holy. Men are born to serve them. That's the law he learned at his mother's breast."

"Astonishing," Kemni said as if to himself. "And the horses—has he many?"

"Hundreds," Pepi said before Iry could answer that. "You can be a stable-lad if you like, and if your stomach will stand it. Then you'll get your fill of them."

That was a little presumptuous, but Pepi did not seem to care. Nor did Kemni. His eyes had lit. So, Iry thought: he found horses irresistible, too. "I doubt anything could sate me, there," he said. "Yes, that would do. That would do very well indeed. Or will I be the only Egyptian who dares do such a thing?"

"There are a few of us," Pepi said. "One more won't be too noticeable."

"Pepi has been master of the stables here," Huy said in the sweet, vague way he could affect when it suited him. "The new lord brought his own man to do that, but as with the lord's cook, he found other occupation."

"Truly?" Kemni laughed, a little incredulously perhaps, but in admiration, too.

"Truly," said Huy. "We're all rebels here, though the Retenu think they rule us."

"How marvelous," Kemni said. "How strangely wonderful."

Pepi shrugged. "It's the way we do it here. Why, did you think we'd tamely submit?"

"Most people have," said Kemni.

"Ah," said Pepi. "Well. They can't help it, I suppose. But this is the Sun Ascendant." He said it as if that answered everything. No doubt it did.

Kemni sprang up. "Take me, then. Take me to see the horses."

Pepi might have liked to linger over his second jar of beer, but Iry caught his eye. He sighed and consented. Kemni did not seem to notice. He was wonderfully eager.

After Pepi had taken him away, Iry sat with Huy for a little while in silence. Then Huy said, "You didn't tell him."

"There wasn't time."

Huy shrugged, and sighed as Pepi had. "He'll find out. I don't suppose he'll be very angry."

"Does it matter if he is?" Iry demanded.

"Probably not," said Huy. "He's not the lord here, nor ever was. But what you are, what the Retenu have made you . . . that might give him pause to think."

"I am still myself," she said. "I am still of the Two Lands. Nothing will ever change that."

"I know, child," Huy said in his gentle old voice. "I do know that. But—"

"Dear old friend," Iry said. She bent over him and kissed his brow. "I'll talk to him again. I promise. Will that make you happy?"

"It doesn't matter if *I'm* happy," said Huy. "Now go, child. They must be hunting high and low for you."

"I'm sure they are," she said. She was deeply reluctant to go, to leave this place that had been a sanctuary since she was small. But she could not stay. She kissed him again, patted his dry old hand, and left him in his private darkness, with his dreams and his stories, and his soul that saw so clearly and so well.

················· **IV** ················

K EMNI HAD NOT intended to linger in the Sun Ascendant. It had been his plan to creep in, discover what he could discover, then withdraw before anyone knew he was there, and make his way to Avaris where Iphikleia had gone to confer with her own people.

But when the gods brought him over the wall at his cousin's feet, some god or spirit had possessed him. To find her alive and so well, unharmed, and so evidently free of the house, struck him strangely. Then to learn that the master of horse here was not only an Egyptian but Pepi, his old friend and sometime ally—it seemed like the hand of a god.

This was not at all as he had expected to find a holding under the conqueror's heel. The house was crawling with Retenu, yes. They stalked about in their robes and their arrogance, fancying that they ruled the world. But they did not rule this house. The kitchens, the stables, the servants' quarters—every one looked to an Egyptian. Even the steward of the estate was the same as he had always been, Teti with his broad shoulders and his brusque manner. His wife Tawit, his daughters the five Beauties—all much the same as Kemni remembered.

Not that Kemni made himself known to them. He had risked enough with Iry and Pepi and the scribe Huy, now sadly blind and terribly aged, but as keen of wit as ever. The stable-lads did not seem to know him. They were content to be told that here was a young kinsman of Pepi's, come in from Memphis after some infraction that no one quite referred to, keeping his head low and doing as he was told, and waiting till it was safe to go home again.

That was true, or as true as it needed to be. The fabric of his fancied life, like one of Huy's stories, spun itself more intricately, and bound him more tightly, with each hour that he spent in that house. When hours stretched to days, Kemni found that he could not tear himself free. There were things that people were not telling him. Glances exchanged, conversations broken off. He had to know—he had to be certain of what went on here, before he could go away.

At least one of the things that people whispered of had to do with the Lady Nefertem. That he determined soon enough. She had been ruling in the women's house, and had not permitted the lord's women to live there—not permitted it, as if she had never yielded her rank even to the conqueror. But something had happened. The new lord, the man whom Kemni had foolishly called soft on first hearing of him, had sent her to his mother. And that one, that lady from beyond the eastern horizon, was no soft creature at all.

"She's greater than a queen," Pepi said that first night, as they shared yet another jar of beer, a loaf and a basket of onions, in the scent of horses and cut fodder. Pepi lived and slept in the stable, as one would expect. Kemni his supposed kinsman would share those lodgings, nigh under the feet of the lord's horses.

Pepi went on to speak of the lord's mother. "She has great power. She's a sorceress, they say. For certain she rules like a king, and commands men. The Retenu are terrified of her."

"And the Lady Nefertem?" Kemni asked. "Has she been harmed?"

"Oh, no," Pepi said. "Not she. But the lord thought to pull her claws, making her his mother's servant. Since, you see, he couldn't make her his concubine."

"He couldn't?" Kemni wanted to laugh, but he doubted Pepi would approve of that. He well remembered his aunt, his mother's sister—her striking beauty, which his mother had had in lesser degree; her air of queenly distraction, and her startlingly strong will. She seemed as empty-headed as she was beautiful, but she was not that at all. Not in the slightest. It was an artifice, like the paint that could not heighten, only illumine her beauty.

"Well," said Pepi, "no, he couldn't take her if she didn't want him, which is a point of honor with the tribe his mother comes from. But they say she tried to rule him, and that he wouldn't have. So he gave her to his mother. The women's house was in an uproar for days. If you want your rebellion, lad, there's the start of it. They'd happily rise up and strike the lord down, for taking their lady away from them."

"A rebellion of women," Kemni said. "Now that would be a marvel for the world to exclaim at."

"Don't laugh," Pepi said. "Those ladies are angry. And the Lady Nefertem . . ." He paused as if to seek the words that would serve him best. "The Lady Nefertem is someone you should talk to. But how to do it, now she's held captive—let me think. Let me think."

Pepi subsided into his beer and his thoughts, nor did he emerge that night. Kemni went to sleep while Pepi was still pondering, slept deeper than he had ever intended, and woke to the morning tumult of horses being brought out, harnessed, prepared for the day's work. When he had roused fully and come out, he understood that the lord had gone as he did every morning, on some errand that duty laid on him. And Kemni had ground to recover: these good servants took a dim view of a newcomer who lay abed till full morning. Small wonder, they muttered, that he had been driven out of his former service, if he was so monstrously lazy.

Kemni found himself compelled to prove the accusation false. He had never labored as he labored here, hard and backbreaking work, and no end to it, either. By sundown he was ready to fall headlong into his bed of hay.

+ +

But Pepi was waiting for him. "Come with me," the old man said.

Kemni suppressed a groan. He was allowed a bit of bread and a sip of beer, but the rest he had to put aside for later. This was no summons that he could refuse, and truly, except for exhaustion, he should not want to.

He had known the house well when he was young. Some parts of it had changed. There was a new house where one of the old gardens had been, a house that was, he had discovered during the day, built by the first foreign lord for his women, because the Lady Nefertem would not let them past the gate of the house that she ruled.

That house was quiet tonight, its women nowhere in evidence, though the halls and courts were clearly still inhabited: lamps were burning, and there were wafts of unguents. Through a door that was ajar, he saw a drift of veil abandoned on a chair.

Pepi led him deep within, to a courtyard open to the flowering of stars. The trees planted in it were sweet with blossom. The pool in its center was home to bright fish: one leaped as he paused to get his bearings.

Two figures waited by the pool. One stood, looming vast and dark: a Nubian, a shadow on shadow, save for eyes that gleamed upon him. He dared hazard a guess as to who that might be. "Nefer-Ptah," he said.

The Nubian inclined her head. "Young lord," she said in her deep sweet voice.

The other, she who sat in silence, was smaller, much smaller, yet regal and erect. The lamp that Pepi had brought to guide them through the dark corridors, set on the pool's rim, cast a faint and flickering light on a face that had changed not at all in the years since Kemni marched away. He had seen beauty in plenty, seen queens and royal concubines, great ladies and great courtesans, and beauties of lesser rank across the Two Lands and on the island of Crete. And yet, beside this, even Queen Nefertari, even Ariana of Crete, paled to a shadow.

It was beauty almost too much to bear, as if she had been a goddess and not a mortal woman. He knelt in front of it, the better to look into her eyes, but in homage, too.

She never smiled. It would have marred that beauty. But her eyes were warm, resting on him.

"Why, child," Nefer-Ptah said above their heads. "You look just like her."

Kemni started, and flushed. Was that laughter in the Lady Nefertem's eyes? Her finger brushed his cheek. "You are lovely," she said. "Do the ladies love you, away in the Upper Kingdom?"

He did not know where to look. She tilted his chin up, so that he had to meet her eyes again. "There, child. We've embarrassed you. We are glad to see you—heart-glad. We had thought you lost long since amid the Field of Flowers."

"I'm sorry," he said. "I should have sent word."

"Maybe," she said. "But that's done. Now tell me. What news do you bring? Will there be war?"

"Soon," he said. "We have allies on the sea: Crete will come when it's time, and sweep the enemy up the river as we sweep down it. But we need help. Can the people of this kingdom fight for us? Will they?"

"Crete?" she said, as if she had heard only that. "Crete will fight for us?"

He nodded.

"Why?"

"For gold," he said, "and for spices. And for a royal marriage."

"Of course," she said. "And yet—of all they hope to gain, is it worth what they may lose?"

"They think so," Kemni said. "It gives them great wealth, and the freedom of Egypt. And makes one of their princesses a queen."

"The queen you serve."

"Yes. She's brought us horses and chariots. She's given us the enemy's weapon."

"That's a great gift," said the Lady Nefertem.

He nodded. "That's why I came here. I heard that there were horses."

"You're not going to steal them."

"No," he said. "But when the war is over—I want them."

"That would be a great prize," she said.

"And a great defense against conquest hereafter." He sat on his heels, comfortable now, if not precisely at ease. "But first, we have to win the war."

"Yes." She folded her hands in her lap. "I am trammeled here, as I am. But what I can do, I will do. When the armies of the Great House come to the Sun Ascendant, the people will be ready."

"And other holdings round about? Will they be ready as well?"

"If they can be," she said.

He bowed his head as to a queen. "That will please the Great House."

"And you?"

"Very much," he said.

"Good," said the Lady Nefertem.

✦ ✦

Kemni could leave then. He had done what he came to do. But he stayed: first because he had no wish to travel at night. Then, in the morning, the order came in to the stable: that the horses and asses be readied, and the chariots, and the great ungainly thing that the Retenu called a wagon, in which the lord's mother and certain of her women would travel. For they were going, the lord's man said, to Avaris, to answer the king's summons.

Kemni needed to be in Avaris. How simple then, and how gods-given a gift, to go as one of a foreign lord's following. Someone after all must look after the horses.

As he set to work among the horses, another of the grooms brought out the lord's pair of dun stallions. They had been gone the morning before—on the lord's errand, whatever that was. Kemni, curious, found occasion to be in the courtyard as the lord came out.

That was the first Kemni had seen of Khayan, lord and conqueror of the Sun Ascendant. He was Retenu, no more or less: big, bearded man in the leather tunic that they wore for riding in chariots. Kemni could see nothing but that he was as they all were, detested and detestable. The one strangeness about him struck as he turned, and Kemni had a glimpse of his eyes. They were startling, golden like a lion's, or a falcon's.

Then another came out from the colonnade, a figure in a white robe, with plaited hair, and Kemni forgot that there was anything odd about the lord of the holding. At first, for disbelief, he did not recognize her. And yet he could not mistake it. That was his cousin. That was Iry in a Retenu robe, stepping into the chariot, looking as haughty as any of them, and sparing no glance about her. The lord handed the reins to her with a smile amid the shadows of his beard, and spoke words that Kemni did not catch. She answered in kind, briefly. Then, as if she knew well the way of it, she turned the horses and sent them trotting briskly out.

Kemni was gaping like an idiot. If he had thought at all, he had surmised that she performed some service in the women's house. Where else might she be? She was safe, that was all he had known.

But this—

Pepi was currying one of the lesser duns who drew the lord's chariot when their brothers were indisposed. He greeted Kemni with a glance.

"Iry," Kemni said. "What—"

Pepi grunted. He smoothed the gleaming gold-brown coat, and added a scratch of the nape, which pleased the stallion greatly. Then at last, when Kemni was ready to strike it out of him, he answered the question Kemni had not quite asked. "He's teaching her about horses."

"But—"

"It's something to do with his mother's tribe." Pepi combed the stallion's tail with his fingers, keeping his eyes on it rather than on Kemni, as if there was something more, but he did not want to say it. "Understand. She would do nothing to betray any of us. But there are more gods than we know in

Egypt, and more powers in the world than some of us ever imagined. One of them has chosen her to be its servant."

Kemni frowned. He who dreamed dreams was hardly one to question such a thing, and yet . . . "What are you saying? Have the Retenu done something to her?"

"Not the Retenu," Pepi said.

Kemni was not going to get anything out of Pepi, that was clear. And it was too late to follow the lord's chariot.

And yet, was it? If Kemni used his wits, surely he could find them. They did not go far. The lord had come back before noon the day before, nor had he looked as if he had been traveling long or swiftly.

It was easy enough after all. Kemni simply asked the guard at the gate he had seen the lord ride through, "Where has my lord gone? I have a message for him."

The Retenu did not even grace him with a glance, but answered clearly enough. "He is with the horses, as he always is in the mornings."

"And that is where?" Kemni asked, holding his breath lest he had betrayed himself.

The guard pointed him down the road to the eastward. Kemni followed it with the carefully cultivated air of a servant on an errand. His back twinged between the shoulderblades, where a spear could drive home and end all his deceptions. But the guard appeared to have forgotten him.

When this holding belonged to its proper lord, the eastern fields had been planted with barley. There were still barley-fields along the road, plowed now and newly planted. The first green shoots gleamed against the black earth.

Over the hill, where the road curved away from a long rolling field, Kemni was reminded of what someone had said of donkeys pastured amid the barley. But these were horses. Hundreds, as Pepi had said. More horses than Kemni had ever seen together, even in battle. Horses of every color, age, size.

And horses of a color he had seen only in dream: white or moon-colored, grazing together apart from the rest. There was movement beyond them.

Iry was riding a moon-dappled horse—a mare, Kemni saw as he made his way toward her. He came as a hunter comes, keeping to what cover there was: groups and clusters of horses, and beds of reeds, for she was riding by an arm of the river. She rode well, as far as he knew to judge, and with an air of one who has studied it for some time.

The lord Khayan was standing in the new grass, with a smoke-colored colt nuzzling his hair. He was giving her instruction, a word here, a gesture there. He was teaching her to ride the mare.

That was even more preposterous than that Iry should be riding out with him at all. He, a foreign lord, a prince, was serving as teacher to an Egyptian slave.

They seemed very amiable. More than amiable, maybe. They had the ease of two who were, if not friends, then allies: comfortable in each other's presence. He addressed her with respect, she with familiarity but no contempt. The language they spoke shifted between Egyptian and the Retenu tongue, and sometimes to one that Kemni did not know, that must be that of the eastern horsemen. It was a little dizzying, and a little confusing. It was, he thought, like a secret tongue, such as kings' spies might choose to speak, or children with secrets to keep from their elders.

The lesson ended with Iry's dismounting from the grey mare and setting her free. She did not run off as Kemni had thought horses did. She lingered, nuzzling Iry's hands, and insisting that Iry rub her neck and shoulders. The lord Khayan said in Retenu, "I can't stay. There's too much to do before we leave for Avaris."

"Then go," Iry said in Egyptian. "I'll follow when I'm done here."

He looked as if he might protest, but after a brief pause he shrugged and went to catch and harness his horses. They, like the mare, came to his hand as if they had been dogs: a thing that Kemni caught himself yearning after. It must be magic. It must. And yet . . .

When the lord had taken his chariot and his stallions and gone, Iry said in clear Egyptian, "Come out of there, cousin. You don't need to hide any more."

Kemni came out slowly, and a little wryly. "I thought I was a hunter," he said.

"The Mare is the hunted," said Iry. She spoke the beast's name and kind as if it were a title, as one would say *Great House* to signify the king. "She always knows what lurks in the reeds."

The gray mare—the Mare—seemed signally uninterested in Kemni. She wandered off as he approached, grazing idly, switching her moon-white tail at the flies. Except for her color and her undeniable quality, she seemed mortal enough; but there was more to her than mortal seeming.

"Have I dreamed you?" Kemni asked her.

She ignored him. Iry eyed him a little oddly. He was not about to explain to her what gift the gods inflicted on him.

It seemed he did not need to. "So," she said. "You still do that. You still dream."

"All men dream," Kemni said.

"Not like you." She began to walk back the way they all had come. He followed her. "You didn't think I knew, did you?"

"It seems everybody knows," he said wearily. "Very well. Tell me what that is, besides a horse of peculiar color."

"A goddess," she answered.

"Of course," Kemni said. "And you are her servant. Pepi told me that. I don't suppose it's intentional."

"Is it ever, with gods?"

He echoed her sigh. "And is it unintentional that the lord and conqueror of these lands is waiting on you like a family retainer?"

"He is that," she said. And when he favored her with a glance of pure incredulity: "Truly. The Mare's priestess stands higher than any man."

"You are . . ." He laughed, not for mirth, but because if he did not do that, he would howl. "Aren't they appalled?"

"Horrified."

"And why—how—?"

"The gods know."

Kemni needed time. He needed to think. "We can use this. We can—"

"You trust me?"

He stared at her. "Why shouldn't I?"

"Maybe," she said, "I've gone over to the enemy."

"You? You'd die first."

"Are you sure of that?"

"As sure as I am of anything," he said. And he was. He could not, walking beside her, believe that she would ever be anything but loyal to her own people.

But if she had to choose between her people and this white mare . . .

That would not happen.

"I wish I could be as certain as you," she said.

"That's faith," he said. "Trust yourself. Be strong. There's war coming. We'll win it—and we'll win it with horses, and with ships from the sea."

"Or lose it and die," she said.

He struck her shoulder lightly with a fist, as he had done when they were children. "Would you rather never try at all?"

"No," she said. "But I'm not sure—you shouldn't trust me."

"And yet I will do it," he said.

She shook her head, but she gave up the argument.

················ V ················

T HEY LEFT FOR Avaris in the morning, the lord and his women and most of the Retenu that had been in the house; and Iry, and Kemni among the grooms. He was not the only Egyptian: Pepi went, too, and another of the men who looked after the horses. Everyone else was a foreigner: bearded man or, startling to Kemni's eyes, veilless and half-wild woman galloping hither and yon on the back of a horse.

It was true. There were women who rode horses. They carried bows, and short spears. In camp at night they stalked about like warriors, and no man offered them impudence. Most spoke the language of the east, and that of the Retenu but poorly, and Egyptian not at all.

They ran in a pack like young men, most often in the wake of a wild beauty with the same golden falcon-eyes as the lord Khayan. That was his sister, the lady Sadana. Kemni asked for her name, not to gain power over her but perhaps to understand her.

She was a fierce, embittered creature. The Mare should have been hers; had been meant to be hers. But Iry had taken it from her.

Iry declared that it did not matter, that Sadana could not oppose the Mare's will. Everyone else watched them when they were near one another, warily, as armies will watch their commanders before a battle.

That first night as they camped in a field outside a village that belonged to this Khayan, Kemni had settled to his bread and beer with Pepi and the other Egyptian groom. He had done well, he thought, in playing the servant. No one challenged him, or asked him if he was other than he seemed.

He was just breaking the loaf and biting into it when someone came to stand over him. He looked up into a foreigner's face: one of the wild riders, who, afoot and with her weapons laid aside, seemed no more than a child, and not a large one at that. She was staring at him as if she had never seen his like before.

He stared back, not caring if it was rude. A smile flickered across her face: bright and wicked, though she suppressed it quickly. That smile almost warmed him to her. It made him think of Ariana.

"Pretty," she said in Retenu, struggling with it a little, but clearly deter-mined to master it. "She says come."

Kemni supposed that she meant Iry. Surely she did not mean Sadana. But he said, "She?"

"Priestess," the girl said. "You understand? Come."

"I understand. Priestess—Iry?"

The girl nodded. "Iry," she said.

Kemni thrust himself to his feet. Yes, this was a small woman for these people: she was not even as tall as he was. Her eyes were frank in their admi-ration of him. He felt himself flushing. It was fortunate that it was night, and that firelight gave every face a ruddy glow.

She led him through the camp, making no particular secret of it, and attracting less notice, maybe, than if she had skulked and crept and tried to conceal him. A few glances flicked their way, but none lingered.

Iry was a person of consequence. She had a tent and a fire of her own, and a company of riders at ease round about. She also—and that he had not seen, or noticed—had the Mare. He had not seen that one among the horses, nor anywhere near Iry as she rode in the lord's chariot, but there was no mistaking that pale dappled hide or that air of royal distance. Somehow, per-haps invisible as gods can travel, the Mare had accompanied her servant on this journey.

It was strange to think of all this as belonging to an Egyptian, to his own kin. And maybe it did not belong to her. Maybe she belonged to it. Maybe she was its prisoner.

She did not seem so, seated in the lamplight in the tent, with a fan blowing a soft breeze across her, and, somewhat surprising, an Egyptian gown to cover her, instead of a foreign robe. Had she done that for him?

She did look well in it. She looked remarkably like her father, who had been a pleasant-looking man, comely if not beautiful. Her mother's beauty had not passed to her. It did not seem to trouble her, nor did it trouble Kemni. He liked to look at her. He always had, even when she was a small and outspoken minnow of a child and he was a lordly not-quite-man.

There was no one attending her. No servant, no guard. The rider had left Kemni at the tentflap and gone to keep her fellows company by the fire. They were not sitting too close, he noticed. It was a pleasant evening for this part of the world; but they were fanning their faces and muttering what must be imprecations against the heat. He was half tempted to suggest, sweetly, that they dispose of their leather tunics and the garment called trousers, and be sensible as Egyptians were sensible.

The tentflap fell with the words unsaid. Iry regarded him unsmiling.

He favored her with his sweetest and most exasperating smile. "Good evening, cousin," he said.

"Don't call me that here," said Iry.

"Why? None of those wild riders understands a word. There's no one else near enough to hear."

"You don't know that," she said. "Sit down."

He was pleased enough to obey, particularly since she had bread and cheese and a bowl of something savory, and better beer than he had been about to drink with Pepi. He greeted that with some surprise. "No wine?" he said.

"Over there," she said, tilting her head toward another jar. "Why, don't you want beer?"

"Beer is wonderful," he said. "Beer is delightful. Now tell me why you had me brought here. Are you trying to taunt our lords and masters with me?"

"In a way," she said. "I've told Khayan that I want an Egyptian escort. He suggested you."

Kemni's eyes widened. "Why in the gods' name did he do that?"

"Because," she said, "I happened to mention that Pepi had a young kinsman here, who knows horses, and who has done a little fighting. He thought that you would do handsomely."

"You're mad," he said. "Or he's playing a game that will end with my body on a hook."

"I don't think so," said Iry. "I think you're better hidden in plain sight. You don't keep your head down well."

"I do, too!"

"Do not," she said. "Now stop that and listen to me. We're going where every word is counted, and every face is examined minutely. You've been lucky that Khayan is a bit of an innocent, and his people are preoccupied with establishing his place and with finding my place objectionable. If anyone stops to notice you while you belong to me, you'll simply be another part of what I am. I'm the safest haven you'll have. Believe that."

"I believe it," he said. "But what if that safety is an illusion? They may decide that we're both worth killing, even with all that you are to them."

"They won't kill me. It would be sacrilege."

"Iry," Kemni said, "when we come to Avaris, I have no intention of staying. Do you understand? I'll do what I meant to do there, and then I'll go, back to where I belong."

"I know that," she said. "I'll keep you safe till you disappear. Do consider the advantage I can give you: while you're with me, you'll be where you can hear everything, and see everything. Your king would command you to do it, if he knew."

He would. Kemni could not deny it. But he said, "I don't want to put you in danger."

"I have the goddess for protection," she said, "and the Mare." She poured a cup of beer and set it in his hand. "Now drink. In the morning I'll be given a chariot of my own. You'll keep me company in it."

"I would rather walk behind it," he said.

"No," said Iry. "In plain sight, I said. The plainer the better. You can drive a chariot, yes?"

"But Egyptians don't—"

"I'm no master, either. We'll be inept together. The horses are well trained, Khayan assures me, and quite docile. They'll not make utter fools of us."

Kemni threw up his hands. There never had been any resisting Iry when she was in this mood. And he could not help it—he was glad that he was to play charioteer, even if it put him in danger.

There was a grand and terrible pleasure in driving a chariot on Retenu land, and living to marvel at it. Surely, if Kemni had been lord here, he would have forbidden any Egyptian to learn of horses or chariots. They were too deadly a weapon.

Arrogance. There was no other name for it.

And yet Kemni did not make the mistake of underestimating these people who had ruled the Lower Kingdom for a hundred years. They had not done it by being fools. They were strong and their weapons were great. They were a warrior nation, which Egypt was not. All their young men were taught from infancy to fight. It was not as it was in Egypt, where most of the men tilled the earth or served in the temples. All of them were warriors. Every one.

And they loved war. They gloried in it. For Kemni as for most of his people, it was a thing he did because he must. It was not a pleasure, or a game. It was grim necessity.

These people fought for the plain joy of it. If they could not fight an enemy, they fought one another. They fought over everything.

Kemni had known this. It was brought home to him rather forcibly that very morning, as he played charioteer to Iry who was, incalculably, a priestess of these outlandish people.

There was always a great deal of running about in this riding, people coming and going, messengers, forerunners, greetings from this holding or that. The wild women could not ride quietly in a column; they were perpetually in motion. And they had their match in the young men who were, Kemni gathered, the lord's kinsmen—or some of them were.

One had been hovering about a great deal the day before. In camp he had been nearby, now Kemni stopped to think—it was almost as if the warrior women had kept him at bay by taking stations about Iry's tent. He had wandered off in the morning, or been headed off by some of the women.

But as Kemni kept to a sedate pace in the middle of the line, tight-backed with the effort of seeming casual, a chariot hurtled toward him across a new field of barley. Insolent foreigner; and idiot, too. That was the winter's provender he was trampling. Not that he would ever think to be sorry for it, he who was set too high ever to know the bite of hunger.

He was riding straight for the line of chariots and people ahorse and afoot. His eyes, Kemni realized somewhat slowly, were fixed on him—on the chariot that he drove, with Iry standing in it, sometimes touching him, sometimes swaying away from him.

They were ordinary eyes, not falcon-eyes like the lord Khayan's: dark, rounder than Egyptian eyes, and bare of paint. There was nothing ordinary about their expression. They were burning with resentment.

Yes, it was that. It was not as strong as hate. Kemni met it blandly, offering no fear, and no anger, either.

The other's chariot veered suddenly, hard, and so fast it teetered on a single wheel. Just at the point of falling, it rocked back onto both wheels, and fell in beside Kemni's own.

There was a pause. In it, so quiet it seemed like a whisper after a crash of thunder, Iry said, "Good morning, milord Iannek. I trust it finds you well."

The young fool opened his mouth, then shut it again, gaping like a fish. Iry had a look Kemni knew well. She meant to provoke this interloper, and she was utterly bereft of mercy.

The young lord Iannek gathered such wits as he had, and let them loose in bluster. "Who is that with you? Who does he think he is?"

"This is a man I trust," Iry said.

"You are supposed to trust *me!*" Iannek cried.

"Trust is earned," Iry said austerely.

"And what has he done to earn it?"

"For one thing," Iry answered, "he doesn't drive a chariot as if all the black gods were after him."

That stopped Iannek for a moment—not long, but Kemni gathered that even that much was extraordinary. "He drives like a blind and toothless old woman."

"He drives like a sane man," Iry said. "And that is why I trust him. Do stop glaring, Iannek. You'll give yourself a headache."

Kemni discovered that he was holding his breath. It was a true measure of Iry's power here, that the foreigner, even as young and headlong as he was, did not sweep out his sword and strike her for the words she said to him. He did not precisely bow his head to her, but he shrank a little, and he said in slightly more subdued tones, "Iry, lady, you know I only want to keep you safe."

"You can't do it by smothering me. Now be sensible and endure this charioteer of mine, because he is not going to go away. And," she added, "if I find that you have so much as looked at him amiss, I will give you cause to regret it. Am I understood?"

"Too well, lady," Iannek muttered.

"Good," said Iry, taking no notice of his reluctance. "Now be a proper guardsman and keep me company, since you insist on it. You can tell me stories."

Kemni swallowed a groan. The kind of stories such a fool would tell would be tedious indeed.

But Iannek was too sulky to be amusing. He drove beside them in silence, conspicuously slow and cautious, though his horses fretted at the pace. He had lovely hands on the reins, Kemni noticed with a stab of envy. They were strong but light, with a clean, sure touch. Kemni would have given much to be so skilled.

"He really is a guardsman?" he asked under his breath.

"Really," she answered, not particularly quietly. "He's the lord's brother, and a scapegrace—but he means well, in his way. The lord appointed him my guardian hound. Not, mind, that he ever asked *me*. I would have had something to say of it if he had."

"I rather think you have said something of it," Kemni said dryly. "So that's what I'm actually doing here. I'm being flung in the lord's face."

"Among other things," she said. She did not ask him if he minded. Nor had he expected her to.

✦ ✦

The Lower Kingdom was a different place from the vantage of a chariot. People kept their distance, and kept their eyes lowered—except those few so bold as to fix a burning glance on the lord who rode so high above them. No, there was no love here for the foreigner. If there was resignation, it veiled a deeper resentment.

They had been telling a story in the markets of Memphis, one that Kemni knew was pure invention, but people told it as truth. And maybe, in its way, it was—as tales of old gods were truth, because they drove straight to the heart of things.

In the story, the king in Avaris had taken it into his head to provoke the king in Thebes. He was bored, maybe, or idle; or his young men were spoiling for a fight. Therefore he sent a message to the Great House in Thebes: "The roaring of the riverhorses in your gardens is keeping me awake of nights. Silence them, if you please, or know the force of my displeasure."

The king in Thebes, the taletellers said, was not pleased to receive so high-handed and so manifestly false a missive from a king whose authority he had never accepted, who slept, when he slept, many days' journey away. Therefore, he had sworn perpetual enmity with the king in Avaris, and determined to destroy him.

That was a tale without an ending. Sometimes it was told of the last king, of Kamose who was gone, and who had fought Apophis but failed to win back the Lower Kingdom. More often now it was told of Ahmose, as a sort of prophecy. People wanted it to be true, perhaps even prayed for it.

Kemni had much to tell when he came back again to the Bull of Re. If he came back. He had to remember that. This hiding in plain sight was a dangerous thing.

The young lord Iannek did not take kindly to a rival for Iry's affections. And that was what it was, Kemni was certain. They traveled together that day in barbed amity. Come evening, the lord's riding paused in one of the lord's own holdings, one that had been under the sway of the Retenu since the beginning, and had no remnants of its old masters to vex his peace. Most of the servants here were Retenu, whether of the foreign kings' people or other cities and nations of Asia. Only those who tilled the fields were Egyptian; and they kept their own counsel.

This was a rich holding, with wide fields of barley and of emmer wheat, and fields of flax, and a village of spinners and weavers. The lord meant to linger a day or two, to inspect the fields and establish his sway over the people, before he went onto Avaris, which was less than a day's journey distant. He had, on his arrival, sent messengers there, and received messengers with whom he was closeted for a goodly while.

They were not, Kemni hoped, informing him that the Mare's priestess had taken a spy for a bodyguard. Certainly no one came to seize him, nor did anyone take much notice of him.

Except Iannek. Kemni took a late daymeal in the stable with Pepi and the young Egyptian groom. He might have dined with Iry, but he left that pleasant duty to Iannek. Or so he thought. Iannek, it seemed, had other intentions.

The young lord accosted him as he went out into the stableyard to relieve himself. The beer here was good, and he had drunk a good quantity of it.

Iannek caught him there, clapping a hand to his shoulder. He whirled, utterly without thought, and had the young fool by the throat before he could defend himself.

By the light of the torch that illuminated the yard, Kemni recognized his fellow bodyguard. He drew back, but rather slowly. "Don't do that," he said in as mild a tone as he could muster.

Iannek swallowed carefully. His eyes narrowed. "You're not a servant," he said.

Kemni felt his heart shrink, grow cold and still. But he kept a bold face. "What else would I be, in this world we live in?"

"You would have killed me," Iannek said, "because I took you by surprise. Where did you learn that? Who are you?"

"A kinsman of Pepi's from Memphis," Kemni said, "who got above himself and was sent away."

It was a bare lie, and would weight his soul terribly when he came to the judgment. But Iannek seemed to believe it. "I can imagine you did," he said, "if that's how you greet anyone who comes on you. What did you do, strike your lord?"

"I would never strike my lord," Kemni said stiffly. "Now tell me. Why are you here? Is she asking for me?"

"No," Iannek said.

"Then who's looking after her?"

That gave Iannek pause, but he recovered swiftly. "She's with my lord brother and my mother and my sisters. How much safer can she be?"

Much, Kemni thought but took care not to say. "And you escaped," he said.

"Well," said Iannek, "it was dull. You've fought in battles, haven't you?"

This was not going to be easy to get out of. Kemni thought of bolting, but he had already relieved himself; that pretext would not do. He answered as best he might, question for question. "Why, haven't you?"

It was difficult to tell by torchlight, but perhaps Iannek flushed. "Are you laughing at me?"

"Not at all," said Kemni. And he was not. "Battles are not such a great thing for us. They're ugly and bloody and often futile."

"Battles are glorious," said Iannek. "Battles are what a man lives for."

"Not our kind of man," Kemni said.

"You are strange people."

"We are what we are."

"So you can fight," Iannek said, returning to that like a dog to a bone. "That's what she wanted you for. And because you speak her language. It's strange for her, being what she is. Egyptian, and the Mare's priestess."

This was a fool, but a strangely perspicacious fool. Kemni saw the road ahead studded with stones, and any one likely to catch and break his chariot wheel.

But he must go on. "One of us should guard her tonight," he said. "Shall we divide watches, then?"

"Yes," Iannek said with a boy's eagerness. "Yes, I'll take the first one. I'll fetch you at middle night."

"Well enough," Kemni said with the hint of a sigh. Iry would be well guarded—too well, perhaps; but who knew? She might actually be in need of protection.

·········· VI ··········

IRY COULD FEEL the walls closing in. Her cousin's presence was a comfort, but he was in danger every moment that he lingered with her. Surely none of these Retenu could fail to see how he carried himself, how he walked like a lord and a warrior. But they seemed blind to him, except as a shadow in her shadow.

When they came to Avaris, he would slip away. That was already decided. He would find his allies where they waited for him, and return by secret paths to the Upper Kingdom.

She would have given one of her souls to slip away with him. But the Mare bound her. She had taken no vows, committed to nothing—but there was no need. The Mare's choice was all the rite and consecration that was required. Through the Mare she was made priestess, and given all the powers that she might hold.

Foreign powers. Powers of a people she hated.

She *would* run away. How could she go on?

"I am not one of you," she said, not caring, just then, what danger she put herself in.

Of all people she might have unburdened herself to, she had not expected it to be Khayan. He should have been preoccupied with duties, with being lord of this holding. But he had seized a moment, late in the second day there, to soothe his spirit among his horses. Iry had had the same impulse, had escaped her guards and her jailers and taken refuge in the stable. The Mare suffered herself to be shut in walls for Iry's sake, though it made her irritable: she was flat-eared and snappish, even went so far as to lunge at Khayan when he drew near.

He calmed her as he knew how to do, born horseman that he was. That had provoked Iry's outburst: the ease with which he moved among horses, the foreignness of his presence, robed and adorned as a prince of his people. But the golden eyes were his own, and the smile he bestowed on her, as if he were actually glad to see her.

"I am not one of you," she said. "I will never be."

"All you need be," he said in his warm deep voice, "is the Mare's chosen."

"No," she said. "No. Today I learned to pray in a language my people never spoke nor heard spoken, a language that was old when my country was a village on the banks of the river. I prayed to a goddess who is utterly alien to me. My ancestors did not know her. *I* do not know her. How could she have chosen me? I'm an utter stranger."

"And yet she knows you," Khayan said, "and finds you worthy."

"Why? What is she doing, besides being contrary?"

"You ask me?"

"Of course I ask you," she said bitterly. "You know everything."

"And you hate me for it?"

She wanted to spit at him, or strike him. The first was ridiculous. The second had begun before she thought. It was meant to be a hard blow, a man's blow, or at least a boy's. But he, warrior-trained, caught her hand before it could strike home. Like a fool she sought to pull free; but he was much, much stronger than her slender and female self.

She had two hands. The second caught him roundly on the shoulder— aiming for the cheek, but he was too tall. He grunted: she had taken him by surprise. It was like smiting a wall, as big as he was, and solid, and honed with years of riding and hunting and fighting.

He caught her second hand. Now she was trapped indeed, but never cowed. Never that.

If he had mocked her or tried to overwhelm her, she would have fought free, with the edge of her tongue if not with the strength of her arms. But he stood still, gripping her wrists as if he had forgotten he was doing it, staring into her face. Had he never seen her before? What had he seen, then?

"What?" she demanded of him. "What haven't you seen?"

"You," he said, like one in a dream.

"Then what *did* you see?"

"A face," he answered. "Eyes, nose, a mouth. A body like a fish in the river, quick and sleek. But I never—"

He trailed off. She wanted to hit him all over again, but he was still holding her arms. "Let me go," she said in a low, still voice.

He obeyed slowly. She lowered her hands. She should leave, she knew it. But there was something about this man and dim places. Moonlight—moonlight became him. And late sunlight through a stable door.

"You can ask," he said.

"What?"

He did not answer. Would not. There was an air about him that she almost understood, that she was not sure she wanted to understand.

"You have to ask," he said. He did not sound angry or dismayed, or disappointed. He was telling her what she should know.

She was not ready to know it. "Please go," she said.

And he did. As simply, as promptly as if she had every right to ask it.

When he was gone, she leaned against the Mare's warm and solid shoulder. The Mare was glad to be rid of him. Males, in her estimation, were worth nothing, except when she was in season. Then she took what she wanted and went away.

That was a very good way to live one's life. It was a pity Iry had not the art. All she had was her ignorance and her stubbornness, and the moon-white Mare.

+ +

Sadana had no patience for fools. And that, she reckoned Iry. It was not about Khayan, as it happened. It was about Kemni. She had conceived an intense dislike for Iry's guardsman.

Or perhaps not dislike. Sadana was hardly proof against that face—Egyptian though it was. "No man has a right to be so pretty," she declared.

"Why not?" Iry wanted to know. "If men are our playthings, why shouldn't they be pleasing to look at?"

"He is not pleasing!" Sadana snapped. "He's a shaven foreigner. If he'd let himself grow his beard like a man, he'd be handsomer to look at."

"I don't think so," said Iry. "Don't you like being able to see a man's face? He can't hide behind a beard, any more than a woman can. He's all the easier to read."

"Why do you think there's anything in a man worth reading?"

Iry shrugged. "Maybe there's not. I'd rather know for certain."

She could not dismiss Sadana as easily as she could dismiss Sadana's brother. In this strange world the Mare had brought her into, women were like men, and men were like servants. And Sadana was a great power here.

She disliked this delay within a day's ride of Avaris. Iry began to wonder if there was something, or someone, in that city whom she was eager to see. Enemy? Friend? Lover?

Or perhaps there was something here that troubled her. She was restless always, but more so the longer they stayed. It seemed she was constantly at Iry to practice with the bow, to go over her lessons in the prayers and rituals, even to exercise herself in riding the Mare, though that was supposed to be Khayan's duty.

Iry did not mind the bow or the Mare, but the endless hours of speaking words in strange languages, and remembering them, gave her a hammering headache. One rite in particular, the death-rite of the Mare's servant, had nothing to do with her at all. The former servant had died before Iry ever knew her. Iry's successor would perform the rite for her.

But Sadana was insistent. "You must know everything," she said. Even the words the initiate must say as she laid out the body, then the thing she must do, that to Iry was deep and heartfelt revulsion: to strip the bones of flesh, and cleanse the bones, and lay them in the earth. All but the skull. That was to be cleansed likewise, polished and set with silver, and fashioned into a cup from which the successor would drink.

"That is sacrilege," Iry said. "I thank my gods I never had to do this— and by all gods that are, no one will do it to me. I will be laid whole in my tomb as is fitting and proper, so that I may come entire to the land of Osiris."

"That is not our way," Sadana said. "It's ill enough that you have no cup of your preceptor's spirit to inspire you and teach you and grant you blessing whenever you drink from it."

Iry shuddered and swallowed bile, but her mind was clear. "Where is it, then? What became of my predecessor's body?"

That gave Sadana brief pause. Guilt? Or simple surprise that Iry should have wits enough to ask?

"She died of sickness here in Egypt, where she had come by the Mare's will. She was buried with all honor."

"Buried whole?"

Sadana nodded shortly.

"You see," Iry said. "So tell me, how is it that the Mare is here? Shouldn't she be in the east?"

"After the Mare's servant died, the elders in the east were commanded by Horse Goddess herself to single out my brother. He was to return to his father's people, and take with him such of the horse-herds as wished to go. Among them were the Young Mare and her kin."

"All of them?"

Again, that sharp nod, as if it offended Sadana to confess to such things.

"Then it seems to me," said Iry, "that the Mare has in mind to change the world."

"I am not in the Mare's counsels," Sadana said.

"Sadana," Iry said, "if I could give you all of this, I would. Am I allowed to make you my successor?"

Sadana's eyes went wild. Her hand swept up, round, down: averting evil, and casting off any temptation to it. "You must not do that! You don't know me at all, nor should you trust me."

"Why not? You know more of all this than I ever will."

"What if I killed you, or trapped you so that you would die? Then I would have what I want. I would have it all."

"No," said Iry. "Not if the Mare wouldn't choose you."

"And what makes you think she would, if you were gone? Or that her own successor would?"

"That's hers to do," Iry said.

Sadana tossed her head like an angry mare. "You aren't making sense."

"I am," Iry said. "If you kill me, you have nothing. If you wait and have patience, you have everything."

"You're younger than I am. You'll outlive me."

"I might," Iry said. "Then your daughter has the office. Is that why you resist? Because you want it all now? Isn't it worth the gamble to accept? I could die in the next fever season, or fall from a chariot, or die bearing a child. Death is beside us with every breath we take."

"And in this country," Sadana said, "it towers above you. What was it with your old kings, that they built tombs as great as cities?"

"They haven't done that for a thousand years," Iry said. "It was something they had in mind to do then, because the gods asked it, or they felt a need to do something grand and mighty, that no one had ever done before. Then that grew old, and their successors hid their tombs, as they do still."

"I know that," Sadana snapped. "But why? Why tombs so rich? The dead need nothing."

"The dead need everything. All that they had in life, they have in death. But they have to take it with them—body, possessions, everything."

"How very cumbersome."

"It's what is," Iry said.

"And you want me to come after you." Sadana shook her head. "No. I will not. I was to be the Mare's servant in this age of the world. The Mare refused me. I'll not be second best, nor wait futile years for a fulfillment that never comes. What I am now, I remain. You successor will make herself known when it's time, just as the Young Mare will appear when your Mare grows old."

"I can't compel you," Iry said. "But—"

"No," said Sadana. "Give me again the prayer you sing when one of the Mare's kin delivers herself of a foal."

Iry drew a breath. That was nothing to do with death—very much the opposite. It was a more comfortable thing to consider, and simpler, once she had groped for and found in her memory the words and the gestures. Sadana did not speak again of death or of successors, nor require that Iry recite prayers and rehearse rituals that she would never need. That had been a test, perhaps, or a slightly cruel whim. Once it was past, as far as Sadana was concerned, it was forgotten.

+ +

It was not death that vexed Sadana, nor, entirely, her long grievance with Iry. Her trouble, Iry discovered, was something quite different. It came to Iry almost by accident at the end of that day's lessons, which had begun to circle and circle as if Sadana were persistently distracted. The end came soon after the changing of Iry's half-unwanted guard. Iannek, who had slept—and snored—through much of that afternoon, wandered off without a word. And

Kemni wandered in, a much quieter and more compact presence, to sit neatly in a corner and entertain his own thoughts while Iry did whatever it pleased her preceptor to have her do.

Sadana's questions grew more and more strange, and less and less coherent. Her eyes were carefully not fixed on the figure in the corner, but Iry caught the dart of glances. He seemed oblivious. His face in that light was striking in its beauty, and strikingly like the Lady Nefertem's, though he practiced no art but that of painting the eyes, which no Egyptian would omit.

Iry went still inside. If Sadana could see—if she began to suspect—

But no. That was not what made her glance return again and then again. Iry had seen a stallion look just so at a mare. It was an odd, intent, almost dreamlike expression, as if Sadana had been taken out of herself.

And it made her angry. In that she was like the Mare. When the Mare came into season, she reveled in it, and yet also she resented it, as if that loss of her body's control and her mind's good sense sparked her temper.

"You should ask him," Iry began to say. But she choked on it. She was remembering quite another face than Kemni's smooth clean-carved one, and a soft deep voice. *You have to ask,* it said.

No, she thought. Oh, no. She was not yearning after the Lord Khayan as the Mare yearned after a stallion, or Sadana—angrily, reluctantly, but beyond a doubt—after Kemni.

No wonder Sadana was angry. Kemni was an Egyptian, a foreigner, and, as far as she knew, a slave. Iry was not angry, oh no. But she would not think of Khayan in that way. Not that great hulking shaggy beast of a man with his yellow eyes and his drumbeat of a voice.

The world was too untidy. Sadana should be wanting one of her own kind—Iannek, maybe, or one of the other young lords who ran wild about this kingdom. Iry should not be wanting anyone. Or if she did, she could want Kemni. He was good to look at, he was pleasant company, he had been her friend since she was a child. He was her kin. She trusted him. But she looked at him, and it was a pleasure, and she was glad to have such a thing; but she did not want to stare and stare as she did when she was in sight of Khayan.

Sadana ended the lesson abruptly, and stalked out in a wholly baseless fit of temper. Iry meant to let her go, but her tongue had other intentions. "Come back," it said. "You're not done here."

Sadana turned her on her heel in the doorway. Her expression would have been frightening if Iry had been a more timid sort. "I am quite done," she said coldly.

"Aren't you going to ask him?"

The high cheeks flushed scarlet. The thin nostrils pinched and paled. "Ask whom? Ask what?"

"You know what I'm saying," Iry said. "Ask. You do want to. Why not get it over?"

"Because I do not wish to."

"Are you afraid he'll refuse?"

"He can't refuse."

"So ask," Iry said.

She was being cruel. She knew it. Kemni could not only refuse, he most likely would. And if he did that . . .

She was putting him in danger. It was like a madness in her. As if she wanted to break the tension that held them all, the delicate and improbable balance of deception and misperception that kept her cousin safe in the midst of the enemy.

But Sadana, who had never yet refused a challenge, refused this one. She spun away from Iry and the room that had Kemni in it, and vanished into the depths of the house.

·········· VII ··········

K EMNI DID NOT understand the quarrel between his cousin and the warrior woman Sadana, nor did he particularly want to. He was glad when Sadana was gone, though Iry paced and muttered and was difficult company for an interminable while. She did not go to dinner as she was expected to, nor would she go when she was summoned. A servant brought her something there, in the room she had been given, which she picked at and insisted Kemni finish; and after she had eaten what little she would, she retreated to her bed.

He supposed he should have asked her what was troubling her. But the glances she shot at him were not encouraging, and he was in an odd mood himself. It had struck him as he guarded her, that it had been a considerable while since he saw Iphikleia, or even dreamed of her. It was as if, once he had come into the Lower Kingdom, where he was born, where he was meant to be a lord and a warrior, the gods chose to vex him by day and leave him in peace while he slept.

But sitting in the corner that he had chosen for its clear view of the room and its ease of access to the door, he saw Iphikleia's face as vividly as if she stood in front of him. He could almost have reached to touch her, or bent to kiss those ripe red lips.

She was sitting in a room he had not seen before, chin in hand, pensive, while Naukrates paced and gesticulated. There were others about them, shadowy figures, Cretan shapes: broad shoulders, narrow hips, the curve of a woman's breast left bare in the fashion of that country. It was a dream, and yet not. He was seeing what passed in this moment, in Avaris as he supposed; and that must be the gathering of Cretan captains there.

Naukrates was lively but not urgent, Iphikleia pensive but not troubled. That comforted Kemni, though his heart ached to be there, to be with them, and not to be trapped here in this game that he had been a fool to play.

If he left now, this very night, found a boat and rode the branch of the river, he would be in Avaris by morning.

But he stayed where he was, listening to Iry's deep slow breathing. She did not need him to protect her, he had no illusions as to that. Yet she needed the comfort that his presence gave her. He was the only one of her people who was allowed so close—and when he came to Avaris, he must leave her. He had his king to serve, and his queen whom he had been away from too long, and Iphikleia who was more to him than king or queen.

A face hovered over him, born as if out of his dream. But it was never a Cretan face. Not this one, with its blade of a nose and its fierce falcon-eyes.

"Get up," Sadana said in terrible but understandable Egyptian. "Come with me."

"I can't do that," he said. "I'm on guard."

"Come," she said.

"No," said Kemni.

She hissed in frustration, seized him and pulled him to his feet. He quelled the instinct to resist. It was better that he stood, if there was to be a fight.

"I must guard my lady," he said carefully. "I cannot leave her."

She hissed again and stalked out as she had done earlier, as seemed to be her way. Kemni sank down again in his corner. Belatedly it came to him what she had been asking; and what she had been speaking of to Iry, that he had taken too little notice of.

And he had refused her. That had not been wise. Not at all.

Ah, he thought; so be it. He would be gone before she could endanger him. And Iry was safe, he could hope. The Mare would protect her.

✦ ✦

He was almost asleep when Sadana came back. Fool that he was, for thinking her defeated. She brought a blear-eyed and stumbling Iannek with her, the import of which was all too clear. "Now come," she said to Kemni.

He did not want to. But those eyes were wild, and perhaps a little mad. He could at least go with her, and hope to appease her. That would be safest for them all.

He sighed and rose. Iannek sighed more vastly and slumped down in the place that Kemni had left. Kemni nudged him with a foot. "Don't fall asleep," he said.

Iannek growled at him. He growled back. Sadana was growing impatient.

He had perforce to leave the drunken fool there, and hope that Iry could do as well with as without him.

Sadana was an odd one. In some ways she was like Iphikleia: brusque, abrupt, and seeming cold. But Iphikleia was warm beneath, and strong. Sadana was like a fire in dry grass.

She led him to a room not far from Iry's. It seemed deserted; it was clean, but there was a drift of dust across the floor. It had lamps, which she lit from the one she carried, all of them, a whole bank of them. Kemni stood where she had left him, just within the door. Perhaps she was daring him to bolt. But he would not do that. He had, in coming with her, made a promise of sorts.

This was a little like his nights in Crete, when importunate and beautiful young women had come to him and bidden him do their will. But they had done it in laughter, for their lady and for their own sake, because they found him delightful. Sadana did not delight in anything, that Kemni could see. She was a creature of oaths and duties. Pleasures were foreign to her.

They were all like that, these women from the eastern horizon. Perhaps that was why she seemed so angry as she turned in the blaze of all the lamps, and glared at him as if she blamed him for making her want him.

Women were incalculable creatures at best. A woman like this could be dangerous.

Danger was a sweetness, like honey. She was beautiful in her way, as a falcon is, or the new moon. Even as forbidding as she was, glowering at him with terrible temper, he approached her steadily, one step, two, across the cool tiles of the floor. She neither leaped on him nor spun and fled.

Her hair was not the blue-black of his own people, or of most of hers. There was a ruddy sheen to it, as if it were not darkest blue but darkest red. There were faint flecks of gold in a spray across her nose, like kisses from the sun. They were charming, and surprising, because the rest of her was so like a sword: keen and hard and brilliant.

Her skin was soft, smooth as new cream, and white as milk. She shuddered as he touched her cheek. He drew back, a little alarmed.

She caught his hand. He went still. She stared at it as if she had never seen its like before.

He began to wonder. Had she never—had she ever—?

Of course she must have. All these women were raised to love men as men in Egypt loved women: early, often, and with pleasure.

And yet, if she had undergone such rites as Iphikleia had told him of, when a girl became a woman, and some wise and skilled man of the people saw to it that she did it in gladness and in as little pain as might be, then perhaps she had not sought that pleasure often since. Her riding and fighting, her duties and oaths, and her long hope and her great disappointment, had preoccupied her till she had will for nothing else.

Maybe he read her all awry. But she was strangely shy, and strangely stiff.

He set himself to gentle her as he had learned to gentle her brother's horses. He moved softly; he moved slowly. He let her ease to his touch on her cheek before he ventured to free her hair from its plaits. It was wound as tight as she was, and bound fast. Patiently he worked it free.

She suffered it with a kind of quivering resignation. He stroked her hair with his fingers, smoothing it. The ripples of it, once freed, flowed about her face, and gave her quite a different beauty: much softer, and much gentler.

But her eyes were still wild. He ventured a boldness, reaching for the fastening of her tunic, and teasing it free. There was a long row of such fastenings, bits of intricately carved bone slid through a loop of leather. They could be maddening, or they could be a pleasant and prolonged game, a slow unfolding of her hidden beauty.

Her heart was beating hard. Her breath came quick. He did not hasten for that.

There was a tunic beneath the tunic, fine linen, damp with the heat of her body. And no wonder, if she would trammel herself so in the sowing time, when the heat was both heavy and potent. The undertunic was fastened with laces, simple indeed to undo. He slipped it from her white shoulders, baring the small pink-tipped breasts. So lovely, and so tender. They rose high above the arch of her ribs, her flat belly.

The belt of her trousers tempted him, but not yet. Not while she tensed anew, shivering with something other than cold. Her eyes had closed as if she could not bear to look at him.

He bent to kiss the tip of her breast. She gasped. He circled it with his tongue, lightly, oh so lightly. Her hands snapped into fists.

He smiled, bent down where she could not see, even if she opened her eyes. She was rousing wonderfully, but tight, so tight still.

He circled each breast with kisses. There was not a great deal of either, but what there was, was sweet. Then when she had arched her back and reached to clutch at him, he slipped free the clasp of her belt and let it fall. A cord bound her trousers. It gave way. Her trousers slipped down over hips nigh as narrow as a boy's, but with the same sweet curve as her breasts.

He freed her from them. She was all naked, and all lovely. He told her so, in words spoken soft lest he frighten her, and slow so that she would understand.

"Get to it," she gritted in her own language. "Just get to it."

It was fortunate for his intent that he chose not to understand any language but Egyptian. He stroked her lightly, long slow strokes, following the scant curves of her. She could seize him if she liked, fling him down, force him to do what she said she wanted. But she did not. He did not think she would. She had given herself to him, though perhaps she was not aware of it. Whatever he wished of her, she would do, or permit.

Men took such gifts for granted in this part of the world. But Kemni who had been in Crete, who had been and still, by the gods' will, was Iphikleia's lover, was not a man to presume any such power over a woman. He moved with great care and great gentleness. She arched at his touch, and opened like a flower of bronze.

And yet . . . not yet. He stroked her with hands and tongue, breasts and belly and the ruddy black fleece of her sex. She tensed and eased, tensed and eased. And when at last the dry land was moist, he entered it. She cried out, but not in pain. He rode her as if she had been one of her own horses, a strong slow gait that quickened only at her will.

The end of it was breathlessly swift. It startled a cry out of him, a shout of astonishment. But what burst out of her was laughter.

Kemni sank down beside her, still breathing hard. She lay on her back, lovely in her nakedness. The sweat-dampened hair clung to her cheeks and breasts. He reached to stroke it away, but she closed against him. He drew his hand back carefully, and lay silent.

After a while she rounded on him. "Why do you not fall asleep?" she demanded in her ragged Egyptian.

"Do you wish me to?"

She glared at him. It was the same glare as before—as if she could not forgive him for being desirable. "You can't be like this," she said. "No man can."

"Not even in the east?"

For an instant he thought she would strike him. But her hands stayed by her sides, clenched into fists. "I was never there."

Ah, he thought. That explained perhaps more than she knew. And from what he knew of the Retenu, they were not gentle lovers—were not lovers at all, Iphikleia would declare. "Some men rut like bulls," she had said to him once. "Three thrusts and a grunt and it's over. I pity the women cursed with such men. The only pleasure they ever know, they find in each other."

Kemni had been rather appalled. But if that was all Sadana had known . . . "No wonder you're so angry," he said.

She was tight, closed in on herself: worse even than before. He regretted that he had said anything. Although he knew that she would clench against him, he brushed her breast lightly, lightly with his finger. The nipple tightened. She shuddered just visibly.

A terrible thought came to him. It must have come from a god, or from a dark spirit creeping about in the shadows behind the light. Iphikleia had told him of that, too: how a woman could learn to hate a man's loving, to shrink from it even when she longed for it.

It could not be true, surely. Sadana was a strong woman, a warrior, a rider and a hunter. She knew the arts of bow and spear and sword. What man would venture—what man would dare—

A man might, if he were of a certain kind. If strength in a woman offended him, if he could only endure it by breaking and destroying it—he well might.

"Someone forced you," he said slowly. "Someone tried to break you. You've never been loved as a woman should be loved. You've only been—"

She fell on him without warning, without sound. Even naked and unarmed, she was a strong adversary, and dangerous. He did nothing to stop her, only guarded himself against her blows. They were hard and they were strong. They rained on his head and his uplifted arms.

Just as he began to fear that she would batter him down, she stopped. Abruptly, breathing hard, breath sobbing in her throat. Her face was stark white. He had never seen such eyes as hers were then, not even in a falcon gone mad in confinement.

"Sadana," he said: knowing that her name could send her into madness indeed, but trusting—praying—that it would touch the true heart of her.

Names were power. She blinked. She came back, a little, to herself. She stared at him as if he were an utter stranger.

"Sadana," he said again. Her head shook a fraction. But he had done it. He had touched her. "Sadana," he said a third time.

She struck him, one hard, backhanded blow. He dropped like a stone.

She stood over him. He lay with ringing ears and throbbing cheek. "How dare you," she said in a terrible voice. "How dare you know me?"

He had no answer for that.

"Yes," she said. "Yes, someone tried to break me. Someone thought he succeeded. I never told anyone. Not even my mother—not even my sister. And above all, not my brother. How could you know? How could you see? *What are you?*"

That he could answer, but he did not choose to. She dragged him to his feet. He staggered, but she held him up. She was little smaller than he, and nigh as strong. "It was a man in the court. A man the king loved, a great power in the kingdom. He laid an ambush for me. He fell on me, and did— did what he pleased with me. That would teach me, he said. That would show me what the gods think of a woman who rides and fights like a man."

And she had never told anyone. Of course she had not. Her brothers would have wanted to kill the one who did it, but they would have punished her, too, for the dishonor to their family. She would have gained nothing, and lost all the pride she had left.

"You killed him yourself," he said.

"They thought one of his enemies had caught him," she said. "I killed him with his own sword. I hewed his head from his shoulders. I hacked off the organs that had violated me, and fed them to him, dead as he was. They said it must have been someone whose wife or sister or daughter he had dishonored—for he was a great raper of women, that one. They never thought that it might have been one of those women."

The words had flooded out of her. When she stopped, she was breathing hard, as if she had run a race. Her eyes on him were wild. "What are you? Are you a magician? What spell have you laid on me?"

"No spell," he said gently. "I'm only a man. I have no arts or powers."

"You have great arts," she said. "Tell me who taught you!"

"Women," he said. "They're like horses, you know. Gentle them, they come sweetly to hand. Beat them, they fight back. Ride them as they best like to be ridden, and they give joy in return."

"Your people know nothing of horses," she said.

"I learned," said Kemni—daring perhaps too much, but she was intent on him. "Horses are new in this country, but women have been here for many times a thousand years."

"Our men know horses, but they know nothing of women."

"The more fools they," Kemni said.

She reached to touch him: a great thing for her, and a gift. Her hand was cold and a little unsteady. "What if I want to keep you? What will you do?"

His belly clenched. "My lady might object to that," he said.

"I'll ask her to give you to me."

"And if she refuses?"

Her lips went tight. "She has everything, doesn't she? Every good thing."

"Don't hate her for it," he said.

"I hate her with all my heart," said Sadana. "But she is the Mare's servant, the priestess, Horse Goddess' own. Never think I'd harm her. Never even dream of it."

"I didn't think you would," he said. "You have great honor. And great beauty. I pray you find yourself a lover you can keep."

"Will you refuse me, then, if I ask again?"

That was the first utterance he had ever heard from her, that was empty of anger. There was only longing in it, and a touch of sadness.

"While I can," he said to that sadness, "while my lady allows, I'll never refuse you."

"Every night?"

"Unless she needs me."

Sadana did not like that, but neither did she let slip her temper. She could accept what she could not change. And she could recognize a gift when it was given. How great a one it was, that perhaps she could not know. But she had no need to know.

W HAT IN THE gods' name did you do to her?"
They had left that house at last, ridden out at dawn in their train of carts and chariots and people afoot, making their some-what leisurely way toward Avaris. Iry had the luxury of private conversation with Kemni, since he was her charioteer. He seemed much as always, but Sadana had been riding like one in a dream. She kept pausing— and almost smiling. And that was unheard of.

"What *did* you do?" Iry demanded. "Did you lay a spell on her?"

"She asked me that, too," Kemni said. He was very busy with the horses, though they were quiet, offering no impudence.

"So did you?"

"I have no magic," he said. "I told her that."

"Did she believe you?"

"I don't think so."

"So what did you do?"

"Nothing at all extraordinary," he answered with a touch of impatience. "Except to her. She didn't know a man could be gentle. Could give her plea-sure."

Iry heard what he had not quite said. Her breath hissed between her teeth. "So they'll even do it to their own."

"Have they done it to you?"

She smiled faintly at his leap to her defense. "No, of course not. Not, sometimes, for lack of trying. But I was in my own house. I knew the ways better than those invaders did. And Mother protected me, before—"

"Before the Mare came."

She let that suffice. She had meant to say, before Khayan came; but they were the same. More or less. Maybe.

"I'm glad you were safe," he said. "These men, they're brutal."

"Not all of them."

"Enough," he said.

He was angry. He hid it well, but his shoulders were tight, and his lips. Strange for a man to care what other men did to women. He must have had teaching of a sort that few men ever had. And from where?

"You went to Crete," she said.

He glanced at her. "And how did you come to that conclusion?"

"Would you understand if I told you?"

"Probably not."

He probably would, but she was not inclined to go to war with him over anything so small. "That's where you've been, isn't it? The Retenu say Cretans are strange people, old people, who've been there for long and long."

"They're kin to the eastern horsemen," Kemni said. "Long ago and far distant, but they worship the same goddess. And women rule them. They remember, dimly, when they were all one, before some went away and heard the call of the sea. Sea of water, sea of grass—it's much the same in the end. Even ships and horses, they told me."

"You went there for the king." She found that pleasing, somehow. He was her cousin. He had risen in the world—higher, she thought, than he might seem, as he played charioteer in a foreign lord's following.

"He needed someone quiet, who could do what needed to be done, and keep the secret from those who might betray it." Kemni glanced about. Iry knew already that there was no one near. The leaders were well ahead, the bulk of the procession well behind. The Mare ran between, white tail streaming. She had been fending them all off, granting Iry this freedom to say whatever she pleased.

The Mare, as Iry had been thinking more often of late, had intentions that the Retenu would not like at all if they knew. In choosing an Egyptian, it seemed she had chosen Egypt. She had encouraged this, and not so that Iry might betray her own kin.

Maybe the gods of Egypt had made common cause with the goddess who lived in the Mare. The conquerors were not horsemen, after all. They were donkey caravaneers, whose chosen beasts of burden were long-eared asses. Horses were rare among them. But Egyptians—some of them at least—found in themselves a potent fascination with horses. Kemni had it, Iry had it. Pepi and the boys he had brought into the stables—they all had it.

What a thought, that Egypt could take horses from the conqueror, and conquer him with them. It made her smile. "Listen," she said to Kemni, "when you go . . . back there, tell him there's one here who may find ways to help."

"I'll tell him that," Kemni said. "If you would do something in return."

"If I can," she said.

"Sadana," he said. "She needs gentleness, and a man she can trust. I can't stay for her. Once I come to Avaris, I'll be called to what I should have been doing long since. Can you help? Will you?"

Iry had had no expectations, but this— "You want me to procure a lover for Sadana?"

He flushed faintly under the bronzing of wind and sun. "You don't have to be that blunt. Just . . . help her find someone to be gentle to her."

"In *Avaris?*"

"Maybe the lord knows someone. Or your other guardsman."

"Kemni," Iry said with great and careful patience, "can you honestly imagine that I would ask men of the Retenu to find a lover for their own sister?"

"They might surprise you."

"Khayan might," Iry admitted. "But I think not. I can try to do this, somehow, if you insist. I can't promise to succeed."

"If you try, it will be enough."

"Well then," Iry said with a sigh. "I'll try. Because you ask it, mind. And because she is easier to endure when she's less tight-drawn upon herself."

"Good," Kemni said. "Good. The gods will love you for this."

"I only hope they won't hate me," said Iry.

❖ ❖

They came to Avaris in the morning, having camped for the night not far outside of it. The walls seemed low in the wet shimmer of the Delta's heat, but as they drew closer, the city loomed larger, till it showed itself both lofty and forbidding.

It was a fortress, a strong holding within a conquered country. And it was vast. It was the greatest city in the world, the Retenu boasted. Larger than Thebes, larger than Byblos or Tyre, larger than Ur or Babylon. Larger than any of them, and vaunting in its strength.

It stood on the eastern edge of a tangled skein of river and land, on that branch of the great river of Egypt which flowed toward Pelusium in the east of the Lower Kingdom. It guarded the eastward gate of the kingdom, and stood athwart the best of the ways on both water and land, both to and from the sea. Its harbor was crowded with ships. Its walls were packed tight with houses, men living on top of one another, spreading out where they could, but clinging to their walls and defenses. So dense were the throngs living within, Iry had been told, that the dead had no place of their own. Any who died in that city was buried in the court of his house. How his kin and descendants bore it, Iry did not know. At night, when the dead walked, the city must be even more crowded than in the light of day.

Khayan's caravan of chariots and carts and servants on foot, with or without laden donkeys, was granted the privilege of the processional way, the wide street that directed itself toward the loom of Baal's temple and the lesser and battlemented loom of the king's palace. Lesser folk kept that way clear, so that high ones could come and go unhindered. Iry could see the common people down side ways and in sudden squares, a seething throng of them, like an anthill opened suddenly to the sun.

So many people. And so many Retenu. The few Egyptian faces that she saw, belonged to ragged and sharp-boned creatures who must be slaves, or even beggars. Though why any child of the Lower Kingdom would wish to beg in Avaris, she could not imagine.

Kemni was motionless beside her, except for such movement as the chariot or the horses forced upon him. She felt the tension thrumming in him. As steaming hot as the air was, and reeking with it, his body's warmth was not entirely welcome, but she was glad of his presence nonetheless. She needed an Egyptian face amid these alien walls. Already they were closing in upon her, and she had not even come to the great fortress and prison that was the palace.

She came terribly close to ripping the reins from Kemni's hands, turning the chariot about, and bolting back the way she had come. But even apart from the fact that the bulk of the lord's following filled the road behind, she was not enough of a coward—not prudent enough, or sensible enough. If she had been, she would have refused to leave the Sun Ascendant at all.

It was done. She was bound to enter those walls within walls. The gates rose before her, warded by what seemed an army of guards. They were all big men, huge men, bearded Retenu and coal-black Nubians, so tall that their eyes were level with hers as she stood in the chariot. Some were even taller.

Kemni held his head a fraction higher as he rode though that deep and echoing gate. So, for pride, did Iry. She wondered if he was as stark with fear as she, or if he saw those walls as cutting him off from all the world he knew. Now he was within them, he might never go out again. If anyone marked him, if anyone betrayed him . . .

She would protect him as she could, while she could. As for herself, she would be safe enough. Her rank protected her, and the office the Mare had laid on her.

So she told herself as the palace of the Retenu closed in upon her. They were to be given chambers within it, and servants to tend them, and a haughty chamberlain to conduct them to their lodgings. He was perhaps half an Egyptian: he was smaller and slighter, his features finer, his lips fuller than if he had been entirely Retenu. He wore a beard as every male among them must, but he clipped it almost indecently short, so that one could see the shape of his face. But the hair in its topknot, the golden collar and armlets, the elaborate and heavily embroidered robe, were all of outland fashion. High and courtly fashion, she could see. Her own simple shift, her hair indifferently plaited, and her utter lack of ornament, earned her a glance eloquent of scorn.

She had no fear of courtiers' contempt. These courtiers above all, whom she would gladly sweep out of Egypt, she would greet with all the arrogance she could muster. They would only admire her for it. That much she had learned of courts, in what little time she had spent in or near them.

They settled in the chambers with some crowding and no little squabbling. Even as vast as the city was, it was full to bursting, and the palace likewise. People on top of people was the way of the world here.

She at least was granted a room of her own, a tiny and airless cell, but it was hers. It was no worse than the cell she had had as a slave in the Sun Ascendant—and it was close by a stair that led to the palace gardens.

The gardens of this palace were a wonder and a marvel. They stretched along the great outer wall and meandered inward among the courts. Those nearest the wall were gardens of trees, a forest indeed, green and richly scented, with little rivers trained to run among the trees, and fountains, and pools of bright fish. There was a menagerie—little enough, Kemni told her, to what the king had in Thebes, but to her a marvel. There were lions, of course, and jackals, and sly and slinking hyenas; oryx and gazelle, ibex, and strange beasts out of the lands beyond the Upper Kingdom: elephants, long-necked visions called giraffe, and creatures like horses, or like shorter-eared asses, but striped black and white in eye-blinding patterns. There was a pool of riverhorses, and even crocodiles; aviaries and pools of fish and cages full of baboons and mon-keys and sad-eyed apes. And, past these, creatures from the northern outlands: wolves panting in the heat, a vast aurochs bull with horns spread as wide as a processional way, even a bear lying limp in a shallow pool.

She had wandered there to escape the crush in the guest-chambers, and perhaps more than a little because, for a brief while, she seemed to have been forgotten. The Mare was nowhere within reach. She had left the riding before it came to Avaris, wandered away unnoticed as Iry had done just now. Iry had made no effort to stop her. The Mare came and went as she pleased. That was her privilege.

Iry did not share it, but for this little while she was free. Or as free as she could be, with Iannek in her shadow. Kemni had handed her over to that annoyingly loyal young man, then arranged to vanish. He would be finding his allies, she supposed, and conveying to them all that he had learned.

Iannek managed at least to be quiet, a virtue he had not cultivated before; but he had not been her guardsman, either. Sometimes she caught him on the verge of his old relentless chatter, but he mastered himself, bit his tongue and was silent. She caught herself almost liking him, Retenu though he was. When he was not leaping about chattering like a monkey, he was quite bearable. In fact he was rather charming.

There were other people in the menagerie, walking about as she walked, Retenu all, some in robes, some in Egyptian kilts. It was odd to see those here—odd and somewhat dismaying. Those even addressed one another by Egyptian names, in their uncouth accents, as if it were a fashion they affected and were excessively pleased with.

Iannek growled at that. She raised a brow at him. He sucked in a breath, thought anew of silence, but yielded to the invitation. "So that's back in fash-ion," he said. "It goes in and out, you know, like floods on the Nile. And of course the king takes an Egyptian name, so that people will know he has a right to rule here. But these kilts—and did you see that man? He shaved his face!"

"Appalling," Iry agreed blandly.

It was a moment before he caught the irony; then he glared. "Well, to you it's not. But he's not one of you!"

"No," she said. "He's not."

She paused in front of a cageful of baboons. They were wise creatures, the old stories said, living images of the god Thoth as the Mare was of Horse Goddess. They were also dangerous, with their long sharp fangs and their uncertain tempers—as gods could be. Two of them now were mating, the female nursing her child while the male sired another with an expression of intense concentration. Perhaps he was pondering great mysteries as his body performed its duty to the race.

Someone else had come up to watch the baboons. It was a man, not young, though not yet old, robed in fine linen embroidered with gold, and escorted by a pair of discreet guards. By that, Iry knew he was a lord of consequence, though he affected no airs, nor did he come closer to the Egyptian fashion than the lightness of his robe.

He watched the baboons with calm interest and an air of one who came here often. "Do you see that one?" he said to Iry. "That's the father of the tribe. He mates with all the females, and drives the young males away, or kills them if they're importunate."

"He's much like a lord of men," Iry observed.

The man laughed, a warm deep sound. It reminded her of Khayan—which made her cheeks grow hot. And why that should be, she did not want to know.

"Men are very like apes, when it comes to it," the man said, seeming oblivious to her discomfort. "See, there the lord goes, off to court another lady. He has his favorites, and that yonder is a great one, a queen of the tribe. I watched her beat a younger lady once for importuning the lord. It was a terrible battle, as terrible as any in the queens' house."

"And was there bloodshed?"

The man nodded. "The young hussy lived, but she was never the same thereafter. In the end she went to a menagerie in Tanis, where she could live alone without fear or rivalry."

"You must come here every day," Iry said, "to know so much."

"I come as often as I can," the man said. "It takes me out of myself."

Iry nodded. "I do much the same," she said, "except with me, it's horses."

"Indeed?" the man said. "Horses need open spaces, and sky. They're not themselves inside of walls. Those of us confined to palaces . . . we take other pleasures, such as we may."

"I could never be confined to a palace," said Iry. "It's a pity you must."

"Ah," said the man. "Well. But that's as the gods will. So I visit the menagerie, and I watch the animals. It's rather more amusing than watching courtiers, and often more civilized."

"You know all the animals, then," Iry said. "Tell me about the striped ones, the ones who are almost horses. Are they from Nubia? Are they horses?"

"They come from south of Nubia, from great grasslands that stretch away to the edge of the world," the man said. "They're called zebras. They aren't horses—they're more like wild asses. It's very difficult to train them, if anyone is minded to try. They don't have the minds that horses have, or our tamed asses, either."

"Pity," said Iry. "A team of these zebras would be a fine novelty for a prince."

"A prince or two has thought so," the man said, "and failed miserably in the trying."

"Maybe the gods want them to stay wild," Iry said.

They walked down the path, past the baboons' great cage and a cage with a lion sleeping in it. The guards had fallen back, Iry noticed out of the edges of her eyes. So too had Iannek. He looked odd, as if something he had eaten had suddenly disagreed with him. She thought of sending him away to rest, since she was safe enough here, but her new companion was regaling her with stories of the lion and the elephants, and the aurochs bull grazing peacefully on cut fodder. "They live in forests far to the north," the man said, "crashing through the trees with their great horns gleaming. They are terrible to hunt, as strong as they are, and huge, and fast on their feet."

"Like elephants," Iry said.

"Rather like," the man agreed. "Whole tribes will hunt them, with packs of huge dogs, and chariots, and vaunting bravery. The man who kills an aurochs is a great hero, and is given rich rewards: the best of the food and the women, and the aurochs' hide and horns for his tent."

"And they brought one here," Iry said in wonder. "What army of heroes was it who dared that?"

"Ah," said the man with a deprecatory smile. "No great army. He came as an infant, a calf no larger than a large donkey. Someone, we suppose, killed his mother and took him from her side, tamed him as much as an aurochs can be tamed, and sent him here as tribute to the king."

Iry was a little disappointed, but also a little relieved. The thought of anything so vast rising up in rage was disconcerting to say the least. But it seemed the bull was a placid enough creature, and tamed. He came to the man's call, and took a bit of sweet from a hand he seemed to know well. He was no more threatening than an ox, nor any less interested in sweetness than Iry's own imperious Mare.

He let her touch his broad wet nose, and lightly rub his jowl. He lowered his head so that she could do it, for he was far taller than she. He loomed above her like a mountain in the desert. Such a beautiful great black beast with his ivory horns. He was almost as beautiful as the Mare; and that was as high praise as she knew to give.

She went away well content, with her companion bearing her company as far as the outer cages. He would linger yet a while, he said; but she had wandered apart long enough. There would be a hunt out for her soon, if there was not one already.

Still with Iannek in her shadow, she found her way back to the guest-chambers. Iannek was even more silent than before, a silence so profound that she came close to rounding on him and demanding to know what he was so patently not saying. But even if she had been inclined to unbar those gates, the outriders of the hunt had found her, a pair of Sadana's warrior women with faces even grimmer than usual. They were not taking Iry prisoner, they made that clear, but they were not inclined to let her out of their sight thereafter.

Iannek's trouble, if trouble it was, was lost in Iry's return to confinement. She was not to go out again, it was made clear, without Sadana and a guard of warrior women. Her young male guardsmen were not enough. She must be protected, and closely, in this of all places.

No less a personage than the lady Sarai told her this, receiving her in a chamber that had become her own with miraculous speed. It looked, in fact, precisely like the one in the Sun Ascendant in which she received guests and entertained scapegrace priestesses. Her expression was no more than wontedly severe, and she did not seem angry at all—quite unlike Sadana, whose expression was thunderous. But Iry was to know that she had overstepped her bounds.

"In this place," Sarai said, "no one is safe. Not even the king. Every passage has its web of intrigue, and every gathering its hidden currents. A word spoken unwisely in the morning is shouted from the rooftops before the sun reaches its zenith. Men have died for a slip of the tongue. And you, child, are not best known for your discretion."

Iry kept her head down and her lips together. She would not quarrel with this of all women, but neither would she swear oaths she did not intend to keep. She took her rebuke in silence, and when it was over, accepted her dismissal. It seemed to satisfy Sarai. It set Iry free, somewhat; she could not go where she pleased, not any longer, but she was allowed to seek her own closet of a room, and rest there. There was no punishment laid on her, beyond the burden of Sarai's disapproval.

It would do. Not well, but it would suffice.

IX

KEMNI SLIPPED OUT of Avaris' great fortress and stronghold with almost disturbing ease. Even here, Egyptians were simply not seen. They crept about in shadows, performed tasks that Retenu would not do, ran errands and conveyed messages and, for all he knew, spied on the lords, all unnoticed.

Kemni was but one of the many. He passed once more beneath that deep and echoing gate, into the teeming throngs of the city. Where he was going, he was not entirely certain, but it seemed reasonable enough that he should seek the river and the harbor. That Iphikleia might not have waited so long—

that all his king's allies might have left—he refused to consider. They must be waiting. Or they would have left messages, and safe paths for him to follow, back to the Upper Kingdom and safety.

It took all that remained of that day, fighting crowds and beating the streets about the harbor, but at last he found *Dancer* drawn up on the shore, and crewmen who greeted him with joy that seemed genuine. One of them guided him to a house nearby, such a one as the Cretans favored, poor and shabby outside but splendid within. It was empty of any but servants, but those assured him that Naukrates would return as soon as might be.

They did not speak of Iphikleia, nor did he ask. He was a coward, he supposed. He whiled the time with a bath and a drowse in a cool and airy room, surrounded by images of ships and the sea. He slipped easily into a dream of sailing on *Dancer*, breasting the waves in a dash of cold spray, while dolphins leaped all about the ship, and a fair wind blew him toward a distant island.

Her face shaped itself out of wind and spray, her hair like the blue-black gleam of the sea in storm, streaming down about him, and her eyes both dark and bright, drinking him in. How, before the gods, had he ever thought her cold? She was the wildfire that could run up a ship's mast and dance along the rigging. She was the lightning out of a roiling heaven. She was the cold kiss of the sea, and the fierce hot stroke of the sun on blue water.

Then all words were gone, and there was only the meeting of body and body. He woke into it, and it was all real, all there, her warm familiar presence in his arms, her scent, the way she fit just so, taking him inside her and holding him deep. Her arms were strong, as if she would never let him go.

For all their urgency, they prolonged it as much as they might, a long, slow, easy swell and surge like a quiet sea. There was beauty in it as much as pleasure, and a joy that deepened the longer it went on, till surely he must burst with it.

She gasped and stiffened and gripped him with bruising force. He let go then, at last. They rode the last long swell down into stillness. And there, for a while, they rested.

✦ ✦

Kemni woke with a small start. He had not meant to fall asleep. Iphikleia was still there—no dream, thank the gods. She lay watching him, her face as unreadable as it had ever been before he learned to see the heart of her. He smiled and fitted his palm to the curve of her cheek. "I missed you," he said.

"I should think you'd have been too busy," she said in a tone of surpassing mildness.

"Never too busy to love you," he said. "Never for a moment."

"Such pretty words." She turned her head till her lips touched his palm. Then she drew away—slightly, but enough. He let his hand fall. "You were away a long while."

"I was discovering great things about the Lower Kingdom—and about the men who claim to rule it."

"And the women?"

"Are you jealous?"

"Should I be?"

"No," he said. "No, you should not."

"Even the one whose hand I feel on you?"

His heart clenched. Which was silly of it, but he was only in part its master. "If you mean my cousin Iry, she was never more to me than a kinswoman should be. If you mean—another, then I can only remind you that it was you who trained me to approach a woman only if she asks. And that one had great need of a man who would do such a thing."

"Tell me about her," Iphikleia said. She was not offering him a choice.

He gathered his wits and his words. There was more here than a woman's jealousy. He could feel it in the air. What he told her would matter, and how he told it. "Her name is Sadana," he said. "She rides horses and carries weapons and knows how to fight like a man. Her mother's people come from the east, where the horse-tribes are, but she has never been there. Her brother was sent instead, because their goddess asked for him. Then when he came back with the white horse, the Mare, who is a goddess, Sadana was supposed to be chosen to be the priestess, but she wasn't—she had more to bear than human woman should."

"You pity her, then," Iphikleia said.

"No," he said. "No, I don't pity her. But the gods haven't been kind to her. She didn't know that a man can be gentle. She only ever knew force."

"Poor thing," said Iphikleia. "And you left her."

Kemni drew himself up as best he could while lying flat in a tumbled bed. "First I'm an ill creature for touching her, now you upbraid me for leaving her? I asked my cousin to help her. It was all I could do, with all I had tugging at me. Ariana has been waiting overlong for all of us."

"You don't think I mean to be reasonable, do you?" Iphikleia asked him.

"Of course not," Kemni said.

"Good," said Iphikleia. "You still should not have left her. Or should never have gone near her at all."

"She asked," he said.

"How difficult." Iphikleia slapped him lightly—for the transgression—but then she kissed him. "Because," she said, "you are what you are."

Kemni did not pretend to understand her. It was enough that she understood him.

✤ ✤

He had meant to return to the palace late that night, redolent of beer and bad wine. But Naukrates was sailing in the morning. Another day and Kemni would have been left to fend for himself.

The gods had spoken, as had Naukrates. Kemni would have to vanish then, and hope to be forgotten.

He surprised himself with regret. As little time as he had spent in that household, he had made himself a part of it. It had been home to him when he was a child, and even broken and conquered, it was still in a way his own.

But he must return to the Upper Kingdom, to his king and his queen and his manifold duties. When he came back to this place, he would come back in arms—or die in the trying.

✦ ✦

Kemni was gone. Iry had expected that, but not so quickly, or without a farewell. She was angry—foolish, but she could not help herself. He must have been swept away by his allies. But what if he had been captured or killed? She might never know.

She had to trust that he had found his Cretans, and that they had taken him back to Thebes. Meanwhile she was left with only half her complement of guardsmen, and no simple explanation for it.

The first day at least, there were distractions. From even as little as Iry knew of courts, she knew that kings never received anyone at once, even ambassadors from great kingdoms. A king made people wait upon him. It was one of the things that made him a king.

And yet, almost before she had risen and dressed and greeted the sun as the Mare's servant was supposed to do—but in her heart she sang a hymn to Re, who was the sun of Egypt—there was a messenger at the door, a lofty and self-important one, with a summons to the king. Unlike kings, kings' subjects must not keep others waiting. Iry was given no time to eat the breakfast that had been laid out for her. She was summoned. She must go now.

Alone then, for Iannek had not come yet to his day-duty, and Kemni of course was gone, Iry followed the king's chamberlain. It occurred to her, briefly, that this might be a trap and the chamberlain an impostor, but if that was so, she would almost welcome the danger.

She was in an odd mood. Her cousin's presence had given her something very like comfort: the nearness of kin in a world gone strange. And now he was lost again. The Mare, whom she could trust, was out beyond the city, doing whatever it pleased her to do. Here in these walls, in the hands of her enemies, Iry was all alone.

And she was almost glad of it. It was like leaping from a high wall into endless space, or for that matter, essaying the back of a horse, and riding wherever the horse wished to take her. Which was, just now, deep into the palace, into the heart of those high walls. Everything about her was odd, not quite Egyptian, but not quite Retenu. The images painted on walls and carved in stone were sometimes altogether alien, but often Egyptian or almost Egyptian. Kings in the Two Crowns and the proper royal kilt, carrying crook and flail, but bearded like Retenu; or men carved in the scribe's pose, seated cross-legged, but no scribe had ever worn his hair cropped above the ears in that preposterous way. Sometimes the gods painted or carved were Set in his own image, but sometimes they were something else that seemed meant to signify Set—Baal, that would be, the Skyfather of the Retenu, whose temple they had built in the city's heart, vast as a mountain. There were other gods, and the gods of her own people, too, but those were the greatest and the most often seen.

Far inside the palace, in a maze of corridors, the chamberlain brought Iry to a pair of tall doors watched over by men in polished armor. They eyed her from the shadow of their helmets, but bowed and suffered her to pass in the chamberlain's wake.

She had come, of course, to the king's chambers. They went on and on, a maze of rooms and passages, all seemingly deserted, but the shadows were full of whispers. She could feel the eyes on her, though she never caught any of those who stared.

In the heart of those chambers was a room of surprising smallness. It had windows, which rather surprised her. They looked out on the central court of the palace, a deep space of pillars that made Iry think, somehow, of a bed of reeds made vast and set in stone. Or a forest such as Khayan had described it to her, pillars of trees that marched on and on into green shadow.

This room was high above it, and must be near the roof of the palace. There was no one in it, but there were chairs to sit in, even a couch if she had a mind to lie at ease, and wine and cakes to tempt her, and a bowl of flowers to regale her senses.

She should sit, she knew, and be patient. But she had been expecting to see the king, not be forced, after all, to cool her heels until he deigned to see her. She paced, pausing with each turn to gaze down and far down into the courtyard. People passed below, sometimes alone, more often in companies. She amused herself trying to guess what each person was, whether lord or soldier, servant or commoner wandering gape-jawed through the palace.

Sometimes there were dogs, alone or on leads, wanderers or hunting dogs or, once, what must be the warhounds she had heard of but not seen. They were large even from this vantage, grey as wolves, in collars spiked with bronze. Their handlers struggled a little against the tug and surge of them.

No cats, she thought. She had not seen one since she passed these walls. Retenu did not like cats. Wicked, uncanny creatures, they said, given to creeping about and startling passersby with a leap and a sudden slash of claws. Which was perfectly true, but that was what made them cats and not simply very small dogs.

Iry did not like dogs. She particularly did not like the warhounds, even seen from so high and far away. She was glad when they were gone.

She had by then become very comfortable in the deep embrasure of the window, curled like a cat herself, with warmth all about her from the sun as it rose above the walls. She let herself drift and dream, till a gnawing in her belly reminded her that she had not eaten since she woke in the morning.

The cakes were not as good as she might have had in the Sun Ascendant, but they were pleasant. The wine, well watered, was of royal quality.

Just as she sat licking her fingers, wondering if she could finish another cake, footsteps sounded—not at the door, but above. She looked up startled. The footsteps passed, grew dim, paused. Then she heard the sound of feet on a stair.

A chamberlain, not the one who had brought her here, opened the inner door. "You will come," he said in the soft light voice of a eunuch.

Eunuchs, like warhounds, were a thing she had heard of but not seen. Neither of the lords she had been slave to had had eunuchs.

She had heard that they were gross and vastly fat, and warbled like birds. This was a very tall, thin, elegant personage, and his voice was higher than a man's but low for a woman's. He reminded her of an ibis, as tall as he was, and as gangling-graceful. He did not look like a woman, except that he was beardless; but Egyptian men did not grow their beards.

She followed him more because she was fascinated than because she was obedient to his summons. He led her out into a passage and up a stair. The top of it was blinding sunlight and the broad expanse of a roof. Much of that was cleared for ease of defense, but not far from the stair, someone, king or queen, had made a garden. It was small, and nestled against the foot of one of the four tall towers that warded the corners of the palace. A low wall surrounded it. Greenery overhung the wall, and a torrent of flowers.

Within, there was no sense of smallness at all. Everything was green, and dizzying with scent. Above it Iry could see the grim face of the tower, but veiled and softened in leaves and bright petals. The center of it was, as always in this land of desert and precious green, a pool: here, rimmed with stone and glinting with fish. Lotus grew there, flowers like moons floating on the water.

A man sat by the pool. The same guards who had attended him the day before attended him now: favorites, they must be, and trusted as she had trusted Kemni and—yes—Iannek.

Of course the man in the menagerie had been the king. She remembered clearly Iannek's face—he had known but not spoken, the idiot.

King Apophis, against whom she had sworn perpetual hatred, smiled at her and said, "Good morning, my lady. Did you rest well?"

"Very well, majesty," Iry said. "And were the rest of the animals as entertaining as always?"

"Quite so," he said. "One of the lionesses cubbed in the night—I was visiting her, or I'd not have kept you waiting."

Gods, she thought. It was ghastly difficult to hate this pleasant man who loved his animals. And yet he was Apophis of the Retenu. He ruled the Lower

Kingdom. He was the conqueror of conquerors, king of the foreign kings. All that she hated, all that she had sworn to fight against, was embodied in him.

She could only do a thing that she had learned to do when the old lord seized the Sun Ascendant after her father died. She divided her souls. That part of her which hated, she laid aside. The rest could be cool if not dispassionate, could listen to him and converse with him and be as civil, even as amiable, as she had been to the nameless man in the menagerie.

That nameless man was the one she spoke to. Names were power; everyone in Egypt knew that. Without a name, a man could not live forever, could not be immortal.

And so, to her, the king of the foreign kings was simply a man. He had no name, and therefore no strength to stand against her if she chose to do battle with him. "Did you see the lion-cubs?" she asked him.

"No," he said rather regretfully. "The mother was not ready to bring them out of her den into the world. But when she does, would you like to go and see them with me?"

"I would like that," Iry said. And she would. This man without a name was very good company, and wise in the ways of beasts. Except horses. Those, he had confessed, he did not know well.

She did not think that she would teach him. And indeed, as if he had read her thoughts in her eyes, he said, "So you are the Mare's servant. Do you know how surprising you are?"

"I would think the proper word would be 'appalling.'"

He laughed, rich and deep. Iry wondered if he and Khayan were kin. It was possible. Why not? "Yes, there are those who have called you appalling. I might have thought so when I first heard of you. But you are not as any of us might have expected."

"What did you expect?" she asked him.

"Fear," he answered. "Defiance. Mockery of us all."

"How do you know I don't feel every bit of that?"

"Maybe you do," he said. "But you have mastered it. Have you not? You are what you are. You do what you must do. The Mare chose you for that."

"I'm glad you see so clearly," she said. "Not many of your people do."

"Kings are taught to see clearly," he said.

"Even through clouds of flattery and the sleights of courtiers?"

"Especially through those. The king who fails in that is weak, and his kingdom may suffer for it."

Oh, Iry could hate him now—for being wise; for speaking the words of a good king. He must not be a good king. He was a conqueror, an invader. He must be cast out of Egypt.

And yet he sat in that garden on the roof of his palace, under a sky that his people had never been born to—but he had; he was born in this country as Iry herself had been—and he smiled at her, and said almost gently, "You wish I could be weak. Don't you?"

"Does it matter what I wish?"

"The Mare's servant is a great power in this kingdom. Surely you know that. What you wish matters very much."

"Why?"

He must be accustomed to difficult questions. He was barely taken aback. "A goddess chose you for her own. She speaks through you. What you do, what you think, signifies more than if you were a simple mortal woman."

"So they tell me—those who've taken it on themselves to teach me. So you're all afraid of me?"

"Some are in awe of you," he said. "Some think you quite dangerous. A person of your nation, given such power as the Mare gives you . . . you could destroy us."

"And you would say such a thing?"

"I'm sure you've thought it," he said.

"Do you think I would do that?"

"I think you might." He seemed unperturbed by it.

"And you won't try to stop me?"

"I never said that."

There was a pause. Iry had been warned. His expression was as calm as ever. He even smiled a little. He liked her, she could see. But he was a king. Kings could destroy even what they loved, in the name of their kingship.

When she spoke, she spoke carefully, but taking no great pains to be circumspect. "I can promise nothing. Except this. Whatever I do, it will not harm the Mare. Whatever comes of all of this, it will be as she wills. Not as you will, lord king. Not for the good of your kingdom. But for her—whatever she ordains, I will do."

"She is ours," he said.

"She chose to accompany you for a while. She comes from another tribe than yours, and another world."

That silenced him. Iry might have condemned herself, but she thought not. She had seen how he looked at her. He was remembering what she was. Not a slave, not an Egyptian, but the Mare's servant. The goddess' chosen.

She still had not fully understood what that was; what it meant. Sometimes she thought she never would. And yet she could use it. She used it now, to face the conquerors' king.

And what, she wondered, if he had no fear because he knew what she could not face? What if, for the Mare's sake, Iry turned on her own people? That must be what he hoped for, even expected. As of course he would.

Never, she thought. *By the gods. Never.*

But doubt niggled at her. Maybe it had troubled Kemni too—and hence he had vanished without telling her when or where he was going.

Enough. She was still in front of the king, and he had eyes that could see both far and deep. For him she must be strong, and not waver. He must never see her doubts or her fears, nor know that she had them.

She smiled at him, not too brightly, and not too shakily, either. "Tell me more about the animals," she said. "The spotted ones whose necks go up and up, till they tower like trees—tell me about them."

He might have been inclined to press her on the subject of the Mare, but it seemed that he too saw the wisdom in turning aside from it. He answered with no apparent reluctance, in fact almost eagerly. The rest of the audience was pleasant, and perhaps prolonged; until a chamberlain came and hovered, and reminded him that he had duties in the greater palace. Then Iry was let go. She was not sorry to go, but neither was she in excessive haste.

She did like him. What he was, she hated, to the heart of her. But the man without a name, the pleasant companion who knew so much of so many animals, she could think of, in a way, as a friend.

X

KHAYAN IN AVARIS remembered anew why he had been so glad to be sent away to the steppe, far from the courts of kings. In his own domain he was happy enough; he was born and bred to rule, and he did it well. But he was not born to be a king.

"You were born to serve kings," his sister Maryam said. She had taken on herself the management of the suite of rooms they were all crowded into. Of them all, she seemed the most content.

"I can serve kings outside of the court," Khayan said. He had not exactly come looking for her; he had been seeking refuge from the importunings of people who seemed to think that he had influence with the king. But she had been overseeing the servants on their washing-day. Amid the scents of fresh-washed linen and damp wool, he paused to whimper at his sister. It was no more than that, he knew it, but he had been doing much the same since he was young enough still to seek his nurse's breast.

Maryam had always indulged him but never spoiled him. She went on about her smoothing and folding, with a very pretty maid to help her. The maid slanted glances at Khayan that he could well read. If he should happen to remember her later, she would be delighted to oblige him.

He might, at that. Barukha was a jealous woman, but in Avaris she had had perforce to return to her kin. Protestations that she was a priestess in training, that she could not be spared, had been set at naught by Sarai's gracious granting of leave. Sarai was perhaps glad to be rid of her. Khayan was somewhat surprised by the extent of his own gladness. Barukha heated his blood wonderfully, but she was neither a restful nor at all a safe companion.

He was free now to cast his eye elsewhere. That was quite to his liking. He allowed himself to meet one of the girl's glances, and to bestow on her the hint of a smile. She took it as he had meant. Her eyes sparkled as she bent diligently to her work.

Maryam's voice pierced through the distraction. "You'll be leaving here soon enough. Surely you can bear to be a king's man for the little while between."

Khayan sighed gustily. "I'll have to, won't I?"

"Yes," she said. "You will."

She had dismissed him, so smoothly and with such tact that he was well away from her before it struck him what she had done. He paused then and laughed ruefully. Maryam kept his house wherever he was, but she did not serve him or any man—no matter what she might want him to think.

He should be in one of the courts, gathering with others of the lords who were in the city, to speak of things that they had spoken of endlessly before. Matters of the kingdom, the latest embassies, and of course, always, the question of war. Some of the young hotheads, Iannek's agemates, were yelling to be allowed to conquer the south of Egypt. They and their forebears had been yelling for it for a hundred years, and no doubt would be doing the same in another hundred. It was not practicable, that was all. Khayan knew it. The older lords knew it. But the boys and children would not hear it. They wanted what they wanted. They did not care what it cost, or how difficult it might be.

Khayan had been as young as that once. He was not so old now. But he had been riding the steppe when he might have been ramping and snorting with the other boys. The women of his mother's tribe had kept him in hand, slapped him down when he got above himself, and taught him to master his temper.

It was a pity, rather. He might have liked to be an idiot for once. Idiots were happy creatures, as far as he could see. When they were thwarted, they professed to misery, but even that had an air of good cheer about it.

In that frame of mind, he made his way through the crowded and bustling rooms. People kept stopping him with this trouble or that. Most he could send to Maryam, a few to his mother—though they blanched at that. The rest he put off till evening. It would make for an interrupted dinner, but that in turn would spare him the need to attend one of the court banquets.

For the moment he was as free as he could be in the heart of this prison. He considered hiding in the room that he had, bless the gods, to himself. But he happened on his way up to it, to collide with Iry on a stair. She was hurtling down it just as he began to go up.

He was a middling large man and she was a small woman, but her speed came near to knocking him flat. Only good fortune and battle-quickness kept him on his feet, albeit winded and counting his bruises. She clung to him lest she tumble past him down the stair.

Somehow and another it seemed most sensible to swing her up into his arms, light weight that she was, and carry her up the way he had been going. The passage it led to was long and very dim, with his own door at the end of it. Hers, he knew, was somewhat nearer. But he passed it, and she did not try to stop him.

He began to wonder if she had injured herself somehow. She was so very still. Her eyes were shut. He quickened his step, kicked open the door at the end of the passage, and nearly dropped her as she came to life and wriggled bonelessly out of his grasp.

She seemed quite unharmed, after all. She looked about at the room, which was smaller than he had grown accustomed to but still rather larger than a tent among the tribes. The bed was discreetly hidden behind a drapery, but she could not but know where it was. The rest at least was harmless enough: a gilded couch in the Egyptian fashion, a table and a pair of chairs, a chest for such of his clothing as the servants saw fit to keep close by him, and a quite incongruous graven image of an Egyptian king.

"King Dedumose," Iry said, tracing the characters of his name with her finger, then enclosing it within the carved cord of the cartouche. "He must have been king before you people came. There was a city here, you know. You found it and built it high, but it was ours before it was yours."

"That's the way of conquest," Khayan said.

She shot a glance at him. "Do you expect me to love you for it?"

"No," he said. She stalked round the room, frowning at the walls, which were hung with fine weavings. There were painted revels underneath, he knew, but she did not look to see them.

After a little while she halted by the window, leaned deep into the embrasure and peered out. Her voice sounded strange, coming from within: muffled, yet with an echo in it. "The king has a window, too, but on the other side, and much higher."

His brows rose. "You're high in favor, then."

"Or the Mare is." She slipped backwards out of the embrasure, with little care for the way her robe slipped up, baring her leg to the thigh. Khayan had carefully refrained from thinking of anything while he had her in his arms but that she might be hurt. But under such excessive provocation, his manly parts leaped to attention. And never mind that he had seen every part of her that there was to see.

She did not even notice the altered quality of his silence. She said, "You've been there, too."

He needed a moment to recall what she meant. That flash of thigh had driven everything else out of his mind. But it came back, if reluctantly. "I've been in the king's favor, yes. Only those he trusts implicitly are allowed into those chambers."

"He shouldn't trust me," she said in a low voice.

He bit his tongue before he asked why she would say that. He thought he knew. For all the lessons she had been given, the words she had learned, the rites and prayers, the arts of war and peace, she was still Egyptian. She could not even wear her robe as a woman of the people might. Either it was rucked up or slipped down at an immodest angle, or she was carrying it as if it had been a burden.

His mother, he knew, expected that Iry would become one of the Mare's children, with time and teaching and sufficient stern discipline. But Khayan, looking at her now, knew that this spirit would not yield. It would learn all it might, and do whatever it must. But it remained itself.

That was a dangerous thing. And yet he was not afraid. He said, "You'll be asked to show yourself to the court, and likely soon. Are you prepared for that?"

She tensed, perhaps. But she said calmly, "I suppose I am as ready as I may ever be."

"I won't be far from you," he said, moved to it by he knew not what. "If it becomes too much to bear, come to me. Will you remember that?"

She looked at him strangely, as well she might. But she only said, "I'll remember."

He nodded. "That's well. Yes, very well."

And there was another silence. There were often silences between them, but this, to Khayan at least, felt different. He was thinking, quite apart from any volition or sense, that there was a bed yonder, and she was remarkably close to it. Her body in the rumpled robe seemed as scant as a boy's, but he knew what sweetness was hidden beneath the embroidered linen.

She must not know. That was his first thought, and perhaps his only one. It was not fitting that he should presume to look on the Mare's servant in this manner.

Belatedly he recalled that he stood in the door; that he must move before she could leave. He stepped aside.

She did not escape as he had thought she might. She looked from him to the door, shrugged almost too slightly to see, and turned again to gaze out of the window. "I have no window," she said. "Are you hungry? Would you like to send for something?"

In fact Khayan would, but he paused to marvel at her. She had gall, he had known it. Still, she could surprise him.

He sent for food for both of them. She never left the window while they waited. "Look," she said. "More warhounds. I never saw them before I came here—and now I've seen whole packs of them."

She beckoned. He came more obediently than perhaps he should have. The embrasure was close quarters for two of them, as broad as his shoulders were. Her arm was warm against his. He knew exactly where each part of her was, and how close it was to him, even through his robe and hers.

It was an effort to look out, to see what she wanted him to see. A handful of men passed through the court, each with a brace of the great fierce dogs that were, to some of the lords, a fashion and an affectation.

"You don't have warhounds," Iry said, "nor did your father. Why is that?"

"My father used to say that every animal should be of use in peace as well as war. A dog once taught to hunt men is good for nothing else. He gets the taste of manflesh, you see, and craves it over after."

"That's what they say of lions," she said, "and crocodiles, and riverhorses. Manflesh is sweet. Too sweet."

"Mind you," said Khayan, "for some lords, that might not be an impediment. The greatest hunt of all, they say, is the hunting of men."

She shivered. Before he had thought, he circled her with his arm and drew her even closer. She did not stiffen or resist. For an instant, too quick almost to catch, she melted against him.

Then she was separate again, standing on her own. He let his arm fall. She said, "The men they hunt would be my kin. My people. Do I have that power? Can I forbid it?"

She had surprised him. He forgot, or never entirely remembered, all that she was. He had to think about what she had said. "I suppose you could disapprove of it," he said, "and let it be known. But the Mare's servant has always taken care not to interfere overmuch in men's fashions and follies."

"The hunting of innocents for their blood is a fashion?"

"Iry," said Khayan, "you don't know what they would ever do that, or that they would do more than think of it. You can't forbid what no one has been proved to do."

"But you said—" She stopped. "Khayan," she said.

Her tone had changed. He could not have said exactly how it was different, and yet it was. "Yes?" he said.

"Khayan," she said again. "Khayan. I name you. Three times I name you."

It was a magic. He shivered as she had not long before, but she did not move to comfort him.

Her eyes on him were dark and a little cold. Eyes like the night sky behind the stars. "You spoke my name," she said.

"I . . . meant no harm by it," he said. The words did not come easily. They came out of his pride, and his fear, too.

"Say it twice again," she said.

"But—"

"Say it."

"Iry," he said. "Iry." Such a little bit of a name, but so strong. So very much a part of her.

She nodded at each repetition, as if he had, in some way, satisfied some need of hers. "Three times you said it," she said. "And now we are equal. Your power over me is the same as my power over you."

"Is that a good thing?" he asked.

"Do you want it to be?"

"I want . . ." he said. He shook his head. "I don't know what I want. Is this an Egyptian rite? Should I be wary of it?"

"Would I tell you if you should?"

"It's a little late, now it's done."

"That is so," she said. "But because I am generous, I tell you that you may have something to fear—if you fear me. If you trust me, then you can trust that I would never hurt you."

"May I trust you?"

"I can't tell you that."

Of course she could not. His people had conquered hers. She would never forget or forgive.

"I am going to do it," he said. "I will trust you. Because you have my name, and I have yours. That is what it means, yes?"

"Yes," she said, and not too willingly, either. "That is what it means."

"Good," he said. And it was. How, even why, he did not know; but it was.

HORUS OF
GOLD

I

THE PLAIN WAS wide and barren, beaten down by the sun of Egypt. Horus' falcon wheeled against that bitter light. Beneath them both, a line of chariots waited. They were as still as men and horses could be. A hot dry wind plucked at the horses' plumes, and tugged at the kilts of the charioteers.

Kemni stood in the center of the line. The reins were quiet in his hands, but he could feel the horses' eagerness thrumming through them. On either side of him the line stretched away. It had seemed little enough in the muster, half a hundred chariots, a hundred men, and himself to lead them, but from the center it seemed a goodly number.

Away across the plain, a gleam of gold marked the king's pavilion. Servants had pitched it there before dawn, and the king established himself in it by full morning, borne up from the river in his golden chair. Kemni, who had camped out of sight of the king and his train, knew from messengers that it was an illustrious if small and secret gathering which had come to this place not far from Thebes. The king was there, and the chiefs of his ministers, and the priests of Amon and of Osiris.

Kemni met the glance of the charioteer on his right hand. Ariana favored him with a wide bright smile. She knew, too, and she did not care. She had announced that she would ride, and ride she had, with Iphikleia in the warrior's place. They were a striking sight among all the Egyptians, kilted like them, helmeted, and armed as if they had been fighting men. But there could be no doubt at all that these were women. Not in the slightest.

The falcon wheeled at the zenith, lazily, like the god's own blessing. Kemni drew a breath. Yes. Yes, it was time.

He slipped a fraction of rein. His stallions were ready, waiting for the signal. They leaped ahead. The rest of the line surged behind him, a long sweep backward on either side, like the track of geese in the sky, or a wake on the river. It was not the best way to fall on the enemy, but for vaunting before a king it was splendid.

In a pounding of hooves and a rattling of wheels and a chorus of shouts and whoops and war-cries, the first chariotry of Egypt swept upon the royal camp. Kemni drove not for the pavilion but for a point past it, bending in a swift arc, while the two wings of chariots behind him drew together. A doubled line of them circled the camp, till the outer ring bent again and swerved and reversed its direction. There were two rings still, but one galloped sunwise, the other against it, round and round in a dizzying spiral.

They halted as they had rehearsed, close in about the royal pavilion, with Kemni himself roaring to a stop full before it. He vaulted from the chariot and ran to kneel at his king's feet, breathless, stifling laughter.

Ahmose the king spoke above him in a voice warm with mirth of its own. "Marvelous," he said.

Kemni lifted his head. The king was smiling.

"Show me how to drive your chariot," Ahmose said.

There were gasps among the courtiers, some not as quickly suppressed as others. The king, the god, the son of Horus, was never to act on a whim, nor to depart from the carefully ordered round of his days.

But Ahmose had commanded. Kemni could only obey. He rose and bowed and followed the king to where his chariot waited. His stallions, whom Ariana herself had trained, were standing obedient, though their sides were heaving. It would be well to walk them out, and well indeed if the king was minded to learn how that was done.

The rest of his chariotry left its circle to follow. The king had a great escort; and beside him, calmly and without expectation of rebuke, the newest of his queens.

Kemni had not seen any women about the king. But there had been a curtain behind him, and Kemni was sure that Nefertari and her ladies sat behind that. Perhaps some of the gasps he had heard had been theirs.

There would be a price to pay for this. But for the moment Kemni allowed himself to indulge in the pleasure of it: the open plain, the company of his men and his queen and—yes—his lady Iphikleia, and his king beside him showing not too ill a hand with the reins. Ahmose seemed as lighthearted as a boy, even when he surrendered the lines and laughed and said, "I have no art in this. Show me how a master does it!"

"For that, my lord," Kemni said, "you should look yonder." He pointed with his chin toward Ariana, who had drawn somewhat ahead.

Ahmose sighed. "Ah," he said. "Yes. Oh, yes indeed."

"If you wish to learn this art, my lord," Kemni said, "you could have no better teacher than that."

"I do not doubt it," said Ahmose. "But if it were known that I was learning the way of the chariot under the tutelage of a Cretan woman, what would the rumormongers say?"

"Since all that we do here is a secret, sire, and since the woman is your lawful wedded queen, they're not likely to say anything at all."

"That is true," said Ahmose. "And after the war, when all is won, there need be no secrets."

Kemni should have held his tongue. But he said, "My lord, if you have a desire to ride to battle in a chariot, then you well may. Only find yourself a charioteer, and learn to fight from behind him. Later is soon enough to learn to ride and fight, both."

"It would be more kingly to do that," Ahmose mused. "Still, since that may not be done in the time we have, I have found myself a charioteer. Will you teach me to fight from behind you?"

Kemni had not meant to put himself forward at all. If anything, he had been thinking of Seti, who had a great gift for both horses and chariots. But if the king chose him for this thing, he would not refuse it. It was a great honor.

Great danger, too. The king would be the focus of any attack, its greatest prize and its most natural center. But Kemni was not afraid of danger. Not enough to turn away from it.

He nodded, bowing as low as he could with the reins in his hands and the horses fretting against the tensing of his fingers. "I would be glad to teach you, sire," he said.

+ +

The king, who had left Thebes under pretext of hunting lions in the wilderness, chose to linger a day or two on that plain above the river. Some of his escort did indeed go hunting lions, and gazelle and whatever other quarry presented itself to them. They ate well in camp that night, and the night after that, of gazelle, ducks and geese from along the river, and a fine catch of fish.

In those two days, while Kemni and his men gratified the curiosity of the king and his lords as to the way and manner of driving and fighting in chariots, the king's ladies never once showed themselves. They must have had to go out if only to relieve themselves, but if they did it, they managed to do it in secret. Kemni began to doubt that they were there at all. In the night, it was Ariana who kept the king company in his bed, and gladly, too, as far as Kemni could see.

But on the third morning, when the king showed still no inclination to return to his city, Kemni was on his way to fetch his stallions and his chariot when a servant stopped him. It was a man, a scribe, small and nondescript, with an unassuming manner; but Kemni had not seen him before. "My lord," the man said, "my lady would see you."

"Your lady Nefertari?"

"Yes, my lord," the scribe said.

Kemni let himself be led, with hammering heart and sweating palms, behind the curtain that divided the pavilion.

It was much the same on the other side, no darker or more confined. But as all the people without were men, all those within, except for a scribe or two and one who must be a priest, were women. Kemni had no difficulty recognizing the queen, even veiled and seated among several likewise veiled. Her carriage, the way she sat, the way the others sat about her, marked her as clearly as if she had been clothed all in gold.

He bowed to her, low and suitably reverent. With a gesture that in another woman he might have called reckless, she cast off her veil. Her face was exactly as he remembered it, beautiful beyond the measure of simple mortal women—though the Lady Nefertem, he could not help thinking, was more beautiful still. But she had not the air that this one did. She was a lady of good family. This was queen and goddess.

She looked down at him, at the awe he made no effort to hide, and perhaps she was pleased. Or perhaps she merely found his face pleasant to look at. Iphikleia had told him, much more than once, that he should learn to accept that, if he could not understand it.

It still made him blush to be stared at, and women always seemed to stare. He could not speak, either, without sinning greatly against propriety. He must wait for her, and she was in no haste to end his discomfort.

But at last she said, "Good morning, man of the Lower Kingdom."

"Good morning, majesty," he said after a pause to gather his wits.

"It will be better when we leave this place," she said, "and return to the city. But that is not a thing that I have power over."

"No, majesty?" Kemni asked—biting his tongue too late. It was not that he meant to be impertinent. But whatever his gift of tongues, he had no gift for the language of courtiers.

She knew that. Did she smile? If so, it was a faint and shadowy thing, but it colored her voice as she said, "I suppose I might, if I set myself to it. But some battles are not worth winning."

"He'll not linger much longer, lady," Kemni said. "He knows that. He is a dutiful king, though at the moment he may not seem so."

"I do know that," she said a little coldly, and he knew that he had been presumptuous. Again. But she did not seem angry. "He has made you his charioteer. Are you content with that?"

"I am the king's charioteer. Could I be less than content?"

"Some might be," she said. "It is an office without precedent. Our world is rich in precedent—rife with it. How are we to live when so much is new?"

"That is the fault of the Retenu," Kemni said. "We had never been invaded before, and never conquered. We have never had to win back a kingdom. But we will do it—with their own weapons, and ours, and our allies'. However we may."

"Surely," she said. There was a silence, which Kemni was not bold enough to break. Then she said, "Keep him safe."

That was not at all what he had expected. It left him speechless.

She smiled. Yes, she smiled. "Poor child. Are we ever what you expect?"

"I suppose not," he said after a pause. "Lady."

"Good," she said. "Now you begin to be wise."

Wisdom was desirable, but he thought perhaps he was too young to cultivate it. He began to say so, but she spoke before him. "I would like to speak with the Cretan woman. Will you fetch her for me?"

Kemni could well have pointed out that he was no slave, to be sent on errands, or that she had ample servants of her own who might have been given the duty. There was a reason, surely, why he had been set this task. He bowed and did as she bade.

✦ ✦

Ariana had a tent just outside of the king's encampment, within the circle of the charioteers. It was a warrior's tent and not a queen's, for she had come here as an advisor in war, not as a lady of the palace. Her only concession to rank was the pair of maids who kept the tent and saw to her person. They smiled brilliantly at Kemni when he came to the tent. It was their fondest hope that, just once, he would forsake his Cretan priestess for their welcoming arms.

Maybe someday he would. But not today. Ariana was within, they assured him, and he was free to enter.

She was preparing for the day: dressed, her hair in a plait, her face painted lightly, running through the roster of the chariot-wing with, of all people, Ahmose himself. Kemni stopped short and nearly fled, but they had both seen him. Ariana's smile was as brilliant as ever. "Kemni! We looked for you, but you were nowhere to be found. My lord wants to know, can we double the number of men, and have them ready to fight by harvest time?"

"This year or next?" Kemni asked: the first thing that came into his head.

"This year," Ahmose said.

Kemni frowned. "That's not long at all."

"But if each of those we've trained to fight were made a charioteer, and the new men were taught to fight—could we do it?" Ariana asked him.

"It would be difficult," Kemni said.

"But possible?"

"If the men were the best to be had, and willing to work day and night— yes. But have we enough horses? Enough chariots?"

Ariana nodded.

"Good," said Ahmose. "Very good indeed. Have them ready just before the harvest begins. We'll harvest men, and take back the Lower Kingdom."

Kemni bowed. Almost he had forgotten why he came here; and it was delicate, with the king sitting beside Ariana. But he did the best he could. "My lady, the Queen Nefertari . . ."

Ariana raised a brow. "Go," the king said. "I'm well enough here."

He had dismissed them both. Kemni doubted that he had been meant to follow Ariana back into Queen Nefertari's presence, but he chose to do it. It happened that, as they walked back through the camp, Iphikleia met them. She did not say anything, simply took a place in the procession. Kemni was glad of her; he suspected that Ariana was, also.

Ariana had not had audience with the Great Royal Wife since her wedding in Thebes. They had managed to avoid one another with great ease, since

Ariana had hidden herself away in the Bull of Re, and Nefertari had kept her place, as always, by the king's side.

Queen received queen with rather more ceremony than Kemni had had. There was a graceful dance, an exchange of pleasantries, compliments and finely framed words that signified little. Kemni was lulled almost into a drowse. He had to struggle to listen, to catch the subtle shift, the moment when Nefertari began to come to the point.

They were speaking of the Bull of Re, how Ariana had rebuilt part of the house and added greatly to the stables, and made the holding into a haven for the king's charioteers.

"That is a great work," Nefertari said. "What you do will be remembered."

"Memory is a great thing here," Ariana said. "Is it not? Remembering the name. Remembering the life."

Nefertari inclined her head.

"Where I was born," Ariana said, "the name matters little. I am the Ariana—that is my title and my office. What name I had when I was a child, I set aside, and it was forgotten. When I grow old, I shall take another name, another office. And when I die, I shall go to the breast of the earth my mother. Who I was, what I did, will matter nothing then. The earth will hold my bones. The air will bear my spirit."

"Then who you are, what you are—your self—it matters nothing?"

"What I do," said Ariana. "That matters. That I did it, and no one else— when the seasons have turned, and all who live now are gone to the earth, who will care that *I* did it?"

"Your name is your immortality," Nefertari said. "We must give you one, so that you may live forever."

"Whatever name you give me," Ariana said, "I remain what I am."

"Yes," said Nefertari.

Ariana smiled her quick smile. "If it will make you happy, you may do it. It's of little matter to me. I'll go on, and do what I do, and help you all to win this war."

"And why will you do that?"

"Because," said Ariana, "it's what I was born for. When we are young, you see, when first our women's courses come to us, we go into the womb of the Mother, into the deeps of the earth. There we dream what we will be; what we will do in this turn of the seasons. I dreamed sun hotter than I had ever known, and a falcon poised against it, and a river of life through the dry land. I dreamed Egypt. The falcon came to me and folded his wings about me and made me his own. And I knew that when it was time, I would come to Egypt."

"Then you are blessed of the gods," Nefertari said. She said it slowly, as if she must consider all sides of it, all meanings of the words.

"Do you do such things?" Ariana asked. "Do you lay yourself open to your gods, and ask that they show you what they intend for you?"

"No," said Nefertari. "Not . . . in such a way. The priests speak to the gods, and the king, who is a god, speaks for all of Egypt. For others, there are prayers and dreams, and for some, the blessings of priesthood, or service to the gods."

"That is very practical," Ariana said. "Do people ever wonder what it would be like to talk to the gods? And to be answered?"

"The gods are far above us," Nefertari said.

"Surely not above you," said Ariana. "Are you not queen and goddess?"

"I am that," said Nefertari.

"And do the gods speak to you?"

"Sometimes," Nefertari said slowly, "I dream dreams."

Kemni, mute in shadow, woke suddenly and fully.

"Do you now?" Ariana said. "Do you indeed? Are they dreams that others should know?"

"I never speak of them," Nefertari said. "But . . . they come to me often, and weigh on me sorely."

"Dreams of war?"

"Dreams of war," Nefertari said, "and dreams of peace. Dreams of long ago, and dreams of what is yet to come. In my dreams the gods walk. The priests say that they dwell beyond the horizon, but in my dreams the world is full of them."

"When you dream, you live in the gods' country," Ariana said. She sounded as close to awe as Kemni had ever heard her. "Oh, you are blessed! Are they beautiful? Are they terrible?"

"They are both," Nefertari said. "They speak to one another, but never to me. Once . . . I dreamed that one of them came down to a duller world, this world of ours, and saw a woman of such surpassing beauty that even he— even a god—stood mute in astonishment. He knew then what it was to worship a thing, mortal woman though she was. Then he took on the face and semblance of her husband, and went in to her, and set in her a spark of divine fire. And that spark grew, and swelled her belly, and was born in blood and pain as mortal children are born. And that child—that child had my face."

Ariana nodded as if she had expected just such an ending. "The gods come often to mortal women," she said.

"Not ours," said Nefertari. "They are not given to such excesses. That a god—that Amon—should do such a thing—"

"Then it is a very great thing."

"Or a very ill one."

"No," Ariana said. "It is never that. Does he speak? Does any of them? What is it they ask of you?"

"They never speak to me. But I see the Two Crowns in their hands, and my husband waiting, ready to be crowned."

"That is an omen," Ariana said.

"Or a great and wishful hope." Nefertari shook her head slightly. "If it should be of use, I will use it. But if not . . . not."

"Yet you told me," Ariana said.

"Your world is full of gods. To you, it would seem neither strange nor mad."

"I would understand it." Ariana nodded. "Is that all you ask of me? Understanding?"

"I ask nothing of you," said Nefertari, "but that you serve the king faithfully, and obey him in all that he bids you do."

"Of course I will do that," Ariana said.

"That is well," said Nefertari. "He is pleased with you. Most pleased."

"And you? Does that distress you?"

"No," said Nefertari. "You are not as other women. Nor am I. We are worthy of him."

"You do me great honor," Ariana said. She did not speak with humility; it was truth, that was all. "And yet you still don't entirely approve of me."

Nefertari's lips thinned a fraction. "Do you require my approval?"

"No," Ariana said. "But I should like to know why."

There was nothing to compel the Great Royal Wife to answer her, and yet she did so. It was courtesy. And perhaps, Kemni thought, it was a seal of alliance. "A queen in Egypt," Nefertari said, "does not ride in a chariot like a man, bare-breasted and bold-faced before the world. Are you dreaming that you will ride to battle? That you will fight?"

"No," Ariana said, but she said it slowly, as if with reluctance. "I know better than to think that I will be allowed to ride into battle. A king risks himself because he is the king. A queen is ill advised to do so. When the war comes, I will keep to the tents and the baggage like a proper woman. You need have no fear that I will run wild among the fighting men."

Nefertari nodded once. She was perhaps relieved. Or perhaps she had expected this answer, but had desired to hear it from Ariana's own mouth. "That will do," the queen said. "I am content."

And perhaps that was true. Ariana took it as a dismissal, bowed and withdrew quickly enough that if Nefertari had been inclined to call her back, it would have been difficult to do gracefully.

Kemni was not at all averse to making an escape. His head was aching, and his shoulders were tight. Nefertari frightened him. He did not know why. Ahmose was king and god, the living Horus, and yet Kemni was at ease in his presence. Immortal though his spirit might be, in this life he was a man like many another.

Nefertari, as she had said to Ariana, was not like other women. Maybe it was true. Maybe a god—Amon himself, as she had dreamed—had begotten her.

II

ETI THE CHARIOTEER was troubled. He was the most insouciant of men, with a light heart and a wry wit and eyes that had seen everything there was to see. But when he came to Kemni, not long after they had returned to the Bull of Re from that plain north of Thebes, he was unwontedly grim.

He found Kemni in the workroom of the charioteers' house, going over accounts and wishing himself very, very far away. Kemni had no objection to scribes' work, in fact read well and wrote not too badly, but accounts made his head ache. Seti's arrival was a godsend, a rescue from the long crabbed columns and the endless figures.

Seti, the fool, saw the scribe for the charioteers and the scribe for the Bull of Re, and retreated as rapidly as he had come. Kemni abandoned his captors to their heaps of dusty papyrus, and set off in pursuit of his second-in-command.

Seti had not gone far. He was slumped against a pillar in the court, glaring balefully at a cat who made her insouciant way across the sunlit space. Seti in his wonted self was very like the cat. It was strange to see him scowling.

"Very well," Kemni said from behind him. "Who is she, and why did she bid you begone?"

Seti spun. "I would die for the queen, but what does that matter to anyone? She doesn't know. And even if she did, would she care?"

"She would care," Kemni said. "She does. I'm sure of it."

Seti shrugged, sullen and glowering. "That's not my trouble."

"Then why are you glooming about so mightily?"

"It's nothing," Seti said. "I was a fool to trouble you. I'll go; I should be getting ready for the first of the new recruits. There's a boatful coming in a day or two."

Kemni knew that, and Seti knew he knew it. It was chatter, no more. "Tell me what's troublesome enough that you'll come looking for me. If it's not a woman, then what is it? Some worry over the recruits? They're picked men, the king assured me."

"I'm sure they are," Seti said. He looked as if he would like to bolt, but had thought better of it. He glanced about. "Not here. Let's go where there are no ears to hear."

That, in Seti's estimation, was as far away from the Bull of Re as possible. Kemni had been intending to ride among the herds in any case, to count them and to ponder whether there were enough horses, with sufficient training, to do what the king had asked of him. He took Seti with him as charioteer. As simply as that, and rather quickly, they escaped the confines of house and courts, and turned toward the hidden valley with its growing herds.

Kemni's bays were fresh and a little headstrong. They were not the gentle creatures he had first driven under Ariana's tutelage. These were younger beasts, stronger and more fiery, more inclined toward a good gallop than a sedate trot through and about the valley. He gave them rein at first, let them run down the straight and well-leveled road, until, near the valley's entrance, it narrowed and grew winding and steep. They were not so unwilling to be prudent then, though they tossed their heads and snorted with suitable ferocity.

In among the herds at last, with the team settled to its work, after a fashion, Kemni could not help remembering the great herds at the Sun Ascendant, and the Mare and her servant, and the Retenu lord and his kin who had found themselves afflicted with an Egyptian priestess-queen. Iry did well, Kemni hoped; and Sadana, that wild creature with her bold face and her shy heart.

He had almost forgotten what had brought him here, between memory and reckoning the count of the horses that Ariana and the king had gathered. He would have given gold to have the herds that belonged to the lord Khayan, the mares and foals as well as the teams of war-stallions. But those were far away and in another kingdom. What he had for his use was here.

It was not an ill gathering of horses, for a beginning. He said as much to Seti.

"It will do," Seti said. He was not pressing to be heard. Maybe he hoped that Kemni would not ask him why he had asked that Kemni come here.

But Kemni was not one to let go a thought for long, once it had taken hold. "Tell me," he said.

Seti sighed. "It may be nothing. Really, my lord."

"And yet it eats at you," Kemni said. And again: "Tell me."

At last and with an air of casting it all at Kemni's feet, Seti said, "When we went to show the king what we had done, while you were occupied with the king and the queens, I had occasion to go wandering about. I'm a great idler, you know. Everyone says so." He said that with a flicker of his usual wit.

"I happened, as I idled here and sauntered there, to come across several of the king's men. They were keeping close by one another, sharing a jar of beer and waiting for the king to have need of them. They weren't happy about that: they were very lofty personages, to be kept waiting about like servants.

"They were unhappy about a great deal more than that. There are factions in the court, it seems, who don't approve of the king's war. They think that he should stay at home, tend to the Upper Kingdom, and do nothing to provoke the foreign kings' anger. We'll be destroyed, they said. We've survived so long by the blessing of the gods, but if the Retenu are reminded too forcibly of our existence, they'll sweep up the river and conquer the whole of Egypt."

"Cowards' counsel," Kemni said.

"Craven," Seti agreed. "But in certain things they're terribly bold. They were talking, when I happened by, of finding ways to stop the war. Those who have his ear were to bend it, of course, but others said that that wouldn't be enough; that something more should be done. They were talking of sending messengers to the Lower Kingdom, and warning the Retenu of the war that's been prepared against them."

"But won't that force the very thing they're most afraid of, and bring the enemy down on us?"

"They thought not. They said that an early warning would let the Retenu stop the invasion at the start, and keep them from pressing it backward into its own country."

"That's ridiculous," Kemni said. "And Crete—did they talk about Crete?"

"Oh, yes. And the horses, too. Everything."

Kemni drove for a while in silence, circling the outer limit of the valley. The bays had quieted considerably; were content to trot smoothly out. There was a great pleasure, even with such thoughts as clamored at him, in the lightness of their mouths through the reins, and the roll of wheels beneath him, and the wind in his face.

But the things that roiled in his belly would not long be ignored. He said to Seti, "They're going to betray the king? How can they do that?"

"For his own good, they said. To save his life and the freedom of the Upper Kingdom. To prevent us all from being enslaved."

Kemni shook his head hard enough to dizzy him briefly. "They can't believe that. One of them, or more, must be a traitor—must be taking Retenu pay."

"That's possible," Seti said. "One or two seemed to say the most, but they might simply have been the most inclined to talk. Except that one . . ."

He trailed off. Kemni waited, but he did not go on. "Except that one . . . ?" Kemni asked.

Seti shivered behind him. "It may have been nothing. I wasn't there to hear the beginning, and I certainly wasn't privy to the whole of their conspiracy. If that is what it was."

"You know it was."

"I don't want it to be." Seti's voice snapped out. "There was one who seemed to be leading them. He argued most strongly against the war. Then someone—someone said, 'What if the king can't be dissuaded? What do we do then?' And he said, 'Then maybe the Upper Kingdom has need of a new king.' "

"He can't have said that," Kemni said before he thought. "The king is a god. No one can kill him. It would be sacrilege."

"Suppose that someone had a dream," Seti said. "That he dreamed a god spoke to him, and told him that he, and not the living Horus, was meant to be king."

"I would say that his dream lied," Kemni said. In spite of himself he remembered what Nefertari had said to Ariana, how she dreamed of gods, and a god, maybe, had been her father. That was not a lie. He had been there. He had heard her. She had spoken from the heart.

What if this man had done the same? No; it was unthinkable. "Who was it? Was it one of the lords of the nomes? The chancellor? A priest?"

"A prince." Seti said it as if from a core of pain.

There had been several of the princes in the king's camp. Gebu, of course; he was a charioteer still, and not a bad one, either. One or two of his brothers of the same mother, and a number of sons of concubines, and the royal princes, the sons of Nefertari, and Amonhotep the heir foremost. A dozen, perhaps. Maybe more. And one of them, or more, contemplated betraying his own father.

Small wonder that Seti was so troubled. Kemni reined in the horses, wound reins round the post, and turned to face his second. This was a man whom he had thought he knew; not from childhood, not even from the wars, but since he began this venture with horses. They were comrades in arms, not yet battle-brothers, but that time would come—if this conspiracy of princes did not stop it.

"We should go to Gebu," Kemni said. "These are his brothers. He should know what they've been plotting."

Seti's face went still. "No. You don't want to go to Gebu."

"But who better? I have no power to stop them, but Gebu—"

"Gebu led them!"

Kemni stopped with words half-formed on his tongue. "What? I don't understand—"

"Of course you understand!" Seti snapped. "You don't want to, but you do. Gebu was playing ringleader."

"No," said Kemni. "You misheard him. Or heard someone else. Some of his brothers sound remarkably like him."

"It was Gebu," Seti said stubbornly.

But Kemni was equally stubborn. "Gebu could not do such a thing. He's one of us—he's a charioteer. He's my battle-brother. I have no better friend in the world. Of all the princes, he is the most honorable, and the least inclined toward intrigue. How can you accuse him of such a thing?"

Seti's lips set tight. "I heard what I heard. Maybe he's all of that. But if he's afraid, and if he wants to be king—he might bend to others' persuasion."

Kemni did not want that to make sense. And yet, in a terrible way, it did.

He turned from Seti, closed himself away, though they were close together in the chariot, and set the horses in motion once more. They walked sedately forward, but the pause had restored them. In a moment they were trotting, and then cantering; and then, with a toss of the head, they had surged into a gallop.

And Kemni let them. He made no effort to slow them, only to keep to the smoother ground, and to veer somewhat away from the herds. Some of those caught the stallions' urgency and swirled into motion, running with them round the broad sun-parched valley.

The wind was burning hot, the wind of Upper Egypt that blew like the blast from a furnace. It could scour flesh from bones, if it chose. But it could not scour thoughts from a man's mind, not such thoughts as these.

Gebu. No, not Gebu. If truly there was a conspiracy of princes, Gebu was the last man to indulge in it. He was a simple man, as princes went. He was known for his loyalty to his friends and his refusal to play the game of courts. Most of the fiercer players discounted him because of that, reckoned that he had little desire to be anything but what he was: royal and princely but, as the son of a minor wife, unlikely to come close to the throne.

And he was content with that. Kemni would have sworn it before the gods. What he had done in coming to the Bull of Re, in joining the ranks of charioteers, was a gift to his battle-brother. He had said so, more than once. He was not a great horseman, but he had a gift for fighting from a chariot. With one of the more skilled men for charioteer, he was formidable in the practice battles.

He could not be plotting to stop this war, and worse, to overthrow the king and set himself on the throne. Not Gebu of all the princes. Gebu wanted the war. He wanted his father to be lord of the Two Lands, king of Upper and Lower Egypt, Great House of a reunited people. That was as much honor as he needed, and as much ambition as he had.

Kemni convinced himself, in that long wild gallop, that Seti had, somehow, misheard, or misunderstood. There was no other way to explain it. Unless Seti himself conspired against them all, to weaken them with lies—but that too was inconceivable. Seti had proved to be a strong second-in-command. He had offered his place to Gebu, in fact, but Gebu had refused it. A prince could be a charioteer, but he could be second to no one but the king himself.

Seti did not say anything at all even when the horses tired at last and slowed to a canter and then to a jarring trot, and finally to a hard-blowing walk. Kemni had nothing to say to him. They returned slowly to the Bull of Re, rubbed down and stabled the horses together, but before Kemni was done, Seti had vanished.

Kemni had further duties, exercises mounted and afoot, and at day's end, as the light grew long and heat bore down like great and heavy hand, a mock battle between two of the chariot-wings. He commanded one. Gebu commanded the other.

There was nothing furtive in the prince's command of his men, nothing cowardly. He kept to the fore, and fought splendidly with his blunted sword, holding off the full force of Kemni's charge. Such a man would never shrink from war, nor would he creep and skulk and slink along the traitor's way.

Gebu's wing won that battle, with great and whooping glee. Kemni's own promised a terrible revenge, but later. This evening, in the swift fall of dark and sudden cool of desert night, they gathered in the charioteers' hall for an uproarious feast.

Gebu sat beside Kemni, and Kemni, as the defeated captain, had to serve as his cupbearer. Gebu was warm with wine and victory, and expansive, giving gifts of gold and gems to those of his wing who had fought most well. If he labored under a burden of guilt, he showed no sign of it.

No; Gebu was not a traitor. Kemni willed himself to ease, to forget what he had heard. Seti had not been lying, not as he understood it, but he had not seen the truth, either. He could not have.

····················   **III**   ····················

"TELL ME WHAT troubles you," Iphikleia said.

Kemni had not thought that he was troubled at all. He was tired. It was a great work, to receive the king's recruits, to bring them into the ranks of the charioteers, to see that they had proper training and swift training, but not so swift that they broke and fled. He rose before dawn and fell into his bed long after dusk. He had no time to brood over anything.

But Iphikleia had caught him as he stumbled in somewhat earlier than usual, having managed to bed down the latest boatload of recruits with no more than half a dozen greater mishaps or half a hundred lesser ones. He had nothing on his mind but sleep; though her presence gave his body somewhat else to think of.

She lay beside him without inviting him to do more, propped on her elbow and regarding him steadily. Her face was as drawn as his must be, hollow with exhaustion, but her eyes were clear. "You're troubled," she said. "You've been half among us for days."

"I've been doing the king's duty for days," Kemni said a little crossly.

"More than that," said Iphikleia.

He was not going to tell her. There was nothing to tell. But his tongue had a mind of its own. It told her what Seti had told him, every word of it, as preposterous as it was, and as perfectly and manifestly false.

She listened in silence, without change of expression: no surprise, no horror. When he had finished, she did not speak at once, but narrowed her eyes a little, as if deep in thought.

He had nearly slid into sleep when she said, "No wonder you look as if something with sharp teeth has been gnawing your liver."

He started awake. "It's not true. Nothing he has ever done or said has betrayed a sign of it."

"And yet it eats at you."

"It *can't* be true."

"Have you dreamed anything?"

He shook his head hard. "Nothing. Not one thing."

"Ah," she said, and was silent for a little while. Then: "You could ask him," she said.

He stiffened. "Are you mad?"

"You would know if he lied," she said, "or if he told the truth."

"I can't do that," Kemni said. "He would be well justified in killing me for accusing him of such a thing."

"Still," said Iphikleia, "if he loves you as a brother, he'll forgive you."

"No," said Kemni. "He's guilty of nothing except, maybe, keeping ill company. I don't doubt that a good number of the lords and princes would be pleased to stop the war, or that some of them might even be conspiring with the Retenu. But not Gebu."

"Whether he is or he is not," Iphikleia said, "if there is a conspiracy at all, the king should know of it."

Kemni lay very still. If he moved, he would cry aloud. Fool and worse fool. Of course she had the right of it. And he, blind to everything but Gebu's innocence, had never thought of the danger—of what it all signified.

"You should tell Ariana," Iphikleia said. "She'll get word to the king."

"Yes," Kemni said. "Yes. In the morning, before I do anything else. I'll tell her."

"Good," Iphikleia said.

✦ ✦

He slept well, better than he had in a long while. But out of sleep he emerged into a dream, a harsh and vivid light like the light of noon in the Red Land. There was desert all about him, stark stone, bare sand, and at great intervals, a brown and shriveled thing that once had been green.

It was not the plain on which they had shown the king their chariotry, but a dream-image of it. There were the stark hills, the level land, the descent to the river. And there was the camp, both smaller and larger than in life, with the king's pavilion gleaming like a sun come to earth.

Kemni knew in his bones where the dream would take him—and he did not want to go. But the dream, or the gods, ruled him. He flew like a falcon against the blue heaven, spiraling down and down, till at last he came to earth within the king's camp.

He must be standing where Seti had stood, concealed by the corner of a tent, able, if he peered, to see the circle of men passing the winejar round, and able to hear them clearly. They were oblivious to him—fools, with such things as they were saying, such enormities as they professed to contemplate.

He did not want to look. He did not want to see. But it was laid on him. When he resisted, he was again a falcon, or perhaps his own *ba*-spirit, hovering in the air above the heads of the gathering.

There were perhaps a dozen of them. He knew them all, some—those who were princes—rather well; others by name or face. They were not the greatest lords of the court, nor the highest of the princes. They were sons of lesser wives, followers of the great ones, even a man whom Kemni had seen close by the chancellor of the Upper Kingdom. No one of them held great power, but together they could muster a remarkable amount of influence.

The leader, the one they all looked to, the one whose words began and ended the circle, was hidden in a darkness of dream. But Kemni was not to be given mercy. He knew the voice. He knew the face when it was brought before him in that bitter light.

He knew the lines of it, the set of the brows, the long nose, the square chin; the body stocky for an Egyptian's, though slender enough if he had been Retenu. But the expression, the way in which he said the words, Kemni had not seen before. This was a stranger wearing Gebu's face, a man whose spirit had gone hard with old anger and old fear. When he spoke of the throne, his hands twitched, fingers opening, closing, as if to clasp the crook and flail of the Great House, the Pharaoh.

"King of the Upper Kingdom is half a king, some would say," he said, "but my father looks to be king of nothing, if he forces the Retenu into a war. They'll kill him and set up a vassal king, one of their own—give him a name of our people, a royal seal, all the trappings of the office, but he will still and always be Retenu."

"Unless one of us can win them over," said the chancellor's servant. "There is that. Let the king lose the war, or let us lose it for him. Put us all out of our misery. They might even be glad of a vassal who comes of the old king's blood. The people will accept him, and he'll owe them too much to betray them."

"Maybe," Gebu said. "I would rather not be a vassal king. King unchallenged of a kingdom that, though halved, is extraordinarily rich—I would prefer that. Let us stop the war, then. Let us do whatever we must do."

"Even to . . . remove the king?" the chancellor's servant asked with a twist of distaste. But no fear; no horror. He had thought the unthinkable, and found it less than difficult.

Gebu, too. Gebu nodded, with no visible reluctance. "Whatever we must do. Send a messenger to the Retenu. Then let us see what we will see."

They all nodded, every one, as conspirators must. None shrank from it, or protested it. It was decided. It was done. The king was betrayed. The war . . .

Maybe not yet. Kemni knew how difficult it could be to pass undetected into the Lower Kingdom. These traitors would not use Cretan ships—that way was not open to them. How, then? A fisherman, again? Another ruse?

The dream swirled and shifted about him. He had soared up again, far into the sky, till the plain was shrunk to nothing below him, and the river wound serpent-supple through the narrow ribbon of the Black Land. He hovered at the zenith of heaven. And as a god might, as Horus of the noonday sun, he saw all below both remote and close, high above it and full within it. There was the north of the Upper Kingdom, the Black Land narrow still, but ahead of it, the broad green branches of the Delta, and the Red Land held far at bay. The Lower Kingdom was a different world, a world of wet and greenery, tangled skeins of river, great beds of reeds, grasses, fields planted thick with barley and wheat, onions, lettuces, green things both pungent and savory.

But he had wandered far afield. His flight brought him circling back to the harsher land south of the great surging sprawl of Memphis and the loom of the old tombs. There were boats in the river, many of them, and caravans on the roads, and an endless train of people on foot.

The eyes that he had been given, the eyes of a god, fixed on one of all the multitudes below. One man, nondescript, trudging beneath a laborer's burden. But inside the bundle, wrapped deep in noisome rags, was gold: a collar of honor, that was his passage to the conquerors' king. The symbols graven on it, shaping words of praise, were a message also, subtle perhaps beyond the wits of a foreigner, but the messenger would be instructed, surely, to make them clear to him.

The messenger's progress was slow, as it must be. He was some considerable distance still from Memphis, and far yet from Avaris. He was—

By all the gods. He was close by the Bull of Re, on the stretch of road no more than a day's journey south of it.

The gods had given a gift. If it was true. If it was not his own wishing shaping the dream.

But this was a true dream. The light in it, the inevitability of it, convinced him of that.

He could wake. He must wake. He must take chariot and ride. He must find that single man among all the men on the roads.

He clawed his way out of sleep into the dark of deep night. Iphikleia slept beside him in a tangle of hair. Her arm lay heavy across him. He slipped from beneath it, taking great care not to disturb her.

She started awake in spite of him, glowering as she always did on first waking, but sharply and fiercely alert. "You dreamed," she said.

Kemni glared back at her. "You, too?"

She shook her head. "But I can feel it in you. The air is full of gods' voices."

"Ill spirits walk the night," he said.

"Surely. But these are gods." She rose, raking hair out of her face. "Where are we going?"

"You are staying here," he said. "I am going out."

"We are going out," she said. She rummaged in the clothing-chest. Mostly it was his, but she had left a garment or two there, by chance or design. One was the tunic she wore for riding in her chariot, and the fillet with which she bound her hair.

She was dressed before he was, though he had less to put on—a kilt only, and sandals. Almost he forbore to put on his eyepaint, but habit was strong, and some vestige of sense. As dark as it was now, come morning the sun's glare would be fierce. So too its heat, though the chill, now, made him shiver even in that closet of a room.

Iphikleia dropped his Cretan mantle about his shoulders and said, "I'll fetch bread and beer. You go harness the horses."

He could do worse than to obey her. The stable was dark, but he had brought a lamp, which though dim was enough to see his way to his stallions' stalls. Falcon was awake and alert, Lion curled in sleep, but he roused as his brother trod softly out to be fed a bit of fodder while he was brushed and harnessed. Falcon went on with his breakfast, calmly, while Lion underwent his own toilet.

When both were ready, Kemni led them out to the court of the chariots. The chariot they usually drew was heavy, a war-chariot; but Kemni sought out Ariana's, which was lighter and therefore faster. Lion and Falcon snorted and champed the bits at the feel of a different chariot behind them, tugging at the reins, eager to run.

Just as Kemni knew that he could hold them in no longer—and was ready to let them go, so that when he came back he would protest to Iphikleia that he had tried, he had really tried, to wait for her—she appeared with two bundles wrapped each in a cloth. One was smaller, round and soft. The other was long and narrow and hard. It looked like a bow in a case, or two, and a quiver of arrows; and possibly a sword.

They were weapons, indeed: they clattered to the floor of the chariot. The other must be the bread she had promised, and she carried a jar, which she laid carefully between her feet. "I had to wait for the bread," she said.

It was warm against Kemni's foot, even wrapped in its cloth. He gave the horses their heads, and let them find their own way out of the court. The outer gate gave them pause, but the sleepy guard would not defy Iphikleia or his own commander. He opened the gate for them.

It boomed shut behind them. The road stretched ahead in the grey dawn. Kemni let Lion and Falcon find their own pace, which was steady enough once they had run out the excitement of the lighter chariot and the strange hour and his own thrumming urgency.

Iphikleia was silent behind him, leaning lightly against him, which she need not have done, but he was glad of it. The air was cold in this hour before sunrise, blowing fresh in his face. If his dream was true, and he was not pursuing the track of a shadow, he was some distance yet from the princes' messenger. The man would have found a place to hide and sleep; when the sun rose, he would rise with it and go on.

And if there was no messenger, if Kemni had come on a fool's errand, then he would be glad. Need all his dreams, after all, be true? Might he not dream a mere dream, but as vivid as life?

He did not turn back for that thought, nor for any of those that galloped on its heels. There was truth to be found on this journey, whether his own or Seti's or another altogether.

The road bore him through villages still asleep, but some in them had risen and set to baking the day's bread. The warm scent of it followed him. The nearer morning he came, the stronger the scent grew, till it mingled with the sharper one of beer. Children were up by then, running about in the half-light, stopping to gape at the chariot as it passed.

It dawned on him, much too late, that these people had seen neither horses nor chariots. All that passed to the Bull of Re had come through the Red Land, or hidden in boats on the river. No charioteer had ridden openly through the villages as Kemni in his madness was doing.

But if he turned aside, if he sought the desert, he might not come to his destination in time. He had to risk the stares and murmurs, and hope that the children's tale would be disregarded as whim or fancy.

He was close now. So too the sunrise. But not, thank the gods, any town or village. In his dream the messenger had taken shelter in the ruin of a house— a farm abandoned long ago, when the river's flooding shifted and left it in a corner of the Red Land without the yearly renewal of black earth that made a farm rich.

The lie of the land was as the dream had shown him. He could see where the river had shifted, eating into the farther bank, carving a steep descent, but here the Red Land had crept in, a field of sand and stones where must once have been wheat and barley. The ruin stood far back in it, too far to run water, though there were remnants of old channels eaten away by the wind of years.

A man on foot, with a need to hide, could walk there easily enough, and conceal himself through the night. The walls of mudbrick still stood, though the roof had tumbled in.

Kemni left the horses near the river, dropped the stone weight like an anchor that would keep them from wandering with the chariot, and unwrapped Iphikleia's larger bundle. There were two bows and a sword, as he had suspected, and a quiver of arrows. She took a bow and the quiver, leaving him the rest. Without a word, soft on her feet as a hunter should be, she made her way toward the ruin.

Kemni followed somewhat belatedly but with equal softness. The sun was close now. The eastern horizon had flooded with light. A wise messenger would have left long since, but this one was weary and perhaps ill. He had been coughing in the dream, as he trudged bent under his burden.

The ruin was silent, not even a bird to rouse it to life. But as Kemni drew near, he heard a sound like the clatter of a stone falling—or the hard dry cough that someone had once, in Kemni's hearing, called the song of Egypt. This was no simple fever. This was the lung-rot, the cough that killed.

But not quickly, not, sometimes, for years. Foolish to send a man so ill on such a journey, but then, if he had hopes of surviving till his message was delivered, he could die thereafter and so keep his secret. It was an odd, cruel choice of messenger, but not altogether improbable.

There was more to the ruin than Kemni had thought. It had been less a peasant's farmstead than a small holding. It must have belonged to a man of substance in the region, a man wealthy enough to own a house with half a dozen rooms and a small courtyard, and an orchard now parched and dead, and a byre and granary fallen in upon itself but the lines of it still clear to see. There were touches of beauty in it: a painting on a wall of cattle and a herdsman, a lotus pillar holding up the fallen lintel of a door.

Just as the sun climbed above the horizon, Iphikleia slipped into the darkness of the house. Kemni was hard on her heels.

It was very dark within, but enough light slipped through the doorway that Kemni's eyes, after a brief struggle, came slowly into focus. The room was empty. So too the one beyond that. Past that was the court, pale gold with morning light, and in it, again, nothing.

But as Kemni raised his foot to cross the court and search in the rooms beyond, the sharp bark of a cough brought him about.

What he had taken for a corner of deep shadow was a man. He might have hoped to remain in concealment, but his sickness had betrayed him.

Kemni altered his step to move toward the man. He surged up and bolted.

But Iphikleia was there, braced to catch him. She was not as strong as a man, but he was wasted with illness. She held him long enough for Kemni to reach them both, to seize him and haul him away from her—and none too soon. A knife gleamed in his hand, stabbing at Kemni. Kemni struck the hand aside, caught the wrist and wrenched hard. The man gasped. Kemni swung him about and against the wall. He crumpled down it in a renewed spate of coughing.

"I," said Kemni, "would have sent a man in better health."

He dragged the messenger out into the court, the better to see his face. It was the one he had seen in the dream, thin and nondescript, the face of any man in Egypt. He blinked in the light, peering up at Kemni. "Sir," he said. "I regret—you woke me—I didn't mean—"

Kemni frowned. "You know me?"

The man nodded. As his eyes cleared, he stood a little straighter, and eased visibly. "Yes, sir, my lord. He sent you, didn't he? He said someone would come from the holding. Have you brought the things that I was to carry?"

Kemni's mind had begun to race. That the messenger should pass this way—yes, he would have had to pass by the Bull of Re, though not near, not except by design. But that meant . . .

Not now. He must not tangle himself in denials. The messenger had mistaken him for a messenger himself. "Yes," Kemni said, "I was sent." And never mind by whom. "I've nothing with me, but they're at the holding. I'll bring you back with me."

He held his breath. But the messenger did not seem suspicious. He nodded. Kemni kept a grip on him as he retrieved the bundle that he had carried so far, and left the house and went back down to the chariot. Iphikleia followed in silence. She had her bow strung, an arrow in her hand. Her face was white and set.

Kemni dared not speak to her lest he betray them. The messenger seemed to have judged her harmless, though he eyed her a little oddly. As indeed he might, if he thought Kemni one of the circle of traitors.

The chariot, ample for two riders, held three only with difficulty—and with the messenger's bundle, it was impossible. Iphikleia, still silent, sprang calmly onto Falcon's back. He shied a little and rolled an eye back at her, but she stroked and murmured to him until he quieted.

"So it is true," the messenger said. "There are women who ride on the backs of horses."

"And carry weapons," Kemni said, "and fight like men. Yes."

"Marvelous," said the messenger. His eyes on Iphikleia were hungry, the eyes of a man who had not had a woman in much too long.

Kemni would have loved to strike those eyes out of his head, but he was too valuable alive and unmaimed. When the chariot started forward, he clutched wildly at the sides, just as Kemni had done the first time. With somewhat of evil intent, he let the restive horses choose a fast pace, not back the way he had come, but round and into the Red Land as he should have done when he began. The messenger asked no questions. He was too busy holding on, and, from the look of him, refraining from shrieking aloud with terror.

This was a mad thing that Kemni did, but all of it was mad. Iphikleia riding Falcon ahead of him, perched amid the traces. The messenger in his arms, because it was safer there than behind him and able to leap out. The thing he did in letting the man believe he was—yes, that he was Gebu's servant, and part of the conspiracy.

He went back to the Bull of Re, for lack of better inspiration. He did not know what he would do when he came there. The way he took led to the valley in which the horses were hidden, passing out of sight of the holding, and indeed of any habitation.

It was well on in morning now, and fiery hot. The messenger had gone limp. Asleep, Kemni hoped, and not unconscious or dead.

There were men among the horses: Seti and some from his wing, capturing colts to be broken to harness. And, with them, Ariana in a tunic with her hair bound up, just as Iphikleia's was.

The gods had ordained this. Kemni was sure of it. He rode straight through the herds out of the Red Land, having descended the steep narrow cleft with little memory of how he had done it, and halted before Ariana. "I brought you a gift," he said. And flung the messenger out of the chariot at her feet.

Seti, bless his quick wits, was on the man before he could come to his senses and bolt, binding his hands with a rope meant for one of the horses, and holding him fast.

And that was well, because Ariana was not looking at him at all. Iphikleia had slid from Falcon's back and fallen lifeless to the ground. Much, much too late, Kemni saw the dark stain on her tunic, the blood that had flowed and then dried, but had begun to flow again, seeping through the leather.

She had said no word. Not one. Kemni had thought that he had deflected the knife; but he had been too slow.

He leaped toward her, but there were others there before him, Ariana foremost. They would not let him through. "Fetch Imhotep," Ariana said. Her voice sounded remote and very cold.

Imhotep, whose name was in fact something else altogether, was the king's best gift, in Ariana's estimation: a physician trained in the high arts, and reckoned worthy to serve the king himself. He was a personage of no little consequence; and for him to be fetched, rather than for the fallen to be fetched to him, did not bode well at all.

Indeed, Seti protested. "Won't it be faster if we take her to him?"

"She's ridden enough," Ariana said. "You—you—you. These horses are exhausted. Set them loose and harness another pair. Now! Quickly!"

Lion and Falcon were let loose to drop and roll and make their way eagerly toward water. A different team, a pair of chestnuts whom Kemni vaguely recognized, were harnessed in their place. Then one of the men sprang into the chariot and drove them off at a gallop.

Silence fell. Seti stood guard still over the captive, who was alive and awake—Kemni saw his eye roll white. Kemni bent down to him. "If she dies," he said, "I will hang you from the wall with spikes."

The man did not speak. Kemni would have smitten him silly if he had tried.

At last they would let Kemni near Iphikleia. She was not dead. He saw her breast rise and fall. He dropped on his knees beside her. "I did this," he said. "I did this to her."

"Stop that," Ariana said, so like Iphikleia that Kemni gasped. "Now. Tell me what this is."

There was no brief way to tell her. But they had time. It would be some little while before Ay came back with the physician. He supposed he should be careful, should not speak where so many could hear, but he could not make himself care. Either they could be trusted or they could not. If they could not, he would kill them.

"This is a messenger," he said, "from a gathering of princes who have in mind to stop the war. We caught him upriver from here, and surprised him. He had a knife."

"I can see that," Ariana said. "How did you know where to find him?"

"The gods told me," Kemni said. In front of so many people he said it. "I dreamed that he was coming, that he was on his way to the Lower Kingdom with messages and tokens for the king there. The bundle beside him—there is gold in it. Open it and see."

Seti was already moving to do it, cutting the cords that bound it, folding back the reeking rags that Kemni had seen and smelled in the dream, freeing a flame of gold.

It was gold of honor, yes; a massive plated collar graven with symbols, enameled in red and green and blue. Only a prince could have ordered such a thing. Even a lord had no such resources, or the power to command goldsmith or scribe. The smith might have been allowed to live, but Kemni could not imagine that the scribe had.

"There are other things," Kemni said in a voice that sounded, to his own ears, very far away. "He was coming to the Bull of Re, to fetch them."

"Here?" Ariana frowned in puzzlement. "Why would they be here?"

"Because," Seti said—daring greatly, and he should pay for it, save that he had spared Kemni the need—"the master of the conspiracy is here."

"Gebu," Ariana said. She said it without hesitation, and without surprise.

Seti did not seem astonished that she knew. He, like the rest of the men, was in awe of her, and madly in love. If she had sprouted wings and soared up to heaven, he would have reckoned it no more than proper. "Shall I fetch him, lady?" he asked.

"No," she said. She went on kneeling beside Iphikleia, stroking the pale brow. "No. Wait."

Seti opened his mouth as if to protest, but he clearly thought better of it.

Ariana smiled at him, casting him into confusion. "Good," she said as if he had done something worth her praise. "Good."

There was nothing to do then but wait, and pray. One of the men had found Kemni's Cretan mantle among the baggage cast out of the chariot, and fashioned a canopy propped on spears. It offered a little shade, enough to keep the sun from Iphikleia's face.

She seemed unaware of it. She was deathly pale, breathing shallowly. Kemni would not, could not think of where the wound was, how it had pierced her belly. That was the worst of wounds, save only a stroke to the heart.

The gods must protect her. They had brought her to this place. They could not take her. Not so soon, or for so little cause.

I
T SEEMED A very long time before Ay returned in the chariot, with yet another fresh team, and Imhotep the physician clinging grimly behind him. Imhotep was not what one might expect of so august a personage. He was young, not greatly older than Kemni, with a long, pleasant face and a crooked smile, with which he was rather generous.

There was no sign of it now. Even before the chariot had rolled to a halt, he had sprung from it, stumbling but keeping his balance, and waving away the hands that reached to support him. He had no eyes for anything but the figure lying on the ground, supported in Ariana's lap. Then one could see the gift that the gods had given him, the utter and perfect concentration of all his souls, his body and his mind, in the art of healing.

He knelt beside her, and paused for a moment, taking in what there was to see. Kemni wanted to howl at him. But he would not be hurried. Blood had dried and bound tunic to undertunic, and undertunic to flesh. With exquisite care he worked them all free of one another.

There had been a terrible lot of blood. The wound itself was narrow, and had gone in low in the belly. Imhotep frowned at that, and murmured to himself, words that Kemni could not catch. They were an incantation, perhaps, or a prayer to the gods.

The wound bled still, a slow seep of blood. Iphikleia's skin was the color of milk, with a grey cast beneath. Her lips were blue.

Ay the charioteer had brought from the chariot the box that went with Imhotep wherever he was, his box of medicaments. Imhotep opened it without looking at it, reached in with a sure hand, and brought out a selection of vials, rolled bandages, and an oddment or two for which Kemni could see no purpose. He cleansed the wound carefully, filled it with a grey powder from one of the vials, and wrapped it close in the bandage. He held another vial to her lips and coaxed her to drink, even as unconscious as she was, and said to Ariana, "Now you may move her. Take her where she can be in complete quiet. See that she has strong wine when she wakes, and such meats as I instruct. And pray, lady. Pray hard. This wound is in an ill place. If anything is pierced, if I've not seen all there is to see, no art of mine will be of any use."

Ariana regarded him with the solemn stare of a child. "She could die?"

"She could die," Imhotep said.

Ariana bent her head. But it was not in to collapse in tears, though Kemni would have been glad to do as much. She looked up with sudden intent. "We'll take her back. But quietly. Do you all understand? No chatter. No taletelling. My cousin collapsed in the field. The sun was too strong for her, perhaps; or she's taken ill of a fever. Ay: did you speak to anyone before you fetched Imhotep?"

"No one, lady," Ay said. "The others were out doing whatever duty bade them do. I had to fetch Imhotep myself; there was no one to run the errand for me, except a lad or two in the stable—and I thought it better for them to tend the horses."

"Excellent," Ariana said. "Now remember, all of you. Fever, that's all."

"And this?" Seti nudged the prostrate messenger with his foot.

"This comes back as baggage," Ariana said grimly. "Keep him hidden. Bring him to me when I've settled my cousin."

Seti bowed. He would do it, Kemni knew. As did Ariana. She nodded and turned her attention back completely to her cousin.

✦ ✦

The world should properly then have shrunk to Iphikleia and nothing more. If she lived, he would live. If she died . . . he did not know what he would do. Life was strong in him, and beautiful, but she had become the heart of it.

But he was not permitted such luxury. Once she was settled in Ariana's own wide airy chamber, with Imhotep beside her and Ariana's maids and servants all about her, and the best of the guards on the door, Ariana beckoned to Kemni. Kemni had meant to stay on the other side of Iphikleia, face to face with Imhotep. Ariana's will rolled over his and overwhelmed it with ease that recalled to him how she was, after all, both queen and goddess.

She took with her only Kemni, and she went by ways that were frequented by servants, walking apart from the broader, brighter corridors and the open courts. Kemni had not realized how many such ways there were, or how secret they could be. Anyone not a servant might never know how easily the servants came and went, or how invisibly.

Ariana clearly did. She moved quickly and with the air of one who knew those ways well. In very little time they had traversed the house and come near the walls, into one of the guardtowers, no less. At the top of it they found Seti, and the messenger bound and set against a wall. He rolled eyes at the newcomers, but could not speak: Seti had gagged him.

Ariana stood over him. "She lives," she said to him, "through no fault of yours."

He stared up at her. Maybe he contemplated defiance. She bent down, and ripped the gag free. He gasped and sucked in air, and coughed convulsively. Blood stained his lips. She wiped it free with the gag, not particularly gently. "Now talk," she said. "What were you to fetch here?"

He set his lips and would not answer.

She drew a knife from her belt and laid it lightly, oh so lightly, not against his throat, but against the faint bulge within his loincloth. "In the country to which you were going," she said, "both kings and queens enjoy the service of eunuchs. I shall send them another, if you wish it. It's yours to choose."

It was not an empty threat. He must have known it. He held for a moment longer, but her blade edged closer by a fraction, and pressed just a little harder. "I was to fetch—I was to fetch letters. And tokens. To admit me to—to certain houses."

"Lordly houses?"

He nodded a little painfully. Her knife had not lifted. If he moved his body, he well might do to himself what she had threatened.

"Why letters and tokens? Wouldn't the gold be enough?"

"That's for the king of kings. To keep safe till I came to him. The rest is for others."

"And who was to give these things to you?"

"A—a messenger." He yelped. Her blade had drawn blood. "A prince! There's a prince here. He was supposed to—"

"I see," Ariana said. And so did Kemni.

"Letters that would betray him," Kemni said.

"Possibly," said Ariana.

"Shall I go?" he asked.

Her brows drew together. "Can you be circumspect? Are you strong enough?"

"Maybe not," he said, "but I can try."

He watched her consider denying him and sending Seti. If he had been Ariana, he would have done just that. Seti could be calmer, could think more clearly.

But Kemni could more plausibly be seen in Gebu's rooms, could seem to have gone in search of the prince, or to have conveyed a message to or from his battle-brother.

She nodded. Like Iphikleia, she always knew what he was thinking. "Go," she said.

+ +

Gebu was not in his rooms. Kemni had bargained on that. He also gambled, and maybe without hope, that the letters and tokens would be there and not on Gebu's person, or on that of one who served Gebu. The messenger had been clear: he was not to fetch them from a hiding place. He was to be given them from a living hand.

Gebu could have no reason to know he was suspected. He might leave the things in plain sight, the better to conceal them. Just as he had done with himself, establishing his presence in that of all places, not so very far from the border of the Lower Kingdom.

It was all a gamble, a pattern of guesses and hopes, and the memory of a dream. Gebu's door was not guarded. There was no need for guards, if he was not there. Kemni walked into rooms that he had come to know rather well, where he had spent not a few evenings sharing a jar of wine or beer, tossing the bones, or talking of trifles. Once they might have shared a willing maid or two, but here, when Kemni had Iphikleia, that was not a thing he chose to do.

For her sake he did this, for her life that could even now be ending. Kemni could blame the gods for that, or himself. Certainly he blamed the messenger. But the man who had sent this messenger, the leader of the conspiracy—if there was blame to bear, he bore the brunt of it.

Anger kept Kemni on his feet, though he struggled to keep his mind clear of it. The worst of all sins was betrayal. He must remember that; must never forget it. A man who would betray his father and his king would hardly hesitate to betray a friend.

If Kemni wanted to hide letters and tokens in plain sight, he would do it quite simply: in a scribe's box, with the inks and brushes and the palette of the trade. Gebu had such a box. Not all of the princes had schooling, but Gebu had had a leaning toward it. He did a little reading still, and a little writing, for the pleasure of it.

Indeed, there was his box, beside his bed as it had always been. It was plain, with little ornament, but beautifully made as was proper for a prince. Kemni hesitated to touch it. As if, somehow, there might still be some hope.

He steeled himself and raised the lid. The inks were there, the brushes, the stone palette. And no more.

Before he collapsed in relief or despair, it little mattered which, his fingers had found the palette's edge and lifted it carefully.

There. Papyrus in small rolls, folded tightly, and a packet wrapped in linen. The letters were not sealed, though Kemni suspected that they would have been when the messenger came for them. With beating heart he unrolled the first that came to hand. It was nothing exceptional, at first glance: a prince's letter to a lord with whom he would confirm alliance. But that lord's name, though written in the Egyptian characters, was a foreign name, and he was bidden to win to the cause such of his fellows—both Egyptian and otherwise— as seemed to him trustworthy.

Two more of the dozen letters said much the same. The packet amid them proved to contain a handful of scarab-seals, each of a different stone, but all carved with the same name: Gebu's princely name, by which he would be known to the gods after he was dead. To it was added a second name, an epithet of the god Re. And that was circled with the cord of the cartouche, as if it had been the name of a king.

Kemni stood with one such in his hand. It was carved of lapis, deep blue like the sky over the Red Land. It held the weight of a world, and the chill of folly.

No man with his wits about him, no man who was not at heart a fool, would dare to write his name so, not unless he was the king. Had someone urged this on Gebu, perhaps? Perhaps someone who had in mind to destroy him and take what he laid claim to? Yet he had allowed it. Out of blindness or pride or simple failure to understand the consequences, he had let these stones be carved, and kept them here, till they could be sent to strangers who might also betray him.

It must have been the spirit that wove about these things, that darkened Kemni's heart and caused him to do what he did. He kept the lapis scarab, but wrapped the rest as they had been before. He laid them with the letters in the box, and set the palette over them, carefully, lest he disturb the arrangement of the inkpots and brushes atop it. He closed the lid on it all, and with the scarab still in his hand, burning his palm like a living coal, he left those rooms and returned the way he had come.

+ +

Nothing had changed, that he could see. Iphikleia lay like the dead, with Imhotep seated beside her. Ariana sat across from him. The crowd of servants was gone, but they had not mattered before and did not matter now.

Ariana raised her head at Kemni's coming. He knelt in front of her, took her hand in his—great daring, but she did not resist him—and laid the scarab in it.

She examined it, turning it in her palm, frowning at the carving on its underside. Her fingertip brushed the oval of the cartouche. "A king's name?"

"Gebu's."

"Ah," she said. It seemed she understood. "Is this all you found?"

"No," Kemni said. "There were a dozen of them. And letters."

"And?"

"I left them," he said. She raised her brows. "I thought . . . we should conspire against the conspiracy. If they think that a messenger has come and taken the letters and gone, how soon will they understand that no man of theirs ever came to the Lower Kingdom? Whereas if we uncover it all now . . ."

"Yes," she said. Only that, but it was all the praise he required. "Will he know who was sent here? Or believe in a stranger?"

"Surely we can find a man with the coughing sickness, who looks enough like the messenger to pass muster. If he learns his lesson well, says the words he's bidden to say, then is last seen walking away northward, he well may persuade the traitors that their errand is done."

"And what will you do with him when he's finished?"

"We could kill him," Kemni said with a cold heart, "or we could reward him lavishly for his silence and send him somewhere suitably remote. It's a risk, but so is all of it."

"What in life is not?" Ariana nodded abruptly. "Do it. Do it quickly."

Kemni swallowed a sigh. It had been too much to hope that he could linger here, counting Iphikleia's breaths and praying that she would heal. Maybe Ariana thought it better for him to be up and doing, however weary he was, and however much he yearned to rest. It would be like her to care for such a thing. But it would also be like any queen or king, not even to notice how great was the burden that she laid on him.

Nevertheless he carried it. Seti would know where to find such a man as they needed; and indeed, when Kemni told him what was afoot, he made no secret of his glee. "My lord! That is *clever*."

"And I'm not usually clever?" Kemni asked dryly.

Seti was never one to blush at a misstep. "Well, my lord, as to that, lords are lords, and what with people wiping their noses for them all their lives, and wiping their arses, too, and doing most of their thinking for them . . . well, they can plot and they can scheme, but real cleverness isn't usually their habit."

"I think I shall be flattered," Kemni said. "I can't be insulted, or I'd have to beat you senseless. And I need you."

"Of course you need me," Seti said. "And that's clever of you, too, because you know it."

Kemni growled and made as if to strike him. He danced away grinning. "I'll find a messenger for you, and never you worry. You'd best go now and be commander of the charioteers. They'll have expected you to be distraught, what with the lady being so ill of a fever, but you're best advised to drown your sorrows in work."

That was intensely annoying but inescapably true. He must play out the game, however long it lasted.

+ +

Seti found a man who looked eerily like the one who was still a captive in some hidden part of the holding. In fact when Seti brought him into Kemni's workroom, not long before sunset, Kemni could have sworn that it was the same man. But the other had been a little older and a little smaller, and his voice had been less deep. And this was a stronger man, less far gone in the coughing sickness.

"This is Amonmose," Seti said. Kemni inclined his head. The man bowed low as was proper for a man of low birth before a lord. His eyes, Kemni noticed, were bright and alert. This was not a dull-witted man.

"Amonmose knows what we need of him," said Seti. "He's willing to do it."

"Are you?" Kemni asked the man directly.

He nodded. "It's for the queen," he said, "and for the Great House."

"And for gold?"

"And for gold," Amonmose said. "My wife is dead of the coughing sickness. My sons died of it. I'll be dead soon enough—but not before I do something of worth in the world. When they weigh my soul against the feather of Ma'at, when I come to the judgment, I would like one thing to give it substance."

"This thing will weigh you down with blessings for all of the life after life," Kemni said.

"I do hope so," said Amonmose.

"Are you ready, then?" Kemni asked him.

"As ready as I can be," he answered.

"So," said Kemni. "Let it begin."

Seti was already gone. While they waited, Amonmose was silent except for an outburst of coughing. Kemni lent what aid he could, which was terribly little. As Amonmose got his breath back, a step sounded without. Kemni steeled himself not to stiffen; composed his face into a smile of greeting for Gebu.

The prince brought with him a breath of the outer air, dust and sun and the last of the day's heat. He was still in his charioteer's garb, as if he had come direct from the field. "Brother!" he said. "The lady. Is she—"

"She lives," Kemni said, though it caught in his throat. "She's very ill; she may not recover. But for now, she lives."

"Ah," said Gebu with every appearance of honest relief. "That's well. May the gods grant she recovers completely."

Kemni bowed his head to that. But he lifted it almost at once. "Brother," he said, and he did not choke on the word. "This man is a messenger, he says, from Thebes. He's asked leave to speak with you."

"That's well," Gebu said. No flicker of guilt marred his face, nor did he seem perturbed that Kemni knew of the messenger's existence.

And why should he? Messengers came from Thebes often enough, and some claimed to bear messages that the prince must hear in solitude. Kemni left him to this one as he had a time or two before, with every possible appearance of goodwill, and a promise to join him in a little while for the day-meal.

Once he was out of the room, he slipped into the one behind it, which happened—and not by coincidence—to be well within earshot of what passed in the workroom. Such rooms, Kemni knew, were common in palaces: places from which the ladies might listen to the affairs of their lords, either for their own advantage or so that they might offer advice without the intrusion of their presence on matters of state. "Or," as Iphikleia had said once, "betraying to fools of men how much of the world is ruled by women."

It served Kemni well now. If he shrank from it, he remembered Iphikleia, and the knife that had struck her down. He sat very still in that airless box of a room, ear pressed to the wall.

The voices came clearly, perhaps more clearly than if he had sat in the room with them: Amonmose's somewhat thin and interrupted with coughing, Gebu's deeper, stronger, and somewhat peremptory. He was not affable to this man as he was to those he reckoned his equals. "Tell me," he said, "why you came so publicly, when you had been given orders to come to me in secret."

"My lord," Amonmose said with a degree of trembling, but firm enough for all that, "I did try, but there was no way in but through the gate, and the guards are watchful. I thought it best to be public then, and so avoid suspicion."

Gebu grunted. "The gods protect fools. And there's no harm done. I'll see you housed for the night, and set on your way in the morning, with the things you were to carry with you."

"As my lord wills," Amonmose said. "But it might be best if I did what I came to do, and left in the night. There's a place nearby where I can wait till morning; then go on with no one to notice."

Kemni held his breath. If Gebu ordered Amonmose to stay, he would have no choice but to obey. That would harm nothing, but it would prolong the game, and sharpen the risk of discovery.

But Gebu said, "Very well. Some would call you a madman for daring the things that walk the dark, but worse things might walk the daylight, after all."

"You think anyone here suspects?" Amonmose asked—the fool, the reckless fool.

Gebu answered him calmly enough. "I think not. What is there to suspect? I'm the good prince, the loyal son and servant, the novice charioteer."

"Good," said Amonmose, and Kemni remembered to breathe again. "I was asked to be sure of that. For safety's sake, you understand."

"I understand," Gebu said. "Very well, then. I'll fetch what's needed. Stay here and wait. If anyone comes, tell him you're waiting on my pleasure. I'll have food and drink fetched, to make it more plausible."

"My lord is generous," Amonmose said.

Kemni heard Gebu go: the footsteps receding, and Amonmose's long, audible sigh. Kemni thought of speaking to him, but thought better of it. There might be a spy, or Gebu might return unexpectedly. Conspiracies bred suspicion.

Safest then to keep silent, and to wait as Amonmose waited, though the time seemed endless. A servant came with food and drink—fortunate for Amonmose; Kemni's stomach growled like a dog, demanding its own dinner. But that he could not give it until this thing was done.

More than once Kemni knew that Gebu had guessed that all was not what it seemed; that the true messenger had been found, or had escaped; that—worst of all—Iphikleia had died while he sat there in useless stillness, waiting for the game to be ended.

He was perilously close to leaping up and bolting when Gebu's steps returned. They were brisk, no slowness of reluctance, and he was alone as before. No guards to destroy the impostor.

"My lord," Amonmose said, with a rustle as if he rose from where he had been sitting.

"Sit, sit," Gebu said. "Here, I've brought what you're to carry. Be sure you keep it safe."

"As always, my lord," Amonmose said.

"Well then," said Gebu. "The gods protect you, and favor your journey."

It was a dismissal—and such a one as to knot Kemni's belly. As if any god could favor such treason. As if any god would.

·············· V ··············

A MONMOSE LEFT THE room as he had been instructed, and let Gebu think that he had found his way out through one of the gardens with Gebu's guidance. But once Gebu was well deceived, Amonmose found Kemni where they had agreed to meet, in a stable outside the wall, new-built and occupied by only a handful of horses.

Seti had gone to drift for a while in Gebu's shadow, to be certain that no suspicion tainted him. There was no one in the stable at this hour of the night. The one man who should have been on guard had been lured away on an errand that would keep him occupied for a little time.

Kemni was alone, then, and Amonmose found him among the horses, resting for these few moments in their peaceful presence. The man's eyes rolled white at the sight of them; he stopped short, as if his feet had failed him.

Kemni had forgotten what fear the rest of his people had for these great gentle creatures. He left them regretfully, but Amonmose was too stark with terror to be coaxed closer. He breathed a long sigh when Kemni came to stand in front of him. "My lord, it's done," he said. "I have the letters."

And so he did, wrapped in the pack with the golden collar. "Did the prince say anything," Kemni asked, "about the number of tokens?"

Amonmose shook his head, a shift of shadow in the light of Kemni's one small lamp. "No. He gave me the packet, that was all."

Kemni breathed his own relief. "He never looked. Thank the gods. Here, I'll take these, with thanks to you for winning them. You'll go as we bade you, yes? Rest as you can where you told the prince you would, and go some distance in the morning. Seti will come to you on the road and set you on your new way. You are still determined to go as far as Nubia?"

"I always wanted to see it," Amonmose said. "If the gods grant I live that long, then I'm content. And if not, I've earned a reward with this thing. I'll ask that my spirit complete the journey."

Kemni regarded him half in amusement and half in respect. "Well, and why not? I'm sure they'll grant what you ask. But go now, and may the gods protect you—the gods of good faith and loyal service."

"And the gods of gold," Amonmose said with a flicker of wry laughter. "Don't let your man forget that part of it."

"By my name, he will not," Kemni said.

Amonmose was content. He and Kemni between them restored the weight of his pack with stones that Kemni had brought for the purpose and bound it anew. He shouldered it then, grunting a little for it was heavy, and slipped out into the night.

When he was gone, and no sound to be heard above the night noises, or beneath them either, Kemni allowed himself a moment's boneless collapse. But he could not linger. Though he craved sleep, he must not succumb to it. Not till he knew what he must know.

✦ ✦

She lived still. Lamps were lit about her, many more than were strictly needed, but the light was blessed. Imhotep had gone—to rest, Ariana said, though her own eyes were hollow, her voice thin with exhaustion.

"You let him go?"

Kemni must have sounded grimmer than he knew. Ariana bridled a little, though she was too tired for anger. "There's nothing he can do that I can't do as well. It's all in the gods' hands."

"I pray that's so," Kemni said. He sank down beside the bed, in the chair that, he remembered vaguely, Imhotep had claimed for himself while he was there. "It's done. The messenger has gone. In the morning Seti will complete the plan. And then . . ."

"And then," she said, "we go on."

"I don't know if I can," said Kemni. It came to him as something he had been thinking of for a long while, though he had not even shaped the thought before. "I know we agreed. We'll let him think all's well, and betray nothing of what we know, until the time comes when we can destroy him."

"After the war has begun," Ariana said, "when there's no danger of its being stopped. Unless there's more to the plot than we know."

Kemni shook his head. "I can't do it, my lady. I can't pretend to be his brother, to love him, trust him. Not knowing what he is, and what he's done."

"You've known it for rather a while," she said, "and he's not suspected."

"But now I *know*," Kemni said. "Lady, please. I can't do it."

"That is difficult," she said. "I can't let you run away again—I need you here. And I can't send him away without a plausible excuse."

"Might not the king summon him to Thebes? He is a prince. Surely there's something that he's required for, away in the city."

Her eyes narrowed. "Wouldn't you rather he was here, where we can keep him in sight, than there, where he can plot the gods know what?"

"But there," said Kemni, "the king can watch him, once it's known that there's something to watch for. And he won't learn any of our secrets here."

"He and his fellows were plotting under the king's very nose. Do you think it would be any better in Thebes?"

"I wonder if the king knew, but for some reason chose to let it continue. Maybe he expected us to stop the messenger?"

"He is a god," Ariana conceded. "But—"

"Suppose," said Kemni, "that you contrive a summons from the king—and while you do that, send a messenger to Thebes with word of all that's happened here. Then when the prince comes there, the king will know what there is to know, and be prepared for him."

"And what if the king won't do as we ask him?"

"I think he will," Kemni said—which was a great presumption, but he could not help it. He had trusted Gebu with his life, and Gebu had become a traitor. What if the king had no more honor than that?

The king was the king, the living Horus. Kemni must trust him, or trust nothing in the world.

Ariana pondered what he had said. While the silence stretched, he bent toward Iphikleia who lay unmoving as she had done since he came there, and laid his palm softly against her cheek. Her skin was cold, though not quite as cold as death. She breathed, but faintly, almost imperceptibly.

Imhotep had warned him that she would lie so; that the potions he had given her would bank the fire of life in her, and cause it to burn low—the better, he had said, to preserve her body's strength. She was all pale and shrunken, her face too still, its beauty leached away. And yet he loved her more than he ever had, loved her with force that shook him to the soul.

She would have died for him, for his dream that she had believed in even more strongly than he had. She might still die. Death's claws were sunk in her heart. Imhotep's art and his magic might not be enough to win her free of it.

Kemni had only love to offer her. Love, and anger. If the gods had any care for that, then maybe they would let her live. And if not, not.

It was a cold world. Cold and dark, if she was not to be in it. His brother a traitor, his kin dead or conquered—what did he have, anywhere, but this one woman?

Ariana spoke beyond her, startling him out of his maundering. "If I do as you ask, promise me something."

"If I can," Kemni said.

Her lips twitched. "Or if you will? Very well. Promise me, if you can or will, that you will stay in this world. No matter what happens."

"Even if there is nothing left for me?"

"I would hope that I am something: I and our king."

Kemni lowered his eyes. Her tone had not been aggrieved, nor was she rebuking him. And yet he felt most thoroughly chastised.

"May I take that for a promise?"

He nodded.

"Then I will do my part. That one will leave here as soon as I can contrive a message—and his father will know what I did and why. Whatever consequences there may be for that, I take on myself."

"But—I don't ask you to—"

"But you did," she said with composure. "It's no matter. You, I need. He's better disposed of where his father can keep watch over him."

"He won't be killed?"

"Not yet," she said, "nor by my asking."

Kemni sighed a little. "It might be best if he were. But . . . not for my asking, either, or by my doing. I never wanted this."

"The gods shape us," said Ariana, "and Earth Mother brings us forth. What we do thereafter, we do of our own will. He will pay whatever price the gods—or the god his father—will set. Not you. Not I."

Kemni bowed to that. There was little else he could do.

✦ ✦

It was a long night, endless as he might have thought, measured in Iphikleia's slow breaths. Ariana had gone away at Kemni's urging, to rest; and she had promised that she would see to the matter of Gebu before she came back. He kept watch alone. Now and then a servant came, to bring food or drink, or to see that Iphikleia was tended. None of them stayed. In the hours between, the silence sank deep.

Somewhere in the deep night, Kemni stretched out on the bed, close by her but not touching, save for his hand that he twined with her thin cold one. He did not sleep, he was sure of that. Nor did he dream. He had dreamed enough for one lifetime.

As the hours darkened toward dawn, and the cold crept in, the cold of the Red Land that overcame the Black Land then and most strongly, something changed. Kemni lay unmoving, as if any motion, any sound, might disturb whatever had roused him.

It was silent. Utterly silent. The only sound was the beating of blood in his ears.

No breath. She was not breathing. She had stopped.

A great cry welled up in him, welled and crested and held just short of bursting free.

She gasped. Convulsed.

He caught at her. She was breathing hard, but breathing deep, and her eyes were open. They were not quite empty of self. He watched them fill with his face.

"Beautiful man," she said with the whisper of a breath.

"Don't die," he said. He was not pleading with her. It was a command.

"I'll try," she said.

"Don't talk, either."

But that, she would not obey. "Tell me what—" She shifted, and gasped. "I hurt!"

"You *are* alive," he sighed.

She lay very still. "I remember—he had a knife. I didn't want you to know—"

"Idiot."

"Yes. But it would have distracted you. Is he—"

"Ariana has him. He'll be dealt with."

"Killed?"

"I don't know. I haven't asked."

She nodded. Her eyes closed; she sighed, carefully. She was still awake. "And . . . the rest?"

"It's ended."

"Tell me—"

"Later. When you've rested."

"I've been doing nothing but rest."

Kemni did not answer that, nor argue with it. He moved a little closer, till his body rested lightly against hers. She sighed and let him take her in his arms, with great care, because even that little movement caused her pain.

"Only tell me," she said, "how bad is it? Will I live?"

"I pray so."

"Of course you do." Her lips brushed his shoulder. "Beautiful man. I love you immoderately."

"You're babbling."

"While I babble, I'm alive."

She was frightened. Bright, strong, indomitable Iphikleia, who had never been afraid of anything, was afraid of this; of the dark that took every living creature, if not sooner, then later.

"You won't die," he said to her, putting into it every scrap of power or conviction that he could muster. "If any prayer of mine has ever mattered, or any word I've spoken, or any rite or duty or service to the gods, they will not let you die. On all my souls I swear it."

"Why," she said. "You do love me."

"You doubted it?"

"No," she said. She let her head rest on his shoulder, and yawned as a child will, wide and unabashed. "I'm sleepy. Will you watch over me?"

"Always."

"Then I can sleep," she said. "Promise you'll be here when I wake."

"I promise."

She nodded against his shoulder, sighed and yawned again, and slipped into sleep.

It was sleep, not death. Deep and healing sleep, within the circle of his arms.

GEBU LEFT ON the second morning after Iphikleia was cut down. A messenger had come to him, purporting to be from his father, and commanding his presence at once in the court of Thebes. Kemni's fear, that Gebu would suspect at last that he was unmasked, seemed unfounded. The prince prepared to depart with suitable though not excessive speed.

In the evening before he left, he sent a man to Kemni, inviting him to share a farewell feast. Kemni declined, politely. "The lady whom I serve," he told the servant, "is still very ill. I've promised not to leave her side."

The servant bowed to that, which was manifestly true.

Kemni was not greatly surprised, some time later, to find Gebu himself at the door like a supplicant. Iphikleia was asleep, as she had been much of the time—healing sleep, Imhotep said, and forbade anyone to disturb it.

Kemni hated to leave her. But Gebu was not going to go away. Nor could Kemni escape him. To do that would be to betray everything.

He could keep a bold face for an hour. Surely he could do that.

He went to the door therefore, set finger to lips and tilted his head toward Iphikleia, and let Gebu follow him back into the outer room. Gebu's expression mimed sympathy exceeding well; and it allowed Kemni to forswear a smile, or any warmth of greeting.

"Is she well?" Gebu asked as they sat in the light of the lamp-cluster, and a maid brought wine.

"Not well," Kemni answered, "but she lives. Imhotep thinks she may recover."

"So sudden a fever," Gebu said with a sigh, turning his cup in his hands, gazing down into the swirl of wine. Kemni tensed, but Gebu did not tax Kemni with the lie. "I pray it leaves her quickly."

"So do we all," Kemni said.

He let the conversation stop there, leaving it for Gebu to resume if he pleased. Exhaustion was his excuse, and fear for his lady.

Gebu obliged willingly enough. "I leave in the morning. My father has matters for me to settle, matters of the war and the kingdom. I'd ask you to come with me, but they tell me you're needed here. And," he said, "I know you'll not leave her."

"No," said Kemni. "I won't. I can't."

"My poor brother," Gebu said with more warmth than pity. "I'll pray for her in Amon's temple, when I come there."

"I thank you," Kemni said.

"It's the least I can do," said Gebu. "Have you any messages for me to carry? Any word you'd like to send to anyone? My father, even?"

Kemni tensed. Here if anywhere would be betrayal—would be suspicion. "Just tell them," he said, "and him, that I do my best for the war and the kingdom."

"I'll do that," Gebu said.

Kemni bowed his head; let it droop, in fact, with weariness that was not at all feigned. "May I—"

"Yes," Gebu said. "Go back to her. Fare you well, brother."

"Farewell," Kemni said. He could say that much, in a fading whisper of a voice.

"Rest," Gebu said. "Be at ease. She will live."

Kemni bit his lip before he cried out against this liar, this traitor, this speaker of false words. His flight looked, he hoped, like a weary plod back to his lady's side. He did not embrace the man who had been his brother. When the door shut, it shut with Gebu on the other side of it. And if the gods were kind, he would not again force Kemni to wear the face of amity when all below was hate.

✦ ✦

Gebu was gone. Iphikleia recovered slowly. Much sooner than Kemni would have wished, she pressed him to return to all of his duties, not simply those he could not pass off to whoever was convenient. The closer the war came, the more of those there were, and the more completely he must devote himself to them.

Every morning he woke in dread that she would take a turn for the worse. Every night, as he fell into bed beside her after a long day's labor, he prayed that he would wake to find her yet alive. She had had a fever, as if to prove the truth of the story that people were to believe, and it had weakened her terribly; but she had rallied. She was, Imhotep insisted, improving. But slowly, so slowly. Breath by breath and day by day, till she was a pale shadow with great dark hollow eyes.

"Wounds in the belly are the worst," Imhotep said wearily, one morning when Kemni should have been doing a dozen things at once, but lingered instead to fret over Iphikleia. "They fester most often, and too often, when you think the patient has recovered or near to it, he dies all unlooked for. But," he said before Kemni could cry out against the words, "if she were going to do any of that, she would have done it a good while since."

"Then why is she still so weak?" Kemni demanded. "Why isn't she getting better?"

"She is getting better," Imhotep said. "The wound and then the fever weakened her greatly. It will take time for her to be strong again."

"How much time? The rest of her life?"

"I do hope not," Imhotep said. "Now go, before you wake her. Don't you have chariots to drive? Wild horses to tame? Recruits to beat into submission?"

Kemni sucked in a breath of pure rage.

"Go," said the man who was, people said, the living image of the healer-god Imhotep—who had also, once, been a mortal man. "Train your charioteers. Trust me to keep your beloved alive."

There was nothing Kemni could say to that, that Imhotep would listen to. He turned on his heel and stalked out.

Anger carried Kemni through much of that morning. He knew that people were walking shy of him, but he did not care. While he did what he was required to do, that was enough.

Unfortunately, anger could not carry him through with the horses. They took it from him and returned it tenfold, in rearing and fighting and bitter resistance. For them he had to put anger aside; to be calm, to speak softly. In spite of himself, he left the anger behind somewhere, lost on the trampled field amid the turning of the chariot-wheels.

In that state of hard-won calm, he saw a messenger coming at the run, one of the lightfoot boys who ran errands about the Bull of Re. This one's eyes were so wide the whites showed all around them, and he was desperately out of breath, as if he had run without stopping all the way from the river. It was a while before he could speak. And when he could, Kemni understood that that was indeed the case: he had come up from the river with profoundly startling message. "The queen," he said, "the Great Royal Wife—Nefertari—she—"

Queen Nefertari had come down from Thebes, in secret, on no less a ship than *Dancer*. Her appearance and attendance were those of a woman of good birth, but certainly not royal—as if she had taken passage to visit kin downriver, and the Cretan ship had been convenient, and its captain perhaps a little smitten with her, so that he offered her the best of his hospitality.

So much secrecy. So many ruses. Kemni knew that he was bitter, but he was in no mood to care. He had difficulty even being glad to see Naukrates, whom he was fond of. The captain was sailing back toward the sea, intending to catch the Cretan fleet.

For the war was beginning. It was sooner than Kemni had expected, still some time from the harvest, but the king was determined, Nefertari said.

She spoke to them after the feast of welcome, sitting in Ariana's garden in the fading daylight: Ariana and Naukrates, Kemni and, by no one's summons but with everyone's acquiescence, Seti. In this guise of a lady of high birth but mortal breeding, Nefertari seemed a warmer, more human creature; but Kemni still could see the hard bright light of divinity behind those eyes.

"When you sent back his son with word of his betrayal," she said, "my lord undertook to search out the roots of it, and discover its branches. He did nothing, as you so wisely suggested, choosing rather to let them flourish in ignorance for a yet a while. But it made him think. They might have failed in this one thing, but there must be others that had succeeded, or were in train. He determined then to move more quickly than anyone expected. To press for the war now, while there is still some chance of surprise."

"But are we ready, lady?" Kemni asked, since no one else seemed inclined to. "Can we fight the war so soon?"

"Can you?" she asked him, question for question.

He began to say that he could not, but some vestige of prudence made him pause. So many preparations, so many things still to do, and the recruits— the horses—the chariots—

"I think . . ." he said. "I think, if I must, I can. But it will be difficult."

"But not impossible."

"No," he said. "Not quite."

"Then you will do it," she said. "In a month, at the full moon, the army will come past the Bull of Re. You will be ready for it."

So soon. Sooner even than he had expected. He breathed deep, to steady himself, and prayed the gods that it could all be done in time. The king would expect it. Kemni must, somehow, grant him what he wished.

"And will you stay with us?" he asked the queen.

She nodded. "The war's heart will be here, hidden for the moment, but beating strong. When my lord comes, it will go with him into the Lower Kingdom. Then all will be as the gods decree."

"Do you think," Kemni asked after a pause, "that this can remain a secret even so long?"

"I rather doubt it," she said. "But the later the discovery, the better for us."

He nodded. So he had thought. "And the prince. The traitor. What has become of him?"

She did not rebuke him for the impertinence of so many questions. "The king has sent him on an errand," she said, "that will keep him away from the city and from knowledge of the war until the army is ready to march."

"And then?"

"And then," she said, in a manner that warned him to ask no more, "it will be as the gods will."

Kemni bent his head. He could imagine that the gods—among them the king and the queen, god and goddess—would ordain for the king's son who had betrayed his father. There was no sentence for him, in the end, but one.

+ +

Iphikleia was awake when Kemni came to bed late as always, for after his audience with the queen he had had duties still to perform, and things to do that could not wait till morning. It was deep night when he dragged himself away, yawning and stumbling, to the lamplit room and the wide and welcoming bed, and her eyes upon him, open and alert as they had not been since the gods knew when.

He stopped halfway from door to bed, swaying a little on his feet. "Beautiful man," she said. "Have you been at the wine again?"

"I've been at my work again," he said. His heart had risen and began to sing: for her voice, though weak, was her own, a little sharp, a little wry; and her expression was nigh as vivid as it had always been.

"You look as if you haven't slept in a month," she said.

"Maybe," he said. "I don't remember."

"Come here," she said, "before you fall over."

He was happy to obey. It was all he could do to lower himself gently beside her, and not fall flat on his face. Her hand—so thin and so frail, with a tremor in it—brushed his cheek. "Poor lovely man. You're working yourself to death."

"You're awake," he said. "You're talking. You're twitting me."

"Of course I am," she said.

"But it's been so long since—"

Her fingers pressed to his lips, silencing him. "Imhotep told me. I dreamed . . ." She shook her head. "No. That doesn't matter. I'm awake. When I sleep again, it will be a plain and mortal sleep. I'm going to live, my love, whether it pleases you or no."

He could not find words to answer that. He gathered her in his arms and held her, all bird-light bones that she was. She sighed and rested there, but she was far from asleep.

"Tell me," she said. "I didn't dream it, did I? My uncle is here."

"Yes. And *Dancer*."

"The war's beginning?"

"Soon."

She sighed again. "Then I have to recover, don't I?"

It was a moment before he understood. "You are not going to the war!"

"I am not staying here."

"You can't—"

"I do intend to," she said.

He bit his lip. They could argue it later. That she was awake, stubborn and contentious and insisting on doing the maddest possible thing—the joy in him was so piercing that he thought he would die of it.

WITH THE GREAT Royal Wife in residence and the war approaching with terrible speed, the Bull of Re forsook sleep, and forsook quiet. The armorers, the harnessmakers, the captive chariotmakers in their shop that was half prison, labored day and night to prepare for what must come. The last gathering of recruits found itself pressed to learn more swiftly and more thoroughly than perhaps human mind and body could bear. But Kemni had no mercy. He could allow none.

They hated him. Hate could be a good thing. It sharpened the spirit and strengthened the will. They would learn faster, fight better, because they detested him so cordially.

It was a different hate he met when he ventured into the chariotmakers' workshop. Amid the scents of new-planed wood and fresh paint and the sharp hot reek of metal shaped in the forge, the captives and their Egyptian apprentices built chariots for the king. They built well—Ariana made sure of that, and Iphikleia had done so while she was able to walk about. But they did not build willingly.

Four of them, in the end, had come back to the Bull of Re from the Lower Kingdom. The master was not the eldest, but he seemed, for his rank, to cultivate the longest and most luxuriant beard. Kemni found it fascinating that he could keep it out of whatever he worked at, nor ever caught it or stained it. The others cropped their beards close, and the youngest had none: a sullen and remarkably pretty boy who spoke the most Egyptian, but seldom saw fit to display it. Even as young as he was, he labored in the shop beside his father, and it was he who drove the chariots as they were finished, to ascertain that all was well.

Although Kemni had not brought them to this place, they seemed to have decided that he was the lord here, and to have concentrated in him all their hatred of this captivity. It had a reek like hot bronze, and a force like a blow whenever he came into their workshop. And yet he visited often. He found their craft fascinating. They had perfected a way of building many chariots at once: taking each a portion—body, axles and wheels, shafts—and overseeing a company of workmen who completed each part according to instruction. Then the master himself oversaw the putting together, the completion—and no weakness anywhere, no frail spot on an axle or a wheel, no flaw in the body so that it would break when its rider needed it most.

Kemni had asked him why he did not do such a thing. He had regarded Kemni in utter contempt, and said, "Because I have my pride."

"Your chariots are worth more to you than the preservation of your people?"

The man spat. "Don't twist my words! I build chariots. My chariots are the best of all. I will not build one that is flawed, simply to gratify an urge for revenge."

"Even if it would protect your people?"

"Do you think," the chariotmaker had asked him with a curl of the lip, "that half a hundred chariots, however well made, will even begin to oppose the king's hundreds?"

"Probably not," Kemni said. "But even a little is something."

This day, a handful of days after Iphikleia woke and came to herself again, they were completing one of the last of the chariots. There were guards on all the doors as always, and the apprentices were loyal to the king. Some of the commanders would have preferred that the master at least be kept chained, but Kemni would not allow that. It was an insult that would, he knew in his belly, compel even that proud craftsman to break his word and bolt.

The master, whose name was Ishbaal, greeted Kemni as he always did: not at all. He was overseeing the painting of the body, frowning as one of the Egyptian artists painted it in the style of the Two Lands. "Ugly," he muttered, still not acknowledging Kemni, but no one else was close enough to hear.

"It may be ugly," Kemni said amiably, "but it's ours. And how are you this fair morning, sir?"

Ishbaal snorted. "Don't 'sir' me. I'm a slave."

"You are not," Kemni said—as he had said often before.

"Then I may go?"

"Of course not," said Kemni. "We need you."

"What will you do when I'm done, then? Shut me up in a box? Kill me?"

"Keep you at work building chariots," Kemni said. "What else would we do?"

"Dispose of me," he said. "I'm difficult. I'm miserable. I've taught these fools everything I know."

"Not your years of mastery," Kemni said, "and not your incomparable eye. Come now, admit it. You're not miserable. You thrive on this: despising us all, building chariots day and night, being the first master chariotmaker in the Upper Kingdom."

Ishbaal snarled. "You! Fool! Not that way. This way." And he stalked off to correct the turning of a spoke for a wheel.

"We could let him go," Ariana said from beside Kemni, startling him, for he had not heard her come in. "Once he's done, he has the right of it: his apprentices will do well enough."

"I think not," Kemni said.

"Have you ever reflected," she asked him, "that by stealing him, we might have done great harm to his family? Caused a wife to grieve, or children to go hungry?"

Kemni bit his tongue on a sharp rejoinder. "This is war. Would you rather we lost it out of pity for this man's children—who are no doubt well looked after, if in fact he has any at all besides yonder glowering child?"

"How like a man," she said, "to say such a thing."

He stared after her as she walked away. She was always odd; she was the Ariana of Crete. But this was odder than usual.

He lingered only a little longer among the chariotmakers, to satisfy himself that all was going as well as could be expected; then, as he turned to go to the next of his myriad duties, he turned a little further instead, and followed where Ariana had gone.

It was not perhaps a wise thing to do. She was on her way to confer with the Great Royal Wife. Still, she did not order him away when he established himself a step behind her. She simply said, "You were slower than I expected."

"Sometimes I stop to think," he said.

"Amazing," she said.

"Is something troubling you?" he asked before he could think better of it.

"No," she said. "Why do you ask?"

He shrugged. "One would think you had regrets about this war."

"Hardly," she said. "Egypt reunited will serve Crete much better than Egypt half-conquered."

"But the war itself—you dread it."

"Don't you?"

He did not answer at once. "I'm not a coward. I'm loyal to my king. I want this war, and I want to see it won. I'll do whatever I must to accomplish that."

"But you dread it."

"No," he said.

"Men," said Ariana.

Kemni paused, but quickened his step again before she drew too far ahead. "What message did the king send you through Queen Nefertari? Did he command you to stay here when the chariots go out to the war?"

She would not answer. But her expression was clear enough.

"Will you defy him?"

"He's the king."

"Will that stop you?"

She stopped, spun, so that he nearly collided with her. "What is it to you?"

Temper from her was vanishingly rare. Kemni regarded her in some startlement, not least for how closely, just then, she resembled her cousin. "Someone has to hold the Upper Kingdom behind us," he said.

"The Great Royal Wife will do that," said Ariana.

"Not alone."

"No, not alone. In the company of a hundred lords and scribes and priests and servants."

"And you."

She shook her head slightly, not to deny what he had said, but as if to cast off the thought and the rebellion that it aroused in her. She never had thought as Kemni expected a woman to think, nor accepted the lot that was given her sex. Perhaps it came of being from Crete, where the greatest of the gods was a goddess.

She walked the rest of the way in silence, with Kemni behind her as before. The Great Royal Wife had been given a house of her own within the encircling wall, displacing a flock of servants and a handful of the charioteers, for whom Kemni had had to find room wherever he could. The guards at the gate would not have let Kemni pass, but Ariana spoke sharply to them. They subsided, albeit with dark glances and fingerings of their weapons. They were eunuchs, Kemni happened to notice. Men entire were not common in Nefertari's house.

In the courts of Asia, Kemni had heard—and certainly in the courts of the Retenu—a man who walked in the women's house without the king's leave could be carried off to join the ranks of eunuchs, or actually put to death. That was not, he hoped, the case here. Whether Ariana was glad of him or merely tolerated him, she kept him with her even into the elder queen's presence.

Nefertari was not, for once, waiting for them in hieratic immobility. She was sitting in a small cluttered workroom with a pair of scribes, with ink on her fingers, and no more state to her dress or her person than a noble lady might affect in her own household. It dawned on Kemni that Nefertari might be regarding this venture as an escape—a brief taste of freedom from the strictures of court and palace. The king welcomed such escapes. Why not the first of his queens?

Kemni looked at her somewhat differently then, though with little less awe. She was still Nefertari.

She looked up from the heaps of scrolls and written scraps of papyrus, frowning faintly as if she paused to capture and pen a thought before she turned her mind to her visitors. With a slight shake of the head, she smoothed the frown, though she did not smile. "Good morning, lady," she said to Ariana. And to Kemni: "Commander. Welcome."

He flushed and resisted the urge to shuffle his feet. He had not expected to be acknowledged, or to be granted his rank, either.

She rolled a scroll neatly and with the deftness of long practice, fastened it and handed it to one of the scribes to be tagged and put away. "It looks better than I thought," she said, "if not as well as it must. We must be ready within the month."

"We will be," Ariana said, sparing Kemni the need. She sat in a chair across from the worktable, easily, without asking leave. "Tell me something."

Nefertari raised a brow.

"Did you find and root out the whole conspiracy? Every bit of it?"

"We can hope so," said Nefertari. "Why? Is there a thing that we should know?"

"No," Ariana said. "I was only thinking . . . what if we told them false things? Let them send a messenger in haste to the Lower Kingdom, to tell their allies there that we come to the war sooner and in greater disarray than we actually are?"

"And have them ready and waiting for us when we come?"

"Not likely," Ariana said, "if we let it be thought that we begin the war elsewhere than we intend to. Suppose that they're waiting on another branch of the river, for a different kind of attack—say that we move toward Tanis instead of Pelusium, or attack north and west of Memphis instead of round about Avaris. And that, instead of armies in boats, they expect armies on the march. And more—that the Cretan envoys in Thebes feign a quarrel and a departure in dudgeon, with a withdrawal of all their alliance. Can this be done?"

"It can," Nefertari said slowly, "but it would have to be done now, and from here, and in great haste. My lord king is in Thebes, mustering the last of his armies. He might not—"

"You know," said Ariana, "that the king will bow to anything you bid him do."

Nefertari raised her chin a fraction. "He may. But there are matters of policy, and of appearance. People must think only what we wish them to think."

"That the king rules, and not the Great Royal Wife?" Ariana shrugged. "Well, don't do it, then. It's likely the traitors will have sent messengers of this new and swifter war, and that we'll not have caught them. It was the gods' will and fortune that we caught the one who came near the Bull of Re. When we come to the Lower Kingdom, we'll find the enemy waiting—maybe not in all his armies, but he'll be expecting us."

"I never said we should not do it," Nefertari said. "It can be done. But carefully. And quickly. Who is the best of your runners?"

"That would be Nakhtmin," Kemni said when Ariana's glance bade him speak.

"Bid him come to me within the hour," Nefertari said, "and be quiet about it. I will give him the words to say—I and my sister queen."

Kemni bowed. Nefertari's eyes rested on him for a disconcerting while, as if she took simple pleasure in the sight of him. Then, as abruptly as the shutting of a door, she let him go.

✤ ✤

"She would like you in her bed," Iphikleia said. She was up and sitting in a chair, white and gaunt but determined, when Kemni found a moment to look in on her. He had not meant to tell her of his audience with the Great Royal Wife, but what with one thing and another, with pausing to talk and being plied with the breakfast he had altogether forgotten, he found himself chattering more perhaps than he should. She was hungry for news—the servants, she complained, told her nothing, and Imhotep was oblivious to all but his work.

"She wants you," Iphikleia said. "There, stop shying like that! She'll never take you—no more than Ariana will. But I'm sure she loves to look at you."

"Every woman in the world can't be wanting to take me to bed," Kemni said crossly. "I'm not *that* good to look at."

"You don't think so?" she asked. "No, maybe not all women, after all. Only women of taste and discernment."

"And you aren't raging with jealousy?"

"Should I be?"

"Women," Kemni said, in much the same tone Ariana had used of men. "Stop tormenting me now, and be sensible. For by the gods, one of you women has to be. Ariana is going to try to smuggle herself to the war, I can see it as clear as the sun at noon. Gods know what the Great Royal Wife intends to do, but I'll wager she won't be sitting here like a proper and submissive royal subject, doing her king's bidding and not a fraction more."

"Do you think she'd betray the king?" Iphikleia asked.

"No!" said Kemni. "She terrifies me. She makes me want to turn and bolt. But she's loyal. I'd wager my souls on it."

"So would I," Iphikleia said, "if I had the whole rank of Egyptian souls, and not the simple one we Cretans are given. But you think she has more on her mind than her king's wishes."

"I think," he said, "that when the gods look down from the horizon on this kingdom, and ask one another whose will rules most strongly in it, some of them would declare by their very divinity that while Ahmose is king, Queen Ahmose Nefertari is the one whose word matters most in the counsels of the kingdom."

Iphikleia did not recoil from that thought, nor seem to find it at all shocking. "Well, and what of it? The kingdom is well ruled, everyone agrees on that. Does it matter who actually does the ruling?"

"But Ahmose is the king!"

"Ahmose is a wise man, who knows what he has in the chief of his wives. I admire him. Every man should be so sensible."

"You women are all appalling," Kemni said. "And you are all *here*. Maybe I shall invent a messenger of my own, and run away to hide behind my king."

"You won't do that," said Iphikleia. "Come here, kiss me. Then go. You've dallied here long enough, and I want to sleep."

Kemni was glad to kiss her, even in his fit of temper—and a long, deep, splendid kiss it was, too, with a promise in it of more. But not now, and not tonight. She was weak still, and more than ready to rest.

Soon. If the war allowed. If his king and his queens and all the rest of Kemni's tormentors permitted it to be so.

VIII

T HE KING'S ARMIES had begun to come down the river. Those that had gathered in and about Thebes were behind. These were the lords and nomes of the north, coming to Queen Nefertari in the Bull of Re, and mustering along the river to the south and north of the holding.

There was no Cretan ship on the river now. *Dancer* had left the day after it brought Nefertari, sailing as quickly as it might toward the enemy's country and past it, the gods willing, to the sea. All the boats were Egyptian boats, a great jostling fleet of them. Yet more had come bearing provisions, supplies, weapons. Those came and came again, emptying the granaries and storehouses of the Upper Kingdom, pouring all they had into the king's war.

It was a mighty undertaking to gather them all, not so soon that they grew restless, nor so late that they missed the muster. The stream of runners and messengers never stopped or slowed. They all came to the Bull of Re, to the two queens in the heart of it, who held together all those myriads with an ease that surely must come from the gods.

Kemni, with twice a hundred men and chariots, with all their grooms, healers for both men and horses, servants, armorers, and men under orders to maintain and repair the precious chariots, reckoned himself much beset. Nefertari and Ariana between them did all of that for many a thousand. He tried to compose himself as he saw them do, always calm, never visibly frazzled, and not raising their voices even to chastise great error. And chastise they did, even to death, if such was the penalty they reckoned fitting.

His charioteers, gods knew, were no better or worse than young men ought to be, but their infractions were minor. They kept apart by the queens' order, indeed had removed the horses and chariots from the holding and retreated to the valley of horses, as the army began to gather. How much of a secret they were, Kemni was not certain, but if they could remain but a rumor, it would serve the king's purpose.

They camped in the valley therefore, kept watch as if they were already at war, and kept up their spirits in wondrous fashion. Kemni had no need to hunt for ways to keep them occupied. Horses took a great deal of looking after, and horses with chariots were almost excessively engrossing. In moments of despair, Kemni knew that they would never come to the Lower Kingdom; they would be trapped here forever, grooming and tending horses, repairing chariots, and discovering how very much of the art they still were ignorant of.

He had tried at first to come back to the house at night, but the third time he found himself still in the field long after the sun had set, the messenger he sent to Iphikleia returned with a message of her own: "Never mind that. Stay with your people. They need you."

He had got out of the habit of sleeping alone, but as exhausted as he was when at last he could snatch a few hours' sleep, he had little enough time to fret over the absence beside him. There were women if he had wanted them: girls from the villages, maids from the holding, who seemed untrammeled by duties and unconcerned by secrecy.

Kemni took one to his bed one night, a bright-eyed young thing with a supple body and a quick tongue. She was far from the first to let him know that she would not be averse to a night in his company; he was the commander, after all, and there was that damnable face of his.

"Oh, not only your face," she said as she slipped his kilt from about his middle and stood back to admire. "Beautiful man! All the others will be oh so jealous."

His body had warmed to her of its own accord, as well it might: it had had no taste of a woman since Iphikleia was struck down. But as she set about stroking and fondling him, he went cold. Her hands were not the hands he wanted. Her voice, though pleasing, chattered on endlessly. Her face was pretty, but pretty was not enough.

She did her best with lips and hands, with unwavering patience and good-will. At last he set her hands aside and slipped away from her lips. "Enough," he said as gently as he could. "You are lovely, and I regret . . . but not tonight."

She did not laugh. That much grace she gave him. She sighed and patted his limp organ, which quivered faintly but could not bring itself to rise, and said, "Never mind. I understand. You can't help it. She's put her spell on you—and wisely, too. If I had such a lovely man, I'd want him all to myself, too, and I'd make sure I kept him."

She left him then, he hoped not to tell the tale to all her fellows, nor would she take the necklace of lapis stones that he offered her. "It wasn't for pretties I did it," she said.

"Still," he said, "don't you want something for your trouble?"

"You were no trouble at all," she said. "But this, I will take." And she took a kiss, a long and luxurious one, before she slipped out into the night.

He slept alone that night, and the nights after. Sometimes he thought the women about the camp stared and giggled as he went by, but he told himself he was fancying things.

Until Seti said to him one morning as they shared bread and beer and the rolls of accounts, "Tell me what you did with Meritamon the other night."

Kemni looked up from a blur of numbers. "Merit— Who?"

"The pretty one. Breasts like little green melons. Never stops talking."

Kemni remembered her perfectly well, once he had been reminded. "What's she saying I did?"

"She's not," Seti said. "She walks about with a smile on her face and a dreamy look in her eye. When she deigns to lie with one of us, she's only half there. She's got all the other women dreaming and mooning about, too, but they're all singing laments of the 'beautiful unattainable.' "

Kemni came nigh to choking on a swallow of beer. "They're doing *what*? They're mad."

"I'd say so," Seti said. "They're not refusing the rest of us, at least— though we're made to feel like very poor seconds indeed."

"I did nothing with her," Kemni said through gritted teeth.

Seti stared at him. "You must have done something."

"Not one thing." Kemni glared in the face of Seti's disbelief. "I swear on my name. She said my lady put a spell on me. Maybe so. I only know I wanted no other woman."

"Astonishing," said Seti. "They really are making love to a dream."

"Or mocking us all."

"No," Seti said, toying with a pen, scribbling on a scrap of papyrus as if he had known how to write. "That's like women, you know. Nothing's as good to them as the man they imagine. They can't have you, and so the rest of us are nothing beside you. Some of the men would kill them, and want to kill you, for that."

"So don't tell them," Kemni said with a growl beneath the words.

"Why not? You're already half a myth."

"Nonsense."

"Really," Seti said, spreading his hands as if to swear an oath. "Look at yourself. You dreamed a dream, and the king sent you away across the Great Green. You came back with a queen for him and a priestess for you and an alliance that might, by the gods' will, win us this war. You dreamed another dream, and it gave us chariots, and made us lords of horses—us who were conquered by chariots, and frightened to death of horses. The Great Royal Wife speaks to you as to a great prince—and she speaks to no one except the king and her fellow queens. The gods know your face, people are saying. And the gods only know kings and priests. Since you're neither, you must be something else—either one of them, or one of their chosen."

"That *is* nonsense," Kemni said. "And worse than nonsense, if people start thinking I really am a god. That's treason."

"People think what they want to think," Seti said. "They don't make a habit of telling kings what's tumbling around in their bellies."

"I'm supposed to be comforted by that? If they start invoking me when they swear at one another, someone is going make sure the king hears."

"The king loves you. What's more, he knows you. He won't be alarmed, and I doubt he'll be angry."

"His own son," Kemni said, "turned against him and thought to make himself king. I'm that son's battle-brother. Do you think he'll forget that?"

"I think the king knows the difference between a handsome liar and a man who'd cut off his own rod before he'd lie to his king."

"So much you know of kings," Kemni muttered. "Set's black balls! This is unbearable."

Seti goggled at him. Kemni as a god or a god's child barely perturbed him. Kemni swearing like a lowborn soldier took him utterly aback. "Sir! Where did you learn to talk like that?"

"You know perfectly well where I—" Kemni bit off the words. "Are you trying to drive me mad?"

"I'm trying to make you laugh." Seti looked doleful. "I'm not doing very well. Aren't you even half tempted to find this all a grand joke?"

"It's all a grand mess."

"Oh, now, it's not as bad as that. A commander ought to be a bit of a myth—it keeps the men sharp."

"It also keeps greater lords on edge, and makes them want to dispose of him," Kemni said grimly.

"You should have thought of that before you started entertaining gods in dreams," Seti said. "Here, my lord, drink your beer and finish your numbers. We've got exercises in the field; the men will be waiting."

"Of course I must not keep the men waiting." Kemni downed his cup of beer and glared at the columns of figures. "This says that unless we march soon, we'll be needing more provisions than we've gathered. How long before everyone's mustered?"

For a moment Kemni thought that Seti would resist the change of subject, but he had, after all, begun it himself. With a faint sigh he said, "Three days, I heard. The lords from the outlying holdings are coming in. There's been a little grumbling—a few aren't delighted to be called to their duty. But nobody's dragging his feet too badly."

"Three days." Kemni shook his head. "That's five or more before we can take the road. And the king comes when?"

"Three, four days. Five at most."

"Close," Kemni said. "Damnably close. But that's not to be helped. We'll make the best of it."

Seti bowed his head to that.

"Go on," Kemni said. "See that the men are ready. I'll be out as soon as I'm done with this last bit."

✦ ✦

The men were as they always were, waiting in their ranks: those who drove and fought alone, those who drove but did not fight, and those who fought from behind the charioteers. As always for simple exercises, they had left off the horses' plumes and ornaments and put on plain kilts in place of their bronze armor, but their harness was clean, their weapons in good order, and the horses brushed till they shone. They were a handsome company, and proud.

Kemni expected that they should look to him with obedience. But with awe? He did not see it. They were strong men. He knew each one by name, and knew a little of each—his family, his friendships, what pleasures he liked to take. A commander knew these things. It made him stronger, and bound his men to him more firmly.

He rode through the ranks, meeting eyes here, matching a smile there. If they had made a myth of him, they were not letting him see it. No one shrank from meeting his stare, or fled at his smile.

They were all in order, ready and honed and eager. They would stand down after this, rest, prepare to march; but today, for all their spirits' sakes, he put them through their paces, from slow march to rattling, thundering gallop, in companies and all together, hub to hub across nigh the width of the valley. Then they broke and scattered and indulged at will in mock battles with headless spears and blunted swords, and much whooping and yelling and brandishing of weapons.

Kemni paused on a hilltop, reining in his restive stallions, and watched them with pride and singing pleasure. Seti's words were nigh forgotten.

One of the commanders of ten, with a handful of his men, came roaring up below and paused to breathe. They all grinned at Kemni. He grinned back. "Well, Rahotep," he said to the captain, "are we ready for war?"

"As ready as we'll ever be, my lord," the captain said. He sheathed his sword, slapped it into the scabbard and wiped sweat from his brow. "So then, my lord. What's ahead for us, then? Will we win?"

"That's with the gods," Kemni said.

"Surely, my lord," said Rahotep. "But surely you can see. Is it victory? Will we all come out alive?"

"I would hope so," said Kemni. He was beginning to grow uneasy. It was the way Rahotep was looking at him, the odd and unwonted intensity.

"But *you* know," Rahotep said. Then he shrugged. "Well; but that's not for simple mortals to ask, is it?"

"I'm as simple a mortal as you," Kemni said sharply.

"Why, surely, my lord," Rahotep said, but not as if he believed it. "Not that it's my place to ask, but . . . will *I* live? Will I come home unharmed?"

"If the gods are kind," Kemni said, which was not an answer.

But Rahotep took it as one. He smiled broadly and bowed and whipped up his horses, and went galloping back into the nearest tangle of gleefully brawling men. His own men paused, regarding Kemni with—gods, yes, that was awe—before they sent their horses in pursuit.

Kemni snarled to himself. Out of a few vague words they would build a whole prophecy.

And was that not what an oracle was? A cryptic utterance, a word that could be taken in any of a dozen ways—and there, out of nothing, a foretelling of what would be.

Even if Rahotep died, which the gods forbid—they would say that that had been the deep meaning of Kemni's words, the significance that they, simple men, had failed to comprehend. Kemni knew too well how men schooled themselves to speak of gods, or of the gods' beloved.

He sent his horses back down onto the field in a fine flash of temper. There were men in plenty willing, even eager to cross swords with him. But none would give him an honest fight. They all bent, bowed, yielded after a stroke or two. The harder he struck, the more quickly they gave way.

Only the rags of prudence kept him from beating the last man senseless. He turned instead, shouted to the horses, gave them leave to run as they would.

And they followed, the whole ten score of them, men and chariots, as geese will follow their leader, or sheep the shepherd. They were bound to him indeed, inextricably. And there was nothing that he could do—not one thing— to free himself from them. He could not even want to. He was theirs as much as they were his.

IX

WHEN THE KING was but a day's journey from the Bull of Re, all that could be prepared was done. The household was ready, the armies encamped, fed and given a light ration of beer, for they must be as keen as swords before the king's eyes.

They all rested in quiet, with little revelry. Kemni even found himself free to rest, and not so long after dark had fallen, either. If he had been wise he would have stayed in his tent among the charioteers, but wisdom had little to do with wanting. He took his stallions and harnessed them to his chariot, and in moonlight nigh as bright as day, rode back to the Bull of Re.

The holding was quiet, the great circles of camps asleep. They had grown since Kemni saw them last, till the whole plain of the river was full of them, and their fires shone as innumerable as the stars. He rode through them in a soft rattle of wheels and a thudding of hooves, unseen as if he had, like a god, the gift of passing invisible. But he was no god. He was only Kemni of the Lower Kingdom, the king's charioteer.

At the gate he found the guard awake, but it was a man he knew, who greeted him and let him pass. The empty stables daunted him a little; still, there was cut fodder, and a clean stall large enough for the stallions to share. They were content to rest there, to eat their fodder and idle and dream their stallion-dreams.

Kemni hoped for better than a dream. He trod softly through a house asleep, to the room in which he had left Iphikleia weak and ill though likely now to live.

She was not there. Her belongings were in their places, the bed made ready as if to receive her, but no one lingered there, not even a servant.

She was with Ariana, perhaps. Or in the bath. She loved a bath in the evening, when the air had cooled a little and the water's warmth was pleasant. A jar of wine was waiting for her, and a basket of cakes. Kemni ate and drank a little, washed away the dust of the road in the basin by the bed, and thought of going in search of her. But she would come back. He set aside kilt and ornaments and the sword that he wore at his belt, and sat on the bed to wait for her. In a little while, in such comfort as he was, he lay flat; and in a little while more, he was asleep.

✦ ✦

He dreamed of battle. There was no great terror in it, no more than there should be among the rains of arrows and the stabbing of spears. It was battle; fear was part of it, and a wild joy, too. It might almost have been one of his battles when he was younger, for he was fighting among men he knew, and Gebu among them, his old friend and battle-brother. They were all on foot, but Kemni rode in a chariot above them, swifter by far than they, and stronger.

Gebu was not a traitor here. There was a strange and piercing gladness in that. He fought as they all did, bravely. All of them—the living, and yes, the dead. He saw his uncle, that gentle man who was so fierce in battle; his cousins arm in arm and singing as they fought; and yet, nearby them, Rahotep of the charioteers, and a handful of his men, and one or two of the other commanders of ten. And there beyond them, rising above them on the back of a night-black mare, Iphikleia with her bow, taking aim over their heads, felling the bearded ranks of the enemy with her swift hail of arrows.

She was riding toward him, slowly for the press of men was thick, but there was no mistaking it. Now and then, if she could pause, she caught his eye. Once she smiled. His heart warmed in the light of it.

"Kemni," she said.

She was beside him suddenly, then above him—looking down at him. He was lying in her bed. She was bending over him, dressed not in armor of scaled bronze but in the fashion of a lady of Crete, many-tiered skirt and painted breasts and armlets like the coil of serpents. She was awake and alive and nigh as strong as she had ever been, only a little gauntness left to recall her wound and her long sickness.

Kemni sat up so quickly that his senses reeled. The dream scattered and fled. The thing that he had been about to understand, the thing that the gods wished him to know, was gone before he could grasp it.

He made no effort to pursue it. She was here, warm and living and wonderfully supple in his arms, laughing as she devoured him with kisses. "Beautiful man! Don't tell me they let you go."

"I let myself go," he said when she would let him speak. He clasped her so close that she gasped, then set her a little apart from him, drinking in the sight of her, assuring himself with his hands that what his eyes told him was true. "You're healed! But how—"

"Imhotep is blessed of the gods," she said.

"And may they bless him for a thousand years." They tumbled together into the bed, losing her garments somewhere, but not her jewels.

He rose up over her. Naked, but still with her hair in its elaborate coils and curls, and her body gleaming in necklaces and earrings and armlets, she made him ache with wanting her. And yet he took his time about it. He kissed every fingerbreadth of her, lingering round the sweetness of her breasts, and the cup of her navel, and most of all in the narrow, livid scar that was all her remembrance of the messenger's knife.

She seized him with sudden strength, and overset him, and took him by storm. He gasped with the shock of it, then laughed. "There was never a woman like you," he said.

"I should hope not," she said. Then there were no words left in either of them, only the dance of the body.

✢ ✢

Kemni had not slept so well since before he could remember, nor waked so well content. Iphikleia was still in his arms, curled against him with her head on his shoulder. He hated to disturb her, but it was nearly sunrise—long after he should have been up and in his chariot and on his way back to the camp.

She opened her eyes and smiled drowsily. "Beautiful man," she said. "Love me again?"

"We can't—"

For a moment he thought she would insist—and he would surrender. But she sighed and yawned and kissed him regretfully. "Go, go," she said. "Maybe tonight . . ."

"Maybe," he said without much hope. Tonight the king would be there. Then who knew when he would see her again? They would march to the war, and she would remain behind, as women had done from the beginning of the world.

He stooped to kiss her before he went, and nearly forgot all his resolve. But she pushed him away. "Tonight," she said.

It was not as late as he had feared. He had time to gather and harness the horses, and to make his way back to the camp before the sun brightened the

sky. Then there was no rest for him; for today they were to show themselves
before the armies of Egypt.

The runner came at midmorning as expected, with the word he had been
waiting for. The king had come. His fleet had come in, crowding that which
waited already along the river's edge. The armies were gathering, the muster
proceeding apace—and that was somewhat unexpected. The queens had prepared a royal welcome, feasting and foregatherings for a day or two or three,
before the armies were to move.

"He wants us to move tomorrow," the boy said. "The Great Royal Wife
said come now. Come in arms, with the baggage, and everything you can
gather. You'll camp by the river tonight. At dawn, you march."

Already the camp was astir, the tents falling, men at the run, breaking
camp and harnessing horses and rounding up those who would go as reinforcements. Kemni found himself trapped in his tent with a pair of the servants
insisting that they must dress and arm him. "All Egypt will see you today,"
they said. "Don't shame us."

Of course he must not shame the servants. He let them do as they would,
but in and about their fussing and primping, he managed to order both march
and departure.

At last they let him go. And none too soon: the tent was ready to fall. The
chariots were mustered, every man in armor, gleaming like an image cast in
bronze. They raised a cheer as Kemni came out, a roar of joy and pride, and
a welcome, and a promise. They were his. They would serve him to the death.

✤ ✦

They came out of hiding in the strong light of morning, not far from noon,
when the heat was rising and the sun beating down on the bronze of helmet
and armor. They suffered, but with pride, because they were the first who had
ever ridden to war in chariots for the Great House of Egypt.

The road was clear before them, but the fields on either side of it were
thronged with armies. The river was crowded with boats. The center was a
flame of gold, the king's own barge with its golden hull and golden canopy,
and its ranks of golden oars. He himself sat on its deck, lifted high on a throne
of gold and lapis and blood-red carnelian. His armor was washed with gold.
From so far he seemed no living man at all, but the image of a god.

Kemni allowed his stallions to stretch their stride. A murmur followed him,
swelling to a roar as the armies understood what hurtled toward them. That
roar bore him up. It made light the feet of his horses, and lifted the chariot as
if on wings.

By the time they came down to the river, all the world was one vast swell
of sound. Kemni was dizzy with it and with the heat and with the speed of his
coming. Lion and Falcon had the bits in their teeth. He battled for control of
them before they ran from land into water—and perhaps, as swift as they were,
full onto the king's barge.

They came to a rearing, plunging halt just short of the river. Kemni met the king's eyes across the brief stretch of water. Some dim and distant part of him knew that a mere lord and commander did not do such a thing; that to do it was to profane a god. And yet he could not help but do it.

The king was smiling. Not with his lips: his face was composed into a proper and royal mask. But the eyes in their warding of paint, beneath the blue crown of war—those were near to laughter.

He rose from his throne, uncrossed his arms from his breast and laid down the crook and flail of his kingship, and beckoned imperiously. Servants ran to his bidding. They bore him down off the ship, set him in a boat of remarkably plain and ordinary aspect, and delivered him onto the land.

Then on his own feet, like a mortal man, he walked toward Kemni in his chariot, and sprang lightly in.

The roar of the armies, that had died almost to a whisper while the king did that utterly unwonted thing, mounted again until it shook the sky.

As he had on the plain north of Thebes, the king rode with Kemni for his charioteer, circling this far vaster army. The sight of the king in a chariot, far from outraging them, swelled their hearts with pride and a fierce yearning for battle. To take the enemy's own weapon, to turn it against him—however small or feeble it was in truth, in the heart it was a mighty and powerful thing.

The king felt it. He stood taller. The light struck him more strongly. He was a god indeed, strong in his people's belief.

Belief, thought Kemni as he drove the horses in the king's shadow. Belief made a god. And if his men believed that he was a god . . .

He must not. The king and only the king was the living god of this kingdom.

With the king, the living god, he raised the army's spirits, and showed them a face of victory. When they had circled the whole of the army that was on the land, they returned to the river and the golden barge, to find the queens waiting: Nefertari at last in her proper and glorious state, and Ariana clad as an Egyptian royal wife. The truth of that, then, would wait for yet a while.

The queens accompanied the king in his chariot, through the massed ranks toward the Bull of Re. They came likewise in a chariot, with Ariana as charioteer: such a sight as Egypt had never seen, nor perhaps had the Retenu, king and queen side by side in golden chariots, their horses running neck and neck up the road to the holding.

✦ ✦

There was a feast that day, as was expected; but king and queens left it early, just after the wine had begun to go round. They let it be thought that they went to rest. But in truth they gathered for a council of war.

Kemni did not put himself forward, but when the high ones took their leave, Ariana caught his eye. *Come,* her glance said.

He lingered for a little while, to divert attention. Gebu was there, and others of the princes; Kemni had been hard pressed to avoid them. But he let them catch sight of him then, and greet him with every appearance of gladness, and insist that he share a cup of wine.

"I hope you left a chariot for me," Gebu said, as warm as ever, pulling Kemni into a half-embrace. Kemni did his best not to shrink from it; to remember what this man had been to him for half a score of years before treason tainted him.

"You still want a chariot?" Kemni asked him. "What does your father say to that?"

"He gives me his blessing," Gebu said.

"Well then," said Kemni, "if your highness will submit to my command again, I'll do what I may."

"Excellent!" said Gebu in open delight.

It was difficult, so difficult, to remember what this man had done. Ten years of love and trust against a season of mistrust and growing hate—the balance lurched and swayed. Kemni was glad to plead a bursting bladder, to escape to the relative safety of the queens' house.

They had not been waiting for him. Of course not. But when he came, with lowered head and suitably modest demeanor, Ahmose greeted him as gladly as his son had, and beckoned him to a chair among them. There would be no ceremony here, clearly. They had all put off their finery, the queens—and Iphikleia, who sat beside Ariana—for plain linen gowns, the king for a kilt and his own cropped greying hair. Kemni in festival clothes felt out of place, until Ahmose's words made him forget such frivolities.

"I still am not assured that the enemy is ignorant of this war," he said. "He's had ample opportunity to send and receive spies. There can be no doubt that I've mustered my armies, nor any at all as to where I've directed them. Nubia is secured behind me—or as well as it can be; I'll not repeat my brother's error, there, and lose the Lower Kingdom because I failed to remember the kingdom at my back."

"Still," Nefertari said, "he'll not be as ready as he might be."

"Maybe," said Ahmose. "But he will close the gates of the Lower Kingdom, and fortify Avaris against a siege. That would be the most sensible course, yes? My brother won by driving straight down the river to the capital."

"You have another plan?" Ariana asked.

"I had been thinking," said Ahmose, "that we might attack from another direction. The enemy's strength comes from Canaan. His kin are there, his people, his trade and his wealth. Whatever he needs that Egypt cannot or will not give him, he takes from the land of Retenu. Suppose," he said, "that we cut him off from his native country. The gate is at Sile. If we take that gate and hold it, he'll be taken by surprise—or so we can hope—and with all his forces drawn away to the inner parts of his kingdom."

"Sile." Nefertari frowned. "Yes, that's the gate to Canaan. But it's well past Avaris. Are there river routes to it that the Retenu aren't guarding?"

"There is the sea," said Ahmose. "Suppose that we keep the fleet in abeyance just south of the border into the Lower Kingdom, and take a strong part of the army—and my chariots—toward Sile. If the Cretans come to us there, and we take that city by both water and land, then hold it with Cretan aid, the enemy will lose his reinforcements. He'll have only himself to rely on, and such of his people as are in the Lower Kingdom."

"And those are few." Nefertari nodded slowly. "Then, when Sile is fallen, let the fleet sail on down the river and lay siege to Avaris. Will you command the fleet, my lord? Or the attack on Sile?"

"I go to Sile," Ahmose said. "As for the fleet . . . my ladies, do you think that the bold river-sailors of the Upper Kingdom will look to a pair of queens for their command?"

Kemni had been looking for the sudden light in Ariana's eye, but it was Nefertari who lit like a lamp. "What, my lord," said the elder queen, "have you no sons or lord commanders to take that office?"

"Well," said Ahmose, "I'll give you an admiral or two, and more than enough princes and lords to keep the men in hand. But I need someone I can trust, to be overlord to them all."

Nefertari inclined her head. "If they will accept me, I will do all you wish."

"They will accept you," he said amiably, but there was the strength of stone beneath.

Kemni wondered if Ahmose had noticed that Nefertari spoke of *I* and not of *we*. If he did, he chose to ignore it. And so, it appeared, did Ariana.

Ahmose rose with an air of satisfaction. "Good, then. It's all settled, and will be seen to. Now I advise that we sleep. Tomorrow begins before dawn. We'll march and sail by sunup."

"As you will, my lord," Nefertari said with no evidence of dismay.

.... X ....

I T WAS NO great matter for Kemni to alter the direction of his chariots' march. A march was a march, whether direct to Avaris or roundabout to Sile. But he had another concern, which he must settle before he slept.

Iphikleia did not try to keep him in the house. He would have been sore tempted if she had. But she kissed him and pushed him away. "Go. We all have much to do."

Even then he would have lingered—for if the queens were commanding the fleet, then Iphikleia would come to the war in the end; but not till after Sile was taken. He might not hold her in his arms again for a long season;

perhaps even longer than that, if the war proved more difficult than the king expected.

But she had never been one to linger over farewells. She was gone even as she spoke, striding in Ariana's wake, and leaving Kemni alone and heart-cold.

He called himself to order. It was not so very late—just barely past sunset—and that was well; he had a long night ahead. He went in search of his charioteers, who were, for this night, housed again inside the Bull of Re, except for those who stood guard beyond the walls, warding the much enlarged herd of horses.

Seti was, as he had hoped, still awake and still unblurred with either wine or beer. He was passing round a jar in the guardroom and playing at hounds and jackals with what seemed to be a conspiracy of charioteers. There were wagers and laughter, and a girl or two.

They quieted somewhat at Kemni's coming, a hush he knew well from other times: *The commander comes,* it said.

But they remembered their insouciance soon enough, with Seti for ring-leader. "My lord!" he called. "Come here, lend me your wits. I'm sore out-numbered."

"Surely," Kemni said, "if I may borrow you a moment first."

Seti betrayed no reluctance. "We'll return and conquer you all," he promised as he left them.

Kemni's old workroom was cleared of its clutter now, the heaps of scrolls put away or packed for the march, the table unwontedly bare. The lamp at least was there still, and primed with oil. Kemni lit it from the lamp in the guardroom and set it on the table. He did not sit, though Seti perched on a stool, waiting with a servant's patience for his lord to deign to speak.

It was almost insolence—but then most of what Seti did was like that. "Help me with a thing," Kemni said to him. "Prince Gebu is here. He wants a chariot; and the king hasn't spoken to forbid him. Who is unwaveringly loyal, strong with the horses, and willing to serve as both guard and charioteer to a prince who may be a traitor?"

"*May* be?" Seti shook his head. "Well. He might have changed his mind, after all. Let me think."

Kemni was happy to do that. He wished he had brought wine or a jar of beer from the guardroom; he was suddenly parched. But there was nothing here but a locked scroll-case and the empty table, and a stool or two.

Seti did not take overlong to run over in his head the muster of the chariots. "There's one man," he said, "rather young, but steady. His name is Ahmose, like the king's. People call him Ahmose si-Ebana—Ebana's son. He's asked for a change of companion; he was matched with one of the recruits, who's proved to be a poor fighter. If you'll shift that one to the reinforcements, the prince can ride behind si-Ebana."

"And will si-Ebana stand fast if there's sign of treachery?"

"I've found him trustworthy," Seti said, "and rather interesting, too. He was a scribe before he came into the army. He can read, and he writes well. If the treachery takes the form of anything written as well as spoken, he'll be able to read it."

"Bring him here," Kemni said. "Let me speak to him."

Seti was not visibly insulted that Kemni had not taken him at his word. But then very little dismayed Seti. He went to do Kemni's bidding, leaving Kemni alone, dry, and regretting his decision to linger.

The boy who brought bread and beer would never know why Kemni laughed. Seti the wise, Seti the perspicacious, had seen Kemni's distress and set about disposing of it—and without a word spoken, either, that Kemni had heard.

Just as Kemni had downed most of a cup of beer and begun to gnaw on the hard barley bread, Seti returned with a young man behind him—a boy, in truth, whose cheeks barely knew the razor. But he had the eyes of a much older man, weary and wise.

In that, he was very like Seti—who could not have been past a score of years himself. He bowed to Kemni, not too low, but low enough for respect. "My lord," he said in a youth's light voice.

"Ahmose si-Ebana," Kemni said in return. "Has Seti told you what I need?"

The boy nodded. "A charioteer, my lord, for a prince who has ambitions to be a king."

"And are you incorruptible?" Kemni asked him.

The world-weary eyes lit with a spark of amusement. "My lord, no man is incorruptible. But reward me well and command me fittingly, and I'll be yours till the gods release me from my oath."

"What reward will you take?"

"I'd have to think on that," he said.

"You'll be paid in gold," said Kemni, "and the king will honor you. Will that content you?"

"It will do," said Ahmose si-Ebana.

✦ ✦

They marched in the morning. The army was divided as the king had ordained, the fleet embarked down the river for yet some distance, to a haven where it would wait to be summoned into the Lower Kingdom. The bulk of the fighting men, and the chariots, set off on the long road to Sile.

Kemni was the king's charioteer. If he had thought at all, he would have expected that the king would be borne in a chair as kings in Egypt had gone to battle for time out of mind. But Ahmose was not one to be left behind in the march of years. "When I come to Sile," he said to Kemni that first morning, as he mounted the chariot, "I will know how to fight from this thing. Will you teach me?"

"Gladly, sire," Kemni said, he hoped not too dubiously.

The king grinned like a boy. It was his grand pleasure to take the head of the march as no Pharaoh had done before him.

The queen, in a chair as was much more proper, rode with her husband to the edge of the holding's lands. Ariana was not to be seen, nor Iphikleia. Nor did they appear in the ceremony of farewell. It was all Egyptian: the priests, the princes, the words and prayers that would set the king on his way. And when that was done, when the king and his Great Royal Wife exchanged embraces, as formal as the ritual in a temple, no Cretan faces appeared among the throng that had gathered to watch.

Kemni's heart sank. He barely heard the words that the queen spoke to the king, soft words and strangely tender. "Go with the gods, my lord and my brother," she said, "and return to me in triumph."

"I will bring you greater victory than our brother brought, ten years agone," Ahmose said. "That I swear to you."

"Yes," she said. "What you have taken, be sure that you hold."

"Farewell, my lady," said Ahmose.

"And you, my lord," said Nefertari.

Then they parted, and the army marched, the whole long column of it, soldiers and servants, baggage, weapons, trains of oxen bearing what men would not carry; and even here, in this land that belonged to Ahmose, companies of guards afoot or in chariots. They might not be needed till they had passed into the Lower Kingdom, but best, as Ahmose said, to begin as they meant to go on.

Kemni drove his chariot blindly, even while he upbraided himself for a fool. It had been wise of Ariana to keep herself hidden, and not to intrude on the king's farewell to the first of his queens. And of course Iphikleia had remained with her. There was more than enough to occupy them at home in the Bull of Re.

And yet, neither had given Kemni any farewell. Not even a word. That Ariana had taken leave of the king in private, he did not doubt. From Iphikleia he had had nothing. And if he died in this war—and war being being war, that was likely—he would never see or speak with her again.

Foolish. Worse than foolish. What they had, had no need of words or of rituals. He would live to see her in the conquest of Avaris, or he would see her in the gods' country. Even if his gods were not hers, and her death would not be as his was—surely, by the gods of both Egypt and Crete, they would find a way to be together again.

With that thought in his mind, he turned himself resolutely to the task of commanding his chariots and ordering their march and being the king's charioteer.

Ahmose si-Ebana, by Kemni's orders, followed not far behind Kemni's own chariot, in the first wing of charioteers. Gebu the prince was safely settled in the chariot at his back. For a man who must know by now that his attempt to halt the war had failed, he seemed remarkably cheerful. Or did he expect that the Retenu would be waiting for them on the road to Sile?

Maybe he did not know which road they took. The men would have been told that the army was divided—they could see it for themselves. But Ahmose had not stood up before them to tell them what he would do. He had simply ordered them to march.

Kemni gathered his courage. It took a goodly while, but they had the whole of the day. At length he spoke. "Sire."

"Yes?" said Ahmose behind him, a soft calm voice like the voice of a god.

"Sire," Kemni said. "Your son—does he know where we go?"

"He will know it," Ahmose said. "There's no help for that. But now . . . no. He knows only what the rest know, that we march into the Lower Kingdom."

"Do you think," Kemni asked, "that he'll try anything? Once we've passed the border?"

"I hope not," said Ahmose, as calm as ever, but with perceptible chill.

And that, Kemni understood, was for Kemni to accomplish. Come evening he would speak to Seti, and to si-Ebana.

Then the king said, "He has been under guard since he returned to Thebes. He remains under guard. If he speaks to anyone, approaches anyone, I know."

"You could have put him to death," Kemni said.

"I could," the king agreed.

"Yet you didn't."

"It was of greater advantage to let them all be, to let them think I knew nothing. It is even more so now, when we go where no one expects."

"He doesn't know?"

"He's not meant to."

"Will he ever?"

"That's in the gods' hands." Ahmose sighed faintly, scarce to be heard above the wind and the rattle of chariot-wheels.

Kemni did not press him further. How it must be, to so contrive that a prince of Gebu's rank and intelligence should know nothing of the web woven about him—Kemni would not have been a king for all the gold in the world.

And now it was Kemni's task to see that Gebu continued in ignorance. The first wing, Seti's wing, was well placed to shield the prince from aught that he should not know.

But in the end he would know. What then?

Kemni could ask, but he chose not to. He had no desire, just then, to know the answer.

✢ ✢

Seti, and through him the first wing, already knew what the king wished done with his son. Kemni should not have been surprised. He had been caught up in fretting over women, or he would have been much quicker to understand.

They marched through the Red Land, camped at night far from cities, and so advanced into the far east of the Lower Kingdom. These were desert places, bare of greenery and empty of habitation. But as they advanced, the land changed. It grew marshy, buzzing with flies and biting things; and bare sand and barren rock gave way to strings of lakes thick beset with reeds.

By then even the dullest of wit must understand that they had not marched toward Avaris, not at all. In the way of armies, who managed to know everything in short order, it was widely understood that they had marched east and then north; that they advanced upon the eastward gates of the Lower Kingdom.

"Sile," Kemni heard men say round the campfires at night. "It has to be Sile. That's where the road into Canaan begins."

Wise men, to see so clearly. They could, if Kemni lingered, map out the whole campaign, and conceive it as clearly as the king ever had.

Even Gebu. Kemni came upon him one night under the stars of this wetter land, in a mist that had risen off the marshes. He was sitting by the fire, shivering with damp, while certain men of the wing took their ease nearby. He was a prince; he must not find it strange that there were always people where he was, and always eyes upon him.

He greeted Kemni with a wan smile and a doleful sneeze. "Good evening, brother," he said.

Kemni squatted on his heels by the fire. "Are you well?" he asked.

"Well enough," Gebu said, though he belied himself with another sneeze. "We're not going to Avaris, are we?"

"We are," Kemni said. "Just not—"

"Just not the shortest way." Gebu warmed his hands over the flames. "So it's true? We're taking Sile?"

Kemni nodded. It was a direct question, after all; and Gebu was under guard. If he succeeded in betraying them after this, then he was a greater master of intrigue than Kemni had ever taken him for.

"That's clever," Gebu said, "cutting off the lifeline before taking the heart. Have you thought of what it would have been like if my uncle Kamose had thought to do that? And if he'd secured Nubia in back of him?"

"He did neither of those things," Kemni said.

"He was young," said Gebu. "Older than we are now, but . . . young. He should have listened to his mother when she told him how to fight his war. But he shut his ears to her. 'War is for men,' he said. 'Stay at home, lady, and rule as you are best fit to rule.' "

Kemni remembered the Queen Ahhotep, who had been mother to Kamose the king, and to Ahmose the king after him, and to Queen Nefertari, too. If any woman could be greater or more terrible than Nefertari, that one had been.

And yet she had yielded to her son's will—reluctantly, as Gebu professed, but in the end obedient.

"Maybe she should have defied him," Gebu mused. "She would have won the war."

"Would you have wanted her to?"

Gebu slanted a glance at Kemni. "If she had," he said, "we wouldn't be camped in this marsh, and I would not be vexed with a rheum in the head."

"Would you stop the war if you could?"

That was a dreadful question, and pure folly. But Kemni's tongue had a will of its own.

Gebu turned to face him. "Why would I want to do such a thing?"

Kemni shrugged. "Because you could?"

"That's mad."

"Not if it gained something. Power. Wealth. A throne."

For an instant Kemni knew that he had done it: he had pierced that mask. There was darkness beneath, black as the space between stars.

Then the mask was whole again. Gebu said with practiced ease, "I have wealth and power. I was born to them. A throne is for the gods to give."

"Would you take one, if it were given you?"

"Wouldn't you?"

"No," Kemni said. "Not if Amon himself offered it. I've no desire to be a king."

"Fortunate man," said Gebu.

+ +

"Madman," Seti said. He had been listening, of course. Most of the wing had been.

"What can he do?" Kemni demanded. "He's under full guard."

"He can think," said Seti.

Gebu was out of earshot, safe in the tent he shared with si-Ebana and two others of the wing. Kemni had in mind to seek his own bed in his own and solitary tent, but he lingered by the dying fire. "A man may think as he pleases," Kemni said. "I catch myself thinking—maybe it's all a deception. Maybe he never did any of it. Even when I saw and heard . . . it might have been a dream or a false seeming."

"It was true," Seti said.

"Then why is he so calm? Why does he seem so pleased to be a charioteer?"

"Maybe," said Seti, "because while he wants to be king, he also wants to drive a chariot. And maybe, when he finds opportunity, he'll try to take the chariot he's been riding in, and bolt for the enemy."

"He won't get far," Kemni said a little grimly. "He's a poor horseman at best, and si-Ebana's team is inclined to be headstrong."

"I had noticed," Seti said. He sighed, yawned, stretched. "I'm for bed, my lord. Will you stay here yet a while?"

"Not long," said Kemni.

"Sleep well, then, my lord," Seti said.

Kemni watched him go, idly, thinking of little but his own bed. The burden of worry, even that which was closest, the man who had been and was no longer his brother, had faded somewhat. He was all but asleep where he sat.

And yet he saw how Seti walked on past the tent that was his, and slipped away into shadows. Without thought, Kemni was up and in pursuit. When he did pause to think, it was that he had seen his second-in-command in odd places before, walking apart from the wing. It was not treachery, surely. It might be a woman. There should have been none among the army, but Kemni knew there were a few smuggled among the tents and the baggage. There always were, in armies.

Kemni wanted to sleep, not to follow Seti to an assignation. And yet he did not turn away from the pursuit. He trusted Seti. He had trusted Gebu; he still wanted desperately to do that. And Gebu was a traitor.

Seti did not go far. In the interlocking rings and squares of the camp, tent was sometimes pitched almost on top of tent, and one wing blurred into the next. This tent might have belonged to either the first or the fourth wing, or to neither. It was pitched out of the light, near a bed of reeds, so that anyone who came or went might not easily be seen.

There was a woman inside, or women. Seti scratched at the flap; a soft voice answered, too high and sweet for a man's.

Kemni knew he should turn and walk away. It was no concern of his if there were women among the charioteers, unless they bred contention. And he had heard not one word of such.

But he had not laid eyes on a woman since he left the Bull of Re. And maybe he had a small and not entirely laudable desire to tax Seti with his deception.

Seti had slipped inside the shadowed tent. There was light within: it gleamed forth briefly as the flap lifted, then vanished again. Kemni guided himself by his memory of that, advanced soft-footed in the dark, and found the flap where he had thought it would be. He paused there, ears sharpened.

There were voices within, but not what one would expect of an assignation in the night: low, intent, no lightness to be heard.

This was a night for the body to do as it pleased in despite of the mind's prudence. Kemni lifted the flap as Seti had, and slipped into a blaze of lamplight.

It was dim in fact, but brilliant after the dark without. Kemni's eyes cleared quickly enough, while he stood dazzled, peering at three shapes that sat decorously in front of him. One was Seti. The others . . .

He was not astonished. He should have expected precisely this. Their absence from the king's farewell; his own abandonment, and never a word or a sight of them. And no wonder, if they had smuggled themselves into the army.

"How?" he asked: the simplest question he could think of.

"Baggage," Ariana answered with equal succinctness. "Who notices servants among the oxen? Or an extra bag or two among the rest?"

"The king will have your hide," Kemni said.

"He may," she agreed, unperturbed. "But he's going to find he needs me when we come to Sile. I can speak to the Cretan captains for him, and win from them respect that he, for all his godhood, would never gain. They'll follow his orders if I'm there to strengthen them."

"Why? Is Crete contemplating treachery?"

"Of course not," she said, nor did she seem offended. "But we have our own ways and our own gods. They'll listen to me where they'd argue with your king."

"I hope he believes that," said Kemni.

"Are you going to drag us in front of him tonight?"

Kemni would dearly have loved to, but after all he had a little sense. "Not tonight," he said, "but sooner than Sile. He'd best know where you are before he begins the battle."

"Why? So that we can distract him?"

"So that he can keep you safe." Kemni sank down to a floor that was rather richly carpeted—part of the concealing baggage, he supposed—and took a moment to simply stare at his queen and her priestess. Iphikleia seemed determined to ignore him. And why she should be angry at him, when she had deliberately flouted the king's own command, Kemni could not imagine. It was a woman's thing, surely. It was always a woman's thing.

But there was a man's thing amid all this, an affair of Kemni's own command. He fixed Seti with a hard stare. "You have earned yourself a whipping for this," he said grimly.

Seti winced, but he shrugged. "So I have, my lord. May I ask that you be a little gentle? You do need me to keep your charioteers in order."

"There is nothing gentle about the rod," Kemni said.

"A few strokes," said Seti, "for those I've earned—but the men will want to know why. Surely you won't—"

Clever, wicked Seti. Of course the men would ask why their commander had flogged his second with right and proper severity; and if Kemni answered, he would betray the women. Which he should very properly do, but he knew that he would not.

So too did they. Ariana smiled at him. Iphikleia turned her eyes upon him at last, and that warmed him even more than Ariana's smile. He should not be so easily subdued, but there was no help for it. No hope, either. Nor could there ever be. He was too utterly hers.

HARVEST

IRY HAD THOUGHT that her time in Avaris would be brief, but it seemed that once the king had got hold of a thing he was reluctant to let it go. Khayan and Iry between them delighted him immoderately. They were, Iry realized, favorites.

She would much have preferred to be disliked intensely—for if she had been, she would have been sent away long since. As it was, she was trapped here in this great mountain of worked stone, in the palace of the conqueror king. She had not even the solace of the Mare. The Mare, like any sensible creature, had refused to enter either city or fortress. She was somewhere amid the fields and marshes of the Lower Kingdom, waiting for Iry to be freed from this captivity.

There was some diversion at least in remembering her promise to Kemni to find a lover for Sadana. Iry was no courtier, least of all of this court, but as the Mare's priestess and the king's favorite, she could go wherever she pleased. If that was to walk among the young men at their drinking and fighting and dancing, so be it. She might have gone among them at their whoring, but they were too shy for that.

She had no honest expectation of finding what she looked for. Sadana was not likely to thank her even for the search. But it was preferable to sitting in the room she had been given, going slowly out of her wits with boredom, or else suffering Sarai's less than tender instruction in the arts she believed the Mare's servant should know. That had not stopped or abated simply because Iry was in Avaris.

But the rest of it, the lessons with Khayan, the instruction with Sadana, had stopped: Khayan's because the Mare was gone, and Sadana's because the warrior woman had not been in evidence since Kemni vanished. No one knew where she was. Iry hoped that she had not gone looking for him—or, gods forbid, found him and discovered what he was.

She must trust that he had escaped, that he had returned to the Upper Kingdom with all that he had discovered. His disappearance had attracted notice, but not too much; people believed, or said that they believed, that she had sent him back to his kin in Memphis, though Iannek would have liked to know why.

"He didn't stay long," he said soon after Kemni's departure. "Was it that easy for everyone to forget whatever he did?"

"Evidently," Iry said in her most dismissive tone.

But Iannek was not to be dismissed. "Don't you find it strange? That as soon as he came here, he went away again? Is there someone here he didn't want to see?"

"That's possible," said Iry.

"It's inconvenient is what it is. I don't suppose anybody is going to take his place?"

"Should anyone?"

That gave Iannek pause. "Someone's got to protect you."

"Why, from what?" Iry asked. "From myself?"

Iannek shrugged uneasily. "You don't know what people here might do. Not everyone's happy to see an Egyptian so close to the king. And since you insist on tramping about, everybody sees you."

"Everybody sees me and grows accustomed to me," she said a little sharply. "Isn't that to my advantage? I've become familiar. I'm no longer anything to marvel at."

"But you might still be something to dispose of." Iannek sighed gustily. "I suppose there's no hope for it. I'll have the servants spread a pallet tonight in front of your door. It's not what my rank calls for, but it is the safest thing."

"You don't have to do that," Iry said. "There are guards everywhere in this part of the palace, especially at night."

Iannek set his jaw and looked obstinate. "You don't know whose guards they may be. And my brother commanded me—"

"Your brother saw a simple way to keep you out of mischief," Iry said.

"And isn't it succeeding?" said that maddening creature. "Maybe he only did it to rein me in, but who's to say you don't need me?"

Iry threw up her hands. "Oh! You'll drive me mad."

"But you'll go mad in safety," said Iannek.

✢ ✢

Sometimes Iry thought she truly would forsake her wits; that she would break and run screaming in search of something, anything, that was not Retenu; that was plain and honest Egyptian. She had the run of that palace, but she could not pass the outer gate. She did try. The guards politely, respectfully, but firmly denied her escape. She was a captive indeed, for all her rank and her freedom within the walls.

At that she stopped. Simply stopped. Sat in her chamber and refused to rise, to eat, to dress, to move. If she was not to claw the walls, she would do nothing. Whatsoever. She would not answer Sarai's summons to her daily lessoning. She would not attend the king when he asked. She would not do anything at all.

People tried to vex her, but for once Iannek proved useful: he kept them out. Not without excessive vexation of his own, but she was inured to that. She could ignore it.

She did not know how long she sat in that dim room. After a while her stomach stopped asking to be fed. She would drink a little water, if her mouth grew parched. It was rather peaceful, once Iannek began to hold visitors at bay. She lost count of those, nor cared who they were. Iannek said once that even the king had come, but had been turned away. "And that won't endear me to him, you can be sure," he said.

She shut the door on him then, and barred it. Then she was blessedly alone.

For a while. Of course these people would not leave a woman to her sulks. They began to hammer at the door, to call out to her, and worse, to consider coming in through the window, even as high and small as that was.

She clapped hands over her ears and buried herself in the coverlets of her bed. It did little good, but it was something to do.

When the door came down, she was half in a dream in which the Retenu had never taken the Two Lands, and her father was alive, and her brothers; and she was the lady of her own household. It looked a great deal like the Golden Ibis, and the man who stood beside her in the dream looked a great deal like Kemni. Except that he was much larger. And no Egyptian had ever had such a face, carved as if with a blade, or a nose like the arc of the new moon.

He did not, in fact, look like Kemni at all, except in being young and male. He looked very much like the face that hovered over her as she started out of her dream, if that face had not been thick with black curly beard.

The door was open behind him, the bar broken. There was no one else with him, not even Iannek. Iry blinked at him. "What did you do to your brother? He only did what I asked."

"I sent him on an errand," Khayan said.

"To repair the door?"

"Among other things." Khayan reached in among the coverlets, got a grip on her, lifted her as easily as if she had been a child, and set her wobbling on her feet. He held her there, which was well, or she would have fallen. "Now tell me. What's the cause of this?"

"Walls," she answered.

He frowned, but not with incomprehension. "They won't let you out?"

"Not past the outer gate."

His frown deepened. He lifted her suddenly, startling her into immobility, and carried her out with a long and purposeful stride.

Just before she had made up her mind to struggle, she saw where he was taking her: to the baths of the women's quarters. They were not empty. Iry saw a blur of faces, none of which she could put a name to, and heard the shrieks of alarm. "Out," Khayan said in his deep voice. It would not have swayed Iry, but these creatures of veils and confinement obeyed as they had been trained to do, and fled.

When they were gone, totally without ceremony, he dropped her into the pool. She sank like a stone in her Retenu robes. The water closed about her. She struggled wildly, thrashing, bursting into the air, blessed air, gasping and choking and spitting water. She lunged at Khayan in pure mindless rage.

He caught her wrists as she clawed at him, pinned them, and set his free hand to the damnable robes. She stopped struggling to glare at him, but did not resist as he stripped her out of all the wet and clinging wool and linen. She had no modesty to constrain her, and no love for these robes, either.

Free at last, and clean, she stood in the pool and still, implacably, glared at him. His eyes did not waver from that or from the sight of her body. "I could have you flogged for this," she said.

"Surely," said Khayan. "But it woke you up. And you are much pleasanter to the nose."

"I was not—"

"Oh, not so bad, no," he said amiably, "but this is better. Will you come out?"

He held out his hand. She glowered at it. It did not fall. She reached for it, but not quite far enough. He leaned to meet her own hand. When he was as far as he could go, she caught hold, and pulled hard.

He tumbled headlong into the pool. Just as she had, he thrashed and struggled and came up gasping. But he was laughing.

She only wanted to wipe the laughter from his face. With grim intent she gripped his robes and tore at them. The wool was strong, but the fastenings gave way. As he had done to her, she stripped him, and left him standing in a puddle of water and wool and linen.

His laughter died, but not into the horror she had hoped for. He was as beautiful as she remembered, a beauty that was nothing like Egyptian beauty.

And he let her look at it. He made no move to cover it. The plait of his hair had fallen over his shoulder. She unbound it. That made him shiver. Someone had told her, somewhere, that no one touched a man's hair among these people but a servant or a lover.

She was not his lover. It could be said that she was his servant—or he, perhaps, hers. She stroked the heavy locks out of the plait, which was as thick as his wrist. Thick and curling, and night-black, but with a faint, ruddy cast. Her fingers loved the touch of it.

His eyes closed. He was doing nothing to stop her. And why? Because he dared not? Or because he had no desire to?

A man, like a stallion, cared little who a woman was, if only she was a woman. Iry bade her hands thrust him away in disgust. Somehow they ran down his breast instead, raking lightly through the crisp curling hair. He shivered, with pleasure it seemed. Certainly his manly member thought so. It was a magnificent thing, small enough beside a stallion's, but for a man's, more than ample for the purpose.

"If I asked you," she said to him, "would you?"

His eyes opened. They were always a little startling under those black brows: amber gold, sun-clear when one expected the dark of deep water. "Do you know," he said to her, "that legend says that when the Mare's servant first rode out of the dawn into Earth Mother's country, she asked that same question of the great queen's son?"

"And what did he answer?" Iry asked.

"He answered," said Khayan, "that if she had chosen him, he could do no other than accept."

"But did he choose her?"

"It's said he did," Khayan said, "and did everything in his power to persuade her to choose him."

"Is that how it's done in the east of the world?"

"Yes," he said.

"And you? Are you like that? Or are you like the rest of the Retenu?"

"If I were like the rest of the Retenu," he said, "I would have taken you that first night in the Sun Ascendant, and had my will of you."

"Even though I proved to be the Mare's servant?"

"I didn't know that then," he said. "And if I had, it might have slowed me, but not for long."

"You could be killed for that."

"A man of the Retenu, doing what a woman clearly asked for? A foreign woman without kin and therefore without honor, even one whom a goddess has chosen? I might be flogged for it, or sent into exile, but no more."

Such words should have wrought cold distance between them. But as they spoke, they moved imperceptibly toward one another, till they were almost touching. Iry was aware of the heat of his body, and the scent of it, salt and musk and sweat, and the lovely pungency of horses. He was so much larger than she—and yet, so were horses. She had no fear of them, not any longer. She had learned not to hate them.

She could never learn not to hate the Retenu. And yet, this man was not entirely of them. His mother's people had never conquered the Lower Kingdom.

He was a lord of the Retenu. He had fought and killed to take that rank. To rule in Egypt; to set his foot on the necks of a conquered people.

And she did not care. Not so close to him, body just apart from body, and no move from him unless she asked it first. Impossible for a man to show such restraint; and yet he did. It was a torment: she saw how he quivered, and how he breathed short and fast. But he was master of himself as of his horses.

If he had broken, if he had seized her, she could have fought him. This stillness, at such cost, broke down all her defenses.

She only had to ask. But if she asked—what then? What would he expect of her? Or she of him?

If she could be like a man, if she could take as a man did, for the moment, and let the rest look after itself—would she take this man?

In an instant.

She closed the space between them. Body to body then, flesh to flesh.

He gasped as if in pain. She could feel the hard hot thing between them, swollen as if it would burst. It was a wonder it had not done that already.

"Do it," she said. "Finish it."

He shook his head. His beard brushed her forehead. Something swelled deep inside her, rose up and grew and bloomed like a flower. But he said, "I can't."

"You *can!*"

He was not going to. Maddening, contrary man.

She knew what a man did, and what a woman did. She had seen it often enough, but never done it. Never wanted it. Never known a man from whom she wanted to take it.

Till this one. This enemy, this lord of a hated people.

"I am asking you," she said. "You have to accept. Yes?"

"No." But it was not an answer; it was more a groan of pain.

She struck him with her clenched fists, hard, on the breast. He grunted but did not fall back. "What is it?" she cried out at him. "You don't want me? Is that it? I'm ugly? I'm little? I'm not one—of—your—own—kind?"

Each word was a blow; and these did drive him back, step by step, till he caught the edge of the pool and fell ignominiously onto the rim. She swooped over him, still pummeling him. "I hate you!"

He gasped and flung up his hands, but not to thrust her away. He pulled her close, too close to strike. So close that there was nothing in the world but that big warm body, and the hot and urgent thing between. There was somewhat that one did—that the body did. One opened. One shifted. One took—with a gasp, and a long moment of impossibility—so large, so very large, she so small. And there was pain, but the urgency was greater. She must do this. She *must.*

The pain mounted till she could not bear it, till she must retreat.

Not retreat. Surrender. Open, ease, allow. And there was still pain, but not so much. It was almost—it was—pleasure.

They lay in a tangle on the pool's edge. He was inside her, filling her to bursting. His eyes were wide. Appalled?

No. Astonished. Maybe afraid. But not appalled.

"Show me," she gasped. "Show me—what—"

To that he was obedient. Even joyful. And gentle. That, she had not expected, even knowing how he was with his horses. He was so big and so strong, like a stallion. But he moved gentle and slow, careful of the pain, waking the beginnings of pleasure. He stroked her, and traced her face and shoulders with kisses. He roused all her body, not only the part that held him within itself, till the simple brush of lips across her lips made her gasp.

Then he began the dance that she had seen but never known, slow at first, but quickening as she learned the way of it. It was like riding the Mare from walk to trot to canter to gallop, the same lift and surge, and the same pure delight in the body's motion.

But there was more than that. Some dim part of her remembered—there was something that happened. Something . . .

This. Like the swell of a wave. Like the hawk arrowing up into the vault of heaven, poising at the zenith, and plummeting like a stone. Down and down and down, headlong, blinding fast, full upon the prey. And the strike, hard and swift, the explosion of feathers, the sudden, enormous, breathless stillness.

Her body throbbed from the center to its outermost extremities. She lay limp along the length of him. He was still inside her, though softening, shrinking. She tried to hold him, but he slipped free.

He was all slack, as she was. She raised her head with great effort and looked into his face. She had half expected that he would be asleep, but his eyes were open. When she met them, they warmed so suddenly and so completely that she nearly wept.

Tears always made her angry. "I suppose you smile like that at all your women," she said nastily.

"Only those who make my heart sing."

"All of them," she muttered.

He shook his head. He was still smiling. Laughing at her.

If she pummeled him again, the rest of it would happen again; and she hurt too much for that. She kissed him instead. His lips were twitching. He gusted laughter through the kiss. She was stiff with fury—and yet she caught that laughter, caught it and could not let go of it. It flung her to the cool tiles, rolling and kicking, roaring for no reason at all, except that the world was one grand and glorious jest, and she was the butt of it.

·········· II ··········

KAYAN WAS BEWITCHED. Ensorceled. Taken altogether by surprise, and altogether by storm.

What Iry thought . . .

His mother and his brother Iannek were merely grateful that, whatever he had done, Iry had come out of her retreat. He doubted that they could imagine how he had done it, or that they would be at all pleased to know. The Mare's servant was not enjoined to any laws but those that bound the women of the tribe, and those set her as free as a man to love when, and how, she pleased. Nevertheless this was not as other Mares' servants had been.

Sarai had told him already: "I will keep her as straitly as any father his daughter, and protect her against any who might prey on her. She is an innocent. I will not have her corrupted."

And Iannek, of course, was Iannek—as headlong a young idiot as ever sprang from a noble house. He would try to hunt down Khayan and kill him, or something equally ridiculous.

Iry, corrupted, dishonored, and robbed of her maidenhood, after succumbing to fits of laughter, sat up hiccoughing and fighting off gusts of giggles, and seemed to realize just then that she had fetched up beside him. She stared at him, all of him, and then down at herself. Her eyes widened a little. "I—I'm—"

She touched the blood that stained her thigh. For an instant he thought she would cry, or scream. But she only stared.

With all the gentleness that was in him, he brought water from the pool, and a soft cloth, and washed the blood away. She let him do that, unresisting, till he began to draw back. Then her hand fell over his, stopping it on her thigh. His breath caught. She did not want him to think what he was thinking—surely she did not.

"You may want," he said carefully, "for a day or two, to do what you would do in your courses. Because sometimes—"

"Sometimes it goes on." She nodded. "I know. I had that lesson. Since, your sister said, I likely wouldn't have learned it from my own mother."

"My sister? Maryam?"

"Sadana." Iry took his hand in both of hers and lifted it to rest between her breasts. Her heart was beating a little quickly, her breath coming a little shallow, but she was remarkably composed. "I'm not going to command you to come back. But if you should wish to . . . you may."

"And will you welcome me?"

Her breath shuddered as she drew it in. "I—if you want me—"

"How could I not want you?"

"But I'm not—"

"Stop that," he said. It was not perhaps a wise or a respectful thing to do, but he gathered her in his arms, drew her in like a child, curled in his lap with her head on his shoulder. She did not resist, not at all. She sighed in fact, and nestled against him.

"What do we do now?" she asked. Her voice was lighter than usual, as childlike as her comfort in his lap, but he knew better than to think that her mind was a child's.

"What do we do?" he echoed. "Why, whatever you like."

"No," she said with a hint of impatience. "Tell me what I should do. Should I walk away? Should I pretend that this never happened? What is proper? *Is* anything proper?"

"In the east," he said slowly, "you would have several choices. You could send me away as unsatisfactory. You could express yourself pleased, and invite me back into your bed. You could even, if you were truly delighted, order me to move myself and my belongings into your tent."

"And you? Would you have any say in it at all?"

"I could refuse to come back, though I might not insist on coming if you forbade me."

"What if I ordered you to move into my—not tent; my rooms, then. What would you do?"

"It would be a scandal," he said.

"Would you refuse?"

"No," he said. He did not know what he would say until he said it, but that was the answer that came to him. It was not the reasonable answer, or the sensible one. It was the one that his heart spoke, as he met that clear and level stare.

"What if I ordered you to go away and never speak to me again?"

In spite of himself, his belly clenched. "I . . . would obey."

"Willingly?"

"You know I wouldn't."

"Do I know that?" She frowned slightly. Her head tilted. "You don't lie, do you? Many in this court, they live in a fabric of lies. Everything they do is false, sometimes a little, sometimes entirely. They dance a long dance of words that are not true, and faces that are masks, and smiles that never reach the eyes."

"That isn't so in an Egyptian court?"

"I've heard it's so wherever there are kings," she said. "But you tell the truth. You must be well hated."

"Am I?"

"I haven't noticed," she said.

Of course she had not. She was above the petty maneuverings of the court.

Khayan was, he realized, utterly besotted with her. It struck him with the force of a revelation, though it had been clear enough for a while that he found her more than merely interesting. As he looked at her now, his heart melted, and another part of him would have been delighted to continue what they had begun not so long before.

She did not notice that any more than she had noticed whether Khayan was loved or hated in the court of Avaris. Women were like that. They could think of a dozen things at once, and ignore the one that, to a man, was most important.

He sighed faintly.

She heard that. "You must have somewhere to be," she said.

He shrugged. "Nowhere more important, or that I'd rather be."

"That's charming," she said, "but I'm sure you're wanted in many more places than this one. If I promise to behave myself, and go to my lessons with your mother, will you go where you were going before you rescued me?"

"Was it a rescue?" he asked.

"From myself," she said. She paused as if to gather courage. Then she said, "Tonight we both should rest. Tomorrow night . . . come to me. If you will. And only if."

"I will come," he said. "My word on it."

The light in her face almost felled him. It was all he could do to dress—with her help, which flustered him far more than he ever wanted her to see—and make order of himself, and gather his wits to face the greater world.

She all but pushed him out the door, with a promise to follow after a judicious while, properly and modestly attired. That, from her, was no small promise.

It was almost pain to walk away from her, to become a lord of the people again, to think as a man and a warrior, and not as a lover. He had to pause once, in a corridor mercifully deserted, and lean against the cool stone of the wall, and simply breathe.

Women did not do such things to him. He had loved, so he thought, and more than once: a priestess of the tribe, a chieftain's daughter, and yes, the lovely and wanton Barukha, whom—thank the gods—he was not likely to find in his bed tonight; her father was keeping her close. He had had great pleasure of them, and great joy. But when he was not with them, he seldom thought of them, except when his manly organ grew weary of waiting for him to notice their absence.

This woman he thought of often. He always had, even in the beginning, when she was a baffling and excessively forward child, a slave among his slaves. And of course once the Mare chose her, he had to think of her. He was one of her teachers. But what he was thinking of teaching her now had little to do with chariotry, or with the mastery of horses—unless that were of mares in season.

He had to stop this. He had to clear his mind. It was late, but not so late that he could let himself slip out of the thing that he had been set to do when his mother sent for him and bade him rouse the Mare's servant from her decline. He sincerely doubted that she had intended him to do it as he had, but she would surely be pleased with Iry's new diligence.

And if Iry told his mother what he had done . . . why then, he could only die once.

With a short bark of laughter, he thrust himself upright, shook his robes into place, and strode onward with new and firmer purpose.

✦ ✦

The gods, it seemed, had been kind. The king's guards greeted him as amiably as always. One, who had shared a jar or three of wine and a game or six of the bones with Khayan, grinned at him and said, "You're in luck, my lord. He was out later than he expected; he's just come in. There's men with him, but he said to send you in when you came."

Khayan breathed a sigh of relief. "Ah. That's well."

"We've got a game in the offing tonight," the guard said. "Come and play with us if the king lets you go."

"I'll do that," Khayan said willingly enough. If he was not to go to Iry, a game in the guardroom would do.

He passed the guards with a smile and a nod, into the rooms that he had come to know well since he came out of the east. The king would be in the smaller audience chamber, if he was entertaining guests; and indeed, there he was, with a larger gathering than Khayan had expected. Khayan recognized most of them: the chancellor of the kingdom, one or two commanders of the armies, the master of horse, and a gathering of nobler courtiers. Khayan was hardly a minor lord, but in this company he was both the youngest and the least.

He thrust himself past that moment's hesitation. The king had asked for him. It was awkward to come in so late, but Apophis betrayed no anger. He rose, in fact, and beckoned to Khayan, bidding him sit at his own right hand, and calling the servants to bring him whatever he desired.

Those signs of great favor could hardly go unnoticed. Khayan marked whose eyes slid, and whose face went a little too still. *Young puppy,* these august lords must be thinking. But they maintained expressions of civility, and made no effort to challenge him. There was time for that later.

Once Khayan was settled with a cup of wine, the council—for so it was—returned to the deliberations that he had interrupted.

"You do believe this?" Apophis asked his general of the armies.

That old soldier, who had lost a hand in some battle long ago but who was still a deadly fighter, nodded his scarred and grizzled head and said, "Ten years ago this city was almost taken by the Egyptians because we were caught off guard. But for your foresight, my lord, in bidding Nubia remember its alliance, we would have lost this kingdom that our fathers conquered."

"The Egyptian was driven back," one of the lesser lords said. "He died not long after, fighting Nubians, it's said. His brother, who took the throne—his brother has never offered us even a skirmish. He's ruled by women, they say: first by his mother, then by the wife he inherited from his brother."

"She's his sister, I'm told," said the man next to him. He shuddered. "Barbarian, to bed his own father's child."

They all murmured at that, except Apophis and the general Khamudi, who were intent on the greater concern. "I do believe," Khamudi said, "that the rumors are true. The Egyptian is mustering his armies. Have you had word from Nubia since last the moon was at the full? Have you sent messengers there? It's been silent, my lord. As if the Egyptian has cut us off from our allies."

"How can he do that?" the minor lord demanded. "Or if he's done it, maybe he's marching into Nubia. It's rich country, and everyone covets it. Why not the Egyptian?"

"Because," Khamudi said with an air of sorely strained patience, "the

Egyptian would find it more satisfying to attack us and take back what his predecessors used to hold."

"Rebellion," said the master of horse. He sounded unsurprised. "Yes, I've heard rumors, rumblings in the earth. These people are servile, but some of them are proud. Those would pay dearly to drive us back the way we came."

"*We* came from this very country," the chancellor said. "I was born in this city. I'm as Egyptian as any of these alleged rebels."

"Remember what the late pharaoh said," said Khamudi, "when he stood in front of these walls and taunted us with his victory. 'Vile Asiatics,' he called us. 'Dogs of foreigners.' "

"And he fled," said the chancellor, "and died soon after. Surely his people understood what the gods were telling them."

"And yet rumor is," the king said, "that his successor is marching toward us."

"Rumor only," the chancellor said. "I've sent out spies and runners. There's word of a fleet well south of Memphis, but no one has seen it sailing northward. If it exists at all, I suspect that it is there simply to taunt us. The Egyptian is hardly strong enough to challenge our armies—and he has no more than his kingdom will supply, while we have the might of Asia at our backs."

"Suppose," Khayan ventured to say, "that he had found a way to cut us off from that. It's a narrow ribbon of road that binds us to our people. What if he managed to cut it?"

They all regarded him as if he had been a child piping up in the council of his elders. Even the king looked on Khayan with more patience than credence.

"How would he cut off the road to Asia?" the chancellor demanded. "We hold all the ways to it. And even if managed that—what strength would he have? We have great armies. He would have no more than he could spirit through the desert or across the marshes and fens, which are impenetrable. His attempt would be feeble and doomed to fail."

Khayan shut his mouth carefully, though words in plenty begged to tumble out of it. They were all nodding, some smiling at him with pitying expressions, others looking much too pleased at what they reckoned his folly.

Maybe it was folly. It would be a ghastly undertaking, and impossible to sustain, even if it could be done at all. But if he were the Egyptian king, he would look for a way to do it. Particularly if he could rely on the Egyptians within the kingdom—whose numbers were vast, and Khayan's own people terribly few—to rise up and fight for him when he came.

"So," Apophis said in the stretching silence. "No one has more than rumors. All's quiet within the kingdom. If the fleet moves, if it exists—we'll know, yes?"

They all nodded. Khamudi said, "Most rumors I'll ignore, my lord. But this one is worth our attention. If it's false, well, our young men could use a dose of marching and guarding. A sufficiency of days in the sun and nights in the fens, with hardships enough, and maybe a skirmish—that would keep them quiet for a while."

"Then you would take a company or two southward," Apophis inquired, "and investigate these rumors of a fleet?"

"Perhaps three large companies," Khamudi said, "or four. A show of strength would not be amiss."

"Do it," said Apophis.

Khamudi bowed in his seat.

"Sire," Khayan said. "If it's as simple a matter as that, and as little a thing, why not send a company to Sile, too? If nothing else, the march will give them occupation, and they can visit their kin in Asia if they've a mind."

Apophis considered that. Khayan granted him as much. "It might not be an ill thing," he said. "But if attack comes upon us, it will come from the south. Best not to dissipate our forces by sending a portion of them into the north."

"But if the attack is from the north—"

"My dear young cousin," Apophis said warmly, but with a warning beneath, "your concern is admirable. But there is no danger from the north."

Khayan bowed his head. "Then . . . sire, might I take my own men, and only those, on a training-march? And perhaps we may pause at Sile, and assure ourselves that my fears are unfounded?"

"In time," said Apophis, "perhaps. For now, I prefer you here."

There was nothing Khayan could say to that. This was the king, and these were the wisest of his counselors. If they saw no merit in what he proposed, then perhaps, indeed, it was only silliness.

The council ended so, with Khayan set aside, and Khamudi bidden to march into the south in search of the Egyptian king's fleet. Khayan would have left with the others, but Apophis kept him there with a word and a glance.

That was not excessively well received. But Apophis took no notice. When the last of the lords had passed the door, and there were only the servants and Khayan remaining in the suddenly empty hall, Apophis said, "There, lad. No need to sulk. Are you tired of this city already?"

"No, sire," Khayan said. "But—"

"I understand," Apophis said, and smiled. "Come, then. What would you say to a few days' escape? A hunt—we'll hunt for whatever the land will give us."

"May we hunt northward?" Khayan asked—daring greatly, but he did not care.

Apophis laughed. "O persistence! Yes, we may hunt northward, if that's your whim. Go on, choose your companions. We'll leave tomorrow."

Khayan stopped short at that. "Tomorrow, my lord?"

"It's somewhat late to begin today," Apophis said.

Khayan began to correct him, but though better of it. What could he say? The truth? *Sire, I have debauched the Mare's servant, and she commands me to attend her tomorrow night. If you will only put off the hunt for a day—*

No, the truth would not do. And Khayan, as Iry had said, did not lie. He settled on silence. He bowed, accepted a blessing on his head, and let himself be dismissed.

·········· III ··········

I RY DID NOT believe it when she saw it. Their chambers were in an uproar. All the men were leaving, it seemed—riding off in the morning to hunt with the king. "A great hunt," one of the young idiots half-sang in an ecstasy of delight. "Days and days. Maybe a whole month—riding and living in a tent and hunting whatever quarry the gods bring."

"And whose golden inspiration was that?" she demanded.

The boy goggled at her. The last he or anyone had known, after all, she was shut in her room, pining away for who knew what cause. But he was obedient enough to answer her question. "Why, lady, the Lord Khayan's."

"Khayan—" She broke off. "Not the king's?"

"I'm sure I don't know, my lady," the boy said.

"But tomorrow night he—"

That was not anything this child needed to know. She let him go where he was clearly desperate to go, on some errand or other involving a great deal of speed and enthusiasm.

Some said the king had ordered this expedition, but most laid it at Khayan's door. Iry hardly needed to ask why. So: he had not wanted her after all. How clever of him to persuade the king to take him away before he could be forced to lie with her again.

She was not angry. Oh, no. She was too intent on murder to be angry.

Of course they were taking no women with them. This was a men's hunt. Though no doubt there would be maids and servants, and suitable pleasure for the evenings. Of which he would take his ample share.

She was not going to lock herself in her room again. No. This time she would take refuge with the Lady Sarai. That formidable woman appeared content to accept Iry's renewed diligence and her heightened attention to lessons that grew steadily more complicated. This was the art of statecraft, the manifold skills of ordering tribes and nations. She might have had no head for it, except that she needed something, anything, to take her mind off that horrible man.

But her body remembered anything but horror. Kisses as deep and sweet as his voice, and hands that knew how to wake such sensations as she had never known. It remembered the warmth of his arms and the thick softness of his hair, falling over his shoulder and brushing her breast.

Such memories should have distracted her sorely; but in turning away from them, she focused all the more intently on the proper protocols for addressing each level of envoy from a foreign king, from princely ambassador to lowly message-runner.

"I'm not a queen," she said. "Why do I have to know these things?"

"Because what you are is higher than a queen," Sarai said as calmly as always. "Whatever a queen can do, you must do better."

Since that was true, Iry held her tongue and set to learning what she was set to learn. And ignoring the tumult without, which seemed quite excessive for as small an expedition as it was. They were not mounting a war; they were simply going hunting with the king.

That tensed her spine, but as far as she could tell, none of them knew that there was, in fact, a war coming upon them.

She was deep in the intricacies of yet another ritual—this one of birthing, and yet also of dying—when she heard a voice without that she knew too well. Khayan had come to muster the troops, with much laughter and easy camaraderie, as there always was when he was among his men. It struck her that such a thing was not usual. He had come as a stranger, an interloper, who had grown to manhood in a foreign land; and he had made himself beloved of his father's people. That was not an easy thing to accomplish.

And she was not in a mood to admire him. He stayed away from his mother, at least, and from the women. That suited Iry very well.

Very well indeed. Yes.

✦ ✦

In the morning they left, the whole uproarious lot of them, filling the courtyards with shouting and clatter. All the pomp and state that accompanied a royal hunt in Egypt was little enough in evidence here. The king was remarkable only in that his scale-armor was washed with gold, and his chariot bright with gilt. His weapons looked well worn and rather plain, like the man himself.

Iry had not intended to watch them go, but she happened to be near a window when the clamor began. She saw them all with their chariots, most drawn by asses, though the king's and of course Khayan's rolled behind a team of horses. Khayan was close by the king, and by no means the largest or the most imposing of all those big bearded men, and yet there was something about him that drew the eye.

She had no desire to follow him with her gaze, and yet her eyes had a will of their own. It was the body again, remembering.

If one meeting of body to body was enough to rob a woman of her wits,

then no wonder so many women were fools. Iry turned her back on the window and on the great riding that streamed out of the court, and went back to
her lessons in the arts of priestesses who were more than queens.

✢ ✢

Khayan tried thrice to gain admission to the women's quarters before he left
on the king's hunt. But the Lady Sarai had forbidden ingress to any man for
that day and night, because, the door-guard said, she was engaged in teaching
the Mare's servant one of the great rites.

That might even have been true. Or perhaps she had guessed what Khayan
had done with Iry. Women knew. It was a magic of theirs.

Even a messenger, even one of the maids, was not allowed to pass. Without
help and without forgiveness, then, Khayan left the palace of Avaris.

He was almost cravenly glad to leave those walls and to be free of that vast
and crowded city. The king's riding had all the road free before it. Passersby
fled his coming. Caravans hastened to open the way. Lesser lords and princes
either drew back or called out, "Sire! Where away?" And when they had their
answer, some of them joined in the riding, either right then and there or later
in the morning.

Khayan did not forget Iry. Never. But among these men of his own kin
and kind, he could ease his spirit, and smooth away the tightness of too long
a time within walls.

At night in the camp, he would remember her, lying alone on his blanket.
Many of the men had brought women for their pleasure, packed among the
servants and the baggage. They would happily have shared with him, but he
smiled and refused. Wine, companionship, dancing and song, he would take,
but women . . . no. They were not Iry.

Oh, he was besotted. He laughed at himself while he lay there, listening
to the sounds of pleasure outside the tent's walls. When he slept he dreamed
of her; not true dreams or dreams of prophecy, but memories all the sweeter
for that they were so brief.

When at last the king allowed him to return to Avaris, he would make his
amends to her as he could, and love her with all his heart. But now, while
there was no hope for it, he would ride and hunt as the king wished, and be
as happy as his spirit would let him be.

Wherever the king was, runners came and went, messengers bringing word
of things that even on a hunt the king must be aware of. Khamudi's company of
picked men had gone away southward. They had not, as yet, found any sign of
invaders, whether on the river or on the land.

"Did they look in the desert?" Khayan asked at that.

"Nothing," the runner said. "It's quiet. The young men are not pleased."

"I can imagine," Khayan said dryly.

With such news to ease their hearts—though Khayan was on edge still, like the fool he no doubt was—they made their way north and somewhat west, into the depths of the marshes where the hunting was gloriously rich. So too were the swarms of stinging flies, and the crocodiles in the braided streams of the river, but those were little enough to deter the men of the people. All day they hunted, and in the evening they ate the fruits of the hunt.

On the day when they met the great herd of riverhorses, and the king himself brought down the great bull—and lost a loyal servant doing it, the hapless man torn in two by the great jaws and the ivory teeth—a messenger came to them from a new direction. North, he came from, and east. He rode in a chariot behind a pair of stumbling and nigh foundered asses, wounded himself, and haggard as if he had ridden day and night without rest or nourishment.

"Sile," he said. "They're taking Sile."

The king's glance flashed to Khayan. For an instant Khayan feared that it was suspicion—that he might be accused of being a spy. But the king taxed him with nothing. He simply said, "We stop here. Send for the servants."

+ +

Wine from the king's own wineskin, and bread and onions and a slab of cheese, restored the messenger remarkably. He would not rest in the camp they made a safe distance from the riverhorses' pool, until he had told the king all he knew.

"He's laid siege to Sile," he said. "The king from Thebes—the Egyptian. He came out of the empty lands, with his armies—and chariots, sire. He came with chariots. He has a whole great herd of horses, and—"

"Horses?" the king broke in. "Not asses?"

"Horses," the man said. "Good ones, fast, well trained. But they're not all he has. He has a fleet. A vast fleet, sire, of ships that ride on the sea."

"Ships that ride on the sea?" Apophis repeated. "But Egypt has no—"

"Crete does," the messenger said.

The king had been on his feet, pacing as he listened, as he liked to do. It helped him think, he said. At that, he stopped, wheeled, and nearly fell. He groped his way to his chair, and sank into it. "Crete? They've made pact with Crete?"

"Those are Cretan ships, sire," the messenger said.

"Sile," Apophis said as if to himself, "and Crete." He lifted his head, frowning at the sky. "Gods, what fools we've been. What arrogant fools."

"Sire," Khayan ventured to say. "We're numerous enough here, and armed. If we leave as soon as we can, we might be able to—"

"No," the king said. And to the messenger: "Tell me the rest of it."

The man bowed in his seat, drank deep of his wine as if to gather courage, and said, "The army came from the empty country, and the fleet from the sea. They surrounded us before we knew what we had seen. We were able to man the defenses and to barricade the walls, but their numbers are great, and they've cut off the road in back of us. They'll hold back any who try to come from Canaan."

Apophis nodded. He could see it if Khayan could, though he had refused Khayan leave to stop it before it began.

Khayan spoke again. "Sire, if they've laid siege—how long ago? Two days ago? Three?—there's time. We can win the city back and crush them before they move south."

"They will be coming down the river," Apophis said as if he had not heard him. "There is a fleet in the south, even if Khamudi can't find it. We're threatened on both sides."

War. Khayan did not know who first said the word. But in scarce a dozen heartbeats, it had hummed through the camp. *War. We've found us a war.*

But the king was not to let them have it. Not all of them. After that first moment's prostration, he was on his feet again, as strong of will and wit as he had ever been, snapping out orders almost too fast to follow.

Those of the lords who had joined the hunt on its way, and those with holdings nearest this country and toward Sile, he bade return home with all speed, and muster every man of theirs who could fight. As soon as that was done, they must make of themselves a wall to the south of Sile, and prevent the Egyptian and his seaborne allies from advancing deeper into the kingdom. The one he set in command of them was not Khayan. It was one of the generals who had been in the council, sitting in Khamudi's shadow.

The rest of them, and Khayan, would return to Avaris. "I need you there," Apophis said before Khayan could voice his protest. "You'll get your fight, I promise you. This war will come from south as well as north. I want you with me when the second attack comes."

Khayan had no choice but to bow his head to that. There was no reward for foresight, after all, and no advantage in having seen before anyone else, how the enemy would choose to fall on the kingdom.

✦ ✦

So quickly it all changed, from hunt to war. The young rakehells in the king's following were beside themselves with gladness. Most of them, Khayan noticed, were let go with Khamudi's lieutenant. The steadiest and the most sensible, such as they were, remained with the king.

He supposed he should be flattered to be counted high among them. And it was true, there would be war enough for everyone.

In very short order, those who would ward the borders of Asia had gathered weapons and baggage and gone. The king was not in quite so much haste, but neither did he see fit to camp in that place. He paused only to take the great ivory tusks of the riverhorse. The rest he left for the crocodiles, and for the vultures that had been circling since the hunt began. When the sun had passed the zenith, they had taken the road to Avaris, with messengers sent ahead in swift chariots to warn the city of what would come upon it.

Khayan he kept at his right hand. Khayan hoped it was for liking, and not for mistrust.

Khayan's mood was vile. He was being a fool, and he knew it. He had no need to ride to Sile. But to be given the command of that venture—that would have been an honor, and one he would have been glad of.

Many would have said that he was more greatly honored to be kept so close to the king and admitted to all his counsels. Apophis in the face of war was no longer the easy and affable man who had taken such delight in his menagerie. This was a hard man and a king, and a great commander of armies.

Armies which he must gather, and prepare in haste. As he rode toward Avaris, his runners ran tirelessly to all the lords and holdings, and bade them gather their fighting men.

By evening, in the way of such things, the news had run ahead of them. The kingdom had roused. Its lords were gathering their weapons. The lesser folk, the conquered people, labored unregarded, except perhaps by Khayan. War or no, there was a harvest to get in, wheat and barley and the lesser fruits of the earth.

"Sire," Khayan said as they rode at speed through fields of ripe barley and little dark people cutting it with sickles. "This harvest—can it be got in faster? If the enemy comes so far, and finds only empty fields, he'll find nothing to feed himself. And if the harvest is gathered and stored well apart from his advance, and guarded with as much strength as we can spare . . ."

"Indeed," Apophis said. "That's well thought of. See that it's done."

Khayan bowed to that: to the trust as well as the command. It was a gift, whether the king knew it or no. Khayan chose to take it as such.

················ **IV** ················

O
N THE THIRD day they came back to Avaris, the king and his much diminished hunting party. Behind them was a kingdom in uproar, lords mustering troops, men arming for war. And far behind them, on the borders of Asia, the war itself had begun and continued.

The city seemed, at first sight, to be no more or less crowded or tumultuous than it ever was. But the crowds were impenetrable, the tumult deafening. Everyone who could had come seeking shelter within those high walls, under the king's protection.

Apophis rode in to a thunder of cheering and a torrent of gladness. Khayan could feel the strength pouring into him, even from in front of him, struggling a little with the stallions, who though weary with long marching at a hard pace, tossed their heads and pranced at the roar of the crowd. The people's love was a strong drug, stronger than wine. It made him dizzy.

The palace walls cut off the worst of it, though it surged still without, like a roar of the sea, as the rest of the army made its way through the city. There was fear—war always brought that, fear of death, fear of pain—but not fear of defeat. That, Khayan's bones knew. They were a strong people, and they had ruled in this land for a hundred years. They would win this war.

"And this time," Apophis' princes said in council, "we win it forever. Let us crush the Egyptian and all his armies. And when we have done that, let us pursue him even to Thebes, and do what we should have done years since: take the other half of Egypt, and make it our own."

Always before when Apophis had heard such counsel, he had pointed out, with crushing logic, that they were strong but they were few, and the great length of Egypt, with all its crowded people, was a hard prize to hold with such numbers as they had. But now he only nodded. "We have to consider that," he said, "yes. Or they'll keep coming back, and keep defying us, till they manage to destroy us."

Then he sent a strong force to Khamudi south of Memphis, to block the fleet when it came down the river. So guarded in the south as well as the north, with his own city strengthened greatly between, he settled to wait, and to rule the kingdom while his generals waged war far afield.

Khayan came late to his rooms, very late indeed, and stumbling on his feet. He had gone direct from march to council, and had dined with the king after—astonished at Apophis' tirelessness. When he left the hall, Apophis was still in it, passing round the wine and ordering the disposition of his armies.

Khayan had his own orders. His levy from the Sun Ascendant was to stay where it was, on guard over the herds of horses—such of them as would not be sent to one or the other of the generals for use in the war. He would be very well paid for that, in lands and treasure.

And he was to stay with the king. He was the king's charioteer. It was an office of great honor, and great power if he chose to take it. Which he might well do. He had drunk from the king's cup, out in the city. He would not be averse to another taste.

Dangerous thoughts, he told himself wryly as he passed the guard at his own door. He stopped in the outer room, yawning hugely. There was no servant waiting to undress him. At last: the palace servants had understood that Khayan preferred to look after himself before he slept, though he was glad enough of help in the morning. He dropped his robes and his ornaments with a sigh of relief, leaving them for the servants to find, and stretched till his bones cracked. Another yawn seized him as he half-walked, half-stumbled into the inner room.

The lamps were lit, the nightlamp in its niche and the cluster by the bed. They cast a soft glow across the coverlets. Those were fresh, scented with some green herb. Someone had scattered petals across them, as if he had been a prince. He shook his head at that, and lay down with a sigh that was half a groan.

He should rise again, blow out the lamp-cluster. But the bed was marvelously comfortable. Sleep toyed with him, hovering just out of reach. Memories flickered behind his eyes. The king's face, the great riverhorse dying, the messenger and his staggering team, shouts and cries and the dim clangor of war.

Soft hands stroked his back. Warm breath tickled his nape. A supple body fitted itself against him.

He was suddenly and completely awake. All through the hunt and the beginning of war, he had kept memory at bay, had let himself forget that he had left Iry without a word. But it seemed she had forgiven him. Her hands stroked down his breast and belly to grasp his wakening rod, tightening softly round it, stroking and teasing, knowing just where to—

Iry would not know *that*. Only one pair of hands would tease him precisely so.

He tensed to turn, but she held him fast. "Barukha," he said. "I thought you were with your father."

"My father has gone to fight with Khamudi in the south," she said. "He gave me leave to go back to your mother. Aren't you glad? Aren't you delighted to have me back again?"

"You should not be here."

"Silly man," she said indulgently. "Of course I shouldn't. But aren't you glad?"

His manly organ was in bliss. The rest of him, insofar as it had wits to think, could only see one face. And that was not Barukha's.

Somehow, he never quite knew how, he worked himself free. He stood swaying. Barukha lay in his bed, naked and beautiful. She stretched, and wriggled a little, arching her back till her breasts jutted boldly at him.

"Go," he said to her. "Let me be."

Her smile did not fade. She raised a knee and let it fall lazily to the side, opening herself to him, black curly hair, moist pink lips like the petals of a flower.

He tore his eyes from that secret place. "I said, go."

"My dear sweet man," she said, "what's come over you? Did some outraged papa catch you, one night on the hunt? Did he whip you? Let me see— let me kiss the memory away."

"Barukha," he said, his voice so low it was a rumble in his chest. "I want you to go."

At last it seemed to dawn on her that he was not toying with her. Maybe she had not seen his face at all, only his body. And that had obliged him by going cold. She was beautiful; she was alluring. He did not want her.

Then she looked up past it. He did not know what she saw in his face, but her own went still. "You really—want me—"

He nodded.

She shook her head slightly, once. "You can't do that."

"I am doing it."

"I said, you can't." She rose to her knees amid the coverlets. "Tell me who she is."

Khayan set his lips together. He should deny any knowledge of another woman. He knew that. But he could not lie. He never had been able to. Therefore he resorted to silence.

"Tell me," Barukha pressed him. *"Tell me!"*

He would not.

She sank back on her heels. "That shouldn't matter. Should it? All women have to share. Men take as many as they like. I'll share you. I won't like it, but is the way the world is. Isn't it?"

"I don't want to be shared," he said. His heart was as cold as his voice. It was true. He did not. He had not expected that. Barukha was beautiful. She was a marvelous lover. And gods knew, he was far from the first that she had ever taken, nor did he expect that he would be the last.

He did not want her. Perhaps he never truly had. What he wanted was a slip of an Egyptian girl with neither art nor skill, but sweetness beyond any other he had known.

He could not say that to Barukha. "Go," he said. "If you won't be commanded, I beg you. Surely there's another man who can give you what you look for. He might even be prettier."

She did not smile at that. She wore no expression at all. "You're casting me out."

"I'm asking you to go. For your safety even more than my own. If your father hears—"

"My father." She laughed. It was a strange sound, light yet brittle. "Do you know what I did, Khayan? Do you know what happened to me? When I was shut up in his house, wrapped in veils till I was like to suffocate, and no servants near me but women and eunuchs, I knew that I could never live like that. I couldn't be some old man's harem ornament. I need a young man, a strong man, a man who will let me have the free air. Then I knew. It came to me like the voice of a god. I wanted you. No other man. You. When my father comes back from the war, you must ask him for me. You're rising high in the kingdom; the king loves you. My father will find you worthy. You'll see."

"Barukha," Khayan said in a kind of despair.

"It will be a very suitable match," she said. "Even my father has to see that."

"Barukha," Khayan said. "I can't—"

"The bride price is high, of course. But you can pay it. You're a royal favorite. You can ask the king for whatever my father demands."

"Barukha!" Khayan said sharply—with a small start as it struck him. A name spoken thrice: so Egyptians gained power over one another.

Barukha was not one to be ruled by any man, except by force. But she stopped her babbling. She stared at him.

"I will not marry you," Khayan said. "I will not bed you. Come, where are your clothes? I'll take you back to your rooms. You sleep in my mother's chambers, yes?"

"Yes," she said rather faintly.

"Good," said Khayan. "Good. Here." Her gown was close by, gods be thanked: crumpled in a heap beside the bed.

He lifted it and shook it out. She made no move to take it. With a sigh he laid it about her shoulders, lifted her unresisting arms to slip them into the sleeves, reached to draw the front of it closed. She stirred at his touch, turned a fraction, till her breast filled his hand. He drew back quickly. The robe gaped open. She made no effort to cover herself. Quite the opposite. Her hand rose to cup her breast, stroking its nipple to tauten it. "I'm beautiful, aren't I?" she said.

"Very beautiful," he said, but stiffly. With greater care then, he drew the robe across her breast and belly, lapping it over, fastening it as was proper and modest. "Come; I'll take you back where you belong."

"Yes," she said in a voice that was half a sigh. "Do that."

He knew better than to think that she had surrendered. But she had yielded, he thought, to the inevitable. Somewhat belatedly he remembered to put on a garment of his own. The first thing that came to hand was a night-robe like hers, light and open. He fastened it with a cord, and reckoned that it would do. He was not about to parade either of them through the public ways of the palace.

They went the way she must have come, through a small inner door to a passage that led, in time, to his mother's rooms. It was a servants' corridor, narrow and ill-lit, but there was enough light from a lamp or two in a niche, to find his way. Barukha clung to him, stumbling a little. It might be a ruse, but truly, it was dark. He let her find her balance against his body.

It was not far at all, but more than far enough, in Khayan's estimation, before she said, "Here. My room is here."

The door opened on a surprisingly large chamber, with an ample bed in it, and a golden lamp. Barukha stumbled on the threshold and nigh went down. Khayan caught at her. Her arms locked about him.

He struggled free. She flailed at him, clawing, spitting, diving for his eyes. He flung up a hand to defend himself. It struck flesh—her face, as if she had cast herself in its way. He drew back appalled, but she pursued him, hammering at him, till he seized her and pulled her to him to make her stop.

She melted against him—briefly, before he gathered himself to pull away. Then she erupted anew. Struggling. Shrieking. Shrilling like a mad thing. "Let me go! *Let me go!*"

He was trying desperately to do just that, but every move she made clutched him the tighter. He clapped a hand over her mouth. "Idiot! Do you want to—"

She bit him. He cursed. She screamed all the louder.

The outer door burst open. Faces—eyes—staring, gaping, weapons gleaming as guards poured into the room.

Then at last, and mercifully, she ceased her shrieking. She slumped in his arms, hands fisted in his robe. As she sank down, she took it with her, leaving him bare to all the staring eyes.

She lay at his feet. Her own robe had given way, baring a long lovely leg, a round white breast. It was scratched and torn. She must have done that, somehow, in her struggles.

He looked up into the crowding faces. The shock in them mirrored his own. He found his voice somewhere, enough of it to speak. "Someone fetch a physician. She's taken a fit, I think."

His words fell dead in the silence. They were all staring, not at her, but at him. And no wonder, with his robe at his feet, and the poor mad creature sprawled on it. He bent to retrieve it.

Like hounds on the lion, the guards fell on him. They bore him back and away from her, and flung him down with force enough to knock the wind out of him. He tried to protest, to struggle, but there were too many. They were too strong.

It only came to him once he was down and pinned, with a guard's sword pointed at his throat and another at his manly parts, what they must think they had seen. A man in the women's quarters at night, locked in struggle with a woman, and he naked and she nearly so. If he had seen it, he would have thought exactly the same.

He stopped fighting. They hauled him up, not gently, and bound his hands behind his back—wrenching at his shoulders till he gasped. "Serves you right," one muttered. "Son of a dog."

He clenched his jaw against a spate of words. Barukha was still lying where he had left her, in a flock of chattering women. Those kept glancing at him— glaring murderously, though some let their eyes linger.

He would have to try to understand. Somehow. If there was time; if he was let live for violating a lord's daughter in her own chamber.

Or was it? He did not recognize these women. They were all strangers. Unless his mother had cast off all her maids and servants, these were not his mother's women.

The guards dragged him out before he could ask the women who they were. He set himself to go limp, to offer no resistance. They grunted as they took the brunt of his weight, but it was better for him than fighting.

They did not cast him in prison, perhaps because it was a very long way down from these heights to the stronghold's foundations. They thrust him into a room and left him there.

There was no light in the room. It was black as the pit of Set's heart. Khayan lay for a while on his face where he had been flung. But his shoulders were crying in pain. He rolled and struggled and scrambled, and somehow got to his knees; then, with a grunt of effort, to his feet. He almost fell again, but somehow managed to stay erect.

He stood for a moment and simply breathed. Then he moved. Carefully, foot sliding in front of foot, groping his way round that space. It was larger than he had expected. He barked his shin painfully against what must have been a chair, or perhaps a chest.

There was an inner door. It yielded to the thrust of his shoulder.

Light. It was dim, the reflection through a window of a torch below, but it was enough to see that he was in a set of chambers much like those in which he had been living.

He sat on the bed, because it was closest. He could not lie down. There was nothing in the room to cut his bonds, no weapon, nothing edged or sharp.

He sat, therefore, and let his head hang, till his shoulders objected again. If he could have beaten them into silence, he would have.

Somewhere amid the struggle with Barukha, amid her shrieking and carrying on, she had said something. He had not remembered it then. It came back to him now, vivid to the point of pain. "If I can't have you, no one will."

He had never thought that she was mad. He knew she was reckless, and cared little for consequences. If her temper was roused, if she was wild with jealousy . . .

Could jealousy compel a woman to destroy a man?

Foolish question. And the more fool he, for walking into the trap. If he had simply sent her away, she could not have done this thing; not without explaining why she was in his chamber.

He was not dead yet. Nor had they gelded him. He was intact, all but his honor.

✢ ✢

They came for him much sooner than he had expected. Again he was dragged, this time a greater distance, but up into the higher reaches of the palace rather than down into the prisons. He knew these corridors: they led to the king's residence.

Of course the king would judge him. There was no higher authority, and Khayan had been his man. Was still, if anyone knew it.

For this hour, which must be well short of dawn, the passages were remarkably full of people. All of them stared as he stumbled past, and whispered to one another. Next to the war, this would be the greatest scandal they had seen in an age. A lord of high rank and great favor caught assaulting the maiden daughter of a fellow lord—delicious. Appalling.

The king was waiting for him. Apophis looked as if he had not slept; and

perhaps he had not. His robe was a nightrobe, as if he had been abed or about
to go there.

Khayan hoped that he would never have to look into such eyes again. Eyes
that had seen all there was to see, and gained from it nothing but sorrow.

The guards kicked Khayan's feet from under him. He fell hard, on bruises
from the falls before. He did not try to rise. It was not that he lacked heart to
do it. He simply could not see the use in it.

"Unbind him," the king said above him.

The guards were not happy with that. The man whose knife cut the bonds
was not careful; the blade nicked Khayan's arm. He felt it dimly, though his
arms had gone numb. They fell lifeless to his sides.

"Lift him," said the king.

Hard hands dragged him up. They had to hold him: his knees had turned
to water. But he could lift his head. He could do that.

The king looked him up and down. He supposed he was a shocking sight.
The guards had made certain that he struck every stair on the ascent. The
heedless swing of a fist had split his lip. One eye was swelling shut. He did not
even remember what had caused that.

"Set him in a chair," the king said, "and go."

That was not at all to the guards' liking, but the king had spoken. They
had perforce to obey.

There were still people about. Servants. A guard or two. No lords or
princes. In that absence, they were as much alone as they could be.

"Tell me why," said Apophis.

Khayan could not answer that, not in any way that would be honorable.
He sat in the chair that the guards had brought, aching in every bone and
struggling not to slip ignominiously to the floor, and said nothing.

"You were found," the king said, "in the midst of the chambers allotted
to my queens, forcing the virtue of a lady of considerable rank. The lady is
prostrate. She will not tell us why she was there, some distance from the rooms
in which she should have been sleeping. It is all too clear why you were there,
and what you were doing."

Khayan closed his eyes. If he defended himself, he dishonored Barukha.
Dishonor for a woman was worse than for a man. No man of rank would take
a woman who pursued and seduced a man. Whereas a woman who had been
forced—she might be forgiven, and absolved through swift marriage to a man
of impeccable honor.

Silence was his refuge. He had no other.

"Why?" Apophis asked him again. "Why, Khayan? You of all men—this
is the last crime I would ever have expected to find you guilty of. *Are* you
guilty? Or is there something that we haven't been told?"

Khayan let his head fall forward. He could, if he let go even a fraction
more, have fallen headlong into the dark. But he was too stubborn for that.
He did not want to wake and find himself a gelding.

A strong hand, but not a harsh one, tipped his head up. He looked up blurrily into the king's face. "I should have you killed," Apophis said as if to himself, "but not for this thing which I begin to doubt you did. For being such a blind and perfect idiot. I don't suppose you'll name the man who laid this trap for you?"

No man laid a trap for me. The words were there, on the back of Khayan's tongue. But they would not speak themselves.

"You understand," said Apophis, "that if you won't defend yourself, I can't defend you. The woman's family is out for blood already. Her father has been sent for. When he comes, he'll want your jewels for a necklace. Tell me why I shouldn't let him have them."

"Mine." That word obliged Khayan by letting him speak it. "They're mine. He can't have them."

"By law he is entitled to them," Apophis said.

"No," Khayan said. "Can't have them."

"If I let you keep them," said Apophis, "and give you what it is you seem to want, what will you give me in return?"

"Loyalty," Khayan said.

"Yes," said the king. "That is a valuable thing. What if I take your rank with it, and your holdings?"

Khayan shrugged, though the pain nearly cast him down. "If you're wise, you'll not call my brothers back from wherever they may be hiding—where for all I know, after all, they may have had something to do with this. If you will, my lord, of your kindness, let my mother keep them in your name. She'll rule them as you would best prefer. Whereas my brothers, or Barukha's father . . ."

"Barukha's father is a truculent fool," Apophis said, "and he is going to deafen me with his bellowings when he makes his way here. Of your brothers, the less said, the better. Yes, I can make your mother regent for your holdings, and protect them against any who would take them from her. But what am I to do with you?"

"Send me to war," Khayan said.

There was a pause. Apophis' eyes blazed. "Is that why you did it? Is *that* why?"

"No," Khayan said.

"I don't believe you."

Khayan sighed. His breath caught on a spike of pain. He waited till it had passed before he spoke. "Sire, if you want to believe that I would commit such a crime in order to be sent to battle, you well may. You are the king."

"So I am," Apophis said. "If I give you that—if I send you to the north— will you be glad?"

"How will I be sent to the north?"

"At the head of a company of footsoldiers. You'll be a commander of a hundred, my once proud young lord. No more than that. There will be commanders over you. The general above them will know that you are in disgrace. What he chooses to do with you is at his discretion. Will you still go? Or will you give me a way to exonerate you from this appalling charge?"

"I will go," Khayan said steadily. "And I thank you, my lord. This is most generous, and most merciful."

"Merciful? I've likely sent you to your death."

"I don't intend to die," Khayan said. "I intend to defend this kingdom against its invaders. I'll help drive them back, my lord. Then when they're defeated . . . maybe there will be a pardon for me. Do you think that's possible?"

Apophis shook his head. "Young fool." His voice was rough, but strangely tender. "Blazing idiot. I should throttle you with my two hands."

"Leave that to the Egyptians," Khayan said.

Apophis laughed, a bark almost of pain. Khayan tried to echo him, but it was dark suddenly, and he could not find his voice. After a while, neither could he find the light, or Apophis' face, or anything but oblivion.

················ **V** ················

IRY HATED KHAYAN. She hated him with a perfect hate. He had gone away from her, left her aching and bleeding, and never spoken a word. Then he had come back, and that same day, that very day, not only tumbled into bed with a woman of notoriously supple virtue, but managed to be caught at it and condemned for it.

"You don't honestly believe he did it," she said to the king. She had gone to him as soon as the sun came up, and been admitted remarkably promptly, which after all was her privilege; she was the Mare's servant. The king was haggard and worn, but he still found a smile for her, and offered to share his breakfast. She declined as politely as she could, but her mind was elsewhere. "He didn't rape that woman."

"Child," said the king wearily, "don't you think I know that?"

"Then why—"

"Consider," said the king of the Retenu, "that the woman involved is the daughter of one of my greater lords. He can muster a thousand men and half a thousand chariots. If he is told that his daughter, for whatever reason, lured and entrapped a young man and cried rape against him, the dishonor will force him to go to war against me. I need him, child. I can't afford to lose him. And your young lord knows that, too."

"He is not *my* lord," Iry said somewhat more firmly than was strictly necessary. "And I doubt he's thinking of you. If he's true to himself, he's shielding the woman. Protecting her. Defending her honor."

"I'm sure he is," Apophis said. "And I would happily throttle him for it."

She had to pause, to breathe, before she could speak again. "What will you do to him?"

"Exile," he answered, "after a fashion. I've taken his rank away from him and sent him to the war in the north. If he does well—and I expect that he will—he'll win it all back again. In the meantime, I keep it, with his mother as regent."

Iry sagged in the chair, briefly, before she remembered to stiffen her spine. "Will the woman's father know this?"

"He need only know that Khayan is sent into exile. If he reckons that I've returned the boy to his kin in the east—well, and the road there is blocked by Egyptian armies. . . . He can hardly be faulted for joining in the war."

"He could die."

Apophis bowed his head. "Yes. As could any man."

"I think," Iry said after a pause, "that the king, to salvage the woman's honor, might do two things. He might marry her to a man of suitable rank and strength of will. And he might send her as far away from the young lord as she can go."

"What, should I marry her off to a man in Memphis?"

"That would do. Or," said Iry, "would your general Khamudi be pleased to accept a wife whose honor is besmirched but whose beauty is incontestable?"

"My general is in the midst of a war," Apophis said.

"I know that he took a dozen of his women with him. Why not send him another, with your compliments, and with her father's blessing?"

Apophis frowned. It seemed he did not like it that she was thinking like an abandoned lover. If this Barukha was married to the general Khamudi, who was aged yet strong, and famously jealous of his wives, she would never set foot outside the women's quarters again, nor lay eyes on another man but her husband.

It was a fitting punishment, in Iry's estimation. She opened her mouth to say so, but Apophis overrode her. "I will consider it. The woman meanwhile is in close confinement—for her own protection, as she has been told."

"Good," said Iry.

He eyed her a little oddly. Whatever he thought, he did not speak of it. And that was well. She took her leave, abrupt perhaps, but she did try to be polite.

+ +

Khayan left the palace without fanfare, hidden in a company of men who were being sent to the war. Iry told herself that she was glad to see him so reduced, limping on foot, with his face battered and swollen and his back as stiff with pain as with pride. It might have been merciful to keep him imprisoned until he was healed, but it likely would not be safe; not if Barukha's father descended on the citadel in a proper and paternal rage.

"There's a chariot waiting for him half a day's walk northward, and a hundred men for him to command."

Iry started and turned in the shade of the colonnade. "Sadana! I thought you were—"

"I came back this morning," Khayan's sister said, "on the heels of this uproar. Mother and Maryam told me everything. Don't pity him too much. He's getting what he wants; and he never was one to set great store in niceties of rank and station."

"No," Iry said coldly. "He never was."

"What, you can't forgive him for being a fool?" Sadana sighed. "Nor can I."

Iry turned and walked away. Sadana was kind enough not to follow. Or else she simply did not care. And that was well. Iry had no desire to tell anyone why she was so angry at Khayan. It was no one's affair but her own—and his, if he ever troubled to remember it.

+ +

He was gone. Barukha was sent away, borne on the wind of her father's wrath, to be married in haste to the general Khamudi, and given a name and rank and honor apart from the scandal that still exercised the court in idle moments. Iry had not been able to resist seeing her go. She went veiled and in a curtained wagon, but before she did that, she had to walk through the women's quarters. Iry saw her then, saw how erect she was, and how high she held her head. That was rage, Iry would have wagered. Rage and a kind of fear. Barukha hated confinement, the women whispered. She had sought Sarai's service because the lady of the tribes allowed her greater freedom than was granted to women of the Retenu.

This to her would be prison, and unbearable. And Iry was glad. If Barukha had simply bedded Khayan, that would have been almost bearable. But to bed him and then try to destroy him . . . Iry could not forgive that.

They were gone. And she was shut in these walls nigh as closely as Barukha's new husband would confine his wife. She was the Mare's servant; for that she had great rank and respect. But she was also Egyptian. No one spoke of betrayal or mistrust, but the guards on the gates, the eyes on her wherever she went, told her all that she needed to know. She was accused of nothing. But she was to be allowed no freedom to turn against the Retenu.

She could not retreat into herself as she had before. Khayan had ended that. She had no refuge. None within these walls, where every thought and word was of the war against her people. None in the lessons that she was compelled to learn, that were shaped by and for the women of a tribe beyond the edge of the world.

She needed the sky. Even more than that, she needed the Mare. She needed that warm sweet breath and that strong back, and that mind which cared nothing for the follies of human people.

The Mare was far away from this anthill of a city. And Iry was trapped within it. Foreigners surrounded her. Every one was her enemy, and her people's enemy.

For a hand of days she endured it. She did as she was bidden, performed her duties, attended the king in those brief moments when he could turn his back on the war.

She was in his roof-garden on the fifth day, alone but for the silent and half-drowsing Iannek. The king had come up to share a moment's peace with her, but a messenger had called him away—some matter of the war.

She wandered out of the garden to the roof's edge. The parapet was high, but the crenellations let her look out on the city below. Far below.

There was one escape. She knew that as she stood there. One long wingless flight, a moment's blinding pain—and then, nothing. Or the gods' country. Would she see that to which her own people went, or would the Mare's people claim her?

She climbed into the crenellation and knelt there. It would be simple to lean forward till she overbalanced. And then—

Hands dragged her back. Iannek's—and Sadana's.

Iry lay on the sun-heated stone of the roof and stared at the warrior woman. "Are you my guardhound now?" she asked.

"It seems I may have to be," Sadana said. "What were you thinking of?"

Iry shrugged. "I wanted to look at the city."

"You wanted to fall on the city. Why? Is life so intolerable here?"

"Yes!" Iry had not meant to shriek the word, but it had burst out of her like a cry of pain.

They were both staring. Iry had not realized before how much alike they were. Their father had stamped both their faces, though their mothers had shaped the rest.

She should keep it to herself, all that roiled in her. But she could not make it matter. "I need the sky," she said. "I need the Mare. I've been cut off from her—gods, for months. I must see her."

"We can bring her—" Iannek began.

"We cannot," Sadana broke in. "The Mare never enters cities, except for the greatest need."

"This isn't great need?" Iannek demanded.

Sadana sighed. "Maybe it is. But she'll not be commanded by any of us."

"Then Iry has to go to her," Iannek said with sublime simplicity.

"The king has ordered that she be kept within the palace," Sadana said.

"And isn't she above the king?"

Sadana opened her mouth, then shut it again. "She can't just walk out. The guards obey the king. And the king has ordered them to keep her in."

"He can't do that."

"And yet he has."

Iry found it fascinating to be discussed as if she had been invisible. She might have let it continue—its direction was most pleasing—but she was too much a fool for that. "You can't be thinking of disobeying the king."

"Why?" Sadana asked her. "Aren't you?"

"If death is disobedience," Iry said, "then yes. But I'm Egyptian. I've never sworn myself in service to him. I never will."

"You can't die," Iannek said. "We won't let you."

"Then let me go."

Iry should not have said that. But there was nothing reasonable in anything she was feeling. She wanted the Mare. The Mare—the Mare wanted her. But that proud bright spirit would not enter so great a city. Not alone. It would break her.

She scrambled up and dived again for the parapet. She had some thought, dim and half-formed, of trying to see past the city, to see if she could find one distant white shape in the fields beyond. But they must have thought she wanted to finish the leap she had begun.

Again they dragged her back. This time Sadana sat on her, shaking her till she was dizzy. "Stop doing that! There is a way, and you needn't die for trying it. If you'll let me—"

"Where?" Iry asked. "What way?"

"It's a postern," Sadana said. "At night, with care, we might—"

"How do you know I can trust you? Or," Iry said, fixing her stare on Iannek, "you?"

"I am your servant," Iannek said.

"And I," said Sadana a little slowly, as if she had to think through the words before she spoke them, "belong to the Mare, though she would not have me for herself. I swore oath to her when I was a child. I never swore oath to any man, or to any king."

"And if I choose to betray the king of this city?" Iry asked. "Will you kill me? Confine me?"

"You are the Mare's servant," Sadana said.

"And you hate me for it."

"No," said Sadana.

Iry might find her own way out, once she knew there was one. But these two would watch her more carefully even than the king's guards had done. If she could trust them, if they would help her, she well might succeed. If she tried to do it alone—they might stop her.

She had not thought about what she was doing, or what she would do once she had won free of that prison. But the answer was plain enough. Egypt had risen. She was of Egypt. But these two—she could not—

She would find a way. Somehow. And if these were not to be trusted, or if they turned against her and killed her, then so be it. It was better than living trapped in walls, surrounded by enemies.

✦ ✦

It was hardly strange to walk softly and keep secrets, or to conspire against the Retenu. But this time Iry's conspirators were Retenu themselves. Or Iannek was. Sadana was something different.

Iry considered that this might be Sadana's way of destroying the interloper who had taken the Mare from her. But what did that matter? Whether she leaped from the walls or took an arrow in the back while escaping through a postern, it was all the same. And the postern might truly offer escape, whereas a leap from the walls offered only death.

"Give me two days," Sadana said to her. "Then go into seclusion. Invent a rite if you must, that will keep you cloistered for as many days as you can manage. Three will do. Seven would be better."

"But your mother—" Iry began.

"Leave my mother to me," Sadana said. "Tell her nothing."

Iry would hardly confide in Sarai. Even more than Sadana, she was of the Mare's people, her blood untainted with the blood of the Retenu. And yet she had cast in her lot with these people. She had brought Iry here and colluded in her confinement. She was no friend, nor anyone Iry trusted.

The habits of slavery served Iry well now. Silence and lowered eyes and mute obedience. It was nothing different than she had given Sarai before.

And on the second night, as Iry lay in her bed, open-eyed in the night-lamp's glow, Sadana slipped through the door. "It's time," she said.

"But I haven't told the king—" Iry began.

"The king will be told," said Sadana.

Iry sat up, regarding her narrow-eyed. "I don't know if I trust you."

"Then stay here," Sadana said.

Iry shook her head. "No. But if we're caught, I'll know you've betrayed me."

"I haven't betrayed you," said Sadana. "Are you coming?"

Iry rose from the bed, pulled on the dark robe Sadana had brought her, and shouldered the bag of belongings she had gathered for herself. Sadana had more: food, a waterskin, and weapons. A bow for each of them, and arrows, and long knives on baldrics. Iry took her share. Without a word then, Sadana led her out through the servants' passages.

Iry knew these ways. They had been her only escape while she was trapped here. But the postern Sadana knew of—that, she had not found before. It was well hidden in a fold of the wall, seeming part of the wall itself, till Sadana set hand to it and opened it into the redolence of the midden.

Which, indeed, explained why no one knew of it. Iry drew her mantle over her nose and tried to breathe shallowly.

There was a wan moon, enough to see where they walked, picking their way among the heaps of refuse and the odorous pools. Sadana was a tall cloaked figure ahead of Iry. She spoke no word, nor seemed to care if Iry followed her.

When Iry stumbled and fell into one of the pools of filth, she never stopped or slowed. Iry scrambled up, gagging and choking, and half-ran to catch her, but with care lest she fall again.

Past the midden was a stretch of open land, parkland and garden, dark under the moon, and the broad branch of the river that flowed past the whole of the city. They were to go north, Iry knew, along the river for a while, then away from it lest they be seen and captured.

The Mare waited ahead of them. Iry could feel her like a warmth on the skin, strongest when she faced the north, weaker if she turned away. That warmth gave her strength. She did not even want to pause to wash off the stench from the midden, but she did that for prudence, and for Sadana's sake. With wet and clinging skirts and dripping hands, she pressed on past Sadana, toward the North Star.

✦ ✦

When morning was close and the city well behind, Sadana caught Iry as she strode onward, tripped and felled her. She lay winded but already struggling to rise. Sadana set a foot on her breast. "Stop," she said. "Be quiet. Come with me."

She let Iry up, but kept a grip on her arm, dragging her into the reeds that bordered the river. Iry tried to protest, to remind her of crocodiles and snakes and swarms of biting flies, but Sadana clapped a hand over her mouth. "Quiet," she breathed.

Iry stopped struggling. Then she heard what Sadana must have heard long before her: hoofbeats on the road, approaching at speed. Her heart leaped. If it was the Mare—

But the Mare was ahead of her. This one came from behind, from Avaris. She crouched low in the reeds.

It was a chariot drawn by a pair of horses, and a single man in it. Iry bit her tongue. It was Iannek.

"I ordered him to—" she began.

Sadana's hand stopped her mouth again. He rattled swiftly past, unaware of them, intent on the road ahead. She strained to hear, but no one followed him.

When he had been gone for a long count of breaths, Sadana let Iry rise at last, and continue—as it happened, in the direction he had been going. She could walk no faster. She could run, but she would exhaust herself before she ever caught the man in the chariot. If he was riding to capture the Mare, then he would fail. If he went to betray her, he might succeed.

She was armed. She was making all speed that she might. It must be enough.

Grey light washed slowly over them. Moon and stars faded. They must leave the road soon, before they were seen on it. Traffic northward had faded to a trickle except for the king's runners and his armies, but traffic southward was an unending flood.

Sadana turned aside from the broad and beaten track into the fields beyond. The barley had been harvested and taken away. They made what speed they could through the stubble. There were copses of trees beyond, orchards, a vineyard.

Daylight found them walking among the pruned and tended trees of an orchard, keeping to cover and out of sight of the road. Iry was aware, dimly, that her feet were blistered and bleeding, and that her body was stumbling. But she had to come to the Mare. She had to find Iannek and stop him—from whatever he was doing.

She was leading Sadana as she had done since they left the palace gardens. Sadana had voiced no complaint, expressed no exhaustion. She was made of bronze, maybe, or honed to a keener edge than most women knew was possible.

Iry could not go much farther. Her body knew that. Her spirit was beginning to acknowledge it.

Just as she knew she must stop, crawl into hiding, and sleep like the dead till night came again, the orchard ended. Wild land lay beyond, marshes and tangled thickets, rich ground for hunting, and for hiding in.

A pale shape glimmered amid the green. Iry forgot weariness, forgot pain, forgot even fear. She began to run.

The Mare called out to her, a clear and piercing call, and burst out of the thicket. They met on the field's edge, the Mare pounding to a halt, Iry all but falling against her neck. The Mare was sweating, but lightly. Her mane was brushed and smooth, not in the knots Iry had expected. She looked, in fact, as if she had been freshly groomed, her feet trimmed, her body pampered as it well deserved to be.

A patchy-bearded face grinned at her from amid the tangle of shrubbery. "Good morning, my lady," Iannek said.

Iry would have leaped on him, but the Mare was in the way. She settled for a murderous glare. "I told you to stay in the city. What made you think—"

"I had older orders," he said, "to stay with you no matter what happened. I was never released from those."

"Convenient," Iry muttered. "Now get you home. And pray the gods no one asks what you were doing riding north alone in a stolen chariot."

"It's not stolen!" he protested. "A friend borrowed it from another friend. I promised to return it. Which I did. The man who owns it has a house not far from here."

"And the horses?"

"Well," he said. "Wouldn't you rather we could all ride, and not just you?"

"Gods," Iry said. She glanced about. She could hardly stand on the edge of a field, instructing this perfect fool in simple prudence. She turned her face toward the thicket. As she had expected, the others followed, Iannek and the Mare, and Sadana at a little distance, as if she had at last succumbed to exhaustion.

He had made camp deep in the thicket, where a clearing offered space; from the look of the edges, he had widened it till it was large enough for three horses and three people. The pair of dun stallions stood together in hobbles, one grazing, one drowsing, though the Mare's arrival roused them both.

Iry knew those stallions. They were Khayan's own, his darlings, whom he had bred in the east, and raised from foals. Their dam, he had told Iry, was one of the Mare's people, their sire the king stallion of a great queen's herd. He doted on them as if they had been his children.

The elder, who had a star on his brow, whickered at the Mare. The younger, whose brow bore a crescent moon, kept his head low. He must have offered insolence and been corrected for it.

The Mare ignored them both. She set to grazing where the grass was not too badly trampled, and left Iry to confront Iannek unhindered.

Iannek seemed unaware of his danger. Even when Iry advanced on him, he stood his ground. He smiled. He said, "There's bread. And beer. Yakub, the man with the chariot—he says it's the best beer in the Delta."

"A Retenu would know?" Iry stood face to face with him, or rather face to breast. When had he grown so large? He was as large as Khayan.

He was still a flaming fool. She jabbed a fist in the hollow of his belly. With a faint wheezing sound, he crumpled to his knees.

She kept him there with her hands on his shoulders. "You rampant idiot. Look what you've done. You've stolen these horses, you've advertised your presence by returning the chariot, and now you think you can travel with us? They'll be hunting for the horses, you can lay wagers on it."

"They won't, either," he said, aggrieved, and still wheezing slightly. She hoped he was glad she had not struck lower. Then he would have been in genuine pain. "I was supposed to have sent them back to the Sun Ascendant. The rest of the horses can go to the war, but Mother wanted these kept apart."

"And were you to be sent there as well?" Iry demanded.

"Well," he said, "no. But I let everyone think that's where I was going. If they look for me at all, they'll look to the south."

"Or to the north, where your brother went—since you were known to have returned the chariot by this road. Your brother to whom you are famously loyal, to whose exile you've been heard to object in no uncertain terms."

"Maybe," said Iannek, "but if they look where the army is, they won't find me, will they? They're busy with the war, lady. They won't take the trouble to hunt me down, if I'm known to be on a simple errand for my mother."

Iry could argue with that, and began to, at length; but Sadana broke in on them both. "Give it up, lady. If we send him away, he'll simply follow.

Best we keep him with us. We might even be able to keep him out of trouble."

Iannek glowered at her. But when he turned back to Iry, he was his insouciant self again. "Well? Where *are* we going? To the army?"

"To the army, yes," Iry said. "The Egyptian army."

Neither of them flinched or seemed surprised.

"Will you still follow me?" she asked them. "And be loyal to me?"

They nodded.

"You understand," she said, "that if you do this, you're traitors to the king in Avaris. If he captures you, you'll die."

"I know that," Iannek said. His voice was steady. "My brother ordered me, lady. Protect her, he said. Stay with her. I have to do that."

"But you," said Iry, "swore oath to the king."

He shook his head. "I didn't. I swore oath to my brother, as my lord and commander. I swore to obey him in everything, to do whatever he bade me do. That's how we do it, you know that. Then the higher lord swears to the king. Khayan has to serve the king. I serve Khayan. And because Khayan ordered me, I serve you."

Iannek's logic always made Iry's head ache. "It doesn't—trouble you—?"

He winced a little. Did his head ache, too, then? "Honor is simple. It isn't always easy."

Iry sighed and shook her head. "Then it seems I'm bound to you. I hope you don't live to regret it."

·············· VI ··············

THE ARMIES OF the Upper Kingdom descended on Sile utterly by surprise. The long march had gone through empty places, but through towns and villages too, and never a one had betrayed them to the conquerors. Indeed they had shared their harvest, and sent the Great House on his way with prayers and blessings and the worship proper to one who was both king and god.

The gods were with them. Kemni needed no greater proof of it.

But the war was far from won. They had still to come to Sile and engage the enemy. And Crete had to be there, waiting at sea, till the proper time. If there was a storm, if the waves of the sea ran against them and they could not come to shore . . .

The enemy, after all, had gods of their own. They had claimed Set the destroyer, the enemy of Horus and Osiris, and made him their lord and patron.

His temple loomed on the horizon of Sile as it did over every city that these Retenu built. Great ugly blocky thing that it was, within walls built high and broad, it had neither beauty nor power. It was merely massive.

They descended upon it out of the empty lands, eaten alive by the biting things that dwelt in the marshes, seared by sun and wind, and worn down with long marching. They found the great gate open, caravans streaming in and out, the markets humming with commerce, the walls but lightly guarded. The governor of the city, the king's spies said, had gone to take the waters in an oasis in Asia, taking with him half a dozen of his favorite women, and his newest and most delightful wife.

Such arrogance was entirely to be expected, and yet it amazed Kemni. For a people who built walls as strong as these, who lived for the arts of war, they were remarkably disinclined to believe in war when it came upon them.

"Not from us," Ahmose said. He had bidden Kemni drive his chariot from the middle ranks, where all the army could rejoice that it protected him, to the head of the march. He was in his golden armor, crowned with the blue crown of war, and all his weapons were gleaming with gold. Still they were weapons and not ornaments, keen-edged and well balanced, and he knew how to wield them.

As they sped past the van to the open field, Ahmose said calmly, "They think of us as servile, even after all my brother's victories. We are a nation of slaves, a conquered people. And how could we attack *here*? All our strength is in the south. This is the northern gate of their conquest."

Kemni nodded. And yet, he thought, they had grown careless. Had there been no raiders out of the desert, no reivers from Canaan?

It seemed not. Their coming cast the city into disarray. Men—and women and children, too—swarmed on the walls. The gates swung ponderously shut. Travelers and caravans caught without ran about in panic. The caravans at least remembered good sense, gathered together and posted guards and cast about for an avenue of retreat. There was none: Ahmose's army came on in a wide arc. Those who broke and ran either met the points of spears, or cowered on the shore of the lake that opened on the sea.

And from the sea came a vast fleet of wine-dark sails, ships with long bright eyes, and crews of warriors who laughed as they rode the waves on wind and oar. The great ship that led them, the flagship, bore on its sail a golden bull and a great double axe; and its prow was horned like a bull. The admiral on the deck raised his weapon as he came on: a double axe, bright-gilded and flaming in the sun.

Ahmose's army raised a roar of delight, which met its echo from the ships. They closed the vise on land and sea, surrounded the city of Sile, and mounted siege outside those towering walls.

Not too long a siege. That was the king's order. They must break the gates down quickly and take the city, and secure the road to the north, close it off against reinforcements from Asia.

Ahmose on the march had begun to show his age. He was not a young man, and though he was strong of will, his body was beginning to yield to the years. But in front of Sile, in the camp that they had made behind the line of the siege-engines, he won back his youth.

The Cretan admiral had come down from his ship to speak with the king. He was a great prince, a lord of the sea-warriors, high and proud—and yet, for all of that, he was still the captain whom Kemni had known on the voyage to Crete. Naukrates in his proper rank and station dressed more richly— much—but put on no greater airs, nor scorned to acknowledge a mere commander of a hundred, a king's charioteer.

In fact he was most particular in his greetings to address Kemni with warmth and welcome, as a friend and kinsman. Kemni did not need to feign gladness in his response. "My lord! You came in excellent good time."

"Of course I did," said Naukrates, draining the cup of wine that he had been given with his welcome, and holding it out to be filled again. They were feasting in the camp, Egyptians and Cretans sharing what they had; and for the king's following, that meant dining on fish of the sea and on the flesh of a fat ox that the supply-parties had taken as tribute from one of the carvans.

Naukrates drank from his refilled cup but did not drain it. "Now tell me," he said. "How fares my niece? Is she well?"

Kemni's throat closed. The king still did not know who traveled hidden among the baggage and camped at night amid Kemni's men, hidden and protected. He could hardly tell Naukrates that Iphikleia was not only in the camp, she was shut in a tent that her uncle could, if he but lifted his eyes, catch sight of amid a thousand others.

Nor was Kemni inclined to tell Naukrates that she had been wounded, or how or why. Gebu was too close, laughing uproariously in a crowd of princes. Kemni settled for a few empty words: "She's well, as far as I know."

"Indeed," said Naukrates. "She's not here?"

Kemni bit his lip.

Naukrates' eyes narrowed. "Ah," he said. "The king forbade?"

"The king bade his queens command his own fleet in the south. They will have begun to move northward when we move south."

That seemed to satisfy Naukrates. "That's wise. Yes, wise indeed. And you—you look splendid. Is it true what I hear? You're charioteer for the king?"

Kemni nodded, with a faint sigh of relief that he had escaped the difficult ground of Iphikleia's whereabouts. "The king is most pleased with his chariots."

"Good!" said Naukrates. "Here, aren't you thirsty? Drink up! There's war ahead of us."

"And war all about us," Kemni said as he lifted his cup.

"May the gods favor our victory," said Naukrates.

✦ ✦

Maybe the women had been listening, or maybe they had simply decided that it was time. As the servants brought in the great savory hulk of the ox, pungent with onions and herbs, there was a flurry beyond the tent: voices murmuring, muffled cheers.

Ariana had come as the Ariana of Crete, the living goddess, priestess and queen. Her skirts were the height of fashion in Knossos, a full dozen tiers of finely woven fabric embroidered with gold and silver. Her vest was studded with jewels, gold and jewels about her throat and her waist and her ankles, golden bells chiming in her ears, and golden serpents coiling about her arms. Her hair was piled high and held in a crown of gold.

Every eye fixed on her. Every man in that place gaped like a rustic at the blaze of her beauty.

Kemni tore his eyes from it to watch Ahmose. The king seemed not at all surprised. Nor, gods be thanked, was he angry. He rose as she approached, as splendid in his trappings of war as was she in her trappings of the court. He held out his hands. "My lady," he said in the enormous silence. "Welcome."

So, Kemni thought. He had known. Had he been angry when he discovered his queen's disobedience? He showed no sign of it.

She came to him, smiling her wonderful smile, with such warmth that Kemni heard more than a few long sighs. Ahmose took her hands and set her in his own chair, standing beside her, smiling at his lords and generals, his princes, his commanders, and yes, his servants. "My lords," he said, "I give you my lady and my queen."

There was a moment of further silence—astonishment, surely, though there must have been rumors. Then, all at once, a shout went up, a great roar of greeting and gladness.

So, thought Kemni. She had aimed for this moment. Of course she had. There was none better—and none more perfectly calculated to deflect the king's wrath that she had disobeyed his order. If indeed he was angry. For all Kemni knew, he had expected it.

Iphikleia, lost in her lady's shadow, sat calmly beside Kemni and reached for his cup of wine. Her uncle, on her other side, embraced her so tightly that she gasped; but she did not rebuke him except for spilling the wine.

He laughed and filled the cup again. "Well met, sister-daughter. Well met! And are you well?"

"Very well," she said, and truthfully too. She had thrived on the march, grown strong, even gained flesh. And if Kemni had had anything to do with that, then he was glad. Gladder perhaps than she would ever know.

Servants brought her a cup of her own, but she was content to share Kemni's plate, and no shame if everyone knew what it meant that they sat so close. As why should there be? In Crete it was perfectly acceptable.

✦ ✦

"That was a bold thing you did," Kemni said.

She nestled in his arms, stroking him lazily. He was all limp, even the part of him that wanted most to rise and worship her. "Bold? I? What did I do?"

"You and Ariana," he said. "Coming to the king as you did."

"How else should we have done it?"

"You should have stayed where you were told to stay."

"Ah," she said, a sound of disgust. They had fought that battle days ago, and she knew it as well as he.

"Ah," he echoed her, drawing it out till she slapped him to make him stop. He grinned down at her face in the hollow of his shoulder. "Very well. I admit it. I'm glad you came. I'm glad to have you here. I'm more than glad to have had you—"

This time she silenced him by holding his rod hostage. But she could not stop his laughter. "Gods," he said. "Gods, I love you."

"Beautiful man," she said. "Show me how you love me."

"I've shown you and shown you and—"

"Show me more."

"Cruel woman," he said. There was little left in him but kisses, but of those he had a myriad.

⚬ ⚬

In a siege there was little enough use for chariots. But the king was not about to let them stand idle. He sent them out as scouts, in small companies, to find provisions which larger companies on foot could bring back, and to hunt down escapes from the city, and to range wide in the army's defense. Their speed, and the distances their teams could cover, delighted Ahmose to no end. "Old kings dreamed of this," he would say when Kemni brought back word of the day's explorations. He loved his chariots; he was like a child with a toy, wielding it in every way he could think of, playing to his heart's content.

The siege went well, for a siege. The city was cut off. The road into Asia was shut, with an army across it. But the people within the walls were holding fast. No doubt they preferred starvation or death to the life of captives.

Kemni could understand that. The Lower Kingdom had lived so for a hundred years.

He rode out with the rest, though as commander he was not required to do it. It was relief from the boredom of the siege, long days of sitting in camp while the engines hammered the walls, and the archers shot off fire-arrows from both the ships and the land. Those who would fight when the gates fell had nothing to do but wait, unless they were fortunate to be sent out as Kemni's men were.

He ranged wide to the south, till he knew all the villages within a day's ride of Sile. Word had gone to Avaris, he knew; they could not keep every messenger from escaping. But likewise the Retenu could not prevent the army from learning what passed in the south. The king in Avaris had sent armies to the defense of Sile. And yet, said those of his men whom he had sent out, they were traveling slowly. They seemed in no haste to reach the city.

"They're not coming to Sile," Seti said. "They're outriders from Avaris—they're defending the kingdom's heart."

Kemni could not argue with him. As few as the enemy were, lords set over a foreign land, they could not spend their men in defending the outer cities. If they would retain their power, they must retain it from the center, from their strongest places.

The king was not minded to engage them. Not yet. First he would take Sile. Then he would advance into the south.

················ VII ················

K EMNI'S OUTRIDERS HAD found the foreign king's army. As Seti had foretold, they were not attempting to rescue Sile. They had camped two days south of the city, and set to building what looked like a fort across the road.

They could not build a fort across the river. Kemni found he almost pitied them, poor mariners that they were, and not given to thinking of water as well as land—even after a hundred years.

He went out hunting on a morning when it seemed the siege was close to ending. He had shot a fine flock of geese, enough to feed a fair few men, and the men with him had chariots full of fat quarry as well. Time, he thought, to turn back, though the day was young. If they surrendered their prey to the cooks, they would have time after that for battle-exercises.

They paused to rest and graze the horses, in a field near the branch of the river. Some of the men ate and drank, taking their ease, though they kept their weapons close to hand, nor let their horses stray. One or two had wandered afield, he supposed to relieve themselves, or to while the time.

A shout brought him to full alert. None of them ever forgot that this was war. He strung his bow and fitted an arrow to the string, but stayed beside his chariot. His bays had lifted their heads to stare at the field's edge. Their nostrils flared. Falcon, who was always the leader, snorted explosively. Lion pawed the ground. Suddenly, deafeningly, he whinnied.

Seti and one of the others—Ay, that was his chariot, with the ibis painted on it—drove slowly over the hill. There were others behind them, men of the fourth wing, Kemni saw, whom he had sent to keep watch on the enemy. They rode in a circle about something else. Three horses, and three riders on the horses.

Riders, not chariots. Two of the horses were ordinary enough, if very fine: golden duns. The third was as pale as the moon.

Kemni had not even known that he was running, till he was half across the field. The others had not moved. They were all staring, waiting for Seti and Ay and the fourth wing to come to them.

The riders were captives, they could be nothing else, but neither they nor their horses were bound. Two were Retenu. One of those two—by the gods, one was a woman, a tall fierce creature with falcon-eyes. And the third . . .

"Iry!" Kemni called, and never mind who heard, or what he thought. "Iry! Cousin!"

She lifted a hand. She was as he remembered her in Avaris, as calmly self-possessed as ever, until he met her eyes. Then her smile broke free, wide and white and irrepressible. "Kemni!" she called back. "Cousin! Well met! Well met!"

Everyone was goggling. They must think these were spies for the enemy. Kemni could not think how to explain, not in haste. Orders, for now: "Let them go," he said. "They're friends."

His men did not want to, but the habit of obedience was strong. He brought Iry and the others back to the rest of the chariots, to bread and beer and as fine a welcome as he could manage. The other woman he knew quite well indeed, but she seemed not to remember him, or to be lost in a kind of dream. The man had been a great gawk of a boy when Kemni saw him last, and was now a large man and strong, with great bull's shoulders and the beginnings of a handsome beard, but there was no mistaking that wide and deceptively foolish grin. Iannek of the Retenu and his sister Sadana had followed Iry into the north. Followed, not led. That much he could well see.

Preposterous. And yet there they were. "You *are* friends?" he said to Iry.

She nodded a little impatiently. "Of course we are. Yes, the others, too. They belong to me. How far is it to Sile?"

"Half a morning," Kemni answered, letting be for a moment the thing that she had said, that she was mistress to a lord and a lady of the Retenu.

"So close?" She sighed. For a moment he saw how weary she must be, and how far she must have traveled. "Thank the gods. I'd begun to think we'd never come there."

That too Kemni let be. Time enough to hear it when he had brought her to the king.

He appropriated a chariot from one of the men, and set Iry in it with Iannek. Of necessity, Sadana rode with him. The horses followed: the duns on their leads at the tail of Kemni's chariot, the Mare free, but keeping close.

There was much to think of, and much to remember. Kemni had not seen the Mare so close before. She looked, at first glance and except for her color, like a rather ordinary, rather heavy-bodied, short-legged mare of a kind quite unlike the slender-legged stallions that the king had brought out of Libya. And yet in motion she was splendid, a beauty to stop the heart. She had eyes for no one but Iry. It was striking, that intensity; fixed on her servant as if there were no one else in the world.

For the matter of that, the same could be said of the two humans who followed his cousin. Iannek was as devoted to her as a dog to its master. Sadana . . .

She had not spoken since she came in front of Kemni. When Iannek took the second chariot as charioteer, Iry had got in as a matter of course; and wisely enough, if he might think of escape. Kemni doubted that he ever would.

And that had left Sadana to ride with Kemni. She still had not acknowledged him, even with a glance.

Was she angry, then? "I'm sorry," he said as the chariot left the field for the smoother surface of the road. "I'd not have left you like that, if I could. But—"

"That's what you were doing," she said, abrupt as if she had chosen to enter into the middle of a conversation. "You were spying."

"Yes," he said.

"You're not a servant at all. I thought so. You put on too many airs for a slave."

"Not a few slaves in this kingdom have been born to rank and station."

"And what is yours?"

"Commander of the king's chariots," he answered, not without pride. "King's charioteer. But before I was that, I was heir to the Golden Ibis, not far from the Sun Ascendant."

"And her cousin."

Kemni glanced at Iry. "Yes. Our mothers were sisters."

"Where I come from," said Sadana, "that would make you as close as brother and sister, and bind you together from birth till death."

"That's almost true," he said. "I used to run wild with her brothers. She followed us when she could, though she was so much younger. She was just the same then as she is now, only smaller."

"I imagine she was a very self-possessed child," Sadana said coolly.

"She was that." Kemni let the horses go on for a while. Then he said, "You're angry at me."

"Why do you think that?"

"I left you."

She laughed, a brief, sharp sound. "How like a man! So you think that one night's pleasure has made you the center of my world?"

"Not at all," said Kemni. "But I never went back. And I never spoke to you."

"You had to go," she said. "Spying."

"Spying," he said a little wearily. And something else, but he was not about to speak to her of that. Iphikleia had been waiting for him. He could hardly tell a woman that he had left her for another, or that he had barely thought of her since, in the light of that other's presence.

Sadana did not speak again. Nor did she touch him except as the chariot's motion compelled her.

He wondered if Iry had been able to find her a lover who could stay with her and be gentle to her. Probably not. It had been a ridiculous thing to ask, and impossible to accomplish. None but Sadana could find a man who loved her. If Sadana did not want him, or did not want to find him, then that was her choice.

She would hate him if she knew what he had asked Iry to do. It smacked of pity, and of condescension. And she deserved neither.

He almost apologized again. But that would gain him nothing. He drove in silence instead, back to the plain and the city, and the king in his great camp amid the hammering of the siege-engines.

The gates had buckled. Soon they would fall. Kemni found the king just behind the great ram, seated under a canopy with a flock of his lords and generals, and a fair company of priests who had been invoking the gods' names with each blow. They had, when Kemni came, run through the Ennead of the Two Kingdoms and begun on the lesser deities.

Between the priests' chanting and the thunder of the ram, there was no lull in which to speak. But Ahmose did an unwonted thing: at Kemni's coming, he rose from his golden chair and walked on his own feet into the sun, and bellowed in Kemni's ear, "Come with me!"

Everyone was staring. It was a mark of enormous and potent favor for a mere lord to be approached by the king. But Ahmose was taking no notice. He led Kemni and his three guests or captives back to the relative quiet of his tent. The gaggle of followers was shut out, and none admitted but a single quiet servant.

There, in scented dimness, Ahmose said, "Well met, lady of horses. Well met at last."

Iry inclined her head. She seemed immune to the awe of kingship. "You were expecting me, my lord?"

"I had a foreboding," Ahmose said with the hint of a smile. "And my Great Royal Wife . . . she is closer to the gods than most. She told me that I might expect such a guest. And such an omen."

"I suppose," said Iry, "I am that."

"The white Mare of the conquerors chooses for her priestess a conquered Egyptian," Ahmose said. "She suffers that Egyptian to return to her own people. It might be said that she has, in so doing, shifted her favor from the conquerors to the conquered."

"It has been said," Iry said, "and will be."

"Then it must be true." Ahmose's smile escaped its bonds. "Welcome indeed, then. Welcome in great joy."

✦ ✦

There was a great deal to be said for a god-king's favor. It won Iry and her two silent shadows a tent of their own, the best grazing for their horses, servants to attend their needs, and unquestioning—if sometimes teeth-gritted—acceptance from the king's people.

It was, as Ahmose had said, a great omen. Greater for that, even as he spoke with Iry in his tent, the ram broke down the gate of Sile. The army was caught almost off guard. But they mustered quickly, formed their ranks and took their weapons in hand and swarmed over the broken timbers into the city.

City fighting had little room in it for chariots. But Kemni had been a footsoldier long before he became a charioteer. He found a company that would be glad to take him, under a commander he had known since he was a boy. He stormed the city with the rest of them, in a kind of black delight. At last—at last, reparation for all the years of servitude, for the victories under Kamose that had turned in the end to defeat, for slavery and humiliation and the conquest of the Two Lands by barbarians out of Asia.

They fought, and yes, they killed. The enemy fell back before them. Kemni kept no count of the blows he struck, only of the steps of his advance, street by street to the center and the citadel.

There he was halted, as they all were. The citadel was open. Its commander had surrendered in fear of his life.

Kemni came to himself as if out of a dream. Surrender—terms—the king!

He had not known he had strength in him to run through the whole of that fallen city, through massed armies, past the broken gate and the silenced siege-engines to the camp and the king.

And none too soon, either. The king's chariot was almost ready. Iphikleia was standing by it with a jar that proved to be full of excellent beer, and a basin and a heap of cloths. With some, as he drained the jar, she cleansed him quickly of dust and blood and sweat. The rest resolved itself into a fine new kilt wrapped about his best ornaments and the wig he kept for festivals. She clucked her tongue over wounds he had not even known he had, but they were scratches only. They needed no tending.

The king was ready in his golden armor and his blue crown, crook and flail held crosswise over his breast, and even the false beard that he was seldom inclined to trouble with: all perfectly the Great House of Egypt.

Kemni sprang into the chariot and took up the reins. The horses were fresh and a little headstrong. Kemni was hardly fresh at all, but the beer had filled his parched and empty spaces, and Iphikleia's cleansing—and her presence, and the touch of her hands and, slyly, her lips—had roused him to life again. He was as ready as he could be, to see the king borne in his chariot to the citadel of Sile.

✤ ✤

The commander of the garrison surrendered to the Great House in the court-yard of the citadel. He was not the governor; that worthy was still absent, and unlikely to return. This was his second-in-command, the man who, Kemni was sure, had actually ruled the city in the governor's name: a gnarled and grizzled soldier, not tall for a Retenu but thickset and strong. He neither wept nor quailed in front of the king. He handed over his sword with regret but no hesitation, won freedom to gather his wounded and to tend the dead, and agreed—as if he could have argued with it—that once all that was done, he would take his men and leave his weapons, and withdraw into Canaan.

"On foot," the king said. "Your chariots and your teams, we keep."

That was blow: the commander flinched just visibly. But he bowed his head. "Sire," he said, "I can hardly resist you. But if you would leave us enough pack-beasts to carry our baggage and our wounded—"

"You may have oxen," the king said, "and such of the asses as we can spare."

"That will be enough," the commander said, "sire. And I thank you for it."

Ahmose inclined his head. He could afford to be gracious. His victory was complete. He had won far more than a city full of booty. He had won the northward way, and the road into Asia.

················ **VIII** ················

S ILE HAD FALLEN. Khayan could not imagine that anyone had not ex-pected it, and yet the howls of dismay as word flew through the army were both lengthy and loud. Surely at least a few of these bellowing bullcalves had understood that Sile was a sacrifice, a gobbet of fresh meat cast in front of the crocodile, to give the king time to fortify the center of his kingdom.

And yet it did not seem so. Khayan had been reckoning himself, if far from happy, at least not unhappy. The misfortune that had cast him here had a habit of haunting him in the nights, but in the daylight he was as content as he could be. He had rank, to a degree. He had men who seemed willing to fight for him. He was not too terribly humiliated, all things considered.

So he had been telling himself. But all the folly that he heard in the army made him yearn to be a lord of high degree again, a royal favorite—because a commander of a hundred foot was not entitled to speak before the council of the generals, still less to upbraid them for fools.

They had built this hasty fortress athwart the road from Sile, with no apparent concern for the fact that the enemy had simply to sail past in his Cretan ships. Or, for that matter, if his army was too numerous for the ships, they could ferry him across to the far bank, and he could march lightly on his way, grinning and baring his brown behind at the idiot barbarians.

And now they wanted to abandon their stronghold and fall back to Imet, not far from Avaris. It was a city, they said to one another, or at least a town of respectable size, and its walls are higher and stronger than anything they could erect here. They said no word of fighting, only of retreating. And had not the king told them to stand their ground?

He was not even supposed to be present at the council within the hastily erected walls. But it was not under guard, and he was not prevented from hanging about beyond the circle. Others of the lower ranks seemed to have succumbed to the same curiosity. Was it as morbid as his own? Lords, he had learned, were regarded by the lesser commanders as a necessary evil, a pack of fools whose orders, in the main, had nothing to do with reason or sense. For that, one needed a commander of ten or a hundred, a man who knew what the men were thinking, and could see to it that they lived to fight in the next battle their lords' foolishness flung them into.

Khayan, once a high lord and now, for his sins, a commander of a hundred foot, had yet to earn the trust of his fellows. But they were free enough in their speech when he was in earshot.

Some of them were listening as he was, rolling their eyes at one another where the lords could not see, and muttering, "Lords. All hot for a fight one instant, all cold and shivering the next. And it's never the thing we should be doing."

"What should we be doing?"

Maybe Khayan should have kept his tongue between his teeth. But he had heard too much, and was too far out of temper.

"Well, young cub," said the scarred veteran who was nearest—who was hardly older than Khayan, perhaps, but ancient in battles—"if you think about it, maybe your belly will tie itself in knots, or maybe it will tell you."

"We should stand, not run," Khayan said.

They all saluted him, the half-dozen who loitered about. "By Set's black balls!" rumbled the largest of them, a giant indeed, like a vast and shaggy bear. "The puppy can think."

"That's probably why the puppy got knocked down to trooper," said the scarred man. "Not just for plucking some lord's pretty flower."

That in its way was true. Khayan shrugged. "Does it matter? The kingdom's being lost in front of us. Shouldn't we do something about that?"

"Certainly we will," the great bear said. "We'll keep our boys together, we'll make sure they're fed and have places to sleep, and if we can, we'll make sure they stay alive."

"We could enter the council," Khayan said with swelling surety. "If we all go, as many of us as we can muster, surely they'll have to listen to us."

The big man regarded him in what could only be pity. "Where did you learn to think like *that*? No, don't try to answer. I remember. You used to be one of the warrior women's pets, before they gave you to the king. They rule one another like that, yes? Anybody can speak in council and be heard, no matter what the rank. All that plain good sense—the gods must hate them."

"Horse Goddess loves them," Khayan said. "Come, why can't we do it here? We're not so far from the tribes ourselves. If we all go and present our arguments, surely they'll listen?"

"They'll throw us out on our arses," the scarred man said, "and flog the ringleaders. No, puppy. This isn't a tribe here. This is an army. The lords give orders. We carry them out. The men obey."

"But if the orders are—"

"Orders are orders," the scarred man said.

Khayan bit his tongue till it bled. "And if I try it? You won't back me up?"

"Puppy," the big man said, "you'll have to find someone else to patch your back for you after they're done whipping you. We'll be gone. Obeying orders—and keeping our backs clean."

They left him there, returning to duties, no doubt, and following orders. Khayan stood alone beyond the circle's edge. Inside it, the lords were coming to an agreement. Imet it would be, the town on the road to Avaris. The rest of the north they would abandon. "After all," they told one another, "when we win the war, all this will be ours again. But to win it, we need Avaris and the cities in the south. We can do nothing here."

Folly. Rank folly. Khayan actually moved to step into the circle, but something—whether prudence or cowardice—held him back. He would not mind a flogging for a cause, but to stripe his back for nothing—no. He could not do it.

He was a coward, then. He would do as he was told.

+ +

They prepared to abandon the fort, but none too hastily. There was time, the lords said. The enemy was enjoying the fruits of his victory, taking his ease in Sile. Long before he came south, they would be gone, safe within the walls of Imet.

Khayan could not oppose their orders, but he could take what precautions he could—as could all the commanders of his low rank. He saw to it that he was posted with his men, on guard outside the fort, watching the road to the north. Surely the lords' spies and messengers told them the truth, but his belly, round all the knots, was not easy with it. Would not the enemy wish the lords to think such a thing? He had already surprised the kingdom with the taking of Sile. Why should he not surprise it again with the speed of his advance?

It was not unpleasant duty. The hunting was nearly gone, but there were fish in the river. And the air was clean, untainted by the stinks of too many men shut too close together for too long. They elected to camp in the field that night, while the fort continued its leisurely preparations to depart.

Night was always the worst. Khayan tried not to dream, and tried not to remember, but his heart was a stubborn thing. Again and again he saw Barukha's face as she cried rape against him, and heard her hiss in his ear when he was captured: "If I can't have you, no one will."

Sometimes, if he was fortunate, memory turned to dream. He was lying with Iry, nearly always in a field of flowers—such a field as Egypt had never known, but the steppe knew well. Horses grazed about them. White horses, grey horses, dark foals that would be grey as they grew. The Mare's herd, and the Mare among them.

Iry was smiling. He had seldom seen her smile in the waking world. She was not a somber person, but she was a serious one. Her smiles were never given lightly.

She gave it as a gift to him now. He reached to touch it, to cherish it. It was as elusive, as insubstantial as a flame. And like flame, when he came too close, it went out.

✦ ✦

Khayan woke with a start. It was morning—later than he had wanted to sleep, grey dawn and one of his men bending over him, Shimon the swift runner, who ranged farthest of all the scouts. He looked as if he had been running all night.

"Lord," he said, for he insisted on calling Khayan that, "Captain, I've seen—they're coming. The enemy are coming."

"How close?"

"They stopped when it got dark, though I waited to see if they'd go on. I could run the distance in an hour."

"As close as that?" Khayan sat up, raking his hair out of his face. "And it took you this long to find me?"

"I found them much farther from here," Shimon said a little sullenly. "I needed to see how close they'd come. I sent Lamech to tell you. Didn't he do it?"

"Lamech never—" Khayan's mouth shut with a snap. "They caught him."

"But how could—"

"Boats," Khayan said. "There are always boats on the river, fishing and trading. I'll wager half of them are spies outright and the other half are in Egyptian pay. They caught Lamech. But not you. Maybe because they knew you'd get here too late to be of any use?"

"There's still time to fight, my lord," Shimon said.

"So there is," said Khayan. He said it with a kind of satisfaction. "So. We stand our ground here after all. The lords are not going to be pleased."

"You are pleased," said Shimon, whose rebellion had always been less than subtle.

"But I," said Khayan, "can't be a lord, can I? I can think."

✦ ✦

The Egyptians fell on the fort at sunrise, from the land and from the river. There were a great many of them—more than any of the scouts had counted. Their own kind had rallied to them, it seemed, from all over the north. And of course there were the armies from Thebes and the ships from Crete. A rather insulting number of those sailed on past as the battle raged in and about the stronghold. As strong as the Retenu might be on the land, they never had mastered the river. And that, Khayan knew as he stood in the line, watching the enemy surge toward them like a river in flood, would be their downfall.

He had brought his men back to the walls, but the gates were shut. There were others outside of them, camped in a great circle, brought in so that they might march in a day or two or three, when the lords decided that it was time.

He had sent a runner ahead to raise the alarm. This was the response: barred gates, men shut out. The lords, of course, were safe within, and most of their picked troops, too. All those without were ordered to do what they could to keep the enemy at bay—so that, Khayan supposed, the lords could escape through the southward gate and run toward Imet.

He had no particular desire to turn tail and run. His mood was strange. It had been strange since he walked out of Avaris. He cared if he lived or died, but not enough to save himself. And after all, he had men to look after, and a battle to fight.

Without lords to interfere, the commanders had set up as best they could a plan of battle. The fort was at their backs. Archers with fire-arrows lined the river's banks to hold off the ships. The chariotry, such of it as the lords would give them—the rest were occupied with running south—ranged in front. The mass of the foot stood behind: swordsmen, spearmen, archers. The archers too were few, and the rest of them running after the chariots. Mostly there were spearmen and swordsmen, a wall of bodies between the enemies and the fort.

Khayan, as one such body, took as much ease as he could while the morning brightened about them. He could hear the drums beating on the ships, striking time for the oars. The deep rhythmic roll of it echoed far up the river. Their hearts seemed after a while to echo it, beating strong and slow, as the horizon spread and darkened and began to move. The sun, in its rising, caught the heads of spears and set them aflame.

Most of war was waiting. And the worst waiting of all was that of the soldier commanded to stand while the enemy advanced. The sun beat on Khayan's helmet. Sweat ran down his back and sides. His mouth was dry, but he dared not drink too heavily from his skin of water. It had to last, perhaps, for all of that day. If he drank at all, he drank a sip at a time, rolling the warm leather-tasting liquid on his tongue, savoring every drop.

The enemy came on. There were chariots in front and to the sides. So: that was true. They had horses and chariots. Some of the horses were of the Asian strain, but many were not. They were Libyans, deceptively delicate, more like deer than like the sturdy beasts Khayan had known from his childhood.

The charioteers did not drive too badly, for men who must never have stood in a chariot before this year began. They had no art, but they had skill enough.

The army marching behind them was large. Very large. And the fleet came up beside it, wind in the sails, oars stroking the water, carrying the black-hulled ships against the current of the river. The drums had become the world, beat and beat and beat.

Hold, Khayan's orders bade him. *Let the enemy come to you.* Easy enough for a lord to command—a lord who could not himself have endured to stand unmoving while an army marched toward him. But soldiers lived to do as their lords bade them.

When the first rain of arrows fell, Khayan had been expecting it. It still took him by surprise. It looked so harmless; and yet a man within his arm's reach, staring skyward at the deadly rain, fell without a sound. An arrow had pierced his eye.

"Shields!" Khayan bellowed to his own men and to whoever else would listen. "Up shields!"

Shields swung up, too late for some and too little for others, but they did what they could. And the enemy kept coming. The chariots had drawn aside, leaving the archers and the spearmen a clear field.

The battle had begun when the first arrow flew. But when the spears left their wielders' hands, blood paid for blood. The defenders began to fight back.

Khayan saw his spear bite deep in the body of a slender brown man with painted eyes. He wore no armor. The shield he carried was light, and hardly large enough to protect him. His expression when he fell was one of profound surprise.

Khayan's shield deflected a spear. It was bristling with arrows. Some of the arrows broke. The weight of them dragged at Khayan's arm. But he did not drop the shield. He was not fool enough for that.

It would have been useful to press forward against the enemy, to try to drive him away from the wall. But the orders were clear. They were to hold their ground, neither to advance nor to retreat.

Therefore they stood. When their spears were spent, they drew swords.

In most battles there were lulls, moments of quiet in which a man could stop, breathe, rest his sword-arm. But whether because the enemy was irresistibly fierce or because this part of the wall took the brunt of the enemy's assault, there was no pause, no rest. And no reinforcements. The enemy had rank on rank to fling against the wall. The defenders had only themselves.

Now that was irony: the invader from far away had men to spare, but the defender in his own country had only those who stood about him. It made

Khayan laugh as he drew his sword. There was no distance between the armies now. The world was full of little brown men. They were as numerous as rats in a granary, and as pernicious. And they kept coming for Khayan, or for the wall behind him.

The wall was his refuge. He kept watch as he could over the men in his command, kept them together, kept them fighting in ranks, those in front shifting to the back when their arms grew tired. The enemy never seemed to tire; and he had many more ranks than Khayan did.

Men were falling. Of his own, not so many; he had done his best to train them well, and it seemed they had remembered. The cries of the wounded were piercing, but after a while the ear stopped recording them. Worse were the screams of the horses. Khayan flinched at those. He had not struck any himself. All those who came at him were on foot. And he was glad. He hated killing horses. Even in sacrifice, even for the gods, he hated it.

His arm ached terribly. He shifted to the left hand for a while, but his aim was less certain, his strength less great. People kept trying to tell him to move to the rear, to take what shelter there was, and let the ranks behind do his fighting for him. But he was in command. He had to be in front. That was what a commander did.

It was his own stupidity that ended it. He knew it even as it happened. A fresh wave of Egyptians came at the line. Khayan, in front of it, tripped over his own feet and fell to his knees. An Egyptian, running past, reached down almost casually, and thrust with his sword.

The pain did not come at once. Khayan finished falling. Feet trampled all about him. Some jostled him. Then there was pain, but remote, as if it belonged to someone else. Night was coming. How strange. He could have sworn that it was still morning. But time in battles could run otherwise than by the sun's time. Maybe after all the sun was setting. It was lovely, the darkness, soft and warm and quiet, and empty of stars.

.... IX ....

THE BATTLE WAS going well. Most of the defenders outside the walls were felled or taken captive. Those within had nearly all fled. Ahmose himself had secured the southern gate through which the last of the enemy were escaping.

It was all won by late morning, all but the last brief flares of fighting, like flames from embers. Ahmose had had the fleet come close in to shore, bringing the servants and the baggage, and the physicians for the wounded. They made camp somewhat apart from the fort and away from the battle, but close enough for those whose duty was to bring in the wounded and the dying.

Kemni, as the king's charioteer, drove hither and yon at the king's command. The king did not fight unless he was forced to it; it was not the way of kings in Egypt. Nor, it seemed, of lords among the Retenu.

Kemni's men had fighting enough to occupy them, chasing down escapes and pursuing the lords in their own chariots. One such escape had, out of blindness or malice, fallen on the camp with a sizable force. Maybe their commander had in mind to strike a blow against the Great House before he fled into the south.

Ahmose was far away from the camp but in full view of it when the attack came. He did not need to command Kemni. The chariot wheeled. The horses were tiring, but they had speed enough at the crack of the whip over their backs.

Others in the king's following pounded behind, chariots and foot, but the chariots soon and far outpaced the footsoldiers. The camp was guarded, but the attack was strong. Ahmose's forces were occupied elsewhere, those closest outnumbered.

Kemni had no thought in him but to reach the camp before the enemy took it. There would be little enough in it to content him; no wealth and no booty. That was all on the ships, which rode well out in the river. But there were the wounded, and the servants. And the physicians, among them Imhotep the king's favorite, who was worth a kingdom's weight of gold.

Ahmose's chariot was somewhat ahead of the rest, flying behind its strong and eager horses. They were his Libyans, who would race the wind for the plain joy of it. Even after a long morning's battle, they were glad to stretch their legs and gallop.

The camp's defenders cheered as the king's chariots roared down on them. The attackers stood their ground briefly, but they were on foot, and the chariots rolled headlong over them. Those who could, broke and fled, scattering past and about and even through the camp. Those wrought such havoc as they could: hacking at tent-ropes as they ran, and stabbing at bodies that stumbled in their way.

A small company had managed to stay together, had rallied behind a giant of a man and struck for the tent where the wounded were lying. They were trapped behind and trapped ahead. They would do what harm they could before they were captured or killed.

Kemni in the king's chariot saw them go, traveling close together while all about them scattered at will. He saw them burst into the tent with its open flaps, and fell the healers and servants who ran to stop them.

He was too far, too far. Even if he leaped from the chariot and ran, he could not—

"Go," the king said at his shoulder.

He did not ask what Ahmose meant. One last time he cracked whip above the horses' heads, while Ahmose called his men to him, afoot and in chariots.

The horses' leap was not as strong as it had been before, but their great hearts bore them onward through the wreckage of the camp.

Kemni could fight in the chariot—but not with the king behind him. He could only drive the horses and leave the rest to Ahmose, and pray that it would be enough.

The horses pounded to a rearing halt in front of the tent. It was a melee within, even the wounded rising—those who could—and wielding whatever came to hand.

Ahmose sprang down, tossing something into Khayan's hand as he went. It was the king's own sword. Ahmose had a throwing spear, shortened in his fist.

Kemni left the horses as they were and ran in pursuit. The king's sword was beautifully balanced in his hand, like a live thing, lovely and deadly. It whirled almost of its own accord and cut down a bearded barbarian who had stooped over one of the most sorely hurt. He dropped. Kemni kicked him aside from the unconscious Egyptian, thrust the sword into his throat and wrenched. The Retenu gurgled and convulsed and died.

Kemni waded onward. There were women among the healers, he saw, and not cowering in corners, either. They had set hands to the prostrate wounded and dragged them out of harm's way, as much as they could in such confusion. One or two were even armed. Sadana—Sadana was fighting her own people over the body of a man he doubted she had ever seen before. Iry had a spear. And past them, Ariana wielded a sword, and Iphikleia in her charioteer's tunic, though she had been sailing on her uncle's ship.

Or had she been? He had not seen her on the field, nor recognized her chariot or her horses.

He fought his way toward her. It was not anything he needed to ponder before he did it. The king was moving in much the same direction. Most of the attackers were down. A few, their giant of a captain among them, fought on with trapped ferocity. They fought on toward the women, as if they had some hope even yet of taking hostages against their escape.

It all came together in that small and crowded space. Battle hand to hand, hand to throat. Kemni grappled with a man almost as large as the captain. But the captain was beyond him, stronger than any Egyptian, bellowing as he flung them aside. They were like children about him, armed and deadly children, but children nonetheless.

Kemni saw the giant break through. Heard him grunt as Ariana's blade bit his arm; grunt and raise the great sword that in his hands seemed little more than a long knife, and hack at her in return. But there was another between them, a body flinging itself against his blade, driving it back with all of its weight and speed. Driving it full into Kemni's sword.

The king's beautiful blade bit deep, clove up beneath that coat of boiled leather, through flesh, veering off bone. The giant roared in agony and writhed, twisting against the keen-edged bronze.

Kemni's arm alone could not have driven that blade as deep as the giant's struggles. The huge body toppled, nearly taking Kemni down with it. He staggered aside. The giant fell full on the sword; hung briefly as it caught in his flesh and bone and against his breastplate; then sank down with a kind of sigh. A broad handspan of notched bronze protruded from his breast, bright with heart's blood.

Kemni barely saw. Someone else had fallen too, someone far smaller and far lighter, but no less terribly wounded.

He caught her before she struck the ground. Her eyes were open. They saw him. She frowned as if to ask him what he did here when he should be out on the field, finishing the battle. But when she opened her mouth to speak, the words were lost in blood and foam.

He sank down slowly with Iphikleia in his arms. She was all over blood. His mind was empty. As empty as her eyes. She was dead. He knew that. He did not try to deny it. But there was nothing real about it.

People kept trying to take her from him. Some of them seemed to think she lived; could be saved. But she had died even as she recognized him.

The battle was over. The giant had been the last to die—and much too late for Iphikleia. Kemni felt nothing. Not grief, not rage. Not the terrible irony of it, that she should have been wounded again so soon after she had nearly died, as if the gods truly were determined to take her to themselves. Not anything at all. And he would not let her go.

Even the king tried. Kemni recognized Ahmose. He bowed as much as he might. But he held fast. Imhotep came and told him, with little patience, that he was in the way. He took no notice. Ariana stood over him and wept. He would have comforted her if he could, but he had no comfort for himself.

Even Iry came, but not her guardian hound—not Iannek, who would have been killed if he had walked in that place in that hour. Kemni might have yielded for her, if he had had any yielding in him. She had the right of it; they did need the space he was sitting in, and Iphikleia should be taken, tended, made seemly for her journey to the gods' country. The embalmers were there already among the dead, wrapping them and carrying them away.

They would not have his beloved, the half of his soul. Not until he had mourned her.

A clear voice spoke through the clouds of grief. It was not Iphikleia's, no, never again. And yet it was the same kind of voice, sharp, keen-witted, and unforgiving of nonsense. It scattered the people about Kemni. It sent them all away, even the king—who after all, as the voice said, had a victory to oversee.

Sadana sat on her heels in front of him. She had been fighting: she was filthy, and there was a bruise on her cheekbone; and from the way she moved, he thought she might have a wound somewhere, perhaps more than one. She did not say anything. She set to cleaning her sword instead, carefully, lovingly, with a cloth she must keep for the purpose. Then she brought out a stone and began to sharpen it.

Her concentration was remarkable. Healers plied their trade about her, but did not trouble her—not as they had hounded Kemni. She was like a stone in a flood, and the flood parting before her.

"You fought for us," he said.

"I fought for the Mare's servant," she answered, never lifting her eyes from her task. She was meticulous in it, and painstaking.

"Against your own people?"

"My people are in the east, beyond your horizon," she said.

"My lady is dead," Kemni said.

"Yes," she said.

That struck him with a thought. "You knew?"

"Everyone knows." She sharpened her fine bronze blade, sharpened and sharpened it. When she was done, it would draw blood from the wind.

"But I never told—"

"We knew."

"So you know—why—"

"I know what she was to you." Sadana tested the edge against her arm, shook her head slightly, went back to sharpening the blade. "You should let her go. Her spirit is gone. That is her shell you cling to."

"No," he said. "No. She needs it whole. For when she passes into the gods' country."

"Then shouldn't the embalmers see to her, before she rots?"

"She won't—she won't be allowed to—" His breath caught in his throat. "She's from Crete. They *burn* their dead. And priestesses—priestesses are taken away forever, their names, their selves, everything they were. They're given back to Earth Mother. The embalmers will give her to the Cretans. I know they will. Then I'll lose her. Do you understand? I can't lose her!"

"You've already lost her."

"Not if I find a way," he said. "There must be one. Maybe if the king commands? But will her spirit know where it was supposed to go? What if it goes to her own gods' place? I can't go there. I don't even know where it is."

"But can you learn?"

His eyes widened. He had not thought of that. He had only thought of the terrible thing, the thing that emptied him of everything else: that they could not be together in death. Their gods were different gods. The life-in-death that she expected was nothing like that to which he had been raised.

And that was unendurable.

"You can learn," Sadana said. "Let her people take her. Let them set her on her way as they know how to do. Then let them teach you the path. When your time comes, you can follow her."

"It won't be Egypt," he said slowly. "It won't be—"

"It will be with her."

He looked at her. She was the first thing he had truly seen since Iphikleia fell, except for Iphikleia's face. This was a very different face, with its odd yellow eyes and its fierce bones. That difference gave him something like comfort— if he could ever know comfort again.

He nodded. His arms loosed their grip. Hands took her from him, gently, as if she slept and they had no wish to wake her. He knew how heavy she was. Death weighed a body down, turned it, as it were, to stone: cold and stiff and still.

She was dead. If she had been Egyptian, he would have had the threescore days and ten of her embalming to find tears for her. But she was from Crete. They would build her pyre at evening, and destroy the flesh that housed her spirit. That set it free, they said. If they left the body whole, the spirit was trapped inside it, rotting with it, unless it mustered strength to torment the living.

If he was to follow her, he must learn to think that way. He did not know that he could.

But it was too late to call her back. When he tried to rise, his knees would not obey him. Not all the blood on him was hers. He was hurt, not badly, he did not think, but enough to weaken him.

He would not die of it. Which was well. He had to learn. He had to school himself to go where she had gone. Or else there was no life for him, in this world or any other.

·········· **X** ··········

S ADANA HAD PIERCED through the madness of Kemni's grief and per- suaded him to let the Cretan priestess go. That was well, Iry thought. It was a terrible thing that the enemy had done, and a terribly unwise one. Ahmose might have been inclined to be merciful toward the captives of this battle, even to set some of them free. But when their kinsmen attacked his wounded and killed a great lady among his allies, he sent out the order. All the worst wounded were to be killed and burned on a pyre with their dead—terrible retribution for an Egyptian to take. Those who were whole or but lightly wounded, he had confined without food and with but a little water. They would be made an example, he said. He would bring them to Avaris, and there under the eyes of their king and their kin, he would slay them.

His advisors rose up against that. Most would have had him kill them now, rather than be a burden on the army. A few pointed out that for men of that nation, to be shorn and whipped and enslaved would be a terrible punishment, more terrible than death.

"That is true," Ariana said in the council. She had wept for her kinswoman, and would again. But as a queen must, she had gathered her wits and firmed her will to face what must be faced. "It is true—for them, there's honor in death, but slavery is the worst dishonor. Strip them of the hair they're so proud of, and the beards that mark them as men; flog them till they scar; and set them first to disposing of their own dead, and then to the most menial labor you can think of—and they'll wish to all their gods that they had been fortunate enough to die."

Ahmose was more like his great enemy Apophis than he would ever have wanted to know: affable as kings went, and warmer than most of his kind were known to be. But today he was a king, as hard as forged bronze, tempered with anger. His eyes had narrowed as his councillors and then his queen spoke. They had found the gate into his anger, Iry could see.

"Yes," he said. "Yes. That to them would be worse than death. And if the enemy sees them—some of them his lords, even a prince or two—then he will know how terribly he has offended against us."

So it was decided. There was a darkness in the camp, even through the songs of victory. It was not the death of one Cretan priestess, though that was a terrible thing. It was that men had waged war against the wounded and the dying, and their lords had fled like cowards and fools, leaving those of low estate to rampage at will.

Some of those lords were captured, either because they had left last, or because their long-eared asses were not as swift as the king's horses. They were kept a little apart from the lesser captives, still in their fine armor, though their jewels and gold were long gone: ripped from ears so that they bled, torn from fingers and about arms and necks.

Iry was there when the king's command was carried out. They began with the lords, haughty creatures that they were, braced for death or to be paraded in chains before the Egyptian king. Those would have been acceptable fates. They were shocked, and then appalled, to be taken by strong men, stripped naked and dragged to the center of the camp, where the barbers waited with their razors sharpened and gleaming. They were sure, Iry could see, that this was a new and painful way to die.

Some broke and tried to flee. Some stood taller, brave to the last, though that was somewhat weakened by the way they all shuffled with their hands covering their manly parts. None escaped. They were dragged kicking, fighting, shrieking into the circle, flung down and pinned, and the barbers went to work.

Then even the brave ones bellowed like bulls. The Egyptians roared with laughter, mocked them, stripped off kilts and waggled organs in their faces.

Nor did the barbers stop with hair and beards. They were under orders to strip the captives utterly, from crown to toe. It was a great undertaking, as shaggy as these foreigners were, and as persistent in their struggles. Not a little blood flowed; though one clever barber found a cure for that: he let his blade slip just a fraction while he shaved a man's jewels. The man shrieked as shrill as a woman.

He must have thought he was being gelded. It silenced the rest, for a while; and that was well, in Iry's estimation. The Egyptians did not even pause in their chorus.

At length they were all shorn like strange sheep. Ahmose's soldiers dragged them up again, a dozen white peeled wands of men, big men still and massive, but greatly diminished by the shearing.

It was purely cruel, and a great vengeance. Iry should have been more pleased with it than she was. Her time in Avaris had changed her—corrupted her. These were men to her now; some whose names she even knew. She could not hate them as perfectly as she wished to.

She had been intending to leave when the lords left. Many of the other high ones did, though the king's soldiers gathered in even greater numbers to see men of their own rank brought low by so simple a thing. Nor had she seen the one she had half expected to see. He was dead, or fled.

No. Dead. Khayan would not run away as the others had. It was not in him. She should go, search among the dead. Or she should send Sadana, or call Iannek from the ship where he sulked in furious exile—there was no safety for him here, where any bearded foreigner was killed or captured on sight.

But she lingered. She hated Khayan. She did not want to see him dead.

The lesser men were not shorn completely as their lords were. There were too many of them, and they were of too little account. The barbers settled, with them, for stripping them of their garments and shaving their beards and cropping their hair close, as quickly as could be. It was still a great shame to them to be made like Egyptian slaves. One or two tried to trick the barbers into slitting their throats, but the barbers were too deft with the razors, and too much on their guard.

There was one near the end who drew her eye. He was walking wounded— surprising; most of those had been killed. Maybe he had concealed it until he was stripped naked? He was young, and large; no giant but tall enough, and leaner than some, less bull-broad. He looked—like—

As if she had spoken the thought aloud, he raised his head. His face was a blank Retenu face, pale arch of nose thrusting from amid the thicket of beard, but the eyes she knew. No other man of that people had such eyes, golden as a falcon's. They were blank now, as if he had gone blind. He did not seem to see her, or if he saw her, to know who she was.

When the guards took hold of him, he did not resist. His spirit had gone away. They threw him down and held him as they had the rest, as casual now as shearers with the sheep. The barber finished sharpening his razor—ignoring bystanders who encouraged him to do no such thing; to let the blade go dull, the better to torment the prisoner.

A faint sound escaped Iry as the man set blade to that thick and beautiful hair. But she did not move, did not try to stop him.

It was over in a few deft strokes. The guards hauled him to his feet.

He was—very good to look at. Very good indeed. Almost as lovely as

Kemni, and Kemni was the greatest beauty she knew, who was not a woman. His eyes seemed all the stranger now that they stared out of a face and not a black shadow of beard.

She spoke then. She moved forward a step. "That one," she said. "I'll take that one."

At first she thought she would be ignored. But everyone knew who she was. The guards glanced at one another and at their commander. There was no lord of greater rank here now; even the king had gone to other duties.

"I'll take him," she said, "as recompense for what was done to my kin and my holding."

Some of the soldiers standing about grinned at one another and remarked on her taste. "He's a pretty one," one of them said with a leer. "And a fine young bull of Baal, too. You'll get good use of him."

Iry had always been able to keep her face cold, even when the blush flamed inside. It was a gift, and she was glad of it. If any of them had known what he was to her . . .

What he was no longer. He did not even recognize her. No doubt, to him, all Egyptian women looked alike: too small, too thin, and hidden behind their masks of paint.

"You," she said to the guard who held the rope that bound his hands. "Bring him behind me. If your captain can spare you?"

The captain bowed low. He was hiding a grin, she could see. She would exact a price for that—later. At the moment it was enough that he had given her one of his men.

She had no expectation that Khayan would escape. He had the look of a man who had retreated into himself, far and far, until he felt nothing, saw nothing, heard nothing. Beneath the shorn black curls, she thought she saw a swelling, and perhaps a glisten of blood.

For that, and for the clotted and oozing wound in his side, she had him taken not to her tent but to the healers. They had begun to recover from the battle. A new tent had been raised for them, and their instruments and their boxes of medicines recovered as much as could be, and more brought from the ships. The dead were taken away, the wounded looked after.

When she came, Imhotep was just finishing with a limp and unconscious man. Acolytes hastened discreetly away with a bundle wrapped in a cloth.

The man had lost his leg. Iry shivered and swallowed bile. Now the embalmers would take it and do what they did, letting that part of him go before, so that when he died he could be reunited with it.

Imhotep smiled at her. He had taken a liking to her from the first, for what reason she did not know. Maybe because she knew a little of the healing arts, and asked to learn more. He did not keep secrets, did that one, though others of his order frowned to see him instructing her.

His smile faded however as he saw who followed her. She drew aside to let him see.

Khayan obliged them both by crumpling at their feet. Imhotep stepped neatly aside to let him fall, then bent down and arranged the long scattered limbs, frowning as he did it, counting grazes, bruises, and of course the most obvious wound; but he went on. When he came to the head, he paused. "Blow to the head," he said, with a glance at Iry.

She nodded. She had thought so.

The long clever fingers searched amid cropped curls. "Nothing broken. But the brain might be . . ." The rest subsided into a murmur.

Iry kept silent as Imhotep sent acolytes for this medicine and that, and set one of them to cleaning and stitching and binding the gash in Khayan's side. Only when Imhotep had drawn back and paused for breath did she ask, "Is he badly hurt?"

Imhotep shrugged. "With blows to the head, one never knows. The rest is nothing, unless it festers. I've done as much as I may. If you should be inclined to pray, that would be useful."

Iry could pray. She wanted this man alive. Not because she loved him or wanted him happy. She wanted him to suffer.

Imhotep sent Khayan away, and Iry and the guard with him. "Watch him," the healer said. "If he sleeps too long, if he seems confused, if he acts strangely—bring him back to me. He should wake in the morning with a hammering headache, but no more than that."

"And maybe a little wound-fever?"

"I hope not," Imhotep said. He had already turned away toward another who needed him.

She let him go. The guard was willing to continue with his charge, at least until he was settled in Iry's tent. As for what she would do then . . .

There was little to do, at least with this captive, aside from see a pallet spread for him and mount guard over him. Iry sent the guard away, over his protests—which rather startled her. Even after she had given him a bit of silver, he wanted to stay. Odd man. But he had a captain waiting for him, and duties that had nothing to do with the Mare's servant or her sudden prisoner.

She mounted guard herself, then, though there were other things that she could have been doing. Khayan slept uneasily, stirring and murmuring. His brow was cool; no fever. His face was pale, but so was the rest of him. He was whiter-skinned than anyone in Egypt, white as milk where the sun had not touched him.

She hated him. He had bedded her, left her, forgotten her. Then he had, like a blazing fool, let himself be condemned on that preposterous charge. No one had believed it, except the woman's father. And for that, he had lost his rank and his honor, and now, his freedom.

"Idiot," she said to him. *"Idiot."*

He did not hear. She settled comfortably, prepared to wait for as long as she needed to. Part of her knew that she should leave this task to a servant and go out to be an omen, and to help as she could. But the Great House had servants and subjects in rather astonishing number. Khayan had no one. Not that he deserved anyone, but it did not seem right, somehow, to leave him to the care of strangers.

She would have to summon Sadana. Eventually. And Iannek, too, she supposed. They were his close kin. But not until he had got over whatever horrors he would need to get over, once he woke and discovered what had become of him. She did not do it out of concern for his spirit, she told herself, but out of concern for theirs. He was their brother. Whatever shame fell on him, to a degree they shared it.

She slept, perhaps. The day darkened into night. The camp quieted slowly, though the sounds of singing and revelry went on. The king would have to pause for a day or two, so that his men could recover.

That would serve her well enough. She roused with a start, to find that his eyes were open. They were clear—startling, a little. "Don't tell me I dreamed it all," he said.

It was strange to hear that rich familiar voice out of that stranger's face. That beautiful and unguarded face. Why, she thought: a man who had a beard to hide behind might never learn to conceal what he was thinking.

He did not know yet. If he felt strange, maybe there were too many oddnesses, and to many small and greater pains.

"This isn't Avaris," he said, looking about in the lamplight. "This is—are we in camp? Do I remember—I went to war? Then what are you doing here?"

"This is a stronghold south of Sile," she said. "You are in camp."

"I remember . . ." He sighed, and gasped: it must have stabbed him with pain. "There was a battle. I fought. It wasn't a dream, was it? I really did—Barukha—"

"Yes."

"So the king came after all? And brought you?"

"I brought myself," she said. "This is the Egyptian camp. You lost the fight. Most of your lords have fled."

His mouth, which was long and remarkably well shaped, twisted wryly. "Lords. Never enough sense among the lot of them to come in out of the sun."

"I suppose you would know," she said.

He winced. Then at last he seemed to understand that something was odd. His hand crept up. She thought briefly of stopping it, but he had to know. Best to get it over.

His hand explored his face, which surely was as strange to him as it was to her, and his shorn hair. It lowered slowly. He lay very still. "I was fighting," he said quietly, calmly. "Then I woke, and I was here."

"You don't remember anything?"

"Nothing. We lost?"

She nodded.

"Then—what—"

That calm was a thin shell over hysteria. She knew. She had known it herself often enough. "You were wounded. You took a blow to the head. Then you were captured."

"And not killed?"

"The king decided to let all the captives live," she said.

"As slaves?"

"As whatever he needs them to be."

"Slaves." Khayan raised his hand again to his face. "You, too?"

"Oh, no. I'm their omen. I came with the Mare, you see. She brought me to my own people."

"Of course." He should have sounded bitter. He sounded merely tired. But his wits were quick enough. "I suppose I was your share of the booty?"

"I don't know," she said. "I just took you and walked away."

"Why?"

"You'd rather I'd left you where you were?"

"That depends on what you want with me."

"I don't want anything," she said. "You should sleep. Is your headache very bad?"

"Dreadful."

"Then sleep. You'll be better in the morning."

"I don't think so," he said: and that was bitterness. But his eyes closed, perhaps of their own accord.

Iry could have left then. But she stayed and watched him sleep. She was not thinking of anything in particular, though it might be useful to consider what indeed she wished to do with him. She owned him now as once he had owned her. His hand on her had been light—that much she granted him. But whether her own could be as light . . . she did not know.

Tomorrow, she thought. She would think about it tomorrow. Tonight she would sleep as he slept. Part of her babbled that he was feigning it, that once she had fallen into a drowse he would rise and escape; but the rest knew that he would not. Where would he go? How would he dare to show his face among the men of his own people? He had already been dishonored. He was worse than that, now.

No. He would stay. He had nowhere else to go.

KING OF
UPPER AND
LOWER
EGYPT

THE WORLD WAS a strange and shifting place. Khayan, for being a fool, had fallen as low as man could fall. He was a captive, a slave. Far better had he died than be subjected to this.

Others of his people had searched for ways to kill themselves. One even succeeded: provoked a short-tempered guard into running him through with a sword. He was cast into the river for the crocodiles to devour—a terrible fate, if he had been an Egyptian, but no more terrible than what the Egyptians had done to him.

All of that, Khayan knew. And yet he had no desire at all to die. One of the most difficult things he had ever done was to walk out of Iry's tent into the pitiless glare of the sun, where every eye could see his face laid naked to the world. He would almost rather have stripped off the kilt that was given him, than show his bare cheeks.

Still, once it was done, it was done. The Egyptians stared briefly, then ignored him. A beardless man, to them, was a natural thing, far less unnatural than the beard he had been robbed of.

He still could not remember that, nor anything after he took a stand with his men near the fort's wall. They were pulling that wall down now. Of his men there was no sign. Dead, he supposed, or fled. None of them had been taken captive; of that, he was certain.

No one tried to prevent him from walking through the camp. He had waked alone, eaten and drunk what he found beside him—bread and beer and a bowl of onions—and ventured out before his courage failed him. He did not know where Iry was. Was she hoping that he would escape? Did she want him to be killed in the trying?

She was angry with him. He had seen that, though she hid it rather well. This was her revenge on him, this slavery, and perhaps this abandonment, too.

The fort that his people had built was coming down in a great crashing and eruption of cheers. Once it had fallen and been trampled into the earth, the army would go on. All the dead were tended, the wounded seen to. The wrack of battle was all but cleared away.

His fellow slaves had been given the lowest of tasks: digging new privies and burying old ones. More than one bore the marks of the lash. They had not been washed as he had, fed and given a clean kilt. They were all naked and filthy.

There at last he was not permitted to go. A guard with a whip of many thongs interposed himself. The man was half Khayan's size, but the whip was convincing. He stepped back out of reach. The man smiled. It was not a malicious smile, at all. It was as if—

Khayan wandered away, greatly puzzled and uncertain whether he should be angry. When he sharpened his ears and his understanding of the Egyptians' speech—not as easy as he might have thought; the dialect of Thebes was different from that of Memphis—he heard what made him pause. They all knew who he was. *Don't touch that one,* they said. *It belongs to the white priestess.* For that was what they called her, for the white robe she wore and the white Mare she served.

To belong to her . . .

Well. They all did, all the Mare's people. He began to be—not angry, no. Amused. Even a little wild, as if—no, he could not be happy. Relief; he would call it relief. The world was a strange place, and yet he was glad to be living in it.

He found her where he would have expected, near the horses. She was speaking with a man in a plain kilt and a short wig, who still must have been a person of rank: he wore a golden collar. There were other people about, a great number of them, but they were of no account.

Except one. His sister Sadana met his eyes across the stretch of field. He shrank inside himself and came within a breath's span of bolting—but one thing kept him where he was. What in the gods' name was she doing here?

She strode toward him as no woman of his father's people did, with pride and confidence that were given only to men. But she was of the Mare's people, and warrior-trained.

She stopped in front of him and looked him up and down, taking her time about it. He set his teeth and suffered it. Her brow rose. "You're even prettier than you were when you were small. I think I rather like it."

He rubbed his chin, which rasped already with stubble. "I suppose I know why you're here. But why is she?"

"The Mare called her," Sadana answered.

Khayan sighed faintly. He had not seen the Mare when he came, but as he stood there, a herd of duller creatures shifted, and she was there, her moon-pale coat gleaming.

There were others beyond her. Khayan forgot Sadana, forgot even where he was. He advanced a step, set fingers to lips, loosed a piercing whistle.

His dun stallions, his beauties, his beloved, flung up their heads and whinnied back. Moon stamped his foot. Star tossed his head till his black mane flew. They wheeled together and galloped toward him—straight through the crowd of Egyptians.

The little brown men scattered, some with severe loss of dignity. Only the one beside Iry held his ground as she did, and the duns veered round them, as they would have done if any of the others had stood where he was.

They checked as they came up to Khayan, eyes rolling, snorting. He laughed: laughter that was half a sob. "My poor beautiful brothers. You don't recognize me, do you?"

They snorted again, explosively, and approached in delicate steps. He held out his hands. Their soft noses brushed his palms, blowing into them. "Yes," he said. "Yes, it's I."

But they had to be certain. They nosed and sniffed him all over, licking, offering to nip until he halted them with a rebuke. He stroked their heads and necks and shoulders, rubbing their napes were they loved to be rubbed, and combing tangles out of the thick manes. They wrapped themselves around him, shutting him off from the world, so that all there was to see was golden hide, black mane, and the roll of a bright eye.

It was only with great regret that he ended the greeting and looked past them. Sadana was laughing at him. Iry—Iry was smiling. So too the man beside her, a man past his youth and somewhat soft, but who carried himself with a certain loftiness that marked a lord.

Iry's smile faded. Khayan felt as if a cloud had gone across the sun. It was with difficulty that he made sense of the lord's words, which were addressed not to him but to Iry. "So. This is your Retenu?"

"I do own him, don't I?" Iry said. "Yes, that is the one I took from among the captives. Do you want him back?"

"No," the man said. "You may keep him. Only see to it that he behaves himself."

Khayan bridled. Even the memory that he was a slave could not keep him quiet—but Iry's glance clove his tongue to the roof of his mouth. "Come here," she said. "Tell us something."

He left his stallions reluctantly. The Egyptian lord regarded him with calm curiosity—measuring him as if he had been a stallion himself. He set his teeth and ignored the man, and bowed to Iry.

"We've captured a number of horses," she said, "and many more asses. The asses we'll set to carrying baggage. The horses we're very glad of—but we're lacking charioteers. Should we send them north, do you think? And keep them where they'll be safe, until we win back the whole of this kingdom?"

"You may not win it at all," Khayan said, not wisely. He could have been flogged for it, but as he had thought, they were not interested in punishing him for too free a tongue. They ignored that and listened to the rest. "If the decision were mine to make, and I know well that it is not, I would take them with the army. You've not met the full force of our chariotry yet. When you do, you may find you need all the remounts you can muster. Our men are trained, you see. They strike for the horses."

Iry shuddered. "Yes. I do remember that." She glanced at the Egyptian lord.

He nodded. "That's wise enough. We'll keep them, then. Can you spare enough men to look after them?"

"Those we have should be enough," said Iry.

The lord looked pleased, after the fashion of lords. He wandered back round the edge of the herd. All the others followed, and Iry at his side. Khayan walked behind them, with a stallion on either side of him. Sadana he had lost somewhere; he could not see her.

It had begun to dawn on him who this slightly slack-bellied, unpretentious man must be. The flock of people about him, the way they glanced at him, and no one spoke to him but Iry, who was as easy with him as she was with everyone: this must be the Great House of Thebes, the Pharaoh.

Khayan was a little disappointed. The Pharaoh, he had always heard, lived his life as a priest in a ritual, from waking till sleeping, without respite ever. And he was always crowned; he always carried the crook and the flail that marked his office.

Ahmose, it seemed, had not heard that he was supposed to conduct himself perpetually like a king. He was as easy with Iry as she was with him, taking transparent and almost childlike pleasure in the horses. So much, Khayan thought, for the Egyptian hatred of horses and their long-eared cousins.

Still, Ahmose was the king. He could only linger so long before his duties called him away. When he left, he took with him the crowd of his followers, and left Iry and a handful of men who must be the herders of horses, and Khayan.

Iry gave way then, and briefly, to the slackness of exhaustion. Almost as quickly as she had succumbed, she mastered herself. She straightened her shoulders, took a breath. Her eyes narrowed as they came to rest on Khayan. "You! You've been hurt. You should rest."

"Not before you do," he said.

"I can't do that. There's too much to do."

"Just for an hour."

Her head shook. "I can't—" She seemed to come to a decision of sorts. "I can't now. This is all mine to look after. The one whose charge it was— he's . . . indisposed."

"Wounded?"

"To the soul," she said.

"And he has no second-in-command?"

"Yes, but—"

"So send for him," Khayan said. "You need to rest."

"You are not my master!" she flashed at him.

He flinched. She saw. Her eyes did not soften, but her body's tautness eased a fraction. "I'll send for Seti. Though he may not—"

"He'll come if you command that he come."

She nodded. She was not accustomed to giving orders, even now; it was a habit, he supposed, that took time to set in the bone. Whereas he could not get out of it. Even shamed and cast down, he had still been commander of a hundred. It was a long, hard fall from even that lowly rank to the lot of a slave.

She commanded, and the man came: yet another wiry Egyptian, this one more insouciant than most, with the usual raking glance at Khayan, and a gratifyingly abject one at Iry. Khayan doubted that she was aware of it, but this man adored her.

"Seti," she said. "How is he? Is he—?"

Seti's eyes went dark; the mockery vanished from genuine and soul-deep grief. "He's the same, lady. He hasn't changed."

She sighed. "I suppose it will take time. Did you leave him under guard? Did they find any more knives?"

"The men are watching him—and there's nothing with an edge that he can get his hands on. Or rope or cord, either."

"Good," she said. "I'm leaving you in command of the horses and the chariots. Just for a little while. Until I've rested a bit."

"Lady," Seti said, "we're all yours, always. But there's no need for you to wear yourself out with taking your cousin's place. I'll do it in your name. You go rest."

She might have shaped a protest, but Seti waved her away. "Go," he said. "It's done, and will be well done. My word on it."

She let herself be led away then, with a docility that spoke to Khayan of a night, and perhaps several nights, without sleep, and the weight of weariness crushing her down.

Khayan's curiosity was keen enough to cut, but he was not inclined to weary her further with questions. Her cousin? And it seemed the man was in great distress, though as to why, Khayan could not imagine. Who knew what drove an Egyptian to extremity? Perhaps it was only the shock of having, late in life, been flung into the heat and blood of battle.

He settled her in the tent in which he had awakened, found someone who could bring wine and bread, though the jar when it came was full of the inevitable beer, and saw that she ate and drank at least enough to keep a bird alive. She who had never been richly fleshed was almost gaunt. "They're working you to death," he muttered.

"And you care?"

Ah, he thought. Anger. "You may quarrel with me all you like," he said, "but not until you've rested."

"I'll do it now," she said.

He sat on the floor at her feet and made himself comfortable. She stared at him. Maybe, after all, she had never seen him sitting except in chairs in palaces. She had not known him when he lived among the Mare's people.

"You left me," she said, a little distracted, as if she was not quite done with scrambling her wits together. "You went away. You never said a word."

"I sent messages," he said. "Several of them. The door was shut. You were not to be disturbed."

"I never—"

"No," he said. "But my mother would. And, I'll wager, did."

Her teeth clicked together. "Did she—does she know—"

"She might," he said, "though I doubt it. She was keeping you safe, that was all."

"I've been hating you," she said. "I'm not going to stop. What you did to get cast out—"

"I didn't."

"I'm sure you didn't do *that*. But you let her trap you. I thought better of you than that."

"Everyone did," he said. The pain was dull with age and use. He was more wry now than shamed. "I've paid for it, don't you think? I'd say I've paid rather high."

"You chose it for yourself," she said.

That startled him into laughter. "You really don't intend to forgive me, do you?"

"Is it forgivable?"

"I—" He stopped. It struck him, terribly late, that as thin as she was, as worn, and as determined in her anger, she was still surprisingly pleasing to the eye. Not beautiful as her mother was, but something perhaps better than beauty. She was . . .

Beloved. That was not a thought he had expected. And yet, it was the truth.

That was what he had run away from. And yes, he had run. First because the king commanded, then because he could think of nothing else to do. Straight away from her—and straight into her arms.

Which were not at all welcoming. And yet she had taken him away from the grim labor to which he should have been condemned. She must feel something besides anger.

"I think," he said out of all of that, "that you might give me leave to make amends."

"What amends can you make?"

"I can serve you," he said, "since the gods have seen fit to lay me at your feet. We all serve the Mare's servant, after all."

"Your sister said the same," Iry said. "Is it as easy as that for you?"

"It's the hardest thing in the world," he said from the heart.

"Then I'll accept it."

Such an odd person she was. What he offered her, he would have given no one else—no, not ever.

"I think I understand," he said, "why the Mare chose you."

"Why? Because I'm too stubborn for words?"

"That," he said, "and because you don't think as other women do. The goddess sings in you."

"Is that what it is?"

"Could it be anything else?"

"I could simply be very, very obstinate."

He laughed. "That, too. But didn't the goddess make you? And shape you? And choose you?"

"It seems she did."

"So," he said. "I forget—you never knew your predecessor. She died untimely; she hadn't yet chosen her acolyte. The Young Mare was already born and growing into her power, which should have been a warning, but no one elected to heed it."

"No one wanted to," said Iry. "They told me: when the Mare goes her own way, the world is changing. That's never something people want to see."

"I brought her back, you know," he said. "Or she brought me. I would have stayed in the east if I could. But she left it, she and her kin. The priestesses appointed me her guardsman until she came where she wanted to go."

"Here," Iry said. "The Lower Kingdom."

"She was looking for you."

"Yes." Iry grew tired at last of standing. She sat on her heels beside him, calm and contained as she almost always was. She reached and touched him—brushing his cheek with her hand.

The touch was strange, nor did it grow less so with use. He kept looking for the beard that had shielded him so well against the world.

"It will grow back," she said, reading him as easily as she always had.

"Will you let it?"

She tilted her head. "I think you look very well, if rather odd, without it. Surely it's cooler. You must grant it that."

"It is very much cooler," he admitted. "But I don't—"

"You'll accustom yourself to it." She sighed, and yawned. But her attention was on him. "And here you are wounded. You must be out on your feet."

"I don't feel anything," he said. It was mostly true. His side twinged if he moved too quickly, and his head ached with dull persistence. But he had had worse after a hard night in the banquet-hall.

She was still watching him, regarding him narrowly. Horse Goddess alone knew what thoughts ran behind those long painted eyes.

She touched him again, this time more lightly, letting her fingers trail down his cheek to his neck and his shoulder. She looked as if she were trying to remember something she had all but forgotten. "I was hating you," she said. "It was very satisfying. Until I saw you again."

He did not know what to say to that. Except: "I never hated you."

"Why would you? You never even thought of me."

"I thought of you every day. I could hardly help but think of you."

"Prove it."

His wits were slow. He did not, for a long moment, understand what she was asking. Just as she began to remember her anger, he knew. "You don't—"

"I'm not going to force you," she said. "Nor will I command you. This you must choose. If you don't, I'll not punish you. I swear that by my name."

"Iry," he said. "Iry. Iry."

"And thrice Khayan," she said. "Your power for mine, and mine for yours."

"Yes," he said. He took her in his arms. She stiffened. Foolish woman: had she expected that he would choose to spurn her? He could never do such a thing.

She eased slowly, till they lay together on the heaped carpets that shielded the tent against the raw earth. He was weaker than he should have been, but she was weary. It freed them, in its way. It let them explore one another with lips and hands, and learn one another's bodies. She found the spot under his ribs that made him collapse, helpless with laughter. He found one down her spine that reduced her to a limp puddle of pleasure.

She rose over him, sitting astride him as if he had been a stallion she had a mind to tame. She seemed enraptured with his face. She framed it in her hands and kissed it, slowly, thoroughly, from brow to chin.

His hands cradled her hips and the sweet curve of her buttocks. She shifted, coiled, took him inside her with a motion so smooth that surely—oh, surely—

Yet she seemed as startled as he, as if her body had acted without her willing it. She held very still, till he began gently to rock: like a boat on a slow swell, or a horse at an easy canter, long rolling strides over an undulating field. She rode it as she would have ridden the Mare, all of her given up to it, letting herself become the long slow easy motion. He, who was not so gifted, filled his eyes with her body above him, the slender frame, the firm young breasts. Her head had fallen back. Her eyes, he was sure, were shut.

She drank the whole of it, every drop of pleasure. His pleasure was all mingled with hers. He had never known such a thing before: to take as he gave, exactly, moment for moment. To set her pleasure entirely before his. To be—to become—a part of her.

It was strange. As strange as being stripped of his lands and lordship, shorn of his beard, and robbed of his freedom. And yet this strangeness was wonderful. In becoming the mirror of her pleasure, he became pure pleasure.

The gods laughed, surely, as he found his way to the summit, and found her there. Her eyes were open wide. She was astonished. "I never knew," she said, "that this could be."

He kissed her into silence. Time enough after to tell her that he had not known it, either. It was a rarity, a gift of the gods. Of the goddess—Horse Goddess, who had chosen this woman to be her servant.

And did that mean that he was chosen, too? No; that was too overweening of him. If he was anything to the gods, he was their plaything. Not their beloved, whom they had taken for their own.

THE ENEMY'S FORTRESS was broken down, its rubble ground into the earth. The king, well satisfied, gave the order then. By the river road, and by the river itself, they marched upon Avaris.

They met with little resistance. The people who had lived in this land since the beginning either fled at their coming or welcomed them as kin. The foreigners who had conquered them made no stand against them. For warriors who had brought the terrible swiftness of the chariot into Egypt, they were remarkably enamored of their high stone walls and their guarded cities.

"It's Egypt," Iannek said. "Egypt changed us."

He had kept his bright spirit remarkably well, but even he had gone dark as they came in sight of Avaris. The choices that he had made must trouble even that light and foolish heart.

He was still Iry's guardian hound, but he had appointed himself Kemni's watchdog as well. Kemni's heart was ripped from his breast and his souls all scattered, but he still had enough wits to know how he was being watched. Iannek did not even try to pretend that he hung about simply for the pleasure of Kemni's company.

Probably he was wiser than he wanted anyone to know. Kemni's fingers kept twitching toward knives and swords. Sometimes as he stood on *Dancer*'s deck, riding the Cretan ship openly as once he had ridden in hiding, he knew that if he let go, simply let go, he would fall. Then the river would take him, and the crocodiles. And there would be no more pain. But Iannek always seemed to be there, or Naukrates, or one of the crew.

He tried to explain to them that he did not want to die yet. Not only because he had promised Ariana, but because he had to learn the way to Iphikleia's own goddess' country first, then learn how best to go there. That would take time. Ariana, who could best teach him, had other and innumerable duties. And she grieved as he grieved, when she could. It was not time to ask her to guide him where he must go.

The others were convinced that he would go whenever they let him out of their sight. Maybe they saw a truth he was too blind to see. He would not have been astonished. He was good for very little except to go where he was told, and to leave all the rest to the making of their war.

Seti was commanding the king's chariots now. Someone else drove the king's own chariot. Kemni saw them on the riverbank, keeping pace with the

fleet. Sometimes he found in himself a yearning to be there and not here, but
it was dim and far away.

He was being indulged like a child, or like a prince whose whims were
law. The anger at that was dim, too. Everything was dim and remote. Waking,
sleeping—sometimes he could hardly tell which was which. It was all a black
and empty dream.

From the midst of that dream he stood at *Dancer*'s prow, as a strong wind
bore them against the current over the river, up toward the great loom of walls
that was Avaris. From the river it was like a rise of sea-cliffs in one of the isles
of the Great Green, and yet all of it wrought by hands. That too must have
been Egypt changing the invaders from Asia, so that they built larger, wider,
higher, than they ever had in their own country.

There had been battles before this. Imet was strongly defended, till it fell
to the same cowardice that had lost the Retenu that unnamed fortress. They
all seemed devout in their faith that if they retreated to Avaris, they could
somehow win back all the land that Ahmose had taken from them.

Kemni did not think they reckoned on the power of an Egyptian king
reconquering Egypt. For every one of the Retenu there were a hundred, a
thousand people whose grandfathers' grandfathers had tilled this land, or ruled
it, for time out of mind. As easily as they had fallen, as mute as they had lain
beneath the conqueror's foot for most of a hundred years, when they had a
king to follow, they rejoiced to rise up against their foreign overlords.

Kamose had known that, and accomplished it, until the threat from Nubia
and—if Kemni allowed himself to think it—his own failure of will turned him
back from the edge of victory. Ahmose hoped to succeed where his brother
had failed.

Certainly this was a greater force than Kamose had mustered, and a greater
alliance than he had dreamed of, Crete's double axe raised in Egypt's name,
and its ships set at the king's disposal. Naukrates the admiral had bidden all
his captains make a wall of ships, a barrier across and along the braided skeins
of the river. Ahmose's own fleet had done a great thing, had taken Memphis
with scarce a blow struck, when the Egyptians in the city turned against those
few of the Retenu who remained. They sailed down the river in the morning,
as Ahmose's army made camp to the north of the city and began to mount
the siege from the land as the Cretan ships mounted it from the water.

Kemni saw the coming of the fleet, saw the blaze that was the flagship of
gold, like a sun come to earth. High on its deck sat a figure in royal state,
crowned with a marvelous crown of gold, like the downcurved wings of a
vulture, Nekhbet who was queen and goddess. Queen Nefertari had come with
the might of the Upper Kingdom.

They met on the river, the flagship of gold and *Dancer* sleek with new
paint and wine-dark sails, golden ship and black ship gliding side by side. Ahmose wore the crown of the Upper Kingdom, but not, yet, that of the Lower.

He sat on a golden throne, with Naukrates the admiral at his left hand and Ariana the queen at his right, each in the full high finery of Crete.

They well knew that the city's walls were thick with people, wide eyes and staring faces. And men with bows, but the ships were well out of bowshot. Their captains had seen to that.

Still they were close enough for all to see how they gleamed in the sun; how they met and exchanged royal greetings, though only those who were on the ships might have heard what words they spoke to one another. "Well met," said the king, "and welcome."

"Well indeed," said the queen. "Is the north secured?"

"The north is secured," the king answered. "And the south?"

"Well enough," she said.

+ +

They held the feast of welcome on the golden flagship, with *Dancer* moored alongside. The intrepid traveled back and forth, seeking *Dancer's* quieter deck, or swinging across on ropes to taste the queen's good wine.

Kemni kept to the same corner of *Dancer's* deck in which he had traveled to Crete. Someone had brought him food from the feast, and wine. He left them where they were. He had no strength to eat, though he knew he should. He had to live, for a while.

Some of the younger princelings were making a game of swinging on ropes from ship to ship. The king and the queen indulged it; it was harmless, if noisy. Every now and then one would lose his grip, or simply let go, and fall into the water. His fellows would fish him out with much hilarity.

One figure swung across with economy and dispatch, and no headlong whoop of delight in the game. It landed on the deck, rolled, came up beside Kemni.

Gebu, who had once been his brother, sat beside him and investigated the plate and cup and bowl. "Someone loves you," he said. "Even the princes didn't get any of this honey-sweet. There was just enough for the king and his queens."

Kemni did not answer. Gebu shrugged, ate the sweet and drank half the wine, and set the rest of the jar near Kemni's limp hand. He got up then and slipped quietly over the side, away from the golden flagship into another of the boats.

That game too the young men had been playing: leaping from boat to boat across the river. Kemni did not know why he followed. Maybe because he was tired of sitting. Maybe because Gebu went toward Avaris, and Kemni's belly did not care for the feel of it. His belly had felt nothing so distinct in so long that he could only follow where it led.

It was useful for once that he did not care if he lived or died, leaped into a boat or fell into the water. He waited till Gebu had advanced two boats, or three, before he began his own pursuit, moving as quietly as he could. His body was slack with days of lying about, but it remembered somewhat of its strength, and its hunter's cunning.

As he had thought, Gebu made his way toward the eastern bank, somewhat apart from the camp that spread along it, and made his way toward the city. Once or twice he slipped into deep shadow: driven there by the passing of a sentry, or the arrival of a mob of beer-reeking soldiers. They delayed but did not stop him.

Gebu might have been going into the camp. There was that. But the knot in Kemni's belly would not go away. A prince royal had no need at all to creep and hide and slink, unless he did something that even a prince might be ill advised to do.

Gebu slipped past the camp with no pause except for passersby. There was an open space beyond it, at the foot of the walls. He ghosted round the edge of it, away from the loom of the northward gate. Kemni was the ghost of a ghost in his wake.

But there was another behind, a whisper in the wind, a ripple on the sand. Kemni stopped and made himself invisible, unmoving, unbreathing, utterly still. A shadow passed, wary, but never wary enough. Kemni tripped it and sat on it, blocking its mouth with his hand.

In what starlight there was, he could see the shadow of a face. But his hand told him more, and the sense of the body beneath him. It was an Egyptian—a little startling, for he had been expecting Iannek of the Retenu; but this was not that great bearded man. This was Gebu's charioteer, the young man named for the king, Ahmose si-Ebana.

Kemni staggered up, dragging si-Ebana with him. Gebu was almost out of reach, almost invisible. Kemni made what speed he could in pursuit, with si-Ebana hard on his heels. He did not try to stop the young fool from following. A loyal man, a man who knew how to fight, might be useful—if he had the sense not to move until Kemni allowed him.

Gebu advanced less stealthily as he neared the walls. The Egyptian army was behind them. The walls were dark and silent. At wide intervals Kemni heard the heavy tread of a sentry; but the city was asleep, or feigning it.

Round the curve of the wall, not far from the river, was a postern gate. It was hidden between two courses of stone, angled into shadow and well concealed by the stink of a midden, but Gebu knew where to go. It opened to his hand. He slipped within.

Kemni never even paused. Where Gebu had gone, he went also, and si-Ebana, because si-Ebana knew no better.

There was light within, torches beginning to burn low but illuminating a passage through the walls into what must be a portion of the citadel. All that way was clearly prepared, laid open and deserted, which could not have been easy in so crowded a city, and a city under siege.

Gebu was not looking for pursuit, nor, it appeared, had those who opened this way for him. It led up by many flights of stairs, through dim passages, out at last onto a broad expanse of roof under the stars. There was a garden on that roof, small but cunningly made, lit now by a ring of torches. Men waited there, big bearded men in robes of rich embroideries.

Gebu in his kilt of fine white linen, his collar of blue and red and gold, his princely wig, seemed odd, misplaced. But he held himself erect as a prince should.

Kemni made himself a shadow amid the shadows of that garden. si-Ebana slipped into his shadow, leaning toward him, breathing in his ear. "There. I'll wager good beer on it: that's Apophis."

There amid the rest, seated no higher or richer, nor dressed as splendidly as some; but they all sat so that, no matter where he was or what he did, he was their center. Kings did that. It was one of the gifts that made them kings.

He made Kemni think, unwillingly, of Ahmose. He was much the same kind of man, the same age, the same comfort in his office. He wore kingship as easily, with as little need for ostentation—unless, of course, there should be need for it.

He regarded Gebu with a flat dark stare, and no expression on what could be seen of his face beneath the thicket of beard. Gebu did not flinch. He was a brave man, whatever else he was. Kemni had always known that.

Apophis spoke in Egyptian as many of these Retenu could, without either beauty or elegance of phrase, but his words were easy enough to understand. "So, man of Egypt. You have a bargain for me?"

"I might," Gebu said. "Tell me what you need of me."

"No, no," Apophis said. "First you tell me what brings you here. What would lead a prince to betray the king his father?"

"It's said he's not my father," said Gebu. "My mother was a concubine. She died bearing me. Who knows who might have bedded her while the king was occupied elsewhere?"

"Convenient," said Apophis. "They say you resemble him."

"He has brothers," Gebu said. "And he had more, once. I offer you the bargain that Kamose made. The siege breaks, the army withdraws to Thebes."

"And how will you bring that about? Is your king about to waver?"

"There will be a new king," Gebu said.

Apophis blinked once, as a crocodile will, lying in the reeds. "How do I know that I may trust a king who killed a king to reach his throne?"

"A king with such a burden on his spirit would feel obliged to be loyal in all else. Yes?"

"More likely no," Apophis said. "I would ask that such a king give me more than his word. That he swear a solemn oath that he will do as he undertook to do—and that, once he has done it, he will rule in Thebes according to my advice and counsel."

"As a tributary king?" Gebu asked with great calm.

Apophis spread his hands. "No. Oh, no. Nothing so dreadful as that. Say rather that we become allies—for you will be the new king, yes? Will you have your father killed, or will you do it yourself?"

For the first time Gebu seemed disconcerted. "It will be done," he said somewhat brusquely. "How it is done is my affair."

"So it is," Apophis agreed with every appearance of amiability. "I simply wish to secure my half of the bargain."

"I trusted you," Gebu said, "by coming here alone as you asked—and that was not well thought of among my allies. Will you trust me in return, that I will give you what I agreed to give?"

"I suppose I must," said Apophis. "Or I may simply have you killed here and now, and trust that my armies will overcome your father's, and win a clear victory over both kingdoms."

"Do you honestly think you can win this war? Egypt rules the river. The land belongs to it—the people have risen to welcome the Great House wherever he goes."

"I might ask the same of you. If you dispose of the king, and make yourself king, then go away, what will Egypt do?"

"Egypt will submit," Gebu said, "because the king is a god."

"Not if he can be killed."

Kemni, in the shadows, wondered if Gebu heard the threat there. Maybe he did. Or maybe not. He said, "His death will be seen to be the gods' will. I intend nothing as crude as a knife in the back."

"Indeed." Apophis let silence stretch for a moment. Then he said, "Tell me why. Why do you do this?"

"Does it matter?"

"Yes," said Apophis.

Gebu did not like that: he was as close to showing temper as Kemni had seen him. "The gods move me. They set in me the desire to be king."

"So you blame the gods." Apophis shrugged. "Maybe it's even true. Though I think a younger son, the son of a concubine, whose parentage is somewhat in doubt, might find his ambition thwarted unless he took steps to accomplish it for himself. What will you do with your brothers, then? What of the heir—what is his name?"

"Amonhotep," Gebu said. "They also will be dealt with."

"By a conspiracy of—what? Priests?"

"Lords of the Upper Kingdom," Gebu answered. "Some are priests for part of the year."

"And are they still with you, now that your father is succeeding so well in his conquest of this kingdom?"

"Do you think that he can win?"

"He might," Apophis said. "He has gained far more than I thought, though less than he seems to be claiming—or even than you seem to think. He rules one branch of the river and two cities—Sile and Memphis. I rule the rest. Now that all his forces are gathered here, I'll close upon them and crush them. And yet, your erstwhile allies might not see it as I do. You might find them faint of heart and inclined to cling to the king they know, and not trust their hopes to a lesser prince."

"Some of them, perhaps," Gebu said. "But most have other reason not to love the king. Kings make enemies, as you well know. Judgments given against certain men of the kingdom, jealousy of others favored above them, duties given them that are onerous or unwelcome—even the imposition of war on men who prefer to live in peace: no, my lord; these enemies will not turn back to the king who has treated them so ill."

"And they may believe that they can control you, whereas Ahmose has proved that he will submit to no such thing." Apophis nodded, and rose suddenly. "Very well. Swear your oath before these men of my council. Then go, and do as you promise. The way out will be open, as was the way in. Only have a care that you don't stray from it. An Egyptian of apparent rank in certain portions of this city is likely to be killed on sight."

Gebu inclined his head. It was not a bow. "I will swear," he said, "and then go. We'll meet again as king and king, before the gates of this city."

"So we shall," said Apophis. "Only tell me this, before you swear. Has no one suspected this conspiracy of yours?"

"No one at all," Gebu said steadily. "We've concealed ourselves well."

"And yet I'm told that you sent a messenger to us before the war began, offering to stop it. He never came here, and the war went on in spite of you."

"He was one man," Gebu said. "I would have sent more—would have had an embassy, and used the lords in Memphis who were then subject to you. But I was overruled."

"You never thought that the messenger might have been caught and stripped of his secrets, and the conspiracy uncovered?"

"If he had been," Gebu said, "do you think I would have been left alive, and even allowed to ride in a chariot behind the king?"

"That would be very subtle of him," Apophis conceded. "Very well, then. Swear. And then go."

Gebu swore his souls away before the lords of the Retenu council, bound in blood—a barbarian rite, but Gebu submitted to it. He seemed glad of it, as if after all some god was in him, perhaps even Set himself, who was the enemy of Horus. Had not Set destroyed his brother Osiris and fought with Horus for kingship over the Two Lands?

Set was Baal of the Retenu. And it was to Set, and therefore Baal, that he swore. When he had spoken the great words and sealed them with his blood, he was let go. Alone as he had come, he left the roof and the garden, and the king of the foreign kings.

KEMNI FOLLOWED GEBU out of the Retenu palace and city, with si-Ebana silent in his wake. He glanced back once or twice, but he could not read the charioteer's expression.

As they took the narrow and lighted ways, keeping back out of Gebu's sight, Kemni came to a choice. It was coming to king-killing—soon, if Gebu hoped to fulfill the oath that he had sworn. He would go to Ahmose, of course he would. But he would go as he best saw fit to go.

He stopped before they passed the postern gate, so abruptly that si-Ebana stumbled into him. He grunted but did not fall. "Si-Ebana," he said, soft but clear. "Will you do a thing with me?"

"Yes," si-Ebana said promptly.

"But you don't even know—"

"I know." si-Ebana's face wore an expression at last, and it was grim.

"It's dangerous," Kemni said. "He'll never forgive you, once he knows what you've done."

"I belong to the king," si-Ebana said. "Quick now. He'll be gone before we can catch him."

Kemni had more to say, but si-Ebana had spoken rightly. They would lose Gebu if they lingered. With a shrug and the faint gust of a sigh, he slipped out of the postern into the odorous night.

Gebu was still in sight, if barely. Kemni ran as quickly as he could, with si-Ebana soft-footed at his back. The army was close. If Gebu slipped in among the tents, he could lose himself before they ever caught him.

Part of Kemni knew that that was absurd. Gebu the prince could not be lost. But if he gathered his co-conspirators before Kemni reached him, and set the oath in motion, it might go very swiftly—too swiftly. And Ahmose would die.

If Kemni had been wholly in the world, he would have been too appalled to move. This black remoteness of grief made the rest of it, not endurable, but thinkable.

Gebu had quickened his pace. He might be aware of pursuit, or he might simply be eager to finish what he had begun.

Kemni was not as strong as he should have been. si-Ebana passed him, running long and light. He circled wide round Gebu and vanished into the camp.

Kemni stumbled to a halt, gasping for breath. Gebu had passed in among the tents—too easy; someone should see to that, dig a ditch or build a palisade, or the enemy could walk in unnoticed.

Kemni slipped in much as Gebu had, on the edge of a fading revelry, to find Gebu face to face with a middling large, seemingly drunken, and very friendly young charioteer. He dropped a heavy arm about Gebu's shoulders, spraying him with beer from a jar that he had found—gods knew where, but bless the boy, for that was clever indeed. "Friend," he said in a slurred voice. "*Good* friend. Have some beer?"

Gebu was neatly trapped. If he fled, he confessed to guilt. If he stayed, he could not go where he needed to go. And si-Ebana's arm was immovable about his neck.

Kemni did not need to feign the stagger, nor, when it came to it, the sluggish tongue, either. He was distressingly near the end of his strength. He managed to circle as si-Ebana had, to come from within the camp and not from without, as if in search of what he found in si-Ebana's hand: "Beer! Where did you find beer? Everywhere I look, it's all wine."

Gebu must have been grinding his teeth behind his fixed smile. Kemni cried out to him as if to a long-lost kinsman. "Gebu! Brother! So that's where you got to. I looked *everywhere*. You were finding beer!"

"And you see I found it," Gebu said with a flicker of laughter.

"Splendid!" Kemni declared. "Splendid!" He hung about Gebu's neck from one side as si-Ebana hung about the other, by sheer force of ill-balanced weight bearing him away from the camp's eastern edge where he had been aiming to go, and toward the starlit gleam of the river. The fleet was like a shower of sparks, so many lights were in it still.

Near the bank, Gebu resisted at last, digging in his heels. "My friends," he said, still feigning merriment, "It's been a great pleasure, but I must—"

"You must come with us!" si-Ebana cried. "The camp's gone as dull as a dead fish, but look, the fleet is as lively as ever."

"No, indeed," Gebu said. "I had promised—"

"Ah," si-Ebana said with a wave of his free hand that sent the beer-jar flying into the river. "Promises. She can wait. It's early hours yet, and we're out of beer."

"I must go," Gebu said, with markedly less mirth. "Truly, my friends, I must."

"I don't think so," si-Ebana said. His free hand circled Gebu in an embrace that must feel like bands of bronze. He swung his burden up with surprising strength and dropped him with some force in a boat that waited on the bank. Kemni knew better than to think that the boat's presence was an accident. Si-Ebana was proving to be a man of much more complexity than anyone would have thought.

There were coils of line in the boat, since by birth it must have been a fishing-boat. With one of these Kemni bound Gebu's hands, while si-Ebana cast off and began to wield the oars. He was greatly skilled with them, and much at ease in a boat—more so, in truth, than in a chariot.

Gebu lay at Kemni's feet, bound and helpless, but not seeming yet to recognize that he was found out. "Brother," he said, "what is this? Is it a joke? If so, it's in poor taste. Let me go."

Kemni did not answer. Not because he was trapped behind the wall of dream; not at all. Because the wall was broken. He could feel again. And the pain—oh, gods, the pain.

He could not even double up with it. He had to mount guard over the prisoner. Si-Ebana rowed them in among the ships, striking unerringly toward the golden flagship and *Dancer* moored beside it. The lights there seemed softer, the revelry muted. There was music, the deep pure strain of the aulos of Crete and the piercing sweetness of a voice trained in Egypt. It was a song of love and loss, beauty and grief. It came nigh to breaking all of Kemni's hard-won calm.

But he had a thing that he must do. That was always so, and perhaps always would be. As the boat slid smoothly in toward *Dancer's* side, he caught at one of the lines flung over it for just such a purpose, and moored the boat. Si-Ebana, no longer feigning drunken unsteadiness, slung Gebu over his shoulder and hauled himself up over the side. Kemni followed more lightly but less gracefully, a little restored by such rest as he had had in the boat, but exhausted beyond words.

The king was there, and his queens on either side of him, sharing the last of the wine. They were warm with it, but not lost in it.

Si-Ebana dropped Gebu, bound, at their feet. They all gazed down at him, and up at the two who had brought him.

The warmth of the wine left Ahmose's face. "It is done?" he asked Kemni. Kemni nodded.

"Ah," said the king with sadness that seemed almost as deep as Kemni's own. "He wasted no time."

"In what?" Gebu asked from the king's feet. "Drinking to excess, sire?"

"Wanting to excess." Ahmose gestured to the guard who stood nearby. "Raise him."

The man obeyed, raising Gebu to his knees. His wig was gone, lost somewhere between the camp and the ship. His ornaments were all in disarray. But he maintained his air of innocence, the lie that he had lived—for how long? Since Kemni had known him?

"What could I want for, sire?" he asked. "You've always been most generous."

"Except with my throne," Ahmose said. He leaned forward in it. "Give it up, child. I've known from the first what you were doing. Did you never wonder what truly became of your messenger to the lords of the Retenu?"

"Sire, I don't—"

"No more lies," Ahmose said.

And yet Gebu persisted. Almost Kemni would have believed him, except that he had seen and heard the other side of him, the face he showed to the enemy whom he would make his ally. "Have I ever lied to you, Father? Surely—"

Ahmose lashed out like a cobra, swift and utterly without warning. Gebu fell sprawling. "Enough! Your crimes are known, the judgment passed. You have been among the walking dead since first you conspired to dispose of me and take my throne. If you will not confess to it, others have witnessed, and will testify."

"I have enemies," Gebu said. "Do you believe—"

Ahmose struck him again. It was a hard blow, with pain in it, and sorrow even more than anger. So a father struck his son who had sinned against him. "The truth is all lost to you. When your soul comes before the judgment and is weighed against the feather of Truth, the feather will plummet, and your soul will wither and fall into Soul-Eater's maw. Is that what you wish, child? You would have destroyed me in this life. Would you destroy yourself in the next?"

Gebu shook his head. He had, at last, fallen silent. Maybe he was afraid.

And Ahmose said, "Unbind him."

People stared. There were many about by now, caught by the sight of a prince in bonds. But Ahmose took no notice. "Untie his hands."

One of the guards obeyed when no one else would. Gebu knelt, rubbing his wrists, frowning at the air midway between himself and his father. "Are you letting me go?"

"No," Ahmose said. "I am letting you confess."

"Will I live any longer for it?"

"You'll die more quickly."

Gebu shrugged. "I have nothing to confess."

"Then you die slow," Ahmose said.

Not even the guards saw how Gebu moved then. Kemni barely did; but he was closest, and his eye happened—by chance or the gods' blessing—to be resting on Gebu when he launched himself at the king. There was a blade in his hand, gleaming bronze—and a guard's sheath empty, the man standing helpless, as if bound by a spell.

But the spell did not bind Kemni. Perhaps he was too close to the land of the dead already, to be trapped so simply. He flung himself between Gebu and the king. He felt the bite of the sharpened bronze, but far away and of little account, a mere burning along his side. Kemni's hands had leaped of their own accord, to catch the hand that held the blade, to turn it sharply aside. They fell together. Gebu twisted, struggling, fighting with blind ferocity.

All at once he stiffened. Kemni saw his face, as close as a lover's. Its lips were twisted still in a snarl, but the eyes had gone empty. The spirit was gone from them.

He fell lifeless to the deck, sprawling across Kemni, with a dagger plunged deep in his back. Si-Ebana stood over him with empty hands and an expression of profound shock.

The silence broke into headlong clamor. Kemni took no notice of it. He struggled out from beneath that dead weight and stood beside si-Ebana, staring at it as the boy stared. This had been his battle-brother. This had been the king's son. This had tried, in the extremity of desperation, to slay the king.

People thrust the two of them aside, flocking round the body, and gathering, much too late, as if to defend the king. Kemni saw that si-Ebana was shivering. He was giving way to shock, and to a storm of tears. Kemni held him while he wept, wishing vaguely that he had any tears of his own. But he had had none for Iphikleia. He could hardly find them for Gebu the prince.

It seemed most sensible to stay where they were, out of the way of the crowd, huddled together against the curve of the hull. Either they would be remembered in time, or forgotten; and if they were forgotten, they could escape. But not yet. Kemni needed to know what the king would say, and what he would do.

It seemed a very long while before Ahmose's voice rose above the clamor. "Enough! Leave me, all of you. Go!"

They were slow to obey, but his guards advanced on them, driving them back by plain force. They were all driven away, taken on boats to other ships of the fleet, or to the camp on land. Only the queens remained, and such of the guards as had not been sent to capture and kill the rest of the conspirators, and a few servants; and Kemni and si-Ebana in their sheltered corner. And Gebu, lying as he had fallen, sprawled without grace or dignity.

Ahmose rose from his throne and laid aside his crown, and knelt beside his son's body. His face in the light of the lamps and torches was very still, and more grim than sad. "The gods may forgive you," he said. "I doubt that I ever can. And no—not for trying to slay a king. For thinking that you could do it at all. I had never taken you for a fool, my child. What possessed you to do such a thing?"

"The gods make men their playthings," Ariana said behind him. Nefertari had not moved, but Ariana had come down from her own throne. "Who knows what it amusement it gave them, to lead him astray and then destroy him?"

Ahmose shook his head. "No. The gods have great power, but men also have power to choose. My son chose this."

Ariana set her lips together as if she would argue, but had thought better of it.

Nefertari said, "Ambition can do terrible things to a man. This one wanted more than he was ever entitled to."

"Now he has lost it all," Ahmose said. He gestured to the guards. "Take him, and do as I will bid you."

The guards bowed and obeyed.

Then at last Ahmose remembered Kemni and si-Ebana, if indeed he had ever forgotten. "Come here," he said to them.

They came without resistance, and without fear, either. Kemni did not care what became of him. Si-Ebana, he suspected, was as yet too deep in shock.

They stood in front of the king. He examined each of them with close attention, as if he would commit them to memory. "I owe you much," he said at length. "Only ask, and it shall be given you."

"Anything?" si-Ebana asked.

"Anything in my power to give," said Ahmose.

Then give me back my beloved. But Kemni did not say it. He bit his tongue against it.

Si-Ebana answered first. "If I may have whatever I desire, then may I be allowed to fight in the fleet?"

"Not in the chariots?" Ahmose asked.

"My lord," said Ahmose si-Ebana, "I was not a bad charioteer, and I didn't dislike it. But my second—my warrior is dead. I killed him. I had to, but—my lord, that's a memory I'd sooner forget. I was born on the river, and grew to a man on it. I would like, if it can be granted to me, to go back to the ships."

"Then that shall be given you," Ahmose said, "with my blessing. And all my gratitude."

Si-Ebana bowed low, to the gold-washed deck.

Ahmose turned his eyes on Kemni then. "And you, my son? Is there a reward that I can give you?"

There was none that Kemni could think of. Unless . . .

"My lord," he said. "Let me be your charioteer again. Let me fight in the battle that is to come."

"I can't give you that," the king said.

Kemni sighed.

"Because," the king said, "I must be here in the flagship. But I can give you back your chariots, and a charioteer, if you would fight in my place at their head."

He spoke with regret that seemed real—as if he would have preferred to fight in his chariot, and not to rule the battle from the flagship of gold. But a king did what a king must.

And Kemni would fight in the war. Maybe die in it. Maybe not. He cared little. He had lain in the dark long enough. It was time he faced the sun again, and the bitter light of day.

KHAYAN HEARD WHAT everyone had heard, of the king's son who had undertaken to kill the king. It was great anger in the army, which had turned somehow against the Retenu—because, people seemed to think, the Retenu had had something to do with the prince's corruption. Khayan rather doubted that, but he did not speak of it. He was one of the hated enemy, safe while he was known to belong to the priestess Iry, but well aware that wherever he walked in that camp, he was watched. If a prince of the blood could turn traitor, surely a Retenu slave could be expected to do the same.

The one who had killed the prince, the young charioteer, had asked to go to the ships as his reward. He served on the one called *He Who Appears in Memphis*: strange name for a ship, but then Egyptians were strange. He kept his head down and his manner modest, but everyone knew who he was and what he had done. He did not rejoice in it, Khayan had heard. He had been set on watch over the prince while they were in the chariots, knowing even then what the prince was. And yet it seemed that he had come to know the man, perhaps to be fond of him—and to kill him then was grief.

It was never for Khayan to judge. Khayan was a captive. Whatever he did, he could not betray his people. That privilege was taken from him with his freedom.

He forgot all of it in Iry's tent, in the nights, when there were only the two of them. There were no tribes or races or nations then, and never a thought of war.

How strange to have found such joy at the end of all that he was, when he should have been praying to die and be set free. He did not want to die. Not while the world had Iry in it.

He was greatly diminished, everything taken from him, and yet he could not grieve. By day he was her shadow, sometimes with his brother Iannek, often alone, afoot or riding on one of his dun stallions. At night she lay with him in her tent, and professed to be as glad of it as he was. It was hard to tell, sometimes, with Iry, as composed as she was inclined to be, but he had learned to see behind that composure.

He would have given much to be so blessed. Whatever he thought was written large on his face, now he had no beard to hide it, nor would she let him grow it out again. That was the only tyranny she visited on him. She loved his face, she said. She would embarrass him terribly by lighting all the lamps and setting them round the bed, and insisting that he lie there while she drank in the sight of him. If he blushed or fidgeted, she only smiled. When he demanded the same pleasure, she lay placidly in his wonted place, and let him look his fill. She had no modesty to vex her, nor humility, nor anything that would allow him to take revenge.

In the world beyond the tent's walls, the war advanced to its conclusion. The day after the prince Gebu was killed for the ugliest of intentions, to kill a king who was also his father, Ahmose had his body set up like a grisly trophy in front of the chief gate of Avaris. Vultures circled above it. Men guarded it, to keep them at bay.

The walls of the city were always lined with people staring or standing guard or, intermittently, shooting arrows or hurling missiles at the besiegers. On this day, the crowds were thicker, their voices louder. They knew what the trophy was, and why it had been raised. Khayan thought he heard anger in their voices, but most seemed not to care. It had only been an Egyptian. Who could fault their king for taking what he offered? And if it had failed—well, and that was a pity, but so the gods had willed.

Iry stood for a long while so near the city that Khayan held his breath lest some luck-sped arrow, at the far stretch of its range, should strike and pierce her. A few fell about her, but none found its target. Horse Goddess protected her, she would say. It was hardly Khayan's place to contradict her.

Just as he was about to carry her off bodily, she turned the Mare and rode back through the army. The king's men parted before her. Some cheered. To them she was a great banner for the war, priestess of the enemy's own goddess, brought here as an omen of their victory.

Iannek met them when they had passed the line of siege-engines. He had been dividing himself between Iry and her cousin who had sunk into such grief after his Cretan lover was killed. That one had helped to unmask the traitor, Khayan had heard, and had come back to life again in the doing of it.

Iry asked after him, in fact; and Iannek answered, "He'll live now, I think, if he doesn't throw himself on somebody's sword when we finally have ourselves a battle."

"Will you fight for us, then?" Iry asked him.

His face darkened briefly, but Iannek could never be grim for long. "I'll fight for you."

Iry nodded. When she rode on, Iannek followed, walking at the shoulder of Khayan's dun Star. "You could go back in there," Khayan said.

"I don't think so," said Iannek.

"Mother is there," said Khayan. "I rather doubt she's suffered for her children's defection. She could win you the king's pardon."

"No," said Iannek. "I belong to the Mare." He paused. "You could escape. You aren't tainted with treason. You were captured. You'd be welcomed back with open arms."

"After the crime I never committed, but was sent out for?" Khayan laughed shortly. "I think not."

"You've paid for it," Iannek said. "You'll be welcomed back as a great hero. Especially," he said, leaning in close, "if you bring her back with you."

"As a captive?" It rather alarmed Khayan not only that his brother could think of such a thing, but that his own first thought should be of doing it. The Mare belonged to the people. And Iry—

The Mare belonged to herself. What Iry did, she did because the Mare had chosen her. If Khayan went back to his people, he went without her.

And that, he could not do. Any more, it seemed, than Iannek could, or Sadana, or the women who had come to serve the Mare's servant. It was a terrible thing the goddess had done, in dividing them from all their kin. And yet Khayan could not wish it otherwise. No, not even to be a lord among lords of the people again.

"I can't, either," Iannek said in Khayan's silence. "Horrible, isn't it? The gods aren't kind."

"Kindness is a human vice." Khayan shrugged with much more carelessness than he felt. "We are what the gods make us."

"And we love whom the gods give us."

Khayan flushed. Iannek laughed at him. Iannek knew, of course. Everybody did. It only amazed Khayan that no one twitted him with it.

While they dallied so, Iry had gone on ahead. Her face was turned toward the center of the camp, where the king had come off his flagship to confer with his commanders. They were all seated in the pavilion that was raised whenever the king held council, shaded from the sun but open to the airs, and shielded from the stinging hordes of flies by a drift of gauzy draperies.

Iry left the Mare on the edge of that circle of the camp. The Mare snorted and tossed her mane and went her own way, with Khayan's stallion obedient in her wake. Khayan, with Iannek trailing, followed Iry into the council.

He did not usually do that. When Iry was with the king, she was as safe as she could ever be; and he was best advised to stay out of sight. But today, for what reason he could not have said, he stayed with her. Something in the way she moved was a warning.

They were speaking, when she came, of mounting an attack down several of the river-branches into Avaris—wielding the river that was their great weapon, as chariots were the enemy's. But her presence silenced them. She acknowledged them with a glance and a slight inclination of the head. Her eyes, and her attention, were on the king.

He greeted her as he always did, with warmth that he reserved for few. "My lady," he said. "You have a message for me?"

It was always wise to be direct with the Mare's servant. This king was a wise man. Khayan granted him that.

Iry did not bow to him. The Mare's servant was above kings. She spoke

to him with respect however, and warmth that echoed his. "Sire, you are going
to force battle, yes?"

"Yes," Ahmose answered her. "A siege is of no use if it goes on too long.
It saps the besiegers as well as the besieged."

"And it gives his people in Canaan time to take back Sile, and his people
elsewhere in the Upper Kingdom time to rally and fall on you from behind—
while your army weakens with time and inactivity and the sickness that always
comes with a long siege." She nodded. "Yes, you would want to end it quickly.
What if it could be ended without bloodshed?"

"I doubt that is possible," the king said.

"But if it were?"

He met her stare. People here never did such a thing, never looked their
king full in the face, but Iry was what she was. She stood steady.

"Tell me what you would do," he said.

"I would go," she answered, "in the garb of my office, and speak with
the king of the Retenu. He might, for the goddess' sake, withdraw and leave
this kingdom to you."

Somewhere amid the council, someone laughed. He was quickly hushed.
Ahmose did not laugh, nor did he smile. "You believe that can be done?"

"Probably not," she admitted. "But it may be worth the trial. If nothing
else, it would impress on the people in the city that one of their great divinities
has left them."

"They know that already," one of the commanders said. Few of them
looked like warriors to Khayan's eyes, and this was no exception: a slender,
almost weedy man of no discernible age, decked in gold and jewels, with an
elaborate braided wig, and a face painted into an expressionless mask.

Iry spoke to the mask as one who had learned from childhood to see the
face beneath. Her voice was cool, her words precise. "Certainly they know.
But if I make them see, it may dishearten them."

"Now that is true," the king said. "And it makes me think . . . Set is ours,
though they claimed him. Has not Set also come back to us?"

"I know nothing of Set," Iry said. "I only know Horse Goddess. And she
has turned away from them."

"Surely," said another of the commanders, speaking Khayan's own
thoughts—which he could never utter, not in this place—"whatever you can
do, lady, however well you do it, will endanger you far more than it will aid
us."

"Maybe," she said. "I think not. The king of the Retenu is an honorable
man. He would hear me out, and then let me go. And who knows? The goddess might prevail on him to surrender."

"Or he might hold you hostage and compel some surrender on our part,"
the second lord said.

"He'll never hurt me," she said. "None of them would dare. If he holds me, well then, all the better for the war, to feed your soldiers' anger and give them so much the more cause to seize the victory."

"I'm not sure—" the king began.

"I will go," she said. "This is something the goddess bids me do. I would be glad of your blessing, but even without it, I must obey her."

Ahmose shook his head. "Lady," he said, "that is not safe. What if someone does dare to harm you?"

"Then the goddess wills it," Iry said. "Will you give me your blessing, sire? Even if you can't bless what I do?"

"You always have that," Ahmose said. "But—"

"I thank you, sire," she said.

✦ ✦

"Someday," Khayan said when they had come to her tent, "a king is going to forget who you are, and bind and gag you and keep you locked in a cage."

Iry shrugged. "Maybe the king of the Retenu will do that. Does it matter? I have to do this. No man is going to stop me."

"Then I'm going with you," Khayan said.

"You are not."

"You won't stop me."

"But it's not safe for you to—"

She stopped, and wisely, too. "Exactly," he said. "I suppose you're going to do it today? The longer you delay, the more likely the council is to find a way to stop you."

"I would do it now," she said. "But not if you insist on coming with me."

"Good," Khayan said.

She hissed in frustration. "You are a maddening man."

"Then we're well matched." He sat on the chest that held her priestly robes, and smiled sweetly at her. "Since you're not going to do it after all, shall we rest a little instead?"

He did not mean that they should sleep. But she was in no mood to yield to his blandishments. She pushed him off the chest and retrieved her white robe, and all that went with it: the belt of knotted cords, the black dagger in its ancient sheath, the bag of sacred things. In it, he knew, were amulets and images of the goddess, and herbs used in the rites, and other things that were not for him, as a man and mortal, to know.

She put on the robe, belted it as custom prescribed, and hung the dagger from the belt. The bag she set aside. When she went out, she would carry it over her shoulder. But now she took from it a comb of ivory or fine-carved bone, closed the chest and sat on it and combed out her hair. It was not long enough, quite, to braid, but she could bind it with an intricately plaited fillet of white horsehair set with disks of beaten gold. Golden ribbons streamed down the back of it.

Khayan had never seen that headdress on a living head. It was worn only for the very greatest of rites, which had not been his to see. Iry wore it as a queen would, holding her head high, and proud with it, but not so over-whelmed by her own consequence that she could think of nothing else.

She was almost done. If he would go with her—would face his people as he was now, a weight of shame so heavy that it came near to crushing him—he must at least do her no dishonor. He had only one other kilt, which hap-pened to be clean, and a pair of sandals that were new and none too com-fortable, and no ornaments at all.

But she turned at the end of her robing and set a box in his hands. It was very heavy for its size; he nearly dropped it. In it was one of the great collars that the Egyptians favored, and armlets, all of gold. He looked from them to Iry's face. "How—"

"People give me gifts," she said. "These are a man's jewels."

"But I can't—"

"If you insist that you must come with me, in spite of what it will do to your spirit, then you must come with all the pride that you have ever had. They're going to mock you, Khayan. Mock and spit at you. And you must bear it as a king does, as if he were far above it."

"I'm not going to stay behind," Khayan said through gritted teeth, though he would have loved dearly to crawl into the corner of the tent and stay there till she came back.

If she did. That stiffened his spine. He put on the collar, with her help—finding it not so heavy once it rested on his shoulders. The armlets were large enough, which was also surprising. They were graven with a wonderful thing: horses and chariots pursuing one another round and round through a land-scape of reeds. He traced the lines of one with his finger. "This was not a gift," he said.

"But it was," said Iry.

He narrowed his eyes at her.

She tossed her head so that the golden ribbons rippled and danced. "Well then. The gold was a gift, and the smith made it as I asked. You don't like it?"

"It is princely," he said. "And I am not."

"You are my prince," she said. "Now wear it, and hold your head high. The Mare chose me. I chose you. In the east, that would make you a very great lord."

That was true. And yet—

She turned and left him with the armlets still in his hands. He had to thrust them on if he would catch her, and stride long and fast. When he had caught her, he was too breathless to speak any of the words he had gathered to fling in her face.

Which was probably not an ill thing. The Mare was waiting. She was bri-dled as if for a festival, and brushed till she gleamed. Khayan would have won-dered how that could be, if he had not seen Iannek's broad white grin beyond the Mare. Iannek, of course, would never reflect on what danger Iry rode to. Danger to Iannek was both meat and drink.

And indeed he held the bridles of Khayan's own beloved duns, harnessed with suitably princely splendor, and drawing a chariot that must have been one of the king's: it was gilded, and its shafts were tipped with gold. Iannek was in armor, Egyptian no less—and how he had managed that, seeing that he was a bull in a herd of gazelle, Khayan could not imagine. It did seem to fit him well, and he looked well in it, in an odd and barbaric way.

Khayan was to be charioteer, it seemed, with Iannek in the warrior's place. And, as that sank in on him, there inevitably was Sadana with her warrior women, mounted and armored and ready to ride.

They were all together, then, a small riding but a very noble one, and Iry on her white Mare, whom they all served. Khayan would gladly have been her only guard, but these would protect her as no one man could.

They might also be seized and killed. If so, then so be it.

They rode through the camp with no attempt at ceremony, and yet it became a procession. The Egyptians made a path for Iry as they always did, and many followed, murmuring, as she rode toward the gate. The people atop it had seen: their faces were turned toward her, eyes wide, fingers pointing.

No one shot at her. That much power her presence had, and the Mare's moon-white coat that seemed to drink the sun and turn it to cold fire. She rode past the siege-engines into the open space between the army and the wall. The gate loomed over her. It was splintered but not broken. This was not Sile. It would not fall as Sile had fallen. It was the greatest city in the world, and the most strongly warded.

She halted before that gate and raised her hand. "Open," she said, not even particularly loudly.

It opened for her. Not all of it; only the smaller gate within the gate. But that was large enough to admit horses and chariot, and Iry leading them on the Mare's back.

Khayan's heart was cold and still. He was beyond terror. Just so had it been once when he hunted a bear to its cave, and while the hounds swarmed and bayed, made his way into the reeking darkness.

The bear had fallen to his spear. Maybe in this hunt he himself would fall. But not before Iry. He swore to that, in his heart where all oaths were strongest.

As Iry had ridden through the Egyptian army, so she rode through Avaris, down the king's way amid the gathered crowds. The word had spread as it always did. The Mare was in Avaris, where she had never gone. And the Mare's servant had come back among the people.

The palace was open for them, the frown of the citadel little lightened by the gate that stood wide. It looked, to Khayan, like a gaping mouth.

He knew the men who waited. They were princes of chamberlains, the king's own. They met embassies from great allies, and saw to their comfort.

Iry was not looking for comfort. The rest of them left their horses in the first court, but the Mare would not go. She paced beside Iry, hooves echoing on the pavement, through the courts to the king's hall.

After all Khayan's fears, no one appeared to have seen him, still less to know who he was. He was as invisible as the rest. Every eye turned on Iry, and on the Mare.

The king was waiting in his hall of audience, crowned with the crown of the Lower Kingdom that Salitis the first king had taken as his own. His robes were of the people, but his throne, the lotus-pillars of the hall, and its painted walls, were all of Egypt. That was his name painted on the walls in the binding of the cartouche. Khayan did not read the Egyptian writing, that march of beasts and birds and strange shapes and fragments of human figures, but he knew what some of it signified. Enough to recognize a king's name when he saw it.

Apophis had not changed. He looked no older and no more haggard. He was, if anything, at ease on that golden throne. His court had a faintly wild-eyed look, as if it felt the terror of the siege, but he was calm.

His herald greeted Iry as was proper for formal audience, taking no notice of her escort, as was also proper. What was not proper was that all of them carried their weapons still; and that sat ill with the guards whose wonted place was at the door and round the walls. They had drawn in close, poised to leap if any of them menaced the king.

He waved them back, cutting through the herald's lengthy oration. "That will do," he said to the herald, who shut his mouth with a snap, suppressed an expression of purest pique, bowed and withdrew.

The king rose. "You will come," he said to Iry.

Khayan knew the room behind the throne. He had sat in it often in the king's company, or with great lords of the court. When he followed Iry, he was not prevented—perhaps because he was unarmed. The others found them-selves face to face with the guards, and throat to point with their spears.

Iannek at least might have tried to press past, and maybe died for it, but Iry turned. "Stay," she said to him.

He was hardly as docile as a favorite hound, but he was obedient. He snarled and stood still.

Iry had already turned away. Khayan strode after her.

✦ ✦

The king was not alone in that place of private audience. There were guards, of course. And there were a pair of veiled women.

Almost Khayan could not pass that door. A man of the people learned to recognize the shape behind a veil; and those he knew very well indeed.

And they knew him. Their eyes on him were steady, unflinching.

The king's face was rather less difficult to read. He turned in the room, and pulled Khayan into a hard embrace. Khayan stiffened against it, more than half expecting the bite of a dagger in the back; but Apophis was weeping tears of—gods; joy.

What Khayan felt was much less simple. When the king would let him go, he tried to bow low, but Apophis would not allow that. "No, my child. No. No ceremony here. I only thank the gods that they let you live."

"I live a slave," he said.

"You serve the Mare's servant." That was not Apophis' voice. It was Sarai's. She was not one to rise for anyone, even a lost son. But when she held out a regal hand, Khayan had no choice but to take it. She drew him to her. Her fierce eyes searched his face—much as Iry loved to do, but never so tender. "So. The world changes. Are you content?"

"I—" Khayan would have said that he was not. Except that his eye caught Iry, standing quiet as she best knew how to do; and the sight of her made him dizzy with joy. Even here, on the raw edge of pain.

"The goddess gives where she wills," Sarai said, "and chooses whom she will."

Khayan looked down. He was blushing again. He blushed a great deal of late.

His mother laid a cool palm against his burning cheek. She was smiling, maybe. Beneath the veil, it was difficult to tell.

"It would be better," he said, "if you cursed me and cast me out."

"Easier," she said, "for you, perhaps? And how could I do that? You belong to the goddess."

"I am thinking," he said, "that if I had not grown from boy to man among your kin, I would have flung myself on a sword a good while since."

"And you reckon yourself a coward because you did not." She shook her head. "Child, a coward takes refuge in death. A brave man lives the life his gods ordain."

"So they teach among the eastern tribes." He sighed. "Lady, Mother, this is a war. We are on opposite sides of it."

"Surely. And we intend to win." She spoke without doubt or hesitation.

"Even with such an omen as we are?"

"The Mare goes where she goes," Sarai said. "And the people are the people. This kingdom has belonged to them for a hundred years. Should they simply let it go?"

"They are besieged. The river is blockaded with their ships. No reinforcements can come from Asia. The lords away from here—"

"They are still a great people. And they were born here—just as you were. This is their country. If they are driven out of it, where can they go?"

"Back to Asia," Iry said levelly. She had come to stand beside Khayan. "Your time here is ended. We offer you freedom to go, with all your goods and chattels, and even such wealth as you can safely carry."

"We have no desire to carry it away," said Apophis. "We rule here. We intend to remain."

"The Great House will destroy you," Iry said. "He lives in spite of the plot against him. The gods of this kingdom love him, and wish you gone."

"Our priests say," said Apophis, "that Baal, who is Set, will defend us, and crush the armies that march against us."

"Set is a destroyer," Iry said. "Those whom he chooses as his playthings, he dandles and fondles, until he casts them down."

"Are you a priest of Set, that you know such things?"

"I am the Mare's servant," Iry said. "I know what the goddess permits her to know."

"We will not yield," Apophis said. "No, lady; not even for you."

"Even for wealth and life and freedom, and the avoidance of war?"

"War is pleasing to the gods, and to Baal their king," said Apophis. "Blood is their sacrifice. We will give them their fill, and so win back our kingdom."

Iry stared at him as if he had astonished her. Maybe he had. Egyptians, Khayan had come to know, were not warriors, nor did they make a virtue of war. Quite the opposite. Iry could not understand a man for whom war was not a threat but a promise; who had been born and bred to fight in battles.

"You would fight," she asked, "even if you knew that you could avoid it?"

"Avoid it? How? By surrender? No," Apophis said, "I would not do that even if my people would allow me. Even for you, lady—even for your goddess. I cannot."

"You will not," she said, soft and a little bitter.

"That, too," he agreed.

"Then will you hold me here, and make me a hostage?"

"No," he said. And when her eyes widened in disbelief, he went on, "I will let you go. It might serve some small purpose to hold you prisoner, but I see no great profit in it."

"This mercy will not help you, if you lose."

"I never expected that it would." He smiled at her. "This is a praiseworthy thing you do, and brave—braver perhaps than you know. It will gain you admiration among our young men. But no surrender. That would be unthinkable."

"We can think of it," she said.

"Ah," said Apophis, "but you are Egyptian."

"I don't understand you," she said.

"No." He took her hands in his, and bowed over them. "Understanding is not necessary. Only acceptance. When we win this war, my lady, if you choose to come back to us, there will be no punishment; no retribution. It is understood that the Mare does as the Mare pleases."

"I won't come back," she said.

"We shall see," said Apophis.

WHEN IRY CAME out of the city, the battle had already begun. Ahmose had ordered it before she went in, nor delayed it by more than a little for the embassy she had taken on herself. He left that gate alone and the siege-engines silent, but his ships had closed in from the river, battering the city where it could raise no defense.

That was no fight for chariots. But once Iry had come out, white-faced and wordless, and let herself be taken away to safety, the king called out his chariotry to be a wall of living bronze about that side of the city.

Kemni was ready for the summons. All of him that had been given up to grief was given now to war. When he went to fetch his chariot, he found it ready, the horses harnessed, and a charioteer waiting.

"I mean to fight alone," he said—foolish words, and weak, but they were all he had.

"No one fights alone here," Sadana said. "Why? Am I objectionable?"

"No, but—"

"Ah," she said. "I'm a woman. I'm not ill luck, man of Egypt. Trust me in that."

"I never said you were," he said. "But—"

"Get in," she said. "The king wants us out there now, not in a day or three or six."

That was true, and the rest of the chariots were waiting for his signal. Kemni sighed hugely and stepped up beside her.

That was the signal they had looked for. The trumpeter blew the call to advance. The line of chariots rolled forward, toward the city. They were not to go in too close. Along the edges, by the river, Sadana's women rode on their light fast horses. There would be no escape from Avaris, except into death.

The ships attacked the soft underbelly of the city, the riverbank and the canals that ran into the city itself. And the enemy was waiting. He might have fled here, he might have given Ahmose the north, but he had no intention of letting go this city.

It was a river-battle now, the enemy's chariots shut up within his walls. Kemni had little to do but ride up and down and watch and listen, and see the ships' crews do battle with men on land. Sadana's women swooped in and out along the river's edge, darting toward the wounded and the dying and bringing them out as they could, whether toward the ships or toward the open land.

Kemni could have done such a thing, but the king's orders were precise. The chariots were not to be spent wantonly. They would circle and look threatening, and wait. When the king was ready, he would summon them.

There was some small challenge in eluding arrows from the walls, and once they caught a handful of Retenu in flight—men of low rank and less courage, fleeing like rats. Like rats they died and were flung into the river, fed to the crocodiles.

Sadana seemed content to drive the horses up and down, making a show of force but offering none that was real. She was not given to idle conversation. Kemni had been once, till grief changed him. It was almost a comfortable silence, the silence of those who saw no need to fill the air with chatter.

Near sundown the king sent them a summons, but it was not to battle; it was to rest. The morrow would be the same, and the day after that, as long as the Retenu resisted Ahmose's war.

The river-fighters were full of vaunts that night, brandishing the right hands of enemies whom they had killed, and some flaunting the gold of valor that was given only to the best of them. The land-fighters huddled by their tents and snarled. Their time would come—but it was not likely to be soon.

"I don't call it a victory," Iannek declared by Kemni's campfire. He had appeared not long after dark, as pleased with himself as ever, and looking somewhat happily battered.

"You got onto a ship," Seti said. His envy was palpable. "How in the gods' name did you manage that?"

"I got on board," said Iannek. "It wasn't hard. The man who's named after the king, si-Ebana—they've made him a captain of marines. I asked him if he needed an extra hand. He allowed as how he did."

"It couldn't have been that simple," Seti said.

"Things with Iannek are always simple." Sadana startled some of them, if not Kemni: he suspected that they had not seen her sitting just out of the fire's light, knees drawn up to breast, never moving. Until she spoke; then it was impossible to ignore her. "Iannek lives the life of the blessed idiot. Wherever he goes, people take him in."

"I wouldn't call myself an idiot," Iannek said, aggrieved. "Si-Ebana can fight! He took a hand from a dockside lord, and wounded a dozen more. He said they used to take more than the right hand, but in these days the old customs have worn thin."

"Those are your own people you're fighting," Seti said.

Iannek shook his head, beard and heavy braids and all. "I'm fighting where the Mare is."

"And they cast you out." Seti prodded the fire till the sparks flew. "They say you're a good man to have at one's back. Would you fight at mine, if I asked you?"

"If you could give me a battle," Iannek said.

"Someday we may," Seti said with a sigh. "I'm thinking I should have stayed with the boats."

"You men," said Sadana. "It's always about fighting. I thought Egyptians were peaceable people."

"Not when there's a war to fight," Seti said.

Sadana snorted in disgust, but did not add to it.

After a while the two boys—for they must have been near the same head-long age—wandered off. Kemni stayed where he was. He was not so very much older than either of them, and yet he felt as old as the world.

Sadana was still sitting in the shadows, gazing at the campfire's flames. "Tell me something," she said after a while.

Kemni raised a brow.

"Are you like them?" she asked. "Do you live to fight?"

"I think I did once," he said.

"Ah," she said. "Until you discovered that men are mortal. And . . . women."

The pain was so sharp and so sudden that he gasped.

"So now you live to die," she said, seeing far too clearly for his comfort. "Has it occurred to you that if she knows this, wherever her gods and her faith have taken her, she well may be grieving that you grieve so much?"

He surged to his feet in a flare of sudden rage. "What do you know of this? What do you know of anything that is between men and women?"

He had struck to wound, and wound he had. Her face was white in the firelight. Yet she spoke calmly, without the fierce temper that he would have expected. "I know," she said, "that death is a terrible thing, and death untimely is the worst of all. Yet I also know that she was a great lover of life. She would want you to live, and live in joy."

"There is no joy without her."

"Not even in memory?"

"Memory." He spat the taste of it out of his mouth. "Memory is a cold companion in the nights."

"Just so," she said.

He stood speechless. She rose to face him. She was as tall as he, if not actually taller. Her body was all sharp lines and spare angles, its curves somewhat too subtle for his taste. He could, if he let himself, remember how surprisingly sweet they could be.

Never as sweet as the one who was gone. There would never be another like her.

"I think," Sadana said, "that you are wallowing. It surprises me rather. I had always taken you for a man of sense."

"What sense is there in death?"

"Very little," she said, "which is why we wrap it about in ritual—and none more so than you Egyptians."

"She was not Egyptian. She had her own rites."

"Ah," said Sadana.

"Yes, that was pain! But it's past."

"Is it?"

He would dearly have loved to strike her for what she was doing to him. But he found he could not raise his hand. He knew how deadly she was, like a finely honed blade, trained in all the arts of war and the chase. And yet when she stood before his face, she seemed as slender as a grass-stem, and as likely to break.

That was a weapon, and surely she was aware of it. "What would you have me do?" he demanded of her.

"Nothing," she said.

"Don't lie to me."

"Truly," said Sadana. "I want nothing of you but what I would want of any man. That you live; and that you conduct yourself with some semblance of common sense."

Laughter startled itself out of him. "Gods! Dear gods. You sound just like her."

"Then she was a sensible person."

"She could be like a cold dash of seawater in the face," he said, "or like the wind blowing across the pinnacles of the island where she was born. She had no patience whatever with what she considered to be nonsense. Which was most of what men did."

"Most men make very little sense," Sadana said.

"And women are different?"

"Profoundly." The fire was dying. She knelt to rouse it, feeding it with bits of grass and dried dung. Her concentration on the task was wonderfully complete.

He could have walked away, and he suspected that she would not have stopped him. But he stayed. He had nowhere else to go but his bed, where the dreams would come crowding in, and the black grief.

When the fire was burning strong again, she straightened, sitting on her heels. Her plait had fallen forward over her shoulder. It was inky black in this light, but in the sun, he happened to remember, it had a ruddy cast quite unlike the blue-black of his own people, or of Iphikleia's.

She was more foreign even than the foreign kings. He knew a little of what she was, from things that Iry and others had told him. He did not understand her at all.

It did not matter, when he thought about it. There was an ease about her presence, a not quite pleasure in her company. As if they were kin, in some odd way.

He found that he could contemplate sleep, even the dreams it brought, without quite so much dread as before. After a while he rose and bade her goodnight. She nodded, making no move to rise herself.

He paused. "Won't you sleep?" he asked.

She shrugged. "I don't sleep much. I never did."

"But if there's battle tomorrow—"

"I'll be awake, aware, and as strong as I ever am." She tilted her head up, peering at his face above her. "Stop fretting. I'll sleep in a little while."

"Promise?"

"Promise," she said solemnly.

He decided to be content with that. But as he slipped into his tent, he paused, and looked back. She had returned to her contemplation of the fire. It was almost as if she stood guard—but over what? Kemni?

Foolishness. He let the tentflap fall, and groped through familiar darkness to his bed.

············· VI ·············

THE SHIPS WENT on battering Avaris from every branch of the river, till the city was laid waste some distance inland. The Retenu had built a wall of rubble against the unrelenting invasions. It was slow work, tedious and exhausting, fighting for each hand's breadth of land, against enemies who flatly refused to yield.

The chariots began at last to have somewhat to do. Outlying lords had gathered their forces and marched on the city. They were a great army, harried by uprisings among the Egyptians until Ahmose had sent out word: *Let them come. Let them think us weaker than we are.* He had, meanwhile, divided his forces on the land and sent some of them out as if to forage—and that they did; but their chief duty was to seem to have dissipated his strength about the landward walls of the city. Only a token few companies of foot, and his chariots, remained in evidence there.

It was a trap, neatly laid, and Kemni's chariots were the bait. Iry saw them on the day she rode the Cretan flagship, out of curiosity but also to be a banner for the war. The admiral from Crete had thought of that, and the Cretan woman who was one of Ahmose's queens. They believed, for whatever reason, that Iry's presence would hearten the fighters, and perhaps bring them victory.

She had ridden in boats, of course, all her life. But never on a ship built to sail the sea. It was larger and higher, and it was made of hewn wood, which was precious-rare in Egypt; here, boats were most often made of reeds, or of bundled papyrus. She had wandered all over it at first, to the manifest amusement of the crew: slender laughing men with long curling hair, who seemed for some reason to find her delightful. They called her by a name that, Ariana the queen said, meant *beautiful lady,* and brought her gifts when she had settled under the canopy on the deck: a necklace of translucent shells, a fish carved of bone, an odd silvery pearl that looked, if she held it just so, like the Mare when she pranced and snorted and tormented the stallions.

It seemed that Ariana and the admiral had seen clearly: she was more than welcome here. And she was safe, as safe as anyone could be in the midst of a war. The flagship kept well back, overseeing the fight. The rest of the ships, greater and lesser, were ranging up and down the river, hurling missiles from the decks, and dispatching companies of fighting men to rampage through the city.

"We'll win through to the citadel soon," Naukrates the admiral said beside her. He never stayed in one place for long; he was up and about, up and down the sides and the prow and the stern, sending messengers in small swift boats or ordering that signals be sent to this ship or that, or to the whole of the fleet. He had paused just then, peering under his hand at the rise of those massive walls. "Yes, we'll surround it; then we can take it."

"If the Retenu will let you," Iry could not help but say.

He grinned at her. He was not a young man, but he could be as light-hearted as a boy—they all could, these dancers and sailors from Crete. "Oh, they'll let us. We'll sweet-talk them and croon to them and make love to them with our spears and our swords, till they're begging us to have our will of them."

Khayan laughed behind her. He had been remarkably light of spirit himself since they came back from the citadel. She might have expected him to be sunk in sadness, but he had been conducting himself as if a great weight had been lifted from his heart. She had not asked him why; it did not seem a question she should ask.

He had also proved surprising in another way. Warrior and horseman and charioteer as he was, he was also at ease on the water. That was not like the rest of his people. But then he had been born in Memphis, and his nurse had been Egyptian. He was more like her people than anyone liked to admit, even Khayan himself.

He stood at her back as he undertook always to do, more at ease here than he was in the camp—maybe because these too were foreigners, and kin from long ago. He was a kind of prince to them, as she understood it, both because he belonged to her, and because he was the son of a great queen of the tribes beyond the eastern horizon.

Even more than that—here, he would actually rest a hand on her shoulder, a light touch, familiar, and blessed in it; but he would never have done such a thing in front of her own people. She leaned very slightly into it, just enough that he would know she was glad of it.

Khayan and the admiral were peering under their hands now, but not at the citadel; at the sky. It did have an odd look: dark along the horizon, and streamers of cloud overhead. Clouds were not as rare here in the Lower King-dom as in the desert realm of the Upper Kingdom.

Still, these were not like any she had seen before. If they had been closer
to the Red Land, she would have wondered if there was a sandstorm coming
toward the river.

She opened her mouth to ask what such a thing could be, but Naukrates
spoke before her. He spoke not to either of them, but in a voice pitched to
carry. "Signalers! To me."

They came from all round the ship, at such speed as they might, for his
tone was urgent. "Halt the battle," he said. "Call in the fleet. Have it put to
shore beyond the city, as near as is practicable, but far enough to be safe; then
batten the ships. Beg the Pharaoh's indulgence, and ask that his ships do the
same. Quickly."

"Why should he do that?" Iry asked.

Naukrates looked as if he would snap at her, but remembered, almost too
late, who she was. He muttered in his own language, shifting somewhat belatedly to Egyptian. "Yes, he'll argue, too; he'll not likely know."

"Tell the Great House," Khayan said to the messenger who went most
often to the king, "that a storm is coming. It were best his ships were beached
and battened before it strikes."

"A storm?" said Iry. "But there are no storms in this country. This isn't
the sea, or your steppe. This is the Lower Kingdom of Egypt."

"All the more reason to protect against it," said Khayan. "In other countries, people know what to do. Here, no one knows. Few of you at all have
seen water fall from the sky."

"But it can't be—"

They were not listening. Naukrates was turning about, testing the wind.
His frown deepened the longer he went on. Khayan with his heavy brows and
his strong face looked even more forbidding. "If you were at sea," he said,
"you could run ahead of it. But this . . ."

The oars were out, the ship beating its way down the river amid the gathered fleet. The enemy on the shore had stopped their fighting. Some even
clambered to the top of their barricade to stare. A few had raised a ragged
cheer. They thought, perhaps, that the fleet was retreating.

So it was—but not before them.

Word had gone to the army. As the flagship passed the southward edges
of the city, Iry saw the tents fall, the men racing to pack and secure them. The
chariots had come in from the field. They guarded the rear as the army began
to march. They would join with the fleet downriver, and take what shelter the
beached ships could offer, since the city's walls were still closed to them. The
siege-engines they left, in some despair; but the Cretan captains were agreed.
There was no time.

Iry wondered if the king doubted what he had been told, that there was
a storm coming, and a deadly one. If it failed to come, they might indeed find
that they had lost the city and the war. It could even have been a plot far more
clever than the one for which the prince Gebu had died.

But no. She could see the wall of cloud now, advancing from the west: blue-black and shot with lightnings.

The city's gates had opened—astonishing, unlooked for. An army marched out, regiments of foot strengthening with a great force of chariots. Did they not see the storm? Or did they believe that their gods had brought it? Baal was a stormgod. This could be his, this wrath of the heavens. Their priests might even have summoned it, in extremity, at the threat to their citadel. Had not Apophis said that Set would destroy his enemies?

The presence in the heart of Iry's spirit, the bright warmth that, she had been assured, was the great goddess, was still. The Mare was gone; she lived, but Iry did not know where.

Iry had believed implicitly that the Two Lands would be one again; that Ahmose would have the victory, and Egypt would be whole. But now, in a fleeing ship, with a storm like the gods' own wrath pursuing them and the army of the Retenu speeding before it, her faith wavered and began to fall.

The wind had begun to blow from the west, lightly but distinctly. Naukrates bade his sailors run up the sail, but wait on his command; when the wind freshened, he said, they must drop it again. For the moment the wind was their ally, bearing them swiftly down the river. All about them the ships, both Cretan and Egyptian, had done the same. The golden flagship, clumsy thing that it was, rode somewhat in the rear of the fleet, but it was well warded by smaller, quicker craft.

They ran downriver till the city was out of sight, till they had found a place that the pilots knew: a bend in that branch of the river, and a landscape of fields, stripped now by the harvest, and a string of little villages. The people had come running out to see the ships, crying in dismay: "Defeat? Is it defeat?"

"Take cover!" the men on the ships roared back. "Take cover and pray. The wrath of Set is upon us!"

The villagers wailed and scattered and fled. The ships ran up on the banks, their crews battening and stowing and securing as they went, pulling down masts and sails where they could. Fighting men ran to mark the edge of a camp, to surround it and hold it with the weapons that they had, and with the chariots as they came up. It was a madness of haste in a rising wind, a breath of cold such as Egypt seldom knew, damp cold that made Iry think of deep water.

The army on foot was still running, the enemy closing in behind. Kemni's chariots turned in a great arc and bore down on them. A hundred chariots, that had seemed so many in the war's beginning, proved to be distressingly few against the enemy's strength. And yet, from the shelter of the ships, neither the captain nor his charioteers seemed afraid. Sadana's mounted warriors were riding amid the chariots, not far behind the commander, like a guard of honor.

The wind blew strong now, lashing the reeds and the marsh-grasses beyond the fields. Most of the ships' crews had taken shelter behind or beneath careened hulls.

The servants and the baggage came up, staggering with exhaustion—they were not made to run so fast or so far. Those in the rear were wounded, some of them, by the enemy's arrows. He had not caught them, but their rearguard had turned at bay behind the wall of chariots. It was a thin line, perilously thin. It was all they had.

Iry made her way through a freshening gale to the king's ship, where the king was sheltered, and not happily, either. Even as she came, his lords and his queens were remonstrating with him. "I will summon my chariot," he said against them. "If I am to lose the war for this ill choice, then let me lose it from the thick of a battle."

"You haven't lost it yet," Iry said.

It seemed a terribly obvious thing to say, but everyone regarded her as if she had proposed a thing unheard of. Their eyes were rolling white. The sky's darkening even before the sun had come to noon, the wind's howling, the flash and flare of the lightning and the roll of thunder, had reft them of their wits. Even as she stood swaying in the gale, lightning leaped across the sky, branching like the river in the Delta, stream upon stream upon stream, till with a hiss it died. Thunder snarled in its wake, mounting to a roar.

Iry spoke above it, pitching her voice as she had been taught, as priestesses learned to do. "The war is not lost. My lord, stay. Wait. Trust the gods."

That steadied him, somewhat. He still champed and snorted like a stallion shut in walls, but he had stopped insisting that he fling himself into the battle. He was needed here, where the army could see him, and where the runners could come, seeking his commands or his counsel.

But having given him that wisdom, she undertook to slip away herself, only to meet a large and living wall. Iannek and Khayan together stood in her way. She had not known that they were the same size exactly. It was like looking at two images of the same man, one shorn and dressed in the Egyptian fashion, the other all Retenu from his crown of battle-plaits to his booted feet.

They kept her there, as trammeled as the king. She tried to thrust past them. It was like throwing herself against stone.

And the world went mad.

+ +

The wind swept down like a monstrous hand. The skies opened as if an icy river had poured itself out upon the earth. Thunder pealed and pealed and pealed again. Lightning cracked the sky.

There could be no battle in this, except the battle of earth and heaven. Even the greatest of them cowered in whatever shelter they had. The bulk of *Dancer*'s hull barely held off the torrents of water—and it was made to withstand the sea. Iry saw a man plucked like a feather from the boat he had been clinging to, and flung far and hard. She saw lightning strike an upended hull and cleave it in two, and leave the men beneath it stunned, exposed, and drowning in that terrible rain. It stripped kilts from men's bodies, helmets from their heads; wrested weapons from their hands. It had no mercy, no mind or will but to break and flatten and destroy.

Iry in her shelter, sheltered further by two large warm bodies, could only huddle and endure. Strong arms circled her. She would have loved to bury her face in Khayan's breast, but she had to see. She had to know: What this storm wrought. What was coming at her, whether lightning or wind or rain.

It seemed to go on forever. It lasted perhaps an hour of the sun, perhaps more, perhaps less. Such storms, the Cretan sailors would tell her, could last much longer, even for days. But this, for this country, was enough.

When it ended, the silence was so complete that she wondered if that last peal of thunder had deafened her. The rain lightened little by little till it was all but gone. The wind died. The clouds endured, black and boiling overhead, but the western horizon brightened slowly.

They crept out one by one, great lords and warriors reduced to frightened children. They were wet, mud-spattered. Many were naked.

They stood in a field of mud and water. The villages were gone, heaps of rubble and melted mudbrick standing in their places. People crept about them as about the boats and the battered ships. There were wounded and dead.

It was a battlefield of the gods. Slowly, out of it, the army took shape again. It was beaten and battered and white about the eyes, but it had taken fewer losses than anyone feared. Even the chariots: some of the horses had broken loose and escaped, and some of the chariots were broken, or chariots and teams had vanished, but when they had gathered, they were most of them alive, conscious, and not too badly wounded.

But of the enemy's army there were few left standing. A wind of wrath had caught them, and lightning pursued them. Those who lived had fled.

"But they raised the storm," Iannek said, speaking for them all.

"It seems their gods were not pleased to be disturbed," the king said. He was shaken as they all were, but he had mustered his courage and firmed his strength. At his command, men gathered what little of the baggage had survived, and made camp, guarding it with such weapons as they had. Others were set to work taking count of casualties, examining the ships for seaworthiness, and, not least, offering prayers of thanks to the gods that they had been spared. A few even went up to the villages—"For these are my people," Ahmose said. "If I would rule them, I should protect them."

Messengers began to come in before sundown, runners white-faced with shock, speaking of a storm that had swept the whole of the Lower Kingdom from Memphis to Avaris and beyond it. Baal the storm-god, Set the destroyer, had risen in wrath. Avaris in its high walls had suffered less than some, but roofs were torn away, walls battered, and the gate broken where the siege-engines had weakened it. Lightning had struck its bindings of bronze and half burned, half shattered it.

Apophis had not surrendered. "Not yet," Ahmose said.

He could not travel for what was left of that day. But in the morning, all ships that could sail would sail, and all of the army that could march, would march on Avaris. The broken, the hurt, and the stragglers would stay behind. Ahmose would take Avaris, or he would go down in defeat, felled by the Retenu as even the gods' lightnings had not been able to do.

·············· VII ··············

I T WAS A mad thing they did, marching and rowing back through storm-ravaged country on a river that ran strong and high as in the flood time. But if they lingered, their retreat would become the truth. Avaris could restore itself, muster its armies, and repair its gates. And Ahmose would have no strength to take it. More—if the storm had struck the Upper Kingdom as well as the Lower, and rumors said that it did, then he would have to turn and retreat as Kamose had done before him, and go to the aid of his people.

But first, if he could, he would take Avaris. He took the city by surprise: gates open, people clearing away stormwrack, watchers on the walls more intent on the labors below than on attack from an army that they had reckoned fled, and then destroyed.

The fleet, such of it as had come whole from the storm, bore down on them. Ahmose's army on foot and in chariots drove for the broken gate. They had one chance, one battle. That, they all knew. If they lost, they lost the war. There was no strength in them for more, nor provisions, nor weapons to sustain a new siege.

Desperation drove them. This was the end of it, for victory or for defeat. When the sun set, there would be one king in the Two Lands—but it might be Apophis.

Kemni found that he could, after all, care what became of any of them. He had no desire to be a Retenu slave. Not again. Iry, who had been both slave and more than queen to the foreign kings, had found the Mare waiting for her when she woke before dawn, standing white and glimmering in the last of the starlight. She rode with Kemni now, for all that anyone could say. Sadana's women rode as her escort. The two brothers of the Retenu, Khayan and Iannek, had demanded for themselves a chariot—and Ahmose had bidden Kemni give them one. Two charioteers marched with the footsoldiers because of that, and not to his delight, either; but he could not defy the king.

At least, he thought sourly, if the two of them did not turn traitor, they were certainly more skilled in chariotry than any of his own men. After a brief squabble, settled by Khayan's fist, Iannek held the reins, and Khayan, in his brother's armor, stood in the warrior's place. Iannek's eye was swelling already and turning a glorious shade of purple-black. He looked remarkably cheerful in spite of that, and remarkably odd in an Egyptian kilt.

There was a wild joy in what they did, this last cast of the bones, win or lose, live or die. The air was washed clean after the storm's passing, the sun bright as new gold. Broken houses, shattered villages, lands flooded long out of season—they were all one with this descent on Avaris. The Cretan ships had run up their wine-dark sails, riding a wind that seemed intent on driving them into the city's heart. The Egyptian fleet, which had fared less well, followed as it could, the flagship of gold battered but afloat, and the king standing high on it in his golden armor.

The fleet struck the strongest blows, as it well could. They who fought on land served chiefly to bar the enemy's escape and to offer battle to whoever tried to flee through the landward gates. Kemni had the north: that, the king thought, would be most likely to lure Apophis and his court, since northward was their own country, and some hope of escape.

Kemni hoped that Ahmose saw truly; that Apophis would not simply shut himself up in his citadel and hold fast till the Egyptians went away. But there was a kingdom to restore, and that could not be done from a citadel in the midst of a siege. Apophis too, Ahmose thought, would wish to get it over.

The chariots were not to enter the city—that command was explicit. The companies on foot would drive within if they could, but Kemni's men were to hold the open field. They had groaned on being told that; Ay the headstrong spoke for them all when he muttered, "What, we stand about again, and wait again, and lose again all our hopes for glory?"

Not this time. The great gates hung askew. Figures milled within. Women shrieked, children cried. Men's voices bellowed orders.

Kemni touched Sadana's shoulder. She slowed the horses. He raised his hand so that they all might see and do as he did. They rolled to a halt in a long line before the gate and the walls, as steady as they could be amid the wreck of the siege-engines, broken fragments that the camp had left behind, and the pits of the privies still open and reeking and buzzing with flies.

The foot-companies pressed on, so that the chariots guarded their backs. As they neared the broken gates, men began to stream out of it, bearded men in armor of leather or scale mail.

They met with a clash like two swords meeting. Kemni held the line, though his men champed and pawed, as restless as their own stallions. Body collided with body, bronze with bronze.

Kemni watched, alert. Ahmose had been precise as to when the chariots might drive forward.

There. The line of Egyptians swayed back; hung as if in midair; then swung strongly forward.

"Now," Kemni said to Sadana.

His team of bays leaped forward. He clutched the chariot's sides before he pitched backwards out of it—ignominious as that would have been, at the very taking of Avaris. The wind of the stallions' speed sang in his ears.

The footsoldiers gave way before the chariots, opening paths to the enemy. The enemy looked up and saw their death falling on them.

But they had their own weapon—as Kemni had been warned they would. Their chariots had been hidden behind the rubble of the gate. That was a flaw in their plan: they had to come out no more than two or three abreast, and slowly, over broken ground and past the companies of their comrades on foot.

The Egyptian foot closed in behind the chariots and about them, returning to the fighting with renewed strength. The chariots pressed forward—but not as far as the gate. They had their orders. They were a wall beyond the wall. The enemy's chariots could not flee except through them.

Kemni's bow was strung—a Retenu bow, which was the strongest in the world, and needed a strong arm to draw. He set an arrow to the string. *Strike at the charioteers.* That was the order he had been given, and that he had given his men. Not the horses—those, they could use. And not the fighting men, until the charioteers were down.

He raised the bow, aimed, loosed. Even before the arrow struck home, another was set to string. The chariot rocked and veered underfoot. He rode with it, keeping the arrow as steady as he might, focused on the target. Man in leather tunic, beard to the breast. No face to distract him. Simply the shape of his breast and shoulders, and the surety that the heart was there, as it was in every man. Kemni loosed, drew another arrow from the quiver, nocked, aimed.

One more. This one he saw fly wide, the chariot come on, horses wild-eyed and foaming. The warrior in it had no bow—fool, to trust to a spear, which needed closer quarters.

The chariot veered suddenly, rocking Kemni against the side. It half knocked the breath out of him, and let the spear pass harmless where, a breath before, Kemni's body had been.

He breathed a prayer of thanks, and flashed a smile at Sadana. She was grinning like a mad thing, darting among the mingled armies, setting him free to fight as he could. They had gone as far as they might under the king's orders; she turned and sent the horses along the wall. The rest of his people had done the same. The mounted women ranged among them, catching the wounded and bearing them behind the lines, and clearing away the dead. It was a strange duty, the more so for that, if attacked, they would fight, and fight well. But fighting was not all they did.

Close by Kemni, always, were the Retenu Khayan and his brother, fighting for the Mare and for her servant. They fought with great skill. They did not, that he could see, regret the bodies they wounded or the lives they took. They were born to war as no Egyptian ever was.

He must not let his mind wander. He had to know where every man was, and every chariot. They were only to go so far along the wall, then they must go back. The gate was their charge. They were not to leave it.

He signaled the return, curving back toward the gate. Chariots came out of it still, and men. It looked like a wound, the city draining its blood upon the northward road. The river they had never had. The south was Egypt. Where else could they go but north?

They fought harder now. The oncoming ranks were fresh, and his men were tiring. But they must hold. The king had commanded it.

There was no telling how the fleet fared. The bulk of the city lay between. Yet it must have driven in hard: among the warriors now were lesser figures, men unarmed or only lightly armed, children, even veiled women choosing the terror of the chariots over whatever passed within.

Women and children he let pass. Men died. That was the way of war. He rode over them, cut them down with spear or sword. So they all did. No one had forgotten the Retenu who shed new blood among Egyptian wounded and dying.

He was almost cravenly glad to meet another outriding of chariots. These were richer than the last, their charioteers gleaming with gold. They fought harder—for they had more to lose.

"Is it—?" he asked Khayan in a lull in the battle, when they had drawn up side by side to rest the horses.

Khayan was proof to Kemni's mind that Retenu grew their beards not to seem more manly, but to conceal faces that were all too easy to read. Khayan was as transparent as clean water. And his thoughts now were half of anger, and half of guilt—because he reveled in this battle, though he fought against his own people.

He answered willingly enough, whatever his thoughts. "These are lords of the court," he said. "The citadel must be breaking."

"Or broken." Seti halted his horses beside them. His left arm was bound up in a rag, and his cheekbone was split as impressively as Iannek's brow, but he was grinning as if he had no care in the world. "Will you wager we're winning?"

"Not if they keep coming," Kemni said. "There's no end to them. We're all there is."

"There has to be an end," Seti said. "The citadel's only so big."

"It's bigger than you might think." Kemni let himself rest briefly against the chariot's side. His legs and feet were aching—the price every man paid for riding in a chariot. Sadana seemed impervious, but she was not joining in the conversation, either. All her mind seemed focused on the horses. They were weary, standing hipshot, heads low. They would need water soon, and grazing, if they were to thrive.

They all watched a company of footsoldiers overwhelm and drag down a gilded prince in a chariot more elaborate than their own king's.

"That's not Apophis," Seti said.

"No," said Khayan. "That's a man whose wealth comes from trade, and who bought himself a noble wife. The king won't come out till the last."

"You think he'll come here?"

Khayan's face was set. Even what color it had—for he was a white-skinned man, as white as a woman—had drained from it. "Not likely," he said. "If he surrenders, he'll do it by the river, as king to king."

"Unless he means to run and not surrender," Seti said.

"There is that." Khayan shook himself, hunching his wide shoulders, then squaring them so that they seemed as broad as the city's gate. "Look, there's another wave of them. Iannek—"

Iannek had already moved, whipping up the horses, driving them back toward the battle. Kemni's bays followed, and Seti's blazefaced chestnuts. They fell on the advancing chariots with almost their full strength, and bow and spear and sword, and no memory of weariness until the battle paused again.

Earlier charioteers had taken no particular notice of the Retenu among the Egyptians. But these were lords—perhaps even Iannek's old drinking companions. They took his presence as a personal affront. They, and those behind them, each of whom seemed richer than the last, struck again and again for that of all parts of the line. "Keep moving!" Kemni called out. "Don't let them trap you."

Counsel he could well heed himself: after Iannek, the Egyptian captain won the greatest share of their hatred. If they were not intent on merely breaking through the line—and these lords of warriors wanted a toll paid in blood—they struck for Kemni nigh as often as for Iannek. He fought them off with an arm that grew heavier with each attack. If Seti had the right of it, and there truly was no end to them, Kemni would die of exhaustion before he died of his wounds.

He could not think of that. Fight—he must fight. His arrows were long gone. His spear was broken. His sword had grown dull. And still they came. The city was emptying of chariots. They were not turning once they had broken through the line, not going back within the walls. Those that escaped, escaped northward.

They were coming faster now, and some were wounded, stained with bright blood. Kemni's men held—brave fools, every one of them, and the more beloved for it. He called them off at last, pulled them back, left the way open.

Their numbers were fewer—grievously so. Empty chariots, masterless horses, wandered the field. Of foot there were more standing, but those too had withdrawn from the fight. It was a retreat, they could all see—a rout.

Avaris was taken from the river and secured from the land. Apophis came last out of the citadel—but if Seti had been wagering with Khayan, Seti would have won the wager. Apophis did not surrender to the Great House in the harbor. He led the last of his armies to the northward gate, and fought his way out. Even as the Egyptians held back to let him go, his men turned on them, as a boar at bay will turn on the hounds that would herd him toward the hunter's spear.

Kemni rallied his men almost too late, and almost too feebly. This was death. This, at last, was the end he had been praying for: at the hands of a prince of the Retenu, after Avaris was taken and the Lower Kingdom had fallen into Ahmose's power.

But, for that, he could not let himself be killed. He had to see it, to know it was so: that the war was won.

Sadana crooned to the horses, who were nigh at the end of their strength. There had been water for them, the last of the skins, with little spared for Kemni or Sadana. Either they would drink again within the city, or they would die.

They moved forward barely faster than a walk, but as they advanced they found a remnant of speed, enough to meet the king's riding as it passed the broken gate. They fell on it from every side that they could, and the scattered fragments of the footsoldiers among them, so that the ground and the air were deadly, both, and Apophis paid toll in blood for his use of the northward road.

Kemni gathered all the chariots that he could, for one last stroke. He set himself at the head of them and hurled them upon the king and his royal guard. All the hundred years of subjection, conquest, slavery, made weary arms strong, and honed their hate. They smote without care for life or safety, only for an end to the long war.

Apophis' chariots reeled before that charge. But they were fresher by far, and they protected their king. They steadied, rallied, thrust back. "Take the king alive!" Kemni roared to his men. "For all the rest—no quarter!"

He would hardly have known Apophis from that night of spying on Gebu in the garden of the citadel. That quiet, rather ordinary man was becoming a warrior king in a golden chariot, crowned with gold. The beard beneath the helmet was grey, but the shoulders were broad in the gilded armor, the arms corded, strong, wielding a great sword and a heavy-hafted spear. This king of warriors had no fear of war, and though he was well protected within his circle of guards, he thrust past them into the thick of the fight.

Maybe he too taunted the gods, and dared them to destroy him. Kemni pressed toward him, but there was a wall of chariots between, bearded men with flat dark eyes and grim faces. Their stallions challenged his, rearing and striking, daring them to fight as their charioteers did, to the death.

Kemni had taken advantage of a lull to sharpen his sword, a moment or a lifetime ago. It hummed as it wheeled and smote. It yearned for the taste of blood—king's blood.

The battle narrowed to this one man and this one purpose. The defenders between were shadows, albeit shadows armed with bronze. Edged bronze could banish them.

There were others on his right hand and his left. Seti, indomitable, with Ay for his charioteer—that was not how they had begun; Kemni would wonder, later, when they had made such a pact. Most likely when Ay's chariot was broken or his warrior killed. And on Kemni's right, Iannek of the Retenu and his brother Khayan. They hung back by an almost invisible fraction, but only by that.

They were following Sadana. Kemni might not have thought of that, except that the chariot lurched over something—fallen warrior, wrack of the storm—and rocked her briefly against him, and he glimpsed her face. It was white, set, terrible. It was not that she wanted to die, but that she had no pressing desire to live.

And that, he thought distantly, was a pity. She had beauty and strength and courage. She should live in joy, and not die in blood.

And all the while his wits wandered, his arm rose and fell, striking and striking again. He did not see whom he wounded, or who was killed. Only that the way was clear to the golden gleam that was the king.

One more man. One more defender armed with bronze. This one was fierce in defense of his king, and greatly skilled in the arts of the sword. Kemni's strength was failing. Pain niggled at the edges of awareness, and weakness gnawed at it. He was wounded, he did not trouble to determine where.

Take the king alive. His own words, echoing in his skull as if a stranger had spoken them. He reeled, dizzy. He saw the blow come, swayed away from it, but not far enough. It caught the edge of his helmet and flung him aside, tumbling end over end. Hooves flew past him. Wheels roared a scant handspan from his head.

He lay on the tumbled earth in a mire of mud and blood. The battle had passed him by. He was conscious. His head was remarkably clear. He could not hear well: his ears rang like smitten bronze. But he could see. He could even, after a while, sit up.

Apophis was gone, running northward in the diminished circle of his guard. Kemni's charioteers had stopped, their horses gasping, staggering. The men's faces were blank, flat with exhaustion.

Their own people found them there, footsoldiers and mariners in service to the Great House of Thebes, striding out of the city that they had taken.

Kemni by then was on his feet and had found his chariot. Sadana was still in it. She eyed him oddly and tried to say something, but he did not hear her. He leaned against the familiar side of the chariot, as comfortable as he could ever remember being, even without the Retenu king for his prisoner. It did not matter greatly that he had failed. Maybe if he had been Retenu, and had come so close to the enemy's king, he would have fallen on his sword.

But he was Egyptian. His gods had a sense of irony, and a sometimes cruel humor.

There at last was Ahmose, striding on his own feet, in armor that had seen hard use. He seemed to be looking for Kemni. Kemni tried to offer obeisance, but he was too dizzy. He clung to the chariot instead and mustered a smile. "Sire. I regret—I lost—"

"We'll catch him," Ahmose said, brisk and cool, just as he needed to be. He looked about. "You have done well. Very well indeed."

"We did try, my lord," Kemni said. Then, because he had a need to hear it from the king, and from no one else: "It's done? The city is yours?"

"The city is mine," Ahmose said with quiet but enormous satisfaction.

················ VIII ················

APOPHIS HAD ESCAPED, running north, but he had left people in the citadel: his queens, his concubines, ladies of the court, and the formidable lady Sarai, whose children, all but one, had fought for the Egyptian king. They sued for surrender as they could not but do, and through the lordly eunuch who was their messenger, begged leave to follow their lords out of Egypt.

Ahmose received them in the hall of the palace that Khayan remembered well: the great hall of audience with its throne of gold. His heart clenched at the sight of that little brown monkey sitting where the great bulls of Canaan had sat for so long. The throne was too high for Ahmose; his feet rested on a footstool. He had had his servants set him up on cushions, to appear less dwarfed by that throne of giants.

He seemed undismayed by that sacrifice of dignity. By some miracle of servants' art he was clean, clothed in linen of impeccable whiteness, with a splendid collar of gold, and golden armlets, and on his head the Blue Crown of war. People murmured that somewhere, some man of great honor and skill was making for him what had not been seen since the Lower Kingdom fell to the conquerors from Retenu: the Two Crowns of the Two Lands, White Crown embraced within Red. He would wear it, it was said, when he took formal possession of this kingdom, not here in the conqueror's city, but in Memphis of the ancient kings.

But all that was still to come—and Khayan dared still, however unwisely, to hope that it might not come at all. For this day, Ahmose was lord in Avaris, and victor in war. He had the royal ladies brought before him, knowing surely what dishonor it was for them to be seen, even veiled, by the eyes of men and foreigners.

But then, by the laws of war, they were his to do with as he pleased. Had he been one of the people, he would have taken them for his own and led them away into his harem. That he did not do such a thing, that he agreed to speak to them as if they had been men and kings, was strange and perhaps ominous.

Khayan might not have come to this place, nor would Iry have forced him, but he found he could not stay away. He came as what he was, the slave of an Egyptian. They were all there, Iannek, Sadana, such of her women as were alive and well enough to walk. So too the Cretans, those great allies, and the little princess who had wedded the king. She stood beside and somewhat behind him, not seated on a throne brought in and set next to his as the Great Royal Wife was, but close, and in a place of great honor.

She smiled when Khayan, somewhat unwarily, caught her eye. She seldom stood on ceremony unless it suited her. And she liked the look of a handsome man, or so it was said. There was a rumor that while she could never in honor bed any man but her wedded lord, she well might send maidservants in her name, who would give great pleasure to a fortunate few. Kemni the Egyptian was said to have been a great favorite of hers, until he became her kinswoman's lover. Now no woman was known to come to his bed, nor was any wanted there, for he grieved too greatly for his lost priestess.

Sadana was standing close beside him now, by accident or design, just as she had appointed herself his charioteer. When this was over, Khayan would consider the meaning of that.

Now he fixed his eyes on the ladies who came in procession, a long line of veiled figures, all in black unadorned. But many betrayed beneath the veils a gleam of gold or the flash of a jewel.

Behind the guards who preceded them and the eunuch who led them, Khayan recognized the straight back and proud carriage of his mother, and the likeness of her just behind, his sister Maryam. They must be able to see him: he was standing on the dais of the throne, as guard to Iry—and still in Iannek's armor, too, somewhat to Iannek's disgust. He did not try to meet their eyes, which in any event were hidden behind black gauze.

Such division this war had wrought, and all because the Mare had chosen a woman of the conquered people. Khayan could not bring himself to regret the fault that was partly his, for letting himself be prevailed upon to bring the young Mare into the west when word came that the old one was gone. It was all as the gods had willed—pain as much as joy.

Sarai halted at the foot of the dais as the guards drew back on either side. She went down in full reverence. Behind her, all the great ladies did as she did, however stiffly and unwillingly some chose to do it. It was as graceful as barley rippling in the wind.

Ahmose inclined his head, a great concession to the captives of war. "My lady," he said to Sarai. "Rise and face me."

She obeyed without servility, rising as a dancer might, or a warrior. Perhaps she expected that he would ask her to unveil, but he did not do that. He said to her, "You ask leave to depart. If I grant it, where will you go?"

"North, great king," she answered, "into Canaan."

"You do understand that I will pursue your king?"

"I would expect it," she said calmly.

"It may serve you to travel with us for a while, if your companions can endure such speed as we will make."

Her head lifted a fraction, as if her back had stiffened. "Great king, I offer no insult, but if we travel with your army, will we not be captives of it?"

"Say rather that we would be your escort, and that when we found your king and his people, we would surrender you with full honor. That I swear to you by my crown and my kingship."

"That is a great oath," she said after a pause. "Still, great king—"

"If you travel apart from us," Ahmose said, "I can promise you no safety. I can assure you that you will come to your people late, and find them perhaps defeated, and certainly embattled."

"Then you will leave soon," she said, as if she had not expected that.

"On the morrow's morrow," Ahmose said, "I go. My queens will do what it is needed for the securing of these kingdoms. For my honor and my office, I must assure that the Two Lands are never again invaded and never again conquered. That duty, my gods have laid on me."

"So they have," she said, "great king. Very well. On your oath and for our protection, we will accept what you offer. If, which the gods forbid, our men are overwhelmed and taken before we can be given back to them, will you swear me another oath? Will you set us free to find our kin in Canaan?"

That was a great presumption, but Khayan would have expected no less. Nor, it seemed, would Ahmose. His eyes glinted within their mask of paint, as he inclined his head.

Sarai bowed low once more. "You are indeed a great king," she said, "and a great prince of this world."

+ +

"And not of the next?"

Iry had lingered only briefly once the ladies of the Retenu had left the hall. Khayan should have expected that she would follow them, would wait a little while till they could settle again for the last night but one in the queens' chambers of the citadel. Then she went as she had gone so often, to the rooms that were Sarai's.

As with the hall of audience, Khayan was not asked or expected to remain in her shadow, but he could not bring himself to stay away. It was like a boil: he must lance the whole of it, or see no end to the pain.

Sarai was overseeing the preparations to depart, although there was a full day yet, and clearly she had been ready for some time. It was something to do, he supposed: a means to keep the women occupied, and therefore less inclined to succumb to hysterics.

She greeted Iry as if they had never been parted, and Khayan with a glance, no more—but also no less. In that brief flicker she set all that he needed to know, and all that she would give him: every gift, every blessing.

She sat with Iry in a small chamber that had been cleared of every personal thing, though it remained rather richly furnished. There was wine. There was bread, and a pot of honey. Khayan declined them, but Iry professed to be hungry. She ate and drank with her wonted composure.

Sarai shared with her a cup of wine, sipping it slowly. Here, the veils were gone. Her face was much as always; somewhat thinner perhaps, and somewhat paler, but as strong as ever.

"You really will go?" Iry asked her after a while.

She nodded. "It's time," she said.

"All the way, then? Back to the tribes?"

"Yes," Sarai said.

Iry sighed a little. "I wish you might stay."

That perhaps startled Sarai, though not Khayan: her eyes widened slightly. "And why would you wish that?"

"To teach me," she said. "To be mother to your children."

"My children are men and women grown. And you," said Sarai, "have gone past me."

Iry shook her head with a look Khayan knew well: lips tight, long eyes narrowed. "I had only begun my lessons with you."

"Everything I taught you, you can continue, or my children can teach. I should like to see my kin again, and ride the wide sea of grass, and sleep under the sky."

Iry bowed to that perforce. But she had not given up yet. Surrender was not a thing Iry knew the meaning of. "You could go, and stay for a while, and then come back."

"I think not," Sarai said almost gently. "When I go, I go to live out my life, and then to die. I have no desire to wither in the sands of Egypt, or to rot in these fens. I would have a clean death, and a long sleep under the grass."

"Did you hate Egypt so much?" Iry asked her.

"No," she said firmly. "No, I did not. I could say that I loved it. But it was never home to me. You understand that, child. You better than any, how Egypt may welcome guests, but if they seek to claim it for themselves, it turns and casts them out."

"But your children—"

"My younger children were born here. My elder daughter is a daughter of the steppe." Sarai paused, caught by Iry's expression. "What, you never knew? Yes, Maryam was born among the tribes. She came with me when she was very young, when the Mare before yours chose her servant and brought her into Egypt. I was chosen, too, though not to be the Mare's chief servant."

"And when you came here, you were given to a lord of the Retenu." Iry spoke slowly, as if she needed to understand.

"I gave myself," Sarai said. "I chose him. He was beautiful then, and kind. His heir is very like him."

Khayan flushed.

They laughed at him, but not too cruelly. "So," Iry said when the laughter had died, "you will go. I pray you come there safe, and live long under your eastern stars."

Sarai bowed low, lower than she ever had to a king. "From you," she said, "such a prayer is a thing of great power."

There was a silence. Iry rose after a while and wandered off.

Which left Khayan alone with his mother. He was sure that was their intention—both of them. Women were always conspiring in ways that men could not understand. Sometimes he was certain that they spoke from mind into mind, without the interference of mere words.

Sarai regarded him as she often had, with a clear, measuring gaze. When he was younger he had wondered what she found lacking. Now he was a man, he still wondered that, but it mattered less. Whatever his failings, she was gracious enough to forgive them.

"Come here, child," she said.

He came as she asked, and sat at her feet. She smoothed his cropped hair and brushed her fingers across his shaven cheek. He shivered lightly. The wind no longer felt so strange, nor his head so light, shorn of its weight of hair; but at her touch, he remembered vividly how it had been when first he stood naked before the world.

"My beautiful child," she said. "You know we'll never meet again."

"No," he said. "I don't. I lived in the east. What's to prevent me from going back?"

"Why, nothing," said Sarai. "But I am not young, and you are very young. And there is much to do in Egypt."

He opened his mouth to deny that, but he was too clear-sighted: her gift from the womb, and a curse of sorts. "In Crete," he said instead, "they say that the tide of years bears all things away, and seldom brings them back. I wish that were not so."

"As do I," Sarai said. She would never break and weep; that was not her way. But her eyes were suspiciously bright. "You give me great pride, my child."

"Even as I am?"

"Chosen of the Mare's chosen. You will be a prince again, Khayan. The stars have told me."

"I was going to say it doesn't matter," he said after a moment, "but I find it does. I'm male enough for that."

Her smile had a hint of wickedness that reminded him oddly of Iry. "You are male enough for any purpose."

His face flamed again, as it had a habit of doing. She laid her cool palms against it, and tilted it up till he could not but meet her gaze. "I give you no wisdom," she said, "and no advice, either. Except this. Love her, Khayan. Simply love her."

"And remember you?"

"If your heart desires."

"My heart . . ." His throat was tight; he had to force the words through it. "My heart will grieve to see you gone—but be glad, too, because you've gone home."

"You always were too wise to be a man." She set a kiss on his brow and on each cheek and on his lips. "May the goddess love you and keep you for her own."

· · · · · · · · IX · · · · · · · ·

AHMOSE THE KING rode in pursuit of the fallen enemy, leaving behind him Nefertari the Great Royal Wife and Ariana the queen and his allies from Crete; and a great force that had gathered of lords and commons from the Lower Kingdom. Those would restore the wreck of the storm and the wreck of the war: a mighty undertaking, mightier than the closing and barring of the gates of Egypt against the invaders from Canaan, but no more or less vital to the life of the Two Lands.

Before Ahmose departed, he did three things that would be remembered. He crowned himself with the Two Crowns. He took again to wife Ariana of Crete with as much pomp and ceremony as haste and war would allow. And he gave Iry the lands and lordship of the Sun Ascendant, and bade her raise horses there, to draw his chariots. With the Bull of Re in the Upper Kingdom, it would give him a great weapon for all his wars hereafter.

He rode away in a chariot, but Kemni was not his charioteer. Kemni had walked away from the battle in, he thought, as splendid health as could be expected, and passed much of that day in the aftermath of battle. But near sunset he had fallen over. He did not remember that, or much of the hour before it. When he woke again, he was in the citadel of Avaris in the rooms of a prince, and Imhotep the king's physician was bending over him. So, and more to his surprise, was the warrior woman Sadana.

At first they did not seem to see that he was awake. They were frowning at one another as if they had been quarrelling. "Of course you know nothing of that herb!" she snapped in her accented Egyptian. "It grows on the steppes of Asia. It gives dreams and visions, but it also gives healing."

"And it can kill," Imhotep said through gritted teeth. "That, I have heard. You hinted at it yourself."

"Not in this infusion. And not as I will give it. Can you put aside your arrogance for one moment, and admit that maybe—maybe—there are things you do not know?"

"There are a myriad things I do not know. Medicine is not among them."

"The medicine of Egypt. This is not of Egypt. I will give it to him. Now stand aside."

Imhotep stood his ground. Sadana raised a hand.

Kemni stirred and tried to speak. Nothing came out but a strangled grunt.

It was enough. They stared at him, their quarrel forgotten. He stared back. Words were there, if his tongue would shape them. It felt thick and unwieldy in his mouth. "I want—I must—where—"

"Thank the gods!" Imhotep said.

But Sadana's expression did not lighten. "Look at his eyes. He's all addled." She slipped in past Imhotep, cradled Kemni's head in her arm, and poured into him a vial of liquid fire.

He gasped and choked. She held his mouth shut till he must swallow or drown. The potion went down as it had gone in, in a stream of searing heat.

He lay breathing hard, head and heart pounding alike. But his thoughts had stopped jangling and steadied. "What in the name of the gods—"

"Something to help you heal," she said.

"And make me dream?"

"It might."

He groaned and shut his eyes. Of all the things she could have given him, he needed dreams the least.

But the fiery stuff had cleared his head, and even, after a while, made it stop aching. They were both still there, still watching him, as if they feared that he would die between one breath and the next. "I'm not as badly hurt as that," he said to them.

"You had a blow to the head," Imhotep said, "that came near to splitting your skull. The king has informed me that if you fail to recover, my skull will be split in its turn. You are wonderfully dear to the king."

"Gods know why," Kemni muttered.

"Everyone loves your pretty face," Sadana said.

✦ ✦

However that might be, Kemni stood by the gate when the king departed, leaning on a support which happened, just then, to be Sadana's large and amiable brother Iannek. Ahmose had been most clear. Kemni was not to go. He had been wounded and was still barely able to stand.

The king would drive out the Retenu, hunt them all the way into their own country, and take it if he could. He was bent on revenge. But he had not forgotten the kingdoms he left behind him in the care of his queens. "When you are well," he had said to Kemni before he mounted his chariot, "I have a task for you. Will you be my master of horse?"

Kemni was still addled, after all. He could only stare and say, "Master of horse? But—"

"I give you the Bull of Re and the lands about it," Ahmose said, "as I've given your kinswoman the Sun Ascendant. You in the Upper Kingdom, she in the Lower, will begin a thing that will make us stronger than ever. Give me horses, my son. Give me chariots. Make me as strong in them as I am in men afoot."

That was a great charge. Too great for his throbbing head and his many aches and bruises. But he would not stay abed. He saw the king ride out with the strength of his army that remained—much more than Kemni had looked for, with those who had remained in reserve on the ships and those who had come in from round about the Lower Kingdom. The storm had wrought terrible destruction, therefore there were fewer fighting men than had hoped to come, but their numbers were still very great. And though storehouses had fallen and provisions been destroyed by war and storm, there was still enough to bear his army into the land of the Retenu.

Some of the Cretan fleet went with him as far as the river would go, and would then go out to sea, following the coast and bearing provisions as they could. The rest remained in the service of the queen from Crete, and among them the admiral himself, her kinsman Naukrates.

They dined together the night the king departed, no formal gathering, but when Kemni was carried off bodily to the rooms that everyone insisted were his, Naukrates came at the head of a procession of servants with the makings of a feast, and ordered it spread in one of the outer rooms. Kemni was spread with it, as it were: laid on a couch like a lady with the vapors, and served like one, too, by a pair of maids whom he thought he recognized. When under his stare they began to giggle, he knew them in truth. They were Arianas—maids of the Ariana of Crete.

As if that recognition had been a signal, she appeared herself, dressed as he so loved to see her, in the tiered skirts and the vest that flaunted her beauty. The pain of that, of remembering another who had dressed so and smiled so when they were alone, was oddly remote—perhaps because of Sadana's potion, which she had been feeding him in fiery doses.

They dined together in the style to which, Ariana told him laughing, he should become accustomed, "For you are a prince now."

"I've lived with princes since I was little more than a boy." And that was sadness too, to remember Gebu and what he had been and what he had become. Kemni would never, please the gods, fall to the temptation that had destroyed Gebu. He did not want to be a king.

"But you are more than a prince's hanger-on," Ariana said. "You hold the rank yourself."

That was true. Kemni had not realized; his head was still too addled. Master of the king's horse was a high rank, greatly noble, royal perhaps. Why not? He would need as much wealth as the king or the queens would bestow on him, to do as they bade him. And power, too, to command and be obeyed.

It was too much to think of all at once. He ate what he was given, instead; or tried. This feast was like the thoughts that crowded in his mind: delicious, exhilarating, but too rich for his weakened spirit.

He would be strong again. Both Imhotep and Sadana, in a rare moment of agreement, had assured him of that. Tonight he was allowed to indulge his weakness.

Naukrates had been drinking deep of the wine. He was one of those men who grew warmer with it and more expansive, but never more quarrelsome. He laid an arm about Kemni's shoulders and embraced him. "Poor boy! You look overwhelmed. Why not escape from it all? Come with me, take ship on *Dancer*, run away to sea. We'll sail beyond the world's edge. We'll cross wakes with the barque of the sun."

After a few sips of wine, Kemni was even more fuddled than Naukrates. "That," he said with great care not to trip over his tongue, "would be splendid. Shplendish—splendid."

"You can do that," Ariana said, crisp and sharp, "when you've given the king his horses. And not before."

"Not give king horses," Kemni said. "*Make* king horses. Many many many many many—"

"Many horses," Naukrates said helpfully. "*Then* ship."

"Then ship," Ariana said.

+ +

Kemni remembered that after he had recovered from both wine and addlement—a remarkably short time, all things considered. The king had left at the moon's full. By the time of the new moon, Kemni was well enough, and matters well enough in hand, that he could travel with a company of the queens' soldiers and with others who were going to rebuild their holdings, or to take holdings that had been given them out of the booty of war. All over the Lower Kingdom, lordly houses that had been subject to the Retenu were in Egyptian hands again, and were, many of them, in sore need of tending.

This would be the work of years. If Kemni ever ran away to sea, the beard he did not grow would no doubt be as grey as Naukrates'.

But that, as Naukrates reminded him, was not so terribly old. Meanwhile, in his youth, he had a great work to share in.

So too did Iry. She rode with them, and her following at her back: warrior women, lone bearded Retenu lordling, and the shorn one who, everyone knew, was her lover. They would take the Sun Ascendant as Kemni was to take the Bull of Re. And he had in mind to pause there, if he might, for a little while.

+ +

The return to the Sun Ascendant was a homecoming—for Kemni as much as for Iry. It was not his own holding, nor had it been, but he had known it from his childhood.

The storm had battered it, but not as terribly as some. The roof was off one of the houses within the wall, the Retenu women's house, no less. The rest had fared well enough. There were even houses still standing in the villages, and people rebuilding those that were fallen, a vision of industrious labor that would warm any lord's heart.

The horses were well, the herds intact. There were foals already, some born in or about the storm, and most of those ran at the sides of moon-pale mothers. The Mare's people had increased by a blessed number.

Iry would simply have ridden in as if she did so every day, but her foreigners, of all people, would not hear of such a thing. They insisted that she put on her robes and her golden headdress and mount the freshly bathed and shining Mare, and ride home like a queen in procession. They were all in their best finery, the brothers in the chariot that they had appropriated for themselves, with Khayan's duns to draw it; and as had become their custom, Iannek wore the kilt and served as charioteer, and Khayan rode in armor as a warrior should. Kemni had overheard them casting the bones to decide their places; and Iannek had cursed thunderously when he lost the throw. "By Set's black balls! I always lose!"

And Khayan had laughed and said, "So swear by Mother Isis' tits next time, and maybe she'll let you wear the armor for once."

Khayan was not laughing now. Kemni, riding nearby, tried to read that face, to see what he thought of riding back to the holding a slave, who had ridden out of it a lord and prince. But for once his thoughts were not written as clear as on papyrus. He looked like an image carved in ivory, with his arched nose and his firm jaw, and his long mouth, usually so mobile, set and still.

Iannek seemed to regard it as a lark, as he did most things. He sang to himself and crooned to the stallions, filling his brother's silence with cheerful noise. That was a kind of wisdom, Kemni supposed. It lightened hearts remarkably, and made people smile.

The holding was waiting for them. Its gate was open, and people in it: guards with polished helmets, dignified people in good linen with their best ornaments, and young girls and slender boychildren with garlands of flowers. Kemni saw familiar faces, many he could name and a few he could not. There was Nefer-Ptah the Nubian, black and towering amid the little brown people; Teti the steward with his wide shoulders and his air of authority; Tawit his wife and his daughters the five Beauties, chattering like a flock of geese; even Huy the scribe, leaning on the shoulder of Pepi the master of the stables, waiting on the greatest gladness, maybe, that they had ever known: the return of a lady of the old blood, bearing the blessing and the authority of an Egyptian king.

But there was one face he did not see, a face of unmatched beauty. The Lady Nefertem lived; they had been assured of that. So too had they been assured that she remained in the Sun Ascendant, were she had taken back the women's house and ruled it as she always had—even while the Retenu were still lords in the Lower Kingdom.

They were taken in with songs and dancing, in a rain of flowers. Kemni had never seen such joy here, even when he was a child. It struck him strangely—as if he wanted to laugh, but if he did, he would burst into tears.

The courts were full of people, all the servants, the scribes and clerks, the guards, the women. Every one of them must have come out to see the holding in Egyptian hands again, and to celebrate the victory.

The Lady Nefertem was sitting in the second court, the court of the lotus pillars, shaded by a canopy, with her women about her. Kemni smiled to see her. Yes, she would let them come to her. Even her daughter, who was become her ruling lady.

Her beauty was as marvelous as ever. She would not mar it with a smile, but her eyes were brilliant with joy. As they approached, she rose, and did a thing she had never done in her queenly life: she stepped down from the dais on which her chair was set, and held out her arms to her daughter.

Iry eyed her rather dubiously, but stepped into her mother's embrace. It must have crushed the breath from her: she gasped. But she did not struggle to escape.

"My child," Nefertem said. "Oh, my child."

Iry won free at length and left the field to Kemni. Nefertem did not speak to him, simply held him hard and long. The comfort in that, the embrace of kin, astonished him. It nearly broke him.

He would come in the end to the Bull of Re, and be a prince of the Two Kingdoms. But here in the Sun Ascendant, he had come home.

.... X ....

THE LADY NEFERTEM regaled them all with a feast of welcome. She had not been greatly pleased to find herself host to remnants of the Retenu, as she thought of them; or to be informed by her daughter that those remnants would join in the feast. "They are slaves," she had said. But Iry had stared her down.

Iry was still shaking with the memory of that. No one, even lords of the Retenu, defied the Lady Nefertem. Only one man had ever come close. And that one was seated beside her, not greatly willingly, but she would have him nowhere else.

Khayan was quiet and rather pale in this hall that had been his once, before his people's kingdom fell. She regretted, a little, that she had made him come with her; it was costing him pain. But she needed him here: his solidity beside her, the warmth of his presence, his strength that seldom wavered.

Everyone else was dizzy with joy. Even Kemni, who had become a somber man since his Cretan priestess died, was drinking deep and joining in the singing. He was a pleasure to watch: grief had fined his beauty and given it a poignance that caught the heart. Women sighed wherever he went, and mourned when he was oblivious to them.

Silly creatures. It was only a face, he would say so himself. He was the least vain of men, with the most cause to be.

Tomorrow the world would be real again. There were houses to rebuild, people to feed and clothe, horses to breed. The king must come back to a strong kingdom. This part of it was given to Iry to make whole.

Her hand crept out beneath the table and found Khayan's. His was cold, but its grip was strong. She leaned toward him. "Soon. We'll be done soon."

He sighed: a faint lifting of his breast. She wanted to touch it, to stroke the curly fleece, and when he had begun to laugh that wonderful deep laughter, to let her hands wander down and down. And then . . .

Another hand touched her arm, another hand, much lighter, but very firm. Her mother spoke in her ear. It mattered little what she said. It drew her away from Khayan, which perhaps was the intention.

Well enough—for this hour. Tonight they would all be shut in their chambers, and Iry would lie with Khayan, and the world would vanish. It would be only the two of them, and the lamps' light, and the dance that was the sweetest in the world.

She was thinking, perhaps—the gods knew she might be hoping too much, but her courses, which had never failed to come exactly on the day of the new moon, were still not begun, and the moon was waxing night by night. Sometimes when no one could see, she would lay her hand on her middle, and wonder if there was something there—someone, some living creature, a child. Then her heart would be so full that surely it would burst.

It would have begun, if it had begun, the night after Avaris fell, when they lay together in the citadel. He had wept, startling himself; then grown angry and called himself a fool. She had had to comfort him, comfort that went the way it could not but go.

Tonight she gave him such comfort again. The room they lay in had been his once, and his father's before that, and before that, her own father's. None of them had changed it, as it happened. The Retenu had covered the walls with heavy hangings and buried the tiles in carpets. Stripped of those veils and concealments, it was a beautiful room, a little worn with time, its vivid colors softened till they were almost gentle. There were dancers on the walls, long skeins of them, young girls with plaited hair, and young men leaping like acrobats, and even, in a corner, a wicked-faced monkey mimicking the dancer above him.

They had danced their own dance to its completion, and lay tangled in one another, breathing hard. When Iry could move again, she raised herself over him, looking down at his face. He smiled as if he could not help it.

"Does it hurt too much?" she asked him.

He shook his head. "I thought it would hurt more."

"And you still do it."

"Am I given a choice?"

"You could have gone with your mother. Or followed Apophis."

"What, to Sharuhen?" He sighed. "No. You aren't in Sharuhen. You won't ever go to the east."

"I would let you go. If your heart yearned for it."

"My heart is here." He laid his hand on her breast.

She laid her own hand over it. "But every day is pain. Every day you are humiliated. People call you a slave. Sometimes they spit at you. When we came here—I saw how they stared, and how they whispered. If I'd let you go where you wanted to go, to sleep among the servants, they would have tormented you."

"And I would have seen that they never did it again."

She recoiled a little, not for revulsion, but for startlement. More fool she: she had forgotten what, after all, he was.

That pricked her temper. "I should just turn you loose? Let you fight like a stallion, and win the herd?"

"Why not?"

She sat back abruptly. "Yes. Why not? What if you're killed?"

"No one will kill me. I still belong to you."

Was he bitter? She thought perhaps not. That was the Mare's people in him. They could accept what a warrior of the Retenu might never hope to do.

+ +

The Lady Nefertem summoned her daughter to her on the day before the full moon. Some of the servants who had attached themselves to Iry were not pleased: she was the ruler of that domain, and not Nefertem. But Iry was pleased enough to obey.

She met Kemni on the way there, going about some errand of his own. He was lingering, she had noticed, as if he could not bring himself to leave. She wondered if he knew how much that had to do with his frequent companion. Sadana might not be aware of it, either: how they were drawn toward one another. They were not lovers at all; if Sadana had been a man, people would have called them comrades in arms. They were always out and about the horses or the chariots or the boys and young men whom they had begun to train in chariotry. The king needed as many as could be sent on, all the way into Canaan, to the kingdom called Sharuhen, where Apophis had turned and made his stand.

But just now Kemni turned on a whim and said, "I'll go with you. It's been a little time since I paid my respects to your mother."

Iry eyed him a little warily. "Is there something I should know?"

"No," he said. "Except possibly that she should be coming to you. You're the lord here."

"My mother has always made the lord come to her," Iry said. "Why should I be different?"

Kemni snorted. "Yes, why? The gods made her a queen. Men have been somewhat slower to get about it."

Iry stopped. "What are you saying? Should I marry her off to the king?"

"Would you like to?"

It was not as preposterous a thought as it might have seemed. Except . . .

"She'd never share him with anyone," Iry said. "And he has two great queens already."

"Then she'll be queen here. But you can't let her rule you."

"I don't intend to," Iry said.

They had come to the women's house, past the guards who bowed and smiled—they never could keep their faces as expressionless as they should, not in these days. It was great joy to them to bow to one of their own as lord.

She went in to her mother with a daughter's obedience but a lord's heart. Nefertem was occupied as she liked to be, with the accounts of the holding, and Teti the steward with her. She greeted Iry calmly and Kemni without surprise—indeed, with pleasure—and sent Teti politely away. He left without reluctance, with the flicker of a smile at Iry, as if he knew why she had been summoned, and was much pleased with it.

The Lady Nefertem was determined to make this a proper occasion, with food and drink and talk of nothing in particular. Iry sighed but endured. Her mother was not to be hurried, nor could she be compelled to do anything she was not minded to do.

At length—and long after Iry had promised to meet with Khayan among the chariots—Nefertem came to the point. "It has occurred to me," she said, "that while it is all very well that you rule here in the name of your father and brothers, it would be much more proper if this holding looked to a lord of suitable rank and lineage."

Iry declined to be taken aback. "Lady," she said. "Mother. The king himself named me lord here. My office, my position, grant me grace to be more than a woman."

"Still, you are a woman. In days past, after your courses began you would have been matched with a husband. Now the Two Lands are whole again, and a king wears the Two Crowns. It's time we returned to the ways of propriety."

"The Two Lands are whole," Iry said, "and the foreign kings will be forgotten, their names scoured from our earth. But some things have changed. The king rides in a chariot now. Where cattle grazed and barley grew, we raise horses for that chariot. Those horses are my charge. The king has said nothing to me of surrendering them to a man."

She had not meant to be or to sound so angry. Men ruled this world, she knew that. It was what was. But she was the Mare's chosen. In the Mare's world, women ruled. And she could not go back. Not for this.

"I am not asking that you give up your horses," Nefertem said coolly. "But the rest of it, the lands, the lordship—what can be so ill in letting a man hold the title? It's proper, it's accepted, it may serve you in court when you go there. You will go there. Did you think that you would not?"

"I know that I will," Iry said, fighting for calm. "And that court, Mother, is ruled now by a pair of queens."

"In the king's name," Nefertem said with devastating logic. "Come, child. If nothing else, you should give thought to the question of an heir. None but a man can give you that."

Iry's belly clenched round what might be, indeed, an heir. But she was not about to speak of that.

"Do consider," said Nefertem, "what I have considered. There are a number of lords who might do. But long ago, when you were a child, your father and I had spoken of a match that would please him well." Her eyes turned to Kemni. To his credit, he looked as startled as Iry must.

"Yes," the lady said in tones of considerable pleasure. "I see you understand. And why not? You two are kin. You were children together. You hold like rank, and like favor with the king. And you share an office: to give him horses. What better match can there be?"

Why, thought Iry, if one looked at it so, there was none. And the gods knew, he was beautiful, he was pleasing, he was her dear friend. He was everything that a woman could want in a husband.

None of which removed the fact that they both knew, but her mother surely did not: that neither of them had any desire to marry the other. Iry's beloved was out among the chariots. Kemni's heart had died with a Cretan priestess, though Iry thought it might be coming to life again for a woman who rode horses and who fought like a man.

She could not say this. Not yet. She rose abruptly, but she did not care if it seemed rude. "Thank you, Mother," she said. "I will consider it."

+ +

Kemni followed her out, which was as she wished. She led him toward the bit of garden where they had spoken together, that day when he came over the wall to spy on the Retenu. It was as quiet now as then, and as deserted.

She faced him there. He met her gaze and waited for her to speak: an art he must have learned in Crete, or from Sadana. Men never did such things in the rest of the world.

"Do you want this?" she demanded.

He lifted a shoulder: half a shrug, as if he had but half a heart for it. "Do you?"

"Will you be offended if I say that I do not?"

"Maybe a little," he said.

She shook her head in irritation. "Silly man. You don't want me."

"I could," he said, "if it were my duty. Just as you could want me. We were raised to marry as the family bade us. If you don't accept me, who knows what sort of man your mother will find for you?"

That made her shudder. "Don't tell me you don't know why I have to refuse this."

"I know," he said, "that your mother would be properly appalled if she knew what keeps you warm of nights."

"And are you?"

He shook his head.

"And would you be? If we were wedded—would you try to forbid me?"

"Yes," he said without hesitation.

"Yet you would take other women if you were so minded."

He had the grace to flush and lower his head. "It is the way of the world here. Though if you forbade—"

"What, so that we both could suffer?" Her eyes narrowed. "Yes, I would do it. And then we would be miserable alike."

"Maybe not miserable," he said. "We might get on very well. We always have."

"As kin," she said. "As friends. What then of my beloved? Must I send him away? I can't keep him here. Then we truly would be wretched."

"Send him to the south," Kemni said, "to the Bull of Re. He'll be much needed there, and most welcome."

"You will consider this," she said. "You really will."

He spread his hands. "Won't you? It's sensible. It's useful. It serves both our purposes. And it will content your mother."

"Mother must be kept content at all costs." Iry snapped off the words. "You can say such a thing? Knowing what I have? Or is that why? If you can't have yours, I'm not to have mine? Is that what it is? Is it?"

She had driven him back to the wall. He flattened against it, not particularly cowed, but wary of her temper.

And well he should be. She stepped back, letting him go. "Go away," she said, "and let me think."

He obeyed her without a word. She caught herself wishing he had protested. It would have been easier then to stand against this thing.

She did like him. A great deal. Love him? Yes. As a brother, as her close kin. That would hardly prevent them from marrying, not in Egypt, though the Retenu had a horror of it. Was not Queen Nefertari the king's own sister?

But when her heart sang, the name it sang was Khayan's. And that was altogether impossible. He was a foreigner, a captive. He had been lord here, and done well, but the people had hated him—still hated him, because he was Retenu.

Egypt labored already to forget that they had ever been. Their names, the memory of them, would be scoured away, cut from the monuments, buried in the sand and in the black mud of the Delta. The captives who remained, who had not be killed or sold far away, must become Egyptian, as far as they could; as far as he could, whose face would never be anything but foreign.

"Lady," she said to the goddess in the solitude of that place, "could you possibly have chosen a more awkward man for me?"

The goddess refrained from answering, as well she might. She had chosen Iry, too—out of all the women of the tribes and the Retenu, she had turned aside to set her hand on an Egyptian, a stranger to horses, who had grown up hating them. That she would then bind that Egyptian's heart to a man of the Retenu was utterly like her humor.

And now it must end. Egypt must be Egypt again. Iry would take her cousin as her mother ordained, in marriage that was an alliance of princes. So had the Ariana of Crete wedded the king in Thebes. It was the way of this world, right and proper.

She straightened her back and firmed her spirit. She went to duties that had been waiting for far too long while she contended with this folly of resistance.

+ +

And when those duties were done, she did as Kemni had reminded her that she should do. She summoned her mother into her presence.

There were others, too. This was not a formal audience, but what she had to say, she must say in front of everyone who was concerned in it. Therefore she had established herself in the smaller reception-hall, in the chair that had been the lord's for time out of mind. Kemni was there, and Teti the steward and his wife, and inevitably his daughters. Sadana also, and Iannek because he could hardly be kept away, and Huy the scribe, who could remember what he heard, though he could no longer see to write it. And, of course, since all the rest were there, Khayan making himself a large and silent presence at Iry's back.

The Lady Nefertem kept them waiting, but Iry had prepared for that. There was wine, there were cakes as was fitting. The five Beauties filled the silence with chatter, sparing the rest the need to do so. They did not seem to recall that their former lord understood Egyptian; they raked him over with frank appraisal.

"Such shoulders," Mut-Nefer said. "Like a bull's. I wonder—do you think the rest of him—?"

The others collapsed in giggles. "Oh! Oh, I wager!" cried Neferure. "But those eyes, I'm not sure I like them. They're too much like a cat's. Or a hawk's. Hawk's eyes are cold. They're full of killing."

"Not these," said Mut-Nefer. "They're warm, like amber."

"I'm sure he's killed people," Neferure persisted. "They all have, all that kind. With those big hands." She shivered deliciously. "Oh! To feel them on me."

It was fortunate that the Lady Nefertem deigned to appear just then, in a procession of maids, or Iry would have risen up and knocked those idiots' heads together. The lady's arrival silenced them abruptly and mercifully. It took a great deal of time to see her settled in the proper degree of comfort, full in their center, of course, with all of them hovering, waiting on her eagerly.

All but Iry, and Khayan who never left his place once he had established himself in it. He was like the Mare. If Iry was there, he cared little for anything else.

At length the flurry faded. The room had a new center, that luminous beauty and that serene certainty that the world existed to serve the Lady Nefertem. Iry let it indulge itself for a little while—not, she told herself, because her courage was failing, but because her mother seemed so happy in it.

She could not delay too long. The five Beauties were restless already. A moment more and their clamor would begin anew.

"My friends and my kin," she said. Her voice sounded thin in her ears. She firmed it as she had been taught to do, as a priestess must who would speak before all the people. "I have brought you here to tell you of a thing. This morning my lady mother reminded me of my duties and obligations, not only to rule here in the king's name, but to consider the proper rule of these lands and the continuation of the line. She pointed out that in the Two Lands, a woman holds lordship through and by her men; that the king's name alone is not enough, and that certainly he cannot provide her with an heir."

One or two of the Beauties tittered, till their mother boxed their ears. When the cries of outrage had died down, Iry went on. "My mother informs me that, as is proper, she has chosen one to stand beside me in the ruling of this domain." She held out her hand. Kemni took it a little warily, eyes dark with mistrust.

People were beginning to babble, a clamor more joyous than not. But there was silence behind her, silence as large as Khayan's body.

Iry met Kemni's stare. His hand, she could not help but notice, was well fitted to her own. Khayan's was easily twice the breadth, so that if she would take it, she must do it in both of hers. Kemni was a smaller man by far, but large enough as men went in Egypt. They would look well together, matched as to height and breadth, and in looks, too, though Iry was no beauty and Kemni was a great one.

Still with her eyes on his, she slipped her hand free. "I have heard my mother's reasons," she said, to him more than to anyone, "and considered them with care. They are excellent reasons, most fit and proper. No one could possibly quarrel with them.

"And yet," she said, "I can't marry you."

He said nothing. He was—relieved? Maybe. He would still argue with her, if she let him.

Which she did not intend to do. Not with him, not with anyone. "You see," she said, "I was born a daughter of this house, a child of the Sun Ascendant. But when I had come to womanhood, another destiny was laid on me. I was chosen to serve a goddess whom none of us then knew, a power that takes shape as a white Mare. That goddess, in choosing me, laid on me other choices, choices that I cannot refuse. Even if I would, I cannot refuse them. And one," she said with beating heart and a prayer for calm, "is this."

She rose. She took Khayan's hand in both of hers. It did not resist her. He was very, very still. "This," she said, "is the father of my daughter who is to be born, and the father of the children that I will bear hereafter. He is my husband by the law of the tribes, my chosen one before the goddess."

It interested her to see how little surprise there was, even in her mother. But shock—of that there was much. Outrage, indignation, all of that. Even anger.

"That is one of the Retenu!" Mut-Nefer cried.

She spoke for them all, except, Iry thought, the Retenu themselves, and Kemni who was beginning, rather maddeningly, to be amused. If he laughed, she would hit him.

"This is a man of the Mare's people, whose father happens to have been Retenu," Iry said. "He is a great master of horses. He knows the ruling of lands—including these—and the ways of our people."

"He is not Egyptian," Nefertem said in a tone of icy scorn. "Child, truly, he is good to look at, as one of his stallions is, and no doubt he serves as well as a stallion may, but is he fit mate for a lady in the Two Lands?"

"Not at all," Iry said. "And yet he is mine."

"I forbid it."

"You cannot. It is done."

"Then let it be undone. You will take your kinsman as I bid you, and send this young stallion away. There are mares enough for him, surely, wherever he may choose to go."

Oh, she was angry, was the Lady Nefertem, to come so close to the edge of vulgarity. Iry had never seen her in such a temper.

Fear, as Iry had discovered in the war, could only rise so high before it either destroyed one's wits or restored them to a keen and almost bitter clarity. Iry's mind was like bright water, that the wind could touch and ruffle and even shift, but always it flowed back to the stillness in which it had begun.

Khayan's hand was still in hers, her small fingers stretching to clasp his large ones, but well content to be so overpowered. "I will not send him away," she said to her mother out of the deep quiet in her center. "If his presence here offends you, then I will give you a holding of your own, a place where you may rule to your heart's content. For you will not rule here. I am the lord whom the king set over these lands, the ruler whom he has chosen. This is my lord whom I have chosen, with the goddess' blessing."

The Lady Nefertem sat mute. Iry did not know that anyone had ever defied her before. It was a terrifying thing, but Iry could do nothing but what she did.

Nefertem spoke at last in a soft, still voice. "You are determined in this?"

"I can do no other."

"I will not leave," Nefertem said.

"Then you will accept my choice."

Nefertem shook her head. But she did not speak further. Iry took that as assent, or as close as that proud lady was going to come.

⟡ ⟡

"Will she ever accept me, do you think?"

Iry sat in the wide and lordly bed, clasping her knees and enjoying the simple pleasure of Khayan lying naked before her. He had stretched out on his side, lazy as a lion in the sun, but his eyes on her were clear amber, almost gold, and very keen.

"Do you think she ever will?" he asked again.

"Probably not," she said. "My mother is almost as stubborn as I am, and very proud. But she won't conspire against you, or try to have you driven out or killed. That much she'll do for me, because I am her blood kin."

"I'll win her over," he said with surety that in another man would have been arrogance. But Khayan might actually do it. "She may never accept me as your husband, but she might, in the end, grant that I have a right to live here."

"That would be a victory," Iry conceded. Then, after a pause: "Are you regretting what I did? If you don't want to be—"

"That depends on what you're asking me to be. Can a woman here marry a slave?"

"You were never a slave," she said. "Never in my heart. You are my lord and my beloved."

"I am an exile in the country in which I was born. People spit in my tracks when I pass."

"That will end," Iry said with calm conviction. "We shall be bold, you and I, side by side as it is done in Egypt. Will you do that, my lord? Come out with me in the morning, dressed as a lord should be, and walk beside me as proudly as you ever did, and sit in a chair equal to mine as we share the morning's judgments. Side by side, my lord. Hand in hand. Can you do that?"

"I can try," he said.

"You will do it."

"As my lady wishes," he said.

"No," she said. "As my lord wishes. Side by side."

"Side by side." He spoke the words as if he did not quite understand their meaning, but was willing to learn.

She smiled. "Side by side, and proudly."

"Proudly." Now that, he understood. "Yes. I can do that. With joy, even. Bravado. Defy them to hate me. Dare them to love me."

"And when they succumb," she said, "let them see your great heart and your strong spirit. Maybe I've forced you on them—but in the end they'll be glad of you."

"I can hope so," Khayan said, a little doubtfully still; but she knew no doubt at all.

SON OF RE

K EMNI DREAMED. HE was his winged self, his *ba*-spirit, riding the winds of heaven above the visions that the gods wished him to see.

He looked down on white walls, blinding in the sun, and the white mountains that men's hands had made to be the tombs of kings: Memphis at the gate of the Lower Kingdom, and the Pyramids beyond it, rising tall out of the Red Land. It was a day of great festival, the festival at the height of Inundation, when the king came to the white city and stood with the priests of Ptah beside the ancient measure of the river's flood, and marked it with great rite and ceremony.

This was the first time in a hundred years that the king at that rite wore the Two Crowns, white within red, and bore the blood of royal Egypt. The foreign kings were driven out, their kingdom in Canaan defeated, their cities broken. Their names were expunged from the annals of the Two Lands. All that they had done was unmade, their monuments broken or taken back. Even their great city, their capital of Avaris, was given as gift by the king to his queen from Crete.

Ariana was present at this rite, beside and slightly behind the Great Royal Wife, the Queen Nefertari. There was a great crowd of princes about them, lords and ladies and their kin and servants and children. Joy sang in them, the joy of victory.

The wind bore Kemni in a spiral downward, the better to see the faces of those about the king. He found those he looked for, and quickly, too: Iry his cousin in the gown and wig of an Egyptian lady, but the headdress that crowned the wig was the golden crown of the Mare's priestess. A towering figure stood beside her, not behind her, in lordly garb and a great weight of gold. A smaller one clung to his leg: small naked girlchild, her head shaven as children's were, save for the sidelock which, even plaited, let slip a vagrant curl. She looked remarkably as Iry had when she was small, but her eyes were light, almost gold, and her skin was not quite the warm red-brown of Egypt. Instead of the blue bead that children were wont to wear for luck, this child wore an amulet: a plump white horse on a string of plaited horsehair.

They stood close, the three of them, and Kemni could see that in a little while there would be four. Even as he watched, Khayan laid his arm about Iry's shoulders, and she leaned lightly against him.

Kemni's spirit knew a moment's regret, and a moment's jealousy. To see two who loved each other so, and could defy the whole of their nation and kin and blood, and came to joy for it, and he—he had nothing—

He called himself to order. He would be glad to see them so glad. More so for that the Lady Nefertem stood not far from them, and not as one who set herself apart. Indeed, when her glance fell on her grandchild, it grew almost soft. Nefertem might never accept the father, but Kemni would wager that the child was the light of her grandmother's eye.

There were others near them, too. Iannek in armor like a guardsman. A number of Sadana's warrior women. Even Kemni himself half-hidden behind the bulk that was the young Retenu.

The sight of his own body sent him spinning down into it. Eyes that had seen the whole great throng, now saw only what a man on foot could see, and that only what the mind behind them willed. Kemni's spirit had no power over this body.

Still, he could see what it saw, and feel what it felt. It was dizzy with joy, and not only to be present at this rite. Something else had befallen it. Something wonderful. Something to do with the warmth beside it, which it refused to glance at, as if the sight of it would make it vanish. It was a woman, his spirit knew. Who she was, he was not permitted to know.

His spirit stiffened in dismay, and in a kind of horror. The love of his heart was dead. How could he turn to another, even after the passage of years? Was he then so inconstant?

It seemed that, at least in dreams, he was. It was sweet, that joy; sweeter than he had ever thought to know again. He was not even afraid to lose it. That fear had tormented him, his spirit knew as spirits could, but he had grown into calm. What the moment offered him, he would take. He would be a fool to do otherwise.

He was almost sorry to wake; but a voice was calling him. He opened his eyes, blinking, half-blind with sleep.

Sadana stood over him. He gasped in startlement, then in sudden relief. "Is it morning already?"

"It's dawn," she said. "The lame mare foaled in the night. Her sister has been pacing for an hour and more."

Kemni sprang up, staggering but keeping his feet, and scrambled for his kilt. "An hour? She'll have foaled before I come there!"

"I think not," Sadana said. "She'll wait for you."

✦ ✦

She had waited. She was in the stable as certain of the mares were who were nearest their time: favorites, or mares of the Mare's kin. Her sister nursed a fine tall colt, dark and spindly against his dam's moon-pale bulk. She was still pacing, lashing her tail, glaring at her sides.

Kemni settled quietly outside of the stall, as he had learned to do when mares foaled. "Does Iry know?" he murmured into Sadana's ear.

Sadana raised a brow. "Why, should she?"

"These are the Mare's kin."

"But not that Mare," Sadana said. "And she may be preoccupied."

Kemni bit his lip. Preoccupied. Indeed.

Sadana folded her arms on the breast-high wall that marked the stall, standing almost close enough to touch, but not quite. Kemni followed suit, resting his chin on his arms, waiting in quiet for the mare to get about her business.

As he stood there, intent on the white mare but aware in his skin of the presence beside him, it came to him: he had felt this before. This warmth, this presence. This gladness so deep he had not even been aware of it.

In this waking world, he could command his eyes; he could glance at her. She seemed unaware of him. She was watching the mare.

Sadana? Sadana was the woman in his dream?

Well, and why not?

He did not love her as he had loved Iphikleia. No woman would ever have that from him again. And yet, maybe, he loved Sadana no less. It was different, that was all. Love born first in friendship, in the bond between comrades in arms; between warrior and charioteer. She had chosen him once to be her lover, but not again; nor had she seemed inclined to do it. He had never forgotten that night, but neither had it grown into obsession.

In the dream she had loved him as he loved her, and that was the joy of it. But that might have been his own wishing given substance. Certainly she took little notice of him now, nor seemed to care how close he stood, and he near naked.

The mare had gone down, heaving as mares did in the swift violence of birthing. He saw the silver bubble of the caul, and an ivory gleam within it: the foal's foot as it dived into the air.

Sadana frowned. He saw: one foot only where should be two, and the mare straining. Sadana leaped over the wall and dropped at the mare's side, reaching within, searching; pausing. The mare strained again. Smoothly, cleanly, Sadana drew out the body of the foal, dark and wet within the clouded silver of the caul. She folded it back from round muzzle and from ears that curled at the tips, thin wet neck and great square shoulder.

The foal stirred, struggling, pulling itself free of its mother. Sadana sat back as it moved, letting it birth itself now that she had freed it. It tried to crawl into her lap. She cradled it, turned it till it faced its mother.

The mare had raised her head. Her nostrils fluttered. She touched nose to small wet nose.

Sadana's smile was sudden, luminous, and completely unselfconscious. It warmed Kemni like sunlight as he settled beside her, watching the mare greet her foal.

"Colt?" he asked.

"Filly." Sadana sounded greatly pleased. "A mare among the Mare's people. She will be very beautiful."

Kemni was learning to see the seeds of beauty amid all the legs and angles of a foal; but he was still far from accomplished in the art. Sadana, who had learned it as a child, spoke with confidence and no little pride. It was a great thing to bring one of these creatures into the world, so rare as they were, and so dear to the goddess.

They watched together in silence as the white mare's child taught herself to stand, to seek the brimming udder, to nurse. There was no need to speak, to cover discomfort with a veil of words. All that they needed to say, the mare and her foal were saying between them.

Kemni could leave it so, as it had been since Sadana appointed herself his keeper. Or, when the foal had drunk its fill and sighed and dropped down to sleep, and the mare had turned her attention to the fodder that she had disdained the night before, he could say, "Come with me. When I go to the Bull of Re, as I should do soon—come and help me."

She raised a brow. "Is there no one there to do it?"

"No one of the Mare's people."

"Well then," she said, "one or two of my women would be delighted, I'm sure, to ride with you into the Upper Kingdom."

He heard her in a kind of despair. But he would not surrender yet. "I was asking you."

Both brows went up. If she was laughing at him, he would look for a sword to fall on. "What can I do that one of my women cannot?"

"Be Sadana," he answered.

"Ah," she said. And nothing else for long enough that he despaired. She did not want to come. She wanted to stay here, where her brothers were, and the Mare's servant, and the Mare herself. Of course. How not?

Then she said, "It's a friend you're wanting."

"I'm sure I shall find one," he said stiffly, "once I come there."

"No," she said. "No. I didn't mean it so. I meant—"

She broke off, and hissed as if in frustration. "Are you asking me for something else?"

He felt the heat rise to his cheeks. "I wouldn't presume," he said.

"Wouldn't you?" She was watching the mare again, and the foal. "What if I said yes? Yes to all of it?"

"All of it?" he echoed her.

"Everything you ask. What you let yourself think you want of me, and what your heart wants."

His heart, at the word, thudded once, hard, as if it would leap out of his breast. "And yours?" he asked. "Does yours want this?"

"From the beginning," she said.

He was afraid. That was the cold in his skin, the shiver in his heart. He had never been afraid with Iphikleia.

This then was a new thing. He did not like it. Not that it cared for like or dislike. It simply was. To love again so soon, after so much grief—even with the strength of his dream behind him, he could hardly endure it.

The gods had little patience with human maunderings. No more did Sadana. She advanced on him. He stood his ground, as indeed he could not help but do: the wall was at his back.

She trapped him there, with no escape. "Yes," she said. "Yes, I will go."

He had asked no less, and should be glad. And yet he said, "I can't give you the whole of myself. I never could."

"I know that." Her finger brushed his cheek. "I don't care."

"You are worthy of more."

"You don't know that," she said. "I'll take what you have, and take joy in it. It will be enough."

"What if it's not?"

"It will be."

He shook his head. He did not know why he was being so stubborn, but neither could he stop himself. "I'm sorry I asked. If you want to send one of the others, I'll be content. You belong here. Maybe someday—"

"Stop that," she said. "You asked. I've answered. I'll go with you to the Bull of Re."

"Will you go as my wife?"

That took her off guard. But not for long enough. "Yes," she said. "Yes, I will do that." Then she laughed. "Great goddess! Your kin will be appalled. First my brother and your cousin. Now—"

"I'm not taking you because she won't have me. Don't believe that."

"Of course I don't," she said, as if amazed that he could think such a thing. "She's never had eyes for anybody but Khayan. Some women are like that. Some dogs, too. And a mare or two. They only ever care for one man."

"I had thought," he said with an edge of bitterness, "that I was a man for one woman."

"One woman at a time," she said. "I'll be content. Trust in that, beautiful man. I will be happy."

She meant it. Her eyes were shining. He had never seen her so, with all the taut fierceness gone. She was very beautiful, beautiful enough to break the heart.

He touched her as she had touched him, the brush of a finger lightly down her cheek. Her eyes closed. She shivered. He would have drawn back, but she caught his hand and held it. "Sometimes," he said, "I'll grieve. Can you live with me then?"

"We all grieve," she said. "I'll bring you healing."

"I don't want to forget," he said with a touch of sharpness. "Don't make me do that."

"Never," she said. "But the pain—that, I can take away. If you will."

"I want the pain, too. For remembrance."

"Pain you may have. But not to wallow in."

He glared at her. And yet his hand was still pressed to her cheek, and hers over it, warm and strong as many a man's.

"No wallowing," she said. "Except in love. That's the law I'll make you live by."

"And if I won't?"

"You will."

There was a silence. Kemni began to wonder precisely who had chosen whom.

She let go his hand. It slipped down of its own accord, to rest on her shoulder. She made no move to shake it off. "You really will?" he asked. "You really would go with me as my wife?"

"With great joy."

And, he thought, no misunderstanding. She knew him, all of him, heart and grieving souls. Even what was missing, or what he no longer had to give. And she could still be glad, so glad that he could hardly bear it.

There was only one thing that he could do, and that was to be as glad as she. It was less difficult than he had feared. When he opened his arms, she came to them—rare gift in one so proud. She held him as he held her, a little shy at first, perhaps a little afraid. She had had pain, too, and fear, and long sorrow.

None of that would go away, not wholly. But even the deepest of wounds, if it does not kill, in time will heal. She, warrior that she was, would not care if there were scars.

No more did he. He was happy, after all; deeply and wondrously happy. Just as he had been in his dream—but with the prick of guilt, the welling of memory.

She felt his drawing back, and caught him, holding him fast. "Memory," she said, "but no guilt. Never guilt."

"I can't promise that."

"Try."

He shook his head. Her hand stopped it, tilted it. Her lips met his.

There, however brief, was forgetfulness. There was healing, whether he would or no.

He would accept it, and the one who brought it. He would take it and be glad.

He laughed suddenly. Sadana pulled back, breaking off the kiss. She was puzzled, and perhaps a little angry.

"No," he said to that. "No, I'm not laughing at you. I'm laughing at myself. That I've been such a fool; and that it's taken me so long to see what was in front of my face."

"You weren't ready to see," she said.

He opened his mouth to say more, perhaps a great deal more, but she stopped it with her hand, then with her lips. When he could breathe again, there were no words left. Nor was there need of any.

Except one. "Beloved," he said.

"Beloved," she agreed. She bore him back and down. She was conquering him as her father's people had conquered Egypt—but here was neither victor nor vanquished, neither captive nor free. Only the two of them, and the love that was between them, that had grown out of enmity and flowered in war. And now, thought Kemni with what little wits he had left: now, in peace, it would yield its harvest.